BLOOD ROAD

AMANDA McCRINA

BLOOD
OATH
1

Month9Books

Copyright © 2017 by Amanda McCrina

BLOOD ROAD by Amanda McCrina
All rights reserved. Published in the United States of America by Month9Books, LLC.
No part of this book may be used or reproduced in any manner whatsoever without written permission of the publisher, except in the case of brief quotations embodied in critical articles and reviews.

Trade Paperback ISBN: 978-1-945107-88-7
ePub ISBN: 978-1-945107-99-3
Mobipocket ISBN: 978-1-946700-00-1

Published by Month9Books, Raleigh, NC 27609
Cover design by Monika Macfarlane

Month9Books

For Mark, Nidley, and "Two-Buck" Tim

I

He could see the sky in pieces between the tenements, bruised purple now with dusk.

At first he was glad for the darkness, because it meant they would be firing the beacon in the lighthouse at the point. He leaned on his saddle-horns, craning his neck to look down the narrow cross streets, trying to catch a glimpse of the great light burning in the distance. By means of the lighthouse he could reorient himself. But the cross streets twisted away into deep shadow between the tenement blocks, and there was the irksome thought at the back of his mind that if they had wandered so far into the city as not see the lighthouse, then they had wandered so far as to be where Imperial control was more a matter of theory than practice—at least at night.

Earlier, when the young summer sun was glaring white in a blueglaze sky and the air under the awnings still and close and hot enough one could feel one's skin baking in it—the tenements shut out the harbor breeze—the streets had seethed with people: sellers of figs and dates and pomegranates and honeyed almonds and goats' milk and flavored ices and sour wine; and potters and silversmiths and leather-workers and basket-weavers at their shopfronts; and housewives browsing the market stalls; and slave girls with water in sloshing panniers over their shoulders; and naked children playing sticks-and-hoops along the foot-stones; and now and then a mounted official in white linen, shouting and swearing until the crowd shuffled aside to let him pass. Now in darkness they were alone in the street. It was as though the rest of the city had died with the sun. The air was dry and rapidly cooling, heavy with silence like a bated breath. He would not mind the darkness if not for the silence. In a city such silence was unnatural.

"Do you suppose they'll look for us?" Alluin said. "Or just wait until our bodies turn up in an alley in a week or so?"

"I imagine they'll expend the effort for me, if they wouldn't otherwise trouble about *you*."

"So there is some benefit to your acquaintance, after all."

"If not for my acquaintance, you'd be just finishing the first course at the officers' dinner."

It had been his idea to explore the city. Alluin was city-born and indifferent—all cities were the same when you got down to it; there came a point when unwashed bodies and stray dogs and bad wine in dirty shops ceased to be as interesting as bed. But he, Torien, still had a provincial awe of big cities—an itching, impatient need to see and hear and know. He had been determined not to idle away his time in Modigne behind the fort walls. True that he and Alluin had no more than a smattering of bastardized Modigno between them, and that Modigne was a rabbit's warren of nameless, ancient streets, built and overbuilt in incongruous layers—in daylight that had seemed far less important than it did now. In daylight it had been enough to know he was an officer of the Imperial army, and a Vareno nobleman, with sufficient coin on his person for any foreseeable difficulty and a sword at his hip in the event his coin should fail. It was remarkable how in darkness one saw things more clearly.

Certain things, anyway—other things than the way back to the fort or the direction of the harbor light.

The street, so narrow now that Alluin had to rein in his horse and fall in behind, plunged into a honeycomb of tight-packed adobe huts, each no wider than the span of Torien's arms, joined to its neighbors by rickety wooden ladders running an uneven line from flat rooftop to flat rooftop. He took the downward slant for a good sign: he knew, from studying the maps on the wall of the headquarters at the fort, that Modigne, built as it was along a volcanic crater, went down to the ocean like the insides of a bowl, and so for the street to be sloping downward meant it must be working its way however haphazardly to the harbor.

He leaned on the saddle-horns, lifting himself a little to see if he could pick out the lighthouse below.

There was a rustle on the rooftop above. Out of the corner of his eye, he saw a darker shadow take shape against the darkness. He recognized the glint of metal in time to jerk around in his saddle, hauling on the reins as he turned. He took the blade in the back of his left shoulder rather than in his throat.

He had braced for it and did not slip from the saddle, though for a moment he thought he might: his knees, pressed against the horse's ribs, went as weak as water. He lost the reins from his left hand. Above him, he heard very clearly the patter of footsteps as the knifeman fled across the rooftop for the nearest ladder. Just as clearly, he heard the thin cry and the muffled thump as the knifeman lost his footing on the ladder and fell back to the roof.

Silence followed.

Torien brushed away Alluin's hand and propped his right shoulder against the wall. He nodded to the hut. "Bring him," he said—calmly, though his heart was pounding. "That fall won't have killed him."

He saw Alluin's face as a pale blur in the darkness. "Tor—"

"It's nothing. It'll wait. Our friend won't."

In truth, his knees were still trembling, and he was speaking through clenched teeth because he knew if he unclenched them they would chatter. There was blood seeping through his tunic and jerkin, and he was conscious, as he hadn't been at first, of the knife blade sunk to its hilt just beyond the cuff of his shoulder. His body was revolting against the thought, sickness threatening in the pit of his stomach.

Lamplight blossomed inside the hut. Low voices filtered out through the reed curtain in the doorway. Torien dipped his chin again, with effort. Alluin swore and swung from his saddle and drew his sword. He pushed into the hut through the curtain, and Torien heard him issuing orders in a clumsy hybrid of Modigno and Vareno—heard the crash of pottery breaking, the scrape of wood dragging across stone, a child's whimper. A moment later, Alluin's head and shoulders and sword hand emerged above him from inside the hut. Alluin pushed himself up on his hands from the opening, landing lightly on his feet on the roof. Picking up his sword, he vanished beyond the roof edge.

Torien leaned carefully back against the wall. He glanced down the street. There were no other doorways lit, no other sound than the clatter of Alluin's hobnailed boots on the rooftop above. In Choiro, there would have been a crowd by now. Modigne lay as still and silent as a plague city.

Alluin reappeared at the roof edge. He had sheathed his sword. He was handling the knifeman along by the shoulders—no, not a man, Torien thought, certainly a boy: he came barely to Alluin's chest. His arms and legs, silhouetted black against the sky, were thin, stick-like things around which his tunic fluttered shapelessly.

Torien pushed up from the wall and gathered himself together and dismounted. The ground was springy under his feet. He wavered for a moment as his heels touched, swallowing back the sickness. There was a ringing in his ears. He blinked in the sudden brightness of lamplight as Alluin flung aside the curtain in the doorway and shoved the boy before him out into the street. Behind him the hut's occupants—a man and a woman and an assortment of half-dressed children—gathered silently in the doorway to watch.

The boy had stumbled and fallen in a heap of skinny limbs and wool rags. He caught himself on his palms. He adjusted the cap on his head and sat back awkwardly, keeping his knobby legs to the side. In the dim light, Torien could see enough to know the left ankle was broken. There was blood dribbling from the boy's nose, and he was sucking breath low and softly through his teeth. His eyes darted over Torien's face, lingering for a moment at Torien's shoulder. He looked quickly to the ground. He was, Torien judged, eleven or perhaps twelve—not yet old enough to face execution for an assault upon an Imperial soldier. He would go to a slaver's block instead. There would be an examination to determine the guilt of his family.

He caught Alluin's eye and jerked his chin to the sullen family in the doorway. "Wine if they have it. Water otherwise—and something passable for bandage cloth." The pain had started, and he was leaning into his horse's shoulder for balance.

The woman in the doorway said something in Modigno. He recognized the word for wine. He said, "What did she say?" Alluin's Modigno was bad, but better than his own.

"They have wine, but it's for a wedding," Alluin said, "for her sister's wedding—I think."

He was irritated and impatient now. "Water, then. Tell them I'd have paid for wine."

Alluin stood at his shoulder and unbuckled his cuirass while the woman went into the hut. "Do you want to do this inside?" he said. His voice was quiet.

"Not until I know he acted alone." Torien nodded to the boy, who had sat motionless all this while, studying the ground as though he were reading something written there. "You. You speak Vareno?"

The boy looked up incuriously into Torien's face. He had determined not to speak: Torien could see as much from the set of his mouth, the hollowness of his eyes. His thin brown hands were clenched to fists on his lap.

From the doorway, the man spoke up in rapid Modigno.

"He's reconsidered about the wine?" Torien said. The shoulder was hurting fiercely.

"He says he knows her family," Alluin said.

"Whose family?"

There was a moment's silence in which he suddenly understood.

"A girl," he said, stupidly.

"He says he knows her family and will tell us where she lives," Alluin said. "Also, he would appreciate very much his lord's kindness if his lord would consider a pittance in return for the service."

The girl flung up her head suddenly to spit at the man's feet. The man seemed embarrassed. He hunched his shoulders and looked at his hands. The woman came out from the hut with a water jug and a cloth. She held them out to Alluin at arm's length, making a quick, nervous gesture with her hands. Alluin shook his head. "Hold them. *Quedas*—hold them, you understand?"

"Give them to me," Torien said.

"Don't give them to him," Alluin said. "He'll drop them when I do this."

He jerked the knife from Torien's shoulder. Torien folded to his knees. The street swam around him. He heard Alluin's voice as though it were carrying to him underwater. He shook his head. Alluin was prying the cuirass from his shoulder and tugging the jerkin down his arm. The night air through his blood-soaked tunic was sharp and cold; he shivered. The girl's eyes were on him. She was watching with the same flat-eyed incuriosity. There was blood trickling over her lips from her nose, but she made no move to wipe it away.

"Her ankle," Torien said. For some reason, her silence shamed him.

Far above him Alluin said, patiently, "What?"

"Tie up her ankle. And tell the Modigno he can show us where she lives, because I don't trust the word of a coward."

The Modigno walked ahead, self-consciously, shoulders still hunched in embarrassment. Alluin followed on foot, leading his horse by the reins. The girl huddled in his saddle with her hands outstretched to the horns, her face buried in the horse's mane, her bare legs dangling limp against the horse's belly. Torien rode at the rear. The street, which turned this way and that through the honeycombed huts, ran steadily downhill all the while, and he knew they must be close to the water because there was a stiff salt breeze rising to his face. It cut through his soaked tunic like a knife. His fingers were numb on the reins. He had knotted them in the horse's mane to keep himself upright in the saddle.

He could have ordered the Modigno to show them instead to the harbor light, of course, or to the fort itself, and they could have delivered the girl into the prison on the hill, and very soon now he might have been enjoying the comfort of his own quarters and a skin of wine to ease the pain in his shoulder—but it might easily be a month before the girl's case went to the governor, and he was due to report at Tasso in a week, and he had too many questions of his own to let it go like that.

Only after they had gone on for near half an hour, the adobe huts having given way to ramshackle wooden shanties and the street sunk in soft, rank mud, the air heavy with the smell of brine and rotten fish, did it occur to him that most likely the Modigno had no idea about the girl's family and no idea where she lived—had grasped for the chance to make a quick coin and come away with more than he had bargained for, and was looking for the opportunity to dart down an alley and vanish into the night.

He had opened his mouth to say this to Alluin when the Modigno swung about suddenly and said something in his own tongue, gesturing with his hands. The shanty at his back was three-sided, sheltered from the street by a tattered sailcloth curtain, unlit.

"He says it's here," Alluin said.

The girl shifted in Alluin's saddle. A shudder ran through her shoulders, but she did not raise her head.

"Tell him to lift the curtain," Torien said. He was cold and aching and the Modigno was a fool, but that was no reason to abandon caution.

The Modigno lifted the curtain. The shanty was empty. There was a fire pit dug in the bare-dirt floor, but the coals were dead.

The Modigno spoke very quickly in his own tongue, his eyes going from Alluin to Torien and back again.

"He seems to think we think he's lied," Alluin said. "He wants us to ask the girl."

"Tell him the girl's our concern." Torien dismounted, cradling his left arm against his stomach. He was too tired for anger. Anyway, it was pointless to threaten reprisals: they would not find him again if they tried. He fumbled at his belt and withdrew a bronze from his wallet. He flicked the coin in the Modigno's direction. "*Bayas*—go."

The Modigno dropped to his heels to dig out the coin from the mud. He made a mockery of a bow as he straightened: it had occurred to him that they had been essentially at his mercy. His shoulders were straight as he walked away back up the street.

Alluin pulled the girl down from his saddle by the waist and held her before him, as easily as though she were made of straw. "I'll have a look around. The harbor can't be far."

"No. We can spend the night here."

"That shoulder needs more than water, Tor, and sooner is better. Though I appreciate your faith in my medical ability."

"I don't like the idea of splitting up. It won't do my shoulder any good if you end up in the harbor with your throat cut. And I couldn't drag myself back into a saddle right now if I wanted to."

Alluin was silent, studying him. He had the girl's shoulder in one hand, his reins in the other. He let go the girl's shoulder, reluctantly. "*Adienta*—inside," he said. And to Torien: "I'll see to the horses."

Weak moonlight filtered through the roof of the shanty, which was nothing more than a reed lattice tied down with leather strips. The girl sat down against the left-hand wall, stretching her bad leg straight before her. She watched silently and unmoving while Torien crouched on his heels at the fire pit and searched one-handed through the ashes for salvageable tinder. By the time he had built up a decent pile, and had found flint and iron to strike a light, Alluin had ducked in from the street with a saddle on each arm.

"I'd have done it if you'd waited," he said. He deposited Torien's saddle against the right-hand wall and sat down with his own against the rear wall.

Torien unbuckled his helmet and leaned his head back against the wall. He sat with the helmet on his lap, his eyes closed. Beyond the crackling of the fire and the rattling of the lattice in the salt breeze, the silence stretched vast and hostile. "If you speak," he said, "it goes better for you." He opened his eyes and looked at the girl across the fire pit. In the firelight, he could see the details of her bony bronze face. She was older than he had thought at first—older than he'd thought when he'd thought her a boy. It was possible she was fifteen. The smallness of her limbs and the sunkenness of her cheeks made it hard to tell. She was looking into the flame in silence, her eyes half-closed, her face magnificently blank, but he knew she had heard and had taken his general meaning by the way her shoulders tightened

11

against the wall. "Tell me if there were others," he said. "Tell me how many."

When she said nothing, he said to Alluin, "In Modigno. Tell her if she doesn't answer to us now, she'll answer to the governor in court—she and her family."

The girl jerked her chin, suddenly. "No others," she said. "I understand what you say." Her eyes came up to his. Her voice was low but hard. "I do it alone. No family. The *coburte* he lies when he brings you. No family. He says it because he wants your coin."

"Why did you do it?"

She turned her face back to the fire.

"Answer me," Torien said.

"I go to the slavers anyway," she said. "It doesn't matter if I answer you."

"Possibly you'll go to the slavers. Possibly they'll decide you're old enough to face execution. My word means a great deal, either way."

"I do not care," she said.

"My word can spare you an examination."

"I do not care."

He glanced over to Alluin, who shrugged very slightly against the wall. Torien could sense his discomfort in his silence. He looked back at the girl. "Speak now and I'll listen," he said. "Come tomorrow in the city prison, it'll be too late."

She said nothing. He saw there was no use in it. He said to Alluin, "We'd better set a watch."

"I'll watch," Alluin said. He seemed thankful for something to do.

"I'll take it over in a few hours," Torien said. "Wake me if you need to."

He did not sleep. He lay against his saddle, carefully still on account of the shoulder, watching the sky through the cracks in the lattice and waiting for sleep to come, but his mind was moving on and on through the streets of Modigne, and in the silence he was restless. At length, he got up. The fire had died to embers. Across the room, the girl was huddled shapeless in the darkness. He could not tell if she was asleep. He went over to the doorway, where Alluin sat cross-legged against the corner post. "You sleep," he said. "I can't."

"Your shoulder?" Alluin's voice was tight. "You should have let me go for help, Tor."

"It's fine. It's just that I can't sleep and you might as well."

"Next time you'll listen to me. Next time when I say I can see enough of Modigne from the fort walls, and you say—"

"You talk like you're the one who took the knife."

"That's the difference between us," Alluin said. "*I* don't have to take a knife in my back before I recognize a bad idea."

Torien sat with his back against the post, his sword unsheathed across his lap. Through the gap between the post and the curtain, he could see the horses and the moonlit street beyond. He watched a cat come noiselessly down the street. It saw him as it approached the shanty, and it paused and watched him and went on again when it decided he was no threat. Behind him, in the shanty, Alluin was breathing long and steadily in his sleep. It was perhaps midnight or a little past. He heard a noise like a muffled laugh or a cough, and he started, fingers seizing instinctively on his sword grip. At his movement, the noise stopped. Across the room, the girl was struggling to hold herself still against the wall. Her shoulders shook with trapped sobs.

He pulled himself up to his feet, supporting himself on the sword. He crossed the room to her. She heard him approaching and drew herself stiffly up, but she did not raise her head. He knelt beside her. In the moonlight through the lattice, he could see the tear streaks on her cheeks. Leaning on the sword, he said, quietly, "Tell me why you did it."

Another tremor ran through her shoulders. She bit her lip. Alluin's untroubled breathing was loud in the silence.

"Give me the truth and I may be able to help you."

She shook her head, once, sharply, her eyes squeezed shut. "You lie. I know you lie."

"I don't lie."

"All Vareni lie. I know this."

"Maybe. But I'm Cesino blood through my father's line."

"Then to your people you are a traitor."

She said it flatly, without interest, as though it were as obvious as the weather, and he understood the absurdity of trying to explain to her, in that moment, how one could feel loyalty to homeland and to empire without hypocrisy. He said, instead, "I'm trying to help you."

"Why do you want to help me?"

"I care to see proper justice done."

"I know your justice." She lifted her face to his, finally. Her voice

14

was thick with anger and tears. "I know what you mean when you say justice. You take Mahlan when he does nothing wrong. I know what you mean by justice."

The curtain rustled in a draft of cold salt breeze. Torien was on his feet and spinning to the doorway in one motion, his sword ready in his hand. Behind him, Alluin sat bolt upright, flinging aside his cloak. He drew his sword and scrambled up, his back to the wall. The figure in the doorway stood frozen at Torien's sword point. For a moment, there was silence in the shanty. Then Torien jerked his chin over his shoulder and said, "Sit—slowly. *Linta.*"

He kept his blade leveled at the newcomer's throat while the newcomer slid down beside the girl. He said to Alluin, "Light."

Alluin dropped to his knees at the fire pit. There was another stretch of silence while he coaxed a flame from the spent tinder. In the moonlight, Torien could see the newcomer's arms tight around the girl's shoulders, head bowed against the girl's head. He lowered his sword. After a moment's consideration, he sheathed it. He turned on his heel and went to the curtain and looked out into the street. It lay empty and silent as before. The horses stood tethered at the post. He drew the curtain shut. There was a tightness in him that had nothing to do with the wound.

Feeble light sprang over the shanty walls.

"It won't last long," Alluin said.

"Use this." With one booted foot, Torien prodded the bundle of sticks that the newcomer had let drop in the doorway. The girl watched him over the newcomer's shoulder. Her face was set as hard as stone, but he saw the flicker of fear in her eyes. He crouched on his heels, facing her, the fire pit at his back. "No family? So it's not only Vareni who lie."

The girl said nothing. The newcomer straightened slowly against the wall and looked at him. He saw the girl's face in near-exact duplicate, but duplicated as it would be in twenty years' time: bronze skin prematurely lined, lips cracked by the sun, dark eyes sunken with hunger and hardship and grief. There was neither fear nor defiance in the woman's face, but rather a resignation which shook him. "I give you what you want. Do not ask it of the girl."

"You can give me satisfactory answers. Otherwise the girl goes before an Imperial court for sedition and attempted murder."

The woman looked at the girl, the girl at the floor. Neither spoke, but in the firelight Torien watched the color drain from the woman's face.

"Dependent upon her age, the penalty is enslavement or death, so I advise you to consider your answers carefully. Who is Mahlan?"

The woman was silent. The girl raised her eyes briefly from the floor.

"Silence does your daughter no good," Torien said.

"My son. He is my son—Mahlan." Her mouth contorted as though the name pained her.

"Where is he?"

"They take him," the woman said. She swallowed. "This spring when the harbor open they come and take him."

"Who?"

She said nothing. Her fingers were tight around the girl's arms. They were bony fingers, bent and blunted from work, the knuckles swollen, the nails split. The backs of her brown hands were traced over with lines like dry leather.

"Vareni?" Torien said. "Answer me."

The woman closed her eyes. "Of the *jente*."

He did not know the word. He darted a glance to Alluin, who was sitting and watching from the other side of the fire pit. "One of the crime lords," Alluin said, quietly.

Torien said to the woman, "This *jente* took your son?"

"When the harbor open, they take him."

He supposed in her mind and in the girl's the Imperial governing authorities were partially culpable in that they had not stopped it; and he supposed he had made more accessible a target than the *jente* for the girl's retribution. It was a stupid reason to be knifed in the street, and a stupider reason to be executed. He was irritated. "You should have gone to the governor. He might have explained to you the difference between justice and vengeance before the girl need hang for it."

"I go to your courts." The woman flung up her head. "I am a citizen. My daughter she is a citizen. My son he is a citizen. I go to your courts for justice. They say to me I have no case, and they tell me if I am not silent then they will silence me. Always it is the same. Always you pretend you do not see, because the *jente* he pays you not to see. I know what is justice and what is not justice. What you hang my daughter for it is not justice, and you know this too."

17

"How many others besides your son?"

There was a moment's silence. He could sense Alluin frozen behind him across the fire pit.

He said, "You say *always* like it's common practice. How many others?"

The woman drew up a little. Her eyes were flat, her mouth tight. She thought he was mocking her. "There are hundreds the *jente* take. You know—"

"I know nothing. I've been two days in Modigne, and despite the fact I just took a knife in my shoulder, I hope to be shipboard and gone tomorrow." He kneaded his temples with his fingertips. "So the *jente* takes them—why? As slaves?"

"He sells them into the salt mines in Tasso. I hear it from the sailors."

"And you say the governor knows and does nothing."

Anger flashed across the sun-cracked face. "I say because I know. We tell him what happens. We tell him the *jente* he takes us to be slaves in the mines. We ask his protection. 'We are citizens,' we say. 'Help us against the *jente*.' But the ones who speak out he gives their name to the *jente*, and the *jente* he kills them or he takes them to the ships. I have seen this. The *jente* he kills us in the street, and your governor and your courts and your garrison they do nothing."

"Every ship coming into or going out from an Imperial port is inspected—slave ships more closely than the rest. Every manifest is reviewed, every cargo taxed. So many kidnapped citizens would hardly escape notice. It would take more than the governor turning a blind eye. At the least, it would mean the city guard, and the harbor master and his agents, and the harbor master at Tasso, and every level of the administration at the mines. This *jente* can't have bought them all."

"The city guard always they belong to the *jentes*," the woman said. "Anyway, the *jente* he doesn't use the slave ships. I see it myself. In the night they put the slaves on trade ships—hundreds of slaves into hidden holds. In the day they fill the ships with jugs of wine, jugs of oil. That is what the harbor master sees. They put water in some of the jugs so it doesn't show on the manifests that they carry water for the slaves. I don't know about the mines."

Torien was silent. The girl was looking at him over the woman's shoulder—unblinking, contemptuous, as though she were daring him to call it a lie. Alluin sat motionless behind him, waiting for him to speak, because in the end the decision was his alone, but he knew Alluin's thoughts like his own, and he knew Alluin, too, was thinking of the empty streets outside the shanty and the silence like a bated breath—fear hanging over the city like a plague.

He rocked back on his heels and got to his feet. The shanty spun as he stood. "This is what will happen. In the morning, I take ship for Tasso. You'll go with me down to the harbor, and you'll show me the *jente*'s ships, and I'll investigate crew and cargo for myself. If I find nothing to convince me of this slaving business, then I'll leave it for the governor's court to decide your fate. Otherwise I'll do what I can from Tasso to see this thing ended and those responsible made to pay for it—Modigno and Vareno alike. In any case, I swear to you

I'll see justice done. If you've told me the truth, you've nothing to fear by that."

The woman's fingers were tight on the girl's arms. "I tell you the truth," she said. Her voice was low and hard, and in it he heard what she left unsaid: that she knew the value of Vareno oaths just as she knew the value of Vareno justice. The truth made no difference to whim.

He ground out the fire under one boot heel. "I'll take the watch," he said to Alluin. It was perhaps four hours to dawn, and he knew he would not sleep.

II

They left the girl at the shanty, on account of her ankle. He had weighed this in his head and decided there was no need to bring her along: as long as the woman was in their hands, the girl would not try to run. Nevertheless, it took the woman speaking in impassioned Modigno to persuade the girl to stay behind, and the girl had glared at Torien in cold fury all the while the woman spoke, and he had understood then that neither of them believed the woman would return.

Heat came with the cloudless dawn. By the time they had come down to the waterfront, there was sweat gathered under the cheek-pieces of his helmet, coalescing on his eyelashes under the brim of the helmet and trickling down his back between his shoulder-blades. The breeze off the water was pushing the heat into his face like a bellows, and with it the tang of salt and the smell of fish and garlic and the clamor of voices and the shrill cries of the gulls wheeling above. Under the bandage, his shoulder was stiff and crusted with dried blood, but there was little pain if he kept his arm very still. They were on foot in the crowd along the quay, the woman walking ahead, Alluin beside him leading both horses. He stopped to buy a pomegranate off a dark-skinned girl who swung down her bushel from her shoulders and accepted the bronze with a solemn, wordless bow. Torien cradled the pomegranate carefully in his left hand and pared it into quarters with his belt knife. He gave half to Alluin. The woman had turned around to wait. He saw her eyes follow the fruit into Alluin's hand. She saw that he had seen it and turned her face sharply away. The girl had vanished with her bushel into the crowd. Torien sheathed his knife. When he came up to the woman, he took her elbow in his fingers and put the pomegranate quarters into her hand when she turned.

She looked at it in her hand for a moment, frozen, while the crowd streamed heedless around them. Then she shook her head, once, wordlessly. Her mouth was tight. She did not look in his face. She pushed the pomegranate back to him on her palm. He did not take it. "Tell me the last time you ate."

Her eyes were away over his shoulder to the harbor and the sea-line at his back. She shook her head again. The pomegranate trembled on her palm. "I do not ask for it. I do not want it."

"Tell me how you support the girl. What's your trade?"

"I grow up on the sea. I have boat and nets of my own. It is enough for us."

"Neither you nor the girl ate last night or this morning."

"I sell my fish to pay my debt. When I pay this debt, then we eat. It is enough."

He was silent, studying her. There was nothing of pride in her face. Rather, there was a nervousness that came, he supposed, of knowing everything must be repaid one way or another: nothing came freely, not really. He closed her fingers around the pomegranate and pushed her hand back. "Take it as the first part of my payment," he said. "If you've told me the truth, I'll owe you better than that."

She did not eat it. She unwound the woolen scarf from her hair and knotted the pomegranate into it and tucked the scarf into her belt, and he knew she meant it for the girl. When she finished, she bowed to him, quickly, uncertainly, and her eyes came up at last to his and lingered there, for a moment. She searched across his face as though she were trying to read it. Then she turned away again. She said nothing, but there was more in her bow than she might have put into words.

They went south and east along the quay, the city rising above them on the left-hand side of the street, single-masted fishing boats knocking against the quay on the right, the sea running to the sky beyond. In the distance—through the heat-haze curling off the rooftops along the quay—he could see the lighthouse at the point, and a three-tiered Imperial navy galley lying at anchor just off the point toward Epyris, and the gentle blue curve of the world at the sea-line. After one quick, sweeping glance, he kept his eyes from the water. The vastness of it and the emptiness of it made his heart drop to the pit of his stomach. As on the first day, when he had looked out over the water from the fort walls, he had the sudden, inexplicable urge to fall flat on his face and cling to solid earth for fear of slipping off. He was glad he had not eaten the pomegranate.

Beside him, Alluin spat a seed and said, "You've thought about what it means—what we're doing."

"You mean if she's telling the truth?"

"Do you think she is?"

"I think I've given her a better chance at it than she'd have gotten in court. And I think you know that as well as I do."

"Regardless. You'd agree she's got motivation to lie. She's got the girl."

He glanced at Alluin sidelong. "You think I should have given them up," he said. It was not a question, but rather a sudden realization.

Alluin was silent, for a moment. "Because I know you," he said, finally, "because I know the way you think—because if you didn't outright assume she was telling the truth, at least you're going to make sure she gets to prove she was lying."

"I thought that was called justice."

"I want to know if you've thought about what it means if she's lying."

"She and the girl face judgment from an Imperial court. Most likely it'll be execution. I know what it means, Alluin."

"I'm not talking about the court. I'm talking about this—now.

You've all but asked her to introduce you to the *jente*. You didn't give any thought to the fact that she can, that she agreed to do it. For all you know, she's on the *jente*'s coin herself. I'm not sure you could have given her an easier way to be rid of you if you'd tried. Whether or not he's smuggling slaves, I doubt the *jente* will appreciate your investigation into his ships, and I imagine he has his own way of dealing with nuisances."

"She doesn't eat well enough to be on the *jente*'s coin."

"Then she owes him money, and she figures you're worth enough as a hostage to make it up. Even if you *are* Cesino blood."

The woman had stopped and was watching them over her shoulder as she waited.

"You can wait for me at the fort if you think you can find your way back," Torien said.

"You can go to Hell," Alluin said, "but I want you to remember that I'm speaking as the one who hasn't been knifed. Every once in a while you might listen to me."

A line of trade ships lay moored at the quay ahead of them: tall sailing ships and long, low galleys, rising and falling gently against their mooring stones in the hot salt wind. The quay crawled like an ant hill. Streams of slaves, stripped to the waist under the sun's glare, flowed up and down the gangplanks from quay to ship-holds and back again, shoulders bent under jugs of wine and oil and bushels of grain and bolts of silk and linen cloth. Merchants and clerks crowded under the awnings at a short remove from the water's edge, ledgers in hand; ship masters and pilots huddled together in clumps

over navigational charts and cargo manifests. A little way down the
quay, a group of slaves bound for auction sat chained at the foot of
a gangplank, silently waiting, while their ship master haggled prices
with a dealer and a harbor official hovered by to collect the sale tax.

From out of the crowd, someone tugged at Torien's left elbow.
The blood cracked and welled up fresh. Pain lanced down his arm.
He sucked a breath through his teeth, stumbling against Alluin,
reaching belatedly for his sword, but Alluin had already dropped the
horses' reins and pushed past him to jerk a stunned Modigno boy
forward by the arms. The boy's unslung skin of milk slipped from his
hands and burst open on the paving stones.

Around them, the crowd withdrew at once, falling back in a
wide circle. The woman stood at the far edge of the circle, her hands
cupped over her mouth. Down the quay, the ship master and the
slave dealer looked up from their haggling at the sudden silence.

Alluin let go the boy's arms. The boy dropped wordlessly to
his knees and folded over to press palms and forehead against the
paving stones at Torien's feet. Torien met Alluin's eyes over the boy's
shaking body. After a moment's hesitation, Alluin dipped his chin.
He bent down and drew the boy up and crouched beside him with
an arm around his shoulders. He spoke to him in awkward, broken
Modigno: "No matter, no matter, it'll be all right—"

Torien picked up the horses' reins. There was a sickness inside
him. Of necessity, the boy must cower. Of necessity, the boy must fall
on his face against the street and wait wordless for judgment, because
it was in his, Torien's, power to open the boy's throat and send his

family to a slaver's block for the mere offense of his touch—and no matter how they might speak of justice, they all of them understood that, deep down.

He said to Alluin, "Ask him how much in compensation for the milk."

Alluin pulled over the dripping skin with his free hand and showed it to the boy. "*Cuenta?*"

The boy shook his head against Alluin's shoulder.

"An eagle," Torien said to Alluin. He looked into the boy's tear-streaked face. "*Sente*," he said. "I'm sorry."

The circle was breaking around them, the crowd spreading out again over the quay. Alluin came to take the reins. "Enough. You need a surgeon, Tor."

"When this is done."

Alluin's eyes ran down his arm. Torien followed his gaze. There was blood dribbling in a thin line from his sleeve down to his hand, over his wrist-guard. He shook his head. "If the *jente* kills me anyway, it doesn't matter."

"If that's the kind of logic they teach you in Cesin, I begin to understand how we made such short work of your people under Taigo."

"I have to do this, Alluin."

"Because you're an idiot," Alluin said. "I know."

When they reached the woman, Torien said, shortly, "How much further?" He did not want to talk about the boy, and particularly he did not want to talk about his shoulder.

The woman said nothing of either. Perhaps she saw it in his face. "The two-masted ship it sails today. I see them load the slaves in the night."

He could see it moored further down the quay, lying a little way out on account of its draft. It was full-laden and riding low in the water: a deep-hulled sailing ship, bigger by far than the ships which came up the river to dock at Vessy, but he recognized the shape. "Wine?"

"The harbor master he thinks so."

He studied the ship. The gangplank had been taken up; he could see the crew moving about on the deck. The ship was waiting for the tide. "If I inspect cargo and manifest, I'll find less wine and more water than I should—provided you've told me the truth."

"Yes."

"If cargo and manifest are equal, then I can assume you've lied to me."

The woman hesitated. Then she said again, "Yes." Her voice was low but firm.

"The boat," Torien said to Alluin.

There was a single-masted fishing boat tied up at the quay below them. The boatman and a boy who must be his son sat cross-legged at the water's edge, mending their nets. Alluin looked at the boat and the bent-headed pair, then at the ship beyond. His mouth was a thin, tight line. "I'll go—and the woman."

"We'll all go," Torien said.

Alluin was silent, for a moment. When he spoke again it was in

Cesino, which he spoke well but carefully. "One of us should stay behind. Otherwise this is suicide."

"Stay behind, then."

"Listen to me, Tor. On land, it would be different. On land, we'd have an outlet, however bad the odds. This way they've got us against a wall from the start."

"If you're right and the woman is on the *jente*'s coin, then we've a hostage."

"If I'm right and she owes him the tunic off her back, then she won't make a difference to them."

"I'm valuable to them—you said so yourself. They'll keep me alive any way it goes. *Logically*, if either of us stays behind, it should be you."

There was another stretch of silence between them. He could see in Alluin's face both the counterargument and the realization that it was useless. The woman, who had understood none of the exchange but had guessed its meaning, shifted on her feet, uneasy. Alluin swore at last in Vareno and put the reins in Torien's hand. He went down to the water's edge to speak with the boatman.

They left the horses in the boy's keeping. The boatman kept the sail furled and sat in the stern to row. They moved out slowly and rhythmically across the water, the little boat rising and falling on the waves in the stiff wind. Torien sat at the prow, gripping the sides of the boat in white-knuckled hands, keeping his eyes fixed on the stretch of floor between his feet. When they came up beside the ship, the boatman rested his oars and leaned out over the water to knot a line on one of the mooring rings. He stood and called up to the deck in Modigno. A dark head appeared over the railing above them. Another line came tumbling down into the boat. The boatman caught it and drew it taut and stood holding it while the boat settled gently against the ship.

Alluin was first up the ship's side, casting a savage glance to Torien as his feet left the boat. He moved slowly and carefully up the holds and swung over the railing, vanishing onto the deck. The woman followed him. Torien stood, unsteadily. His heart was quivering in his stomach. He took a bronze from his belt and held it out to the boatman. "*Bayas,*" he said. It was effort to speak; his mouth was dry.

The boatman bowed and took the coin, still holding the line. Torien pulled himself up one-handed onto the holds. He clung to the ship's side with the boat bobbing a foot below him, the deck railing unbearably far above him. He fought the sudden panic and made himself move. He lunged and got his right elbow over the railing and hung for a moment kicking against the ship's side, scrabbling with his feet for a hold. He found a ledge under his toes and pushed himself unceremoniously over the railing. He landed on his knees, his right hand spread flat against the deck, his left cradled against his stomach, the blood pounding in his head.

He stood, blinking in the bright sunlight. Someone took his elbow to steady him. He thought it was Alluin, but when the dizziness cleared he saw Alluin standing with the woman a little way across the deck, flanked by two armed crewmen. The man at his elbow was Modigno. From the quality of his dress, Torien took him to be the ship master. His bearded face was as brown and blunt and humorless as weathered wood. His fingers around Torien's elbow were thick and stubby, but even so Torien could tell he knew the use of the curved blade hung naked at his belt.

The Modigno said, in smooth Vareno, "You're a fool to come, Commander."

There were two more crewmen watching carelessly from the foremast. Otherwise the deck was empty. If this was an ambush, it was a poor one. "I could put your own sword through your gut before you let go my arm. You're a fool to stand so close."

The Modigno smiled. He dropped Torien's arm and bowed, ironically. Torien darted a glance to Alluin over the Modigno's head. Alluin was scowling. Beside him, the woman was as rigid as a spear shaft.

The Modigno straightened. He waved a hand. The two crewmen, moving quickly, took the woman by the elbows and flung her to her knees on the deck. In one smooth motion, one of them slipped his blade from his belt and cut her throat.

Torien stepped forward out of instinct, reaching for his sword. He froze in mid-step when the woman fell, still fumbling one-handed at his sword hilt, and for a moment he stood blinking dumbly at her crumpled body. He saw it in peculiar detail—her coarse black hair spilled loose over her shoulders; her arms spread wide; her head turned on one cheek against the deck; her blood crawling across the boards from the red gash grinning under her chin. He straightened, slowly. Alluin had managed to get his sword from its sheath; it dangled loosely in his limp fingers. There was white shock in his olive-skinned face.

Torien swallowed. He let go his sword. "She was to be kept alive."

The Modigno pushed past him toward the quarterdeck. "You may carry my apologies to the fort."

"You misunderstand the nature of my business here."

The Modigno swung around to look at him from the foot of the quarterdeck steps. His face was blank, but his eyes on Torien's were sharp and cool. "Explain to me, then, the nature of your business."

"You're to give me passage to Tasso. I've horses on the quay. You can send one of your boats for them."

Alluin had recovered himself. He sheathed his sword and stepped carefully over the spreading blood to Torien's side. The Modigno followed Alluin's movement with his eyes. "I've no room for horses."

"Put some of your cargo overboard. Do you think I care?"

The two crewmen, who had taken up the woman's body by the arms to drag it to the railing, paused at their work.

"I imagine you know the cost of refusing me," Torien said.

A flicker of emotion passed over the Modigno's face: hatred, fear. The Modigno jerked his chin to the crewmen. "Finish it. Ready a boat."

Something dark and wet dropped beside Torien from the railing. He turned to see the girl pulling herself up against the railing, seawater puddling at her feet. She threw herself at him, limbs flailing, heedless, screaming in Modigno, sobbing intermittently. He caught one of her wrists and held her away from him while Alluin slid his arms around her from behind. He let go her wrist. She squirmed in Alluin's grip like a caught fish, twisting against his chest, kicking his ankles with her sound foot. "Bastard! *Cobarte*! I tell her you lie!" There were tears mingled with the seawater on her face. She slumped exhausted against Alluin's chest. She bowed her head over his arm. "I tell her you lie," she said. Her voice was broken. Her shoulders shook. Alluin let her go, gently, and she sank to her knees on the deck and folded over to weep softly and bitterly into her hands.

The Modigno had come down from the quarterdeck. He knelt beside the girl and lifted her up from the waist. He brushed back her dripping hair from her face and knotted his fingers in it, jerking her head up. He ran a finger over the girl's cheek and said something in his own tongue.

Torien said, "Enough."

The Modigno let go the girl's hair. He stood. "Fool. Do you think I'd lay a hand on her? She's worth a thousand eagles or more untouched."

"If she were yours to sell."

The Modigno's face hardened. "My payment. In return for doing your dirty work."

"That you and your kind aren't hanging on the fort wall is payment enough. The girl is mine."

He half expected the Modigno's blade across his throat in response, and judging from Alluin's face Alluin expected the same, but the Modigno only looked at him. At length, he bowed, too deeply and too long. "As my lord wishes."

"Tell one of your crewmen to show us our berths," Torien said.

The Modigno's lip curled. "This is a trade ship, Commander, not a pleasure boat on the Breche. You'll berth with the crew."

"We'll berth in your cabin," Torien said, "and you can lodge a complaint with the harbor master."

"You realize," Alluin said, when he had drawn the curtain across the cabin doorway, "how easy it would be for you and I both to take a sudden fever and die between here and Tasso?"

Torien slid down against the bulkhead with his helmet in his hands. There was pain hammering a steady rhythm against his temples, pulsing black in his eyes. "Fever?"

Alluin came over from the doorway and knelt beside him and started loosening the buckles of his cuirass. "I mean you didn't exactly make a friend."

"I don't exactly want him for a friend. But if he were going to kill us he'd have done it already. Why wait and let the inspectors see us? He's not going to kill us. He's too afraid to kill us. Afraid of the fort? Of the governor? I don't know. Afraid of someone more important than we are." He flinched as Alluin's fingers worked at the shoulder buckle. "Anyway, you keep—keep forgetting how valuable I am."

Alluin tugged the cuirass down his arm and spread open the jerkin underneath. He studied Torien's shoulder without touching it.

His mouth was tight. He sat back on his heels. "I'm going to see if these pirates have a doctor among them."

"Wait." Torien indicated the girl with his chin. "Bring her here."

She had sunk down against the opposite bulkhead when Alluin had first let her go and sat now with her knees drawn up, her cheek pressed to the wall, her hair falling loose over her looped arms. She had stopped crying. She was sitting very still and tense, her eyes flat, but when Alluin reached for her arm she lunged away from him with a choked cry. He caught her by the elbow, pulling her back. She made to get to her feet. He slid his left hand easily under her knees, his right across her shoulders. He brought her in his arms across the room and put her down on her knees in front of Torien. He sat behind her with his arms around her, his hands clamped over her forearms to hold her still. "Quickly," he said.

Torien looked into the girl's face. She met his eyes unblinking, though she was shaking with anger, muscles fluttering in her jaw and throat. Her hands were clenched to trembling fists under Alluin's hands. He said, quietly, "It'll be dark enough when we pass the point that you can swim for it."

"*Cobarte.*" Her voice was low but bitter. "If you want to be rid of me, then you must kill me, and if you do not kill me I swear I find a way to kill you. I swear it on her body. I swear I open your throat. I do not care what they do to me for it."

"Opening my throat isn't justice for your mother any more than opening my shoulder was justice for your brother."

"You bring her to them. You let them kill her."

"If I'd known what would happen, I wouldn't have made her come. I was trying to help her."

"I hear what you say to them. I hear you say to them I am yours."

"It was pretense. If I hadn't said it, you'd be down in the hold with the rest of their *cargo*, bound for an auction block in Tasso. I swear to you I'm trying to see justice done."

"There is no such thing as justice."

He sat up from the bulkhead. He took her upper arms in his hands, ignoring the twinge in his shoulder. "Listen to me. I'll speak to you plainly because you deserve as much. I will see this thing ended, or I will die in the attempt. I promise you that. I ask you give me the chance for it."

The girl said, very softly, "Vareno promises are nothing."

"It isn't a Vareno promise." He let go her arms. He unsheathed his belt knife and laid the edge of the blade on his left palm. "Vareni don't swear oaths in blood. This is a Cesino promise."

Alluin said, "Tor." But he said nothing else.

Torien opened the skin across the breadth of his palm. He had seen the chieftains of the hill tribes do it when they came down to Vessy to swear fealty to his father and to the Empire. He had seen, too, the reckoning for the breaking of a blood oath—the earthly reckoning, at least—because when the Dobryni had risen in failed rebellion five summers ago, and the survivors had been brought by the allied chieftains to Vessy, his father had let the chieftains execute their own manner of justice, and he had watched at his father's side while they did it.

He waited until the blood had welled up in a dark line. Then he held up his hand for the girl to see. "My body to Death," he said, "my soul to Hell, if I do not keep my word."

The girl looked at his hand in silence, her jaw clenched. Then she raised her eyes to his face. She searched it over as the woman had done on the quay—as though she were trying to read something written there. He waited, unmoving, the knife against his thigh, the blood running in thin ribbons over his palm. Through the curtained doorway, he could hear the ship master shouting orders from the quarterdeck and the shuddering groan of the ship's timbers as the anchor was drawn up.

Alluin shifted at the girl's back. "Torien," he said.

The girl said, "It is your name—Torien?"

"Torien Berio Risto. My father is Lord Risto of Cesin."

"To know a name is to know a person true. Among my people we say this. We do not give our names so easy." The girl swallowed. There was a tear slipping down her nose to her lips. "My name is Lida," she said. She pulled her hand from Alluin's hand. She reached and touched Torien's palm, tracing the gash with her fingers. "I accept your oath, Torien Risto."

III

"I don't foresee a shortage of camels anytime soon," Alluin said.

They were standing together at the edge of the quay—or Torien was standing, glad for the feeling of solid rock underfoot. The crossing had taken the better part of a week, and he had spent most of it retching into the pot in the ship master's cabin. Alluin had deposited himself onto a coiling of heavy ship's cable piled up unused at the water's edge. He had taken off his helmet and was draped along the coils with his hands behind his head, fingers laced together, long legs stretched out and crossed at the ankles. Through half-closed eyes, he was watching a camel driver assemble his train a little way down the shore, southward past the arched harbor gate. "Wonderful animals," he said, "and fierce in battle."

"I'll recommend your transfer to the camel troops when we reach the fort."

"Camel troops," Alluin said. He sat up, suddenly, swinging his legs in. "My father would be proud."

There was a thin edge of bitterness to his voice—inaudible, perhaps, to other ears, but Torien heard it. He cast a sidelong glance to Alluin's face, but Alluin was looking down the quay and his face was blank. "When do you suppose the offloading happens?" he said. Despite the clamor of traffic on the quay, he spoke quietly.

"Night," Torien said.

"You think he's paid up with the city guard?"

"Possibly. Not necessarily. If not, he's paid up with someone who knows how to make a diversion."

"Figure the camel man knows anything about it?"

"It's worth finding out."

Alluin's fingers slipped down absently to his sword grip and drummed a swift, silent rhythm on the ivory. "Now?"

Torien shook his head. "No. I don't want our Modigno friend getting wind of it. The fort can handle it."

"Unless he's paid up with the fort."

Torien darted another glance to Alluin's face, uncertain whether he had meant that as a joke, but the question never left his lips: just then Alluin nodded to the ship and pushed himself up from the coils. "The horses," he said. He reached for his helmet. "I was beginning to think they'd tossed them overboard for ballast."

They went on foot along the quay and out from the city through the harbor gate and then, mounting, westward over the open sand from the waterside, keeping the city walls close. They would make better time this way than through the city. Besides, he wanted to get a sense of the terrain. Here by the shore, the sand was as bronzed and hard-packed as clay; further out, the wind was kicking it up in swift spirals along the sunburned tops of the dunes—the dunes themselves stretching to the western sky, as far as the eye could see.

The fort lay due west of the city at a distance of perhaps two miles. A strip of wide paved road led between them, running a straight line out from the western gate of the city, flanked at intervals by bone-white stone markers like rows of broken teeth. The road passed close under the southern wall of the fort; then the paving ended and the markers marched on alone westward into the sand. That was the Salt Road. Back at Vione and away from official ears they called it the Blood Road, and he understood this was not only because it poured life into the city Tasso like a heart vein, but also because so much blood had been spilled on it and for it. The Imperial presence here had accomplished little in that regard. The tribes had been slaughtering each other over this salt-rich strip of desert for centuries, and Torien supposed it was typical Vareno arrogance to imagine they would lay it aside by reason of one Imperial fort.

He studied the fort as they approached. It had been built with the administration and defense of the Road as its immediate object; accordingly, it was laid out on a north-south line, its main gate opening southward onto the Road, its heaviest defenses arrayed along the southern and western walls. It was, in fact, an imposing structure—the walls of sun-bleached sandstone blocks wide and deep as he was tall, wind-blasted smooth and seamless as marble, tall enough to be near unscalable. The towers at each corner were half again as tall as the walls. There would be a clear view of the harbor from that height, and of the desert for miles and miles around.

He ran his eyes along the fort's near wall, the eastern wall, lingering a moment at the base. There were date palms and brushy scrub trees overspreading a broad, shallow basin close by the foot of the wall. He recognized the presence of water. He reined in and glanced back over his shoulder to the city, then in a swift arc across the barren sand around them.

Alluin reined in alongside him. "What is it?"

"Look at the wall."

"The trees?"

"Fresh water—the only source of it I can see."

"Convenient."

"For us."

"You don't think the locals appreciate our watch-care over their water supply?"

"I don't imagine they've much choice."

"Such an elegant way to ensure we are hated as well as feared," Alluin said.

Torien had expected—in the mind's-eye image he had been building since Vione—that the Tasso garrison would have the sour, brittle air of men left too long on the fringes, their discipline corroded in salt and sand, their dignity forgotten if not their technical ability in itself. He had seen it before, in men come back to Vione from terms spent on the frontier. They had not forgotten how to fight—in fact, they fought more bitterly and bloodily than before—but they had forgotten why they fought, and that was worse. But—looking around now, as he and Alluin passed beneath the gate arch onto the broad, guttered thoroughfare running north-and-south from gate to headquarters—he saw the fort well-ordered, functioning as smoothly as an oiled blade, weapons and gear polished and ready, men quick to attention, and he was conscious, all at once and painfully, of his own appearance—of the smell of brine and sweat soaked deep into his tunic and cloak and the leather of his jerkin and cuirass; of the fact he had not bathed properly since his first night in Modigne, a week ago.

But there was nervous excitement in him just the same, remembered for the first time since that night in Modigne, as they swung down from their saddles at the headquarters steps. He had asked for this commission, after all. There had been other postings available to him, better postings—more prestigious postings, at least. He might have stayed on to train cavalry at Vione. They had offered him so, and a yearly bonus to the sum of two thousand eagles, and that was nothing in comparison to the bonus offered him by Maris Pavo, High Commander of the Imperial Guard, for accepting a Guardsman's commission. He had turned down both offers in favor of Tasso. Part of that had been because there was a foolhardy, boyish desire in him for action, for the opportunity to unsheathe his sword and prove his worth in blood, but deeper down and unspoken it was because the Empire had been built not by the Guard nor by the instructors at Vione, but by ordinary folk who did their duty without thought for what they stood to gain from it.

A young lieutenant, in full harness and crested helmet, was waiting for them at the top of the steps.

"Commander Risto," he said, "Lieutenant Senna." His voice was assured, proper, but tinged with the provinces. From his blunt-nosed bronze face, Torien suspected he was not full Vareno blood—half Modigno, possibly, or of the islands. He saluted them with a swift upward flick of his right hand, appraising them both in turn. His dark eyes were as keen as a surgeon's probe and startlingly cold. "I am Lieutenant Tarrega, Commander Espere's adjutant. The Commander has asked me to show you to his office."

He had built a mind's-eye image of Espere, too: a stout, petty, middling officer, shunted away to the frontier because he was no use elsewhere—the sort of man to spend his career behind a desk if he had stayed at Vione. He had begun dismantling the image inside the gate, and he discarded it now completely. Espere was a tough, sun-browned veteran, his stocky legs bowed from long days in the saddle, his fingers deft for the handling of weapons. His tight, wiry black curls had gone to silver-gray here and there; Torien judged him to be perhaps mid-way past forty. He was leaning against his desk when they entered the office, his right leg stretched out straight to the floor, his left propped up and knee-bent on the edge of the desktop, foot swinging carelessly. He had his service knife in his right hand, a bowl of raw red meat balanced on his thigh. He was cutting up the meat in long strips and flinging it down piece by piece to the floor. A giant spotted yellow cat lay at his feet, tearing at the meat in silent fury, head bobbing, jaws pumping. Its whiskers and the paving stones around it were flecked with blood.

Torien's hand, racing up in salute, faltered a little. He brought it quickly back down before Espere could see.

Espere did not raise his head from his work. He made no move to return the salute. "Your voyage was uneventful, I hope."

Alluin found his tongue first. "Yes, sir. Thank you."

"You were lucky." Espere cut another strip of meat and slung it from his knife-point. The cat lunged for it, rattling the silver chain around its neck. "The Modigno ship was a foolhardy choice. I do not tolerate foolhardiness in my officers. I trust you will remember this in the future."

Torien risked a glance sidelong to Alluin. Alluin's eyes met his very briefly, and Torien saw the question there. He shrugged, as openly as he dared. He did not speak. A thin lash of annoyance flicked over him: Espere was deliberately toying with them.

Alluin turned his eyes back to Espere. "Sir, how did you—?"

"The harbor master is under orders." Espere put the empty dish down and reached for the finger-cloth bundled up beside him on the desk. He wiped his hands and his knife blade. He sheathed the knife at his belt and stood up at last to face them. "He sends me word: every ship, every itinerary, every manifest. I've found it a necessary measure in curtailing smuggling and piracy." His eyes passed dismissively over Alluin and came to rest on Torien's face. "It's your custom to let your adjutant speak for you, Commander Risto?"

"Now and then I let him speak his own mind, sir."

Espere's face was like stone. "I assume—perhaps too generously—

you appreciate the risk to you, Commander, as the son of a noble house—a pointless risk, and one which may well have threatened Imperial security. You're aware of the sort of demands which might have been made upon your father in exchange for your life?"

Annoyance licked over him again. "No, sir. Perhaps you could elaborate for me, sir."

"You think this occasion for flippancy, Commander?"

Alluin intervened—dependable, as always. "Sir, we intended to speak with you on the matter of the ship."

Espere's eyes did not stray from Torien's face. "Did you so?"

"Yes, sir. We discovered certain discrepancies in the Modigno's cargo manifest, sir."

"Explain."

"He's smuggling slaves, sir."

There was a moment's silence in which Espere's eyes swiveled at last from Torien to Alluin.

"We're not sure how many—or where he plans to market them, sir." The latter was, Torien had decided, necessary falsehood. They had only Lida's word now on the mines, and to produce the girl as a witness might well be to incriminate her for an attack on a soldier. "But we know he only paid harbor taxes on three thousand jugs of very bad Galleno. The wine should be criminal in itself, sir, as Commander Risto can attest. He made an uninformed decision to partake and spent the next three days regretting it into a pot."

Espere had turned away on one heel. He picked up a tablet from his desk and read it to himself while Alluin spoke, his eyes going quickly back and forth across the lines, his face blank. He snapped the tablet shut and swung back around. "You've seen these slaves, Lieutenant? Or is this guesswork?"

"We haven't seen them, sir." Alluin was unfazed. "We counted the crew. Twelve deck crewmen, the pilot, the cook, the master himself, five slaves. Commander Risto and I were the only recorded passengers. You know harbor regulations require two jugs of drinking water per head per day. A six-day voyage, twenty-two souls aboard— not quite three hundred jugs in total, sir."

"Yes." Espere's voice was cool.

"Sir, the ship quit the harbor at Modigne with nearly eight hundred jugs of water stowed, and considerably less than three thousand jugs of wine."

Espere's chin came up.

"He might have a hundred slaves aboard," Alluin said, "maybe more: it's highly unlikely he feels compelled to abide by standard water rationing with regard to his contraband."

Espere's eyes were narrowed. He was impressed or he was contemptuous; Torien was not sure which. "And how does he intend to dispose of his contraband, Lieutenant?"

"We think he means to move them off the ship tonight. He'll have bribed the harbor master or the guard, possibly both, or he'll have arranged a diversion—and I've my suspicions about the intentions of the camel driver waiting directly out the harbor gate, but on that matter Commander Risto felt it was best to defer judgment to you."

"Lieutenant," Espere said.

Torien had forgotten Tarrega's presence. The lieutenant was standing half-hidden and noiseless in shadow just inside the office doorway. He drew himself up sharply to attention. The tail of his helmet crest rustled stiffly across the shoulders of his cuirass as he straightened. "Sir."

"Take a column of twelve horse down to the harbor and have a look at the ship. And at the Lieutenant's camel train. I'll expect your report in two hours. I'll expect it to be worth my while."

Tarrega's face was blank. "Sir," he said. He flicked back his cloak and turned to go.

"Commander," Torien said.

Espere looked at him; the lieutenant, too, pausing in the doorway to throw a glance over his shoulder.

"Sir, it's more than a matter of the harbor tax. There's a chance some of them are free-born citizens."

Espere did not blink. "You mean some of this contraband, Commander?"

"Yes, sir."

"You think some of them may have been abducted."

"Yes, sir."

"You have evidence?"

It was laid down like brickwork in his head, piece by piece to the inevitable conclusion. He could make his case, and he could do it well and soundly, and he could count on Alluin to support him—not only because Alluin would stand stubbornly at his side for anything, but because Alluin knew the truth of it, too—and in the end none of it would matter, because none of it would hold up before a court, and he knew that just as surely as Alluin did, just as surely as Espere would.

"I've no verifiable evidence," he said. "But I recommend they be allowed to make their own pleas. At the very least, I recommend the master and his crew be examined upon arrest."

Espere tilted up his chin. "You suspected all this before taking ship."

Torien said nothing.

"It is, in fact, the reason you sought passage on this particular ship—come now, Commander." Espere smiled, but his eyes were cool and hard upon Torien's face. "Or did you choose the tub for its seaworthiness?"

If Espere recognized this part of it as a lie, he might be forgiven for believing the same of the rest. "I had some suspicion, sir," Torien admitted.

"A witness?"

"Yes, sir."

"And you judged it advisable to take the matter into your own hands rather than present it to the authorities in Modigne?"

"Yes, sir."

"Having already decided to dispense with Imperial justice at that point."

"According to Imperial justice there is no case, sir."

"Yet you expected I would act upon it, even so?"

"The only thing that would matter to Imperial justice is that the witness put a knife in my back to draw my attention. The rest of it becomes incidental."

Espere's voice dripped mockery. "You are very open-hearted, Commander, to go under a knife and think first of the grievances of the knifeman. Doubtless the rest of us could stand to learn—"

"The Imperial authorities in Modigne are directly involved in the abduction and enslavement of Imperial citizens. That was the grievance. For my part, I could understand violence as the recourse. An Imperial court wouldn't—not a Modigno court, at any rate, and I saw firsthand how they go about shutting this thing up in Modigne."

It was Espere's turn to be silent. Out of the corner of his eye, Torien saw Alluin shift his weight from foot to foot. The lieutenant was frozen in the doorway.

Espere said, "Lieutenant Senna." His face was inscrutable.

"Yes, sir," said Alluin.

"I am interested in your opinion on the matter."

"Commander Risto and I are of the same opinion, sir." He said it calmly, without hesitation, but Torien saw his shoulders stiffen, as though he were bracing himself.

Espere was silent, his eyes going back and forth between them. "You realize, both of you," he said, finally, "the seriousness of the accusation, the penalties incumbent upon you should this go before a court and the ruling come down against you—as it almost certainly would."

"So you'll do nothing," Torien said.

"I will do what I can, Commander, and you will accept it as enough. Is that understood?"

Pride kept him from dipping his chin, lowering his eyes. He felt his face heat up. "Sir," he said, too quickly, too vehemently. Alluin shifted again beside him.

"Lieutenant." Espere spoke past him to Tarrega. "I've changed my mind. I'll handle the business at the harbor myself. You may acquaint Commander Risto with the fort in my absence, if he feels he has the strength for it."

Tarrega said, softly, "Yes, sir."

Alluin's eyes came briefly to Torien's. "Sir, with your permission—"

"If I require your assistance, I will send and ask for it." Espere's voice was cool. "As far as you and Commander Risto are concerned— until I determine otherwise—the matter has been settled. Do I make myself clear?"

Torien said nothing. Alluin said, more loudly than was necessary as though to cover his silence, "Abundantly clear, sir."

"Dismissed," said Espere. "All of you."

Torien kept his eyes fixed upon the stretch of bare sandstone wall above Espere's right shoulder as he saluted, because he knew if he met Espere's gaze the anger would spill out perhaps uncontrollably, and because he knew Espere was expecting as much, and he did not want to give him the satisfaction. He darted a glance to Alluin as they left the office. Alluin's shoulders were still stiff, his harsh mouth pressed tight. He was uncharacteristically silent—conscious, perhaps, of how very fine a line they trod, and of the lieutenant going before them up the corridor, but either Tarrega sensed their hostility and wished to remove himself as its object, or else he meant to signal his own contempt, because he deliberately distanced himself from them as they walked.

Only when they had come out onto the steps in bright sunlight, the iron-bound doors rumbling shut behind them, did Alluin say, in an undertone nearly lost on the wind sweeping east-to-west across the face of the building, "I believe that was a threat."

Torien did not answer. From where he stood, here at the top of the steps, he could just see over the fort's eastern wall. He could see, with startling clarity in the dry air, the Road like a pale scar tracing back eastward over the sand to the city, and the sea beyond—a narrow ribbon of indigo between sand and sky, breathlessly still save for the pinpoint flash of gulls' wings in the sunlight. He could not see the quay, but he knew the ship was there. Frustration and the stark realization of his own powerlessness gnawed at him like a cancer. How simple it should be to take a column of twelve horse and settle this thing. He had supposed that was how it would happen, and he knew now that had been his failing—his alone, not Alluin's, because Alluin had pressed for immediate action and he, Torien, had counseled against it.

"Whatever you're thinking, Tor," Alluin said, quietly, "we can't do much until we lose our watchdog."

Tarrega was waiting for them at the bottom of the steps. He was showing himself politely disinterested, his face half turned away and hidden in shadow under the brim of his helmet, his right palm resting with measured carelessness on the pommel of his sword. Absently, Torien wondered whether he were any good in a fight. From sheer observation, he would not guess so—the lieutenant was too rigid, too decorous, like the young officers of senatorial stock on the parade ground at Vione—but he was unwilling to discount the possibility. If Espere weren't the sort to tolerate foolhardiness among his staff, neither was he the sort to tolerate incompetence.

"We could leave him trussed up in the granary," Alluin said. "Leave the quartermaster to find him come supper time."

Torien smiled. "Tempting but unnecessary."

"Unnecessary but worthwhile," Alluin said, "if only for the expression on his face."

"Espere said he'll do what he can."

"And you trust him? Because I've the feeling he'd have given you piece by piece to his cat if you'd shown him any more cheek."

"I don't know that I trust him. What I *do* know is that we can't do anything until tonight, at the earliest—not if he's going down to the harbor himself."

"And if by tonight we're too late?"

Torien shook his head. "We've got the Modigno on the harbor tax. Espere can't deny that—if for no other reason than that disposal of the contraband falls to him by default, and a handsome cut of the profit. And no matter his own inclinations he won't be able to keep a ship-hold of kidnapped citizens quiet. At some point, he'll have to give the Modigno up for examination or risk suspicion of guilt himself."

"You assume he won't slip a blade between the Modigno's ribs for simplicity's sake."

"I assume he'll want to avoid the sorts of questions that would raise."

"What you fail to realize," said Alluin, "is that no one besides us seems to be asking those sorts of questions."

They walked the perimeter of the fort. For most of it, Tarrega was silent. Perhaps he thought their attention had gone down to the harbor with Espere. Perhaps it was a clumsy attempt at insubordination, in solidarity with his commander against the presumptuousness of newcomers. He hung back in the street while Torien and Alluin went down the stable row. A cavalry troop was just coming in to the stable yard from the Road. It was an irregular troop, not a standard column—scouts, judging by their light harness. Torien stood and watched with Alluin while they dismounted. He had supposed them to be local auxiliaries, as scouts typically were, but when the dust had settled he picked out Vareno faces among them, and one face that might have been Cesino, though he could not tell for sure. One man's eyes fell briefly on Torien's, across the yard. His gaze was hollow. In his dirt-streaked face, Torien recognized the same look of resignation as had been in the woman's face that night in the shanty in Modigne. The scout turned his head away without saluting.

When they rejoined Tarrega in the street, Torien said, "Auxiliaries?"

Tarrega said, "*Signi.*"

Torien's steps slowed. He looked back over his shoulder to the stable yard.

Tarrega said, "You've never seen *signi* before?" As an afterthought, he added, "Sir?"

"They don't post *signi* to Vione."

"But to Cesin?"

Perhaps to the Outland, to the furthest reaches of the mountains where the rebellious Brycigi still thrashed against the Imperial yoke; Torien did not know. "Is the Road so dangerous, then—that you use *signi* as scouts?"

Unexpectedly, Tarrega flashed a cool knife-blade smile. His teeth were very white. "The Mayasi," he said, "make it their peculiar habit to leave their prisoners stripped and staked out in the sand and dead of thirst or sun sickness or jackals, whichever comes first. Or they hold them alive, for interrogation, and from what I've seen of the few poor souls we've recovered—better to die in the sand. So the *signi* are useful twice over."

Torien looked at him. "They aren't citizens," Tarrega said. "It doesn't matter how they die. And they don't know anything to give up under torture."

By the time they had finished their circuit of the fort, the sun was hanging low and blood-red in the western sky, night shadows searching like long blue fingers between the barrack blocks and along the intersecting streets. In his quarters, he paused only long enough to rid himself of his helmet and boots and splash his salt-crusted face and cracked lips with water from the wash basin. Then he collapsed still in full harness on the cot. There was a stiffness in his left shoulder that spread all the way down to his fingertips, a lingering twinge of pain when he closed his hand. The mark of his oath was purple and scarring across his palm. The dry desert air would heal shoulder and hand quickly: the old Epyrian slave woman who had dressed the wounds for him on the ship had assured him so. The desert air was marvelous for the healing of wounds.

He heard the call from the gatehouse when Espere rode in from the city, and the tattoo of hoof beats up the thoroughfare. A little while later, he heard booted footfalls coming down the corridor. There was a voice at his doorway: "Commander Risto."

He sat up from the cot. He propped his elbows on his knees and rubbed his eyes with the heels of his hands. "Enter."

Tarrega ducked in through the curtain. He straightened to salute. "Commander Espere requests your presence in his office, sir."

"My adjutant has been likewise informed?"

"I was not instructed to extend the request to Lieutenant Senna, sir."

Torien turned this over in his head. He was irritated; underneath he was uneasy. "Your duties usually involve running messages, Lieutenant?"

"My duties involve anything the Commander requires of me, sir."

Torien bent to drag his boots across the floor. "He enjoys your unquestioning loyalty, I'm sure."

"And I enjoy his trust, sir."

He looked up at Tarrega's face. The knife-blade smile touched the corners of Tarrega's mouth. The dark eyes were blank. Tarrega said, "I'll wait at the door, sir, if you've no further need of me."

There were charcoal braziers lit on the gate wall and along the thoroughfare when they went out from the barracks. In the gatehouse and the corner towers, the guard were changing for the first watch of the night. The sun had slipped beyond the rim of the desert. The dunes stretched vast and silent under a cloudless sky, lit pale and shaded by starlight and the rising moon. Underfoot, the paving stones were still warm with the day's heat, but the air was clear and cool and there was a breath of wind coming in from the sea and the smell of jasmine and almond blossom carrying from the infirmary garden. Light and voices spilled from the officers' mess adjoining the headquarters on the main cross street. The headquarters lay empty save for the sentry posted at the vestibule, dark save for the thin sliver of lamplight coming out under the curtain at Espere's office doorway.

Espere was at his desk, still in full harness from his ride. He had tablet and papyrus spread open before him, and he was transcribing a letter in ink onto the papyrus by the light of the lamp sputtering at his right elbow. The spotted cat was stretched out long and lithe in the far corner of the room, tail lashing back and forth across the floor tiles, yellow eyes glowing like topaz in the darkness. Espere acknowledged their salutes with a quick nod but did not speak until he had finished writing. Then he tossed his quill aside and looked up. The lamplight cast his face in deep shadow. He looked older, and tired. "I owe you an explanation, Commander," he said, "and an apology."

In the time it had taken to walk from the barracks, Torien had imagined any number of things Espere might say. This had not been one of them. He blinked, stupidly.

"It was necessary subterfuge," Espere said. "I needed to know whether you were mine or theirs." He turned up his chin and smiled a fleeting ghost of a smile. "You understand it's a lucrative venture—not just for the governor of Modigne. The roots run deeper. I don't know how deep, for sure. I know I'm expected not to interfere. I've been instructed so: look the other way or lose my commission. You wouldn't have been the first of their spies sent to test me."

"Do you look the other way, sir?"

"You notice I haven't lost my commission." Espere's voice was dry. "You appreciate the delicacy of my position. Should I do as justice requires—take a detachment of horse down to the harbor and seize the ship and its cargo and subject master and crew to the punishment befitting their crime—Modigne has only to remove me from command and replace me with a man more suited to their purposes. Tell me what that would accomplish."

"The governor of Modigne doesn't have the last word. You'd have recourse."

"I told you I don't know how deep this corruption goes. Certainly it goes beyond Modigne. Possibly it goes all the way to the capital. To strike here, now, to settle for what we can immediately grasp—it's not enough. We must wait and watch until we can cut this thing off at the neck."

"In other words, you do nothing and let Imperial citizens pay the price."

"Commander Risto—"

"Let me deal with the Modigno, sir. Give me twelve horse and let me take him. You can hang it around my neck. You can tell them I was insubordinate. I don't care. But I gave my word in Modigne I'd see justice done—with or without official sanction."

"Your word to the bastard who knifed you? You feel compelled by your oath, I'm sure. But you forget you were already a man under oath. Your duty is to the Empire and to me as your commanding officer. Anything else comes at a distant remove." Espere tested the ink on the papyrus with one fingertip. "The ship and its cargo are no longer your concern. Do not try my patience on this, Risto."

When Torien said nothing, Espere looked up. "You are young," he said, "and you haven't yet learned to count costs. That doesn't mean you're the only one in the Empire who cares to see justice done. Have I not convinced you I'm doing what I can?"

"Tell me why you've decided suddenly to trust me, and I'll tell you whether you've convinced me."

The faint smile went around the edges of Espere's mouth again. "So you can exercise caution when it suits you."

Alluin would laugh, if he were here. "Curiosity more than caution. The only thing I've proven to you is that I know more than I should of Modigne's business. I fail to see why that should earn me your trust."

"I've informants aboard every trade ship plying between Modigne and Tasso. If you were acting on Modigne's directive, I'd have known it as soon as I went down to the harbor. We'd be having a different sort of conversation, you and your adjutant and I." Espere rolled up the papyrus on a pin and tied it with a length of cord. "Which brings me to another matter—of curiosity, if you wish, not caution. I'm interested in your adjutant. He was your choice? Or was he recommended to you?"

"My choice. Always my only choice."

"You trust him—knowing the manner of his disgrace and the circumstances?"

"I daresay I know more of the circumstances than you do. I trust him with my life."

"He feels for you the same loyalty you feel for him, I hope."

"We've finished, sir?"

"No. It wasn't idle curiosity, Commander, and it wasn't meant to cause offense. There's a reason I asked—a reason I needed to know for sure. If I intended to keep you here in the fort, it wouldn't much matter to me whether you were taking coin from Modigne, or whether the former Lord Senna deserves his rank and your trust. But I've need of you in another capacity." Espere held out the scroll over the desktop. "I need you as my eyes on the Road."

Torien took the scroll very slowly. He did not open it. "I thought you had *signi* for your eyes on the Road."

"I have *signi* for dying. Right now, they're not worth a damn for much else. They're undependable at best, outright traitors at worst. I need reliable intelligence on the Mayaso rebellion, and to this point neither the *signi* nor our native allies have been able to give it to me."

"And you think I can?"

"Vione recommended you to me as a risk-taker."

"You don't need a risk-taker. You need someone who knows the desert, knows the Mayasi—"

"The *signi* have the knowledge. What they don't have is the discipline to put it to use. You know how to command men. That's what I need of you."

"I've trained with heavy cavalry. I've no experience with scouting or with *signi*."

"Technicalities that may quickly be learned."

"Else I may quickly be dead?"

"You've demonstrated initiative and creativity. I wouldn't ask this of you if I didn't have confidence in your abilities and desperate need for them. I'm aware it's a disgrace of a command."

"It's a pointless command. You'd do better to recruit a man from among the locals, or to choose an officer from among the *signi* themselves. Perhaps you'd find them better motivated under the command of one of their own."

Espere's eyes had narrowed on his face. "You are very free with your tongue, Risto."

"Did Vione not tell you?"

"The native population is useless to us. Most are Mayaso blood. They still consider the Road and the mines theirs by historic right. If the majority are too complacent now to take up arms against us, neither does it much bother them when the more volatile minority do. And the Asani who hold the mines are more interested in exploiting

Imperial rule than in helping sustain it."

"One of the *signi*, then."

"With the promise of his freedom if he serves to satisfaction? I've tried as much. He took the opportunity to sell his services to the Mayasi. At their behest, he betrayed and murdered a high-ranking Asano—one of their nobility, one of our most important allies."

Torien did not say anything.

"If you are unwilling, Commander," said Espere, "perhaps your adjutant, as a chance to prove—"

"Is he still alive?"

Espere blinked. "Who?"

"The *signo*. I assume you kept him for examination, considering he was in contact with the rebels?"

Espere looked at him. Abruptly, he turned his eyes up over Torien's shoulder. "Lieutenant."

Once again Torien had forgotten Tarrega's presence; once again Tarrega stirred up stiffly to attention from the shadows behind him. "He's alive, sir."

"I'd like to examine him myself," Torien said.

Espere's voice was contemptuous. "You've had much practice examining prisoners?"

"As much as I've had at scouting."

Espere was silent, studying him.

"I'll take the command," Torien said, "but I won't do it blindly. I want to know what this *signo* knows—of the Mayasi, of the desert, of his own men. You owe me that much. I want to examine him myself."

IV

"The question isn't whether he means to kill you," Alluin said. "The question is why go to such trouble about it—to send you out into the desert in the vague hope the Mayasi will do it for him? It's wasted effort. He might have done it with a pen-knife in his office last night."

In the cold gray pre-dawn, they were alone on the thoroughfare which ran between the barrack blocks to the guardhouse and the southern gate. "The Mayasi or the *signi* themselves," Torien said.

"The point is, it's for someone else's benefit. He doesn't just want you dead—he wants you dead at a certain time and in a certain way. Anyway, I don't see why we should give him the opportunity. We could be gone with the tide in three hours."

"We've no evidence against him that would matter to a court martial."

"Neither will this *signo* matter to a court martial."

"No. But right now I want answers as much as evidence. He may know something about this business with the mines."

"You think Espere would have given him to you for examination if he did?"

"I don't see how he could have refused me without admitting his guilt. And if he's already arranged for us to die in the desert, I don't imagine he much cares what the *signo* knows to tell us."

In the guardhouse common room, the captain of the watch stood up quickly beside the fire pit, shrugging back his cloak to salute. "Commander Risto," he said. There was a scarlet lieutenant's braid on his shoulder. "Lieutenant Chareste, sir. I'll bring the prisoner out to you."

Torien was surprised. "Commander Espere told you I'd be coming?"

"Lieutenant Tarrega did, sir, last night."

"I'll see the prisoner in his cell. There's no need to trouble yourself bringing him out."

Chareste hesitated. "The prisoner is in isolation, sir, on the Commander's orders."

"My business won't take long."

"I mean that he isn't being held in a cell, sir."

There was distaste in Chareste's face, and an equal measure of shame. Something turned over in Torien's stomach. "Show me," he said.

He expected another hesitation, or perhaps an excuse. Instead

Chareste complied at once and wordlessly. They went in file down into the cell row. Chareste went ahead with a torch. The row was unlit save for the torchlight splashing over raw sandstone walls, the air cool and damp and bitter with the smell of must. At the end of the row, the corridor turned down another flight of steps and came out through a doorway into a low, close room.

At first glance, it reminded Torien of the family crypt back home in Vessy, and he felt for a moment the fear and gravity which one feels in the houses of the dead. But this was profane rather than sacred fear. His insides turned again and tightened as the light of Chareste's torch went around the room. There was a fire pit dug in the far corner. Above it on the smoke-blackened wall hung branding irons and an array of other instruments whose purposes he did not know and was glad he did not know. A low trestle table fitted with restraints stood at the center of the room, a three-legged stool beside it. In the torchlight, he could see bloodstains on the tabletop and on the sand-swept floor below.

Chareste put his torch into a bracket on the wall. He took his key ring from his belt and fumbled with it in the half-light. There was an iron grating bolted across the wall at his knees, and behind the grating a low cavity hollowed out from the stone, gaping black like an empty eye socket. Chareste found the key and knelt against the wall to open the grating. He leaned head and shoulders into the cavity. He dragged out a limp, dark thing which Torien recognized only belatedly as a body.

He thought at first the *signo* must be dead. The *signo* lay face-down and unmoving against the floor at Chareste's knees. His head was hooded but the rest of his body was uncovered, and in the torchlight Torien saw the lattice of whip weals over his back and shoulders and the open sores which the irons had left on his arms and legs. Chareste turned the *signo* carefully onto his back and bent over him to slip off the hood. The *signo*'s fingers twitched against the floor, searching for a hold. The tattooed number, the *signone*, marking him by law nameless and rightless, marched indelibly across the back of the *signo*'s hand.

Chareste lifted the *signo*'s head and tugged the hood free. He sat back on his heels, the hood in his lap. "It takes some time for his eyes to adjust," he said. His voice was as dead as ashes.

Torien looked at the *signo*'s face. It was an obscene mockery of a face grinning up at him like a skull in the torchlight: flesh shriveled with hunger, bones jutting. The scalp was shaven, the skin nicked and gouged and knotted with scars. At the corner of the right eye, skin and flesh were stripped or burned away entirely, the cheek gaping open, the bone exposed to the ear. The eyes blinked and streamed and darted here and there frantically in the torchlight. The lips were cracked and crusted black with dried blood and peeled back slightly so Torien could see the teeth clenched beneath. It had been a young face when it was whole, a young body. It was a desecrated corpse now through which the last nervous impulses still spasmed.

He knelt, slowly, too unsteady on his feet to stand. "How long?"

"Under examination? More than a month."

He sat on his knees, looking at the *signo*'s body. He watched the *signo's* skeletal ribs rise and fall in slow, shivering breath. The rest of it was dead on his dry and aching tongue. He looked up, finally, to see if Alluin might have words. Right then he was in desperate need of Alluin's words. Alluin shook his head without speaking. His jaw was knotted tight, the muscles in his throat moving as though he were swallowing back sickness.

Torien shut his eyes and opened them. "You've had charge of it?" he said to Chareste.

"Lieutenant Tarrega, sir." Chareste's voice was very quiet.

"He hasn't spoken?"

Chareste said nothing.

"He hasn't spoken through a month of this, and you suppose it's doing any good?"

"The Commander may suppose it does some good, sir."

They looked at each other across the *signo's* body. Chareste swallowed. His shoulders were stiff. He twisted the hood once in his hands and leaned forward to slide his fingers under the *signo's* head.

"Don't," Torien said.

Chareste looked up, the *signo's* head in one hand, the hood in the other.

"Take him up to a cell and send for the surgeon. My orders. You may tell Commander Espere so, if he asks."

There was a stretch of silence. Then Chareste said, in a deliberately empty voice, "Yes, sir." His face was as empty as his voice, but his shoulders loosened.

On the thoroughfare, Torien said, "I mean to take the *signi* on patrol tonight." Dawn had broken above the eastern wall. There was wood smoke on the air, and the murmur of voices from the barrack blocks.

Alluin did not look at him. His eyes were somewhere distant. His face might have been carved from stone. "You know he's going to kill you, and you know he's going to use the *signi* to do it."

"Possibly."

"Don't be an idiot."

"The mines are our only chance for solid evidence against him. Show me they aren't, Alluin."

"A spear between your shoulder-blades is solid evidence. It won't much matter to you, by then."

"The *signi* have no conviction of loyalty to Espere."

"Nevertheless, I've just seen one convincing reason why they might feel compelled to obey."

"Or one convincing reason why they might be compelled to turn."

Alluin looked at him now. He said nothing.

"Give the word to the quartermaster after muster," Torien said. "We leave at sundown."

"I want Tarrega with us," Alluin said.

"As a hostage?"

"As a casualty."

"He may prove useful in court, at some point."

"You understand that, and I understand that," Alluin said, "but I wouldn't much mind if it were lost on the *signi*."

He went to headquarters, after the muster, to see about getting a map of the Road. He found the office empty except for the spotted cat. Upon inquiry, he was informed by the sentry in the vestibule that Espere had ridden out into the desert to inspect a string of Asano horses.

"The Asani supply our cavalry horses?"

"No, sir. For racing. The Commander has a stable down to the city."

Torien absorbed this for a moment, silently. "Did the Commander give any indication when he'd be back?"

"No, sir. It won't be before noon, sir. They took the meal with them."

In the office, he drew the curtain shut across the doorway. The spotted cat watched him lazily from the far end of the room. He searched through the codices on the shelf above the desk, pulling out each in turn: the pay register, the quartermaster's inventory, the log. He held the latter in his hands, considering. A smaller codex slipped to the floor from between the pages. He bent to retrieve it. He took both over to the desk. He spread open the log and read it through page by page, finding nothing. He opened the smaller codex and ran his fingers down the row of numbers set forth along the left margin. For each number there were corresponding jotted notes under various headings across the page: date, age, birth place, crime. In a few places there were addenda—behavioral issues, disciplinary methods used to what effect. He searched through the pages as he had done the log, pausing at intervals to read entries, noting the entries that had been struck through and the brief explanations which accompanied them: *killed in battle—killed in battle—captured—executed—suicide.*

A shadow fell across the desktop. Torien looked up from the codex into Tarrega's face.

Tarrega laid the muster list on the desktop. Wordlessly, he eased the codex from Torien's hands. He turned the pages under quick fingers. "Sixteen," he said, "born in Puoli, convicted of murder. He's eighteen now, or close: the registry is two years old. He had the command because—alone of the lot—he could read and write."

He put the codex down. "Or is that not what you were looking for?"

Torien said nothing.

"It's lucky I should find you here," Tarrega said. "We can talk, you and I."

"I've nothing to say to you, Lieutenant."

"Then I'll talk, and you can listen. I've a warning for you—and advice, if you'll have it. Also, I've a favor to ask of you."

Torien stood, pushing back the chair. He put the codices back on the shelf. "You can tell Espere I'm taking the *signi* on patrol tonight."

"He means to kill you," Tarrega said, "you and Senna both. The *signi* are already under orders. I imagine you can appreciate the *signi* do not refuse his orders."

Torien turned to look at him across the desktop, one hand still outstretched to the shelf.

"They'll wait till you're on Mayaso ground. It will look routine in a report: *killed in battle with Mayaso rebels. Commended for valor,* perhaps, if he's feeling charitable."

Torien lowered his hand very slowly. "Why?"

"Why do you think? You and Senna know too much. You went in over your heads in Modigne."

"I mean why not just kill us here?"

"He needs this war with the Mayasi—else he has to admit the mines are Mayaso by right, and he needs the mines. If you die at Mayaso hands, it gives him further excuse to push the Mayasi off the Road."

"Tell me why I should trust you."

"Maybe if I hadn't found you behind a curtain in his office trying to read his guilt into his log books, then you could afford not to trust me. As it is, you don't have much choice."

"I could kill you and make it look like the cat did it."

Tarrega smiled. "Unlikely," he said, "and pointless anyway. Listen to me, Risto. We're fighting the same fight, you and I, but I've neither the time nor the means to prove myself to you. Nor do I much care whether you believe me or not. I've no real need of you. You, on the other hand, have very great need of me."

"We'll see."

"At least listen to me."

"Before a court martial, when they stay your execution long enough that you can testify against Espere—I'll listen. Until then, I've no interest in anything you have to say."

"I can save your life and Senna's on the Road tonight. I can see you safe aboard a ship for Istra by low tide tomorrow morning."

"We'll take our own chances."

"For the *signo*'s sake, then."

"What has the *signo* to do with any of it?"

"I ask that you take him with you. Tell Espere you want to make use of his knowledge of the Road. Tell Espere anything—I don't care. I'll arrange for—certain friends to meet you on the Road and take him off your hands. After that, you and Senna may die as you please."

"This is out of your concern for his life?"

"For a number of reasons," Tarrega said, "none of which are of any interest to you, as I'm not presently standing before a court martial."

"He can't sit a saddle. Right now, he can't crawl of his own strength. You must know: Chareste told me it was your work."

Tarrega's face was expressionless. His eyes were very dark. "An hour," he said, "two at most. That's all I ask of you—of him. The surgeon can at least ease his pain that long."

"How am I to know your friends?"

"The locals avoid *signi*. To them *signi* are dishonorable, outcast, lower than slaves. So they'll be either my friends or a particularly bold Mayaso raiding party." Tarrega shrugged. "But it's very rare the raiding parties come so far north."

The *signi* were not allowed weapons off-duty, on Espere's orders, nor were they permitted on leave to the city, but they were allowed the use of their horses on the parade ground, under guard. He came down from the headquarters and stood alone under the western gate to watch. He watched for two hours, the sun white-hot overhead and the heat wisping off the flat, hard-packed sand. They did not push the horses very hard, on account of the heat. It was noon now and they were moving off the parade ground and coming up on foot to the gate under the watchful eyes of the guards, leading their horses. Torien stood up from against the gate wall as they approached. He reached a hand to the bridle of the first man's horse. "You," he said. "Wait."

They stood aside stiffly and wordlessly as he picked them out. He picked twelve of them. He had watched them and decided on them individually. He knew horses, and he knew you could know much about a man by the way he handled a horse. The corporal who had charge of the guards came over to stand with him under the gate. "They're afraid," he said. He smirked a little. "They think you're picking them out for punishment."

"Take their horses," Torien said.

"You don't require our assistance, Commander?"

"You and your men can go."

The twelve *signi* stood in a line, waiting. They did not look him in the face. They stood very stiffly and looked at the ground. They were shaven-headed, and they wore undyed wool tunics like field-slaves' tunics and low, thin-soled sandals rather than boots. He could see they were afraid. In two days' time, when they had come down onto Mayaso ground, they would kill him on the Road; until then they must be afraid of him.

"My name is Risto," he said. His name did not matter to them, as their names should not matter to him, but there was comfort in the formality. "Commander Espere has given me command of you and orders to patrol the Road. We leave at sundown. I've instructed the quartermaster to prepare your gear. I'm aware the Commander has already given you—certain other orders."

"And you've come to beg your life?"

One of them raised his eyes to Torien's. His freckle-strewn face was pale but hard. His shoulders were braced very straight, his hands clenched. "Go ahead and beg. I'd like to hear it."

"I know the consequences you face for refusing him, *signo*."

"Doesn't matter to you, does it?"

"You're dead either way. You can't testify before a court, but you might still loose your tongue to someone who can. He can't afford that. He'll kill you when you've carried it through the same as he'd kill you for refusing."

"Not the same." The *signo* shook his head. "Not the same."

"Are you offering better?"—another *signo*, older and calmer.

"Your freedom, if you go with me to the mines."

"Freedom does us no good—not from you, not as long as Espere is in command."

"Take me to the mines and Espere won't be in command much longer."

The *signo*'s face was blank in a practiced way. "Modigne won't hear a case against him."

"Choiro will."

"What do you care about the mines, anyway?" the freckled *signo* said. "It's such as you making a profit of them."

"Then it'll take such as me to right the wrong. I swore I would, in Modigne." Torien peeled off his glove and held up his hand so they could see the half-healed gash splitting his palm. "I don't break my word."

They considered his hand. They looked at him in silence. It was not a hostile silence now, but it was an uncertain one. Then someone said, "It's a better chance than we've got from Espere."

"Either way it goes," the older *signo* said, "it's got to be all of us or none of us. I've had enough of killing our own."

"I've had enough of being used," the freckled *signo* said, "by Espere or otherwise."

"He'll be at our mercy on the Road," the older *signo* said, "unless he's an uncommon quick learner." His eyes were cool on Torien's face. "Tell me which of us is using which."

It was a clear, bright night but a windless one. Even after the sun had gone down beyond the rim of the desert, the heat pushed up into their faces from the sand. There was a young moon hanging just over the horizon, stars turning slowly above. He recognized the stars, though he could not remember all the names. He could see the Wolf, the summer star, which Vareni called the Dog, and he wondered if they could see it that night in Cesin. He wondered if they saw it burning so brightly.

His father had always been uneasy when the Wolf rose. He had not understood it as a boy. The Wolf was *theirs*, the sign of the Risti, running rampant on the arms of their house, and the rising of the Wolf meant winter was done at last, and if it rose particularly clear and bright it meant a good wheat harvest and a mild winter to come. There were, Tauren Risto had explained, certain Cesini who might make trouble at the rising of the Wolf. It was superstition, and foolish, but Cesin had once won a great victory against Varen under the Wolf, and the Wolf had afterward been the sign of the Cesino kings, and even now there were those who thought the rising of the Wolf portended the day Cesin would be free of the Imperial yoke.

Five years ago, the chieftain of the Dobryni had died screaming as much. Torien remembered it very clearly. He had been fourteen years old, almost but not quite a man, still young enough to be bored and restless all through the trial, resentful that he must sit for hours to watch and listen (what did it matter to him, anyway? He was the second-born, the soldier son; Taure as the heir was the one who must learn to judge and pass sentence)—but the Dobryno's death had impressed and scared him. In Cesino fashion they had hanged him with a leather rope from the branch of an oak tree, and while they were putting the noose around his neck his frost-gray eyes had come up to the governor's seat, and for some reason he had found Torien's eyes and fixed his gaze there. "Remember this, boy," he had shouted. "One day the Wolf will rise, and on that day they will hang you before the doors of your own house. Remember my words. Each time the Wolf rises, remember *this* is the penalty for blood traitors. Remember—"

Tauren had signaled one of his guardsmen, then, and the guardsman had reached over swiftly and silently with his belt knife and cut the Dobryno's throat. They had pulled him up on the branch already dead. There were other executions afterward. Torien remembered none of them so clearly. Tauren had taken him by the arms when it was done and said, in a low voice, "Superstition, Torien—comfort only to those who fear death, do you understand?" And he had dipped his chin and said, "Yes, sir," and they had neither of them spoken of it again. But each time the Wolf rose he remembered.

It was, he supposed, something of a reassurance: if he were to hang as a blood traitor before the doors of the house in Vessy, he could not very well die here in the desert with a *signo*'s spear in his back.

They rode loosely in file. Two of the *signi* rode ahead: the older *signo*, whose name was Nerix and who had murdered a senator's son in Salina, and the younger, hot-headed, freckle-faced one, Miro, a thief. Torien rode behind them. The rest of the *signi* followed in pairs. Alluin brought up the rear alone. Mounted at Torien's side, so close their knees were almost touching, the *signo* from Puoli lay against his saddle unmoving. They had tied his wrists one to each of the saddle's fore-horns, tied his ankles together with a rope beneath the horse's belly. A tether ran from his horse's bridle to the fore-horns of Torien's saddle. The *signo*'s head was hooded, his feet bare; beneath his loose tunic his body was swathed in bandage cloth. He had made no movement or sound since they had lifted him into the saddle at the fort. Except for the fact that his hands were clenched to white-knuckled fists over the saddle-horns, Torien would have supposed him dead.

At first there was other traffic on the Road: salt-laden mule trains coming up from the mines, or camel trains bearing figs and dates and almonds and spice and silk cloth. In the last of the twilight, they overtook a chained slave train working sluggishly south and west. The driver recognized Torien's harness and hailed him. Torien raised a hand in return. The driver urged his horse over and fell in at Torien's left knee. Torien guided his horse aside to let the rest of the column pass on his right. Under his headscarf, the driver's face was sun-cracked and humorless, all harsh angles as though wind-blown sand had carved it from stone. His eyes went briefly over the slumped *signo*. He said, in fluent Vareno, "You're headed into Mayaso territory, Commander?"

"My understanding is that the Road passes through Mayaso territory, yes."

"Take care, Commander. There are raiding parties on the move. I've had word."

Torien ran his eyes along the slow-moving line of slaves. They were not mine labor—were not, therefore, the Modigno's contraband. Most were women and children. All seemed to be Tassoan; he did not know enough to distinguish further between Mayaso and Asano. "No concern to you, I take it."

The driver's lips split in a swift smile. His fingers brushed aside the loose folds of his outer robe to reveal the sword at his belt. "I know how to deal with Mayasi."

Torien dug his heels into his horse's ribs. There was a sourness in his mouth. "My thanks for the warning."

The driver reached a quick hand to the cheek-strap of the horse's bridle. He leaned in low and close at Torien's shoulder. "Beware your *signi*, Lord. Men with no tribe are men with no honor. They've taken Mayaso coin before."

"I've no need for a slaver to school me in the meaning of honor."

For a moment, the driver was frozen, his fingers tight around the bridle strap. Then he let go the strap as though it had seared him. He straightened and bowed very stiffly. He kicked his horse away without another word.

"Made another friend?" Alluin said. The column of *signi* had gone past. They were alone at the column's tail, he and Alluin and the *signo* from Puoli.

"I'm about to lose one," Torien said, "unless he shuts up."

After that they met no traffic. The air was still and hot, the desert silent. The moon and stars were very bright, and by their light the column cast long blue shadows over the dunes. The *signo* beside him had been either asleep or unconscious and came awake with a start, jerking awkwardly in his saddle. He struggled frantically with his hands for a moment before he seemed to remember his wrists were tied. He lowered himself in his saddle, rested his hooded head against the horse's neck, and was once more still.

Nerix dropped back from the head of the column. "It will be good to rest soon, Lord Risto," he said. He kept his face turned away. They had all of them so far deliberately avoided looking at the Puolian. They seemed determined not to notice his presence. They had made no mention of it at the fort or since. They assumed, perhaps, that he had been brought along as a reminder—as a threat.

"Pass the word," Torien said.

They had come down the southern slope of a long, low dune to the scrubby mud flat at its base. There was a breath of wind coming off the slope. Eastward, over the shoulder of the dune, he could see a low bank of cloud building at the sea-line, black against the indigo sky. Dismounting, he unbuckled his helmet and took it off and held it in his hands, tilting his head back against his saddle. He closed his aching eyes and let the wind cool his sweaty face. He was thick-headed and tired. The cuirass was as heavy as an iron casing over his chest. He opened his eyes unwillingly. Alluin was coming up on foot, leading his horse. He had forgone his helmet entirely and had instead draped his cloak over his head and around his face, leaving nothing uncovered but his eyes. The narrow strip of visible skin was caked with sweat and sand. "You can ride rear guard after this," he said. "I've had enough sand in my face. I'm practically a portable dune."

Torien picketed his horse and the *signo*'s and took down his pack from the saddle. "You'll ride rear guard for as long as I deem it entertaining."

"Consider this," said Alluin. He threw his reins to Torien and unwrapped his cloak and shook it out. "Consider that we're in the middle of the desert with a detachment of *signi*, none of whom much care about that braid on your shoulder; and consider that I offer them equal share of the ransom I've demanded of your father."

Torien knelt to loop the reins around the picket. "This is how you've occupied your mind for two hours?"

"I've been thinking about it in some fashion since Espere's office—he's the one who gave me the idea. But I hadn't realized the immediate practical benefits until now."

"Help me with the *signo*," Torien said.

They untied his feet, first, then his wrists. Alluin, who was taller, pulled him out of the saddle by the waist. Between them they brought him away from the horses. When they let him go, he sank to his knees in the sand, leaning forward on his hands to steady himself. He sat back on his heels, dragging two fistfuls of sand with him. Torien crouched before him. The *signo* sensed him through the hood and flinched violently and then was very still. Torien leaned over and lifted the hood away. The surgeon had salved the side of the *signo*'s face that had been burned, and in moonlight now the sight of the face was not as jarring as it had been that morning in the guardhouse. Torien could see the shadow of the *signo*'s face as it had been, or he could imagine it with less difficulty: always a bony face, wide at the cheekbones and narrow at the chin, the mouth small and straight and solemn, the nose slightly hooked—a peasant's face, sun-tanned, expressionless by habit. The *signo*'s eyes were closed, his teeth clenched. Torien untied the water-skin on his lap and lifted the *signo*'s chin with his fingers and held the skin to his lips. "Drink," he said.

The *signo* opened his eyes and looked at him, blinking. Slowly, as though it pained him, he parted his teeth and drank. He closed his eyes again as he drank. His thin shoulders were drawn up very tightly, his fingers still curled to fists in the sand. Every now and then a shudder went through him, and his eyes came open briefly and warily upon Torien's face.

Alluin, watching, said, "When were you expecting Tarrega's friends?"

Torien let go the *signo*'s chin. He sat back on his heels. He lifted the skin to his own lips and drank, swirling the first mouthful around his teeth and spitting it out to rinse away the grit. When he was done, he handed the skin to Alluin. He shook his head. "By now, if they were anything more than a fiction of Tarrega's."

Alluin had tilted his head back to drink, holding the water-skin in both hands. He paused and looked at Torien sidelong over the skin. "Was that your working assumption—that it was a fiction of Tarrega's?"

"I didn't make assumptions. I've no interest in Tarrega, whatever his intention, whatever his reasons."

Alluin poured water into his mouth and lowered the skin to his lap. He tied up the skin while he swallowed. His face was suddenly and carefully blank. "You had your own reasons, of course."

Torien jerked his chin to the *signo*. "You think I should have left him in Tarrega's hands?"

"All right," Alluin said, "all right, but don't act as if Tarrega and his reasons don't matter."

"In all honesty, I don't see how they do."

"*You* don't see?"

"It was my decision. I am in command, after all."

"I thought we'd better trust between us than that."

"Ask the *signo*," Torien said. "Maybe he can tell you what Tarrega wanted, provided he can remember how to put words together without the encouragement of a cattle iron."

Alluin said nothing. His mouth was a thin, tight line. His eyes were cool and distant as they always were when he was angry.

Torien dropped the hood over the *signo*'s head. He got to his feet. He buckled his chinstrap and bent to take the *signo*'s arm. "Come on—let's go," he said to Alluin.

They lifted the *signo* to his feet between them. "It would be more a mercy to cut his throat," Alluin said. He was looking away over the slope of the dune.

"Take the head," Torien said. "The *signo* and I will ride rear guard." The thought had crossed his mind more than once since they had left the fort.

They rode down the flat, between the dunes. The wind came in from the sea, carrying the clouds with it. The air was cool now and the sky dark, and they rode close together and slowly so as not to lose each other. At the head of the column, Nerix was turning this way and that in his saddle, trying for a glimpse of the stars behind the clouds. Alluin dropped back. "He's afraid we'll lose the Road," he said. In the darkness and in profile under his draped cloak, his face was unreadable.

"Does he recommend we stop?" Torien said.

"If the wind keeps up, it might clear."

"Ask him if he recommends we stop."

Something flew between them in the darkness on a sudden breath of wind. Alluin dropped against him. Torien's horse shied away and Alluin slid from his saddle, his reins slithering loose from his limp hands. He landed awkwardly on his right hip and shoulder, his right arm curled under his body, his left arm flung wide, feet splayed apart. He lay face-down against the sand, unmoving. He had been unconscious when he first fell and had made no noise. The spear which had grazed him had been deflected to the sand and was sticking up at an angle in the sand at his feet.

Torien slipped from his saddle by reflex. He thought, at first and dazedly, it must have been a *signo* who had thrown, and he reached the spear in the sand and hoisted it up and stood stupidly with the spear in his hands while the column of *signi* rode ahead, heedless. His head cleared very slowly. The spear was unfamiliar to his fingers. He held it up and looked at it closely in the darkness. It was not an Imperial spear. The shaft was smooth, oiled wood, long and light. The head was thin steel hammered wide at the neck where it joined the shaft, tapering along a curve to a fine tip like a palm leaflet. He looked up. A lone horseman was silhouetted at the ridge of the eastward dune. As the horseman urged his horse down the slope, more horsemen crested the ridge to join him. They came at a rising gallop down the slope, flinging up sand in a trailing sheet.

The *signi* had heard them and seen them now. Torien shouted to the *signi* above the thunder of hooves: "Form up! Form up! Get your shields up!" It had occurred to him with a jolt out of the darkness that they might run. He could see them turning in their saddles to look at the oncoming horsemen, then twisting further to look back at him. He stood with the palm-blade spear loose in his hands. He was on foot and could do nothing if they chose to run.

One of the *signi* jerked his reins and kicked his horse around and came riding back down the sand. Torien caught a glimpse of his face when he came close—Nerix. The *signo* reined up at the foot of the dune, his face to the horsemen, his shield slung on his left arm, spear hefted at his right shoulder. The rest of the *signi* followed him. They formed up on either side of Nerix, closing a circle around Torien and Alluin and the *signo* from Puoli. They couched their spears and waited.

The horsemen rushed down to the foot of the dune and swept up to the circle and broke against it like a wave, falling back and then rushing down again, battering the circle until it broke. One of the *signi* was carried out of his saddle by a palm-blade spear and lay kicking to stillness in the sand, the spear through his chest just below the hollow of his collarbone. The circle buckled then. Torien lifted the spear to his shoulder and let fly at the first horseman to push through the gap. The horse stumbled in a shower of sand. The rider fell, sprawling.

After that it was useless. He drew his sword knowing it was useless: a sword was no good against mounted spearmen in daylight and certainly no good in the dark, but he had the stupid thought that he would at least die with the sword in his hands. A horseman bore down on him, hoisting a spear to his shoulder. Torien faced him and waited. The horseman drew back, preparing to loose. His arm dropped, abruptly. The spear swung down from his hand. There was a *signo*'s spear coming out below his ribs. The horseman slid from his saddle almost gracefully, the spear slipping from his fingers.

Torien bent to pick up the horseman's spear. Something solid and heavy slammed into his stomach as he straightened. His knees buckled. His sword went flying. He staggered back, dazed and gulping. He lost his feet and landed flat on his back beside the dead horseman, his throat closed, his breath gone.

After a moment, he pushed himself up on his elbows, blinking away blackness, feeling with stumbling fingers across his middle, finding nothing. He flung out an arm. The horseman's spear was beside him in the sand, and another spear which had glanced off him harmlessly—poorly thrown and too lightweight to penetrate the steel-braced leather of his cuirass. He snatched up both spears, one in either hand, ducking a horseman's swung sword as he rose; the horseman rode past, unable to check his momentum. Another followed. Torien thrust a spear at him, and the horseman caught the shaft in a quick hand and jerked it from Torien's hand and jabbed it back into his face. Torien reeled away. The spear butt crashed against the cheek-piece of his helmet and sent him spinning.

He hit the sand face-down this time and lay still on his spread palms while the world exploded in red above him. He spit blood and a broken tooth. He shook his head. He made himself move. He found his other spear in the sand and pushed himself up on it to his knees.

A heavy blow fell on the back of his neck. He sprawled flat on the sand again and lay now very still, dribbling blood over his numb lips. His throat was closed and he could not swallow. He turned his cheek on the sand and lay looking at the dead horseman. The wind had stopped, and it was very quiet except for the pounding of blood in his ears. He thought the clouds must have cleared a little, because he could see, very clearly, the details of the dead horseman's face— and he could see now, blinking at it in the half-light, that it was a woman's face, bronzed and solemn, marked across the brow and cheeks with concentric lines of blood-red paint.

At length, and at a very great distance across a painful space, there were voices.

He felt the spear being eased from his unresisting fingers. The fingers felt detached from the rest of his body, his body from his mind—discrete pieces joined only by a thread of pain. Someone knelt beside him in the sand and pushed him onto his side and unbuckled the chinstrap of his helmet, lifting the helmet away. Lukewarm water ran over his face, between his lips. He dribbled it back out. His tongue refused to cooperate. The voices conferred. Strong hands jerked him up by the arms and dragged him across the sand.

They settled him on his knees. Fingers under his chin forced his head up. There was white-hot pain splitting his skull behind his eyes, pounding with the pulse at his temples. He squeezed his eyes shut against the pain and felt the need to be sick. He leaned over his knees and vomited on the sand. They let him go while he vomited, but when it was done they pulled him back up by the arms and held him, tightly. He opened his eyes. He was kneeling at Alluin's side. One of the horsemen was turning Alluin onto his back and unwinding the cloak from Alluin's head. Across Alluin's right brow, the skin was split clean to the bone in a long, furrowed line from the bridge of the nose to the hairline. Blood had gone in ribbons over Alluin's face. The horseman traced the furrow under his fingers. He leaned over Alluin's body and unbuckled Alluin's sword belt and pulled it aside. He unbuckled the cuirass. Another of the horsemen knelt to help him. Between them they stripped the harness away by pieces. Torien watched, blinking. While the first horseman unlaced Alluin's jerkin, the second spread Alluin's arms wide across the sand and unstrapped the vambraces from Alluin's wrists.

In that moment, he understood what they meant to do.

He fought. He tore away from the hands holding him and struggled to his feet, fumbling for his belt knife. Someone snaked a strong arm around him, pulling him close, pinning him. Fingers pried his fingers from the hilt and loosed the knife from his belt and flung the knife away across the sand. They kicked his feet from under him and put him back down on his knees. They jerked his head up and forced his arms apart. He continued to struggle, twisting under their hands, trying to push up on his ankles from his knees, to wrench his head free, until from sheer exhaustion he fell still, trembling from frustration and anger, sobbing for breath in his thick throat, blinking through hot tears.

He was sick again before it was done. This time they did not pull him up from the sand but let him lie. He lay on his stomach, his face buried in his arms, his fingers clutching sand. He was in too much shock and pain now for tears. He waited. It seemed to be very much later when they got him up to his feet and pushed and jostled and kicked him along to a horse and shouldered him against the saddle and indicated with many rough hands that he should mount.

The sky had cleared. The moon had set, and the air was bitter cold. The Wolf still shone brightly enough that he could see the bodies of the *signi* where they had fallen at the foot of the dune. He watched dully while they tied his wrists with bowstrings to the saddle-horns. Someone prised his seal ring from his finger. When they were satisfied with the knots at his wrists, one of them raised a spear and smashed the butt into his face.

He woke in daylight and with the wind on his face.

He was on his stomach on cool, shaded sand and he thought, for a thick-headed moment, that he had come awake at the foot of the dune. He said, "Alluin." He twisted against the sand, trying to rise. He struggled for a while and came very slowly to the realization that his hands were tied at his back. His ankles were tied. He was barefoot and stripped to his tunic. With movement came pain. There were needles pricking at his left shoulder, at his elbow and wrist, down to his fingertips. There was a smith's hammer pounding nails behind his eyes. He eased himself back down against the sand and lay still, his head throbbing, teeth clenched. He blinked into morning sunlight.

He was in a tent, and the sunlight was streaming through the open flap, which faced east. Out through the flap—if he squinted his aching eyes nearly shut against the light—he could see in silhouette two spearmen standing guard, and the desert running flat and empty to the horizon. They had come away from the dunes in the night. It was close on the seventh hour, judging by the angle of the sun. He could feel early heat on the wind through the flap.

Shadows fell across him. With his cheek against the sand, he had a glimpse of sandaled feet. Someone jerked his head up by the hair and dragged him up to his knees, sliding heavy arms over his shoulders and across his throat. He closed his eyes. His head throbbed as though it would burst.

A voice floated, disembodied, far above him. The tongue was unfamiliar, quick and harsh, but he knew the words must be meant for him, because the arms wrapped around him jostled him impatiently when he did not answer, snapping his chin up and down. The voice rang in his ears. He said nothing, because he knew nothing to say and because of the pain, and this time at his silence he was shoved face-first into the sand, his arms twisted up in their sockets, his bounds hands wrenched over his head. He writhed, gasping. A spear butt dug between his shoulder-blades, pinning him flat against the sand. His left arm popped in its socket and he screamed once and then bit his tongue until it bled to keep from screaming again. Finally his arms were let go. He lay shivering against the sand, sucking breath through his teeth, while a bout of unintelligible discussion went around the tent above him.

He was hauled up again to his knees. Something heavy was flung down against him; someone that was not him drew a low, quick breath in pain. He opened his eyes. He looked dumbly, blinking, into a blurred face. It was a bruised, bloody face and for a moment, tight-hearted and desperate and stupid with pain, he thought it was Alluin's face, but though there was blood in ribbons over the tanned skin there was no furrow splitting the brow. The right cheek was torn open to the bone. There were patches of new, dark stubble where the scalp had been shaven.

The *signo* from Puoli said, "They want to know why he sent you, Lord—why the C-Commander sent you." He was bent forward at the waist, trembling visibly with pain or exhaustion or the effort of speaking. His eyes were fixed on the ground at his knees.

Torien could not speak. He stared at the *signo*. His throat was tight, his tongue a dead weight against his teeth.

The *signo* shifted on his knees. He did not raise his head, but Torien saw him lick his cracked lips and swallow. "They know you are n-noble-born, Lord. They want to know why the Commander sent you out with s-*signi*."

Torien shut his eyes. He poured his concentration into forming words. He said, "What do they care?" He had intended it to come out coolly and firmly. It came out instead in a clotted whisper, as though it had been cut from him with a knife.

He listened while the *signo* spoke in Mayaso—it must be Mayaso, he thought, or perhaps Mayasi and Asani spoke the same tongue and it was all of it Tassoan; he did not know. It seemed suddenly an incredible failing not to know. It seemed one in a long line of failings that had led here to this place in this moment.

The *signo* said, "They want to know if he'll ransom you—if he c-cared so little as to send you out with—"

Anger pushed the pain from his mind. He opened his eyes. The words came in a rush. "If it was for ransom, they were stupid to kill Alluin. Tell them that, *signo*. If it was for ransom, they should have staked you out for the jackals and let Alluin live. Tell them how much your life is worth."

The *signo* swallowed again. "They know what my life is worth, Lord."

The anger in him went suddenly clear and cold. "I'd forgotten you were theirs."

"It was proof of their resolve," the *signo* said, "what they did to the Lieutenant. That was why they—m-made you watch, so you'd know—"

"Tell them there is no ransom."

"They say you'd best p-pray there is."

Torien laughed. "Tell them go ahead and send for it, then, if they've a particular desire to die. I don't care."

"I'm to ride back to the fort at sundown," the *signo* said. "I'm to give your seal to the Commander. They have—demands which the Commander is to meet. If he refuses to meet them, they'll send you back to him piece by piece on the Road until he changes his m-mind."

"All this provided you can make it back alive to the fort in the first place. Am I to pray for that, too?"

The *signo* said nothing. Torien watched his face. "As long as they've got me, Espere won't lay another hand on you—is that what they think? Or does it not much matter to them what he does with you?"

The *signo* was studying the ground. "They've p-promised me fair incentive, Lord—to go."

"Worth another month or so in Tarrega's keeping?"

The *signo* looked up, blankly. "Poison. Venom of a sand viper. If I wish to have the antidote, I must return with the Commander's sealed pledge of good faith. Of course it d-doesn't matter to them if I return, but they think they've m-made sure I go, at least."

Torien realized, in that moment, that the *signo*'s wrists and ankles were bound as his own were.

The anger shriveled up in shame. His throat was tight. "They think?" he said, quietly.

"It takes two days to kill—the venom. You are vomiting blood by the end." The *signo* did not look at him now. "For most people, it wouldn't be a mercy."

Through the morning and into the afternoon, they were alone in the tent. The flap was closed and it was mercifully dark, but without the wind through the flap the air grew heavy and hot. Torien lay on his stomach, keeping his weight off his bound hands, pressing his forehead into the sand to relieve the pain behind his eyes.

Across the tent floor the signo lay carefully on his side, his face turned onto his undamaged left cheek. His sunken eyes were closed, but from the way he breathed Torien knew he was not sleeping. The silence was worse torture than the rest. In the silence, his thoughts kept going back to the foot of the dune—back to Alluin, who would not be dead yet unless the jackals had come at dawn, who would be dying slowly now of thirst and the heat. Possibly, if only possibly, he might be found alive. They had not been so far off the Road. There would be trains passing by, if not this morning then tonight. Alluin was strong. He could last so long. God knew he could last the hours until darkness.

There would be carrion birds gathered for the dead.

Torien squeezed his eyes shut against the sand. "*Signo*," he said.

There was no answer. He had not been expecting one. He went on, anyway, because it was easier to talk than to think. "Tell me what they really wanted of you—Espere, Tarrega. Espere told me it was because the Mayasi had bought you."

The *signo* said nothing. Torien opened his eyes. He turned his chin and looked at the *signo* across the sand. "Who was he—this Asano you killed?"

The *signo*'s eyes had drifted open. He was silent and very still, his shoulders hunched. He had drawn a barely perceptible breath and was holding it as though by doing so he hoped to go unnoticed.

"One of their nobility," Torien said. "That's what Espere told me. An important ally."

The *signo* said, "I don't know his name, Lord." He did not look at Torien. He was looking away to the far side of the tent at nothing in particular. His voice was low, but steadier than earlier. In the *signo*'s voice now Torien could hear the Vareno hill country so clearly that closing his eyes he could see it: broad oak woodland running up to dry brown hills, and the young Breche in its stony bed coming down from the mountains. He had not seen Puoli, but he had gone hunting in the hills above Civiparro, close by.

"So that part of it was true," he said.

The *signo* said nothing.

"Why did you kill him—if not for Mayaso coin?"

"If it ever mattered to you, Lord," the *signo* said, "it does not matter now."

"Why shouldn't it matter now? Maybe it matters the most now." He was talking simply to talk, and he imagined the *signo* knew it. "Tell me why you killed him."

The *signo* said, not looking at him, "Maybe I've forgotten, Lord, without the encouragement of a cattle iron."

Torien grinned, bitterly. "Does it still matter that you call me 'Lord'?"

"I don't know how else to call you, Lord, unless you wish me to call you by rank. But we've been—instructed not to speak as if we're soldiers."

"Espere makes you call him 'Lord,' then? He's not noble-born. He could lose his head for that."

"Only if I were a citizen, Lord."

"True." With *signi*, as with slaves, Espere could do as he wished. Torien was silent for a moment, considering. "You've a predilection for killing nobility, *signo*?"

"Lord?"

"It must have been nobility you killed in Puoli. Else they wouldn't have stripped you of citizenship. Peasants killing peasants is nothing particularly remarkable. They'd have put you to road-mending for a month."

The *signo* said, "Yes—nobility."

"Why? Or does it not matter now?"

"It doesn't matter now."

"What was his name? I might have known him in the capital. Though if I had I suppose I'd have heard he was murdered by one of his peasants."

The *signo* said nothing.

"You understand I'm just talking, *signo*," Torien said.

"Yes, Lord." The *signo*'s eyes were traveling blindly around the tent. "I understand."

"What's your name?"

The *signo* looked at him now.

"Your name," Torien said, "your family. Tell me about Puoli. Tell me about home." There was an ache in him that had nothing to do with his head or his shoulder or the ropes at his wrists and ankles.

"My lord is just talking?" the *signo* said.

"I'd like to know."

"They are dead," the *signo* said, "my family." He spoke with studied detachment. He might have been speaking of a failed beet crop.

Torien examined the *signo*'s face. "Part of your punishment?"

"Dead of the Fever. My father and mother first. Then my sister. I lived."

"When you were young?"

"It was the winter I was full-grown."

"Three years ago?"

"If my lord says so."

"According to your register, you're eighteen."

"There are no seasons here," the *signo* said. "I do not know."

It was a farmer's way of reckoning things: by seasons, not by calendar months. Torien said, "Tenant farmers, your family? Or hired hands?"

The *signo* shifted on his side and turned his head down into the sand, but not before Torien saw an odd spasm go over his face. "My father's farm, Lord," he said, in a hollow voice. "Three hundred and fifty stadia for his service and his wounds in Volenta."

"Your farm, once he was dead."

The *signo* swallowed against the sand and said nothing.

"You worked it yourself?" Torien said.

"In a good year we hired help. We'd no slaves."

"I mean when your family were gone. Did you work it alone that year?"

The *signo* said, "Alone." His voice was tight. "Please, Lord. I have tried to forget."

He had not meant to cause the *signo* pain. He said, "I'm sorry." He rested his forehead against the sand and shut his eyes and said, "*Signo.*"

The *signo* said, "Lord."

"When they took you. Last night. You were conscious?"

"Yes, Lord."

"You and I are the only ones they took alive?"

"Yes, Lord."

"And none of the rest made it away?"

"If they did, Lord, I did not see it."

"You saw what they did to—the Lieutenant?"

The *signo* said, "Yes, Lord."

"You could find the place when you go tonight?"

The *signo* was silent, for a moment. Then he said, "Yes, Lord."

"If he's there," Torien said, "if he's not already dead—if there's no other way." He could not finish it.

The *signo* said, "I will do it if I can, Lord."

It was not yet dark when the tent flap opened. The heat swept in like a blast from a bellows. From the shadows across the sand outside the flap, he thought it might be the sixteenth hour. They had been alone in the tent all day, except for briefly when one of the spearmen had come in bringing water a little past noon. Hands turned him over now onto his back. He blinked up into a dark, veiled face. The Mayaso sat down cross-legged at Torien's feet and slipped a knife from his belt.

Sudden panic twisted Torien's stomach. He tried to push himself away with his bound hands, arching his back, thrashing his legs. The Mayaso ignored his efforts and leaned over him and held a bracing arm across Torien's ankles while he cut the ropes. He flung the ropes away and returned the knife smoothly to his belt. Torien lay still and watched the Mayaso put his feet into boots. He recognized his own hobnailed boots. The Mayaso drew the laces around Torien's ankles and knotted them. He stood. He took Torien's elbow and dragged Torien up to his knees, indicating with a prodding foot that Torien should stand. Across the tent, another Mayaso was lacing sandals on the signo's feet. Torien stood, slowly. The Mayaso slipped a hood over his head and shoved him toward the tent flap. Torien stumbled out blindly onto hot sand. The heat rose into his face through the hood and pushed against him like a living thing.

They walked over open sand. He did not know how long or how far, but they moved quickly, and the Mayaso shoved him impatiently forward each time he stumbled. His head was spinning. The pain, which had subsided very slowly over hours in the darkness and stillness of the tent, was stabbing fiercely now at his temples. Abruptly, the Mayaso pulled him back by the elbows. Through the hood, he heard voices and the jingle of horse-harness.

The Mayaso held him by the neck with one hand, loosing the ropes from his wrists with the other. He took Torien's hands and spread them apart and placed them over saddle-horns. He nudged Torien's ankles with one foot and said something in his own tongue.

Torien explored the saddle under his hands. His fingers were numb and trembling, but he knew it was his own saddle, the four-horned army-issue saddle, and—running a hand over the horse's shoulder—he knew it was his horse. He knotted his fingers in the mane and pulled himself up, awkwardly, letting out a burst of breath through shut teeth. His legs dangled against the horse's belly. The horse danced sideways beneath him, and he had to seize the horns to keep from falling. He got his right knee over the horse's back and lowered himself into the saddle, collapsing against the horse's neck. He lay still, biting the insides of his cheeks against the pain behind his eyes. He heard voices as from a great distance. Someone was tying his wrists to the saddle-horns. There was another horse saddled at his right knee. He turned his head against the horse's neck. "*Signo.*"

There was a stretch of silence before the *signo* said, from beside him, "Lord."

"What are they doing?"

"There was a—disagreement, Lord." The *signo*'s voice was tight. "I think it is b-because some of them were against ransoming you."

"These were against it?"

"Yes, Lord."

"Where are they taking us?"

"I don't know, Lord. They're taking you so the others can't ransom you to the fort."

"Taking both of us, wherever we're going."

The horses were moving now. They rode in silence. His head throbbed with each hoof beat, and after a while he could think of nothing but the pain. He passed out and came awake much later in darkness with thirst crawling up his throat and the pain at rest in an uneasy truce. Through the hood, he could see the moon risen over his right shoulder, the Wolf over his left. They were riding south and west, and it was perhaps two hours until midnight.

He lifted his head. "*Signo*," he said.

The *signo* did not answer, and Torien did not speak again. He rested his head against the horse's neck and turned his hands this way and that on the saddle-horns, folding his fingers together, flattening his knuckles, trying to loosen the ropes at his wrists enough that he could slip his hands free. He chafed his wrists raw working at the ropes. He got his right hand free, finally, and reached over, without moving his head, to untie the rope at his left.

He lay still against the horse's neck with his hands free. He knew, from their voices and the hoof beats of their horses, that there were five Mayasi—three riding ahead, two behind. The ones behind would see it if he reached up to take off the hood. Also, it was no good with the horse on a lead. He would have to lean over the saddle-horns and unbuckle the bridle, and they would certainly see that. The only thing to do was to wait until they stopped and take both horses when the Mayaso with his lead had dismounted.

It would be a poor chance even then, and it would mean leaving the *signo*.

He had not thought about that all the while he was working his wrists free. Now he made himself think about it. If the *signo* were his soldier, there would be no question about it, by virtue of his officers' oath: they would both go, or they would both stay. But the *signo* was not a soldier. The *signo* was a murderer from Puoli sent here to Tasso so the Empire might profit from his death. Regardless of his guilt where Espere was concerned, the *signo* was a murderer from Puoli. That was the hard truth of it, and he must think in terms of hard truth now.

On the other hand, they were at least a full night's ride from where he knew the Road to be, and the *signo* knew the lay of the land better than he did. There was no point to his running if he could not make it to the Road. If he rode straight east, he would come sooner or later to the sea, and if he could find the sea then he could find the Road—but to ride straight east he needed a clear sky, and that could not be presumed upon. For sheer practicality's sake, it would be better to have the *signo* along.

They did not stop until daybreak. He lay still between the saddle-horns while the Mayaso ahead of him dismounted and picketed his horse. The Mayaso finished with the horse and came over with his knife, reaching for Torien's hands. Torien threw himself from the saddle. He carried the Mayaso down with him to the sand, ripping off the hood as he fell. He rammed a knee into the Mayaso's stomach and covered the Mayaso's mouth with his left hand, pinning the Mayaso's knife hand against the sand with his right. He dug his knee under the Mayaso's ribs and tore the knife from the Mayaso's fingers. Swiftly, he slit the Mayaso's throat and pulled himself to his feet against the horse, knife in hand.

A voice shouted in Mayaso. Hoof beats pounded toward him in the sand. He ducked beneath the horse's neck and came up face-to-face with the Mayaso who had been cutting the *signo*'s hands free. The Mayaso held up his left hand reflexively, swinging his knife wildly with his right. Torien sidestepped the blade. He caught the Mayaso's wrist and shoved him away and lunged for the Mayaso's horse, which was tethered to the *signo*'s horse by a short lead. He dropped the knife, yanked the picket up, and dragged himself into the saddle. He kicked the horse up to a run, the *signo*'s horse behind him.

The horse stumbled violently beneath him. He slid from the saddle. He hit the sand with his weight on his right arm and his breath gone out of him as though it had been ground out under a boot heel. The horse was dead, prone on the sand with a spear through its flank. The *signo*'s horse was on its feet behind, tossing its head and shying; the *signo* looked very small and still in the saddle. Torien sat up slowly on his knees. He had not thought they might spear the horse. A Mayaso reined up before him and dismounted in a shower of sand and swung a spear butt into his face.

He lay curled unmoving on the cool sand while they tied his hands and feet. Dawn was a long red blade cutting across the sky. They dragged him by the arms back over the sand to the horses. He lay on his stomach and watched, spitting blood intermittently, while they dug two shallow graves: one for the man he had killed, one for the horse. The *signo* sat beside him. His hood was off, his hands unbound. The *signo* hugged his knees and watched the grave-digging, not looking at Torien. The skin was thin and smooth and silvery where it had started to heal and scar over his cheekbone.

The *signo* said, suddenly, "I'd have slowed my lord down."

Torien turned his head against the sand and tried to look up into the *signo*'s face. The *signo* kept his eyes fixed on the grave diggers. His shoulders were drawn up. Once more, Torien had the impression he was holding his breath.

"Pragmatism," Torien said. It was effort to push it out through his teeth. The words were thick and tasted of blood. "I'd have left you if I didn't have use for you. You know the Road. I don't."

"My lord had the command."

It was curious logic for a man who had murdered nobility: my lord had the command, therefore he must know the Road. It betrayed a perplexingly naïve faith in the merits of hierarchy. Perhaps it was mockery. He could not tell from the *signo*'s tone, and he could not see it in the *signo*'s face. "Your lord had the command because Espere needed him dead at Mayaso hands, no other reason."

The *signo* turned his head and looked at him, finally—a long, searching look. The Mayasi had filled the graves. Two of them were unrolling bundled tent-hides over the sand. The other two came over to Torien and the *signo*. The taller of the two was carrying a spear and a length of rope. Wordlessly, he pulled Torien up to his knees and stretched Torien's legs straight and drove the spear into the sand at Torien's back, between his arms. He settled the *signo* against the spear and tied the *signo*'s hands to Torien's hands. The other Mayaso had crouched to watch and spoke now while the first one finished with the *signo*'s hands. The voice was low and hard but unmistakably a woman's.

At his back, the *signo* said, "She says if they didn't need you alive, they would do to you as they did to the Lieutenant. But they need you alive, so this is how you will pay for trying to run."

"I thought you said they were against a ransom."

The *signo* was silent, for a moment. "Against a ransom to the fort, Lord."

Torien looked at the woman. Like the others, she was veiled so there was nothing visible of her face but her eyes—and her eyes, which met his unblinking, told him nothing. "Tell her it was my doing," he said to the *signo*. "They needn't punish you for it."

The woman stood up, suddenly. She spoke in a burst of perfect Vareno. "It is astonishing to me—the Vareno compulsion to control. It is astonishing to me how you consider yourself in a position to dictate what I need and need not do."

He swallowed his surprise. He shook his head. "I ask it of you: spare the innocent, punish the guilty. I didn't think it was an idea peculiar to Vareni."

"It is an idea peculiarly foreign to Vareni."

"The *signo* had no say in what I did. I ask that you spare—"

"He is innocent neither by the standards of your people nor by the standards of mine. But if you care for him, you will think twice before you try again to run."

She was gone before he could reply—away across the sand to the tent. The other Mayaso followed her. They were alone on the open sand, he and the *signo*. He could feel the *signo*'s shoulders braced very tightly against his. He said, "I'm sorry."

When the *signo* said nothing, he said, "Tell me why they want me alive, *signo*."

The *signo* said, dully, "I don't know, Lord."

"Tell me what you think."

"They have spoken of the mines, Lord."

He laughed. "They're going to sell me into the mines? They could ask a better price on a block in Tasso. I can read and write and recite poetry."

"They will sell you to the Asani in exchange for some of their own. There are many Mayasi in the mines."

"The fort's work?"

"My work. All those fit for mine labor. The rest I was ordered to kill."

Torien said, at length and quietly, "Did he give you a reason?"

"He made it very plain to me why I should do what he asked of me, Lord."

"You didn't learn the lesson as well as he hoped."

"Not as soon as he hoped, Lord, though I've learned it fairly well since." The *signo*'s voice was faintly dry.

"Who was the Asano?"

The *signo* shifted at his back. "I swore safe passage to some Mayasi at a watering hole. They had come with their goats. They were not looking to fight. I swore them safe passage. The Asano disregarded it. He said it was not binding, coming from a *signo*. Maybe he was right,

Lord. But I had given my word."

"It was the right thing to do." He was thinking of the girl in Modigne, and the scar across his palm.

The *signo* said, "I wish I knew that it was, Lord."

"Why shouldn't it be?"

"Maybe if the punishment had been mine alone, Lord. I thought it would be. It was my word—*my* word. Otherwise I—don't know what I'd have done. I don't know what was the right thing."

"Espere punished your men?"

The *signo* was silent, for a long moment. "Decimation," he said, finally, "by my own hand. He said—said if I refused it would be the whole troop."

He could feel the *signo*'s shoulders shaking. He could feel the *signo*'s hands clenched to trembling fists on either side of the spear. He slid his fingers around the *signo*'s thin wrists. "It was his wrong," he said, "not yours."

"I wish I could believe that, Lord. But I killed them."

"You saved the rest. You did all you could do."

The *signo* said, "Is it a comfort to you, Lord—to tell yourself you did all you could do for the Lieutenant?"

It hit him like a blow to the teeth. He closed his eyes. "Yes," he said, "a comfort." He knew the *signo* could tell it was a lie.

VII

The sun crawled slowly across the empty sky. He slept the first few hours after dawn, head bowed under the heat which hung like a physical weight on his neck and shoulders and eyelids. He woke near mid-morning with pain bursting through his skull and the heat alive now and powerful, pushing him down against the sand, pressing smothering hands over his mouth and nose, closing his throat. His head spun with the taste of blood and the sharp realization of hunger and thirst: he had not drunk since yesterday noon, and he had not eaten since supper at the fort the night before. It was not yet two days ago, but in the heat and sand and across the gaping, jagged chasm that was Alluin's death, it seemed an eternity.

Without much enthusiasm, and to no purpose, he tested the rope at his wrists. He felt the *signo* come awake with a start behind him, arms jerking, and he wished he had not done it. There was no question of sleeping now in the heat. The *signo* sat up very still against him. "I didn't mean to wake you," Torien said. His tongue was thick.

"Better not to talk, Lord," the *signo* said.

They sat in silence. He watched the shadows at his feet turn slowly over the sand with the angle of the sun. He could feel the heat of the sand through his tunic and the soles of his boots. The sand grew painfully hot against his bare calves, and he sat with his knees drawn up to his chest. His head was swimming, his throat tight. He drew quick, gulping breaths, fighting the stranglehold until his lungs were screaming and his heart beating a panicked tattoo against his ribs. He dropped into blackness. Hands on his hands pulled him sharply back up. There was a voice in his ears, quiet but insistent: "Lord Risto."

He opened his aching eyes. He saw nothing but sand and sky. He opened his mouth to gulp a breath. The hands tightened on his hands. The *signo* said, "Slowly, Lord, and through your nose."

He tried to speak. His mouth and throat were as dry as dust. Nothing came out but a creaking moan.

The *signo* said, "Breathe, Lord, don't speak."

He breathed through his nose, long and unsteadily. Sand and sky were tumbling together at the corners of his eyes. He thought he might be sick. He shut his eyes and bent forward from the spear and rested his head on his knees. He spent the next little while working up saliva enough to swallow. The *signo* held his hands and said nothing. Torien swallowed and sat back up with the spear between his shoulder-blades. "How did you know my name?" he said, thickly.

"I heard it of Nerix," the *signo* said, "the night before last. Don't speak, Lord."

"You never told me yours."

The *signo* said, "I don't remember it." His voice was empty. "Please, Lord. Save your strength and do not speak."

He was bent over his knees again, half in the blackness and half out, when they cut the ropes from his wrists and ankles. They got him to his feet before he went face-down on the sand. There were two of them, one on either side of him, and they dragged him by the arms across the sand and into the tent. They let him go on the tent floor. He went first to his knees, then to his face. He lay numbly still, feeling the cool sand against his face and between his fingers.

Someone put a water-skin to his cracked lips and raised his head while he drank, easing him back to the sand when he was done and pouring water over his face. He blinked up from the floor, eyes streaming. The woman sat back on her heels with the water-skin on her lap. She was unveiled. On her forehead and cheekbones were the same red markings he had seen first on the face of the dead horsewoman, two nights ago. "If you try again to run," she said, "I will kill him."

Torien turned his cheek on the sand. The *signo* was watching from the tent-side. The woman tied up the water-skin and stood.

The thin gold loops around her ankles fell together clinking. "Rest," she said.

He tried to push himself up on his hands. Failing that, he pulled himself across the sand to the *signo*'s side. He lay face-down, holding the sand tightly in his fists to stop the tent spinning. "They gave you to drink?" he said.

"Yes, Lord," the *signo* said.

He slept. He drifted awake to voices and the smell of lamp oil and the flickering light of lamp flame on the tent walls. He turned onto his shoulder. The four Mayasi were sitting in a circle to eat. The woman was sitting nearest, her back to him. Her hair was twisted in a thick braid over her right shoulder, and it left the curve of her neck bare to him. At the nape, he could just see the edge of a slave brand, poorly healed, crusted black on the smooth brown skin. It was a Vareno brand. He tried to read it in the half-light. She turned her head in response to something said, and the braid swung down her back and swept the brand from his sight.

There were almonds and dried dates and soft cheese on a cloth spread over the sand beside him, and milk in a leather cup. He sat up, slowly. He brushed dry sand from his face and leaned his head on his palms. "You've already eaten?"

"I did not want to wake you, Lord," the *signo* said.

"Did you sleep?"

"A little, Lord."

Torien dropped his hands. He took the cup of milk and drank. The milk was warm, clotted, sour. It coated his mouth and throat like thick honey. He very nearly spit it out on the sand. He swallowed it quickly and licked it from his teeth and wiped his mouth with the back of his hand. "Mare's milk?"

"Camel's milk," the *signo* said.

"You care for it?"

"It will do my lord good to drink."

He held the cup in his hands. "*Signo.*"

"Lord."

"I know you said you've tried to forget. I don't mean to cause you pain—further than I've caused you already. But I wish to know what happened in Puoli."

The *signo* did not look at him. His voice was as empty as it had been earlier, but his shoulders were drawn up very tightly. "My lord will have friends in the capital who can tell him what happened in Puoli, if he survives to the capital. If he does not survive, then it will not matter to him."

"I wish to know it of you."

"My lord has no more reason to believe what I tell him of Puoli than he has to believe what I told him of the watering hole."

"And you've no reason to lie to me, given the improbability of my survival."

Footsteps approached in the sand. The woman brought Torien's cuirass over and set it down on the sand at Torien's feet. He watched her lay out his kit, piece by piece: helmet, jerkin, cloak, sword belt, gloves, wrist-guards, braid. She nudged the cuirass toward him with one foot. "Put it on."

"You'll kill the *signo* if I refuse?"

She jerked her chin over her shoulder. "These are for the criminal."

Another kit had gone onto the sand beside the *signo*. He recognized Alluin's kit. He recognized the fist-sized dent on the breastplate of the cuirass where the point of a blunted training spear had broken Alluin's shoulder last year: three inches to the right, two inches up, and it would have snapped his neck. Out of stupid, boyish pride Alluin had not wanted the dent hammered out.

Something went very cold and hard and tight and then shattered inside him. He flung the cup away and took the sword belt and had his sword from its sheath and was on his feet with his knees bent, sword hand drawn back in preparation for the killing stroke, all of it by reflex and thoughtlessly—and in that moment of breathless stillness before the lunge, he saw the palm-blade spearhead leveled at the lower edge of the *signo*'s collarbone.

His head cleared. He straightened, slowly. He turned his blade down and drove it into the sand. The Mayaso lowered his spear but stood watchful. Torien picked up Alluin's jerkin and sat down by the *signo* and flung the jerkin into the *signo*'s lap. The *signo* picked up the jerkin very stiffly. He turned it in his hands and shrugged his arms into it. When he had gotten it around his shoulders, Torien laced it up the front. He did it quickly, fingers flying. He did not want to give himself time to think. He hefted Alluin's cuirass and settled it over the *signo*'s shoulders and buckled it. He pinned Alluin's braid at the *signo*'s left shoulder and clasped Alluin's cloak at the *signo*'s throat. The *signo* sat motionless and silent while he did it. The woman and the spearman watched. Torien finished with the *signo* and started on his own kit.

His hands were shaking now, and he could not work the shoulder buckle of the cuirass. He fumbled with it blindly. There was a knot in his throat that he could not swallow. The *signo* sat up on his knees and fastened the buckle for him and pinned the braid. The *signo*'s callused fingers were slow, steady, careful. His hands were farmer's hands, hunter's hands, equally attuned to weapons as to the plow: it would be so for a man from Puoli. He did not say anything, and he did not look in Torien's face. When he finished pinning the cloak, he sat back down. Out of the corner of his eye, Torien could see the *signo* just well enough in his harness to imagine that he was Alluin. He blinked and turned his head away.

"The criminal is wrong," the woman said. "I am not going to ransom you, Vareno—to the fort or to the mines. I am not a fool. I know Espere meant for you to die on the Road. I do not know the reason for it, but I know that is why he sent you out with marked men. He is careless with lives but not that careless."

She was watching him for a reaction. He supposed she thought he did not know. She had counted, perhaps, on his not knowing. When he said nothing, she said, "Listen to me, Vareno. I will make you a better deal than Espere did. The mines are too well-guarded for my company to enter in secrecy, and we are too few to enter by force. But the Asani will not question an officer of the fort. You will take me into the mines, and when I have finished my business there you will be free to go. I will send you safe across the desert to the port at

Kabira, if you wish. Espere has no authority at Kabira."

Torien listened and said nothing. The woman said, "I ask only this, and I offer you freedom. Tell me I do not make you a better deal."

"My lieutenant was staked in the sand and left to die alone, in agony." Torien lifted his head and looked in her face. "You asked *only that.*"

She was silent, looking at him. Abruptly, she reached and took his right hand and turned it over in her hands, opening his clenched fingers. She put his seal ring on his palm. "When your people answer for what they have done to mine in the guise of peace," she said, "then mine will answer for what we have done in war." She held his hand, for a moment. Her touch was surprisingly gentle. She said, very quietly, "If I had been there, Vareno, I would have taken him alive. It would have been better to take him alive. But I was not there."

Torien slid the ring onto his forefinger. He had seen things very clearly with the sword in his hand. Now he felt dazed and dumb. The ache had come back behind his eyes, and he was thirsty and tired and he did not want to think. He pulled the sword from the sand and buckled the belt on his hip and ducked his head to put the helmet on.

It was twilight outside the tent but still very hot. He stood with the *signo* while the Mayasi bundled the tent and saddled the horses. The *signo* seemed ashamed of Alluin's harness. He stood very stiffly and looked at his feet in the sand. Perhaps he was simply in pain. At the fort, the surgeon had said there were two broken ribs and possibly a separated shoulder. He had not recommended that the *signo* ride. If the *signo* were to heal, he should not ride. Torien had disregarded the recommendation. It was only three days to the mines, and they would be riding carefully. Anyway, it was better than leaving him in Tarrega's hands.

They rode south and west. He rode in front at the woman's side. The *signo* rode behind, flanked by two Mayasi. In the darkness, his mind took the *signo* for Alluin each time he glanced over his shoulder.

VIII

Through the night, they rode down an ancient floodplain, long since dried and shot through by mud cracks hardened to stone. By dawn, there were low yellow hills rising across the plain, southward. Early heat hung shimmering over the plain, and in places the heat puddled like water and burned away as they came close. They crossed the plain and rode due west at the feet of the hills. There was a breeze blowing along the hills westward from the sea, and there was the scattered shade of juniper and gorse.

At length, the sun still at their backs, they turned up the hillside from the plain. Above them, the salt mines were a raw wound splitting the hillside to the bone. The slope of the hill was cut out in tiers behind sheer stone walls. At the lowest tier, two watchtowers flanked a low gate arch. A gravel path traced back and forth from the gate up through the tiers to a walled compound at the hilltop.

Torien rode alone in front as they approached the gate, and he heard the call come down from the watchtowers. The gate doors stood open to the path. Two spearmen sat cross-legged against the wall in the shadow of the gate arch, a dice cup between them. One of them got up and went into the gatehouse. The other, standing, took his spear in his hands but made no further challenge. The first emerged from the gatehouse with a third man whom Torien took to be their officer. The two spearmen hung back against the wall and watched while the officer came out to Torien from beneath the arch. The officer's head was uncovered, his face bare. The jagged line of a scar ran across his mouth from chin to left cheek, not quite hidden by his close-trimmed dark beard. He raised a hand in greeting. His eyes, sweeping along the line of Mayasi to the *signo* bringing up the rear, were cool. "Forgive me, Commander. I was not advised to expect prisoners from the fort today."

"I wasn't advised my mission was contingent on your expectations. So we both seem victim to faulty intelligence."

The Asano did not blink. "If I may ask my lord's name."

"Risto. And my adjutant, Lieutenant Senna. I trust you'll remember for the future."

The Asano looked down the line. He studied the *signo* silently. The cheek-piece of Alluin's helmet hid the welt across the *signo*'s face; Alluin's gloves hid the tell-tale inked number on the back of the *signo*'s sword hand. The folds of the cloak mostly covered the scabbing sores on his arms and legs. "If my lord will wait," the Asano said, finally, "I will send—"

From beneath the gate arch, someone said, "Aidar."

He was in Imperial harness, the newcomer, a lieutenant's braid on his left shoulder, and very obviously Vareno by his olive skin and straight-boned face. He was young—very young to be an officer—and haughty. He came down the slope from the gate. "The fort's business, Aidar, not yours. I've explained this before."

The Asano's face was blank. "Of course. My lord will excuse my foolish mistake."

"You can go," the lieutenant said.

The Asano bowed with dignity, once to the lieutenant and once to Torien. He went back up the slope to the gatehouse. The lieutenant said to Torien, "They forget sometimes how it's just that we let them play at sovereignty."

"As you forget sometimes to salute?"

The lieutenant had the grace to flush. He put up his right hand very quickly. "Sir. Lieutenant Espere. I'm afraid I don't know your name, sir."

Torien looked into the lieutenant's face, startled. He looked for the elder Espere in the lines of the face, in the honey-brown eyes. "The Commander is your father?"

The lieutenant lifted his chin, defensively. "My commission came from Vione, if you are calling into question—"

"Never mind it." He had known there was a garrison here, but he had not anticipated Espere would have it so close in hand. From the way the woman had stiffened in her saddle behind him, he guessed she hadn't, either. "My name is Risto. I've charge of these prisoners, and I've been instructed to deliver them personally to the man Idran." He had asked her who this Idran was. She had looked at him curiously. It was no matter, she said, because the gate guards would know the man he meant. He had not had a chance to ask the *signo*. He wondered if the *signo* had known about Lieutenant Espere.

"Lord Idran is taking his meal," the lieutenant said. "If you wish to join him, I will see to your prisoners, sir."

"I've been instructed to deliver them immediately."

The lieutenant hesitated now. His eyes went over Torien's face. "I'm not sure—"

"If I wasn't clear enough, then I'll put it to you this way: you'll take me and my prisoners to Idran, or you'll return with me to the fort and explain yourself to your father."

The lieutenant flinched. "Yes, sir. I'm sorry, sir."

They went up the path through the tiers, the lieutenant walking ahead less haughtily now. He had been earnest in his apology. He was very young to have a lieutenant's commission. He was sixteen or perhaps seventeen: not technically too young—one could have a lieutenant's commission after a year—but still very young. If his commission had come from Vione, then it had come most likely from a friend of his father's or by virtue of his father's coin. That meant most likely there were men at Vione who knew of this business with the mines. Possibly all the way to the capital, Espere had said. Torien had assumed that was exaggeration for effect. Now he wondered.

At the hilltop, they passed through another gate into a broad gravel yard. On either side of the yard there were low, flat-roofed adobe buildings—barracks and a stable and a long building with shuttered windows, which Torien guessed was an infirmary. Directly opposite the gate, a columned portico ran the width of the yard. They dismounted at the portico, and the lieutenant gave orders to the stable-boys concerning their horses.

It was very nearly noon, the sun beating down on their heads and glancing off the flat white rooftops. The yard and hillside were empty and quiet in the heat. The lieutenant led them across the portico and through an arched doorway gaping into the hillside. Two Asano spearmen flanked the doorway. They saluted in tandem. The lieutenant ignored them. The room within was windowless and quite cool, lit dimly by lamps on tall bronze stands. At the far end of the room, four men reclined for lunch around a low table. One of them, on the left-hand side of the table, was Asano—and of some importance, because there were spearmen standing watchfully behind him in the shadows along the wall. He was lean and hard-looking, with a jutting jaw and heavy black brows; like the watch captain, he wore a close-trimmed beard.

The others were foreigners—Imperial, by dress and appearance. The two at the center of the table, along the wall, were unshaven, sun-tanned, their clothes plain and travel-worn. One had long, sun-bleached hair tied back with a thin leather strip. Both had the look of soldiers, and Torien wondered if they might be mercenaries. The man on the right-hand side of the table was in harness, a commander's braid at his shoulder. He looked up as the lieutenant approached. He saw Torien and the Mayasi. He wiped his hands and stood, pushing back his couch. "Lieutenant, what's the meaning of—?"

He convulsed, staggering back into the wall. He slid limply to the floor. The woman had stepped forward from behind Torien, bent slightly at the waist and knees with one hand outstretched, and Torien realized only as she straightened that she had thrown a knife. She ran to the table. The other Mayasi spread out across the room after her. The Asano was on his feet and shouting. One of his spearmen hurled his spear at the woman, over the table. The spear went wide, clattering on the floor at Torien's feet. He stooped to pick it up, instinctively. The lieutenant put a booted foot on the shaft. He was fumbling for his sword, hands shaking. "Don't," he said. "Stand up—s-slowly."

Torien straightened. The lieutenant held the sword toward him and reached warily for Torien's sword hilt. The sword wavered in his hand. Torien knocked the blade away with his vambrace and lunged, lowering his head. They hit the floor together. The lieutenant was beneath him—stunned still, arms flung wide, mouth opening and closing soundlessly like a fish's. Torien dug his knee under the lieutenant's ribs and reached for the sword, trying to pry the hilt from the lieutenant's clenched fingers. The lieutenant twisted against the floor, thrashing his legs, scrabbling for Torien's throat with his free hand.

He subsided all at once.

Torien looked up into the tip of an arrowhead. He followed the arrow along its shaft to the bowman's hands. He looked up into the bowman's face. He recognized the scarred watch captain whom the lieutenant had called Aidar.

The Asano gestured with the arrowhead. Torien let go the lieutenant's hand and sat back on his heels. The lieutenant sat up away from him, wheezing, holding an arm across his ribs. The Asano lifted the arrow away from Torien's face. He turned on one heel. He said something sharply in his own tongue, holding the arrow still nocked. Spearmen poured in through the doorway from the portico and spread out around him, taking up position on either side of the room.

Silence fell.

At the far end of the room, the woman had turned her chin over her shoulder, looking at the doorway. She had a spear in her hands. The Asano who had been at table was doubled against the wall, holding a sword across his knees, spitting blood. His spearmen were dead on the floor around him. Two of the Mayasi were dead. The third was holding a spear trained on the two maybe-mercenaries, who were standing together aside from the table and who seemed to have made no effort to fight. Out of the corner of his eye, Torien could see the *signo* standing motionless at the near wall.

The woman spoke rapidly to the scarred watch captain. The Asano struggled up to his feet against the wall. The woman swung her spear and put the edge of the spearhead against his throat.

The *signo* knelt beside Torien, bending his head to speak quietly in Torien's ear. "She says if they do not meet her demands, she will kill him."

"Who is he?"

"Lord Idran? The chieftain—the head of all the Asano clans."

"What are her demands?"

"The slaves freed, the garrison expelled. If they will agree, she offers peace. She has no interest in the mines."

The chieftain, Idran, said something low and sharp to the scarred watch captain.

"He says to kill her," the *signo* said.

The captain pulled up the bow in his hands and drew back and loosed in one smooth motion. The woman did not move, at first. Then she took the spear from the chieftain's throat and cradled it in the crook of her arm. The chieftain buckled, folding over his knees. His sword slipped from his hand and fell ringing on the floor tiles.

There was silence while he died. The captain stood and watched, expressionless, the bow loose in his hands. The spearmen around the walls made no move, except one of them put his spear down and went to check the pulse when the chieftain had been still for a little while. He said something to the captain, who nodded, once, shortly. The spearman turned the chieftain onto his back and pulled out the arrow and wiped the arrowhead. He draped a fold of the chieftain's headscarf over his face. He brought the arrow over to the captain and held the captain's bow while the captain broke the arrow in his hands. It had the solemnity of a sacrament. The captain gave the broken arrow to the spearman and took the bow and put it over his shoulder. In Vareno, he said, "Peace is not enough. When the Vareni take their vengeance and you and I are dead, Mayaso, will it be enough to look back and say at least there was peace between us, at least now our people suffer together? And the Vareni will come for vengeance—will they not, Pallo, when your father learns what we have done here?"

The young Espere said nothing. He was frozen where he sat, his sword across his lap.

"You have him as a hostage now," the woman said.

"How many times have you known Commander Espere to barter for hostages?"

"He has never been asked to barter for his own blood."

"The Empire has no claim on the mines," Torien said.

They looked at him across the room, the watch captain and the woman, as though they had just now remembered he was there. Beside him, the *signo* drew a long, low breath. The *signo*'s head was bent under Alluin's helmet, and Torien could not see his face. "By law, the Empire recognizes the mines as Asano property," Torien said. His voice seemed very loud in the silence. "We've no justification for reprisals if you come to a separate peace."

"For convenience's sake, the Empire recognizes the mines as Asano property." The captain's voice was dry. "If they were Imperial property, they would be subject to stricter regulation out of Choiro. Commander Espere profits too well from the mines to let them go by mere reason of law. And he has never needed justification."

"Espere isn't the Empire."

"He is the only part of the Empire that matters here."

"Then if he's removed from command, you've nothing to fear."

They looked at him. Their faces were blank. "Are you proposing to kill him?" the captain said.

"No. Unless he's proven guilty before a court martial, the Empire will consider his death an act of treason or an act of war. I'll take him with witnesses to Choiro."

"With which witnesses? Until he's proven guilty, none of his slaves can bear witness in an Imperial court, and neither the Mayaso nor I are citizens."

"His adjutant will be able to testify—and the Lieutenant."

The young Espere was studying the sword across his lap. He picked it up by the hilt, suddenly, turning the blade in and sliding the point into the crease at the front of his cuirass where the buckles crossed. The captain knelt swiftly in front of him. He eased the sword from the lieutenant's hands and slung it away across the floor, speaking quietly in his own tongue. The lieutenant responded in the same tongue, not raising his head. The captain stood. He pulled the lieutenant up with him. With his hands on the lieutenant's shoulders, he said to Torien, "Tell me what happens if I meet the Mayaso's demands and you fail."

"Wait to meet her demands until I succeed and it doesn't matter."

"There must be guarantees," the woman said. "From you, Vareno, that if you are let go you will return to the fort and do as you have said; and from the Asano, that he will honor my demands if you succeed."

"And from *you*," the captain said, "that you meant your offer of peace."

She lifted her chin. "I did not think any further guarantees were required of me, considering that I am presently at your mercy."

The captain said, "I have sufficient assurance on the Vareno's part that he will do as he says, or at least he will attempt it as best as he is able."

"He has given you nothing but words."

"You gave me his adjutant," the captain said, "three nights ago on the Road."

IX

He was in a cell in the infirmary. They had brought him last night, the captain said. They were hired swords with a camel train headed south for Kabira, and they had found him the day after the attack. The train had gone on southward, but they had turned aside on their own to bring him here to the mines, and he had been recognized as Alluin Senna by the garrison commander who was now dead. He was lying on a reed mat on the cell floor. The cell was warm and silent and he was asleep on the mat and Torien, kneeling beside him, did not wake him. There were linen bandages at his wrists and ankles and across his brow. Oil glistened on his sunburned skin. Torien sat watching the rise and fall of his ribs, listening to the slow, steady rhythm of his breathing. "You knew at the gate, then," he said.

"I knew you were not bringing prisoners," the captain said. "I did not know whether you were acting of your own or under coercion. Of that, I admit I am still not certain."

"A little of both. I meant to come to the mines. I didn't mean it to be quite like this."

"You understand it is the same for both of us: the boy in your hands, Lieutenant Senna in mine."

"Yes."

"You understand I care for the boy. As if he were my own son, I care for him."

"I understand."

"I taught him the use of a bow. I thought I had taught him the use of a sword, but it would seem there is not much distinction in claiming so." The captain smiled very slightly.

"I suppose I should be thankful for that."

"I am familiar with Vareno notions of justice," the captain said. "If his father is found guilty, you will punish the boy alongside him."

"Only in the case of treason. This isn't treason. A court martial will take into account his age, his inexperience, the fact that he was under orders. They'll strip him of rank."

"It will be necessary to examine him?"

"Not if he speaks of his own."

"He will think he owes his father his silence. You see already he tried to silence himself."

"If his father has any thought for him, he'll tell him to speak freely."

"If his father had any thought for him, he would not have put this on his shoulders in the first place. The boy saw his duty. His father saw his use."

"Perhaps if you speak with him."

"Yes, I will speak with him. Whether he will listen, I do not know. He knows I have given him to you, and I do not think he will forgive such a betrayal—nor am I entirely certain that he should."

"I'll do everything I can to keep him from an examination."

"It will be his choice," the captain said, "not yours. Anyway, I do not recommend that you leave tonight."

"No. I'll stay tonight. Also, I want to leave the *signo* here in your surgeon's care when I go. He is to be treated as an Imperial citizen—as I would be treated. I'm giving him my legal protection."

The captain bowed. "I will see that he is moved here to the infirmary. There is a room prepared for you in the barracks, Commander, if you wish to rest."

"I'll stay here a little while," Torien said.

He sat against the wall by Alluin's mat when the captain had gone, his helmet off, his head tipped back, eyes closed. It was warm in the cell but not too warm. There was a breeze coming in with the sunlight through the open window. He fell asleep, at length. He woke to soft footsteps. An Asano girl in a white robe and veil was lighting lamps down the corridor outside the cell. Late-afternoon light slanted through the window. The corners of the cell lay in purple shadow. The breeze coming through the window was cool and heavy with the scent of juniper and almond blossom.

The surgeon came in from the corridor. The girl was behind him with a pan of steaming water. "I'll change the dressings now,

Commander," the surgeon said.

"How is he?"

"The wounds are without complication. The dehydration was more pressing. He'll have the scar above the eye, but I don't believe the vision will be permanently impaired. However, I recommend he goes to an oculist when he's well enough to travel."

"Have you everything you need? Tell me what you need. I'll send it from the fort."

"I'm well-supplied, Commander. Most urgently he needs rest."

The surgeon's voice was gentle but pointed. Torien picked up his helmet. "I'll go," he said. "If he wakes, Doctor, will you tell him I was here?"

"Tor."

"Alluin." He dropped to his knees by the mat. Alluin's eyes were open under the bandage. The right eye was bloodshot and bleary. Alluin turned his head against the mat and smiled, faintly. "I think you look worse than I do," he said.

"*I* haven't been lying abed three days."

"One day," Alluin said. "Two days on horseback with some swords from a camel train. They wouldn't let me ride a camel. I swear to God I mean to ride a camel before I've done with this sandpit, Tor."

"How do you feel?"

"Head hurts something awful and I can see two of you and right now I could drink the Breche. Do you remember that wine cellar, below the fish market?"

"I remember. I'm surprised you do."

"Anyway, that's how I feel."

"You know they give us helmets for a reason."

The surgeon said, quietly, "Commander."

"Don't talk to me about helmets," Alluin said. "If you'd listened to me we'd have been shipboard for Modigne and you'd have been using your helmet as a puke-pot, which is not the intended purpose, at least not once you're past the probation."

"You said you wanted to ride a camel before you went. I was giving you the chance."

"Commander," the surgeon said.

"A moment alone, Doctor, please."

"He needs to save his strength, Commander."

"Give me a moment now, and I give you my word I'll leave him in peace for the rest of it."

"He'll swear it to you in blood, if you ask him," Alluin said.

The surgeon smiled. Alluin said, "You don't believe me, Doctor?"

"I'll take him at his word," the surgeon said. "Very well, Commander. I'll walk the hall and back."

"Can you not profess your undying love in front of him?" Alluin said. The surgeon and the girl had gone up the corridor. "An eagle that he already knows."

"Be serious and listen to me. I've got to leave you here, Alluin."

"As a hostage. I know."

He let out his breath in a low burst through his teeth. "*How* do you know?"

"I've got ears, if I've got one less eye at present. If you didn't want me to know, then you should have picked someplace other than my bedside to do business."

"You were awake?"

"They get me, you get Espere's brat. They've the better end of the deal, I'd say. I thought it was a dream. I didn't think you'd sell me so low in waking life." Alluin closed his eyes and stiffened a little on the mat. It was the first indication he had given of pain. "It's ironic," he said, "all things considered." He opened his eyes again and looked at the ceiling.

"I'm sorry," Torien said.

"Don't be an idiot."

"If you were in my place, and I were in yours—"

"Would I have done the same? I'd have held you for ransom on the Road. I said so."

"That was a joke."

"That's what you think."

The surgeon's footsteps were coming back down the corridor.

"Better leave you in peace," Torien said. He got to his feet, tucking his helmet in the crook of his arm.

Alluin said, "It was the right thing to do, Tor."

He looked down at Alluin on the mat. His throat was tight. "I'll send word from the fort," he said.

The *signo* was lying on his back on the mat below the window in his cell. The surgeon had wrapped his ribs and salved the burns and he was lying quite still in the half-light, but he was not asleep. His hands were folded over his stomach, and he was looking up at the ceiling. When Torien came in through the doorway, he turned his head on the mat and unfolded his arms and started to sit up. Torien said, "Don't." The *signo* lay wordlessly back down. Torien stood at the doorway, looking around the cell. Alluin's kit was in the corner. The cell was bare but clean, the floor of red tile and the walls of whitewashed adobe. From the window, there was a view of the upper gate and the shoulder of the hill below, lit gold in the darkness.

Torien said, "What did the surgeon tell you?"

"That my lord is to return to the fort tomorrow, that Lieutenant Senna is to remain." The *signo* lay tensely, looking at the ceiling.

"I mean what did he say concerning your condition?"

The *signo* spoke quietly and detachedly as if he were speaking of someone else's body. "The ribs will heal of their own. The shoulder must first be rested and then it must be strengthened."

"How long?"

"A month. Sometimes more, he said."

"Maybe I'll have some good news to send from Choiro, by then."

The *signo* said nothing.

"I told the captain I've given you my patronage," Torien said.

The *signo* turned his head against the mat and looked at him. Torien slipped his seal ring from his finger. He crossed to the mat and held out the ring on his palm. "Until I can see your case retried," he said, "in light of your service to me and to the Empire."

The *signo* turned his head away. He made no move to take the ring. "You'll have the privileges of my name," Torien said. "Alluin and the surgeon can bear witness."

"No."

"As long as you're under my patronage, any hand raised against you is raised against me. It will be of great benefit to you in court."

The *signo* was studying the wall. He lay very tensely now. "It doesn't matter to you, does it—what I did in Puoli? I please you or I displease you, and because you're someone's son the court will give you what you want. I've had that kind of justice already. If it meant I were set free and restored to citizenship and allowed to go home, I swear to God I wouldn't take it."

"I've asked you to tell me what happened in Puoli. Until you speak, I've no choice but to act as though it doesn't matter to me."

"You've no way to know that I tell you the truth."

"Were you innocent?"

"My lord knows every man condemned to the *signi* will say he is innocent."

"Were you?"

The *signo* said nothing.

"Answer me. Or do you not remember?"

The *signo* said nothing.

"I suppose you don't remember your lord of Puoli's name, either."

The *signo* swallowed. His hands were clenched to fists at his sides.

Torien put the ring back on his finger. "I'll find out his name in

Choiro. We'll see if he remembers you."

The *signo* said, "Lord Risto."

"Changed your mind?"

The *signo* shut his eyes. There was pain in his face. "It is not ingratitude. I do not want my lord to think I am ungrateful. My lord was under no obligation to bring me with him out of the fort, I—I know that. I owe him my life."

He was irritated, suddenly. "Don't call me your lord. Maybe Espere enjoys it when you cringe to him."

The *signo* turned his head away and said nothing.

Torien said, "It isn't justice, *signo*, to let them silence you. It isn't justice simply to suffer."

The *signo* said, "I do not know anymore." He was looking at the wall.

He had missed the meal in the barracks mess, but one of the kitchen slaves gave him a round of flatbread, a bowl of chickpea paste, and a skin of red wine to carry back to his quarters. It was just now the first watch of the night, but the sky was clouded and dark, and a wind was kicking dust along the barracks row. There was a man leaning against the wall by the doorway of his room, just beyond the cast of light from the brazier at the end of the row. He was in silhouette against the brazier light and Torien could not see his face, but he could see the long hair tied back with a leather strip. "A word, Commander Risto?" said the hired sword. His voice was low and very much of Choiro—the good part of Choiro.

Torien had the flatbread cradled in one hand and the bowl of paste in the other, the wine-skin tucked under his elbow. "Go ahead."

"A private word, Commander."

Torien was silent. His sword arm was occupied with the paste and the wine-skin. Beyond the doorway, the room was dark.

The hired sword said, quietly, "I'm unarmed."

"Go in and light a lamp. I'll wait."

The hired sword vanished through the doorway. Presently lamplight flickered over the walls within and out onto the row. Torien went into the room. There was a low cot against the left-hand wall, a desk and stool on the right. The hired sword was leaning against one corner of the desk, arms folded, legs outstretched. "How is the Lieutenant?"

Torien put the bread and paste and wine-skin on the cot, never turning completely away from the desk. "He'll die of boredom before anything else," he said. He glanced up at the hired sword's face. "The Asano told me I've you to thank that he's not dead on the Road."

"Not really. If we'd gotten to you when we intended, we'd be all of us three days out for Modigne by now."

Torien was untying the wine-skin. He paused, looking up again.

"My name is Stratto," the hired sword said. "Commander Briule sent me to meet you on the Road—ten miles out from the fort, we'd planned. The Mayasi must have been trying for Imperial captives.

They hit us before they hit you."

"Commander Briule?"

"Tarrega, as you know him."

Torien absorbed this. "Guard?"

"We've been in Tasso more than a year. Commander Briule—Tarrega—he's the only one in the fort. The rest of us have the harbor. Only two others of us, now. You saw Valle with me in the hall. I lost two men on the Road."

"I'm sorry."

Stratto shrugged. "They fought well, they died cleanly."

Torien sat down on the cot. "Does Choiro know, then?"

"That the crime lords in Modigne are selling Imperial citizens into the mines while the garrisons turn a blind eye? Certain of the Guard command know. It's being kept mostly quiet until we can figure out exactly where the money's going. It doesn't stop in Modigne."

"So Espere said."

"Listen to me, Risto. I let you say your piece in the hall because otherwise they'd have realized their better chance is simply to bleed out of you everything you know of the fort before they join against us in open rebellion. It's possible they'll realize it yet. But my orders are to take you to Modigne."

"No."

"We've worked too long and hard to let this go to Hell now. If it were only ever a matter of removing Espere from command, he'd have been hanging from the fort walls a year ago."

"Maybe if you'd hanged him from the fort walls a year ago, it would not now be a matter of anything more."

"You think you see it all so clearly. You've only been looking at it a fortnight."

"I should sit on my hands and look at it for a year?"

Stratto's face was blank. "Lieutenant Espere will be examined in Modigne, on your testimony. The Commander goes untouched."

"You forget I'm leaving a hostage here with the promise that I'll see Espere before a court martial in Choiro."

"I haven't forgotten. We make sacrifices in war. For your sake, I made two sacrifices on the Road just now."

"It was your decision. Or it was Tarrega's—Briule's. This is mine. And Lieutenant Senna's life is worth more to me than the opportunity to run away to Modigne."

"You can go under compulsion," Stratto said, "if you'd rather not have the onus of the decision. But you'll go, one way or another."

Torien flung the wine-skin and stood, dropping his hands to his sword hilt. Stratto had closed the distance between them by the time he got his fingers around the grip. Stratto clamped a hand on the pommel of the sword. He pressed a knife against Torien's throat, bracing the blade with his thumb. His hand was remarkably steady. The edge of the blade was thin and cool on Torien's skin. "Don't be a fool, Risto," Stratto said.

Torien let go his sword. Stratto took the knife from Torien's throat and put it away somewhere in his tunic. "We'll leave at the fourth watch," he said. "We can be across the plain before the heat of the day."

Torien said, to Stratto's back, "You'd have saved yourself some trouble to hold your tongue and let me think we were riding for the fort."

Stratto smiled, over his shoulder. "You're threatening to run, Commander Risto?"

Torien said nothing. It was, of course, a foolish threat. He did not know the Road, and there would be no point in running.

X

Stratto and the other Guardsman, Valle, were already waiting with the young Espere in the yard when he went out to the stables next morning. A slave boy brought a horse to him in the half-lit stall row. He recognized the tack as his own, but the horse was at first glance unfamiliar—a tall black, well-tended but unshod and high-strung. He remembered that the woman had ridden a black. It was a finer horse than his own, and he wondered if the stable-boys had made the assumption that it was his. With a hand on the trembling black shoulder, he shook his head and said to the boy, "The brown is mine."

The boy, who spoke no Vareno, blinked at him uncomprehendingly. Torien pointed down the row to his own horse. "The brown," he said. He touched the knee-flap of the saddle and pointed again.

"I told him to saddle this one for you," the woman said, from behind him.

He turned. She straightened against the door post where she had been watching him. She was unveiled, her face unpainted. Her coarse black hair hung loose to her waist. She came over and took the reins from the boy. Holding the horse's head, she ran a hand down the long black nose and brushed away a lock of untrimmed mane from the wide-set eyes. "He is young and has much to learn," she said, "but his is a kingly line."

The boy had vanished down the row. Torien leaned into the horse's shoulder and began unbuckling the girth strap. "I'm not a king. I can't accept."

The woman put a hand on his arm. "A request, not a gift. Without use he will go to ruin, and I have no use for him here. He needs use under a firm hand."

He paused, the strap half out of the buckle in his hands. He studied her over his shoulder. "Did they try to stop you?"

She let go his arm and put her hand instead on the horse's neck. "Who?"

"Your people."

"Did they try to stop me doing what?"—blankly, though he knew she knew what he meant.

"Giving yourself up to be a hostage here. They must have tried. Otherwise it wouldn't have been necessary to steal me away as you did."

"They do not understand this is the only way—always the only way. Some of them think there is still hope in war." She turned her head and lifted her hair over her shoulder with her free hand. She showed him the brand on her neck. Then she let the hair fall again. "I have seen your capital," she said. "I have seen the columns at Vione. I have seen the shipyards at Salina. They have not seen, and they do not know. They will not know until too late, if I do not end it now."

Torien tightened the strap again and buckled it. "I'd want vengeance," he said, "or death, if vengeance were denied me. I would not offer peace, and I would not take it if it were offered me."

"If you had been taken and branded a slave, you mean."

"Yes."

She looked at him. "You think I am a coward—that I live, that I give myself to my enemies in exchange for peace."

He pretended to straighten the saddle-cloth. "I've never been branded a slave. I can't speak for one who has."

"You think it is cowardice."

"I don't know if it's cowardice, but I don't understand it."

"You are Cesino blood, are you not? Though I call you Vareno."

"That's different."

"The brand is different. The brand changes over time. You wear their harness now rather than the mark of their iron on your neck. But you are theirs just as I am. There is Varen in your face. You have learned to live in peace."

"Some haven't. Sometimes I think they're the more honorable." It had been in his mind since the day he had watched the Dobryno die, but he had never said it aloud, even to Alluin. He was not sure why he said it now.

"I have heard of these—the ones still fighting," the woman said.

"I have heard they kill themselves rather than let themselves be taken alive."

"The Brycigi do."

"You think it is honorable?"

"Understandable, at least—the desire to die undefeated if you can't live so."

"I think it is cowardice. It is easy to die. It is harder to live; therefore it is braver. Anyway, it is a myth—to die undefeated. Death is defeat. If it is at your own hand and not theirs, it is still death and they have won."

Torien did not say anything.

"His name is Fihar," the woman said, looking at the horse. "He is not the swiftest, but he is sure-footed and does not tire easily. In the desert, it is these things which matter more than speed."

"I don't even know your name."

"That is according to custom. The chieftains of my people forfeit their own names. It is to remember they are nothing more or less than Mayaso." She stroked the long black neck and did not look at him. "I am the voice of my people for peace and the sword in their hands for war. I have no name." Her voice was as dry as dust.

"I thank you for use of the horse," Torien said.

She held the horse's head under her hands while he mounted, murmuring in her own tongue to the swiveling black ears. The horse shifted under his unfamiliar weight but gave him no trouble. The woman came around to put the reins in his hands. "I have said it is a favor you do for me."

"I ask a favor of you, then."

She looked up from his knee. He peeled the glove from his left hand and showed her the scar across his palm. She ran a finger over it—hesitantly, curiously. "I have heard this, too, of Cesini. It is recent."

"I swore it in Modigne to a girl whose brother was sold into the mines. I swore to her I'd see justice done for him. I couldn't promise her I'd find him alive. It'll be three, four months ago now that he was sold: time enough to have died in the mines, if he survived the crossing from Modigne. She accepted that most likely he is dead. It isn't what she asked of me—to find him."

"You wish to find him, even so."

"To know, at least—to give her that peace." He held the reins in three fingers of his right hand and pulled the glove back on with his thumb and forefinger. "The boy is Mahlan; the sister is Lida. Their mother was a fisherwoman of Modigne harbor—dead now, though the boy won't know it. I don't know his age to tell you."

"It is enough."

"Lieutenant Senna can send me word through one of the garrison messengers, if you find him. Any way you find him."

The woman said, "You swore an oath in blood for the daughter of a Modigno fisherwoman." It was not a question, and he could not tell by her voice whether it was wonder or scorn.

He looked away down the row. "You understand how Vareno words are not enough."

"I have never met a Vareno to whom it mattered."

"They kill them quietly in places where it doesn't," Torien said.

Ostensibly the Guardsmen were his guides. Stratto rode ahead. Valle, who like Tarrega—Briule—was Modigno blood or perhaps Epyrian, bronze-skinned with a head of dark curls, rode behind, holding a spear across his saddle. Torien wondered if that was habit or necessity. He supposed they thought the young Espere might try to run. He had tried to kill himself once already, and it was plausible to think he might try to run regardless of how well he knew the Road. But the lieutenant sat silent and slightly hunched in his saddle, watching the dust clods flinging up under his horse's hooves.

He was in civilian clothes, now—tunic and sandals and cloak. Without the armor but with his hair cropped close, according to army regulation, he looked very young. He had looked young in harness and under a helmet, but he looked like a boy now and he looked dazed, lost. Torien rode close beside him. Valle was riding carefully within earshot, the spear cradled on his left elbow across his saddle-horns, and Torien did not speak to the lieutenant, though he wanted to. The lieutenant would not have heard him, anyway. He was watching the dust at his horse's hooves without seeing it.

They crossed the floodplain by noon and made camp on the open sand above the plain. Stratto chose the ground and issued orders. They were alone and there was no need for pretense now. If the lieutenant noticed it had been pretense earlier, it was obvious he did not care. In the tent, when the horses had been unsaddled and watered, Stratto sat down facing the lieutenant and pulled out from the neck of his tunic a seal ring hung on a thin silver chain. He held the ring on its chain for the lieutenant to see. From where he sat at the lieutenant's elbow, Torien could see the sunburst seal on the onyx face of the ring and the Guard unit number in tall embossed numerals around the edge of the intaglio.

The lieutenant looked at the ring for a long time. He did not look in Stratto's face. The smooth olive skin was sickly greenish across his straight nose and cheekbones.

Stratto dropped the ring back down into his tunic. "I'm giving you time to think on it," he said. "You'll have from here to Modigne: time enough to consider very carefully how much you stand to gain or lose by your silence."

"I'm not afraid of you." It came out in a quick burst through shut teeth.

"I'll disabuse you of the idea your silence will protect him." Stratto had produced his knife from somewhere and was paring off the rind of the hard cheese which Valle had handed him out of one of the packs. "At present, he remains in command because it serves our purposes to leave him in command. He'll hang when we've no further use for him, whether you hold your tongue or no."

The lieutenant darted a glance to Torien. For a moment, there was confusion rather than fear in his face. "I thought he was to be tried."

Stratto did not say anything. He offered a piece of cheese to the lieutenant on his knife-point. The lieutenant spit at it with sudden savagery. His mouth must have been dry; nothing came out. He looked from Stratto to Torien and back again. "He was to be tried. What do you need from me if he's not to be tried? You said he was to be tried in Choiro."

"Commander Risto was under a misapprehension." Stratto tucked his knife away and put the cut cheese on its cloth down on the sand.

"He can't be condemned without a trial."

"Names—to answer your question," Stratto said. "They will ask you for names. Most of the names you give them they will probably already know, but it's possible you will surprise them before they've done with you."

"You can't condemn him without a trial!"

Stratto did not say anything. Valle had given him the water-skin. He brushed the laces clear and lifted the skin in both hands and tipped water into his mouth. The lieutenant sprang to his feet, suddenly. He tore the skin from Stratto's hands and flung it across the tent. Valle, almost as quick to his feet, caught the lieutenant's wrist and slid an arm across his throat. He twisted the lieutenant's arm behind his back and shoved him to the tent floor. Stratto was on his feet now. He rammed hobnailed toes squarely into the lieutenant's gut. The lieutenant's breath rushed out in a long, hoarse gasp. Stratto's boots worked methodically along the lieutenant's stomach and chest. The blows landed quickly and heavily. Rather than curling up to shield himself, the lieutenant tried to rise. Stratto kicked him back to the sand, and Torien heard the crunch of bone and the strangled whimper in the lieutenant's throat.

He stood. "Enough."

Stratto crouched beside the lieutenant, who was lying still and quiet now—face-down, hands spread. Stratto slid two fingers under the lieutenant's jaw to feel for the pulse. Then he straightened. His face was expressionless. "The Lieutenant may have his uses. You're along with us for a favor. Don't cross me again, Risto."

Valle had gone to pick up the empty water-skin. "We will need to be careful about rationing, unless you wish to return to the mines," he said to Stratto. It was the first time Torien had heard him speak. He spoke quietly and with the studied, unnatural precision of one speaking a tongue not his own.

Stratto said, "How much have we left?"

"Another skin, besides what we've got for the horses. This was half our supply."

"The Lieutenant can go without, for now," Stratto said.

They broke camp at dusk and rode straight through the night. They rode in silence, Stratto always ahead, keeping his horse to a brisk pace, Valle trailing just far enough behind that he could use the spear to effect, if need be. There was no need and there wouldn't be. The lieutenant had not spoken since he had fought slowly awake in the tent. He had not spoken when Stratto had very deliberately passed him over for the water-skin before they had ridden out. There was blood dried on his nostrils and lips and chin, and he rode doubled against his horse's neck with an arm across his stomach, sucking labored breaths through his teeth.

The sky was clear and the moon waxing full and a wind pushing against them from the sea. Dawn broke early across the dunes. They rode for several hours afterward, the wind keeping up and the heat not as bad as before. In the distance, north and east over the dunes, there were gulls wheeling. They were making good time. If they kept up such a pace, they would reach the city tonight in the late hours or tomorrow morning early.

They spent the heat of the second day on shaded sand at the eastern foot of a tall dune. There was silence in the tent, except for the lieutenant's breathing. The lieutenant lay on his side away from them. Stratto was oiling the edges of his knife blade. Valle sat at the tent flap, looking out over the sand. Every now and then, he looked back over his shoulder into the tent. He spoke at length quietly to Stratto in a tongue Torien did not immediately recognize. Stratto answered him in the same tongue, and Torien realized, from memory of his own clumsy efforts, that it was Modigno, or more probably a dialect of it.

He did not know what they said. Alluin would have known, perhaps, or might have guessed. Alluin had not only an expensive education but an ear for words. He had not studied Modigno particularly, but he had picked up enough through a week's travel across Modigne to follow most conversations, if he could not yet speak it with any confidence. Torien could follow a conversation as far as it had to do with wine. Stratto and Valle were not talking about wine.

Stratto slept, afterward. Valle sat watching the desert. Torien lay awake, listening to the lieutenant's breathing. He had been hoping for a chance to speak with the lieutenant since they had left the mines, and it did not seem now as if he would get that chance. Briefly, he turned over the thought that Stratto was asleep and Valle sitting away from him. They did not consider him a threat. It would take a fool to contemplate attacking two Guardsmen, and he supposed they did not consider he was such a fool. Stratto would wake if he drew his sword. Valle would sense his movement. He could kill one with his belt knife, perhaps, before the other got to him. He could not kill both at once, and he did not think he could kill a Guardsman in a straight fight. If one took him alive, they would give him the traitors' death in Choiro for killing the other.

Valle stood up at the tent flap. He crossed the tent to where Stratto slept against the tent wall. His footsteps made no noise on the sand. He bent to pick up the water-skin. Torien watched him take the skin across the tent to where the lieutenant lay. Valle paid Torien no attention. He sat down cross-legged beside the lieutenant, the water-skin on his lap. He turned the lieutenant onto his back and washed the blood from the lieutenant's face with water in the palm of one hand. He tipped water into the lieutenant's mouth. The lieutenant spit it back out. Expressionlessly, Valle slid a hand over the lieutenant's nose and tipped the water-skin again and held the lieutenant's jaw and nose shut until the lieutenant swallowed. He did this several times in succession. The lieutenant did not struggle after the first few mouthfuls. He had been more than a day without water, and pride did not last so long in the desert heat.

Stratto was awake now, watching on his back from the tent-side. "You'll make trouble for yourself one day, Dio."

Valle smiled but said nothing. He tied up the water-skin.

"Get him up," Stratto said. "We'll go."

"It's two hours until sundown."

"I want to make the ship tonight."

Torien said, "Espere controls the city guard, and I'll wager they pay closer attention to us tonight with the gates closed than they would in daylight tomorrow."

Stratto was lacing his boots. "You assume we're going into the city."

He had, in fact, been counting on it, and he had counted likewise that Stratto would want to enter by daylight, when the gates stood open and the guards were less inclined toward individual inspections. Tonight, camped on open sand outside the city gates, he might have had the chance to slip away to the fort—with the lieutenant, most importantly. He was fairly sure that neither Stratto nor Valle would put much effort into stopping him if he ran for it on his own. Alone he could do nothing. He needed the lieutenant, and they knew it.

Stratto must have seen something in his face. "Your weapons, Risto."

It had occurred to them he might be such a fool after all. He considered protesting—more for dignity's sake than anything else. In the end, he unbuckled his sword belt and wrapped up the belt around the sheath and handed it over wordlessly, the belt knife with its sheath after. Perhaps knowing he was unarmed they would be careless. It was not likely, but it was some consolation.

Stratto tucked the bundled weapons under one elbow. "You'll have them back aboard ship," he said. Then he said to Valle, "Tie their hands."

Torien felt a flick of anger. "Do you believe I'm that much a threat, or are you simply that incompetent?"

"I believe you're desperate," Stratto said, "and I'd rather not have to kill you for it."

South of Tasso at a distance of perhaps ten miles, the sea had eaten the desert down to bare rock at the shoreline. In the moonlight, Torien saw the long black finger of a cove cutting inland through sandstone cliffs. He heard waves crashing on jagged rock. Distantly northward, across the dark sand, he could see the harbor lights at Tasso.

They rode along the cove on the narrow shelf of sand under the cliffs. He was riding at Stratto's side, the young Espere at Valle's. The ship, rising and falling gently on the swell below the cliffs, was small and single-masted, shallow enough on the draft to be moored quite close along the shore. It was no bigger than the boats which came up the river to Vessy, and besides passengers and crew it must carry stores for a six-day ocean voyage. He said to Stratto, "How many of us are swimming?"

"We'll change ships at Istra."

"Istra's still a long way to swim."

"We'll leave the horses."

There were four men waiting for them at the foot of the cliff where the ship lay moored. They had a small driftwood fire burning on the sand: the cliffs trapped the sea wind, and it was cold rather than cool. The men were wrapped in cloaks. Stratto raised a hand in greeting. None of the men returned it. They stood waiting and watching. Torien had a glimpse of one man's face in the firelight. It seemed familiar, though he could not place it.

Stratto swung from his saddle. He flung his reins to one of the men. "Take the horses," he said. "We're putting out."

Metal rasped on leather. Torien saw the flash of a sword in the firelight. The man who stood closest took Stratto's head off with one swipe of the blade. He felt the blood spray. Head and body tumbled to the sand. He kicked the black horse's ribs and clung to the saddle-horns as the horse lurched forward. The saddle leather was slippery with Stratto's blood. The swordsman caught him by the arm. He slid from the saddle with the swordsman's fingers around his elbow, hitting the sand on his hip and shoulder. Pain burst through his shoulder, down to his fingertips, and just for a moment he lay stunned and winded, blinking at Stratto's body across the sand. The swordsman stood over him, blade raised. He forgot the pain in his panic. He rolled away as the blade came down, and he heard the wet crunch as the blade bit sand.

He hauled himself on his elbows across the sand and caught at one of the burning sticks and pulled it from the fire. Sparks raced up the cliff face, ash drifting like black moths. He flung himself onto his back, facing the swordsman, the stick in his bound hands. There were hoof beats coming up out of the darkness. The swordsman fell at Torien's feet with a spear through his unprotected chest.

Valle slid from his saddle to retrieve the spear. He braced the body with one foot and jerked the spear up and spun on his heel and let fly again, in one smooth motion. Torien snatched up the dead man's sword. He held it between his knees and ran his wrists over the upturned edge of the blade until the ropes slithered away. Valle had drawn his own sword and was fighting the two remaining men at once. He had killed one of them by the time Torien got to his feet. The other was backing away. He had his sword toward Valle, and in the firelight Torien saw the tattoo on the back of the sword hand.

"Wait," he said.

Valle paused, sword raised.

"Put down the sword and you live," Torien said to the *signo*.

The *signo* dropped his sword at once. He went to his knees on the sand. The firelight was on his face, and Torien recognized him: the *signo* had looked at him hollow-eyed across the stable yard on his first day at the fort. "Please, Lord. It was orders."

"You knew to wait for us here?"

"The Commander knew, Lord."

"How?"

"He had the Lieutenant under examination, Lord."

"Tarrega?"

"Yes, Lord."

"Had," Valle said. He was standing very straight, his chin up, his face blank. In the firelight, his eyes were dark. "The Lieutenant is dead?"

The *signo* did not say anything.

Valle said, quietly, "Is he dead, *signo*?"

"He was alive when we left, Lord," the *signo* said, "but that was a week ago this morning."

Valle turned abruptly on his heel. Torien went after him. "Valle."

"The boy is hurt badly." Valle was sheathing his sword. His hands were steady, but even so it took him a moment, when he had wiped the blade, to catch the tip of the blade on the slit of the sheath. "I will need your help."

The young Espere lay sprawled on the sand a little way up the shore. He was unconscious, and in the moonlight his face was white. His left arm was gone below the elbow. The same stroke that had taken his arm had gouged his side above the hip. Valle checked the pulse and said to Torien, "Take his feet."

They carried him between them over to the fire, avoiding the bodies of the *signi* and Stratto's body. They laid him on the sand with his head up toward the cliff, his feet toward the water. His skin was very cold. The front of his tunic was soaked through with blood.

Valle cut away the tunic with his knife. Then he wiped the knife and put the blade on the coals. He looked up at the *signo*, who had not moved from his knees. "More wood if you can find it," he said. He was speaking very quietly and calmly. To Torien he said, "There is wine in the packs, and bandage cloth."

For a while, they were busy and silent. Valle tied a tourniquet above the stump of the arm and rinsed the wounds with wine. Torien held the unconscious lieutenant while Valle dressed the gash under his ribs. By then the *signo* had built up the fire quite large, and the heat was pushing into their faces. Valle took his knife from the coals and sealed the stump of the lieutenant's arm with the flat of the blade. Afterward, Torien laid the lieutenant back down on the sand and felt for the pulse under the lieutenant's jaw. The pulse fluttered faintly against his fingertips. The lieutenant's throat was cold. Torien shrugged off his cloak and put it over him. His shoulder twinged with the movement. He had forgotten it in adrenaline and then urgency. He closed his left hand and found there was no feeling in his fingers.

Valle was watching him. "You are hurt?"

"Nothing."

Valle handed him the wine-skin. "Drink."

Torien took the skin. There was blood on his hand—Stratto's blood, spattered on his hand and his arm and along the left side of his body. He swallowed a quick mouthful of wine and gave the skin back to Valle. He got unsteadily to his feet and went down to the water and knelt in the shallows to rinse the blood away. He sat for a while afterward with his eyes closed, his arms limp at his sides and his fingers dug into the pebbly sand, the warm saltwater lapping gently over his knees.

The lieutenant would die. He had been weak already from the beating and water deprivation, and he would be dead by morning. Perhaps he would never regain consciousness. That would be the most merciful. That would be more merciful than waking to realize his father had sent the men who had killed him. It had been done unwittingly, perhaps, but that would be small comfort to the dying when the dying was sixteen years old and willing for his father's sake to undergo a Guard examination. Perhaps in that case he would accept that his father had sent and killed him. Perhaps he would defend the decision. Torien did not understand. He wondered if Alluin might. Alluin joked about his father, but that was because deep down he had never figured out how not to care, and to joke was the only way he knew how to pretend.

Valle had come down beside him in the shallows. "I have given instruction to the *signo* for the boy's treatment," he said. He held out Torien's bundled sword belt and the knife in its sheath. "I told him we would send wagons from the fort. It would kill the boy to ride."

XI

Dawn had lit the sandstone gate wall white and pale pink against the gray western sky. It was not yet the end of the fourth watch, and there were braziers still burning on the wall. The body was visible on the wall from some distance across the sand. It hung by the wrists, stripped and sunburned, from one of the merlons of the walkway atop the wall, between the gatehouse and the southwestern tower.

From the foot of the wall, Torien could not see detail enough in the face to recognize it as Tarrega's body. He was glad for that—glad to think of it objectively only as a body, not as Tarrega's body. Valle did not look at it. He rode up close under the gate wall. The gate doors were closed. The watch had seen them coming for a while, north and west across the open sand from the cove, but they had been riding with the dawn light at their backs, and Torien did not think the watch had seen their faces. One of the guards called down from the gatehouse for the watch word. Valle said, "Open in the Emperor's name."

Several helmeted heads peered down at them from the wall in a sudden flare of torchlight. Valle slipped his seal ring on its chain from his neck and slung it up over the wall onto the walkway. "Open the gate."

There was murmured conferral over the ring. There was no further challenge. The gate doors creaked inward ponderously. The thoroughfare stretched before them empty and dark down to the headquarters. It was two hours until muster, and the barrack blocks were silent. The captain of the watch was coming out from the gatehouse. It was not Chareste. He had Valle's ring in his hands. He was cupping it gingerly on his palms, as though it were delicate or dangerous. "Sir," he said to Valle. He did not seem to notice Torien. There was a corporal's braid on his shoulder and mingled fear and awe in his face. He was a junior officer of a frontier garrison, and he was common-born, and most likely—to his own knowledge— he had never lain eyes on a Guardsman before. His neck muscles twitched as he suppressed a first inclination to bow. "I'm sorry, sir, I didn't expect—"

"Is Commander Espere in his quarters?"

The corporal swallowed. "Commander Espere is with the prisoner, sir."

Valle dismounted and dropped his reins. He went up into the guardhouse without another word. Torien slipped quickly from his saddle. "Which prisoner?" he said to the corporal.

The corporal noticed him now and recognized him. Torien saw the confusion flit on his face: they would know by now that Commander Risto and his adjutant and his *signi* had been killed by Mayasi on the Road. He saw this pass in an instant over the corporal's face and resolve itself into a hasty salute. "The Lieutenant, sir—Lieutenant Chareste."

"Come with me."

"Yes, sir."

Valle had taken a torch from a bracket in the common room. They went down through the cell row—Valle ahead with the torch, and Torien following, and the corporal bringing up the rear. Valle glanced back over his shoulder. "Is the Commander alone with the prisoner, Corporal?"

"Yes, sir."

"Come here, Corporal," Valle said.

He was standing in the low doorway at the bottom of the steps. He put his torch up and tested the shut door once, gently, with his hand and shoulder. He said to the corporal, "He knows your voice?"

"Yes, sir."

"Tell him there is a message come up from the harbor. Tell him the messenger will speak to none but him."

The corporal went down to the door, nervous but unquestioning in his eagerness to please the Guardsman. He pounded a closed fist on the door. "Commander Espere—sir. Urgent message from the harbor, sir."

Espere's voice came muffled through the door: "I will be in my office presently."

"The messenger can't wait, sir, and he won't give the message to anyone but you."

"He may wait in my office, or he may return when I am unoccupied."

"The messenger comes under the sign of the Boar," Valle said, quietly.

"He is under the sign of the Boar, sir."

There was a moment's silence. Then there was the rattling of a chain and the scrape of wood on stone. The door edged inward. Valle kicked it wide. "Well done, Corporal," he said. He drew his sword and ducked through the doorway. Torien followed him, drawing his own sword.

Espere backed away. He had his belt knife in his hand. He lifted his chin and drew the blade across his throat with a flick of his wrist. He sank noiselessly to the floor. The knife slipped from his fingers and hit the floor and lay spinning to stillness on its haft.

"Corporal," Valle said, into the silence that followed.

"Yes, sir." The corporal's face was gray in the torchlight. He was looking at the body and the spreading blood.

"You are witness that it was suicide. This will be of importance should there be necessity for a court martial."

The corporal swallowed. "Yes, sir."

Torien sheathed his sword. He went over to the table. Chareste was on his back on the tabletop, arms and legs spread, wrists and ankles chained one to each trestle. There was dried blood crusted on his brown face. There were wide, purple bruises in rows across his ribs. He tilted his head back against the tabletop, looking at the doorway. He saw Torien. "Commander Risto," he said. He spit blood and tried to smile.

"Don't speak," Torien said. With a hand on Chareste's arm, he looked up at the corporal in the doorway. "Unchain him."

"I don't have the key, sir. The Commander gave orders. No one else was to handle the prisoners."

Valle sheathed his sword and crouched beside the body, slipping the key ring from Espere's belt. "You know which key?"

The corporal opened the cuffs at Chareste's wrists and ankles and gave the key ring to Torien. "I'll bring the surgeon, sir."

"And a detail for the body, Corporal."

"Yes, sir."

The corporal's footsteps faded away up into the cell row. Valle went over to pick up Espere's knife. He wiped it with his sword-cloth and held it by the blade between his thumb and forefinger, tapping the haft on his palm. He was not really paying it any attention. He circled the room slowly—each time, without looking at it, managing to avoid the pool of blood which had spread over the floor at Espere's throat.

"He said you were dead, sir." Chareste had relaxed his head and shoulders against the tabletop. He spoke with his eyes closed. "Said it was Lieutenant Tarrega's work—said that was why—"

He was having trouble with the words. He shifted and grimaced on the tabletop. "Don't speak, Anzo," Torien said.

"He's innocent, sir—the Lieutenant."

"I know."

"It was for the boy," Chareste said, "for the *signo*. Wanted him out of here. Didn't know how else. Wasn't about the Mayasi—wasn't treason, sir."

"I know," Torien said. "Don't speak, Anzo. There'll be time later."

"Coward," Chareste said, with effort. "Could have eased it for him. He wouldn't let me ease it for him. I should have eased it for him. Coward." There were tears at the seams of his shut eyelids. "I should have eased it for him, sir." He shook with the suppressed tears. He drew a deep breath and gasped, hands flying up to his chest by reflex. He spit another mouthful of blood.

Torien leaned over the table and spread Chareste's arms, bracing them against the tabletop. "Lie still," he said. "Lie very still, Anzo, and don't speak." He held Chareste's shoulders in his hands, pinning Chareste's arms under his arms, and he prayed for the surgeon to come. Surely it did not take so long. Surely the corporal had gone first for the surgeon and afterward to raise a detail for the body.

There were footsteps down the stairs. The surgeon came into the room, a slave boy at his heels. He saw Espere's body slumped at the fire pit. His steps slowed.

"The Lieutenant, Doctor," Torien said. "The Commander has no further need of your services."

"Sir." The surgeon came over to the table. He did not say anything about Espere. "I will look at him now, Commander."

Torien let go Chareste's arms. The surgeon felt Chareste's ribs carefully under his hands. He motioned to the slave boy. The boy put the surgeon's bag on the stool beside the table and dug in the bag and gave the surgeon a glass bottle of some liquid. The surgeon unstopped the bottle and tipped it onto Chareste's tongue. The room was busily silent, and Torien was conscious very suddenly of his own uselessness. He backed away from the table. Someone touched his arm. He started, blinking into Valle's face. "Walk with me," Valle said.

They walked together up into the cell row. "Tell me exactly what you promised the tribes at the mines," Valle said.

"That I would see Espere before a court martial in Choiro."

"And later. You spoke with them privately—the Asano and the Mayaso both. You did not offer simply to kill him?"

"You know that would have done them no good."

"I know it as they know it. And they will know you returned to the fort and Espere is now dead without trial."

Torien stopped in the row, suddenly clear-headed. "They'll think I killed him?"

"You can tell whatever story you want of his death. They know we will be looking for a pretext to take the mines by force. It does not profit the Empire to leave the mines in their hands now that our puppet Idran is dead. What is to stop you from swearing before the Senate that Espere died on the Road with an Asano spear in his back? That is what they will think."

There were boots tramping down the row, coming down from

166

the common room. The corporal and his detail went past, saluting. Torien did not return the salute. "I left hostages, Valle."

Valle was silent.

"I'll ride for the mines tonight," Torien said.

"You are the ranking officer here, and you are noble blood. It would not be wise to put yourself in their hands."

"Our only hope is to give them the truth, and it'll be best coming from me—as the ranking officer."

"Some of them will listen to you. Some of them will be willing to believe you do not mean to use his death against them. Many of them will not. Even among the Asani, not all are eager for peace. Many see peace as disgrace. Why else do you think they would stand aside and let a watch captain kill their chieftain? They can kill you just as easily, or hold you to ransom. Even the more moderate among them will recognize you are too valuable a bartering piece to squander. The radicals will think you are a sign from God that their cause is just. Then it will be full-scale war."

"It'll be war anyway if they think I betrayed them."

"We have some time. As it stands, they expect you to travel to Choiro. That gives us a month, at least."

"A month to do what? Mass troops?"

They had come out from the guardhouse onto the thoroughfare. The gate doors were shut; the guards had gone back to their posts. The sky was pearl-gray, and there was a sea wind pushing over the battlements. Torien followed Valle up the steps to the wall. The men on the wall stood aside to let them pass. A few of them saluted, belatedly and with some confusion recognizing Torien as the corporal had done. None of them spoke. None of them seemed sure of what to do about the Guardsman. Valle went down the walkway toward the southwestern tower. He stopped at the merlon from which the body hung and leaned over the crenellation to look, his hands on the merlons on either side. He straightened, slowly. He glanced back at Torien. His shoulders were stiff. "Again I must ask for your help," he said.

They raised the body carefully on the ropes. They pulled it over the wall and laid it down very gently on the walkway. Torien sat at the feet, trying not to look into what was left of the face. He had caught a glimpse as they pulled the body up, and he wished he hadn't. He blinked and swallowed. He thought it was a trick of his eyes or the light that he saw one discolored hand move against the paving stones, but beside him Valle bent over the body and said, "Nico." Then he looked up at Torien, his hands on Tarrega's head. "Water," he said.

Wordlessly, Torien started to get to his feet. One of the guards, standing and watching with some others a little way down the wall, said, "I'll go, sir."

Torien nodded. The man went at a run. Valle was holding Tarrega's head between his hands and speaking softly in Modigno, his head bent, his mouth close to Tarrega's ear. Tarrega turned his head against the paving stones. Torien sat slowly back down against the wall. Tarrega's face was toward him, and he could not look away, though he wanted to, simultaneously repulsed and ashamed of his repulsion. The nose was a shattered ruin. The eye sockets gaped empty—burned-out holes where the eyes had been dark and cool and keen as a surgeon's probe to match the knife-blade smile.

He felt suddenly that Stratto had been right. It was ignorance, not clarity. One could not know after a fortnight. There was very much he did not know and he had been a fool to think he knew after a fortnight.

The guard returned with a water-skin and a leather cup. He gave the skin and cup to Torien and stood back, uncomfortably. It was obvious he wanted to speak but did not know how to say what he wanted to say. Espere had not had the authority to execute a soldier summarily, and of necessity the guards must be afraid they would be punished for complicity. It was Valle's prerogative to choose; they knew that.

Valle did not pay any attention to the guard. He slid an arm under Tarrega's shoulders and pulled him up gently and held him close, loosening his cloak with one hand to put it over Tarrega's body.

Torien poured water into the cup and leaned forward to put the cup against Tarrega's crusted lips. Tarrega turned his head away against Valle's shoulder. His lips were closed. Valle said something in Modigno, and Tarrega turned his head back, opening his mouth.

His teeth were broken, his tongue cut out.

Torien shut his eyes. There was an ache in him as though he had been kicked. He held the cup to Tarrega's lips, tipping it slowly as Tarrega swallowed. Tarrega flinched, his mouth slackening. Water ran over Torien's hands. He opened his eyes. Tarrega coughed and shivered, curling up under Valle's arm. He sucked a breath, then let it go. His head dropped from Valle's shoulder.

Torien put the cup down and reached with numb fingers to feel for the pulse, but Valle caught his wrist quickly in his free hand. "I will need to speak with Lieutenant Chareste," he said. His voice was calm, but his fingers around Torien's wrist were as tight as a vise. "As soon as it may be arranged."

He heard his own voice say, "I'll inform the surgeon."

Then he was going down the walkway for the gatehouse steps, somehow not stumbling, and Valle was sitting on the walkway behind him, holding Tarrega's body and looking at nothing.

He had remembered, as he went down the steps, that he must send wagons for the *signo* and the young Espere and the bodies at the cove, and he had given charge of it to the corporal, Savio, and he had ordered the surgeon along with the wagons, so that he and Valle were alone now with Chareste in a cell in the infirmary. The smoke of the morning cook fires was drifting through the open window, and the rumor of voices from the barrack blocks. Chareste lay on the mat with his ribs wrapped. He was in pain despite the numbing draught which the surgeon had administered, and he was trying bravely but unsuccessfully not to show it. There was sweat on his face though the cell was cool.

"The morning after you left, Commander Risto. I had the watch.

The Lieutenant took the rolls as usual, and then he was with the recruits on the parade ground. There was a messenger come up from the harbor just at mid-morning. The Commander came to me for a guard detail directly afterward. I gave him the men, sir. I didn't know what he needed with them until they brought the Lieutenant in."

"Did you know the charge?" Valle said.

"He told us it was for treason, sir. He told us the Lieutenant had been taking Mayaso coin."

"You did not believe him."

"I assumed he'd finally realized the Lieutenant had been leading him on, sir."

"About the *signo*, you mean."

"Yes, sir. He'd been making excuses for a month—keeping the boy alive until he could get him out of the fort. There was no opportunity until Commander Risto came."

"He confided this to you?"

"He was a friend, sir. And I think he needed to confide in someone. It tore him apart—what he did to the boy."

"You knew he was a Guardsman?"

Chareste hesitated. "Yes, sir. Not at first, though it had crossed my mind more than once that he must have prior orders—from Modigne, I thought, or maybe straight from Vione."

"Prior orders concerning the *signi?*"

"Concerning the mines. Most of the officers knew that the Commander—well, that he had his own business with the Asani, sir. We knew what he'd commanded of the *signi*. We knew he wanted a war with the Mayasi. We were going to write to Vione. I was chosen to do it. He took me aside, then—this was a month ago, sir, directly after the Commander ordered the *signi* decimated. He showed me his seal. He asked me to give him time."

"You were the only one of the officers to know?"

"Yes, sir. The others thought I'd sent to Vione as we'd planned."

"Tell me about the messenger."

"I didn't pay him much attention, sir. There are always messengers up from the harbor. The Commander required it of the harbor master at each berthing—manifest and itinerary, along with the tax. There were ships come in on the tide that morning."

"You remember very clearly when he came, considering you didn't pay him much attention."

"It struck me afterward, sir. I mean that I didn't pay him much attention at the time."

"You understand there to be a correlation between this messenger and the Lieutenant's arrest."

"Yes, sir. It happened all very directly, sir."

"There are others who will remember the messenger? Or were you the only one to see him?"

Chareste's brow furrowed. "I am sure there are others who saw him, sir."

"Otherwise he becomes very convenient for you," Valle said.

Chareste lay still against the mat. "I would not have betrayed the Lieutenant, sir."

"Perhaps not if you had known Espere would examine you for

the other traitors in his command."

Chareste closed his eyes, briefly. "I can give you the duty roster for that morning, sir. I am sure there'll be others who remember the messenger. I swear to you I did not betray him."

"I will see about the roster. When were you arrested?"

"Four days ago, sir—the morning he put the Lieutenant on the wall."

"It was because you objected?"

"I should have done earlier. He made me swear it to him, sir—the Lieutenant did. He made me swear I would not intervene. It was what he wanted, sir. I swore it to him. I wish I hadn't."

"You had opportunity to speak with him?"

"The second night. We'd had word of attacks on the Road. One of the trains reported they'd found the remains of Commander Risto's patrol. I took the Lieutenant water and wine and a draught of poppy while the Commander went out on a cavalry sweep. He'd left the door open, sir."

"You were alone with the Lieutenant?"

"Yes, sir."

"He said nothing to you of who might have betrayed him?"

"No, sir. He asked the oath of me. That was all."

"And you did not speak with him again."

Chareste did not say anything.

"Did you speak with him again, Lieutenant?"

"Once again—yes, sir. Next morning—the morning of the execution. The Lieutenant couldn't walk. The Commander ordered

Corporal Savio and me to take him up to the wall."

"What did he say?"

Chareste shifted on the mat. A spasm of pain went over his face. "He was—not in his right mind, sir. It was nothing."

"What did he say?"

"He said, 'Forgive me, Valle. It was done at my word.'"

Valle's face was blank. "You are very sure, Lieutenant?"

"Yes, sir."

"Who is Valle?"

"I don't know, sir. I don't know if he knew. He was hallucinating."

"The Commander was present to hear this?"

"Yes, sir."

"Tell me what he said."

"He said he would make sure they knew who had betrayed them, sir."

"They?"

"I don't know what he meant, sir."

"Did the Lieutenant say anything?"

"Not—to that, sir."

"To something else?"

Chareste shut his eyes and swallowed.

"Lieutenant," Valle said, quietly, "it is very important that I know everything he said."

"He asked for my knife, sir—the Commander did. He ordered me to give him my service knife. I would not. God knows I could not. The Lieutenant told me to do it, sir."

"He told you to give Espere your knife."

"Yes, sir."

"He had clarity at that point."

"Yes, sir."

"That was all he said?"

"He did not speak again. You saw what was done, sir."

"You said this was four mornings ago."

"Yes, sir. Others can confirm it for you, sir."

Valle was studying Chareste on the mat. "Lieutenant."

"Yes, sir?"

"It would have been a solace to him—all that you did for him. I am in your debt."

Chareste opened his eyes. He turned his head against the mat to look at Valle. He was trying, perhaps, to see if that had been mockery. "You haven't reviewed the duty roster yet, sir."

"If I believed you betrayed him, Lieutenant," Valle said, "you would be dead already."

"But you believe someone betrayed him," Torien said.

They were walking the corridor. They passed the cell where the infirmary slaves were preparing Tarrega's body for burial. Valle did not look in through the doorway. "There are three possibilities that I can see," he said. "That he betrayed us himself—possibly for gain,

175

more likely for that he was afraid he'd been found out about the *signo*; or that he was himself betrayed, and gave up the rest of us under torture; or that we were all of us betrayed together by someone who knew the Guard was operating in Tasso, who knew the ship we used out of the cove. I find the latter the most plausible—or the least implausible, perhaps."

"You proved very neatly that Chareste wasn't making up those last words out of thin air. Obviously Tarrega was of the mind that he'd betrayed you—and so was the *signo* at the ship."

"The *signo* said they had been at the ship a week this morning. In other words, they were at the ship the morning of the arrest. I do not believe Nico would have broken so quickly."

"Then it was deliberate."

"In that case, why wait so long to arrest Lieutenant Chareste? It is more plausible to me that Espere already knew of the ship when he arrested Nico. The Lieutenant's messenger is significant."

"There has to be a reason for his saying he betrayed you."

Valle was looking down the corridor. "It is possible the Lieutenant is right—that it was hallucination."

"Possible but not likely?"

"No," Valle said, "not likely."

"Anyway, if you're right and Espere knew everything by the time he made the arrest, then what did he need from Tarrega under examination?"

"I do not believe Espere knew everything. I believe he knew there were Guardsmen in Tasso, and I believe he knew of the ship. I do not think he could have known that the Guardsmen who were supposed to be either in the city or with the ship were in fact out on the Road on a near-spontaneous rescue mission."

"Then that was the betrayal."

"Perhaps, though it raises a question of why Espere would execute Nico without waiting to see if he had spoken true. To me, it suggests he had found another way to satisfy himself concerning our whereabouts. Five days ago, he heard from a train that your patrol had been slaughtered on the Road. He went out with a cavalry troop to see for himself. The next morning, he put Nico on the wall."

Torien turned this over in his head. "He thought it had been you and the Guard."

"He would have assumed so when he did not find you or Senna or the *signo* among the dead. After that, he had only to wait. He knew we would need come back for the ship eventually."

"It still doesn't explain away what Tarrega said to Chareste."

"'It was done at my word' could be in reference to a great many things and not necessarily to betrayal."

"Had he something else for which to beg your forgiveness with his last words?"

Valle was not looking at him. "I have seen it before: trivial things which become suddenly more important in the face of death. That much I can understand. What I do not understand is why he should have called me by that name. He only ever called me by first name."

Torien, not knowing what to say, said nothing.

Valle came back from wherever he had gone. "I will go through the Lieutenant's duty roster, for thoroughness's sake. I do not imagine he was lying. We know Espere had informants in Modigne, and we know the messages came and went very openly. We've intercepted them before."

"'The sign of the Boar'?"

"A code—a clumsy one, as you have seen. They had gotten careless."

"Afterward?"

"It is necessary that I go to Choiro. I must speak with the High Commander. He will be able to tell me exactly who among the Guard command knew detail enough of our mission to betray us."

"In the meantime I'm to prepare the garrison for war?"

Valle was silent, for a moment. "Send word to the Asano," he said, finally. "*Send* to him—do not go yourself. Give him the truth. Ask him to grant us time. Reaffirm to him that Lieutenant Senna is in his hands as our pledge of good faith, but remind him also that we have Lieutenant Espere."

"If he isn't dead already."

"I wouldn't include that part," Valle said.

XII

They buried Tarrega and Stratto in the morning, and the *signi* who had died at the ship. They buried Espere, too, because he had not been convicted before a court martial and could not by law be burned. They buried Tarrega and Stratto in full harness as officers of the Guard—Tarrega who was really Nico Briule, born on Epyris, who had taken the Tasso mission as his first command. Valle, in his own harness, spoke their names and the prayer for the dead. There was no one to speak the names of the *signi*, but Torien said the prayer for them, though by strict technicality they were not his soldiers and it was not his place.

Valle left afterward on a trade ship out of Kabira, bound for Modigne. From Modigne he would take ship for Salina, and from Salina he would go by riverboat up the Breche to Choiro. It was still early enough in the summer for the river passage. In another few weeks, the Breche would be shrunken back from wide, dusty banks and shallow enough to cross on foot, and in places dried to cracked brown clay under the Vareno sun. The privileged of Choiro would be gone up to their summer estates in the hills. The Emperor would be at Civiparro or perhaps at Ebre, on the Salino coast. Things went very slowly in Choiro in summertime. It would be a month at least before Torien had word again from Valle, and it might easily be two.

That day went very busily in the mundane work of command to which he must now accustom himself. He divided up Tarrega's and Chareste's duties among the remaining officers and wrote out a lieutenant's commission for the corporal, Savio. On Savio's recommendation, he sent for a man who trained animals for the games to come remove the spotted cat from Espere's office.

In the evening, he dispatched a rider to the mines. Besides what he had written to the Asano, Aidar, he had written also briefly to Alluin and to the *signo*, saying none of the things he wanted to say— only that he had come safely to the fort and would write again when there was news and he had opportunity. He left intentionally vague that he was still here in Tasso. He might as well have said nothing at all. Alluin would sense that something had happened and that he was not being told. Perhaps Aidar would tell him in confidence, and he would understand why it could not be written. Even so, the letter seemed like a lie.

After he sent the rider, he went to see the young Espere in the infirmary.

He hung back in the doorway of the boy's cell, at first, while one of the infirmary slaves did something with the dressings on the boy's arm and at his side. The boy's supper was on a tray beside the mat, and the slave, finishing with the dressings, tried first to push the bread into the boy's mouth and then, failing at it, tried to slip a shallow spoonful of bean broth between his teeth. The boy turned his head away and would not take it. His face was very pale in the lamplight. The stump of his left arm was limp and straight at his side, but there was a thick leather strap running from his right wrist to an iron loop bolted on the wall. The slave tried again with the spoonful of broth, and the boy turned his head away to the other side.

Torien ducked in through the doorway. "I'll do it," he said.

The slave bowed, put the bowl and spoon on the tray, and went out. Torien sat down beside the mat. The boy lay tightly still, watching him and saying nothing—shivering sporadically, though there was sweat on his face.

"It'll ease the pain if you've something in your stomach," Torien said.

The boy said nothing.

Torien looked at the strap at the boy's wrist. "You've been making trouble?"

"They think I will kill myself."

"It would be a stupid thing to do. There'd be no point to it."

The boy swallowed. He looked as though he wanted to say something and could not bring himself to say it. Torien picked up the wine cup from the tray. "I won't make you eat, but you should try to drink."

The boy swallowed again. He shut his eyes but made no other move. Torien slid a hand under the boy's head and put the cup against the boy's lips. The boy opened his teeth, finally, slowly, and accepted a long sip of wine. He lay rigidly back down against the mat, holding the wine in his mouth.

Torien set the cup down. "You have family back in Varen?"

The boy opened his eyes. He looked at Torien. He swallowed the wine and said nothing.

"It's my duty to write them concerning your father's death," Torien said.

"Leave them out of it."

It came out quietly but with a forcefulness that surprised him. "I mean nothing else but to write them, I swear it to you."

"You *swore* my father would stand trial in Choiro."

Torien felt a flick of irritation. "As he would have done if he hadn't put a knife to his throat. There's only so much I can control."

The boy was silent, considering this. He said, unexpectedly, "Can you protect them?"

"They're not culpable for your father's crimes."

"I mean when I go under examination." The boy's face was carefully blank, but he was holding onto himself very tightly. "It won't matter to them," he said, "to the Guard. We're common blood. If I do not answer what they ask of me—you know what they'll do to my family if I do not answer, if I cannot answer—if I do not satisfy them."

"I'm not going to give you to the Guard."

The boy did not seem to have heard. "I'll do anything," he said. "I'll do anything you ask, if you will give them your protection."

"You can tell me who betrayed Tarrega."

Pain and disappointment and hopelessness chased in succession across the boy's face. "I don't know. I swear I'd tell you if I knew."

Torien did not say anything. He had not expected the boy would know much. Espere had bought the boy's commission and put the boy at the mines most likely for that reason—that he would ask no questions, that he would do as he was told quietly and without trouble. It had not been necessary that he know. He was as blind and trusting as a puppy.

The boy mistook Torien's silence. "I'll swear it to you under examination," he said.

Torien got up. "I'll keep in mind that you offered."

"Please, Lord Risto." There was desperation in the boy's voice. "I will pay. I can pay near four thousand eagles."

"Your cut from the mines?"

The boy did not notice the sarcasm. "My year's salary. I can get more if you'll give me time, I swear. I'll sell my horse and gear."

"I wouldn't," Torien said. "You may need them shortly. Anyway, there's something else you can do for me, if it'll make you feel better."

"I will do anything."

"Don't kill yourself. And don't ask the surgeon again to do it for you, though I'm sure he'd appreciate four thousand eagles. At present, you're just about all that's holding together our truce with the tribes. That's a better guarantee from me than you can buy."

There was lamplight coming out under the curtain in the doorway of Chareste's cell, down the corridor. When he ducked in through the curtain, Chareste put down the tablet and stylus he had been balancing against his updrawn knees. "Commander Risto," he said. He was sitting up on his mat, his shoulders braced against the wall. He stretched his legs straight, slowly, not quite managing to hide a grimace.

"I didn't mean to interrupt."

"No, sir. It's nothing—some instructions for Lieutenant Savio. It's very good of you to come, sir."

"How are you feeling, Anzo?"

"I've no complaints about a day in bed, sir, though I'm not so sure about a month of it. I'll have run out of faults to find in Savio's work, by then."

Torien poured two cups of wine from the jug on the table and carried them over to the mat and gave one to Chareste. "You'll still have plenty to find in mine, I imagine."

"It's not so difficult, sir, to command a garrison. It's mainly a matter of delegation." Chareste smiled as he took the wine cup, but Torien could tell by his eyes that his thoughts were elsewhere. "I wanted to speak with you, sir. I know you were busy earlier."

"You should have sent for me."

184

"There were other things more urgent, sir. But I wanted to speak with you about the Lieutenant—about Commander Briule, sir, about what he said to me the morning of his execution. You remember what I told you he said, sir, when the Guardsman asked."

"I remember."

"It wasn't hallucination, sir. I lied to say that it was. He was in pain, but he had clarity. He meant to say it. He meant that I should hear. I'm very sure of it. I was sure of it yesterday, but I didn't want to say so in front of the Guardsman."

Torien sat down against the wall beside the mat, holding the wine cup between his hands. "Then it *was* a confession of guilt."

"It's a code—a name. His betrayer's name, sir. You understand for my sake he couldn't speak it plainly with the Commander there."

"Show me."

Chareste set his wine cup down and opened the tablet on his lap. He scratched out the lines he had written for Savio. He commenced to write again. His hand moved slowly and carefully across the wax face of the tablet. Torien watched over his shoulder as the words took shape: *a Valle perdoname ar'ordenone meo s'ie revaia.* "This is what he said, sir," Chareste said, as he wrote, "word for word."

"Yes."

On a new line, Chareste now made a series of quick strokes across the wax: AVPA'OMS'IR. Then, beneath, he rearranged the letters, drawing the tip of the stylus down in a line from each letter above so that Torien could see the count was straight. Torien read aloud when he had finished: "Maris Pavo."

Chareste held the tablet on his lap and said, "I would have told you yesterday, sir, but I didn't know about the Guardsman."

Torien did not say anything.

"I can't believe it's coincidence, sir," Chareste said, quietly.

"It's no coincidence."

"He might have been mistaken, sir. It might have been just a guess."

"It had to have been someone among the Guard command. We knew that already."

Chareste hesitated. "If this much was done on the High Commander's orders, sir, then perhaps also the rest of it—perhaps also the business with the mines."

Torien did not say anything.

"Sir." Chareste's voice was very quiet. "If it goes to a court martial, and it is your word against Lord Pavo's—"

"I need to speak with Valle."

"Valle is the Guardsman? He may not be trustworthy, sir. He may have been on Lord Pavo's orders himself."

Torien was silent, considering this out of necessity, remembering the way Valle's sword had slipped on its sheath after the fight at the cove and the way Valle had held Tarrega's body on the gate wall. He shook his head. "He didn't know—*doesn't* know. He's gone to ask Pavo's help finding the traitor."

"We can send word after him to Modigne, sir."

"I don't much care to sit and wait two weeks before I know whether the message has even reached him. It'll be better done in person. If nothing else, it'll be quicker. Right now, we need time most of all."

"If it has been Lord Pavo's work all along, then Modigne will know you were meant to die here in Tasso. They'll want to correct that failing, sir."

"Possibly. It's a chance I'll have to take. Listen to me, Anzo," he said. "You've nothing to do with it. You don't know where I've gone, or why. Pavo must not be given reason to think you or any of the rest of the men are involved—at least not of your own volition. You understand he doesn't need the courts. He didn't need a court to kill Tarrega."

"Is there no other way, sir?"

"Not that will save Valle's life."

"Then I ask that you let me go with you, sir."

"Don't be a fool, Anzo."

"It's only the ribs, sir. Nothing that a little wine can't carry me through." Chareste smiled.

"I need you here. You'll have the command in my absence."

Embarrassment flooded Chareste's brown face. He ducked his head. "Sir, I've only a field commission. I didn't come through Vione."

"Vione is for senators' sons playing at soldier."

"There are others here better qualified, sir."

"Command is nothing but delegation. You said it yourself. I have to ask this of you, Anzo. I don't know who else I can trust. If Pavo's in this business, then anyone might be in this business. Pavo's got long fingers—and a deep purse."

"Until you return, then, sir." Chareste's voice was quiet.

"Until I return. With any luck, I'll be back in a fortnight. Meanwhile, I need you to keep Espere the Younger from killing himself. That may be just as important, in the end: he's our pledge of peace from the Asani, or as good as we've got." Torien drained his cup and stood. "If I write out a few letters tonight, Anzo, will you send them for me? Only if I—only if you have word that I failed. Otherwise and hopefully they'll be superfluous."

Chareste looked at him. He looked as if there was very much he wanted to say, but he said only, "If it's necessary, sir, I will send them."

"I'll bring them by in the morning." Torien set his cup on the table. "I'll have the surgeon send in more wine."

XIII

The ship was a double-masted sailing ship which had carried olives and oil out of Modigne and was being reloaded now with grain and spice brought up by camel train on the Road. On foot, Torien guided the tall black horse carefully by the reins through the archipelago of bushels and spice chests dotting the quay below the gangplank. The armed slaves who stood guard watched his progress silently but closely. A pound of cinnamon was six months' pay for a common soldier, an equal weight of saffron better than a full year's, and he supposed they had been trained not to consider anyone beyond temptation.

The ship master was overseeing the loading from the foot of the gangplank. He was a leather-faced Modigno with three gold loops in each ear, and he did not immediately notice Torien. He was shouting harshly in his own tongue to two slaves on the gangplank who were wrestling a bushel up the plank. When at last slaves and bushel had disappeared onto the deck, the ship master turned and saw Torien. Something very akin to annoyance went over his face. His eyes darted past Torien to the guards. "You see that I am busy and cannot speak to you now," he said.

Torien slipped his belt knife from its sheath and dug the point under the Modigno's ribs. "Perhaps you can make time."

The Modigno stood very still, looking from the blade up to Torien's face. "I am a citizen."

"Then you'll know this shouldn't be necessary. You owe me your attention."

The Modigno gathered himself carefully together. "It was of course my mistake," he said. He bowed, delicately. "I am at your service, Commander."

Torien took the knife away from the Modigno's ribs and sheathed it. "The harbor master told me you sail tomorrow."

"With the morning tide," the Modigno said, "provided the loading is done without delay." His voice was cool.

"I must have passage today. For myself and the horse."

"There are other ships."

"None licensed for Modigne."

The Modigno was silent, for a moment. Then he said, "The loading will not be finished today."

"You are required by law to give me passage."

"This is absurd!" The Modigno flung up his hands in frustration. His bronze face flushed darkly. He pressed his lips together and drew a long, low breath through his nose. He licked his lips and said, more quietly, "It is one day, Commander. You must understand I cannot sail before the loading is done. I have creditors to pay off."

"I can make up your losses."

The Modigno was contemptuous now rather than angry. "Have you any idea of the value of my cargo?"

"Some idea," Torien said. "I'll pay thirty thousand eagles if you will sail this morning."

It was too outrageous an offer even to be considered a joke. It was more than half again his year's salary as an officer, and the ship master knew it. He studied Torien's face, saying nothing.

"I'll pay three thousand as surety," Torien said. "You'll have the rest by draft when we reach Modigne."

The Modigno's eyes went from Torien's face to the seal ring on Torien's forefinger. He said, very quietly in disbelief, "It is one day."

"We have an agreement?"

"I will have it in writing," the Modigno said. Torien could see in his face what he thought of Vareni, and in particular of Vareno nobility. The Modigno lifted his chin, suddenly bold. "And I will have six thousand as surety, not three—if you want me to believe you are in earnest."

"I'll seal it to you before the harbor master," Torien said.

He saw to the black horse himself, putting him in traces between two stout posts in the ship's upper hold. He spent a little while in the half-light of the hold, rubbing down the black coat with a piece of sacking: the horse was skittish with the movement of the ship and the commotion of the loading going on below, and there was sweat broken out on the shoulders and flanks. The unshod hooves tapped a nervous rhythm on the floorboards. Torien finished with the sacking and held the long black head between his hands and spoke softly into the flattened ears. "You and me both," he said. There was a flutter in the pit of his stomach and an ache between his shoulder-blades that would not go away, he knew, until there was solid ground beneath his feet in Modigne. "You and me both."

He did not go up on deck to watch the casting-off. For thirty thousand eagles, they had given him the cabin that normally would be reserved for creditors' agents or government officials. He lay in the narrow bunk against the inner bulkhead, and he heard the creak of the rigging and felt the long, rolling weightlessness as the ship slipped out from its mooring stones on the tide.

He squeezed his eyes shut and saw in his mind the burnt red shoreline of Tasso going back in the port-side distance, the wide blue nothingness running to starboard. They would tack along the coast to Istra and then cross open sea and then, sighting Gola, run along Epyris to Modigne. Each leg of the voyage was two days, and apart from the stretch from Istra across to Epyris never more than three miles offshore. Pirates were a higher probability than the ship going down. Alluin had pointed this out to him during the crossing from Modigne. It had not made any difference then, and it was not making any difference now.

At noon, the cook's boy edged in through the curtained doorway with a tray in his hands. There was bread and salt fish and a sticky handful of dried dates, and a jug of wine which the boy was taking care not to spill. Torien sat up against the bulkhead, stomach fluttering. His head ached with sun and salt. His mouth was dry. He shook his head when the boy held out the tray. "Water," he said.

The boy bowed and retreated with the tray and returned with a water-skin and a cup. He poured carefully and held the cup out, holding it so that his fingers would not touch Torien's. His downcast eyes were gray the color of hoarfrost above high, sharp cheekbones made sharper with hunger. The iron ring around his neck sat loosely on his jutting collarbone.

"Look at me," Torien said.

The boy looked up from his bare feet. Even so, he did not look in Torien's eyes but somewhere away past Torien's right ear.

"Which tribe?" Torien said.

The boy said nothing. His thin brown hands were tight on the water-skin.

"Dobryni?" Torien said. The boy was old enough to have been taken in the rebellion. He was perhaps twelve years old. Possibly he was older. With the mountain tribes, it was hard to tell age with any certainty. The boy was small, but all the mountain people were small.

The boy was studying the bulkhead at Torien's back. Torien tipped the cup and drank. The water was slimy and stale and tasted of brine. His stomach roiled against it. His throat jumped. He gave the cup with dignity back to the boy and jerked his chin to the doorway. "Go," he said. The boy bowed quickly and backed away. When he had gone out through the curtain, Torien leaned over the edge of the bunk and was sick into the pot. He wondered if it had been deliberate on the ship master's part. Another day in port and there would have been time to take on fresh water.

He was sick for the rest of the afternoon.

At suppertime, the boy was back with the tray. This time Torien did not sit up from the bunk. His stomach had settled down to a wary peace, and he lay very still with one arm draped over his eyes. "Leave the wine," he said. "Take the rest of it."

The boy came over to set the wine jug on the floor by the head of the bunk. He took the tray back over to the doorway. Torien said, "Wait."

The boy froze at the curtain.

Torien slid his arm from his eyes and flicked his fingers to the tray in the boy's hands. "Sit and eat."

When the boy did not move, he repeated it in Cesino. He saw a sudden flash of recognition. The boy's chin came up, his eyes going almost hungrily over Torien's face. He saw, also, the shields which went up immediately after. The recognition slid into careful blankness. The boy shook his head once and fled.

He had not left a cup for the wine. He had, Torien reflected, followed his orders very literally. Torien considered and dismissed the barbarity of drinking straight from the jug. He dug for his mess cup in his pack and poured the wine in the cup, slowly and carefully so as not to spill it when the ship pitched. The wine was thin and cloudy with impurities and very nearly gone to vinegar. It was not much improvement on the water, but he supposed at least it was antiseptic. He drank enough to sleep and woke much later disoriented in pitch-blackness, the jug cradled at his elbow and his head aching fiercely. He slept again only very slowly, and by the time he had really gotten to sleep the sun was glaring white-hot off the water through the porthole.

The curtain was sliding back on its rings, and the boy was ducking in with breakfast on the tray.

Torien shifted the wine jug and sat up. He motioned for the boy to put the tray on the bunk. He picked up the bread from the tray and tore it in two. He held one half on his lap and held out the other half to the boy as the boy straightened. The boy looked at it hollowly. He swallowed without taking his eyes from it. His arms hung stiff and straight at his sides. His fingers were curled to fists.

Torien gestured with the bread. "Take it."

The boy swallowed again. A muscle jumped in his cheek.

"Take it," Torien said, in Cesino.

The boy reached very slowly, one-handed, and took the bread, careful as before that he did not touch Torien's fingers. With the bread in his hand, he darted a stricken glance over Torien's face.

"Sit and eat," Torien said.

The boy sat down cross-legged on the floor at Torien's feet. He bent his head to eat. He ate very slowly and delicately, tearing the bread with his fingers and lifting it in little pieces to his mouth, making it last, making no noise as he chewed and swallowed.

"Tell me your name," Torien said.

The boy swallowed his mouthful. He held the remainder in his hand. Without looking up he said, softly in the same tongue, "Ædyn, Lord."

"Of which tribe? Dobryni?"

"Of the Charysi, Lord."

"How did you come to be so far from home, Ædyn?"

"They sold me at Arondy port, Lord."

"They—Vareni?"

Ædyn said nothing. His eyes had strayed across the cabin to where Torien's kit sat against the bulkhead.

"Punishment for a crime?" Torien said.

"Yes, Lord." The boy was still studying the kit.

"You're young for a convict."

"I mean it was my father's crime, Lord."

"Explain to me."

Ædyn fumbled with the bread in his hand and said nothing.

Torien bent and took Ædyn's bony elbows in his fingers and drew the boy up to his feet. "Explain to me."

Ædyn said, looking at his feet, "He couldn't pay the tax, Lord. They took me instead."

"Your lord sold you to make up the debt?"

"Yes, Lord."

And did well out of it, Torien thought: a slave went for well more than a dirt-poor Cesino barley farmer owed in the yearly tax. He let go Ædyn's elbows. He took the clump of dates from the tray and held it out. "Here. Eat."

The boy shook his head. The bread was unfinished in his hand. "I must go, Lord."

"Take it for later."

The boy said nothing. Torien took the boy's free hand and put the clump of dates into it and closed the boy's fingers. He kept the water cup and slid the empty tray under the boy's arm. "You might as well eat them," he said. "They'll only come up again if I do."

He alternated the water with wine and in that way managed to get most of it down. The rest he splashed over his face and sore eyes. He took the half of bread down into the hold and held it on his palm for the black horse to lip. With nothing else to do, and no desire to go up on deck, he sat down cross-legged against one of the posts and spent the next few hours oiling and polishing his tack—working at the sand-scuffed leather of the saddle until the horns glowed softly red-gold and the knee-flaps were creamy-smooth and pliable, rubbing the bosses of the bridle until the metal was hot under his fingers.

He went back to his cabin at noon. It was not Ædyn who brought the meal, but a florid, balding, tight-lipped slave whom Torien took to be the cook himself. Torien took a little broth and bread and spent the afternoon in anticipation of bringing it up again each time the ship tossed. It was tossing more roughly now than earlier. Through the porthole he could see the waves like rows of white heads bent against the wind.

The sea was still rough at sundown, and he lay in the bunk listening to the creak and groan of the ship's timbers and the whistle of the wind down the ship walls, not realizing the tightness in himself until the boy came in through the curtain and he had to make a conscious effort to unclench his muscles and sit up. He propped himself up with one hand on the bulkhead. The boy brought the tray over from the doorway, moving slowly and carefully across the banking floor. "We are off Istra?" Torien said.

"In an hour or so, Lord."

"Is it common to be so rough off Istra?"

"Storms build over the point in summertime, Lord. It will be a good wind for Gola."

The floor banked sharply. The wine jug toppled from the tray and broke open on the floor. Wine splashed over the floorboards, running in rivulets down the chinks. Ædyn put the tray down very quickly on the floor. He knelt beside it and bowed over his knees, pressing his palms and forehead to the floor. "Forgive me, Lord. I'll clean it."

He stood with the tray in his hands and put the tray on the end of the bunk. He turned back to the doorway. "Ædyn," Torien said.

The boy spun around quickly. His face was white. "I'll bring another jug, Lord."

"Show me your back."

"The wine, Lord."

"Show me your back."

The boy swallowed, looking at his feet. Very slowly, he turned to the doorway. The back of his loose tunic was striped red with blood from shoulders to waist.

Torien said, at length, "It has been dressed?"

"Yes, Lord."

"Look at me."

The boy turned again and fixed his eyes on the bulkhead above Torien's ear.

"Tell me why," Torien said.

The boy said, studying the bulkhead, "I am not to ask my lord for food."

Torien did not say anything.

The boy bowed and said, "Please, Lord. I will bring more wine."

It was a good wind for Gola. They came into Modigne with the tide on the fifth morning. In the ship master's cabin, while the crew lashed the ship to its mooring stones and lowered the gangplank, Torien wrote out and sealed a draft note to the amount of twenty-four thousand eagles. He gave the note to the ship master. "I've another offer to make you," he said.

"As you will put a knife between my ribs otherwise," the ship master said, "I will listen." They had come into port a full day ahead of schedule, and with the draft note in his hands he was in a good mood.

"Your cook's boy. The Cesino. I've a mind to buy him of you."

"Perhaps I haven't a mind to sell him."

"I'll give you two hundred eagles for him."

"Unlike the passage," the ship master said, complacently, "you cannot demand him of me by law. He is not for sale."

"Three hundred eagles."

"A pittance, considering what I paid for him at Arondy."

In all likelihood, the ship master had paid no more than one hundred for the boy at Arondy. Ship labor was plentiful and cheap. "He wasn't half-starved then," Torien said.

"Neither was he trained for service," the ship master said, "nor could he speak a civilized tongue. These things came of my time and effort."

"Four hundred. Anyone can use a whip."

"He is not for sale," the ship master said. "I've taken loss enough on your account."

"Five hundred."

The ship master smiled over his shoulder as he locked the draft note in his strongbox. "I wish you well in Modigne, Lord."

"And my word as Lord Risto that your docking tax at Vessy will be waived henceforth," Torien said.

The ship master paused. "At Vessy and at Alchys, and the fare for the river passage."

"I will give it to you in writing."

Under the ship master's eyes, he wrote it out on papyrus and signed his name and scrolled the papyrus and sealed it. He handed it over wordlessly. The ship master held the scroll in his hands for a moment before he locked it with the draft note in the strongbox. "A pleasure to do business with you, Lord."

"I'm sure. Give me the key for the boy's collar."

The ship master bowed as he gave Torien the key. "A word of advice for the future, Lord Risto, if you will have it. It pains me to say it, but as an honest man I am compelled."

"Go ahead."

"Hire an agent, Lord, to purchase your slaves and make your travel arrangements. There are those who take advantage of nobility."

"Your sense of honesty has impeccable timing."

"You see I am not only honest but prudent," the ship master said.

He tied a cloth over the black horse's eyes and walked close against the horse's neck down the gangplank and onto the quay, one hand on the halter strap under the horse's chin, but even so the horse was nervous at the crowd and the noise, and it was all his effort to hold the horse in and keep him from tearing his head away. They went up the waterfront, he walking ahead with the horse, the boy following silently. It was mid-morning, and the crowd was thick along the quay, the air ringing with the clamor of voices—Modigno and Vareno and the off-shot dialects of the islands—and Tasso was suddenly very far away and hazy as a dream in the heat.

He took the horse off the street into a smith's shop. Ædyn tagged at his heels like a shadow. The shop was open-faced to catch the breeze off the water, but there were coals smoldering on the wide, open hearth, the heat curling off the hearthstones and hanging heavy on the air under the leather awning. The smith was bare-chested at his anvil. He saw Torien across the anvil and put his hammer down and wiped his dripping face with the back of one hand. He pulled his tunic over his head as he came over to the doorway. He bowed, but he was looking at the black horse. "You will want him shod, Lord, if you mean to use him in the city."

"He won't be long for the city. I came for this." Torien reached with his free hand for the lead tag hung on the collar around Ædyn's neck. He indicated it to the smith, running his thumb over the name etched on the face of the tag. "It can be amended?"

"It is a simple thing, Lord."

"My name is Risto. I want it to read thus."

"For a bronze, Lord."

He explained to Ædyn, in Cesino, "For your protection, until I can file your manumission."

The boy looked as though he had been struck across the face. His skin was pale under the tan. "My lord is the governor's son."

"My mother told him so, anyway. Listen to me, Ædyn. I've business in the city. I shouldn't be long—an hour, maybe two. I'll be back for you here."

The boy did not say anything. He was standing as rigid as death at the horse's shoulder.

Torien put two bronze pieces into Ædyn's hand and closed the boy's fingers over them. "Buy yourself something to eat," he said. "Don't stray too far. These streets can be rough."

XIV

The Guard barracks were built into a stretch of the old city wall which crowned the rim of the hill, the city falling away below and spreading out like a cloak to the water. Beyond the wall, north and east, the hill sloped down to barren flatland and then swelled up again to the mountains. There were cloud-shadows moving slowly on the hot wind across the flatland and chalk dust blowing along the northeast road. The earth was baked red and brown and white in the heat. The street was cool in the shade of mastic groves and quiet except for the trickle of water from the drinking fountains along the wall and the tinkle of shells strung in pieces in doorways and open windows.

At the barracks gatehouse, holding the black horse's halter in one hand, he took off his seal ring and passed it through the slot into the gateman's hands. "For Dio Valle," he said. He had not realized, until then, how very dry his mouth was.

The ring went away out of his sight. There was a stretch of standing and waiting, the tightness knotting up in him, the sweat running down between his shoulder-blades despite the shade of the mastic trees and the wind along the street. Then he heard a bolt being drawn back. The gate doors swung inward to the barracks yard. A black-clad Guardsman was standing just inside the gate. It was not Valle, but a tall lieutenant with an angular, harsh-mouthed, olive-skinned face, remarkably like Alluin's, which Torien knew to mean he was of old Choiro family. If one did not know it by his face, one could see it in the set of his shoulders and sense it tangibly on the air around him. One could practically taste money.

The lieutenant jerked up his chin by way of greeting. "Commander Risto."

Torien walked the black horse in slowly through the gate. He glanced around the yard. There was no sign of Valle. The brick-faced yard was empty and quiet. A stable-boy appeared noiselessly from somewhere and slipped the black horse's lead from his hands. "Is Valle here?"

"I've been instructed to show you to the Commander's office." The lieutenant held out Torien's ring on his palm. "Your weapons."

Torien took the ring and put it on his forefinger. He made no move for his weapons. His heart was thumping against the inner steel plate of his cuirass. "My business is with Valle, no other."

"Your business was finished at the gate. Once inside the gate it becomes our business." The lieutenant's voice was careless. "It wasn't a request. The Commander will speak with you. To what degree it is a pleasant conversation depends very much on your cooperation now."

Out of the corner of his eye, he could see another Guardsman watching from the doorway of the gatehouse, and though he could not see the gate wall he knew there were others watching from the arch. It had been foolish to come, and it would be just as foolish to attempt resistance now. He unbuckled his sword belt and wrapped the belt around the sheath and handed over the sword, hilt-first. He slipped off his knife and laid it on the lieutenant's palm. The lieutenant tucked the weapons under his elbow. He turned on one heel and started away across the yard for the headquarters at the end of the barrack block.

Just inside the headquarters vestibule, he came up so shortly that Torien, following, nearly stumbled into him. With his free hand, the lieutenant unbuckled the chinstrap of his helmet. Holding the helmet in the crook of his right arm, he bowed his close-shaven head to the image of the Emperor which faced them solemnly in white marble across the room. Torien watched and did not move. The lieutenant glanced at him as he straightened. "An inconvenience to bow, Commander?"

"My oath is to the Senate and People."

"As a soldier. As a citizen, your prior loyalty is to the Emperor."

"To the Empire. Not to the Emperor."

"It is an unnecessary distinction. The Emperor is the Empire."

"You've informed the Senate?"

"Commander Risto." A new voice broke in. Another officer emerged from the far doorway. He was grayer and stouter than the lieutenant, but just as obviously Choiro-bred. The lieutenant saluted him stiffly. The newcomer acknowledged it with a languid flick of his fingers. His eyes were on Torien. He turned his chin over his shoulder. "My office, Risto, if you please."

The office was small and austere, the walls of white adobe and the floor of bare, hard-packed earth. There was an un-shuttered slit of a window on the far wall, and through the slit Torien could see the flatland and the chalk line of the road and the distant piney heads of the mountains. The Guardsman shut the door when they had entered. There was no other chair than the stool behind the desk, so Torien stood. The Guardsman crossed the room, limping, and sat down behind the desk. He shut the tablet that had been open on the desktop. The lamp flame at his elbow jumped with the breath of wind. The Guardsman glanced up at Torien's face. "I don't believe you came to argue political theory with Lieutenant Aregne," he said. His eyes were the color of blued steel and just as hard.

"No."

"You wanted to see Guardsman Valle."

Torien noted the use of the past tense. The knots in his stomach drew up tighter. "I thought I might find him here. The harbor master told me his ship came in yesterday morning."

"Tell me why you wanted to see him."

"He's predisposed, I take it?"

"At present. Tell me why you wanted to see him."

"That's his business and mine."

"Guardsman Valle has no other business than that which his

commanding officers assign him. But let us leave that aside for the moment and discuss *your* business, Commander Risto, as ranking officer of the Tasso garrison. We are not officially at war in Tasso, so I suppose it is improbable the Senate will press to execute you for abandoning your post. Nevertheless, they might see fit to strip you of rank. Your presence in Modigne constitutes what seems to me a flagrant breach of your oath *to the Senate and People*." The Guardsman's voice was cool. "I'm left to believe you're at best incompetent, at worst a traitor—an idiot, in any case, to come here. Any reason sufficient to justify your being here is mine rightfully to know. Tell me what you wanted of Valle."

"I'm here at the dying request of Nico Briule."

He did not know what sort of reaction he had hoped for. The Guardsman did not react visibly, at any rate. His eyes were unblinking on Torien's face. "I was unaware you were in contact with Commander Briule immediately prior to his death."

"He left behind a message in code. He named his betrayer."

"It is my understanding," the Guardsman said, "that Commander Briule betrayed his own men, having jeopardized his mission for the sake of a recalcitrant *signo*—in which case he deserved the manner of death he died."

"Espere knew too much too soon for Briule to have been the traitor."

"Anything to absolve him—any which way the logic must be twisted." The Guardsman smiled, cuttingly. "Valle tried it the same. But very well. I will humor you for the sake of argument. If not

Commander Briule, then explain to me who else."

"Someone else who knew there were Guardsmen in Tasso—who knew everything of the mission except that for one narrow window of time Briule's men would be out on the Road rather than in the city."

"One of the command." The Guardsman was pouring oil into the lamp in a thin, careful stream. "Yes—so Valle said."

"Pavo," Torien said.

The Guardsman's hand on the oil jug was steady. The stream did not waver. "You suggest the High Commander has been trafficking Imperial citizens into the mines at Tasso."

He thought he had known, this time, what the Guardsman's reaction would be. He blinked. "Yes."

"This was Commander Briule's belief?"

"And mine."

"You have evidence—more than a dying man's tortured raving, I mean? You realize more than that will be necessary."

"It had to have been one of the command. And Briule's testimony can't be dismissed as tortured raving. He had presence of mind enough to formulate a code."

The Guardsman set the jug on the desktop and wiped a trickle of oil from the rim with his thumb. "You've only this lieutenant Chareste's word that Briule spoke at all. As a friend of Briule's, Chareste has reason to want him exonerated."

"Chareste is trustworthy."

"To your mind."

"There were other witnesses. Lieutenant Savio—"

"Doesn't matter," the Guardsman said, "any more than Chareste does—not to the Emperor, at any rate. I will remind you that Maris Pavo has been His Majesty's favorite since they were boys." He glanced up. "Surely you understand if the High Commander is behind this business in Tasso, it was a risk to come here to this place?"

"I had no choice."

"You had, as a matter of fact, but that is beside the point now. I'm curious as to what you thought Valle might be able to do. He is neither an officer nor noble blood."

"I didn't know what he might be able to do. I didn't particularly care. I meant to save his life."

The Guardsman studied Torien expressionlessly. He said, at length, "He left last night on a ship for Salina."

The knots, which had been constricting slowly inside him, loosened just a little. "I looked for him on the manifests for Salina. I didn't see his name."

"Neither will the command, should they look. He is traveling under an assumed name."

"You can tell me which ship?"

"I can tell you which ship. With a good wind, perhaps you may catch him at Salina. Almost certainly you will catch him on the river." The Guardsman shrugged. "It won't do you any good. Unless you find a way to incapacitate Pavo, you'll still be hanging on the Traitors' Wall when this is done."

"Does it matter to you?"

"Your hanging on the Wall? Not particularly. But I recognize you may be useful—necessary, even, if Pavo is to be eliminated. You've already proven yourself a radical: Aregne can testify as much. It will be easy enough to hang this around your neck should you fail."

Torien looked at him sharply. "Is this still hypothetical? Humoring me for the sake of argument?"

"Commander Briule would not have betrayed his men, willingly or otherwise. This was always beyond dispute in my mind, if indefensible rhetorically." The Guardsman was looking at his hands on the desktop, rubbing the knuckles with his fingers, flexing the fingers as though they pained him. His face was blank. "I care to see Pavo brought down, Risto. If you can't believe it's because I care for justice, then perhaps you'll believe it's because I cared for Nico."

"Did you?"

The Guardsman looked up from his hands. He smiled. This time it was a strained, sad smile. His face broke and it was an old man's face and it had been strong for too long. "He was my son."

Torien closed his eyes, briefly. He saw, against his will, the body mutilated beyond recognition in Valle's arms on the gate wall, and it occurred to him that he had not once thought of Nico Briule beyond the context of Espere, of Tasso. He had not wondered who might be left to mourn him. He glanced away across the room. He did not want the Guardsman to see in his face what was in his mind. "I'm sorry."

"He knew the risks." The elder Briule's voice was steady, carefully so. "Objectively, at least. I do not imagine that to his mind they were anything more than risks. He was a talented officer, rightfully confident in his abilities. It wouldn't have made any difference to him, of course—to know the end. He'd have been willing even so. I knew that of him. I knew his devotion to his work, which is why I—couldn't bring myself to believe he was the traitor, despite the logic—couldn't bring myself to believe that even under coercion—"

He faltered. He fell silent. He bowed his head over the desktop as though a weight had dropped on the back of his neck. Leaning on his elbows, he lifted his hands and spread his fingers over his face. Then he pressed his palms flat together against his lips and looked up at Torien over his fingertips. He smiled again. His eyes were hollow. "We were speaking of your usefulness."

"You want me to kill Pavo."

"You? You wouldn't get close enough to him to shout so he'd hear you."

"Then what do you need from me?"

"I need you to tell what you've told me to the one person in the Empire who *can* kill Pavo."

"You said it would make no difference to him."

"I'll correct myself. There are two people in the Empire who can kill Pavo. I want you to go to the one who will. His Majesty would never. More than once, he's turned a blind eye to Pavo's indiscretions. Informed of this, he'll slap Pavo on the wrist and tell him to be less sloppy next time, and he'll let you or Valle hang for it—probably Valle, because your father has too many friends in the Senate, and His Majesty knows it. No, I want you to go to the one who recognizes the precariousness of his position—who knows there's only so long the Senate will put up with the Emperor's incompetence, and who feels threatened accordingly."

"Threatened enough to kill his father's favorite?"

"If the alternative is to lose the throne—yes. And the Prince knows how to turn his father's wrath."

Torien brushed a hand across his eyes. "I asked for a posting away from Choiro for a reason."

"If you wanted to stay out of Choiro, you should have kept your head down and your mouth shut. You will need to be discreet, as it is. I do not recommend you travel by ship."

"Valle will be dead by the time I've crossed the border if I go over land."

"Go by ship and you will be dead at Salina. You can put on civilian clothes and go under a different name, and still there is the possibility someone will recognize you as Torien Risto—probability, considering the extent of Pavo's network. I will send to recall Valle. Your only concern is to reach Choiro unseen. Pavo will know before the week is out that he has lost Espere. If he learns you've left Tasso, he will guess the reason quickly enough."

"How do you propose I approach the Prince? Through his window at night?"

"Show your face anywhere on the Hill and Pavo will know it." Briule was silent for a moment, fingers threaded together against his mouth. "Your best hope is to work by proxy—and preferably through someone outside the circles of the Hill, someone to whom Pavo normally would pay no regard."

"Yet who has access to the Prince? That may be difficult to arrange."

"Not as difficult as you'd think." Briule's voice was dry. "There is a woman of His Highness's acquaintance who may be of some use. You'll have heard of her, perhaps: Chæla Ceno."

"I've heard nothing. Who is she?"

"Nobody, which is why she's suited to our purposes. A merchant's daughter. His Highness is—fond of her. It has caused some scandal."

"A prostitute?"

"A courtesan, to put it more delicately. She has money, if she hasn't a name. She is an educated woman, and she is ambitious."

"And she's trustworthy?"

"Of course not. But she has His Highness's ear. He has been known to visit the apartment she rents below the Hill. Arrange through her to meet him there. Pavo will think nothing of it."

"I'll have to give her some reason, if I can't give her the truth. For all she knows, I'm luring the Prince there to murder him."

"She is well aware her status depends to a great extent on her money. You may make her aware that her money depends to an even greater extent on her father's illegal activities."

"Ceno has a hand in this trafficking business?"

"He has a fleet in this trafficking business. And Pavo is not such a fool as to protect him should we move against him. As a commoner, he is expendable. The daughter is sensible enough to realize she can't afford to refuse you."

"You assume she cares more for her father than for the Prince."

"I assume she cares more for her money," Briule said. "In Choiro, that is always the safest assumption."

XV

It was past noon by the time he came back down to the waterfront. He did not go immediately to the smithy. He had left the black horse in the barracks stable: Briule had given him two saddle-horses for the journey to Choiro, with the promise that the black horse would be exercised daily on the chalk road outside the city. He rode north and west along the quay, then up the mud streets to the girl's shanty. It was a foolish hope that he would find her there, but even so he was disappointed, when he had dismounted and pulled back the curtain, to see the shanty bare and the fire pit cold.

He considered leaving a note before he remembered she would not be able to read it. Instead, he knelt at the pit and drew the Risto wolf with charcoal on one of the firestones. She would know, at least, that he had been there. She would hear it on the street if she did not find the wolf: he was conscious, as he went back out to the horses, of being watched furtively from nearby curtained doorways. He had bundled his kit behind his saddle and was dressed only in tunic and sandals, but he had his sword belt on his hip and he supposed he still looked soldierly enough, or perhaps Vareno enough in general, to be considered a threat.

Along the quay, the shops were shuttered for the siesta. The street was empty. At one of the wine cellars, the girl was just drawing the curtain across the doorway. She spoke no Vareno, but when he dismounted and pointed here and there on the menu painted on the wall she nodded and held up slim brown fingers to illustrate the price. He paid her in bronze, a coin extra for the trouble, and she brought him a cup of chilled white wine and a skewer of lamb folded in flatbread. She swept out the shop-front while he ate and drank. He finished and gave her back the cup. When she disappeared down through the cellar doorway, he saw for the first time a man standing a little way down the shop-front, leaning against the corner at the shadowed mouth of an alley, watching him across the stretch of empty street.

The man saw that Torien had noticed him. He glanced away. Torien shifted the reins from his right hand to his left and laid an easy palm on the pommel of his sword.

At that moment, an arm slipped around him from behind, pinning his arms. A knife blade slid under his chin. He jerked his head away, panic lurching in his stomach. The blade went over the back of his neck and flicked back across his cheek. Hot blood trickled over his jaw and throat. He snapped his head back into his captor's face, grinding the man's foot under his heel. He scrabbled for his sword as the man's grip loosened. He got the blade from the sheath and twisted against the knifeman's arm and ran the blade in under the knifeman's ribs, shaking off the knifeman's arm as the man fell.

There was movement behind him. The alley mouth was empty. A heavy hand clamped on his shoulder. He braced the first man's body against the street with one foot so he could yank his blade free, and as he did so he felt a knife slide smoothly in under his sword arm.

The coldness and rigidity of the steel shot through him like the thrill of ice-water. He could not move or breathe. The knifeman lowered him gently to his knees and eased the blade from his ribs. He pushed Torien's head down with one hand, slipping the knife under Torien's chin with the other, and though Torien knew in an off-hand way what he was preparing to do, he could not muster any reaction to it. The panic was gone in shock.

The knifeman's hands dropped away, suddenly. The knife clattered away on the paving stones. The knifeman folded to the street. Torien lifted his head, with effort. He looked up, blinking, into the wine-shop girl's face.

She knelt quickly beside him. She pulled his arm across her shoulders and raised him to his feet. The knifeman was in a heap, a thrown dagger through his neck. The quay was empty, and the fight had not lasted more than a few moments. The girl's shoulders were straight and surprisingly strong. She supported him in through the wine-cellar doorway and across the sand-swept floor to the partitioned room at the back of the shop that he understood must be her own quarters.

It was like moving through a dream. The pieces made sense in themselves, but he could not put them together coherently. The girl helped him down onto a straw mat on the floor. He sat cross-legged with his back against the wall. He attempted with stumbling fingers to unbuckle his sword belt, and it occurred to him that he had lost the sword in the street.

The girl put her hands on his hands and said something in her own tongue. She unbuckled the belt and tugged it aside. She took a fold of his tunic between her fingers and said something, gesturing. He nodded. It was painful effort to move his head. He sat with his eyes closed while she cut the tunic away. She went out into the shop, afterward. Bare-chested now, he was deathly cold. He sat shivering against the wall, listening to the girl move around the shop. She was gone for a long time. She came back with a wine jug and a piece of linen. She had his sword in her hands. She put the sword down beside him against the wall. She tore the linen into strips and soaked the strips in wine. She spread one strip over his ribs, covering the wound. She took his right hand and pressed it over the cloth. She dabbed at his face with another strip of cloth. He felt the wine in a stinging line where the first man's blade had opened the skin across his neck and cheek. The blood ran warm. The girl held the cloth to his face and neck until the bleeding subsided. Then she crumpled the cloth and gestured again, indicating the sword, then the street, then herself.

With sudden clarity, he caught her wrist with his left hand as she stood. "Not the fort," he said. He swallowed the urge to vomit. His fingers tightened involuntarily on her wrist.

The girl said, hesitantly, "Help, yes?"

"Not the fort. *Na bayas o*—fort. Not the fort. Do you understand?"

She looked down at him silently. He let go her wrist and leaned over and traced with his forefinger in the sand on the floor. He drew the Imperial sun. He looked up at the girl to see if she understood. She nodded. He swept his hand over the drawing, erasing it. He shook his head. "Not the fort."

She spoke in Modigno, illustrating with her hands something he could not follow. Then she was gone. He heard the shop curtain slide on its rings as she went out into the street.

At first he forced himself to stay awake. He forced himself to think about what would happen if she had misunderstood—or, conversely, if she had understood perfectly well, and had gone to the fort hoping for the bounty on a deserter. But she would not have left him his weapons, in that case. If she had gone to the fort, it was well-intended. It would not make a difference in the end, but at least it was well-intended. On further reflection, he twisted his seal ring from his finger and pulled his sword belt over with his left hand and dropped the ring down the empty sheath. Then he held the sheath between his knees and sheathed his sword. It would not make much difference either—there were plenty of men at the fort who would recognize him, seal or no, Pavo's network or no—but if it were uselessness, at least it was not passivity.

The afternoon wore on, and it was too exhausting to think. He hung in a shimmering place somewhere between waking and sleeping, his head thick with the smell of wine and blood. There were flies buzzing on the wall, and he heard the snap of the shop curtain in the breeze off the water. There was sweat on his skin, and the breeze was cold. His hand slipped of its own from his ribs. The cloth tumbled to the mat. He considered, briefly and dully, the effort to reach and pick it up, but he could not see any benefit to it, and anyway his hand was uncooperative now at his side, his fingers numb. He turned his head against the wall and braced his chin on his shoulder and closed his eyes.

Distantly he heard the rattle of wheels out in the street. He wondered if the siesta were over, and if so how long for someone to call out a detachment from the fort on account of the bodies; then much closer he heard footsteps and a voice he recognized as the girl's, though he did not recognize the words. There were other voices. He heard a voice in Vareno all at once, heavily accented but intelligible: "Lift him—carefully now."

An arm went around his shoulders, pulling him up. Someone knelt before him on the mat. Torien opened his eyes. A figure hovered indistinct in front of his face. He flinched. The arm tightened around his shoulders. A voice at his ear said, "Easy."

He tried to speak. Nothing came out. He licked his lips and tried again and managed only a whimpering groan.

"Quiet, yes?" The man who had spoken first was holding Torien's ribs under his hands, looking at the wound. "You save your strength."

Torien held his tongue between his teeth and sat very still while the wound was washed and dressed. The voice at his ear, a younger man's voice, said, "Can he walk or do we carry him?"

"Carry him, but gently. You think he walks with this?"

The girl said something. The man who had done the bandaging replied in the same tongue. The younger man, his arm still around Torien's shoulders, said, "What is she saying?"

"She says she has his horses. I tell her we take them. Hold him, now. I take his legs."

He was lifted suddenly from the mat, the younger man's hands under his arms, the elder's around his knees and under his ankles. They carried him out through the shop and up into the street. He turned his head against the supporting arm. The bodies were gone, the blood washed from the paving stones. They carried him up into a large closed carriage waiting before the doorway. Inside the carriage, they deposited him carefully onto a long, low bench. "Stay with him," the older man said. "I see to the horses."

In the light coming through the carriage doorway, Torien had a glimpse of him as he climbed down to the street. He was wearing a tunic of plain black wool, ankle-length and belted at the waist with a leather cord. Torien recognized it as a priest's robe. He tilted his head back against the bench and saw the younger man robed likewise. While he was arranging this in his head, the girl climbed up into the carriage. She put his sword belt and tunic on the bench at his feet. She touched his hand with two fingers, tracing the line of his thumb inward to his palm. She looked over to where the young priest sat at the far end of the bench with his hands on Torien's shoulders. She said something in Modigno. The priest said, "She wishes to apologize. It is not customary that her patrons are knifed."

Torien could not push the words off his tongue. She must have seen his frustration in his face. She let go his hand and covered his mouth gently with her fingers. She smiled at him. When she looked back at the young priest, the ends of her coarse black hair brushed across his face. He closed his eyes. He heard the hint of laughter in her voice as she spoke. The young priest said, "She says to tell you there are better ways to avoid attention than to wander about during the siesta."

The girl said something else, and the priest was silent for a moment, struggling with the translation. He asked the girl a question. Then he said to Torien, "If you are ever not a fugitive, she hopes she will have your patronage again."

The old priest was tying up Briule's horses at the back of the carriage. The girl took her hand from Torien's mouth. He watched through half-closed eyes, tight-throated, while she climbed back down into the street. The old priest came in, carrying Torien's kit. He pulled the door shut. Darkness fell. The carriage started with a lurch, and Torien drew a hissing breath through his teeth and gripped the rim of the bench in his fingers.

"Keep him still," said the old priest, from somewhere in the darkness.

The young priest bent over Torien, his hands tightening on Torien's shoulders. "It's not far," he said apologetically.

The carriage lumbered on. Through the walls, Torien could hear voices and the tramp of feet and clatter of hooves along the quay, and he knew the siesta was over. It was three hours past noon. The carriage walls trapped the heat like an oven. The pain had started, and he lay sweating and biting his tongue against the jolting of the wheels over the paving stones. Somehow—out of the gnarl of his thoughts—it occurred to him that the boy was waiting at the smithy and had been waiting more than five hours now. He unclenched his teeth and said, with concentrated effort, "Ædyn."

Above him, the young priest said, "Don't speak."

"Waiting for me. The smithy. Told him only an hour or two."

The old priest observed, over the rumble of the wheels, "He kills himself trying to talk."

"There is someone waiting for him on the quay."

"Another deserter, is it?"

"However he has crossed the *jente*, it isn't for that. Brevade doesn't send knifemen after deserters." The young priest bent down close to Torien's ear. "I will find your friend," he said. "You needn't worry. Rest now."

XVI

He must have passed out in the carriage, because he woke anticipating the lurch and clatter of the wheels beneath him and felt instead solid stone and heard only murmured voices. In the glow of lamp flame, he saw white adobe walls under a tall, wood-braced vaulted ceiling; and a long, empty floor of flagged tile; and arched windows open to blue twilight and a cool breath of wind. His kit and sandals were beside him against the wall; his tunic, he imagined, had been taken for washing and mending.

He ached all through, and the ache blossomed into throbbing pain when he tried to move. He lay very still, listening to the snatches of conversation which drifted to him in echoes off the ceiling. He recognized the voices of the old priest and the young priest. There was an unfamiliar third voice which he heard very clearly: "—give him to the fort and let them have it out of him, since he can't seem to find his tongue any other way."

"It's possible he simply doesn't know." That was the young priest.

"He knows more than he lets on. You—slave. Where was he traveling from—your master?"

There was a stretch of silence.

"You see he chooses not to speak. He would have no reason to remain silent if there were nothing to hide."

"Ædyn." The young priest spoke quietly and patiently. "He'll come to no harm, Ædyn, I promise, but—"

"Unless he is, in fact, a fugitive from justice."

"They were Brevade's men," the young priest said.

"And the girl is Sagrado's. The point is, he wishes to avoid the attention of the garrison. It is to me very obvious—"

Torien pushed himself up on his left elbow. Pain burst against his rib-cage from the inside out. The room swam around him. "Let the boy go."

Four faces turned toward him from the doorway down the room. The young priest had been holding Ædyn by the shoulders, but he lifted his hands away now as though in surrender. The old priest said, "I tell you it is better we do this elsewhere. I tell you he needs rest, and what is it you do but wake him?"

The third man ignored that. He was the chapel father, judging by the gold-thread stripe on the seams of his robe. He reached and took Ædyn by an elbow and hauled the boy across the room and flung him down to the floor beside Torien's mat. "You've trained the dog well, Lord Risto."

Torien considered first the father and then the boy, wondering whether they had forced the name from the boy or whether Ædyn had volunteered it, not knowing any better. Then he remembered that he had paid in bronze to have it etched on the boy's collar. It had not seemed so profoundly stupid then as it did now.

He said, in Cesino, "Have they hurt you, Ædyn?" The thought was his, but the voice was distant and unfamiliar.

The boy had caught himself on his hands and knees. He pushed himself up and sat back on his heels. His eyes ran the raw line across Torien's cheek. He averted his gaze quickly. He said to the floor, "No, Lord."

"I'm sorry I didn't come back for you."

The boy said nothing. The father said, in Vareno, "Since your slave refuses to speak, Lord Risto, I must ask you to explain your business in Modigne."

"It waits," the old priest said, "unless it is that you want to kill him."

"It cannot wait. The Church does not harbor criminals, whatever their name or blood."

Torien laughed. Pain swelled against his ribs. He choked. He collapsed against the mat and lay writhing like an overturned beetle. He was aware of the old priest at his side muttering in Modigno, and of fingers prying apart his clenched teeth, and of something wet and warm and bitter sliding down his throat—then of hands holding him flat and still against the mat. The pain subsided very slowly. He lay still. The room went far away and came back blurred and distorted, as though he were looking at it through fogged glass.

The father's voice drifted down lazily from somewhere above him. "I see no cause for amusement, Lord Risto."

Torien squeezed his eyes shut. His mind wanted very much to float away from his body on the mat, and it was exhausting effort to hold it back. "You think I'm a criminal, Father?"

"It is not dependent on what I think. It is dependent on fact. You run afoul of the *jente* yet refuse the protection of the fort; your slave refuses to speak when asked why. Put together, these facts are cause at least for suspicion."

"You've no right to ask my business of the boy. To press him for information without my consent, when I am uncondemned, is against the law. So the Church harbors at least one criminal that we know."

"You were incapable of giving your consent, at the moment."

"How inconvenient for you."

"If your business is innocuous, it should not matter whether I ask it of the slave. Nor should it matter if we transfer you into the care of the fort in the morning."

The young priest said, "Father—"

"Of course, you may speak now, if you wish," the father said.

Torien did not say anything. He was finding it difficult to focus and in consequence difficult to care. More than anything else, he wanted not to have to think.

"Very well," the father said. "I will listen, Lord Risto, if you change your mind."

His footsteps echoed down the flagstones. When the echoes had rolled away across the vaulted ceiling, the old priest said something in Modigno, low and quick and by the sound of it unflattering. The young priest cleared his throat and said, "Come, Ædyn, we'll find you a place to sleep."

"He stays with me," Torien said.

"It is better if he is elsewhere, Lord Risto." The young priest's voice was quiet.

"You'll forgive me if I hesitate to trust you. The boy stays with me."

There was a pause in which he imagined the young priest and old priest were exchanging glances. Then the young priest said, "As you wish, Lord Risto. I will bring another mat."

The old priest knelt beside him to unwind the bandage from his ribs. "You lie very still now, Lord. It continues to bleed."

"Can you not stitch it?"—chokily, as the priest peeled the dressing away.

"I have fear of infection to close it so soon. In the fort, they do this for you."

"How long for it to heal?"

"A month, if there is no infection and it rests properly."

He wondered at the thought process which led them to treat his wounds and speak of a month's rest and the risk of infection when they suspected he was fleeing Imperial justice and had every intention to hand him over for it tomorrow; but it seemed childishly petulant to say that aloud. He lay in silence, blinking at the ceiling, holding himself tightly together against the pain, while the old priest changed the dressing and wrapped it. By the time the old priest had finished, and was gathering his things together beside the mat, the young priest had returned with a mat for Ædyn. "If there is anything else I can do, Lord Risto," the young priest said. It did not sound like a platitude. His voice was serious.

"You can listen to me when I tell you the girl had no part in it. She saw me in the street, she went for the nearest help. I want this made plain should there be an investigation."

The priest inclined his head. Torien suspected this was to hide the smile which cracked the corners of his mouth, suddenly. "I will tell her, Lord, that this was your concern. It will amuse her."

"It is a real concern. If there is an investigation—"

"She is in Sagrado's pay. It is better protection than anything you are presently in a position to offer her, Lord, if you will forgive my saying so."

"Sagrado is one of the *jentes*?"

"One of the more powerful, and not worth crossing for the sake of two hired knives. Brevade knows this." The young priest hesitated. This time, Torien saw him glance sidelong to the old priest. "The governor knows it as well," the young priest said.

"What I know," said the old priest, "is that you rest now, Lord."

229

He lay awake, watching the shadows move on the ceiling, listening to the tramp of feet out in the corridor and the low chanting of a hymn which came in on the night air through the open doorway and windows. Not quite twelve hours ago, he had been in Briule's office arranging Maris Pavo's death as one arranges the pieces on a draughts board. It did not matter, he thought, how carefully one arranged the pieces if the opposing strategy was simply to reach over and upset the board.

Much later, when there had been silence for a long time in the corridor, he said into the darkness, "Ædyn."

"Lord." So the boy had not been sleeping, either.

"Quietly, Ædyn, and in your own tongue. Does the chapel open to the street?"

"There is a yard and a gate, Lord."

"Stables?"

"Yes, Lord."

The horses would be there. That was unexpected good luck. "The gate is guarded?"

"Barred, Lord, but not guarded."

"And the chapel. You think you can move about without being seen?"

"Yes, Lord."

"Good. I will need some things from the dispensary: bandage cloth and salve, acetum if you can find it. Gut thread and a needle, most importantly. And a light."

He knew only by the whispered breath of air that the boy had gone. He spent the next little while summoning the will to sit up. He pulled himself up against the wall, keeping his right arm curled against his ribs. His stomach jumped with the movement. He leaned his cheek against the cool adobe wall and waited with his eyes shut for the nausea to settle. He heard the rattle of the latch as the boy came back in, shutting the door behind him.

The boy crossed the room noiselessly and knelt beside the mat. Torien heard the rasp of flint as he brought a lamp flame to life. He opened his eyes. The boy set the lamp carefully on the floor. He sat back on his ankles, holding the other things on his lap. Torien unwrapped the old priest's dressing from his ribs and said, with a hand over the wound, "Acetum."

He rinsed the wound with antiseptic, sucking his breath softly through his teeth at the sting. He wiped his fingers and unspooled the thread and dipped it in the antiseptic. His hands were unsteady, and it took him a while to thread the needle in the dim light. He held the lips of the wound together under his left hand and stitched with his right, slowly, pausing every now and then to flex his aching fingers and wipe off the blood. He finished and tied off the thread. "Salve," he said—calmly, though his stomach was fluttering. The boy opened the jar and handed it to him.

Torien spread salve with two fingers over the row of stitches and wrapped the ribs with the fresh cloth. The boy brought his kit over and handed him the spare tunic, then the jerkin. The tunic presented no difficulty, but Torien's fingers stumbled over the laces of the jerkin. His arms felt as though they were made of lead. His heart was beating in his ears. He finished with the jerkin, wiped the sweat from his face with the back of one hand, and shrugged his arms into the cuirass while the boy held it. He leaned against the wall, head tilted back, hands clenched to fists, while the boy buckled the straps. He hissed a breath when the boy pulled at the strap under his arm. Ædyn looked up, white-faced. Torien smiled but did not speak. He was holding the pain behind shut teeth.

The boy pinned his cloak and moved down to put his feet into the hobnailed boots. Torien shook his head. "Bring them," he said. He stood with his right hand on Ædyn's shoulder, his left on the wall. He braced his shoulder on the wall and buckled the sword belt on his hip while the boy gathered the rest of the kit and put out the lamp. They went out in darkness to the corridor. He kept his hand on Ædyn's shoulder. It was conscious effort to move his feet. They went out from the corridor onto a columned portico. From the portico, they went down into the yard.

The stable was a single row of open-faced stalls built into the northern wall of the chapel yard, empty except for Briule's saddle-horses and the priests' placid carriage-horses. He leaned into the rail while the boy knelt to lace the boots for him. Then he nodded across the yard to the gate. "Open it and wait in the street. I'll bring the horses."

He found the tack at the end of the stall row. He brought the saddles back down the row, one on either arm. He set them down on the floor while he lifted the rail. Someone put a hand beside his hand on the rail. He froze. He had not heard anyone over the pounding of blood in his ears, and he had not seen anyone in the darkness. He looked up into the young priest's face.

The young priest took the rail from him and leaned it upright against the wall. "They close the gates at nightfall, Lord Risto," he said, quietly. "The watchmen will be looking for you. Most of them belong to Brevade."

Torien did not say anything.

"Normally it would be possible to buy him off," the young priest said, "but I think someone must be paying very handsomely to see you dead. Otherwise even Brevade would not try to kill a nobleman in daylight in the street, especially on Sagrado's ground."

Torien bent very carefully to pick up one of the saddles. "I thank you for the warning."

The young priest stood motionless at the stall door. "But you have no intention of heeding it."

Torien straightened and slung the saddle over the horse's back, leaning into the shoulder to buckle the girth strap. "I should confess, you mean? Wait and hope for mercy from a court martial in the morning?"

"I mean there is another way out of the city," the young priest said. "A longer way, but unguarded—at least by the living."

Torien glanced up. "There are tombs under the city?"

"The tunnels run for miles. Some have collapsed in earthquake, but a good many remain. They come out above Baralla. During the siege, they served as conduits into the city for food and water from the hills. Since then they house the dead, Modigni and Vareni alike.

In death, at least, we are all equals." The young priest smiled.

"Baralla is on the northeast road?"

"Five or six miles distant, yes."

"Can the horses go by the tombs?"

The young priest shook his head. "In places the tunnels are not tall enough for a man to stand upright."

"No use to me, then. I'll need the horses."

"I will bring the horses to Baralla, and I will wait for you there at the inn."

Torien looked up again. This time, he studied the young priest's face carefully. "Why?"

"I have sworn myself to help those in need."

"Criminals?"

"If you could be convicted justly, Lord Risto, the fort would not need pay the *jente* to kill you. I do not know what you have done, but it is perhaps easier for me, for the old one—easier to understand that justice is not always as our Imperial authorities define it." The young priest smiled again. "We are not Vareni."

"The old one—no. But you?"

"Of Volenta, though I have lived among your people since I was a boy."

"You lost family in the fighting?"

"Not in the fighting. My father and mother were among those who—paid, afterward."

Torien did not say anything. There was only so much that could be said in euphemism. The Imperial garrison at Volenta had been overrun and massacred following some squabble over the harvest tax; afterward four thousand Volenti, ten for each man of the garrison, had been chosen indiscriminately and executed in reprisal. It was fourteen years ago, and he had not been old enough then to know anything other than that it had happened—and even that was a child's knowledge pieced together imperfectly and embellished over time. There had always been a comfortable distance to it, and looking it in the face now he found the argument for necessity less compelling than it had been in the classrooms at Vione.

The young priest said, quietly, "It is easier for us, I think—for the ones who have been defeated. The Empire stands or falls. God's work goes on regardless."

"Dangerous words," Torien said.

The young priest's eyes went briefly to Torien's ribs. "You say this because you know?"

"I'm not doing God's work."

"One need not vow oneself to the orders to do God's work." The young priest turned away. "Come. I will show you the tombs."

XVII

They went by torchlight. More than once they had to stop and struggle with the flint in numb fingers to rekindle the flame: there was a cold sea wind blowing down the tunnel, trumpeting in sudden bursts from the mouths of side-passages. Underfoot, the ground was soft loam washed out to silt through long years of earthquake and erosion; in places, there was saltwater puddled to his calves and Ædyn's knees. Here and there, the brick-faced walls and vaulted ceiling had buckled under swollen sand or had fallen in entirely. The torchlight went over brick rubble and shards of funerary urns and bits of bone and relic strewn across the floor, half-buried in silt. The air stank of brine and seaweed.

It was bitter cold. It was a seeping, wet cold that leached slowly into one's bones. He had given Ædyn his cloak and sandals—the cloak was far too big, but the boy had only his thin tunic otherwise—and even with his own tunic of good stout wool, and the jerkin and cuirass over it, his lips were trembling and his teeth chattering and his feet so numb that he could no longer feel the blisters where the wet bootstraps had rubbed the skin raw; but they did not stop other than to relight the torch. He did not allow himself to rest. If he stopped to rest, he was not sure he could start again.

They had walked perhaps three miles when the tunnel began to slope gently up underfoot. Ædyn's last torch had given out and they were walking in darkness, and if Torien stretched to his fingertips he could touch the tunnel walls on either side simultaneously—bare clay now, not brick-faced sand. The wind was not as cold. The air was drier and cleaner, pungent with pine sap. The tunnel rose steeply and came out all at once through a narrow cleft onto a long granite shelf which jutted like a broken bone from the shoulder of a hill. In moonlight, Torien could see the hill falling away below, bristling with pine trees. In the distance, there were lights that must be the village Baralla at the hill's northern foot. The wind was coming down the hill at their backs, and with it the screech of a wood owl and the reedy chorus of cicadas from the trees.

He kept a hand on Ædyn's shoulder as they went down the hill and across open wheat fields to the village. The road, empty and silver-blue in the moonlight, ran a northeast-southwest line through the hills, the village clinging tightly to it as though otherwise it might wash away in the runoff from the sheer wooded hillsides. Looking back over his shoulder down the road, Torien could see the lights of Modigne very close and bright in the clear night air across the flatland, the harbor beyond like mirrored glass cradled in the black arms of the earth.

They walked along the road. It was suspicious to be anywhere on foot at this hour, but it was less suspicious to be on the road than to be walking through the wheat fields. There were braziers lit at the gate of the inn yard, the gate doors standing open to the road, but the yard was empty and he could see into the open-faced stable from under the gate arch. Briulc's horses were not there. The priest should have been there two hours gone. Ædyn started into the yard, but Torien pulled him back by the shoulder. "We'll go up the road," he said.

The boy did not question it. They walked on the road until the village was gone behind the southward slope of a hill. Then they went up the hillside. Below them, the road snaked back between the hills to the village. He could see the inn yard and the straight line of the road across the flatland, beyond. He let go Ædyn's shoulder. He sat down stiffly cross-legged with his back to a tree. He studied the lay of the land while he unbuckled his helmet and sword belt. There was a good view of the road in both directions, and the sea wind would carry the sound of traffic to them up the hill.

The boy crouched on his heels some distance away, hugging his knees under the cloak. "You think they've killed the priest, Lord."

He had not, in fact, considered that possibility. His first assumption was that the priest had gone to Brevade or to the fort. "I don't know," he said. "I'll watch a while. Try to sleep, Ædyn. We may be walking tomorrow." There was a stabbing pain under his ribs that he had been able to ignore as long as he was moving. He braced his shoulders carefully against the tree and stretched his legs straight. He sat with his heels dug into the clay, his hands tight on the helmet in his lap, breathing long and slowly through his nose—shivering a little in the wind, though it was not particularly cold.

Ædyn was watching him. "Is it much pain, Lord?"

"It's tolerable."

"I'll watch if my lord wishes to rest."

"I'd better watch."

He said it through shut teeth. Ædyn did not say anything. After a moment, the boy lay down on the ground and curled in on himself under the cloak, pillowing his head on his arms. It occurred to Torien only later, in the silence before dawn when his mind was going through the exchange again as a means of distraction, that the boy had understood it as a comment upon himself, as a slave must understand it, and by then there did not seem to be much point in waking him to explain he had not meant it so.

The moon was gone down over the black line of the sea, and the Wolf was faint and far in a gray sky. There was a rooster crowing in the village. The road had been empty all night. He considered and dismissed the idea of sending the boy, once it was light, back down to inquire after the priest at the inn. The priest had betrayed them, or else had paid for his foolishness in trying to help. Either way, there would at some point be searchers on the road.

His memory of the northeast road was so vague as to be useless.

There were other villages before the border, but he remembered nothing of distances and had not paid much attention to the land itself. He had counted on having the horses. Everything had been in his saddlebags, except the acetum and salve and one water-skin which Ædyn had in his pack. He did not want to show his face on the road, and he did not much care to show Ædyn's face, either. A foreign slave attempting on his own to buy supplies for a cross-country journey would draw unpleasant attention at the best of times. If necessary, they could find food in the hills, but he could not remember any water before the border river, Nona, which was at least four days' walk and quite possibly more.

Ædyn woke while he was considering this.

For a moment, the boy lay still and silent, blinking up blankly at Torien from the cloak. He turned his chin on the cloak to look around the wooded hillside. It was not yet a full day since they had come off the ship, and Torien supposed it was the first time in a long time the boy had woken on solid ground.

"Baralla," Torien said. "Five miles out of Modigne on the northeast road."

The boy sat up slowly with the cloak pulled tight. "It is like Cesin."

"Hotter and drier. More politically volatile."

"I mean the hills are like ours. In the dark you can almost think it is Cesin."

Torien unbuckled his cuirass. He was reluctant to leave the harness, but without the horses he did not see much choice: officers did not travel by foot. He would, however, keep his sword. He glanced at the boy. "How long since you've been home?"

"It will be three years at the rye harvest, Lord."

"I would have written your manumission in Modigne, Ædyn. I didn't think it would be like this."

The boy's face was expressionless. "My lord thinks the *jente* was acting on the governor's orders."

Torien shrugged off the cuirass, holding his tongue between his teeth. He set the cuirass beside his helmet against the foot of the tree and laid the jerkin over it. In nothing but his tunic, he felt oddly vulnerable. He did not dare open the dressing to look at the wound. He buckled his sword-belt and got to his feet, holding on to the tree for support. Dawn was breaking over the hills. He could see a lone ox-cart trundling along the road to Modigne across the flatland. He could see the old city wall in a sunlit white line atop the volcanic rim. He shook his head. "On the Guard's orders," he said. He did not think it had been Briule—no matter which way he turned it, that made no sense—but it had been someone in the barracks. He sucked a low breath through his teeth. Pain pushed against his ribs like a caged animal. "We'll keep off the road," he said. "Skirt towns and farms. It shouldn't be too hard, for now. It'll be harder across the border."

They walked that day through the pine woodland above the road. By sundown, he judged they had come perhaps ten miles from Baralla. The hills were marching away into the north. Below them, at the feet of the hills, there was a cluster of adobe huts and goat pens which he thought might be the village Gorazo. Beyond the village there was dry, stony flatland stretching to the horizon. They circled the village along the shoulders of the hills and went down onto the plain and walked until the village was a pinprick of light in the twilit distance behind them, the road away to the south across the plain. They made camp in a shallow wash. They had found no water that day, but there had been chestnuts and red currants and figs in the hills, and they had filled Ædyn's pack because Torien was not sure what they would find on the plain.

After supper, the boy sat on the rim of the wash to watch the road, silhouetted black against the sky. Torien lay shivering under the cloak on the clay floor of the wash. The pain had spread from his ribs all through his body, stabbing sharply and then easing away at intervals, stabbing more sharply now and easing away less often. He was squeezing his eyes shut, holding his cheeks in his teeth to keep himself from crying out, but Ædyn must have heard the groan in his throat because he said, distantly from above, "I'll go up to the village for help, Lord."

"I'll be all right"—through his teeth.

Either the boy was silent or Torien did not hear the reply over the pounding in his head. He opened his eyes to make sure the boy had not moved from the rim. The starlight was as painful as needles.

The world was spinning. He shut his eyes again and buried his face between his arms. At some point, overcome with exhaustion, he slept. He woke in brilliant sunlight. It was mid-morning, and the sun was a hard, white ball of flame burning off the mist from the flatland. There were cicadas singing from a line of juniper trees along the road. Ædyn sat cross-legged across the wash, head bowed over his knees, twirling a long pine stick in his fingers.

Torien sat up slowly against the side of the wash. He had meant to take the watch from the boy at midnight, and he had meant to be five miles gone across the plain by now. "You should have woken me," he said. It came out in a croak. His tongue was thick, his throat dry.

Ædyn absorbed the rebuke without expression. "The old priest said my lord needs rest."

Torien sat up on his knees and dragged the pack across the floor of the wash. His hands were shaking. He said, conscious that the boy was watching, "Any traffic on the road?"

The boy shook his head once. "Farm carts for the city, Lord."

Torien swallowed two mouthfuls of water from the skin. Then he held the pack on his knees while he unbuckled his sword belt. He slipped his tunic over his head and unwrapped the dressing from his ribs. The breath of wind burned like cold iron on the wound. The stitches were sunk in swollen red skin. His hands were shaking badly, but he opened the acetum and dribbled it from his palm onto the raw slit of the wound, flinching at the sting. He spread salve gingerly over the row of stitches. The skin was hot against his fingertips. He wiped his fingers on a tuft of grass and wrapped the wound again, breathing long and softly through his nose, his teeth shut. He tied up the pack and gave it to the boy and put his tunic back on. He buckled the sword belt on his hip as he stood. Squinting against the sunlight, he followed the line of the road across the flatland to the eastern horizon.

The road was empty. The cicadas were singing over the flatland, and he could see gulls wheeling at the coast, distantly southward. In springtime, there would be snow-melt flowing down from the mountains, but the gullies and runlets which cut across the plain to the sea were baked dry under the summer sun. Even with careful rationing, the water-skin would not last them to the Nona. They would either have to give up valuable time to look for water in the hills, or at some point they would have to use a village well.

He tried to weigh this choice in his head while they walked, but instead his thoughts wandered off over the plain—back to the elder Briule's office in Modigne; to the girl's shanty at the waterfront; to the quay with Alluin the day they had come in to the harbor at Tasso. The images tangled together and spun out again into confused half-dreams: Espere was there, and the young Espere lying white-faced on the sand with his arm sliced away, and the Modigno ship master smiling over his shoulder at the offer of five hundred eagles, and Alluin in the infirmary with his head swathed in bandages, and he himself asking if it couldn't be stitched, and the old priest saying it must wait till the fort, and the *signo* saying he must please breathe and not speak, and Chareste apologizing, anguished, that he had done nothing to ease the pain—anything to ease the pain, threefold God.

Something cool and wet ran over his burning face. He opened his eyes. Above him, Ædyn sat back on his heels with the water-skin in his lap.

He was flat on his back on the ground, the cloak bundled under his head. Lifting his head a little, he ran his eyes in a circle and saw the flatland stretching away from him under afternoon sunlight and the wind tugging at the tufts of esparto grass. He could see the road off to the south, glittering in the heat. He dropped his head back to the cloak. He looked at Ædyn but did not speak. The pain was going through him in spasms, and he was swallowing it down and holding himself tightly still against the earth. The boy put the water-skin carefully on the ground at Torien's elbow and reached a hand to Torien's shoulder, then hesitantly to his forehead. The hand was as cold as ice on his skin. Torien flinched. The boy said, "I think it is gone to fever, Lord."

Torien shut his aching eyes against the flood of sunlight. He did not say anything. He felt the boy shift on his heels. "Lord, let me go for help."

He managed to say, in a burst through clenched teeth, "How far—how far to the village?"

"Not very far. Five miles, Lord, maybe a little more. I can be back by nightfall."

Torien did not say anything. The boy either took his silence as consent or else had realized Torien was powerless to stop him anyway. Torien felt the breath of air as the boy left his side. He heard the boy's footsteps pound away across the gravel of the plain. He lay waiting for the silence to follow and understood only much later that the pounding was his heartbeat in his ears.

Through the long afternoon, while the sun crawled down to Modigne, he drifted in and out of consciousness. He woke once thick-headed and thirsty and leaned over on his elbow to the water-skin, but his hands shook so that he could not untie the knots. He let go the skin and lay back exhausted on the cloak and watched a pair of lizards chase each other round and round a tuft of yellowing esparto grass. He slipped away again, slowly, and came back with a start at the sound of thunder over the plain. Far off across the flatland, southward, he could see the sky breaking open. There was a storm building at the sea-line, the clouds like green marbled pillars and the rain like a shot-silk curtain hung between. The thunder rolled over the plain and echoed off the hillsides. Twenty miles, he supposed. The storm would be here before the boy.

It occurred to him that the boy was not coming back.

He would have had reason to come back, as he'd had reason to wait through five hours at the smithy in Modigne, had the wound not festered and gone to fever—but that was the way of it, and a dead man couldn't file a manumission. Anyway, the boy had a better chance now to run than he'd had in the city. If he were foresighted, he would wait and watch in the hills and be back at length for the eagles in Torien's wallet and for the seal ring. Over the mountains in Volenta, they would not care about the collar on the boy's neck or that he was carrying a Vareno nobleman's gold.

The first fat drops of rain were spattering on the gravel. He had not seen rain for more than four months. In late spring, he had ridden to Vessy with his new commission and a month's leave in which to say his goodbyes, and it had been raining off the lake on the day he had come home. Closing his eyes, he could see the black Cesino earth crumbling to mud along the causeway, and the long green fields stretching beyond to the oak wood still stripped bare by winter; and the head of the hill veiled in mist and the river spilled over its banks and rushing onto the lowland; and he could hear the patter of rain on the roof-thatch of the fishermen's huts—Cesin itself pouring into that rainfall, Cesin itself pouring out a libation for him in farewell.

A funerary libation, he thought. The Dobryno had been wrong.

Thunder started from a murmur across the plain, building up slowly to a roar and then falling away to sudden silence. In its wake, there were indistinct voices. Footsteps hurried toward him over the gravel. It had not been thunder but carriage wheels on the road. He opened his eyes, fumbling for his sword. He rolled onto his left arm and propped himself up on the elbow and held his sheath in his left hand while he drew the blade under his stomach in his right. He held himself trembling on his hands, the sword beneath him. He could not push himself up. There were hands on his head and shoulders, and someone was bending down close to his ear to say, "Easy, Lord Risto, you've nothing to fear."

He recognized the voice of the young priest.

He gave up trying to rise. He rested his forehead against the dirt and lay still on his palms. The voices went back and forth far above him. He heard Ædyn's voice. He closed his eyes and let the blackness come.

XVIII

He opened his eyes still in blackness. It was like coming up out of deep water. His head was thick, his throat tight. His body was at war with itself, his lungs pushing greedily against his ribs and the pain stabbing angrily back, and he lay very still, holding his breath and trying to keep the peace, listening to the blood in his ears and the patter of rain and realizing only slowly through the pain that the rain was pattering on a roof above him rather than on his face; realizing just as slowly that there was a smooth, hard surface beneath him; trying to remember where he was and how he had come there—and with whom, because he was not alone in the darkness. There were hands on either side of his neck, holding his head still. When he tried to sit up, the hands held him firmly down. A voice floated out of the darkness: "Lie still, Lord Risto."

Memory came all at once, in a clump of sounds and images. He was silent for a moment, struggling to untangle it and arrange it all into a chronology. He peeled his tongue off his teeth and said, hoarsely, "What time?"

"Not yet midnight." The young priest's voice was patient. "Sleep, Lord Risto. Give your body the chance to repair itself."

"Where?"

"Five miles east of Gorazo, perhaps fifty miles from the border. Ædyn met us on the road."

"You did not come to Baralla."

There was a stretch of silence. The young priest's hands were very still on Torien's shoulders. "No," the young priest said. "I did not come to Baralla." He said it quietly as from a distance. "Sleep, Lord Risto."

He slept and woke again, this time in pale daylight. He lay blinking up at the low, slatted ceiling of the priests' carriage, shivering in the breeze through the open doorway. His body was sore and cramped against the bench. The young priest was gone. There was no sign of Ædyn. The rain had passed in the night and the sky above the flatland was gray the color of pigeons' feathers, the breeze ruffling the esparto and kicking spirals of red dust up to the hills.

Torien turned his head against the bench. Across the carriage, the old priest was scraping something from a mortar into a cup, scraping the sides of the mortar and stirring whatever was in the cup with one forefinger, humming under his breath and unsurprised to look up and find Torien watching him. "Yes, yes, you are awake," he said. He wiped his fingers and brought the cup over. "You drink this," he said, "very carefully. I have opened the wound again. I try to bleed out the infection. You are stupid to stitch it. I tell you this."

"Where is Ædyn?"

"They eat now. You drink this."

"Where are my horses?"

"It is not a time for thinking about horses. You drink this. You sleep. If you do not die, then maybe you think about horses. You owe thanks to God we do not come another day late."

The old priest was pushing the cup against his lips. Torien shut his teeth and turned his head away. "I expected the young one in Baralla."

"Yes, he tries to go to Baralla. They stop him at the gate. They look for your horses, and they see he has your horses. They question him: when does he go? Where does he go? Jovan he tell them you sell the horses. You go on a ship, he says. But they know he lies. They ask the harbor master. They treat him very badly now. They say if he does not tell them where you go, they kill him. But the *jente* Sagrado he stops them. He has—how do you say it?—a debt to pay. He stops them from killing him."

"A debt? To the Church?"

"To Jovan a little. Mostly to me. We save his daughter when she is so small and sick. He has no place else to go. He comes to us. We help him. He owes us this debt. So now his people they bring Jovan to me at the chapel."

"He was badly hurt?"

"They beat him. I dress it." The old priest was prying apart Torien's teeth with his fingers. "You drink this now. He tells me how you stitch yourself and walk through the tombs. You are stupid to do this. He is stupid to let you do this. I tell you there will be infection. It is to me surprising you are not dead when we find you." He tipped the cup onto Torien's tongue. "It is most important to break the fever," he said. "If we break the fever, then maybe you do not die."

Torien said, thickly through a mouthful of honey and basil, "I will pay you to take me to Choiro."

"Yes, yes, the boy he tells us you try to cross the border." The old priest did not really seem to have heard. He was bundling his things together on the opposite bench.

"Listen to me. I will pay in gold. You can name the sum."

The old priest looked up. "Is it how you think of priests in your country? That you buy them with coin?"

"Not only priests, and not only in my country."

A shadow fell across the doorway. The young priest, Jovan, came up into the carriage. In daylight now Torien could see the bruises on his face and the stoop in his shoulders which he was making effort to hide. "Go eat, Antoni," Jovan said. "The horses are hitched."

"Yes, I go." The old priest tied up his pack. He looked up again critically at Torien. "Water only," he said, "until the fever breaks. Then you eat. It is necessary against the inflammation. I think you do not care about this, but I want you to understand that I help you."

He went out through the carriage doorway. Jovan sat down facing Torien on the far bench. He leaned carefully back against the wall. He noticed Torien watching him and smiled. "How do you feel, Lord

Risto?"

"Maybe I do not die."

"I should have been there at Baralla. I'm sorry."

Torien ran his eyes over Jovan's bruised face. "He told me what they did to you, and why."

"It is nothing. Though I would not have minded if Sagrado's people had come a little sooner." Jovan smiled again.

"I said I will pay you to take me to Choiro. Anything you ask—anything it takes to make it worth your while."

"I heard what you said."

"I must get to Choiro, Jovan."

Jovan hesitated. "Have you considered that whoever paid Brevade for your death in Modigne may just as easily pay for your death in Choiro? It may be better not to cross the border, Lord Risto. It may be safer to stay in the provinces—perhaps to pass into Volenta."

"Safety was never a primary concern, in case you couldn't tell."

It was half a joke, but Jovan did not say anything, and he did not laugh. His face was serious.

"A horse, then," Torien said, "if you want no further part in this. Whatever medical supplies you are willing to give me."

"He was a Guardsman," Jovan said, "the man who questioned me in Modigne."

There was silence between them, and the breath of wind through the open doorway.

"You've found yourself on the wrong side of this fight, you mean," Torien said, finally.

"I fear I may have misunderstood the nature of the fight and also the scope."

"My offer holds. I will pay anything you ask for a horse and medicine. You can go back to Modigne and tell them you left me on the northeast road. I won't blame you for it. The boy stays with me. I don't want him in the hands of the Guard."

"You think I fear for myself."

"The High Commander of the Guard wants me dead. I think you've the right to be practical about it."

"It is a little late to speak of practicality. If I cared only for practicality, I would have given you up under questioning. I fear for you, Lord Risto. I fear you make a mistake to go to Choiro. I did not understand, and I fear that you do not. They are powerful enemies you have made. Brevade was nothing."

"Perhaps I've equally powerful friends."

Jovan's eyes fell to Torien's ribs. "They have not been much help to you, so far."

"I have to do this, Jovan. There are other lives than mine in the balance."

"It will be a fortnight before we can get you to the city, and that is if we have no trouble at the border. If Modigne has sent an alert—"

"They'll be watching the gates and shipyards. There are other ways into and out of the city. I know the walls: I spent four years at Vione figuring out how not to spend four years at Vione. I could tell you how to breach the city and take the Hill with two hundred men, if you wanted."

Jovan looked at him curiously. "If *I* wanted?"

"Hypothetically speaking."

"Tell me, Lord Risto," Jovan said, carefully, "if this is not more than a matter of justice for the voiceless of Modigne."

That caught him off-guard. "Why should it be anything more?"

"You are not Vareno by blood."

"Not purely. Cesino enough they can give me the blood-traitors' death and feel justified in it. One of the Dobryni promised me once that they would."

"Cesino enough to carry a grudge?"

He was silent, for a moment, looking at Jovan across the carriage. Then, not sure what else to do, he laughed. "Are you trying to turn me?"

"I am wondering what it would take to turn you, and thinking perhaps the High Commander has wondered the same thing. It is not too much a stretch to imagine you could be a political threat."

"I took an oath, Jovan."

"My people as well, before the uprising."

"Anyway, it's beside the point."

"Maybe it is." Jovan stood. He was silhouetted in the doorway against the overcast sky, and Torien could not see his face. "Try to rest, Lord Risto. It won't do any of us any good if you are dead by the city—any of us but the High Commander, I suppose."

"Jovan."

"Yes, Lord Risto?"

"He offered me a commission not six months ago. The Palace

garrison. A yearly bonus of ten thousand eagles and a private house on the Hill. The only thing changed between us is that I stumbled into his trafficking ring in Modigne. It isn't a question of loyalty."

"I am sure you are right, Lord Risto," Jovan said.

They crossed the border river Nona at a cattle ford north of the customs station. Rejoining the road, they crawled north and east across the broad, sunburned face of Varen. The days ran together in heat and monotony. While Antoni nodded on the opposite bench, Torien watched the spelt fields go by through the slats in the carriage walls, the dust billowing in a haze from the horses' hooves and spinning off into whirlwinds over the fields, jumping wicker goat-pens and stone boundary walls, the yellow spelt husks rattling like dry bones and the olive groves fluttering silver, the heat curling off the red tile roofs of the farmhouses, the irrigation ditches seared white as old scars.

Sometimes in the evenings lightning crackled silently in the distance above the hills, but it did not rain. The dust came in on the wind through the slats and hung in the air as thick as smoke. He woke once in the night with sweat trickling down the sides of his face and between his shoulder-blades under the edge of the dressing, the dust sticking on his skin like wet plaster, the salt stinging his cracked lips, and he grasped very sluggishly in the heat that this meant the fever had broken.

Jovan and Antoni took turns at the driver's bench, now, and he suspected that sometimes, in the long afternoons when Antoni dozed inside the carriage, Jovan gave the reins to Ædyn. Mostly they traveled in silence, on account of the blown dust and the clatter of hooves and wheels on pavement, but every now and then, when he was lying awake in the heat trying to resist the urge to scratch at the dressing, he heard their voices coming down from the bench, the young priest's and the boy's, and sometimes the wind carried the words to him very clearly, and no matter how he tried to focus on the spelt fields and whirls of dust he could not help but hear.

"Very much braver than I am, and certainly much braver than I was"—Jovan's voice, quietly in response to something he had not heard Ædyn say. "It is no reason to be ashamed, Ædyn."

"I broke. I always thought—" There was a long moment of nothing but road noise and Antoni's gentle snoring. Then Ædyn said, in a smaller voice, "I did not think I would break."

"They did not have to break me," Jovan said. "I was a coward. They don't have to break cowards."

"It's different. I was older than you were."

"Not so much older."

"Had you won your spear?"

"My spear?"

"I mean that I had drawn blood already."

"My people are not hunters," Jovan said. "My people are farmers. We have different rites."

"They try to make us farmers," Ædyn said, "the Vareni. They

think if they make us farmers we will not fight."

"I see," said Jovan, mildly.

"Did he free you, then—your master? Or did you run?"

"He sold me to a brother of the Hospitallers. The brother freed me. I think he had some idea I would be his apprentice, but I am afraid he hasn't gotten his money's worth. I haven't proven very adept at medicine, you see."

"Antoni." The boy was silent, for a moment. "Is that why you joined the orders?"

"It's one reason."

"Do you ever think about it now—about fighting, I mean? Now that you are older."

"I think there are many different ways to fight," Jovan said.

They came down into the river valley of the Breche. The road cut across the floodplain and hugged the western bank of the river for a stretch of about twenty miles; then the river bent west, and the road crossed over eastward on a line for the city. Jovan took the carriage off the road before they came to the bridge. They would cross here, below the river-bend, out of sight of the bridge watchmen.

It was noon, and while Antoni built the cook fire, Jovan and the boy unhitched the horses and took them down to the water. Torien could not see the water from the carriage, but he could see the line of elm trees along the bank. Through the slats, he watched Jovan and the boy take the horses out of sight into the trees. A little while later, he saw them coming back up the bank. Jovan left the horses with the boy and came up into the carriage. "There is cavalry crossing the river," he said.

"A patrol?"

"A full column, I think. It is a lot of cavalry." Jovan hesitated. "They saw us on the bank, Lord Risto. I'm sorry."

"You didn't know they'd be there."

"What should we do?"

"Eat, I guess. There's not much else to do. Did you find a place to cross?"

"I think it is a good place. The river is very low. I will go down later and test the footing."

The priests and the boy sat at the fire to eat. Torien lay on the bench, balancing the bowl of porridge on his stomach and watching the road through the slats. The cavalry column moved massively down the road from the river. Mess wagons and strings of spare horses followed the troop. He had never seen a full column mobilized before. It was one thing to know the numbers in your head and another to see a thousand Imperial cavalrymen moving down the road in front of you.

Jovan came back up into the carriage. He had water in a gourd, and he helped Torien sit up a little to drink. "They must be going to Modigne," he said, "if they are crossing the river here."

"The question is whether they're staying in Modigne."

"You think they are for Tasso?"

"They could be hunting cicadas for sport on the sunlit plains, for all I know. If this is Pavo's idea of shutting us up, it isn't exactly subtle."

"Perhaps it is trouble on the Road. Perhaps Tasso has called for reinforcement."

Torien paused with the gourd in his hands. "We'd have seen the beacons lit at the border," he said. It was more for himself than for Jovan, who was looking out through the slats and not really listening.

The column passed by in a cloud of dust. Jovan straightened from the slats. "Antoni will take it as a comment on his cooking that you didn't eat," he said. "Give me your bowl. I'll warm it in the ashes."

XIX

The oldest families of Choiro held the land between the river and the road on the eastern bank. The estates were mostly slave-run but occasionally, when the summers or the politics got too hot, the high-wheeled carriages came whisking down from the city and the scions of the oldest families, sipping chilled wine in their country houses, could flatter themselves that they were farmers, as their forebears had been.

The burden of tradition lay heavier on some than on others: Alluin, he knew, had spent his boyhood on one of these estates—he was not sure which. Alvero Senna was as arch-conservative regarding his firstborn son's education as he was with his politics. Other families, even the oldest families, might be content to leave the administration of their estates in the hands of overseers or freedmen, but Alluin, on his father's insistence, had learned the appropriate arts and skills for himself: accounting and viniculture, hunting and the management of slaves.

In effect, he had grown up in the company of slaves and tutors and hired help and tenants, accordingly lax when it came to social hierarchy. It was not quite what Alvero had intended, and his method of correcting the shear was to put a whip into Alluin's hands and order him to redraw in blood the line between master and servant. This had failed entirely. Alluin had dropped the whip and turned on his heel and left the estate without another word to his father. He had ridden that day to the fort at Vione and put down a false name in the recruiting rolls and was two weeks into the probation as a common foot-soldier before one of the officers had recognized him as a Senna—or as formerly a Senna, because by then Alvero had publicly disowned him.

He had not lost his citizenship, but he had lost his inheritance and any hope for a political career, and unless he won a battlefield commission he would never rank higher than lieutenant. He had done a great deal since then to convince others that really he found it very freeing and there were no regrets in having done it, but no matter how he pretended he had never quite managed to convince himself; and Torien imagined it would be harder and harder to convince himself the older he got—assuming he got any older and was not already dead in the desert as the price of a failed truce. Torien had spent the last few days since the crossing thinking of reasons why there might be a full cavalry column outfitted for campaign on the road to Modigne. None were appealing, but the least appealing was the most likely.

The sun was dipping to the western hills and there were long blue shadows stretching across the road when Jovan navigated the carriage into an inn yard. The river was below, curving back lazily eastward under the city walls. The road ran ahead up the bank to the city. Above the crenellated walls—pausing in the carriage doorway to hitch up Jovan's long priest's robe at his waist—Torien could see the tenements of the River Quarter. In the hazy distance, he could see the Hill, walled in white marble, pushing up from the lower city like a crowned head. A sluggish breeze was moving down the riverbank. Through the doorway, the sound and smell of the city hit him as solidly as a slap in the face. He closed his eyes as he stepped down into the soft mud of the yard: God knew he had not missed Choiro.

He sat cross-legged on the thin straw pallet in the inn dormitory, clenching his teeth and hands so as not to wince, while Antoni dressed and wrapped the wound. He knew Antoni saw it. The old priest's lips were pressed tight and he was shaking his head intermittently as though the stupidity of it were striking him again and again, each time from a different angle; but neither of them spoke. When Antoni had finished the bandaging, Torien pulled his own tunic over his head, Jovan's robe after it. He took his knife and wallet from Ædyn. Tucking the knife at his belt, he shook out his key ring and a handful of bronzes from the wallet. With one hand on the boy's shoulder, he bent to open the collar at the boy's throat. He looked up at the priests, who were watching silently. "One of you will have to file his manumission."

"You must be there to seal it, Lord Risto," Jovan said, gently.

"No. I've signed him over to the Order—a charitable donation. The documents are in the wallet, and enough in gold for the manumission tax."

Out of the corner of his eye, he saw them exchange glances. Ædyn was frozen under his hands. Antoni said, "The gold it is not necessary. I have explained this."

"Also enough for your travel expenses," Torien said, sliding the collar free, "if I'm unable to see him home myself. You understand I don't want him freed just to be put out on the street. He'll be on a block again in a week."

Jovan said, "Of course it will be done as you say, Lord Risto."

"Unnecessary precaution, I hope. With any luck, I'll meet you at the chapel this time tomorrow." He squeezed Ædyn's shoulders. "If I'm unlucky, I would recommend you lose my sword in the river and pretend you've never heard my name. I imagine Pavo will be interested to know who brought me to the city."

"We will expect you at the chapel, Lord Risto," Jovan said.

They were firing the braziers on the city walls when he went outside. The city glowed red-gold like embers in the twilight. A lamp-lit houseboat was slipping by at the middle of the river, where the water still ran deep enough for the draft. He crossed the road and walked on the foot-stones along the leftward embankment toward the city, the river below him.

There was traffic on the road: lumbering mule carts and light two-wheeled flies and tall closed carriages, flanked by mounted guards, bound for dinner parties on the Hill, and a mass of common folk and slaves on foot flattening quickly against the embankments as the vehicles pushed past. Just before the gate, he broke away from the crowd and went down the steps which curved down from the road to the water.

He walked for a while at the waterside, northward along the base of the wall, until the clamor at the gate had died away behind him and he could hear the wake of the houseboat, just ahead, lapping gently on the shore. The wall towered above him. The far bank of the river was empty and dark. The houseboat passed slowly out of his sight under a bridge further down the wall. He dropped flat to the sand and slid on his belly under the grating of a low, arched culvert which carried the drainage of the street above down to the river.

They sluiced the drains with water through the day, and if one handed oneself very carefully along the sides one could keep oneself above the sludge at the bottom, but he had never tried it in a priest's robe before, or with a four-inch gash still healing under his arm, and both these things presented difficulties he had not anticipated. He could not hold his weight on his right arm, and the hem of the robe did not allow for much movement of his legs. He gave up trying to move up the sides. He lowered himself to the floor and felt his way forward on his hands and knees, swearing softly through his teeth. He reached the top and sat dripping and shivering for a moment, looking out into the street.

A huddled figure in a cloak was moving away from him up the foot-stones on the far side of the street. A mule cart was creaking slowly toward him. The cart passed by with a clatter of studded wheels, and he pulled himself out from the culvert onto the street. With some difficulty in the priest's robe, he found his feet and sank into the shadow of the low shop doorway at his back—but the cloaked figure had turned aside into one of the tenements, and the mule cart had vanished around a corner. The street was deserted. He hitched up the robe at his waist and stepped out from the doorway and went a little way northward up the street and then cut eastward on a cross street, putting the river to his back.

He paid in bronze for a private cell in the bathhouse on the next block, waving away the slave who came to attend him, drawing the curtain shut. He stripped off robe and tunic and washed himself using only the tepid water and oil in the cell, careful to avoid the dressing around his ribs. Pulling his tunic back over his head, he came across the near-two-weeks' growth of beard on his chin. He had not shaved since Modigne. His first inclination was to ignore it in the interest of time, but he would make a better case before this Ceno woman if he at least looked as though he might belong to the Prince's circles.

He belted the tunic and tucked his knife at his waist. He opened the curtain and called for the slave to bring a razor.

Afterward, his bare chin still smarting a little and his cheek stinging in a line where the knife cut had not yet scarred, he went out into the street and disposed of Jovan's robe down a drain. He worked his way north and east through the River Quarter toward the Hill. The woman had money enough to move out of the brick tenement blocks, if she hadn't the name to move up on the Hill. Her apartment was on a wide, quiet street running parallel to the river at the Hill's western foot. It was a two-story orange stucco building with wood-shuttered windows and a red tile roof. There were almond trees and fig trees and myrtles in the yard, and a tall stucco gate wall overgrown with ivy. Torien hung back for a moment at the end of the torch-lit wall. He had not anticipated there might be a gateman. He squared his shoulders and went up to the gatehouse. He took off his seal ring and slid it through the aperture. "For Chæla Ceno," he said. "My name is Risto."

He followed a silent slave across the yard and up the steps to the second story. On the landing, the slave peeled aside before the open doorway, and Torien went in alone to the vestibule. He paused there, looking in uncertainly through the archway to the long main room. The room was lamp-lit but empty. There was no furniture besides a dining couch and low table. The couch was dressed in silk, and the table was lacquered ebony. Thin gold leaf glittered in the lamplight on the frescoed walls.

There was a curtained doorway on the rear wall, the western

wall, and four tall windows on the eastern wall facing the Hill. The shutters were open, the sheer sashes fluttering in the breeze from the street. The scent of lavender drifted to him through the archway. He stood looking back at himself dimly in a sheet of gold leaf on the far wall. The curtain parted in the doorway. A dark-skinned woman in black silk came toward him across the room, the gold beads in her braided hair clinking as she walked, the silk rustling at her ankles. Her bare arms were long and muscular, her shoulders broad. She was tall: standing at the archway, she had to look down to him in the vestibule. She bowed. "Lord Risto."

"You're Ceno?"

She pushed back her beaded hair with one hand as she raised her head—deliberately, so that he could see the dagger sheathed on her forearm. "I am Vaiz, Lord. Her assistant."

He eyed the dagger. "Her bodyguard?"

"If need be. My duties are not always so pedestrian." She stood aside in the archway. "Come, Lord. Let me prepare you a drink."

He glanced over his shoulder to the landing. The slave had vanished. He went slowly past her into the room. "For a bodyguard, you don't seem particularly interested in my business here."

She went over to the table. She poured wine into a bowl on the tabletop, holding the jug expertly in the crook of her right arm, the wine falling in a long, sparkling stream from jug to bowl. She brought the bowl to him in both hands, as though she were making a libation. "My business is hers. Her business is not mine. She has permitted you to enter, Lord Risto. Beyond that, I ask nothing."

He took the bowl from her, looking at it in his hands so she would not see the color in his face. He tipped the bowl to his mouth. Over the rim, he saw the curtain part again. Another woman came into the room. She was younger than Vaiz. He guessed she was sixteen or seventeen—younger than he had expected. She was dressed in plain linen, her throat and arms unadorned, her dark-honey skin unpainted, her black hair falling in loose curls to her slim waist. She smiled at him across the room, her lips not quite parting, the corners of her eyes creasing very slightly; she studied him as she smiled. "I am sorry to keep you waiting, Lord Risto. Vaiz has not offered you a seat?"

He remembered, too late, the wine bowl at his lips. He swallowed and lowered the bowl. Wine sloshed over his hand. "I prefer to stand," he said. The wine ran down his fingers and dripped to the floor.

"I prefer you sit," Ceno said, "because I would like to sit. You are the only one here of noble blood. None of the rest of us can sit until you do." She was smiling at him and pretending not to see the dripping wine.

He sat, obediently, on the edge of the couch. She sat down very gracefully beside him in a breath of lavender. Her hands were folded on her lap and he saw, with interest, the long, slim fingers callused, the knuckles reddened—a commoner's hands, accustomed to work. She said, following his gaze, "My mother's people are farm folk. I have the mark of the breed." There was something savage in the way she said it, though the smile had not left her lips. She slid her hands from her lap. "The gateman didn't mention the purpose of your visit."

"I didn't tell him the purpose of my visit."

"He assumed he knew, I suppose." Ceno's voice was dry.

Torien felt the color come back into his face. He looked away to the windows. "I came to make a request of you."

"You're terribly direct, Lord Risto. At least you might tell me how much you're enjoying the wine."

He glanced down to the bowl on his knee, distracted. Ceno laughed. "A joke. To be honest, I find it refreshing. One doesn't often encounter directness this close to the Hill. Make your request, Lord Risto."

"If we could speak privately," he said.

"A sensitive matter, I take it?"

"Political. Not personal."

"You needn't be concerned about Vaiz."

He did not say anything. He lifted the bowl from his knee and swallowed a mouthful of wine. Ceno watched him. "Oh, very well," she said, "but it had better be interesting. You can go, Vaiz."

Vaiz went out wordlessly onto the landing. "Shall I shutter the windows, too?" Ceno said. "Or would that fuel the gateman's misconceptions?"

"I need to speak with the Prince."

She looked at him for a moment, silently. Then she let out a quick, derisive breath through her nose. "Is that what I sent Vaiz out for? Go up the Hill if you want to speak with the Prince."

"I can't. I came to you because I've no other choice."

"Not typically what a girl wants to hear, but admittedly

intriguing." Her eyes lingered on his face, running the line of the cut across his cheek. "Have you killed someone, Lord Risto? Or is there an irate senatorial father at your heels? Or perhaps in combination."

"I was told the Prince has seen you here before."

"You avoid my question."

"It's not the issue."

"How disappointing for both of us. You seem to expect His Highness answers to me like a hound. I assure you, Lord Risto, he will need a reason."

"The only thing that should matter to you is that if you do not do as I ask, your father will be arrested tonight for trafficking Imperial citizens into the salt mines at Tasso. Is that direct enough for you?"

Ceno bent over the table to pour herself a bowl of wine. Her hands were steady and unhurried. "It will do," she said, "but I can do better." She straightened and smiled at him over the rim of the bowl. "You will have to take up the matter of my father's arrest with the Imperial Guard. Commander Pavo is a business partner and a personal friend."

"Three weeks ago Pavo ordered the torture and death of one of his own officers in Tasso. I wouldn't count too much on his friendship, and I would consider very carefully what will happen when your father ceases to be useful to him."

"Meaning?"

"If I expose the sort of business your father is doing on his behalf, I promise you Pavo will press harder than any of them for his sentencing. Or he will kill him himself to stop his tongue."

Ceno swirled the wine in her bowl. She did not say anything.

"Help me now and I will do what I can to protect him," Torien said.

"Or I could have Vaiz kill you," Ceno said, "which would be much simpler."

"There are at least two witnesses to my entering this apartment. That's two others you'll have to—"

"This is Choiro, Lord Risto." Ceno's voice was bland. "No one ever notices or cares about anything in Choiro, least of all about one half-blood provincial lordling making a nuisance of himself among Maris Pavo's clients. Anyway, the gateman is loyal to me and the slave means nothing to a court."

When he said nothing, she laughed. "I'm not going to kill you," she said, "though I like that you know I can—or that Vaiz can, rather. But I think you're far too amusing to kill, and if I'm not going to kill you, I suppose I might as well help you." She put her bowl down on the table and stood. She took his bowl from his knee and refilled it from the jug. Her fingers brushed the scar on his palm. "The mark of the breed?" she said.

He said, quietly, "I'm in your debt, Ceno."

"I'll find a use for that, I'm sure." She put the jug on the table and went out onto the landing. When she came back in, she said, "I told Vaiz to have something sent up from the taberna when she goes."

"It wasn't necessary."

"We might as well eat. His Highness will be at dinner, anyway. He may be hours coming, and I'll have run out of witty things to say by then." She sat down beside him on the couch. She refilled her own bowl from the jug and said, leaning back at his elbow, "So, Lord Risto—why Tasso?"

"What?"

"Tasso. It's an unusual posting, isn't it? For a nobleman—though I suppose you are provincial and unimportant." She smiled, coolly. "Even so, they like to keep your kind here on the Hill. They send peasants' sons to do the dying."

"I requested it."

"A chance for glory?"

"A chance to be away from this place."

"*This place*—said with such superiority. Away from politics, you mean."

"Yes."

"And yet here you are after all."

"I guess it wasn't much of a chance," he said.

"You have no political ambition, Lord Risto?"

"I prefer to look my enemies in the eye."

"It must be nice," Ceno said, "believing you can solve all your problems at the edge of a sword. There is always more blood to spill. Endless opportunity for catharsis."

"At least it's honest."

"What a justification!"

"They spill blood each day on the Hill. They just dress it up in words so you don't have to face it squarely."

"Yes—'no greater threat to truth than palatability.' That's the

Poet, isn't it? So 'land reform' rather than 'subjugation of native peoples and seizure of their property.' If you are going to subjugate native peoples, you demand at least to be honest about it."

"At least."

"I can see the attraction. It is a very clear-headed way of looking at things."

"I like to think right and wrong still play some part in it."

"You'll get over that," she said, dryly, "especially if you stay in Choiro."

"Have you gotten over it?"

"I do what I must."

"Necessity makes an easy excuse. There's always a choice."

They were not joking now, and he saw that it had irritated her. The wine bowl wavered on her palm. "For you. For the son of the governor of Cesin. For a merchant's daughter? You have no right to speak to me of choice, Lord Risto." She was sitting very stiffly on the edge of the couch, her chin up, her free hand doubled to a fist on her thigh.

"I'm sorry," he said.

"Why? You've no more reason to apologize for yourself than I've got."

"I offer you my apology even so."

She let out a breath of laughter. "How terribly old-fashioned—to apologize. Did no one tell you?"

"I'm from Cesin. We still find regular bathing remarkable."

She laughed. This time it was a real laugh, warm and rolling.

She loosened a little beside him. He was conscious, very suddenly, of her closeness and of the clean, smooth curve of her neck and the straightness of her shoulders and the shape of her body beneath the soft folds of linen. He looked down into the wine bowl between his hands. He tipped it up and drank. Ceno watched him. "Have you a girl, Lord Risto?"

He wondered what she had seen in his face. He swallowed. "In every town between here and Tasso."

She laughed again, but she was watching him closely. "No, we were wrong. You've no more choice than I have, do you? They pick it out for you from birth: the girl you'll marry, the life you'll live, the death you'll die. Privilege, choice. It's a lie they tell you, and they do it so well you start telling it to yourself. But underneath you're as trapped as I am."

"Some are. I wasn't raised to see duty as the end. My father has no such conceit."

"Bold words for a soldier. What about your mother? What does your father say when *she* speaks so liberally of duty?"

He turned the bowl in his hands and watched the sediments shift in the clear depths. "I don't know," he said. "She was dead at my birth."

Ceno said, after a pause, "I'm sorry."

It was on his tongue to ask why, sourly. He swallowed it and said nothing.

Ceno said, "Did he love her—your father?"

"He loved her. He doesn't speak of her. For my sake, maybe: he spares me the guilt." He had never talked about it to Alluin, and he had never realized the difficulty of putting it into words. "In Cesin there is a custom," he said. "The wedding ring goes on the right hand when the spouse dies. My father wears his ring on his left hand. It's been twenty years—it will have been, come this autumn."

"I didn't think your kind had the capacity for love," Ceno said.

He looked into her face. She met his eyes. Her eyes were the color and quality of amber, strikingly clear and cold and hard—layers and layers of veneer built carefully up, dead things trapped beneath. She blinked and looked away. "From what I have seen," she said. "It inconveniences the blood-spilling."

There were footsteps on the landing.

It was not dinner up from the taberna. Vaiz came in from the vestibule with a Guardsman behind her. Ceno put her bowl on the table and stood, smiling. "Vigo. I'm sorry to drag you away from your dinner."

The Guardsman, a lieutenant, came over from the archway, one hand on the pommel of his sword. There were more Guardsmen on the landing. Torien could see them in silhouette against torchlight, out through the vestibule. He stood, slowly, the wine bowl in his hands. Ceno had moved shrewdly away from him. There was not much opportunity for his knife. He supposed if he flung the wine bowl in the Guardsman's face, he would have time to cut his own throat. It was a distasteful thought—not least because it would be a waste of wine. He did not move. The Guardsman came over and slipped the knife from Torien's belt. He glanced over the wine bowl.

"You might as well finish it, Commander," he said. "You'll be glad for it in a half-hour or so."

He finished it. He caught a glimpse of her as he tilted the bowl: rigid as a statue, her chin up, her arms straight at her sides. He drained the bowl and set it down beside hers on the table. The dregs were bitter on his tongue. "You've done what you must?" he said.

She said nothing.

"I did enjoy the wine," he said.

XX

They had put a hood over his head on the landing, but he could tell by the slope of the street and direction of the wind that they were going up the Hill. They went quickly and in silence. Around them the Hill lay quiet. His head was pounding and the pain fluttering in his ribs, and he could not think except to stumble forward when the lieutenant shoved him. They turned this way and that through the streets on the Hill. He did not know the lay of the Hill very well, and he could not have kept track of the turns if he'd tried. He knew when they passed through a gate, because he heard the rattle of the bolt and the groan of the doors. Still no one spoke.

There was gravel underfoot now rather than paving stone, and he heard from somewhere the trickling of a fountain. There were more doors and then there was smooth, polished tile slipping under his feet. From the echoes of their footfalls, he knew he was alone now with the lieutenant. The echoes chased away and came rolling back. They were in an enclosed space, and through the hood he caught the scent of lamp oil and smoke. The lieutenant pushed him down into a chair and tore the hood from his head.

He recognized the room, though it took him a moment, blinking in the lamplight after the blackness of the hood. It was a small, square room, close and windowless but not dreary, lined on three walls with bookshelves and on the fourth with maps inked on vellum and stretched on wooden frames. The bust of the Emperor gazed down at him forlornly from one of the shelves. There was a desk in front of him and a quill case and papyrus. A tall, empty chair faced him across the desk. He had sat at this desk five months ago, and the chair across from him had been occupied by Maris Pavo. They had drunk chilled wine, and he had turned down a Guardsman's commission worth twenty-four thousand eagles a year, a bonus of ten thousand, a private house on the Hill.

The lieutenant went out wordlessly, shutting the door behind him, and Torien heard the clink of a chain as the lieutenant locked the door from the outside. He did not, however, hear the lieutenant's footsteps go away across the floor tiles. He reached across the desk for the quill case. Someone had been judicious enough to remove the pen-knife. He shut the case and shoved it back across the desk. He got up from the chair and wandered the perimeter of the room. He picked up the Emperor from the shelf and looked at him in his hand. He turned him over to test his weight. The chain rattled at the door. The lieutenant came in, holding the door wide. Through the doorway, Maris Pavo looked at him across the room.

"Whatever you learned in Tasso," he said, "it was not piety."

Torien put the Emperor back on the shelf. "I learned to make the most of the blunt objects available to me, sir."

Pavo ducked in through the doorway. A slave girl followed at his heels, carrying a salver with a wine jug and two silver cups. "You can leave it," Pavo said. She put the salver on the desk and bowed and went out. The lieutenant shut the door when she had gone and stood silently watching, his feet spread and arms folded.

Pavo came over beside Torien at the bookshelf. He was tall and hawk-faced, thin rather than lean, his face full of hollows in the lamplight, his broad shoulders beginning to stoop. There was an opaqueness in his dark eyes that hinted at blindness to come. There were cancer spots sprinkled here and there on his face and on the backs of his brown, muscled hands. He reached and touched Torien's ribs very lightly. "They told me you offered no resistance."

Torien looked down. There was blood in a half-moon stain on his tunic, spreading under the edge of the bandage. Pavo took him by the elbow back around the desk. "Sit," he said. "I will look at it."

Torien did not say anything. He sat holding the arms of the chair while Pavo opened his tunic and unwrapped the bandage and peeled off Antoni's dressing to look. Pavo's blunt brown fingers explored the edges of the wound very carefully. "This was not your work, Vigo?"

From the doorway, the lieutenant said, "No, sir."

"Tell the girl to bring acetum and oil. Cloth as well—and hot water."

"Yes, sir."

Pavo ran his thumb over the cut on Torien's cheek. "This has healed well. The other is a concern. It should have been let to rest. You've carried it from Tasso?"

"Modigne."

"Overland?"

Torien did not say anything. Pavo did not seem to notice. He laid a hand on Torien's forehead. His skin was rough and dry, like papyrus. "No fever, at least. That is a mercy."

The girl brought the things and put them on the desk and stood holding the bowl of hot water and a towel on her arm while Pavo cleaned the wound and dressed it. Pavo worked silently and skillfully. Torien sat looking at the Emperor over Pavo's shoulder. There was a tightness in him and he knew Pavo could feel it, but Pavo did not say anything. Pavo finished and washed his hands and dried them. Torien slid his tunic back on while the girl cleared the things off the desk. She went out from the room and the lieutenant closed the door behind her and Torien listened to her footsteps going away across the tiles.

Pavo poured wine into the cups on the salver. "From Inumæ," he said, "my own vintage." He put one cup in front of Torien. "What do you think?"

Torien took the cup and held it between his hands and looked down into it. His own face looked up at him from the smooth, dark red surface of the wine. "I was not raised to know viniculture, sir."

"Neither was I," Pavo said. "I have come to it very late. I had neither opportunity nor interest as a boy. Therefore, my efforts are still very much those of an amateur. That is why I'm asking your opinion rather than Vigo's. The Lieutenant comes of very good family in Seragno, and winemaking is to him a matter of ancestral pride."

Torien tipped the cup and drew a long mouthful of wine and rolled it over his tongue and swallowed. His throat was tight. The wine slid down heavily and unpleasantly and settled like a clenched fist in the pit of his stomach. Pavo watched his face. "I await your judgment," he said.

"Maybe Brevade can find a market for it in Tasso, sir."

Pavo took the other cup and sat down facing him in the chair across the desk. He said, "I'm not meant to take that as a compliment, I imagine." His eyes ran a circle from Torien's face to his ribs and back across his cheek. "Brevade's work? It was clumsy of him."

"To leave me alive, sir?"

"I am glad to have you alive. I mean that very honestly. The offer I made you five months ago still stands between us, if you are interested."

Torien looked up from the cup in his hands. Pavo seemed amused. "Did you think I was going to put you on a rack?"

"You didn't seem to have much compunction about Nico Briule."

Pavo paused with his cup at his lips. "What was done," he said, "was done out of necessity. Do not assume, childishly, that it was done without compunction."

"Espere hung him alive on the gate wall when he'd finished torturing him. It took him four days to die."

"Espere was an animal, functional to a specific end. Nico was a casualty of war. I mourn him as I mourn the rest of my dead." Pavo drank and lowered the cup and looked into it. "It is what Vigo would call rustic," he said, "but I am also what Vigo would call rustic, so I do not disdain. However, it is not a summer wine."

"You and I have different ideas of compunction, sir."

"Inevitably. You have held command five months. I have held it forty years. You can spare me the condescension until you've had blood on your hands—and you will get blood on your hands, if you continue much longer in command." Pavo looked up at the lieutenant in the doorway. "Vigo, tell the girl to bring some of the white."

"Yes, sir."

"Have you eaten?" Pavo said to Torien.

"I've been locked in an office."

"And dinner for the Commander, Vigo," Pavo said.

For a while, there was traffic in and out through the door. The girl came to clear the desk and pour white wine in new cups. A pair of kitchen boys brought the dinner on trays. There was a cold duck breast and cucumbers and black olives in vinegar and a sticky honey pastry with almonds. The fist in his stomach unclenched a little, and he remembered how hungry he was. He had eaten nothing but Antoni's barley porridge since his fever had broken on the road. He ate a little of the duck and some of the cucumbers and found he could not eat any more. The lieutenant, Vigo, had come over to the desk to say something into Pavo's ear, and Torien sat looking at the wine cup in his lap and pretending he was not trying to hear. Pavo listened and said nothing. He took out a quill and wrote something on papyrus and rolled up the papyrus and gave it to the lieutenant. "Wait outside," he said, "until I have need of you."

"Yes, sir."

"The Lieutenant shares your sense of compunction," Pavo said to Torien, as Vigo went out, shutting the door. "It was his responsibility to see you did not make it past the gates, therefore a personal failing to find you spent the evening on Chæla Ceno's couch. I have tried to reassure him you and the former Lord Senna made an unrivaled art of slipping in and out of the city. He prefers self-flagellation." Pavo wiped the nib of his quill and laid the pen back in its case. He looked up. "I admit I expected Senna would be with you. As I remember it, you were inseparable."

Torien said, looking at the wine cup tight in his hands, "He's dead. A month ago in Tasso. We met a Mayaso raiding party on the Road."

There was a moment's silence.

"I hadn't heard," Pavo said. "I'm sorry."

"He was a casualty of war. I mourn him as I mourn the rest of my dead."

He felt Pavo's eyes on him like a physical weight. "You wrote his family?"

"By law there was no family. I didn't know the protocol."

"There is a time and place for protocol and a time and place for disregarding protocol. You should have written."

Torien did not say anything.

"I will see to it that his father is informed—or perhaps it would be better if you told him yourself. It will mean more coming from you. Alvero knows you were close." Pavo's eyes were steady on his face. "One question raises another," he said. "Tell me who brought you to the city. Obviously, it was not young Senna."

He heard himself say, distantly above the pounding of his heart, "I came alone."

"Up the river, it must be, with such a wound."

"Yes."

"Impressive. Dio Valle did not make it past Salina. Lieutenant Aregne sent an alert from Modigne."

His own voice again, detached from the rest of him: "Maybe I was more careful."

"I am willing to believe it, though I am pleasantly surprised. Caution has never been one of your greatest strengths. The real difficulty lies in the fact that the river has been impassable for three weeks below Manola."

Torien studied his wine cup and said nothing.

"You did not come on foot," Pavo said. "Even without that little memento from Brevade, you could not have come in two weeks on foot from Modigne."

A fly settled on the rim of the cup. Torien shook it off and watched it glide away over the desktop to land on the uneaten duck.

Pavo said, "Who else besides Salvo Briule knew your business in Choiro?"

"Lieutenant Aregne, apparently."

"Who else?"

Torien did not say anything.

"I have already dealt as necessary with your officers at Tasso, if it interests you," Pavo said. "I will deal with Briule presently."

"I'd like to hear you explain to the Senate why you're taking punitive measures against us without implicating your trafficking ring."

"I'm not taking punitive measures. I have sent reinforcements to put down an uprising among the tribes. They will arrive too late to save the garrison, but I will make sure your men are commended before the Senate for defending their post to the last."

"Your puppet at the mines is dead. I have guarantees of peace from both tribes, and I have made guarantees of my own. Disregard them and you'll have a real uprising on your hands."

"My puppet at the mines is alive and well. The guarantees you gave him are not binding—fortunately for young Senna."

The fly had lost interest in the duck and moved on to the cucumbers. Pavo brushed it away with one hand. "So we are back to where we started. Tell me who helped you to the city."

Torien said, turning the wine cup in his hands without seeing it, "He's alive?"

"Aidar?"

"Alluin."

"He is alive for now. Given your cooperation, he will be still alive in a month. It is not much of a threat, granted, considering your willingness to use him as a hostage. And you chide me for my lack of compunction." Pavo's lips twitched in a half-smile. "So I recognize you may require further persuasion—more immediate persuasion." He spoke past Torien to the doorway. "Lieutenant."

Over Pavo's shoulder, the Emperor was looking down at him sadly from the shelf. He sat rolling the wine cup numbly between his hands, swallowing the tightness in his throat, listening to the door creaking open and closed and the footsteps coming across the floor. There was one set of booted footsteps, Vigo's, and one set of bare, shuffling footsteps. Vigo's footsteps were long and slow and heavy, the others quick and light hurrying along beside, two steps to Vigo's one. Both sets came up to the desk and stopped. Out of the corner of his eye, he saw small, dirty brown feet in front of Vigo's booted feet. He looked up from the wine cup into Ædyn's face.

"He is uncommonly loyal," Pavo said, "for a Cesino. In my experience, Cesino slaves can be difficult—particularly those of the mountain tribes."

Torien did not say anything. He sat looking at the boy's face. In the back of his mind, he was aware that Pavo was watching him for a reaction. He made himself consider the boy detachedly. There was a cloth gag over the boy's mouth and tear tracks on his cheeks above the gag, but he seemed unhurt. Torien did not look in the boy's eyes. He looked back down at his wine cup. He lifted the cup and drank. His hands were numb but steady. Pavo, watching him, said, "He must have been raised in your household."

"Bought off a trade ship in Modigne two weeks ago. I meant to sell him again here in the city"—as carelessly as he could manage it.

His heart was pounding.

"Well, we can dispense at least with the fiction that you came alone from Modigne." Pavo put an olive between his teeth and spat the pit into his cupped palm. "Has he a name? What's his name?"

"I haven't given him a name."

"For two weeks I suppose it would not be necessary." Pavo tore into another olive and pushed the pit out between his teeth. "He means nothing to you at all?"

"Eighty eagles and the sale tax."

"I offered him citizenship—also the chance to kill you personally, if he wanted it. He wouldn't take it. Uncommonly loyal for a Cesino, I thought, but perhaps he is simply dimwitted." Pavo chewed, thoughtfully. He glanced up from the olive dish. "Very well, Lieutenant."

Vigo unsheathed his belt knife. Holding the boy tight against him with one arm, he took the boy's right wrist between thumb and fingers of his knife hand, bracing the blade with his forefinger and slicing through the wrist as one might pare a turnip.

Torien was up from the chair blindly, tripping over the chair legs and steadying himself against the desk, the wine cup clattering away across the floor tiles, the wine splashing over his feet. He drove a fist into Vigo's face, jerking the boy from Vigo's arm as Vigo staggered back. He shoved the boy away behind him. He slid an arm around Vigo's neck and shouldered him to the wall, pinning his arm, pinning his knife hand wide. Vigo twisted beneath him and got his arm free and jabbed quick fingers into Torien's ribs. Pain folded over him like wings. He doubled, gasping, his stomach sloshing up his throat. Vigo kicked his feet from under him, then kicked him flat to the floor. He lay breathing through his teeth and blinking against the tiles, holding on tightly as the room spun, looking across the floor at Ædyn sprawled at the foot of the desk.

Far above him, he heard Pavo's voice in mild rebuke: "I need him able to speak."

Vigo's hands were on his shoulders, pulling him up to his knees. He sat under Vigo's hands, looking at Ædyn below the desk, watching the boy's ribs rise and fall, watching the bony legs twitch on the tiles as the boy came slowly up from blackness. The boy's face was away from him. The severed hand was on the floor at the corner of the desk. It had been a quick, clean cut, and if it were treated directly there would be no complication. Shock would dull the pain. It went through his head methodically, like a memorized prayer.

From the desk, Pavo said, "Tell me who helped you to the city." He was writing again, and he did not look up. He wrote in long, smooth, unhurried strokes, the pen rustling comfortably across the papyrus. There was a fascination in watching him write. He formed his letters with the care and grace of a sculptor shaping marble. He was a freedman and had grown up unlettered, and he wrote as only one such could write—with an eye toward penmanship as a privilege.

Torien shut his eyes. The pen went on steadily. There were footsteps beyond the office doorway, and he listened to them echo over the floor tiles and up and down the walls. He thought it was probably the slave girl waiting to see if she should come in and take away the dinner things. He swallowed. He was finding it difficult to think clearly through the pain and the wine. "The boy goes free," he said.

"Once I am satisfied we have reached the truth."

"And Alluin. I want your written word to Aidar that he is to be released to Modigne. He knows nothing against you. You've no need to consider him a threat."

Pavo, still writing, said, "Your *signo* as well?"

"More than that. His full pardon, his citizenship restored. Legal recognition that he is under the patronage of the Risti."

"One could be forgiven for thinking I am presently at your mercy and not the other way around."

"You need as much of me as I need of you."

"Hold your tongue and give it a month's time," Pavo said. "We'll see which of us has more to lose."

The footsteps were coming closer across the tiles, and he could tell now that the tread was too heavy to be the girl's. The office door opened and closed. A gust of cool night air came in from the corridor. Someone shook out a cloak in the doorway. The newcomer said, languidly, "I am interrupting?" His voice was dry and just familiar enough to be unsettling. Torien opened his eyes and twisted his neck to look up to the doorway. Alvero Senna looked down at him blankly. He was tall and lean and sun-tanned, not yet forty, his olive-skinned, aristocratic face very much like Alluin's face, his thin, harsh mouth very like Alluin's mouth. He folded his cloak slowly over his arm. His eyes left Torien's face and went to Ædyn still prone on the floor, then up to Pavo at the desk. He did not move from the doorway. "Anyone in this house can walk in just as I have done."

Pavo paused to re-ink his pen. "Most have the courtesy to knock."

"Ceno has been arrested."

Pavo tapped the nib on the rim of the ink pot. He glanced up. "Whose orders?"

"Direct from His Highness. Raniere made the arrest."

"You are sure?"

"I was at dinner with His Highness when the order was given."

"It would have been better," Pavo said, returning his attention to his writing, "if you had remained at dinner with His Highness. I will clear this up in the morning."

"They are examining him tonight. His Highness is seeing to it personally."

"Ceno knows nothing of importance."

"His Highness knows you are holding Risto."

Pavo's pen fell still for a moment, poised above the papyrus.

"Raniere is coming to make inquiries," Alvero said. "At present, it is all very procedural. They have the Ceno girl's word that Risto is here. If he is not here, they will have nothing, provided your people hold their tongues. My carriage is ready at the gate. I can get him out of the city."

Pavo recommenced to write. His hand moved slowly and carefully across the papyrus. "If he is found in your hands," he said, "it complicates matters."

Alvero's lip curled. "I am above reproach, and he is a family friend."

Pavo was silent, writing. Ædyn was awake at the foot of the desk. He turned his head onto his right cheek. His face was pale. His eyes were bleary with tears, but he did not make any noise behind the gag. He did not look at Torien. He lay still and looked at the fingers of his left hand clenched in a fist against the floor tiles.

From the doorway, Alvero said, "If it is going to be done, Commander, it must be done now. Raniere will be here in a quarter-hour with a detachment of the Household Guard."

Pavo did not look up. "Vigo."

"Yes, sir?"

"Accompany the Senator."

"Yes, sir."

Alvero smiled a familiar swift, bitter smile. "I will pretend that is not a comment upon my loyalty."

"For your own protection," Pavo said, blandly.

He was being hauled to his feet, and Vigo was pulling his hands behind his back. He got his right hand free and found the knife at Vigo's belt and tore it from its sheath, swinging his hand wide before Vigo could catch his wrist. Vigo hooked a foot around his ankle and shoved him forward. He tripped and fell and caught himself with his hands on the edge of the desktop. By the time he had pushed himself up, Vigo had dragged Ædyn away from him across the floor. Vigo pulled the boy up to his feet, sliding an arm over the boy's throat. Torien flung the knife away, savagely. It hit one of the shelves and fell back clattering to the floor.

Pavo laid down his pen and pushed back his chair and went to pick it up. "Take the boy, too," he said to Alvero. "You may find him useful."

"I see," said Alvero, very dryly.

"I have business to finish with Risto in the morning," Pavo said. "I will be at the river at dawn."

"I will be at home," Alvero said. "If you have finished your business with Raniere, you may send for me there."

XXI

He did not know why or how the boy had come there, or what had become of the priests, and he did not really know why, now, he was climbing up into Alvero Senna's private carriage, which was waiting dark and silent before the gate of Pavo's villa. He had thought it would be finished with Pavo, one way or another, and he did not know what it meant that Alvero was there, except it seemed less and less likely that it was about salt mines in Tasso.

There were four of Alvero's personal guardsmen waiting with horses at the carriage. There was a mist lying over the street. The air was very still and humid. He felt his way along the bench in the dark and sat down in the corner below the driver's seat. Vigo picked Ædyn up by the shoulders and knees and swung him up the steps and put him down on the carriage floor. He started up afterward, one hand on either side of the doorway.

Alvero, behind him, put a hand on his shoulder almost companionably and drew a knife across his throat and eased him down face-first against the steps.

It was done quickly and silently. Alvero wiped his blade and tucked the knife away into his tunic, under his cloak. He said something to his guardsmen. Two of the guardsmen lifted Vigo's body into the carriage and laid it on the floor. Alvero came up into the carriage afterward, and the guardsmen shut the doors behind him.

There was pitch darkness for a little while, and then the bright white flare of a flint spark as Alvero lit a lamp. The lamp hung from the carriage ceiling, swinging back and forth as the carriage started. Ædyn was holding his right arm tightly in his left hand and looking at Vigo's body in a black heap on the floor. Torien took him by the arm and sat him down on the bench. It was easiest to focus on what was immediately necessary. He knelt at the boy's knees and unknotted the gag from the boy's mouth. He pried the boy's fingers gently loose from the stump of the right hand and wrapped the stump with the cloth and tied it off. "Now hold it," he said, "hold it up—we need to stop it bleeding." He held the boy's arms in his hands. The boy was shaking silently. Torien felt the tremors through his fingers. The boy was looking at the stump in his lap. His lips moved soundlessly. Torien squeezed the boy's elbows. "Look at me, Ædyn," he said, in Cesino. "Tell me if the priests live."

The boy shut his eyes. Tears spilled down his cheeks. The words came in a sudden burst. "I swear they live. Please, Lord, I swear I did not betray you. I swear that isn't why."

Alvero, on the other bench, poured wine into a cup and held the cup out to Torien. He indicated Ædyn with a jerk of his wrist. In Vareno, he said, "Make him drink. It will be Hell when the shock has gone."

Torien took the cup, slowly, looking up over his shoulder into Alvero's face. Alvero met his gaze expressionlessly, as he had done in Pavo's office. Torien did not say anything. He took the cup in one hand and looked at it in the half-light. He bent his head and sipped the wine and washed it around his mouth. Alvero watched him. "If I wanted to be rid of the slave," he said, "I would not trifle with poison."

Torien swallowed. He put the cup against Ædyn's lips. "Drink this, Ædyn. It'll ease the pain."

"I did not betray you," Ædyn said. His clenched teeth clinked against the cup.

"I know you didn't. Drink, Ædyn."

"I would have warned you at the apartment. They took me before I could warn you."

"You followed me from the inn?"

"I told Jovan I was going to see to the horses. Do not be angry with the priests, Lord. They didn't know."

"I'm not angry with the priests. I'm angry enough without being angry at the priests. You were stupid to come, Ædyn."

"My lord was s-stupid to go alone." The boy's teeth were chattering.

"You'd still have both your hands if I'd been alone. Drink."

The boy's shoulders, braced tightly against the carriage wall, went slack. His head lolled onto his chest. Torien put the cup down. He held the boy by the arm and felt the pulse under the boy's chin. He stretched the boy's legs straight on the bench and folded the boy's arms over his ribs. He sat down beside the boy on the bench, leaning forward with his elbows on his knees, holding the wine cup between his hands, swallowing dryly. His head ached and spun. He could not tell if the rippling surface of the wine was from the movement of the carriage over paving stone or the shaking of his hands.

Alvero was watching him from the other bench. He started to say something and then did not say it. He said, instead, "Are you hurt?"

"I'll last the night."

"I was not expecting to find you alive. Usually he is more—discreet."

"Usually I would be in the river already, you mean."

Alvero's eyes were keen on his face. "What does he want?"

"You're his business partner, Senator. You tell me."

"Maris Pavo does not have partners. At certain times, certain of us are useful to him. I think you know that." The bitter smile flicked across Alvero's mouth. "It was the wrong question. Where is Alluin?"

Torien looked up from the wine cup. There had to be a trick somewhere, and he was silent, looking at Alvero, trying to figure out whether the trick was on him or on Pavo or somehow on both.

"I thought he would be with you," Alvero said. "The girl could not tell me. She said only that you had been taken. I thought surely he must be with you." He looked away. The muscles in his cheek fluttered. "At least tell me if he is alive. Tell me I have not come too late."

"He wasn't with me. He didn't come with me from Tasso. I left him wounded at the mines after a patrol gone wrong."

Alvero looked back. His shoulders were straight, his face like carved stone in the lamplight. "Then he is dead."

"He's leverage, as long as I'm alive. Pavo gave me no promises for once I'm in the river."

Alvero looked at him blankly. "The mines fell to a joint force of Asani and Mayasi more than a fortnight past. The garrison was massacred, the slaves freed and armed. They are moving to besiege the fort. We heard it on the Senate floor."

"You heard what Pavo wanted you to hear."

"We sent out reinforcements from Vione."

"With orders from Pavo to silence my men at Tasso before they can spill what they know about your business in the mines."

Alvero was silent, studying him. His face was inscrutable. "Once you are in the river," he said, finally, "Alluin is nothing but a liability."

"He has no reason to suspect Pavo's involvement. Or yours. I swear he is no threat to you."

"He will make himself a threat when he learns you ended up down the Breche. He'll have the truth out and justice done for it. You give him too little credit. Pavo will not." Alvero leaned his head back against the wall. "It is foolish to think Pavo will leave him alive, alone of your command. He is by far the greatest threat. He will die with the rest, no matter what Pavo promised or did not promise."

"Does a confession from Ceno mean nothing?"

Alvero smiled, sourly. "He made a cut of the profit for the use of his ships. He doesn't know where the rest of the money went. He thinks he was smuggling slaves. Without you in Pavo's hands, they'll hang him and be done with it."

"Why?"

"Because as much as His Highness would like Pavo's head on a spear, he recognizes he can do nothing without proof. The Senate will tear the Palace down to dust if he moves against Pavo without proof. The Berioni have spit too many times in the face of rule of law. Once more and the Senate will have blood."

"I mean why Tasso? Why citizens, why the mines? Why you and Pavo? For a cut of the profit? If I'm going to die for it, I have the right to know. My men have the right to know. Alluin has the right to know."

The carriage had eased to a stop. They had not ridden long enough to be out of the city. He was not even sure they had come off the Hill. Two of the guardsmen opened the doors at the back of the carriage and took out Vigo's body, holding him under his knees and arms. There was torchlight through the doorway. Torien caught a glimpse of a tall white marble wall and, beyond, the black silhouettes of cypress trees against a wide night sky. He recognized the wall and trees. They were at the southern edge of the Palace grounds on the hilltop. The street curved away back down the Hill. In the distance below, he could see the lights of the River Quarter and the silver thread of the river.

Alvero stood up. He stood for a moment, looking down at Torien on the bench. "My driver has orders to take you to Vione. The slave will need a surgeon tonight if you want him to keep the arm."

"I do not understand."

"His Highness will send for you, when he remembers and can

spare you the time. He will be glad to explain and to reward you for the service you have rendered him."

"Senator—"

"He will be emperor before the year is out." Alvero's voice was like ashes. "He will be such an emperor as history remembers. You could do very well by him, Risto. He could make a name of you. He could make you great, if you wanted it. It will be on offer, and it will be your choice. I want you to understand it should not be an easy choice. With him there is always a cost."

Torien shook his head. "I want justice done in Tasso. I want Alluin's life and the lives of my men. I have a name already."

Alvero was silent, looking at him, his face shadowed. "You'd have the throne," he said, "if there were any justice in the world. Then again, I suppose you would not take it." He smiled again, briefly. His shoulders were very straight. "Goodbye, Risto."

"Senator." There was a tightness in him. "Alluin deserves to know it of you, not of the Prince."

Alvero paused in the doorway but did not look back. "It is the best I can do for him now—to be silent. You will understand. He will, in time. I ask that you do not tell him we spoke this night. You owe me that much for keeping you from the river."

He climbed down from the carriage in the torchlight. Torien watched him go. Two of Alvero's guardsmen closed the doors after him and bolted them. The carriage started with a shudder and a lurch. Ædyn was still unconscious beside him on the bench. He was alone with his thoughts all the way to Vione.

XXII

From the window, which faced east and which was left un-shuttered on the surgeon's orders to let a breeze stir the still air of the room, he had a view of the high road, the eastward road past Gracha to Cesin, the spelt fields yellow for harvest on either side of the embankment, the oak woods turning to gold on the far brown hills.

If he lifted himself carefully on his left elbow, he could see down onto the parade ground just below the fort walls, and he watched the musters at dawn and dusk, and the cavalry exercises and foot drills through the day, and sometimes he just lay and listened with his eyes closed to the instructors' voices and the ring of metal and thud of wooden practice weapons carrying on the breeze through the window—listening to it as though it were a language, horse and sword and spear, knowing how to speak it and not being able. He thought he might go crazy with lying there and listening.

He was to have a week in bed, on the surgeon's orders, and no visitors. Absolutely he must rest. Ædyn was gone to the chapel of the Hospitallers. He had not seen the boy since the first morning, and he had not seen the priests at all. He'd had a letter from Jovan saying the boy was safe at the chapel and his arm healing well. He had been alone in this room three days. The surgeon came at first three times a day and now twice, once in the morning and once in the evening. A slave boy brought him the meals and swatted flies for him and brought him water when he asked and reading material when it was possible to get it past the surgeon.

He read indiscriminately: scrolls of verse, and agricultural manuals, and veterinary guidebooks, and apologies on the moral obligations of the nobility, and studies of water disputes along the Nona, and histories of the development of the Imperial law codes out of ancient Vareno tribal customs. He read with some interest a treatise entitled "On the Administration of the Imperial Province of Cesin." It was dedicated to the Emperor by Senator Lucho Marro, and it argued for the abolishment of the hereditary governorship of Cesin, which in effect created a new Cesino monarchy with only nominal ties to Varen and which would lead eventually to open rebellion instigated by the Risti: *the governorship of Cesin is the last vestige of an antiquated system of nepotistic patronage whose continued existence undermines the integrity and stability of the modern Imperial project.* He wondered if the Emperor had read it. After all, it had been the Berioni whose *antiquated nepotistic patronage* had put Cesin in the hands of the Risti, two hundred years ago. He wondered if his father had read it. His father would laugh, reading it. It was hard to lead a rebellion among people who wanted foremost to hang you as a blood traitor.

In the heat and stillness of the late afternoon, the drills done and the fort quiet for the mess, he was dreaming fitfully of cavalry on the road to Modigne, his head full of hoof beats and the jingle of horse-harness. The surgeon was there inexplicably, saying he could wake him if necessary, and a strange new voice was saying it wasn't necessary and he could wait, and the surgeon was saying he would bring a chair. It did not make much sense for there to be a chair. Torien drifted awake. The room was full of Guardsmen. The surgeon was coming in through the curtain with a chair from the officers' mess. The surgeon put the chair down and bowed and went out again. One of the Guardsmen shut the curtain behind him. Their helmet crests were the tall indigo plumes of the Household Guard. Torien sat up slowly against the wall. Someone put a hand on his shoulder.

"I promised I wouldn't strain you." It was the man who had been speaking with the surgeon. "Lie down, Risto, before you get me in trouble."

He was in his mid-twenties, bare-headed, athletically built, smoothly olive-skinned, with a straight, aristocratic nose and firm chin and wide, dimpled, smiling mouth and a high forehead. His tunic was indigo silk edged in gold. A sapphire sparkled on the head of his cloak pin, another on the pommel of the dagger at his hip. The seal ring on the forefinger of his right hand bore no inscription, only the Imperial sun blazing in its zenith over the flat gold face. None but the royal family wore sapphires, and none but those ascendant to the throne wore the plain sunburst seal.

Torien shifted against the wall, trying to bow. The Prince's fingers tightened on his shoulder. "No need for ceremony between us," he said, "not here, anyway. That's why I came. I want to talk straightly. I don't often get the chance." He let go Torien's shoulder and reached up to unpin his cloak. One of his Guardsmen stepped up to his elbow. The Prince handed off his cloak and sat down in the chair. His dark almond eyes lingered for a moment on the dressing around Torien's ribs. "I know you need your rest."

"I think I may die of rest."

The Prince smiled. "Yes, I've been told you are a man of action. Do you know who told me so?"

Underneath the smile, there was a thin, cool edge to the words. Torien looked away. "No," he said. He wondered if it sounded as much a lie to the Prince as it did to him.

"Pavo's words. I do think he admired you, if he never quite understood you. I think it truly astonished him when you refused his commission. It astonished a lot of people. Maris Pavo wasn't often refused."

"You don't sound as if it astonished you."

"I'll wager I understand you—better than he did, at least. If I'd been in his place, I'd have killed you before you ever took ship for

Tasso. I'd have killed you out of Choiro. Knowing your qualities, he was a fool to let you live so long." There was still a hint of a smile at the Prince's mouth, but his eyes were unreadable. "I told you I came to talk straightly."

"Has he confessed?"

"He confessed. There wasn't any point in holding his tongue once Senna talked."

"No point but honor."

"At any rate, he didn't hold his tongue."

"How many arrests?"

"So far? Pavo and his staff, of course, and Senna. Certain of the command here at Vione."

"Who?"

"Brada, Iolano, Montegne—"

"Montegne?"

"He has not been arrested yet. We've sent the orders after him to Modigne. He'll be brought back here for sentencing, along with the senior command of the Modigne garrison. Also the governor and his staff."

"It was Montegne's column?"

"There are others. I won't bore you with the names and numbers: the crews of the ships, the harbor officials. All of them bought on Pavo's coin or Senna's."

"It'll be a year before you've brought them all to trial."

"In your opinion the wheels of Imperial justice turn too slowly?"

Torien did not say anything.

"Speak your mind, Risto," the Prince said. "I'm interested to hear."

"I thought you knew my mind."

Out of the corner of his eye, he saw one of the Guardsmen shift on his feet. The Prince laughed. "I asked for that, I suppose. Fair enough. I'll tell you what I think you wanted to say, and you may tell me where I'm wrong."

"If you wish."

"Every delay compounds opportunity for the miscarriage of justice. It is frankly inexpedient to allow each of the accused his right to trial in Choiro. You hesitated to say it because you felt there was some risk in pointing out to me deficiencies in a legal tradition my forebears have upheld since the time of the tribes. Also in implicitly suggesting that my courts are open to corruption."

"Your father's courts."

"My father will be dead at the first frost, and they will be my courts. We are speaking straightly." The Prince's voice was cool. "An adequate representation? Or have I missed something?"

Torien did not say anything.

"An adequate representation, then. And I've spared you incriminating yourself."

"Your Highness is merciful."

"Reasonable, at least, I like to think. Mercy is too easily manipulated. I share your concern for justice, Risto. I mean the Empire to know I will not tolerate corruption as my father has done. I mean the Empire to know my vengeance will be swift and uncompromising and impartial."

"Or you mean the Senate to know, because otherwise you fear for your throne."

The Prince smiled. "You think I lack conviction? There is twelvefold proof of my conviction hanging on the Traitors' Wall."

Something twisted inside him. "Senna?"

"All of them. Montegne and the rest will join them presently. If I cared only for the good will of the Senate, I would have had Senna quietly beheaded. Don't tell me I lack conviction, Risto."

"Senna wasn't guilty of treason. Nor Ceno. None of them but Pavo and possibly his officers—any who were complicit in the death of Nico Briule. None of the rest."

"Montegne had orders to eliminate your garrison at Tasso and testify before the Senate that it was the work of the tribes."

"Pavo's orders. Montegne was coerced."

"Do you think so?"

"I know Montegne. And I know Pavo. If Montegne took those orders, it was under coercion. He has a family."

"He took them, regardless. He might have refused. *You* would have refused, of course." The Prince's voice was very dry. "Tell me what you think was Senna's crime."

"The same as Ceno's. He was trafficking citizens into the salt mines, or he knew it was being done. It still doesn't merit the Traitors' Wall."

"Alvero Senna was worth seven million a year. Unless you think him the sort to be blinded to logic by petty greed, he had no reason to be involved in a trafficking ring. Anyway, the revenue was worthless, if you think about it. Any attempt to invest it would draw attention to the source. Why risk himself only to let the profits sit moldering?"

"I don't know."

"Think about it."

"Why does it matter what I think?"

"You are too self-effacing," the Prince said. "Too obviously self-effacing, I mean. You've already guessed. You just don't want to admit I've won."

"It was a coup."

"In its infancy, yes. They didn't yet have as much of the army in hand as they needed. You can pontificate as much as you want on the Senate floor—and Senna did, believe me—but when it comes down to it you've got to have the raw manpower to take and hold the Hill, and the coin to pay for it. Till the moment the blood runs, the coin must be untraceable. Slaves have brands and certificates of sale and a certain amount of economic importance. Kidnapped Modigno gutter rats are very easily made invisible."

"Did they know?"

"Who?"

"The raw manpower. The ones doing the actual work. Pavo wasn't an idiot. They didn't know what he intended. They wouldn't have known until the blood was running."

"That is incidental, to my mind, and insufficient as an excuse. One has the responsibility to know the precise nature of one's business contracts."

"So it's treason for all of them."

"And the penalty for treason, irrespective of rank."

"Their families?"

"Chæla Ceno will live. She gave me her father; I can hardly hold her complicit. Likewise your adjutant Alluin Senna. By virtue of his disinheritance, he is rendered legally immune to his family's disgrace. As for the rest—no one will accuse me of jettisoning tradition, at least."

Torien did not say anything. Tradition meant death by the sword for every member of the traitor's household over fifteen years old, branding and enslavement for the rest, the condemned made to watch while it was done.

"It will take some time," the Prince said. "Senna was shrewd enough to alert his household before coming forward to betray Pavo. The family had opportunity to flee. Senna would not give up their whereabouts either for pain or for the promise of a dignified death. But you can rest assured time will not blunt my resolve." The Prince smiled at him, thinly. "Tell me again it was only because I feared for my throne."

He did not look in the Prince's eyes. He looked away past the Prince's right ear to the far side of the room, where the late-afternoon shadows were crawling up the wall. "Forgive me, Highness."

"I'm not toying with you, you know," the Prince said. "Surprising as it may seem, I don't particularly enjoy watching people grovel. I told you I am reasonable. I accept that you are on principle loyal to the Senate and frustrated with my father—with me, by extension. I hope I'm not fool enough to let it blind me to your quality or your

use. I could make good use of you, Risto. I could make good use of a
man who cares as much for justice as I do."

"What do you want?"

"Also a man with no patience for politicking," the Prince said,
dryly. "I want you in Pavo's place as High Commander of the Guard.
My father will object, of course. You're too young, too inexperienced,
too provincial, too inclined to deed over word—too damnably
plainspoken when you are inclined to word. For the sort of Guard
he tried to cultivate, perhaps that's true. For my part, these are the
reasons I want you. I want a man who is uncomfortable in Choiro
and who can make Choiro uncomfortable in turn. I want a man who
will stand by my side and shake the Empire from complacency."

"I've most of a two-year term left in Tasso."

"The Senate can be prevailed upon to end your term early."

"Surely there's someone better suited."

"You weren't paying attention. I want you precisely because you
are not suited. You see how very neatly I've answered any objection
you can make. But I'll humor you. Name me someone better suited."

He said, almost without thinking, "Salvo Briule."

"Of the Modigne barracks. Nico's father."

"Yes."

"Interesting. I admit his name hadn't crossed my mind, but I'm
not particularly surprised it should have crossed yours. He shares
your holy disdain for Choiro. He's noble-born, you know—very
distinguished family. He went and married an Epyrian farm girl. His
father never quite recovered from the shock."

"He knows the Hill."

"He's nearing retirement. He's been a Guardsman sixteen years and a soldier before that. Another year and he'll be off to his villa on Epyris to breed goats. You, on the other hand—I can have you at your prime."

"I refused Pavo's commission. What made you think I would take yours?"

"Pavo gave you a choice."

Torien was silent. The Prince laughed. He put a hand on Torien's shoulder. "Don't be a fool. It's your choice. But I don't want you to dismiss it out-of-hand. Think about it. Take all the time you need. When you do refuse me, I'll expect a good reason." He squeezed Torien's shoulder and let it go. He stood up from the chair. The Guardsman stepped forward with the cloak. The Prince said, off-handedly, pulling the cloak around his shoulders, "There are other considerations, if you're interested. Pavo's estate at Inumæ falls to the Emperor to dispose of as he sees fit. It's a fine place—good land, good vineyards. I've only to speak the word and it's yours. Five hundred thousand stadia of Vareno land to your name. You won't get a legacy like that from twenty years of army service."

Torien said, "You asked me to tell you where you were wrong, Highness."

"Yes?"

"You were wrong to think you've any more sense of justice than your father has. You were wrong to think it somehow proves your conviction that you can deal death and judgment without a second thought. You were wrong to think I'd stand at your side as your executioner. You were wrong to think we've any modicum of the same mind between us. If we do, I pray God he purges me of it. I pray he takes my life before I give it to you willingly. I pray—"

A Guardsman had jerked him up by the arms and shoved him face-down to the floor before he could finish it. For a moment, he lay stunned and blinking, his cheek against the cool tile, the blood beating in his ears. Then, from delayed reflex, he curled up to shield his head and groin, hugging his knees to his chest. The blows came swiftly and silently. Booted feet pummeled his shoulders and back and arms and legs. He heard rather than felt the crunch of bone as hobnailed toes collided squarely with his face. He heard the Prince say, lazily from above, "Enough." Hands dragged him up to his knees. Someone was whimpering like a kicked dog. He realized the sound was coming from his own throat. He swallowed and was silent.

The Prince knelt in front of him. "I could answer your prayers," he said. Holding Torien's head between his hands, he wiped the blood from Torien's face with his fingers. "I could put you on the Wall with the rest. But I'd regret it. You were wrong about that. I would regret the waste. You're far more use to me alive, willing or no. If it won't be at my side, then it will be at my feet. I'll have my use of you either way, I promise you." He let go Torien's face and sat back on his heels. He jerked his chin. The hands pushed Torien back down to the floor. The Prince stood. "My apologies to the surgeon for your face," he said.

Torien lay still and listened, eyes shut, while they went out from the room. He heard the snap of the curtain closing and the tramp of booted feet going away down the corridor. He was alone in the room, and there was no other sound than the blood roaring in his head. He tested his weight on his palms and tried to push himself up. He held himself trembling on his wrists, realized there was no use in it, and eased himself back to the floor, letting out a puff of breath. He turned himself carefully onto his side, then onto his back. He lay beside the mat, watching the shadows stretch across the ceiling, feeling blood spread slowly over his face from his nose.

After an eternity, he heard someone coming up the corridor. The slave boy came in through the curtain. He had bread and cheese and a wine jug in his arms. He came up short just inside the doorway. For a moment, he stood frozen. Then his arms swung loose. Bread and cheese went flying. The jug dropped straight to the floor and broke apart with a crack on the tiles. The boy bolted through the curtain, and Torien heard his footsteps pounding away at a run.

A little while later, he heard two sets of footsteps coming up the corridor. The boy came into the room with the surgeon at his heels. Between them they moved Torien onto the mat. While the boy picked up the pottery shards in the doorway, wiping up the wine and blood with wads of linen spill-cloth from the surgery, the surgeon sat on his knees beside the mat and spread salve on Torien's bruises. He was a stolid, gray-haired veteran, and his leather-brown face was blank as he worked. He finished with the salve and set about cleaning the blood from Torien's face with a towel. "Whatever it was, Commander," he said, "it was foolish to say."

"Necessary to say," Torien said. It came out thickly. Fresh blood dribbled over his lips.

The surgeon wiped the blood expressionlessly. "Maybe. In any case, you're both lucky you were confined to bed, Commander, and without weapons. You can thank me for that."

"I can thank you for the broken nose?"

"For it being only a broken nose. His Highness can thank me he isn't dead at your damn-fool hand, and you can thank me you're not hanging with the rest on the Traitors' Wall." The surgeon put the towel in Torien's hand. "I'll set it when the swelling has gone down," he said.

XXIII

The morning muster was done and dawn just breaking over the eastern hills. Early heat hung in a haze over the spelt fields. Torien made his way up the gate street from the infirmary. Soldiers in intermittent groups of four or five, walking back from the parade ground to their barrack blocks, saluted him as they passed. No one spoke. The fort had the gray, gutted feeling of a battlefield when the fighting is done and nothing left but the dead.

He turned down the main cross street and went up the headquarters steps. There was a lingering soreness under his ribs which he had labored to conceal from the surgeon. There was a remnant twinge of pain up his spine from the beating. He was sweating under his armor and holding his tongue in his teeth by the time he reached the top of the steps.

The vestibule was mercifully cool and dark. He accepted the salute of the sentry and was halfway to the atrium before he saw the familiar forlorn marble face gazing down at him from a tall pedestal across the room. He paused. He looked back over his shoulder to the doorway and found the sentry watching him almost curiously. The sentry looked away quickly. "Soldier," Torien said.

The sentry grimaced. "Yes, sir."

"I haven't wandered into a Guard barracks by accident?"

"No, sir."

"Explain to me why this is here."

"By senatorial decree, sir. His Majesty's image is to be displayed in every Imperial military installment."

"The Senate ordered this?"

"Yes, sir."

"Are the Senate aware they just decreed their own capitulation?"

"I don't know, sir. I guess they'll find out, sir."

The atrium was empty, and his footsteps echoed loudly on marble as he walked. Fiere had heard him coming and opened the door for him and was back across to his desk before Torien had ducked in through the doorway. "Come in," Fiere said. "Close the door." He was copying lines onto papyrus, and he did not look up. Torien shut the door. In the absence of light and air from the atrium, the office was close and dark and smoky. Fiere's face was thrown into sharp relief by the lamp flame dancing at his elbow. There were deep shadows under his eyes and spidery lines at the corners of his mouth that had not been there five months ago. Torien wondered how long it had been since he had slept.

Fiere wiped his pen and laid it in its case. He snapped his tablet shut. He left the papyrus unrolled to dry and beckoned with one hand. Torien handed his medical discharge over the desk. Fiere took it and tossed it aside without looking at it. "You can stop hiding the limp now," he said.

"The surgeon observed me himself and will testify to my soundness, sir."

"Yes, I've spoken with the surgeon. You've no business walking to the latrines in your present condition, much less resuming active duty on the frontier. The surgeon wrote you a discharge because otherwise it would take an armed guard to keep you confined to quarters, and my men have more productive things to do with their time." He glanced up at Torien's face. He said, more quietly, "Also because I want you out of Choiro before you lose your damn-fool head. It was not wise to anger him—not with twelve bodies already on the Wall."

"Wisdom is groveling before his father's image each morning in the vestibule?"

"Prudence is groveling. Wisdom is holding your tongue until this passes over and we can all of us act on reason, not impulse."

"And if we're so very wise that it doesn't pass over?"

"We decimated Montegne's column," Fiere said, "before we brought him back to hang. The survivors have been reassigned as *signi*. I picked the punitive details sent to deal with his family and the families of his officers. Believe me when I say I've had enough of ducking my head and taking orders without question. But I can do nothing when I'm dead. Martyrdom is never practical."

"Does it ease your conscience to tell yourself that, sir?"

Fiere looked at him. "Twenty years ago, I would have killed you for that. As it is, I have no difficulty understanding His Highness's urge to put a fist in your face."

"It was a Guardsman's foot. I might have damaged His Highness's fingers."

"In answer to your question—no. It doesn't. But it's the truth." Fiere turned the papyrus around with his fingertips and slid it to him across the desktop. "Your orders," he said, coldly. "Allow me to congratulate you, Commander."

Torien picked up the papyrus and read aloud: "Commander Torien Berio Risto will assume command at once of the Imperial garrison at Tasso. His objective is to establish direct Imperial control over the salt mines. He will engage and subdue any native resistance. He will execute any local leaders found to be complicit in acts of treason and sedition against the Empire, and will appoint in their places new, loyal leaders per his own judgment. One column of cavalry is assigned his use to this end. Commander Risto is furthermore given specific instruction concerning the Imperial garrison at Tasso: officers will be executed, regular units decimated. *Signi* will be decimated to the last man. Lieutenant Pallo Espere will be returned under guard to Vione for sentencing before a court martial."

He looked up. He could not feel the papyrus in his hands. "It can be appealed?"

317

"I've tried. When they refused me the first time, I asked if it might at least be amended—if the decimations would be enough. The orders stand."

"If I refuse them?"

"Do you need me to tell you what will happen?"

"This is the Prince's doing. They know what he did to Senna. They're afraid for their own skins. Right now, they'll fall over each other to prove themselves loyal. If it were any other—"

"The fact remains they ordered it, and you swore an oath to obey. As did I."

"This is murder. Besides which it's stupid. Espere's officers were prepared to risk their lives to reveal him to the Senate. His regulars and his *signi* did what they did because he was in the habit of summarily torturing and executing anyone who looked at him sidelong."

"It's necessity. Refuse it, and you leave me no choice. I will arrest you, Risto, and I will convene a court martial, and I will see the sentence carried out, because I must. Explain to me what that will change of any of this."

"None of it but my estimation of you, sir."

"We can all be thankful the Empire does not stand or fall on your estimation of me. Shut up and take the orders, Risto, before you say something I can't ignore."

He scrolled the papyrus around his forefinger and tapped the end twice against his palm to straighten it. He turned on his heel. He wanted suddenly to be out of that room. He needed to clear his head. He needed to think.

"Risto," Fiere said.

He stopped in the doorway. Not looking back, he said, "Sir."

"His Highness requests you pay him a visit at the Palace before you leave Choiro. I was instructed to inform you."

"The reason?"

"I don't know. I doubt it's to apologize for your nose."

"Maybe to congratulate me on my commission? My chance to serve Imperial justice?"

"Listen to me. Hold your idiot tongue just this once. He knows he has only to make you open your mouth. Don't let him bait you so easily."

"If fewer of us had held our idiot tongues, there would not be twelve bodies on the Traitors' Wall."

"If I can't order it of you, then I ask it of you as a friend."

"That doesn't mean much to me as an appeal. I'll be executing friends in Tasso."

"Whatever you must do in Tasso," Fiere said, "will be best done quietly. Hold your tongue, Risto. Let him gloat. Let him think he has won."

He glanced back at the desk. "Whatever I must do, sir?"

Fiere did not look at him. "Carry my regards to His Highness," he said.

There were two indigo-crested Guardsmen waiting for him in the Palace stable yard. The junior of them took Torien's weapons off to the guardhouse while the senior led him wordlessly down the portico to the terrace garden on the western end of the Palace grounds. Past the garden wall, the Hill dropped away steeply. From the terrace steps, he could see across the River Quarter and the river to the wide, flat grain land that was the belly of Varen. It was mid morning, and the garden was cool under the shade of cypresses and tall potted laurels, but it would be hot later. There was a haze over the River Quarter and a twanging chorus of cicadas carrying on the humid breeze up from the water.

The Prince was taking his lunch beside the fountain pool at the far end of the terrace. He was in a plain linen tunic and sandals and had apparently just finished at the throwing post, because a slave was oiling the spears and bundling them together on a leather mat. There was a middle-aged man in white senator's robes sitting with the Prince. He was facing the walkway, and he saw Torien and the Guardsman first. He had been speaking but fell silent as they approached. His eyes took in Torien curiously. They were striking eyes—as bright blue as ice, and just as cold. He was a northerner of the old blood. His people had fought and lost their war with Choiro a millennium before Choiro had first sent an army eastward over the mountains to Cesin.

The Prince followed the senator's gaze down the walkway. His face brightened. "Here he is, Lucho—the man who turned down command of the Guard so he could finish his term on the frontier."

The name sparked a memory: Lucho Marro, who had written so vehemently against *antiquated nepotistic patronage* in Cesin. The ancient blue eyes ran Torien up and down and settled on his face. "The Empire could use more of such men," Marro said. His voice was bland.

"You look much improved since I last saw you," the Prince said to Torien. "The surgeon is to be commended."

"Commander Fiere sends his regards. He told me you wished to see me."

"We needn't proceed directly to business. Sit and wet your throat, Risto."

Torien bowed. He sat down facing them across the low table. He unbuckled his helmet while the Prince poured for him. Setting the helmet on the table, he took the brimming bowl in his hands and lifted it briefly to the Prince. "Your health and your father's," he said.

"Unprecedented," the Prince said, dryly, "for so staunch a republican. Do you drink my health, Lucho?"

"At least as often as you drink mine, Highness."

"Very politic of you."

"It is surprising to me that you should have republican sympathies, Commander," Marro said to Torien. "I'd have taken you for an emperor's man, considering your family's history and your relationship with the imperial household."

"Senator Marro imagines himself something of a historian," the Prince said.

"A student, nothing more," Marro said.

Torien swallowed a mouthful of wine. "It complicates your thesis if I am republican, Senator?"

The blue eyes bored into his face. "My thesis?"

"'On the Administration of the Imperial Province of Cesin.' You argue very effectively that my family has imperial aspirations of our own."

"Yes—well." Marro smiled slightly. "I apologize, Commander. I didn't realize you had read it."

"I don't think anyone is bound by history. My father's choices are his own, not his forefather's. My choices are mine."

"A man who speaks highly of choice is not, in my experience, a man who speaks highly of duty—to his emperor or his senate."

Irritation licked over him. "A man who spends his days sipping wine in gardens in Choiro has no right to preach duty to me."

"Perhaps it's different in Cesin, among jumped-up slave stock." Marro's voice was cold. "In Varen, we teach boys to mind their tongues before their elders and betters."

The Prince said, smoothly, "I don't question your devotion to duty, Risto. Nor does Senator Marro, beyond mere rhetorical exercise."

Marro hesitated. Then he drew himself up a little and bowed. "Your Highness."

"Anyway, you're under a misapprehension," the Prince said. "The Senator is from Puoli. He happens to be in Choiro on business."

Torien said, "Puoli?"

Marro caught the edge in his voice. "You know Puoli, Commander?"

He looked down into his wine bowl. "I know Civiparro. There's good hunting in those hills."

"The Senator is quite a huntsman himself," the Prince said. "Quite a spearman, specifically, as he has just reconfirmed to me. You should have been here, Risto. I imagine you'd have enjoyed seeing me soundly beaten."

Marro was looking at him. "You care to hunt, Commander?"

"When I have the time."

"Your people were renowned as spearmen historically, of course."

"Before we were slave stock. Yes."

"You are familiar with an all-iron spear?"

"The Brycigi use them. Some of the other mountain tribes—the ones who have resisted assimilation."

"You've thrown one?"

"I hadn't," the Prince explained to Torien. "I'd never seen one before."

"I brought one from Puoli, if you'd care to try it," Marro said. "Brycigo. I think it could make an effective boar spear. I'd like to know what you think."

"I haven't done much boar hunting."

"Never mind boar hunting," the Prince said. "Try to throw it. The post is there. The Senator swears to me the Brycigi can throw it at twenty paces. I wouldn't have believed him except he did it himself."

The slave brought Torien the spear. He held it on his lap, turning it in his hands. It was a short, heavy, barbed spear, the shank as thick as his forefinger and middle finger together, the grip as thick as his wrist and grooved to prevent slippage. He picked it up and held it between thumb and forefinger, bracing it on three fingers, testing the weight. Marro watched him. "What do you say to a wager, Commander? To make things more interesting."

"You assume I think I can make the throw."

"It needn't be twenty paces. There must be some possibility in *my* mind that you can make the throw; otherwise the wager is not interesting. Would you say twelve paces presents enough of a challenge?"

Torien swung the spear upright and caught it by the shaft. "Twenty. I haven't used a Brycigo spear, but I've used a Dobryno. It's similar—a little longer. We use them for bear."

The Prince laughed. "You thought you had him neatly in hand, didn't you, Lucho? Twenty paces it is." He flicked his fingers at the slave. "Mark it."

Marro's eyes had narrowed on Torien's face. "Perhaps we should introduce a variable, since the Commander is used to living targets. Tell the slave to stand against the post."

"No."

"Admittedly, it is not quite the same element of risk. Would it be more equivalent if he were armed?"

"I'm not going to throw at him."

"The idea is to throw at the post."

"The wager was that I could throw at the post at twenty paces. No other terms."

"You fear you may have overstated your abilities?"

"My abilities are beside the point."

"It is only a slave."

"*My* slave," the Prince put in, dryly. "I've got some say in this."

"I will offer compensation, if necessary," Marro said. "Surely it won't be necessary. The Commander has thrown against bear. This is hardly comparable in terms of difficulty."

Torien shrugged. His shoulders were tight. "Show me a bear and I'll throw."

"There are so few bears in Choiro these days," the Prince said.

"In Puoli, then," Marro said. "How long is your leave? Perhaps we can arrange something before you return to the frontier."

"You'll remember my orders are effective immediately."

"Of course." Marro tilted up his chin and smiled. "Another time. The invitation is open-ended. We can be thinking of suitable stakes."

Torien leaned the spear against the table. The slave came to take it away. He gave no sign he had heard any of the conversation, though Torien was sure he had. "I do have a question for you on the subject of Puoli," Torien said.

Marro paused with his wine bowl at his lips. "Yes?"

"There was a Puolian among my *signi* at Tasso. A murderer. We gave him command of a scouting unit because he knew his letters. He and his men took to raiding trains on the Road. I executed him for it. I swore to him before I killed him that I would exact full remuneration from his family. Unfortunately, he was dead before I realized we had no record of his name. As lord of Puoli, you would have presided over his trial. Maybe you can help me."

Marro tilted his bowl and drank and set the bowl on the table. "I have presided over many trials. You'll forgive me if I am unable to recall one particular criminal from hundreds."

"It was two years ago. He would have been about sixteen. A veteran's son. I find it hard to believe you have dealt with hundreds of literate sixteen-year-old soldiers' sons on trial for murder."

"Moien," Marro said.

"That was his name?"

"Sere Moien. I'm afraid your inquiry comes a little late. His family were dead of the Fever three years ago."

"He has no surviving relatives?"

"None as far as I am aware. Certainly none on his father's side. His mother was a freedwoman. You understand the line becomes difficult to trace."

"And his own land and property would have been redistributed after the trial."

"Given to the family of his victim, in accordance with custom."

"Who was his victim—out of curiosity? I assume it was nobility. I heard nothing at the time."

"The family requested the matter be kept as quiet as possible."

"Why?"

"You understand the concept of keeping something quiet, I suppose."

"I understand there is very rarely good reason to keep a court decision quiet."

Marro looked at him sharply. "The woman was raped and murdered and her body left to rot in the wood. Silence was the best they could do for her dignity."

"And you had incriminating evidence enough to know it was Moien?"

"I could take offense at your implication. Instead, I will remind you that *you* are the one who executed him."

"For robbery. Not for rape and murder."

"If you are capable of one violent crime, you are capable of another. The woman's jewels were found in his possession. Besides which he spent the night before his trial attempting to strangle himself in his cell. I took that as fair admission of guilt."

The Prince leaned over to refill Marro's wine bowl. "In my opinion," he said, "with apologies for changing the subject—Commander Risto has just illustrated precisely what I was trying to say: a man of his word, dogged in his convictions." He caught Torien's eye. "I've been explaining to the Senator your concern for justice and your usefulness," he said. "They wanted to give Tasso to an older man, a more experienced man, and leave you second-in-command. I convinced them it must be you—didn't I, Lucho? No one better to render justice and see it done properly, I said. What do you say, Lucho, now you've had the chance to hear him for yourself?"

"We were right to defer to your judgment, Highness." Marro's eyes were cool on Torien's face.

"Of course you find a way to turn it to your own credit." The Prince smiled. He bent across the table to fill Torien's bowl. He sat back. "What does the attribution matter? The job will be done. I ask nothing more."

Torien did not meet the Prince's gaze. He pressed his palms flat on the table and bowed. He said, to the backs of his hands, "I pray I will warrant your faith in me, Highness."

"I know you will," the Prince said.

He left the wine bowl untouched. He stood, tucking his helmet into the crook of his arm. "If we've finished."

"One thing more, actually." The Prince held out his hand over the table. There was a ring on his palm, a plain gold loop with a blood-red carnelian face. The seal was a hart outstretched to run. Torien recognized Alvero Senna's seal. "For Alluin," the Prince said. "It seems he will come into his inheritance, after all."

Torien looked at the ring on the Prince's palm. He made no move to take it. His throat was tight. "You've found the rest of the family?"

"Not as yet. Honestly, I am hoping for Alluin's help. The household slaves have revealed nothing of use under examination."

"Alluin knows nothing."

"It was clever—the disinheritance," Marro said. "Seal a document and say the words, and the son is made immune to the treason charge."

"He didn't know."

Marro ignored him. "It may be wise to examine him, Highness, just to be sure."

"You're an idiot if you think he was involved. Right now, he is a hostage in the hands of Pavo's man among the Asani."

"Also curiously convenient," Marro said.

"He very nearly paid with his life to uncover Espere's business at the mines."

"*Very nearly* means nothing when his father was master architect of the thing. Espere was always meant to be expendable."

"*Very nearly* means he was stripped and staked out on the sand and left for whichever scavenging animal got to him first. If it were done to you, I don't imagine you'd think it was nothing, though I'm willing to be proven wrong."

"Calm down, both of you," the Prince said. "The foremost priority is to recover him alive, hostage or no."

"Highness, I swear to you he knew nothing."

"Without a trace of irony now—*Highness*. In fact, you almost approach humility. I'm not sure it suits you. I think I prefer you insufferably arrogant." The Prince smiled. "I'm not going to examine him. I'd like to talk with him, that's all." He gestured with his hand. "As a token of my good faith," he said. "And you can give him custody of Lieutenant Espere. Surely that should put to rest any fear that I consider him accessory to the plot."

Torien took the ring and closed his fist around it. It lay cool and heavy against his fingers. "If I recover him alive," he said.

XXIV

In daylight and on horseback, it was a much shorter trip between the Hill and Ceno's apartment than it had been on foot and hooded in darkness. He dismounted at the gatehouse and slid his ring through the aperture. "For Chæla Ceno," he said. It was by now a little past noon, and he was baking slowly in his harness in the heat off the pavement. The windows on the second story were shuttered. The street was silent for the siesta. A slave girl was sweeping the landing, and the rasp of her broom was echoing down the steps and across the yard.

The gateman pushed the ring back to him. "Not here, sir."

"She's out?"

"She's gone. Apartment's for let."

He stood there stupidly, holding the reins in one hand, blinking sweat from his eyelids. "Do you know where?"

"No, sir."

"The landlord would know?"

The gateman eyed him through the aperture. "He might, sir, but he's gone out to Apulano to look after his mother. He'll be all day, and most like he'll spend the night. It's ten miles to Apulano."

Torien did not say anything. He had counted on her being there. In hindsight, he supposed that had been stupid from the start. She would not have stayed in the city with her father on the Traitors' Wall.

The gateman said, "Shall I tell him you came, sir?"

Out of the corner of his eye, he saw a tall, veiled figure coming down the foot-stones along the gate wall. He lifted his head. "Vaiz."

The veil was pinned to leave her face bare, but the breath of wind down the street was tugging the thin yellow silk this way and that. She held back the veil with jeweled hands so she could look at him. Her face was blank. "Lord Risto."

She made to go past him against the wall. He reached and caught her arm with his free hand. "Please. Wait."

She stopped. She did not say anything. He could feel the stiffness in her. He took her by the elbow a little way up the wall, out of earshot of the gatehouse. "I need to speak with her."

She looked at him sharply. "She gave you what you asked. Do you know what she paid for it?"

"I know."

"Then you must be a fool to think she wants to see your face again."

"I ride for Modigne this afternoon. She need never see my face again beyond today." She very likely wouldn't, unless it were on the Traitors' Wall, but he did not say that aloud. "I wanted to apologize."

"Yes, I know. *You* want to apologize. *You* want her forgiveness. *You* want to clear your conscience. *You* want to be rid of the guilt. All of that in your head at once. You can't spare a thought for her."

He did not say anything. He let go her elbow. She did not look at him now. She had taken her hands from the veil and the breeze was pulling it across her face, but she did not seem to notice. The slave girl had finished sweeping and gone into the building. In the silence, it might have been the two of them alone in the city or in the world. He slipped the reins over the horse's neck and pulled himself up into the saddle. The pain jumped up his spine and slid down again. There was an ache in his throat.

Vaiz said, "Lord Risto." She was looking down the street at nothing. The breeze tugged at the veil. "Three miles up the river road toward Vienta. The farm belongs to the man Serro. He is her mother's brother. He is a beekeeper—you will see the bee houses."

She was gone down the foot-stones before he could reply.

Three miles out of the city northward on the river road brought him to quiet farmland. There were damson boughs nodding low over the embankments. There was no breeze along the road. The air was hot and still and heavy with the smell of ripe plums. Domed clay beehives marched back in rows from the road up the eastward embankment.

He rode up the path through the rows. There was a white adobe farmhouse and a cluster of outbuildings past the beehives. Geese shuffled aside unhurriedly as he rode into the yard. A swaybacked old hound padded silently alongside him to the barn and then vanished through the dark open doorway, his duty apparently done. There was a donkey tethered in traces in the doorway. A slave was sitting on a stool with the right forehoof in his lap. He was rubbing salve into the dry sole of the hoof. His back was to Torien, but he had heard the hoof beats up the path. He slid the hoof from his lap and stood, wiping his hands. He came over as Torien reined up. He reached a brown, callused hand for the horse's bridle. He bowed, his hand on the cheek-strap. "My lord is lost?" he said. He did not look in Torien's face. He was perhaps in his mid-thirties. There was a brand on his cheek, *CHI* for *chirone*, fugitive: he had once tried to run.

"This is Serro's farm?"

"My lord is not lost, then."

"I'm looking for Chæla Ceno."

The slave turned and pointed with his free hand down past the bee houses. "The orchard, Lord. Is the horse to be stabled?"

Torien dismounted. He put the reins in the slave's hand and pressed a bronze into his palm. "Water him when he cools, but keep him saddled. I won't be long."

It was cooler in the shade of the damson trees, but the air was thick with the cloying smell of the plums. He walked along the eastern edge of the orchard, looking down each row. The orchard ran to the northern boundary wall. He found Ceno on the next-to-last row. She was barefoot and standing on her toes at one of the trees, head and shoulders lost in the leaves, and she did not see him. There was a wicker basket at her feet, and she was dropping plums into the basket. There was a young slave girl with her. The girl saw Torien first. She bent to pick up a stray plum which had rolled down the row, and she saw him as she straightened. He knew from her face that the branded slave back in the yard was her father.

Ceno's voice came down muffled through the leaves: "Patra, you'll have to climb up for these."

"Lady," Patra said.

"What is it?" Ceno parted the boughs with one hand. She saw Torien. She stood very still for a moment, holding the branches apart. Then she lowered herself to her heels and came out into the aisle from under the boughs. She dropped a handful of plums into the basket. She brushed twigs and leaves from her hair and shook out her skirt. She picked up the basket and held it out to the girl. Her voice was low and level. "Take this up to the kitchens, Patra, and wash yourself. That's all we'll do today."

When the girl had gone, she knelt in the aisle to lace her sandals. Not looking at him, she said, "How did you find this place?"

"I met Vaiz in the city."

"You went to the apartment?"

"I needed to speak with you."

"We have nothing to say to each other."

"Please."

She finished with her sandals and stood. She looked at him down the aisle. She was holding her arms across her ribs, holding her upper arms so tightly in her hands that the honey-brown skin showed white through her fingers. "What else do you want from me? My father and Pavo are rotting on the Wall, and you've got a new estate at Inumæ for your trouble. What else do you want? Was I part of the promised prize, too? You've come to demand your due, is that it?"

"I didn't want them on the Wall."

"How had you wanted them to die?"

"I didn't think it would be treason—not for any of them but Pavo and his officers. Not for your father, not for Senna. I swear to you I didn't know."

"Is that meant to comfort me—as if you would have done anything differently if you'd known? I am neither a fool nor a child."

Torien lifted a hand and dug thumb and forefinger into his eyelids. His head was swimming with the scent of plums. "I don't know what I would have done. I don't know what was the right thing. I thought I did. I've spent the past week having that ripped out of me and kicked to pulp."

Ceno said, "Yes—I forgot you still worry about little things like right and wrong."

He dropped his hand and looked at her. She was not looking at him. She was looking away across the orchard. There were tears making silvery tracks down her cheeks. She unfolded her arms and wiped the tears with the heel of her hand. "I went to Vione that night," she said, "to the hospital. One of His Highness's Guardsmen told me that's where they had taken you."

He searched her face and found nothing. "Why?"

"It was my fault you had been taken. I suppose I wanted to apologize." She swallowed. "They wouldn't let me see you."

"They never told me you had come."

"I thought it would be both of you." She spoke to the trees, not looking at him. "I thought it would be both of you, and it would be my fault. I thought I'd never have the chance to ask forgiveness. They wouldn't let me see him, either—my father."

"I'm sorry."

She shrugged very stiffly. "I, too."

He touched her arm. She tensed but did not move away. He took off his glove and traced her cheekbone with two fingers, brushing the tears from her cheek. She drew a shivering breath. He turned her head and held it between his hands and brushed the tears from her eyelashes with his thumbs. She stood very still and silently while he did it, her eyes closed, her lips tight. He bent his head and buried his face in her black hair—and she slipped in suddenly under his arms, looping her arms around his neck, resting her cheek on his chest.

Then she twisted against him, tilting her head back to look up in his face. "It's no good," she said. "I can't feel your heart beat."

"It's the plums. I think I've suffocated."

She laughed. He felt it echo through her body. He felt her muscles loosen. Her breath was warm on his neck. "If that's all," she said.

They sat below the boundary wall. She unbuckled his helmet and cuirass and held the cuirass for him while he shrugged it off. She sat against him with her knees folded up on his lap, her shoulders under the curve of his arm. She unlaced his jerkin and bent her ear to his chest. "Better," she said. "And this—just to be sure." She leaned into him and pressed her lips gently to the pulse in his throat. She laid a hand on his ribs. "It's beating wonderfully now."

He kissed her. He sat up from the wall, cupping her head in his hands, and he bent his face to hers and kissed her lips, her eyelids, her forehead; he lifted her chin with his fingers and kissed the hollow at the base of her throat. Her arms were around his neck and her cheek against his and her tears running on his face. He tried to lift her to look at her. She shook her head. Her lips brushed his ear. "Don't," she said. Her voice was thick. So he put his arms around her waist and held her, his head and shoulders braced against the sun-warmed stones of the boundary wall, his chin on her shoulder, and he listened with his eyes closed while she cried.

He opened his eyes at the smell of wood smoke. They were smoking the hives over in the bee field. Over Ceno's shoulder, he watched the smoke trail away southward toward the city. He could see the Hill just visible above the pines in the hazy distance, the Palace and Senate buildings in delicate white-marble miniature—and the moment shattered against it, and there was nothing but Tasso, and the orders in his saddlebag, and the cavalry column mustered and awaiting his command on the parade ground at Vione.

She had felt him tense. She unfolded her arms from his neck and sat up, sliding her knees from his lap, wiping her face quickly with one hand. "Does it pain you?" she said. There was no trace of tears in her voice.

"The surgeon asked me the same question. I'd rather it had been you; he weighs more."

"It was stupid of me. I know you were wounded." She touched his ribs very gently.

He covered her hand with his and pressed her fingers down. "No pain."

"A thought, then."

"Just that five months ago I could not wait to be out of Choiro. Five *days* ago I could not wait to be out of Choiro."

"You aren't staying? I assumed His Highness would want you tethered close." She had his wrists in her hands. Her fingers tightened. Her voice had soured. "Or is this for him?"

"I refused his commission."

She tilted her head to look in his face. "You refused—?"

"I've been given the command at Tasso. I'm to return at once."

She looked at him silently. Her fingers were closed so tightly around his wrists that his fingers were numb at the tips.

"I've the orders in my saddlebag, if you don't believe me."

"I believe you." She said it through her teeth. "Oh, I believe you were idiot enough. And you've no idea how to lie." She closed her eyes. "Why, in Heaven's name? No—don't say it. I know the answer. Anyone else but you would have taken it, for fear or for duty or—"

"Or for five hundred thousand stadia of Vareno land at Inumæ, or for you."

She opened her eyes and looked at him. "Was I on offer, then?"

"If you had been on offer, I don't know that I could have refused him."

"You'd have refused him. I said you have no idea how to lie." She shook her head. "He'll kill you. It doesn't matter your name or your rank or the rightness of it or the wrongness of it. He'll kill you because you looked him in the face and told him no."

He studied her. She did not meet his eyes. She had turned his hands over and was tracing the scar on his palm absently under her fingers. "My father wouldn't. He was a businessman; he had something His Highness wanted. I could help him very much, he said. I was twelve years old, and I trusted him because he was my father."

He did not say anything. She held his hands on her lap and looked up into his face. "He asked me if that was my reason," she said. "His Highness, I mean. He asked me if it was for vengeance—if I was planning such a vengeance for him as I planned for my father."

"He threatened you?"

"He knew I tried to see you that night. He was waiting for me at the apartment. He asked me how long I'd been dealing with you behind his back. All of it coolly and quietly: he doesn't lose his head when he's angry. But don't you see? He hears conspiracy in every whisper, reads it in every word. He's always been afraid, more so now that his fears have been vindicated. And *you* must spit in his face and tell him—"

"What did you say?"

"What?"

"When he asked you if it was for vengeance. What did you say?"

"I said it was for justice." Her voice was cool. "Unlike you, I know how to lie."

"He believed you?"

"If he thought me a threat, I'd be dead. He is not careless. Nor is he merciful. You know that by now, surely."

"What is Vaiz doing in the city?"

"Vaiz would not betray me, if that's what you're thinking."

"I don't know what I think. Tell me what she's doing in the city."

"My frescoes are going to an art dealer this afternoon. She's handling the sale."

"Listen to me. I'll send horses for both of you. Go to the chapel of the Hospitallers. Two of the brothers are settling some business for me in Cesin. You can ride with them and remain at Vessy under my father's protection."

"And you? After all, *I'm* not the proud, stubborn fool who defied the Prince."

"I'll be in Tasso. The Prince will have forgotten me in a month."

"His Highness doesn't forget. You'll be dead in a month, and I think you know it."

"My offer was genuine."

"Do you think Vessy lies beyond his reach if Tasso doesn't?"

Torien did not say anything.

"Anyway, I belong in Choiro," she said. "I belong *to* Choiro."

"You belong to nothing and no one."

"We have spoken of this before—of choice." She smiled, thinly. "Always a choice, you said. I remember. But you will take your choices to your grave in Tasso, and I will live."

"You'll exist," he said. There was a bitterness in him that he could not put in words.

Her fingers were busy at the lacings of his jerkin. She did not look in his face. "Better that way," she said. "Better just to exist. I've learned that over sixteen years. I wish to God I hadn't forgotten it for you."

He found Ædyn in an empty stall in the stable. The boy was sitting cross-legged in the corner with a harness strap on his lap. He was oiling the strap, dipping his hand in the oil and running the leather on his palm and rubbing it between his fingers. His right arm was tied in a sling. He was bent on his work and did not look up until Torien crouched in front of him, blocking the light. He looked up briefly. He did not say anything. The stable was quiet. There were late-afternoon shadows crawling across the floor. The chapel yard was deserted in the heat. "Antoni said you would be here," Torien said. "Where is Jovan?"

The boy sat with his shoulders braced against the wall, holding the strap on his lap. "He took the carriage to have the wheels studded, Lord. Muryn says there might be early snow in the pass."

"Muryn?"

"One of the brothers from Cesin, Lord. There are some others. They are all lowlanders." There was cool disdain in the boy's voice. "Some of them can't even speak Cesino."

"They've treated you well?"

The boy shrugged. He was looking at the strap. "Jovan says he will teach me my letters, if I want."

"You should let him."

"Because I will never hold a sword?"

"Because if you learn the sword all you'll know is the sword. Learn your letters and you can take up any trade you wish."

The boy did not say anything.

"Anyway, you can hold a sword left-handed," Torien said. "I've seen it done."

The boy did not say anything.

"I'm sorry I can't take you home myself, Ædyn. I owed you that."

He waited on his ankles for the boy to say something. The silence stretched on uncomfortably. They were waiting for him on the parade ground at Vione. He had planned to reach Ostre with the column by sundown and spend the night along the river. He took his wallet from his belt and laid it on the boy's lap. "For your family," he said. He rocked back on his heels and got to his feet. "Give Jovan my thanks."

"Take me with you," Ædyn said. He had the wallet in his hand. He lifted his face to Torien's. His eyes were brimming with tears. "Please, Lord Risto. Let me go with you to Tasso."

He sat back down slowly on his knees. "I can't, Ædyn."

"I won't be a burden to you. I'll tend your horse and kit. I'll learn my letters, I swear."

"Your place is with your family. They've prayed God for three years to see you again alive and well."

The boy swallowed and said nothing. He clenched the wallet in his hand. The harness strap had slid forgotten to the floor. Torien squeezed the boy's arm. "My term is done in two summers. I'll find you in Charys on my leave. We'll go hunting."

"I lied to you about my family." Ædyn looked up from the wallet. "On the ship. I lied to you that I am of the Charysi."

"Ædyn—"

"I am of the Brycigi." The boy's face was pale, but his shoulders were very straight against the wall. "I wandered too far on a hunt. A patrol took me before I could end my life. I wouldn't talk. They said they would take me down to the fort and make me talk. They tied my hands and dragged me behind the horses. I slipped my hands free and got away, but I was afraid they would follow me back if I tried to go home. I was afraid I would lead them to my people. I went down to the lowland. That's where the slavers took me. They didn't know I was Brycigo. None of my masters have known—none but you."

He had the boy's elbow tight in his hand. He did not say anything. The boy rushed to fill the silence. "I was going to kill you in Modigne. That's why I waited at the smithy. You were the governor's son. I was going to kill you for my people."

"You didn't."

"I couldn't. You were wounded. You trusted me."

"You should not have told me this, Ædyn."

"I wanted you to know." A tear slid down the side of the boy's nose. He sniffed. "I've shed blood for you. That is a sacred bond between us. I wanted you to know. Not just because you took it from me with torture. I wanted to tell you of my own."

He shook the boy sharply by the arm. "Do you know what I'm doing in Tasso? I am going to execute my officers and every tenth man of my command. The Senate will send someone else to do it if I don't. They'll hang me on the Traitors' Wall. But they would pay anything I ask for intelligence on the Brycigi, do you understand? They would give me the lives of my men."

"I know." The boy's voice was a whisper.

"Do you understand the choice you've given me? It's treason if I let you go."

"I know," Ædyn said. "I mean to spare you the choice."

He pulled his arm from Torien's hand. He fumbled at the sling and withdrew a long, slender steel blade, bone-hafted, which Torien recognized as a surgeon's scalpel. Belatedly Torien understood. He knocked the boy's hand aside. The boy ducked away from him. Torien caught the boy by the shoulders and shoved him to the floor. "Ædyn," he said. He held the boy against the floor, his arm across the boy's chest, his knee in the boy's gut. He scrabbled with his free hand for the boy's wrist. "Ædyn, listen to me."

The boy turned his head against the floor. He clenched the scalpel in his fist and slid the blade under his jaw and opened his neck from right ear to throat.

Dimly he was aware he was shouting, the boy's neck under his hands and the boy's life pulsing out warm between his fingers— swearing and shouting for help to the chapel, to the street, to anyone who could hear, and no one answering, and the boy shivering beneath him, and he not being able to shout anymore because the tears had closed his throat, and the boy lying now very still on the floor and he face-down beside him, pounding his fist on the tiles until the blood ran, feeling nothing; and the silence stretching after, and the shadows creeping steadily to dusk—and much later the ringing of the vespers bell and the clatter of Jovan's carriage coming in from the street.

XXVI

"The Commander will see you in his office," the Guardsman said.

It was mid-afternoon, and the column was camped on the flatland below Baralla. There was a storm over the sea toward Epyris, the clouds hanging low and black-bellied, thunder murmuring in the distance across the water. The air was hot and breathless, waiting. He went alone across the barracks yard to the headquarters and then under the Emperor's eyes down to the office. The door was open, and he could see from the corridor that the man behind the desk was not Briule. He stopped in the doorway. "Pavo told me you were dead."

Dio Valle looked up. "He told you what he thought he knew," he said. "He had faulty intelligence from Salina." He pushed back his chair. "Here, sit. I heard that you took a knife. Also that you did not exactly ingratiate yourself with the Household Guard."

Torien did not move from the doorway. "I came to see Briule."

"The High Commander is on Epyris."

"High Commander?"

Valle looked at him quizzically. "You did not know?"

Torien did not say anything. He spun on his heel away from the doorway. Valle came after him down the corridor. "Risto."

"I made a mistake to come."

"Listen to me, Risto."

"I've got to report. My congratulations on your commission, Commander. At least one of us knows how to ingratiate ourselves."

"Listen to me." Valle pulled him around by the arm so that they faced each other. "You have not been betrayed, nor will you be. You have not lost your friends. Let them help you, if they can."

He brushed Valle's hand from his arm. "For your own sake, Dio, forget that I came."

"I know your orders, and I know why you were given them. None of that matters now. We have lost Tasso."

"What?"

"The tribes allied against us. They slaughtered the garrison at the mines and armed any of the slaves who would fight. They sent two thousand horse against the fort. They sank every ship in the harbor and poisoned the water supply. The garrison surrendered after eight days."

"It was a ruse, Dio."

"It is no ruse. Lieutenant Chareste anticipated the attack. Two weeks ago, he sent a message advising that the tribes had taken the mines and were preparing to move on the fort. He requested reinforcements. Modigne had no officers to spare. Half of them were gone to the Wall. By the time we could get a troop assembled, we learned the fort had fallen."

Torien looked into Valle's face. "There were survivors?"

"A ship's crewman made it on foot to Istra. He told us the tribes are using prisoners as slave labor to tear down the fort. He did not know how many."

"And at the mines?"

"I do not know."

Torien was silent.

"There was at least one survivor," Valle said, quietly. "Someone must have carried intelligence to Chareste. There is hope that Lieutenant Senna made it at least to the fort."

"Have there been ransom demands?"

"Not yet. Not that I have heard."

"If he were alive, they would try to ransom him."

"Not necessarily. It is possible they know he was disinherited. Anyway, they are driven by patriotism, not greed."

"Aidar was on Pavo's coin."

"He served Pavo's purpose as far as it served his own purpose. Pavo put him in the position to assume control of the mines, thereby of the tribe. It was never for the coin."

"So let him have Tasso, if he wants it. He gives us his prisoners, and we never set another foot further south than Istra. Or do we have to kill a few thousand natives before anyone is allowed to mention peace?"

"Two columns have already been dispatched to Istra. You will be ordered to join them. The Empire does not want peace, not now. We want the reassurance of an enemy outside ourselves. Otherwise we have nothing but the Traitors' Wall."

"Is that a threat?"

"I said you have not lost your friends. If you hang, it will not be alone." Valle smiled, briefly. "But remember that your friends would prefer you did not hang."

He knelt at the fire pit in the girl's shanty. A spattering of rain had come through the lattice, and he could not get the wet tinder to catch. He tried to feed the flame with bits of salt grass, but the grass only smoked and curled up in black wisps. He gave up and sat against the doorpost with his helmet off, looking out into the street.

The storm had passed. The air was clean and cool. There was a breeze off the hill. The sun was low over the flat rooftops, and there was lamplight through the edges of the curtained doorways down the street. He heard voices and a burst of laughter. The black horse danced this way and that at his tether, ears pricked. Torien stretched his legs straight across the doorway. For two weeks, he had been in a saddle or on his feet in the daylight hours, flat on his back on the hard, dry earth in the nights. He had not noticed how sore he was until now. He closed his eyes. He opened them at the smell of smoke and the flicker of firelight and the sound of someone moving around the shanty.

It was not the girl, though the resemblance was plain. The boy was the same age, bronze-skinned and hollow-cheeked, not yet full-grown, though his arms and shoulders were knotted with muscle. His dark hair was uncut and tucked behind his ears. There was a long, ridged white scar from a whip weal across his face. He sat cross-legged, looking at Torien across the fire. His hands were clenched on his knees, his shoulders straight, his chin up. He was afraid and was trying very hard not to show it. "Are you Risto?"

Torien sat up slowly against the doorpost. "Yes. Mahlan?"

The boy dipped his chin, very slightly, not lowering his eyes.

"Where is your sister?"

"She fishes the point. It is the best time—after the rain." The boy's eyes were unblinking on Torien's face. "You are Alluin's friend?"

"One of them. You met Alluin?"

"They say we go free if we fight. If we do not fight, then we stay in the mines. I tell them I fight." The boy shrugged. "They say to me, 'guard the prisoners.' Alluin he asks my name. He tells me he see my sister in Modigne." His eyes went to Torien's hands and lingered there, keenly. "He tells me the oath you make."

Torien leaned forward, tugging off his glove. He held out his hand palm-up over the fire for the boy to see. The scar was a thin white line under the calluses on his palm. "Justice," he said, "or else my life in the attempt—and my soul if I broke my word. Blood is holy, Cesini say, so a blood oath binds body and soul." He slid the glove back on. His throat was tight. "Mahlan," he said, "tell me if Alluin is alive."

The boy dipped his chin again. "They give the officers as blood-prizes to the clan chiefs. They kill the commoners."

"Where is he?"

"The Mayaso chieftain she takes him. He is in the camp of the Mayasi. I swear to him I get him out. I, too, do not break an oath." The boy's chin came up, proudly. "We run from them two days. Then his friend he finds us in the desert."

"His friend."

"His friend the *signo*. He takes us to the fort."

"Had he a scarred face—this *signo*?"

"There is a scar here." The boy touched his right cheekbone. "Like the mark of an iron."

"He wasn't at the mines?"

"He comes from the fort."

It had been the *signo*, then, carrying word to Chareste that the mines were lost. Alluin, of course, had stayed. Alluin, by reason of his officers' oath, had stayed and waited to die with the rest of the garrison—Alluin, whom *he* had left to die for no reason at all, because Aidar had never had any intention of holding a truce.

"You didn't see the fort fall," he said.

The boy shook his head, once. "Alluin he sends me home."

"Alone?"

"He sends the *signo* with me. It is almost two weeks."

"He's here—the *signo*, I mean?"

"He goes with the soldiers on the ships to Istra."

Through the doorway, Torien could see the last of the sunlight running up the hill. They would be awaiting his orders in the camp on the flatland. He sat up on his knees and poured a handful of eagles from his wallet into his palm. He held it out to the boy over the fire. "For what you've told me."

"I do not tell it for your coin. I tell it because you are Alluin's friend."

There was the same stubbornness in the boy's face that he remembered in the girl's. He did not press it. He slid the coins back into the wallet. "Give my greetings to your sister," he said.

He rode down to the waterfront. They had fired the beacon at the point. He could see the looming black shapes of the troop ships at anchor off the quay, and the nothingness beyond, all the way to Tasso. The sun was gone down over the sea-line and the Wolf risen hard and bright above the strait, the sky bruised purple now with dusk.

THE END

AUTHOR'S NOTE

Torien's world, the world of the Vareno Empire, borrows from the Christianized Roman world of Late Antiquity, but it should not be read as an exact analogue. Readers will correctly note that Varen, the political and cultural capital of the Empire, is modeled on Roman Italy—but that actually knocks the first hole in a strict analogical reading, because by the time Christianity reached the sort of dominance in the Roman world that Torien's monotheistic religion enjoys in the Vareno world, the political center of the Roman Empire had long since pivoted away from Rome. Once we move beyond the borders of Varen, the analogy starts breaking down completely.

In short, the problems of Torien's world—violence and injustice, racial and cultural prejudice, class and ethnic tensions—are not the problems of one particular historical moment, and should not be read as such. But they should resonate as real-world problems, just the same—maybe all the more strongly, since they can't be relegated neatly to the past.

ACKNOWLEDGMENTS

My thanks, first of all, to my family—Dad, Mom, Nathan, Elizabeth, Imogen, Meg, Zeke, Isaiah. Thank you for your support and good humor and longsuffering, and for doses of reality when I needed them. Special thanks to Mom, Zeke, and Isaiah for slogging through early drafts and giving me invaluable feedback. Mom, I hope you can someday forgive me for leaving Alluin to the jackals.

Thanks to my critique partner Mary Johnson, for your steadfast encouragement, your insights, your patient responses to late-night emails, and most of all for your enthusiasm for this story.

Thanks to Akiko Oshimizu, for always wanting the next chapter. Sorrynotsorry that you missed your subway stop.

Thanks to my agent, Lane Heymont, and to Georgia McBride and the team at Month9Books, for believing in this story even when I didn't.

Thanks to the em dash—I couldn't have done this without you.

Thanks to the wonderful community of readers, writers, editors, bloggers, and otherwise bookish people—friends, "real-life" and online—who have helped and encouraged me along the way: Maureen Eichner, Louise Bates, Alyssa Hollingsworth, Elizabeth Buege, Angela Goff, Eric Martell, Daniel Swensen, Hazel West, Amira Makansi, Sarah Hawkins, Mat Meyer. (And thanks to The Twitter, for bringing so many of us together in the first place—what a fascinating modern age we live in.)

I'd be remiss not to acknowledge the huge debt of gratitude I owe to the teachers who instilled my love of history and literature (and showed me how they fit together)—to Mom, again, for raising a bookworm; to Hélène Ranwez, the only one who's ever succeeded in making me enjoy Shakespeare; to Eric Miller, Professor of History at Geneva College, not only for helping me to understand the importance of stories, but for challenging me to think about the way we tell them and why. My thanks, likewise, to the faculty of the departments of History and Political Science at the University of West Georgia—particularly to Michael de Nie, Timothy Schroer, Daniel K. Williams, Nadejda Williams, Robert Schaefer, and J. Salvador Peralta, each of whom has shaped me as a reader and as a writer.

And, finally—

Non nobis, Domine, non nobis,
sed nomini tuo da gloriam.

AMANDA McCRINA

Amanda McCrina was born and raised in Atlanta, Georgia. She received her BA in History and Political Science from the University of West Georgia. She lives in Madrid, Spain, where she teaches middle- and high-school English at an international school. She writes stories that incorporate her love of history, languages, and world travel. She drinks far too much coffee, and dreams of one day having a winning fantasy-hockey season.

OTHER MONTH9BOOKS TITLES YOU MIGHT LIKE

THE SKY THRONE

MINOTAUR

SERPENTINE

PRAEFATIO

Find more books like this at http://www.Month9Books.com

Connect with Month9Books online:
Facebook: www.Facebook.com/Month9Books
Twitter: https://twitter.com/Month9Books
YouTube: www.youtube.com/user/Month9Books
Tumblr: http://month9books.tumblr.com/
Instagram: https://instagram.com/month9books

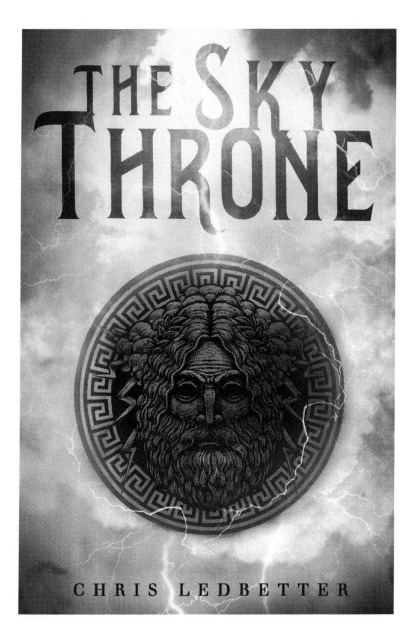

THE SKY THRONE

CHRIS LEDBETTER

SOON THE WORLD WILL KNOW WHAT REALLY
HAPPENED IN THE LABYRINTH.

MINOTAUR

PHILLIP W. SIMPSON

SERPENTINE

"Unique and surprising, with a beautifully-drawn fantasy
world that sucked me right in!" — **Kristin Cashore,** *New
York Times* bestselling author of **BITTERBLUE**

A JUNIOR LIBRARY GUILD SELECTION

CINDY PON

BOOK 1 IN THE PRAEFATIO SERIES

PRAEFATIO

A NOVEL

"This is teen fantasy at its most entertaining, most heartbreaking, most compelling. Highly recommended." –Jonathan Maberry, New York Times bestselling author of ROT & RUIN and FIRE & ASH

GEORGIA McBRIDE

A Gift of Tongues

A Gift of Tongues

Critical Challenges in
Contemporary American Poetry

Edited by

Marie Harris and Kathleen Aguero

The University of Georgia Press
Athens and London

© 1987 by the University of Georgia Press
Athens, Georgia 30602
"Documentaries and Declamadores" © 1987 by Martín Espada
"The Influence of Anxiety" © 1985 by Annette Kolodny
"Caste, Class, and Canon" © 1987 by Paul Lauter

Designed by Kathi L. Dailey
Set in 11 on 13 Mergenthaler Electra with Antique Olive
The paper in this book meets the guidelines for permanence and
durability of the Committee on Production Guidelines for Book
Longevity of the Council on Library Resources.

Printed in the United States of America

91   90   89   88   87   5   4   3   2   1

Library of Congress Cataloging in Publication Data

A Gift of tongues.

   Bibliography: p.
   1. American poetry—20th century—History and criticism.
   2. American poetry—Minority authors—History and criticism.
   3. Canon (Literature) I. Harris, Marie. II. Aguero, Kathleen.
PS153.M56G54   1987   811′.5′09920693   87-1042
ISBN 0-8203-0952-4 (alk. paper)
ISBN 0-8203-0953-2 (pbk.: alk. paper)

British Library Cataloging in Publication Data available.

To all the editors who have brought the work of important and neglected poets into print.

May they flourish!

Contents

Preface

It is the poet's gift to communicate across boundaries created by class and culture. The American poet speaks in a voice that incorporates and echoes, perhaps more than in any other country, many languages and traditions, resulting in an extraordinarily various literature. *A Gift of Tongues* has been compiled to celebrate and evaluate this diversity. The contemporary canon, as defined in anthologies and reflected in critical works, does not, unfortunately, accurately portray this variety. Collections of poetry with titles that suggest they contain the work of our important poets offer disappointingly few surprises: the poets are of similar backgrounds and usually draw upon the shared assumptions of the dominant culture. Likewise, critical volumes attend to these same poets, while those outside the dominant culture are relegated to "special" status and effectively denied the support and challenge serious criticism provides.

We must begin to break down the boundaries that divide our literature as artificially as any map, to introduce to a wider audience some of the poets who have been ignored, and to propose that a new canon be developed that more fairly represents the range and cross-referential nature of American poetry.

Critical responses are learned. We understand those experiences which are familiar to us; we value subject matter and forms that we have been taught to value. The process of enlarging the scope of what is currently considered to be American poetry involves the use of new critical tools to work with a far larger body of work than has yet been acknowledged. We have been taught to hear a narrow band of voices; we can learn to hear many more.

It is not our purpose further to divide American poets into categories. Yet, ironically, it may be that only by drawing attention to poets who have been perceived as falling into this or that category can they be recognized as authentic claimants to a place in a real American canon.

In collecting essays for this book, we have undertaken a task that is far from completed. While these essays grow from many literary and political viewpoints, we are aware that there are traditions not represented here. This collection, therefore, must be seen as a beginning, an example of the kind of criticism needed to challenge the student of poetry—within and outside of the university—to explore further. All the voices that have contributed to the shape of our language, all the traditions that have enriched our poetry must be attended to in order that an integration can be achieved.

The tone and style of the essays are diverse, as is consistent with a poetry and criticism often developed outside academia. Our authors chose their own subject matter within the guidelines of the book. Some discuss problems within the existing canon, some write overviews of particular groups of writers, others focus on specific poets. These last are intended to serve as examples of the kind of detailed consideration necessary to acquaint readers with "uncanonized" poets and are not meant to promote one writer to the exclusion of others.

The work of the poets discussed here is available to the interested reader, but much of it is difficult to locate, consigned as it has been to small publications. We have tried, with the help of our critics, to include sufficient information to make possible the acquisition of the work. We are also planning a companion poetry anthology that will make available in a single volume poetry that has been ignored or underrepresented in anthologies of American poetry.

If it is true that the poet speaks to everyone, it is essential that the listener not hear selectively, responding only to the familiar voice, the expected message. Poets have a gift of tongues. It is our responsibility and delight to hear them when they speak.

Marie Harris
Kathleen Aguero

Acknowledgments

We editors would like to extend our thanks and appreciation to our authors, who stood by this project throughout its labyrinthine course toward publication; to Charter Weeks and Richard Hoffman, who encouraged us to keep going; to Houston Baker, who pointed the way to this book's final destination; to the anonymous reader of all the versions of this book, who provided invaluable criticism and insight; to Annette Kolodny and Joseph Bruchac for their advice; and to Karen Orchard, for her commitment to our project.

The editors and publisher gratefully acknowledge these poets and publishers for permission to reprint the material listed.

Lucille Clifton, "what the mirror said," from *Two-Headed Woman*, published by the University of Massachusetts Press. By permission of the author.

Lucha Corpi, "Como la semilla en espera/Like the seed that waits," from *Palabras de Mediodia/Noon Words*, translated by Catherine Rodriguez-Nieto, published by El Fuego de Aztlan Publications. By permission of the author.

Margarita Cota-Cárdenas, "Soliloquio Travieso," from *Noches despertando en conciencias*, published by Scorpion Press. By permission of the author.

Lance Henson, "comanche ghost dance an impression" and "at chadwick's bar and grill," from *Selected Poems*. By permission of the publisher, the Greenfield Review Press.

Robert Peters, "Ann at twilight, Ann / at dawn," from *The Gift To Be Simple: A Garland for Ann Lee*. By permission of the author and the publisher, Liveright Publishing Corporation. Copyright 1973, 1974, 1975 by Robert Peters.

Wendy Rose, "Walking on the Prayerstick," from *Lost Copper*. By permission of the author and publisher, Malki Museum Press.

Steve Abbott and Rudy Kikel's essay, "In Search of a Muse: The Politics of Gay Poetry," originally appeared in *The Advocate*. Reprinted by permission of Liberation Publications, Inc.

P. J. Laska's essay, "Poetry at the Periphery," appeared in different forms in both *The Arts Journal* and *Hyperion*.

George Ella Lyon's essay, "Contemporary Appalachian Poetry: Sources and Directions," appeared in a slightly different form in *The Kentucky Review*.

Raymond Patterson's essay, "What's Happening in Black Poetry?" appeared in a slightly different form in *The Poetry Review*, published by the Poetry Society of America.

Carmen Tafolla's essay, "Chicano Literature: Beyond Beginnings," was based on a briefer commentary with the same title in *Southern Exposure*.

A Gift of Tongues

The Bones of This Body Say, Dance

Self-Empowerment in Contemporary Poetry by Women of Color

We Were Never Meant to Survive: Resistance to Violence

Anger, resistance, and transformation, sexuality, self-knowledge, and joy, language, memory, and history: all these are crucial aspects of the theme of self-empowerment in the poetry of North American women of color.

Third World feminists have begun to devote their primary creative energies to conversations with each other. The economic, social, and political conditions of their lives appear in their poems as challenges to the institutions of white male privilege. Although Margaret Atwood and others have observed that all women have been colonized under patriarchy, the term "colonization" is often a *metaphor* for white women's experience.[1] It is a historical *reality* for most black women, whose ancestors were slaves and who may themselves have witnessed or been survivors of incidents of racial violence. For Native Americans and Asian Americans, "colonization" refers to the experience of living on reservations or in internment camps; for Latina women, to the economic and cultural exploitation of Latin America by the United States.

For Third World women, the journey to power and selfhood necessarily begins with an unflinching examination of these aspects of racism. The journey to transcendence, to self-celebration, begins with anger at cultural, economic, physical, and psychic violence. Resistance to violence, the determination—even in the face of death—to not be a victim empowers the poetry of Third World women writers. Poems which reflect direct violence against people of color are often appropriately direct in their fury. In June Jordan's "Poem about Police Violence," for instance, the poet demands:

> tell me something
> what you think would happen if
> everytime they kill a black boy
> then we kill a cop
> everytime they kill a black man
> then we kill a cop
>
> you think the accident rate would lower
> subsequently?[2]

In Safiya Henderson's defiant poem "harlem/soweto," the poet denies the separation of the Afro-American struggle against racist oppression from the courage of South African freedom fighters like Winnie and Nelson Mandela, whose spirits remain unbroken in the face of the overwhelming viciousness and violence of Botha's white South African regime. The poem ends with a brilliant sequence of images in which the unity of the spirit world and the natural world empower the unity of a resistance in which possessing one and not many tongues (metaphorically, being of one mind, speaking the same language) acquires a wonderfully visceral actual meaning:

> we are woven
> inseparable as sky
> with one sun
> > one moon
> > one tongue
> > rolled to spit
> > in one
> > eye . . .[3]

Resistance takes many forms. Audre Lorde's "Power" warns that power is not the simple possession of the means of violence. She refuses to accept a vision of power or revolution in which oppressed people turn the tables on their oppressors.[4] In her essay "Uses of the

Erotic: The Erotic as Power," Lorde suggests that power is not a *thing*, a quantity, but an inner source enabling the deepest feeling.[5] Real power—not that fraudulent concoction that passes for power in a racist, sexist, classist society—is not power over other's lives but power over one's own life. Unlike a kind of power that is rooted in physical force, political domination, and economic subjugation, Lorde insists that power resides in individual awareness and integrity; it is claimed by the individual and is something that can be neither bestowed nor wrested away. In claiming that one's "power rises / . . . from the same source / as [one's] pain," Lorde is suggesting in "For Each of You" that real power requires profound self-knowledge, and the process of acquiring such knowledge inevitably causes pain.[6] In this conception, power is a means to individual transformation. Like the Reverend Dr. Martin Luther King or Mahatma Gandhi, Lorde insists that the use of this power *is* the revolution and will engender the muscular, cohesive vision that makes social revolution possible.

Gwendolyn Brooks' "The Boy Died in My Alley" also explores violence by focusing on the issue of individual transformation. In the poem, the literal cause of the violent death of a black boy whose blood, whose body "ornaments [the poet's] alley," remains unmentioned. Indeed, no possible cause is ever speculated about, encouraging the reader to consider the multiple ways in which young black men in this country mysteriously end up dead: deaths that are alcohol or drug related, products of gang warfare, a robbery gone awry, police violence, suicide—all of these are secondary causes to racism, poverty, powerlessness, and despair. The poet acknowledges a sorrowful and determined responsibility for the death of the boy, and in so doing teaches each of us the tragic consequences of "knowledgeable unknowing," of ever failing to act against oppression and violence:

> I never saw his face at all.
> I never saw his futurefall.
> But I have known this Boy.
>
> I have always heard him deal with death.
> I have always heard the shout, the volley.
> I have closed my heart-ears late and early.
> And I have killed him ever.[7]

Brooks insists upon accountability, not self-indulgent guilt; it is that accountability, as well as Brooks' compassion, which transforms the waste of a young man's life into not only the hope for a different world but a call to action.

Lucille Clifton's "Miss Rosie," a poem about an impoverished, mentally confused older black woman reduced in the eyes of the world to bag-lady status, pivots on a similar theme of accountability and commitment. Like the boy who died in the alley, Miss Rosie, a "wet brown bag of a woman / who used to be the best looking gal in Georgia," is a castoff of society, discarded like yesterday's garbage, a parallel made explicit in the poem. This terrible disregard of the value of a human life ignites in the speaker of the poem a fierce and determined resistance fueled by compassion. The refrain "when I watch you," which in its first two usages sets the stage for images of destruction and human waste, is used a third time in the poem but with a twist; the final lines of the poem are an affirmation and a vow, a promise never to stand by and watch the destruction but to stand up and fight against it. With dignity and with love, the speaker announces:

> when I watch you
>
> .   .   .   .   .   .
>
> I stand up
> through your destruction
> I stand up. [8]

In another Clifton poem, "For de Lawd," we see how the capacity to not only survive but aspire, to be "contrary and self-affirming across continents and generations" (what critic Chinosole has referred to in black women as "matrilineal diaspora," the "strength and beauty [black women] pass on as friends and lovers from foremothers to mothers and daughters"), is an important source for Clifton's resistance. [9] A tradition of resistance to oppression, a legacy of will and respect for possibilities, can elicit from characters or individuals a willingness to hold on to what is difficult. The speaker in this poem, like the speaker in many other poems by Clifton, and by June Jordan, Audre Lorde, Alice Walker, and other black feminist writers as well, acknowledges the importance of that historical tradition and names herself part of it. In the face of generations of racial violence, the speaker in the poem refuses to be paralyzed by grief. She draws upon the resolute tenacity and strength of generations of black women across the diaspora, declaring simply:

> . . . I got a long memory
> and I come from a line
> of black and going on women. [10]

Sometimes survival itself in the context of racial violence is sufficient cause for celebration. In "Anchorage," Native American poet Joy Harjo draws a portrait of a woman on a park bench who could be Miss Rosie's sister:

> . . . someone's Athabascan
> grandmother, folded up, smelling like 200 years
> of blood and piss, her eyes closed against some
> unimagined darkness, where she is buried in an ache
> in which nothing makes
> > sense. [11]

Like Clifton, Harjo names the cast-aside of society as family, "claim[s] her / as our own history . . . know[s] that our dreams / don't end here." The poem recounts the improbable, actual story of another survival, Henry's:

> And I think of the 6th Avenue jail, of mostly Native
> and Black men, where Henry told about being shot at
> eight times outside a liquor store in L.A., but when
> the car sped away he was surprised he was alive,
> no bullet holes, man, and eight cartridges strewn
> on the sidewalk
> > all around him.
>
> Everyone laughed at the impossibility of it,
> but also the truth. Because who would believe
> the fantastic and terrible story of all of our survival
> those who were never meant
> > to survive? [12]

The poem, dedicated to Audre Lorde, echoes in its final lines Lorde's "A Litany for Survival," which ends with an affirmation to move beyond fear and silence into language and action:

> . . . when we are silent
> we are still afraid.

> So it is better to speak
> remembering
> we were never meant to survive.[13]

   Incidents such as the 1979 savage murders of thirteen black women
in the Roxbury section of Boston and, more recently, the murder of
twenty-seven black children in Atlanta have inspired poems of anguish
and resistance. The poetic images are as visceral and devastating as the
actual events they describe. Poems such as Jayne Cortez's "Rape,"
Donna Allegra's "A Rape Poem for Men," or Audre Lorde's "Need"
often do not suggest any semblance of conventional poetic diction and
syntax, as if the nightmare being named demands an immediate, unmediated description. These poems derive tremendous impact from
their escalating cadences. As readers are caught up in the increasing
momentum of the poem, they experience viscerally (through breath,
while reading silently or aloud) the horror of the situation, as in the
final lines of Ntozake Shange's "with no immediate cause":

>   . . . "there is some concern
>   that alleged battered women
>   might start to murder their
>   husbands & lovers with no
>   immediate cause"
>   i spit up   i vomit   i am screaming
>   we all have immediate cause
>   every 3 minutes
>   every 5 minutes
>
> every 10 minutes
> every day
> women's bodies are found
> in alleys & bedrooms / at the top of the stairs
> before i ride the subway / buy a paper / drink
> coffee / i must know /
> have you hurt a woman today
> did you beat a woman today
> throw a child across a room
>   are the lil girl's panties
>   in yr pocket
> did you hurt a woman today
>
> i have to ask these obscene questions

the authorities require me to
establish immediate cause

every three minutes
every five minutes
every ten minutes
every day. [14]

In her repeating lines about time (every three minutes, every five minutes), Shange forces the reader to experience *frequency*, not as statistical, but as minute-to-minute time, life being eradicated *while you are reading*, every day.

Ntozake Shange's choreopoem *For Colored Girls Who Have Considered Suicide / When the Rainbow Is Enuf*, like Alice Walker's novel, *The Color Purple*, has unleashed a tidal wave of controversy in the black community for exposing the sexism and violence of some black men. Historically, black male violence, in fact and myth, has been used by whites to foster racist assumptions about black men rather than to demonstrate the pervasiveness, across cultural boundaries, of misogyny. Thus, until very recently, it has been a matter of survival for black women to gloss over their anger and despair.

Audre Lorde has written eloquently on the necessity of black women breaking silence about violence within the black community:

> . . . In this country, black women traditionally have had compassion for everybody else except ourselves. We cared for whites because we had to for pay or survival; we cared for our children and our fathers and our brothers and our lovers. We need to also learn to care for ourselves. Our history and popular culture, as well as our personal lives, are full of tales of black women who had "compassion for misguided black men." Our scarred, broken, battered and dead daughters and sisters are a mute testament to that. [15]

Poems in which women refuse to be victimized by men are not only affirming and necessary for women's lives but for men's lives as well. As critic Barbara Smith has insisted:

> Acknowledging the sexism of Black men does not mean that we become "man-haters" or necessarily eliminate them from our lives. What it does mean is that we must struggle for a different basis of interaction with them. *That if we care about them and*

ourselves we will not permit ourselves to be degraded or manipu-
lated.[16] (Italics mine)

In poetry by Native American women, the refusal to be victimized and exploited often presents itself in metaphors whose contexts are historical and in which the desecration of the land is experienced both as a profoundly personal, spiritual assault and as a metaphor for the violent, urban, technological, compulsively contemporary death culture in which petrochemical products and other poisons replace wool and wood and all that is natural, a theme of Paula Gunn Allen's "Wool Season, 1973." In Allen's "Riding the Thunder," the history of the betrayal and genocide of Native Americans rides the poet's shoulders. Time past and time present merge: "noon, history, night are / stars, are fixed and counted nails / on the doors of hope, the dying bloody dream."[17] In the midst of this horror, not only of violence but of the obliteration of all things sacred, Allen turns to poetry as meditation, as prayer, as solace. Her poems suggest a sense of timelessness, of belonging to an ancient tribal past, of being what all poets once were: shamans, healers, prophets, translators, and transformers of consciousness.

A spiritual heritage of reverence for the smallest living things, the "tiny desert flower / micro beetle bug" inspires Terri Meyette's "Celebration 1982."[18] Ironically titled, given the poem's subject matter (the strip-mining of land, the poisoning of water with radioactive waste, and especially the U.S. government policy of using sacred Shoshone and Paiute Indian land in the Nevada desert for bombing practice), "Celebration 1982" nevertheless *is* a celebration. Meyette celebrates Native American traditional values of reverence "for all of life," and she celebrates as well the writing of the poem, which is itself an act of protest against genocidal U.S. government policies and nuclear madness.

In an untitled poem, Lydia Yellowbird remembers the destruction of her gentle, peace-loving people because the white settlers were unable to see them as fully human.

> When you came
> you found a people
> with red skin
> they were one
> with all living things

But you did not see this
                    beauty
          instead you saw them
                    as animals, primitive
                              savage
Because you had lost this
                    whole
In the progress of your civilization
          look now what
                    your knowledge
          has made them

You ask me to plow the ground. Shall I take a
knife and tear my mother's breast? Then when I
die she will not take me to her bosom to rest.

You ask me to dig for stone. Shall I dig under
her skin for bones? Then when I die I cannot
enter her body to be born again. [19]

The last two stanzas of the poem are a direct echo of the writings of Smohalla, of the Columbian Basin Tribes, who voiced Indian objections to European attitudes in the mid 1800s. [20]

In "Long Division: A Tribal History," Wendy Rose recounts the slow death of her people, who are "bought and divided" by the white colonists. [21] After the destruction of ritual and the magic of song and shamanic healing, all that remains for the poet is the wilderness within her and the wilderness outside. She becomes a legendary figure, the women who "suckle[s] coyotes and grieve[s]."

          . . . we die in granite scaffolding
on the shape of the Sierras and lay down with lips open
thrusting songs on the world. Who are we

and do we still live? Our shamans sleep
saying no. So outside of eternity we struggle
til our blood has spread off our bodies and
frayed the sunset edges; it's our blood that

gives you those southwestern skies. [22]

She refers sarcastically to tourists and white settlers who enthuse about beautiful Southwest sunsets with no awareness of the politics of white claims on that land.

Rose travels geographically and temporally to Wounded Knee, whose massacre is reenacted every time a tourist buys an artifact, a piece of Indian history, unmindful of its human cost. In "I expected my skin and my blood to ripen," the poet becomes the Indian woman who fought in battle only to be stripped bare by the white victors, her clothing sold as curios. She laments the transformation of magic, of shamanic or tribal power, into science and curatorship:

> My feet were frozen to the leather,
> pried apart, left behind—bits of flesh
> on the moccasins, bits of papery deerhide
> on the bones
>
> . . . . . .
>
> My leggings were taken like in a rape
> and shriveled to the size of stick figures
> like they had never felt
> the push of my strong woman's body
> walking in the hills.
> It was my own baby whose cradleboard I held.
> Would've put her in my mouth
> like a snake
> if I could, would've turned her
> into a bush or old rock
> if there'd been enough magic
> to work such changes. Not enough magic
> even to stop the bullets.
> Not enough magic
> to stop the scientists.
> Not enough magic
> to stop the collectors. [23]

While agents of the U.S. government no longer deliberately hand out smallpox-infested blankets to American Indian people, they have replaced that form of attempted genocide with another almost as evil: spiritual annihilation. As Beth Brandt, editor of A *Gathering of Spirit*, a special issue of *Sinister Wisdom* devoted to Native American women's writing, has written, "they take our children to remove the inside of them. Our power. . . They steal our food, our sacred rattle, the stories, our names."[24]

Anger is often spoken of in poems by women of color as an empowering force or a catalyst for movements from racism to resistance

and transcendence. As Native American poet Chrystos explores the
metaphor:

> My sacred beliefs have been made pencils, names of
> cities, gas stations
> My knee is wounded so badly that I limp constantly
> Anger is my crutch
> I hold myself upright with it
> My knee is wounded
> see
> How I Am Still Walking. [25]

"I Walk in the History of My People" alludes to the massacre of the
Sioux people at Wounded Knee and the continuing assaults on Native
Americans by the U.S. government and by U.S. citizens. "Crutch,"
"limp," "wounded"—these words are not often found in poems which
also speak of dignity, of not crawling, of walking "upright." Chrystos'
poem includes both realizations; it neither romanticizes nor denies but
affirms rightful anger and its place in transformation.

Cherríe Moraga's "The Welder" pivots on a similar theme. In this
poem, anger is also seen as engendering social change; Moraga "understand[s] the capacity of heat / to change the shape of things."[26] The
anger in this poem speaks specifically to radical people of color and
feminists who want a sense of unity against oppression so desperately
that individuals' different needs and visions, dissent and anger within
radical movements are often suppressed. Although Moraga includes
herself in the "we" who "plead to each other" . . . "*we all come from
the same rock / we all come from the same rock,*" she also insists on
acknowledging our differences and on the necessity of anger for forming real bonds, not superficial agreements:

> Yes, fusion *is* possible
> but only if things get hot enough—
> all else is temporary adhesion,
> patching up. [27]

In the final lines of the poem, Moraga herself becomes the welder, she
who refuses to smooth things over:

> I am the welder
> I am taking the power
> into my own hands. [28]

Audre Lorde has also written about her desire to heal through her poems, to encourage the profusion of voices within every woman. She alludes to the dialogue among these voices in the title of her 1976 book, *Between Our Selves.*[29] Before our fractured and embattled communities can begin this dialogue, Lorde recognizes that individuals must experience and accept chaos and dissent for and within themselves. In "Outside," a poem from this volume, Lorde celebrates this process as a source of healing: "for most of all I am / blessed within my selves / who are come to make our shattered faces / whole."[30]

In her poem "Epilog," Wendy Rose borrows from Hopi legend to describe her shared political determination in solidarity with other contemporary Native American women writers Leslie Silko, Paula Gunn Allen, and Joy Harjo; the poem speaks to the complexities of change and the power within poets and all people of color to transcend extreme obstacles. The Hopi way is to convert obstacles into sources of strength, and this she promises to do:

> Drop a kernel of corn on a rock
> and say a prayer. It will shoot up
> proud and green, tassel out,
> pull the next crop from the thunderheads.
> That's the Hopi way.
> If the corn doesn't grow
> you eat the rocks,
> drink the clouds
> on the distant plains.
>
> Silko and Allen and Harjo and me:
> our teeth are hard
> from the rocks we eat.[31]

In "A Tribute to Rosa Parks," Alice Walker describes her hopes for all of humanity: our potential for courage, dignity, and love.

> The Cubans have created a word that they call each other in recognition of their common struggle against oppression and their common goal of realizing a common dream. The word is "compañera." It means Sister, it means Comrade, it means Companion, it means Friend. It means we are together. It means we are one.
> I wish we had a word like that. A word that praises the

splendor of our ordinary dignity and courage—and not our biological or religious destinations. A word that reminds us, whenever we use it, that we are together, not separate, and that the
courage and dignity that is possible for one of us is possible for
us all.[32]

In individual acts of self-love and self-empowerment, in acts of
compassion and unity, in poems that reflect anguish, outrage, and
despair as well as the determination to "survive confirmed," the poets
discussed here are proving that Alice Walker's vision is not only dream
but possibility.

In their unflinching gaze into much that is nightmare in American
culture, many of these are not comforting poems. But because they
imagine what Adrienne Rich has called "the possibilities of truth between us," they are poems which chart a new, essential geography, one
whose terrain we ignore only at our own peril.

This is Not Romance/Private Fictions: Redefining the Language, Redefining the Culture

Given not only the poet's traditional relationship to language but also the relationship of silence and invisibility to powerlessness, it is not surprising that finding one's voice has been such a
compelling issue in contemporary feminist poetry generally and especially in poetry written by women of color. Having been denied the
right to speak her truths in a language and form that accurately reflect
her, the Third World woman writer must inevitably seek a language in
which these truths are undiminished. The woman writer in this
culture—whether Afro-American, Chicana, Asian American, Native
American, or white—has written in a language determined by patriarchy as well as racism and thus has a double urgency to redefine
that language, to claim a language and form unfettered by those twin
forces of the dominant culture.

In the preface to *Passion: New Poems, 1977–1980*, June Jordan establishes a relationship among "Black and Third World poets . . .
[generally and] those feminist poets who are evidently intent upon
speaking with a maximal number and diversity of other American

lives." She calls these writers, who range from Pablo Neruda and Victor Hernandez Cruz to Jessica Hagedorn and Margaret Walker, "poets of The New World," and suggests that there is a unifying thread of linguistic interconnectedness among them:

> In the poetry of The New World, you meet with a reverence for the material world that begins with a reverence for human life, an intellectual trust in sensuality as a means of knowledge and of unity, an easily deciphered system of reference, aspiration to a believable, collective voice and, consequently, emphatic preference for broadly accessible language and/or "spoken" use of language. [33]

Those who must forge a literature out of generations of contempt and denial bring to that literature an explosive energy, courage and will, a visionary anger. Perhaps this is when the most incisive literature is made, when celebration is the Janus face of struggle, when a passionate energy soars through the language.

In poems that are as compelling for their ethical vision as for their language, women of color dare to imagine a changed world. And if imagining a changed world will not cause it to come into being, we know the consequences of failing to imagine it.

The very act of putting pen to paper, of giving voice to one's own ideas and dreams, is especially precious in the context of Afro-American poetry, for it is a metaphor for the claiming of one's cultural, spiritual, and emotional existence—one's very right to be. In "In Search of Our Mothers' Gardens," Alice Walker asks her readers to consider the context in which black women have created, against all odds, throughout their history, in this country:

> How was the creativity of the Black woman kept alive, year after year and century after century, when for most of the years Black people have been in America, it was a punishable crime for a Black person to read or write? And the freedom to paint, to sculpt, to expand the mind with action, did not exist. Consider, if you can bear to imagine it, what might have been the result if singing, too, had been forbidden by law. Listen to the voices of Bessie Smith, Billie Holiday, Nina Simone, Roberta Flack, and Aretha Franklin, among others, and imagine those voices muzzled for life. [34]

A poet who to my mind is more lyrical in her fiction than in her poetry, Alice Walker provides in the early pages of her novel *Meridian* what may be the most terrifying and metaphysically accurate paradigm in all of Afro-American literature for the black woman writer whose language has been stolen from her. Louvinie, a slave woman, literally loses her tongue as punishment for the one creative act allowed her: storytelling. Her ghost story, told upon request to the Saxon plantation children, inadvertently frightens the youngest child to death. As a result,

> Louvinie's tongue was clipped out at the root. Choking on blood, she saw her tongue ground under the heel of Master Saxon. Mutely, she pleaded for it, because she knew the curse of her native land: Without one's tongue in one's mouth or in a special spot of one's own choosing, the singer in one's soul was lost forever to grunt and snort through eternity like a pig. [35]

Like Alice Walker, poet Sherley Anne Williams borrows from the slave narrative tradition to emphasize that for the Afro-American woman writer finding a means of articulation is still not only precious but hard-won. A central experience of the narrator of Williams' stunning collection of poems, *Some One Sweet Angel Chile,* is the claiming of self as text, the act of telling one's own story. It is central also to the narrator of a number of Williams' earlier poems, as indeed it emerges as a formal device whose implications are as much thematic as a question of poetics in the work of many Afro-American and other Third World poets. But in the historical context of antebellum slavery and the early period of Reconstruction, the setting for many of Williams' poems, the courage and the power of speech take on much deeper levels of meaning. Consider these lines from "I Sing This Song for Our Mothers," in which Williams takes on the persona of a newly freed black man who announces quietly, surely:

> I was a man full growed
> when the otha folks freedom come, had
> a wife and sons o' my own
> and wa'n't nary-a-one o' us
> eva belongst to no one but us selves. [36]

Odessa's son, the narrator in this poem, knows that through his own resistance and love and through the love and kinship of family and friends he belongs to himself in the deepest sense.

"I Sing This Song for Our Mothers" shifts narrators from Odessa's son to Odessa, following his admonition to black people to carry on the story of freedom by telling it "to yo daughters most especial / cause this where our line come from." Forced to live in a world in which speech and naming are forbidden, even the right to name her own children, Odessa paradoxically claims the power of naming, of living in a world of self-authored meanings and perceptions:

> I say yo name
> Now and that be love. I say
> yo daddy name and that be
> how I know free. I say Harker
> name and that be how I
> keep loved and keep free. . .[37]

In this and other poems from *The Peacock Poems* and *Some One Sweet Angel Chile*, Sherley Anne Williams has sought out the slave narrative as a structural and thematic device for exploring the black woman's quest for freedom, selfhood, and language. The poem contains an actual account of an escape from slavery into freedom as well as a number of traditional slave narrative elements: first-person narrative without the filtering consciousness of an amanuensis; the story of recognition of, resistance to, and the gaining of freedom from oppression; and the chronicling of the social fabric of the community through a chronicling of the life of an individual. Most of all, it celebrates the richness, acuity, energy, and vision of black folk dialect. Here Williams pays homage not only to the first authentically Afro-American genre, but to Zora Neale Hurston's *Their Eyes Were Watching God*, a book whose spirit and language are echoed in this and other poems by Williams.[38]

The self-affirming spirit of Odessa resurfaces in Williams' most recent volume of poetry, *Some One Sweet Angel Chile*, in which Williams again borrows from the slave narrative tradition to create a compelling social and psychological context for the courage and determination of the women who inhabit these poems. The book opens with a series of epistolary poems written in the persona of Hannah, a New

England black woman, who comes to the South as a teacher after the Civil War. Despite Hannah's quiet restraint and dignity, she embodies the spirit of resistance and rebellion. When Miss Esther, the head teacher, is dismayed that Hannah insists on leaving the Big House where the teachers now live to spend time in the old slave quarters among the students and other freedmen, not just for an occasional prayer meeting but to partake in conversation, music, and a shared history, Hannah goes anyway, and recounts:

> It is a stalemate:
> she will not give her permission;
> I go and ask no one's consent. [39]

Despite her respect for Miss Esther, Hannah recognizes the symbolic power of all the ways in which her people have been divided from one another. Paradoxically, in quietly going her own way Hannah is also affirming her solidarity with her community by choosing to resist the unconscious demarcations of power and status which Miss Esther would unwittingly perpetuate.

In another wonderfully understated poem, Hannah refuses the implications of her slave name, Patience, and "answer[s] roughly / some harmless question, My name is Hannah. Hannah. There is / no Patience to it."[40]

The middle section of this collection, exhuberant, boisterous, and sexy, skips sixty years to the 1930s to celebrate a similar spirit of rebelliousness in the persona of famed blues singer Bessie Smith. In these poems Bessie Smith, the "angel chile" in this book, the wild woman of the traditional blues song, is not mythologized but remembered for the ways in which her spirit brought courage, hope, and humor into the lives of others, one of whom comments:

> she touched me; and I
> knowed her. The rest is
> my own memories. [41]

In the final sequence of poems, we hear echoes of Hannah and Bessie in a profusion of contemporary voices. Although the poems in this section seem loosely autobiographical, the narrator of "WITNESS," the opening poem in this sequence, sternly warns us that she speaks not just for herself but for the generations which preceded her and the generations to come: "I give voice to the old stories. This is not romance, / private fictions. . ."[42]

The speaker in Kathy Elaine Anderson's "Keep a Weathered Eye Lifting" also reaches across continents and generations to name herself one of the three defiant, captured Africans on a slave ship bound for America, who "leaped with crazy laughter to / the waiting sharks, sang as they went under." The poem summons the spirit of this rebellion, the courage of Afro-American ancestors, as an apparition and actual hurricane, a wind that fills the sails of ships, a wished-for beacon in a storm-tossed night, a song whose siren call will give its listeners no peace until they acknowledge its compelling beauty and take a similar journey to freedom:

> Listen,
> as they chant stories of lost Griots,
> your language will fall away
> and ours will settle in your mouth.[43]

Mari Evans adopts a strategy similar to Williams and Anderson, that of borrowing slave narrative elements in order to affirm and celebrate not only her own selfhood but the earlier generations of black women whose resistance to slavery, racism, and oppression is indelibly a part of her own struggle and her own empowering. Evans' "The 7:25 Trolley" is not about the demeaning conditions of poverty (although it certainly exposes them) but rather about the determination of black women to transcend their lives' circumstances, to not simply endure:

> ain't got time for a bite to eat
> I'll have to catch my trolley at the end of the block
> and if I take
> my coffee
> there
> she looks at the cup and she looks at the clock
>   (Sure hope I don't miss my car . . .)
>
> . . . .
> I may scrub floors
> but
> I don't
> get on my knees . . .
> and someday
> I won't go at all
>   (Sure hope I don't miss my car . . .)[44]

Evans here uses repetition and line breaks to illuminate an alternating awareness of self in racist society and as dignified transcender. She inserts the line "(Sure hope I don't miss my car . . .)" a number of times in dialogue with a growing awareness on the part of the persona that she someday "won't go at all" to scrub floors. The double awareness of the persona here seems to flash quickly back and forth between realities, creating a tension that moves toward transcendence with the last phrases. Evans exploits the use of short, broken lines to emphasize this aspect of the inner dialogue: "I don't / get on my knees. . . ." The echo is to slavery: the order "get on your knees" is a familiar one in the master-slave situation. The woman in the poem is refusing slavery, but the line is cut in such a way as to deliberately highlight the fact that in former times she *had* to get on her knees. And in fact she still does get on her knees to scrub floors, physically, but the psychic meaning of the kneeling is explicitly refuted.

Refusing to kneel to the dominant culture by refusing to speak in what has been called "the oppressor's language" takes on additional layers of difficulty in American poets whose native language is not English. Metaphors of speech and of translating between languages and cultures surface with exceptional vigor in the writing of Asian American and Chicana poets, who not only write out of a multicultural identity but a multilingual one as well. In *The Third Woman*, feminist critic Dexter Fisher speaks of "translating oneself into understandable terms" as "a major preoccupation" of most of the Asian American women poets included in her anthology. This preoccupation is "symbolized by the literal problem of speaking another language—again the dilemma of being caught between speech and demon silence."[45] The paradox here, of course, is that in "translating oneself into understandable terms" the North American woman of color whose native tongue is not English runs the risk of being increasingly understandable to the Anglo world while becoming increasingly alienated from her own identity.

Such poets may turn to childhood images to clarify the learning and the feelings in these experiences. Diana Chang has written in "Allegory" of the tension between her historical culture and the one in which she now lives; she writes of being the child who is "misplaced / and found again."[46] In "How a Girl Got Her Chinese Name," Nellie Wong reflects on her childhood feelings of blessedness and security when her family and teachers give her two Chinese names, Nah Lei (meaning "where," "which place") and Lai Oy (meaning "beautiful love"). Through this naming she is able to discover an ethnic heritage which had been erased by the demands to assimilate. Wong is restored to a child's sense of omnipotence: "between these names / I never knew I would ever get lost."[47]

The relationship between language and assimilation is also the subject of Tina Koyama's "Next," about a visit to the dentist's office. The poet, whose tongue is literally invaded by the dentist's apparatus, is struck silent as well by the invasiveness of his attitudes and the attitudes of the Anglo world he represents. His questions, pleasantries about the poet's "dog, / undergraduate education, the muffler on [her] car," evade any attempt at real knowledge or understanding. His race, gender, occupation, and class privilege encourage him—and empower him—to formulate not only the questions he poses in his attempts to define her but the answers as well:

> . . . He knows my life can be answered with a nod,
> knows the stoney surface of my tooth
> and the narrow parabola of my jaw
> better than his own hand. He fears
> extraction will be necessary, taps with his mirror
>
> deep cracks that even promises won't fill. Here,
> decisions come in the shape of pliers. I nod,
> swallowing old questions with a numbing tongue.[48]

The poet's "numb[ed]" tongue is robbed of speech by more than novocaine; if the dentist (and the world he represents) has his way, the promised "extraction" will be the forcible separation of the poet from her culture as well as the forcible separation of the molar from her mouth.

The title poem of Fay Chiang's *In the City of Contradictions* affirms in Asian American poets a belief in the essential and necessary power of a nonassimilated mother tongue. Those who shape the world through their own "songs, dreams and dances, / . . . myths, legends, symbols" will make survival in the city of contradictions—metaphor for all of U.S. culture—possible. The poem ends with these affirming words:

> but we with our spirit, our love, our sinew
> we are among the survivors
>
> spread the news.[49]

Sometimes the paralyzing pressure to assimilate comes from within the family. Part of the grief-stricken, charged connection between black mothers and daughters is the heritage of colorism that black mothers often have been forced to pass on to their daughters in the name of their children's survival. In "Prologue," Audre Lorde exclaims:

> . . . When I was a child
> whatever my mother thought would mean survival
> made her try to beat me whiter every day
> and even now the color of her bleached ambition
> still forks throughout my words
> but I survived
> and didn't I survive confirmed . . . [50]

In "Pathways: From Mother to Mother" she adds, "wherever [my mother] wore ivory / I wear pain."[51] The black mother who is clothed in survival clothes—white in "Prologue" and ivory in "Pathways"—wraps her daughter in the same bleached binding rags that she herself has been forced to wear. Audre Lorde's "Outside," Nellie Wong's "When I Was Growing Up," June Jordan's "Poem about My Rights," and Gloria Anzaldúa's autobiographical essay "La Prieta" all focus on Third World parents' attempts to convince their daughters to straighten their hair or teeth and stay out of the sun, or are about obsessions over white skin and cleanliness.[52]

In "Lullabye," Janice Mirikitani examines her mother's apparent acquiescence to the imprisonment of Japanese Americans at Manzanar and Tule Lake during World War II and to the racial hatred that permitted the United States to target the Japanese for atomic destruction at Hiroshima and Nagasaki. The poet concludes that she will remain orphaned, "parentless," until her mother's political consciousness is born. But Mirikitani plays with the Japanese attitude of resigned acceptance: "shikata ga nai / it can't be / helped."[53] She interposes her own "waiting, / waiting" with the patience and waiting of her mother to make it clear that she is not just waiting but *willing* her mother to be born, to be free.

The poetry of women of color is more focused on themes of healing, bonding, and nurturing between Third World mothers and daughters than on rupture and anger. There has been a healing between mothers and daughters, and that healing has been an essential source for Third

World women poets "hearing themselves forth from silence," of returning to deeper sources. [54] In a letter to Barbara Smith, Cherríe Moraga writes of this process:

> I went to a concert where Ntozake Shange was reading. There, everything exploded for me. She was speaking a language that I knew—in the deepest parts of me—existed, and that I had ignored in my own feminist studies and even in my own writing. What Ntozake caught in me is the realization that in my development as a poet, I have, in many ways, denied the voice of my brown mother—the brown in me. I have acclimated to the sound of a white language which, as my father represents it, does not speak to the emotions in my poems—emotions which stem from the love of my mother.
>
> The reading was agitating. Made me uncomfortable. Threw me into a week-long terror of how deeply I was affected. I felt that I had to start all over again. That I turned only to the perceptions of white middle-class women to speak for me and all women. I am shocked by my own ignorance.
>
> Sitting in that auditorium chair was the first time I had realized to the core of me that for years I had disowned the language I knew best—ignored the words and rhythms that were the closest to me. The sounds of my mother and aunts gossiping—half in English, half in Spanish—while drinking cerveza in the kitchen. And the hands—I had cut off the hands in my poems. But not in conversation; still the hands could not be kept down. Still they insisted on moving. [55]

In "For the Color of My Mother," Moraga writes of returning to the words and rhythms closest to her; the "white girl" who "[goes] brown to the blood color of [her] mother" speaks for both of them when she returns to the tongue they share. [56] Moraga describes the mutilation of the spirit that accompanies the mutilation of one's own speech. Aurora Levins Morales writes of a similar mutilation of her mother: "the fear of racist violence that clipped her tongue of all its open vowels, into crisp, imitation British." [57] In Moraga's poem, her mother is forced to speak a different kind of English but also a language of subservience, of "yes," of "stoop" and "carry." Both mother and daughter have been mutilated: the mouth that is not allowed to speak its own language becomes a wound, a gaping hole, a gash, central images in the poem.

I am a white girl gone brown to the blood color of my mother
speaking for her through the unnamed part of the mouth
the wide-arched muzzle of brown women

At two
my upper lip split open
clear to the tip of my nose
it spilled forth a cry that would not yield
that travelled down six floors of hospital
where doctors wound me into white bandages
only the screaming mouth exposed

the gash sewn back into a snarl
would last for years

I am a white girl gone brown to the blood color of my mother
speaking for her

at five, her mouth
pressed into a seam
a fine blue child's line drawn across her face
her mouth, pressed into mouthing english
mouthing yes yes yes
mouthing stoop lift carry
(sweating wet sighs into the field
her red bandana comes loose from under the huge brimmed hat
moving across her upper lip) . . . [58]

The ragged gash of the daughter's mouth is contrasted to "the fine blue child's line" of her mother's mouth, which becomes increasingly distorted. Even at five years of age, the mother's mouth is "pressed" into colonized service, literally in stoop labor, metaphorically in having to begin to adopt the language of yes, of oppression. In the stanzas that follow, the thin line widens to become the lipstick-smeared mouth of a fourteen-year-old, pushed into a sexuality she is not yet ready for; finally, at forty-five, her mother's mouth literally stretches into a bleeding ulcer.

The poem explores multiple injuries and multiple healings. The poet suffers both literal and metaphoric wounding. Her scream of outrage and pain, "spill[ing] forth a cry that would not yield," is simultaneously literal and metaphoric, like the white bandages in which she is swathed, which cover her brownness. She is robbed of her mother's tongue and also of her mother.

The wound of the daughter becomes an emblem of defiance, its blood-red color a return to her mother's darkness. In the final lines of the poem, Moraga invokes shamanic power to cast a ritual circle in which women of color are rejoined through the reclaiming of their mothers.

> *I am a white girl gone brown to the blood color of my mother*
> *speaking for her*
>
> as it should be
> dark women come to me
> > sitting in circles
> I pass through their hands
> the head of my mother
> painted in clay colors
>
> touching each carved feature
> > swollen eyes and mouth
> they understand the explosion the splitting
> open   contained within the fixed expression
>
> they cradle her silence
> > nodding to me.[59]

Moraga names herself a priestess, a healer. Through compassion for her mother and an understanding of her mother's enforced silence, "the splitting / open contained within the fixed expression," Moraga is restored to speech, as to her mother *speaking for her / as it should be.* Moraga intends a double meaning: she is speaking for her mother, and this is as it should be—both as it ought to be (a future one wishes for, in which daughters and mothers share the same speech, the same vision) and as it is proper (a present now attained, at least for the speaker in the poem). The line enjambs forward as well as backward to read: "as it should be / dark women come to me." Again, a double meaning is implied: Moraga envisions a future in which she is a woman who brings women of color together, and this is fitting, proper, "as it should be." The poet offers the healing wisdom of this poem, an explosion out of silence into naming. It is a sacred offering, like the altar-sculpture of her mother, which is passed with reverence from hand to hand.

I Am / a Dark Temple Where Your True Spirit Rises: Resistance to Colorism

Like resistance to speechlessness, resistance to colorism (the mapping of Anglo standards of beauty onto people of color) empowers the vision and the poems of women of color.

In a poem of astonishing loveliness, Native American poet Wendy Rose apprehends, on the deepest level, the beauty of "Julia the Lion Woman," a sideshow freak, "the ugliest woman in the world." By extrapolation, Rose apprehends as well the beauty of all those destined by the racism, colorism, cruelty, and clouded vision of others to be invisible, unfully seen.

> . . . Beauty twisted within
> and pushed your pain against you
> to be nailed like a bronze wolf pelt
> on your bones.
> They called you the ugliest woman in the world,
> the woman with a face like a lion or
> an ape, the woman whose long fur swirled
> like a shawl around her
> in a land where even the wolves
> run naked.
> I call you
> the most beautiful she-wolf,
> the highest flying canary,
> the most ancient song,
> the most faithful magic.
> I call you
> my mother and my sister
> and my daughter and me.[60]

Healing and essential to both self and community, such a re-visioning in the lives of people of color is not to be taken lightly. Consider, for example, the degree to which destructive ideas about physical beauty shatter the community in Toni Morrison's novel *The Bluest Eye* and eventually succeed in driving Pecola Breedlove, one of its members, insane.

Lyric re-visioning is one of many forms of resistance to colorism. Others are more plainspoken, understated, but no less effective. In a poem from Sherley Anne Williams' "Letters from a New England Negro" sequence, set in the period immediately following the Emancipation, a black school teacher confronted by white children taunting "'Nigger!'" responds, unruffled (laughing, in fact), "'and / a free one, too,'" thus indicating to the children as well as herself that the naming of her blackness no longer has the power to hurt her.[61] And in her series of poems on Bessie Smith, Sherley Anne Williams creates a Bessie who refuses the terrible legacy of white racism: the belief that lighter is better, is more beautiful; Bessie bewitches even those black men who "bragged [they] didn't deal in coal" into her bed.[62]

As an antidote to colorism, novelist Maxine Hong Kingston, who describes fear and alienation as "the white ghosts," and other Third World writers have for some time used whiteness as a negative qualifier. Lucha Corpi and Audre Lorde among others reverse the conventional association of whiteness with goodness and purity. In the opening poem of Corpi's bilingual volume *Palabras de Mediodia/ Noon Words*, whiteness becomes a metaphor for those things which hold the poem back from flowering into creation, out of silence:

> Como la semilla en espera
> de la benevolente lluvia
> el verso sediento calla.
> Su quietud se desparrama
> en los adentros y me asusta.
> su sequedad mustia y blanca.

> Like the seed that waits
> for gentle rain
> my poem is silent in its thirst.
> Its quietude scatters
> inside me and I am frightened
> by its withered whiteness.[63]

Other recent poems speak more directly to black women's changing consciousness about skin color. In "I Used to Think," Chirlane McCray first describes herself through the distorted lens of an internalized racist self-image: "A nappy-headed, no-haired / fat-lipped, / big-bottomed Black girl," wanting to be pecan-colored instead of black. By the end of the poem she is transformed, able to recognize her own ebony beauty, "the woman in darkness / who flowers with loving."[64]

As Audre Lorde's poems shift from metaphors of earth brown to coal black, a fierce and articulate voice emerges. The title poem from *Coal*, written twenty years ago, invokes a powerful and joyous recognition of self and of the beauty of blackness:

> I am Black because I come from the earth's inside
> now take my word for jewel in the open light.[65]

In a kind of linguistic reclaiming, Lorde reverses the racist stereotypes connoting darkness with fear, hatred, and death; in many of her poems, she associates darkness with strength, integrity, beauty, vision, and magic. In "Black Mother Woman," Lorde announces,

> look mother
> I am
> a dark temple where your true spirit rises
> beautiful and tough as a chestnut
> stanchion against your nightmares of weakness.[66]

In "For Each of You" she entreats all people of color to claim the majesty of their darkness, to tell their children

> you are the offspring of slaves
> and your mother was
> a princess
> in darkness.[67]

And in a poem from *The Black Unicorn*, "From the House of Ye-manja," Lorde again imbues positive associations of blackness with the healing power of the motherbond.

> Mother I need your blackness now
> As the August earth needs rain.[68]

In these three poems Lorde speaks as a mother, a daughter, or as both at once. She calls on these female kinship ties for access to the redemptive love of her blackness. In this way she extends maternal/ familial love to all people of the earth. She implores all of us to "speak proudly to [our] children / Where ever [we] may find them."[69]

Perhaps more than any other poet, Lucille Clifton's poems trace the transformation in consciousness enabling black women to delight in their own physical beauty, to celebrate their skin color, their nappy hair, their sometimes ample hips. In a poem from the early 1960s,

Clifton glances backward to an earlier, more repressive time and re-members "The Way It Was" to be "a nice girl / not touching / trying to be white."[70] But in Clifton's recent award-winning volume of poems *Two Headed Woman*, she describes not only a change in her own indi-vidual consciousness but a shift which has taken place among black women in general. In "homage to my hips," Clifton sings of her big hips that "Have never been enslaved / . . . that go where they want to go / and . . . do what they want to do."

> these hips are mighty hips.
> these hips are magic hips.
> i have known them
> to put a spell on a man and
> spin him like a top![71]

In "homage to my hair," Clifton celebrates the nappiness of her hair as a source of erotic pleasure both for herself and for black men:

> when i feel her jump up and dance
> i hear the music! my God
> i'm talking about my nappy hair!
> she is a challenge to your hand
> Black man
> she is as tasty on your tongue as good greens.[72]

This poem also reverses the conventional association of aging and asexuality for women. Instead, Clifton suggests that as black women become older, the essence of their racial consciousness increasingly shines through their bodies as well as their spirits. The final lines of "homage to my hair" conclude:

> the grayer she do get, good God,
> the Blacker she do be![73]

Finally, in "what the mirror said," Clifton carries the theme of self-affirmation a step farther. While both "homage to my hips" and "homage to my hair" pivot to some extent on black male recognition of black female beauty, in "what the mirror said" Clifton articulates the profound sense of self-acceptance, self-esteem, and self-love that ema-nates from black women's newly evolved delight in their own physical characteristics. The poem draws a parallel between the physical terrain of the body—its "geography"—and the terrain of the psyche; knowledge and love of one leads to knowledge and love of the other.

> listen,
> you a wonder.
> you a city
> of a woman.
> you got a geography
> of your own.
> listen,
> somebody need a map
> to understand you.
> somebody need directions
> to move around you.
> listen,
> woman,
> you not a noplace
> anonymous
> girl;
> mister with his hands on you
> he got his hands on
> some
> damn
> body![74]

I Will Be Black Light as You Lie against Me: Joyous Sexuality

Poetry by women of color is rich with metaphors of sexuality, passion, and love. These poems often are rooted in the same experiences that give rise to other celebrations of tribal or revolutionary culture and affirmation. Sometimes sexual metaphors and images are used to describe feelings and encounters that belong to a wider definition of erotic than we usually employ; in other poems, sex itself is a theme for women of color as for almost all feminist poets. The fracturing and expanding of the conventional definitions of "sexual" are not surprising for a movement that has claimed, as Adrienne Rich states in "Tear Gas," that "the will to change begins in the body not in the mind / My politics is in my body."[75] Affirming one's sexuality in a culture that despises the erotic while glorifying the pornographic, as Audre Lorde and others have observed, is an unmistakably political act.[76]

Third World and white women must contend with different kinds of sexual repression. Aurora Levins Morales, a Puerto Rican and Jewish New York poet, describes one aspect of this repression in an article entitled, "'. . . And Even Fidel Can't Change That!'"

> . . . if I'm in a Latin [Salsa] scene I freeze. I can't make my hips fluid or keep my feet from tripping. It's the perversion of sexuality that frightens me. It's the way the women around me exude a sexiness that has nothing to do with the heart. Of course Latin women love as well as any other women . . . but while the chilliest Anglo-Saxon repression of sex pretends it simply doesn't exist, Latin repression says it's a filthy fact of life, use it for what it's worth . . . shake it in his face, wear it as a decoy. It's all over the floor and it's cold and savage. It's the hatred of the powerless, turned crooked.[77]

While the poems of Third World feminists (and white feminists as well) by no means conform to a single world view, they tend to depict a sexuality that reflects the capacity for joy and deep feeling. And as Audre Lorde has insisted:

> . . . once we begin to feel deeply all the aspects of our lives, we begin to demand from ourselves and from our lives' pursuits that they feel in accordance with that joy which we know ourselves to be capable of. Our erotic knowledge empowers us, becomes a lens through which we scrutinize all aspects of our existence, forcing ourselves to evaluate those aspects honestly in terms of their relative meaning within our lives. And this is a grave responsibility, projected from within each of us, not to settle for the convenient, the shoddy, the conventionally expected, nor the merely safe.[78]

Ntozake Shange's recent small press book *From okra to greens* is filled with vibrant expressions of sexuality, often playful but also acknowledging to the lover feelings so profound that there isn't a language "big enough / to say your name."[79] In "okra to greens / an aside on amsterdam avenue," the speaker literally transforms her lover into that heart-dish of black culture—mustard greens and collard greens—

and delightedly admits to having a "greens overdose."[80] These lines are a sensual delight and a poetic delight, like the joyous eroticism of Nikki Giovanni's "Beautiful Black Men" in their "fire red, lime green, burnt orange / royal blue tight pants that hug / what I like to hug."[81] But when examined contextually, they are all the more moving. For as June Jordan has noted, "affirmation of Black values and lifestyle within the American context is, indeed, an act of protest."[82]

The poet Ai insists, "I do not write about race, social comment, etc., but about people, life, suffering, and am now trying to bring about the transfiguration of men and women in my poetry."[83] In "Before You Leave," Ai assumes the persona of a woman who is powerfully strong, not traditionally "feminine":

> I set the bowl of raw vegetables on
>   the table.
> You know I am ripe now.
> You can bite me, I won't bleed;
> just take off my kimono. Eat, then go
>   ahead, run.
> I won't miss you, but this one hour
> lift me by the buttocks
> and press me hard against your belly.
> Fill my tunnel with the howl
> you keep zipped in your pants
> and when it's over, don't worry, I'll
>   stand.
> I'm a mare. Every nail's head
>   in my hooves wears your face,
> but not even you, wolf, can bring me
>   down.[84]

And in "Twenty Year Marriage" she takes the persona of a woman who compares her own body to a pickup truck and huskily informs her husband that he should "hurry" because she has "nothing on under [her] skirt":

> . . . get inside me, start the engine;
> you'll have the strength, the will to move.
> I'll push, you push, we'll tear each other in half.
> Come on, baby, lay me down on my back.
> Pretend you don't owe me a thing

and maybe we'll roll out of here,
leaving the past stacked up behind us;
old newspapers nobody's ever got to read again. [85]

In this poem, sex becomes a passport for these two lovers to take leave of the past and make a fresh start together.

The determination to direct her own erotic energy also motivates the speaker in Asian American poet Cyn Zarco's "Saxophonetyx." Jubilantly acknowledging her erotic attraction toward a saxophone player, she nevertheless is determined not to be victimized by her own desire. Warned not to fall in love with musicians because they "take love / don't give love / 'cause they're saving it for the music," she envisions a surreal and fantastic solution to the problem at hand. To transform the saxophonist into a lover who can give love as well as receive it, she transforms herself—literally—into the music he's "savin it for":

. . . when I slowly closed my eyes
I saw his fingers wrap around my waist
my spine turn into saxophone keys
my mouth become his mouthpiece
and there was nothing left in the room
but mercy. [86]

Transformation, fantasy, and dream-vision are also crucial to Native American poet Linda Hogan's "Wall Songs," a poem of astonishingly lovely lyricism and enormous shamanistic power. The speaker in the poem names that fragile covering of the body, her skin, as "the real life / of love and sorrow," thus affirming sexuality and the physical apprehension of a beloved as crucial to the deepest levels of emotional understanding. The walls here are material and actual: roads which separate jungles, wire fences, ledges "embedded with green / and broken glass." In the face of the things which divide us (race, class, and sexual preference), in the face of danger and violence, "the singing of machetes," the speaker utters a prayer for healing, for the dissolution of boundaries—geographical, physical, and those of the heart. A priestess, a shaman, she claims the terrain of the body and the cartography of compassion, friendship, sexuality, and love as a force to transform divisions into bridges, to create a community, a world at peace:

. . . Sometimes a lover
and I turn our flesh to bridges

and the air between us disappears
like in the jungle
where I am from.
Tropical vines grow together, lovers,
over roadways men have slashed,
surviving
the sounds of those lost inside
and the singing of machetes.

May all walls be like those of the jungle,
filled with animals
singing into the ears of night.
Let them be
made of the mysteries further in
in the heart, joined with the lives of all,
all bridges of flesh,
all singing,
all covering the wounded land
showing again, again
that boundaries are all lies. [87]

The valuing of self as well as the refusal to be categorized by the tenets of traditional romantic love often characterize lesbian poetry by women of color. Some of the most extraordinary love poems by feminists of color celebrate love between women. Sometimes this love is explicitly sexual. But just as often it is embedded in what Mary Daly has called "radical female friendship."[88] These multiple meanings and expressions of love are mutually inclusive and perhaps equally valued. They testify to the richness of intimacy and affection which has surfaced from feminism for Third World and white women alike.

June Jordan's poetry reveals her belief that love is the central emotional force in her life and work. In a recent essay "Where Is the Love?" Jordan defines her life commitment to ending "those tyrannies, those corrosions of sacred possibility [of human love]."[89] In the title poem of *Things That I Do in the Dark*, Jordan explains her poems' urgency in lines which evoke the power of desire:

These poems
they are things that I do
in the dark
reaching for you

> whoever you are
> and
> are you ready?[90]

Sexuality is not separate here from the passionate impulse that infuses her poems, the impulse to discover, in all of their complexities, both self and other, "whoever you are / whoever I may become."[91]

Paula Gunn Allen writes of a spiritual and psychic geography embedded in the New Mexico skies and the deserts of Cubero and Albuquerque. Her poems are sinewy and delicate, a poetry of the lacunae and mergings of double consciousness. Allen's love poems to women smell of persimmon, sweet orange, shiny pears, bitter seeds, but most of all they evoke rain, renewal, an end to spirit thirst.

Political as well as spiritual vision empowers the love poetry of lesbians of color. As black lesbian poet Cheryl Clarke suggests in "Lesbianism: An Act of Resistance":

> . . . If radical lesbian-feminism purports an anti-racist, anti-classist, anti-women-hating vision of bonding as mutual, reciprocal, as infinitely negotiable, as freedom from antiquated gender prescriptions and proscriptions, *then all people struggling to transform the character of relationships in this culture have something to learn from lesbians.* . . . The lesbian has decolonized her body. She has rejected a life of servitude implicit in Western, heterosexual relationships and has accepted the potential of mutuality in a lesbian relationship. . .[92]

Clarke's poem "Of Althea and Flaxie" celebrates a nearly thirty-year-long span in the life of a lesbian couple and suggests the way in which women's erotic autonomy empowered their ability to claim other forms of autonomy: of dress and work as well as of resistance to the established codes of such institutions as welfare, jail, even funeral homes. Part of the power of the poem is that it dares to celebrate an explicitly butch-femme relationship, but not the stereotypical one. Althea, "very dark / very butch," is a welder who wears suits and ties, but she also "love[s] to cook, sew, and drive a car."[93] Her lover, Flaxie, may wear tight dresses and high heels, but she also "love[s] to shoot, fish, [and] play poker"—not exactly the sort of hobbies usually ascribed to femme women.

> Althea was set up and went to jail
> for writing numbers in 1958.

> Flaxie visited her every week with gifts
> and hungered openly for her thru the bars
> and did not give a damn who knew she waited for a woman.
>
> When her mother died in 1965 in New Orleans
> Flaxie demanded that Althea walk beside her in the funeral
>   procession
> and did not care how many aunts and uncles knew she slept
>   with a woman.
>
> When she died in 1970
> Flaxie fought Althea's proper family not to have her laid out in
>   lace
> and dressed the body herself
> and did not care who knew she'd made her way with a
>   woman. [94]

The poem is one of the few examples in feminist writing that brings to the poetry a radical feminist analysis of butch-femme relationships, an analysis first begun in print by Joan Nestle, who a year prior to the publication of Clarke's poem wrote an essay called "Butch-Fem Relationships: Sexual Courage in the 1950's," in which she declared:

> Butch-fem relationships, as I experienced them, were complex
> erotic statements, not phony heterosexual replicas. They were
> filled with a deeply Lesbian language of stance, dress, gesture,
> loving, courage, and autonomy. [95]

Refusing the split between personal and political, refusing romance, which, as Judy Grahn has stated, "is so much / easier and so much less / than any of us deserve," Audre Lorde's love poems also insist on the primacy of self-empowering. [96] In "Meet," the relationship between love and power, between healing and revolution, is exquisitely revealed. "Meet" is a vow from one lover to another:

> Woman when we met on the solstice
> high over halfway between your world and mine
> rimmed with full moon and no more excuses
> your red hair burned my fingers as I spread you
> tasting your ruff down to sweetness
>
> . . . .
>
> I will be black light as you lie against me
> I will be heavy as August over your hair
> our rivers flow from the same sea

and I promise to leave you again
full of amazement and our illuminations

.   .   .   .

you will be white fury in my navel
I will be sweeping night
Mawulisa foretells our bodies
as our hands touch and learn
from each others hurt.

.   .   .   .

now you are my child and my mother
we have always been sisters in pain.

Come in the curve of the lion's bulging stomach
lie for a season out of the judging rain . . . [97]

These lovers are priestesses on the solstice night; they draw a ritual circle in which the changing season is celebrated. But their lovemaking is also an act of healing, a place where black and white women meet.

The title of the poem, "Meet," has several meanings, each of which is important here. A meet can be a contest, a challenge, and so the women challenge each other ("no more excuses") to their fullest power. To meet also means to face without avoidance as well as to be united, to concur. "Meet" can also mean proper—Lorde here claims that nothing in their loving is wrong. And finally, of course, "meet" is a verb, meaning to come together, to greet. In this final sense there is a deep, powerful, and proper meeting between the two women.

"Meet" also draws power from the tension produced by ambiguous line breaks, which permit the poem to reveal its meanings slowly. The conventional ideology of romance promotes the fear of abandonment by one's lover. When Lorde endstops a line "I promise to leave you again," she fills the poem with a subtle tension until we read the next line, "full of amazement and our illuminations." The pause between these two lines also encourages the reader to consider what it would be like for lovers to promise one another leavetakings, separations, and independence.

In the line "I will be black light as you lie against me," Lorde's body is a metaphor for beauty, blackness, and luminescence, all qualities engendered by the juxtaposition of these two psyches, two bodies, touching, adjacent. However, the word "you" can also refer to the world at large, not just a single lover. In this second reading, the world is filled with ignorance and cruelty as well as love, and the verb "to lie" means to utter a falsehood, not the resting of one body against another. The poet vows to resist the lies uttered against loving and the censure and denial of lesbian relationships: she will be transformed into oxymoronic black light, incadescent darkness.

This poem can be read at yet another level, which emphasizes the intertwining of sexuality with other aspects of female power. As critic Harriet Desmoines suggests, Lorde ". . . envision[s] the tentative beginnings of a common language between black women and white women, according to the prophecies of the Dahomeyan mother of the Vodu, 'high over halfway between your world and mine / rimmed with full moon and no more excuses. . .'"[98] Lorde borrows from the legend of Mawulisa as a prophecy for the possibility of the deepest healing between "black light" and "white fury," a healing in which "hands touch and learn / from each others hurt."[99] This is the revolutionary vision of love between women that Lorde offers in "Meet." It is a vision of integrity and certitude. The deepest meanings of power and empowerment have been restored to the readers of this fierce, astonishing poem which both questions and embraces the meanings of power.

Remember the Sky that You Were Born Under: African and Native American Memory, History, and Myth

History, myth, and legend, as well as individual and collective memory, infuse the present in the poetry of many women of color; metaphors of transcendence and community in the poetry of Third World women span continents as well as time frames. Although some black poets (like Nikki Giovanni, for example, in "They Clapped") have claimed that American blacks have romanticized Africa and their relationship to it, both ancient and present-day Africa remain crucial sources for poets like Donna Allegra, whose powerful identification with African culture gives rise to poems like "When People Ask":

> When people ask who you are
>
> . . . .
>
> Say that you are Africa
> who birthed the rainbow children

and that they who ask must also remember
the house of sisters

Africa—a spirit risen
not from the dead
but a life run underground
now swelling to the surface
in your children's dreams now awakened
Say that you are Africa come calling
Say it until the children of every house
can give the same answer
Say it so that there's never again
the question denying
Who you are
Say: You are Africa.[100]

The poem is an incantation and a vow; its cadence sweeps over the reader like the rising crescendo of voices calling out "Amen! Tell it brother," in a black Baptist church service, or the distant drumbeats heard above the African plains. Africa provides identity, affirmation, pride.

Perhaps more than any other contemporary Afro-American woman poet, Audre Lorde has unearthed in African myth and culture images which provide for what Harriet Desmoines has called "the recovery of essential knowledge."[101] In a review of *The Black Unicorn*, Desmoines observes that

[Lorde] reaches back across an ocean and centuries of atrocity to the country of the Dahomeyan Amazons, a homeland rife with imagery, with magic, with legend, with female Power. . .

The Black Unicorn connects black women with each other through the common imagery of their finest past, the Dahomeyan Amazons, witches, warrior queens of the southern continent, the first home of human culture.[102]

In "125th Street and Abomey," Lorde draws from the myth of Seboulisa, the "mother goddess with one breast," the strength to face the aftermath of a mastectomy as an Amazon warrior. In the final lines of the poem, Lorde entreats Seboulisa, the Abomeyan creator of the world, to gaze upon her own spirited courage as a tribute to the ancient myths. As the poet is a daughter to the old legends, so she will become mother to the new.

see me now
your severed daughter
laughing our name into echo
all the world shall remember.[103]

Lorde again uses a powerful double entendre: your *severed* daughter as
the one separated from you but now returning home; and your daughter with the severed-off breast, like you physically, the same. She thus
highlights this double experience of simultaneous belonging and ex-
patriation, of difference and identification.

Lorde is a contemporary feminist speaking an American diction that
draws from linguistic sources and images that are more often white and
urban than black. But she is also an African whose sources are ancient,
female, and black. The poet describes her alliances to cultures separated by time and geography as ammunition for impending battle:

Bearing two drums on my head I speak
whatever language is needed
to sharpen the knives of my tongue.[104]

And in "A Woman Speaks," another poem from *The Black Unicorn*,
Lorde again asserts her geographic and transtemporal bonds:

I do not dwell
within my birth nor my divinities
who am ageless and half-grown
and still seeking
my sisters
witches in Dahomey.[105]

For Lorde, ancient Africa is reality as well as metaphor. Like a
shaman or a witch, she travels between the worlds, visiting past lives
for the knowledge they contain. In "Harriet," she returns to a childhood friendship, one embedded in an ancient past and a tribal past
before the pain of slavery taught black women to keep their distance,
even from one another.

I remember you Harriet
before we were broken apart
we dreamed the crossed swords
of warrior queens
while we avoided each other's eyes

and we learned to know lonely
as the earth learns to know dead
Harriet Harriet
what name shall we call our selves now
our mother is gone?[106]

In her poem "For James Baldwin," white poet Kay Boyle describes how the knowledge of African culture and history has transformed and revolutionized the lives of black Americans:

> . . . Young blacks saw Africa emerging
> And knew for the first time, you said,
> That they were related to kings and
> To princes. It could be seen
> In the way they walked, tall as cypresses,
> Strong as bridges across the thundering falls.[107]

In a similar vision of power and certitude, Mari Evans names herself the towering cypress tree in "I Am a Black Woman":

> I
> am a black woman
> tall as a cypress
> strong
> beyond all definition still
> defying place
> and time
> and circumstance
>   assailed
>   impervious
>   indestructible
> Look
>   on me and be
> renewed[108]

The "I" here stands alone and "tallest" in the poem, itself like a cypress tree in a concrete way.

In an untitled poem by Thulani Davis, first published more than a decade ago in *Third World Women*, the poet embraces her African heritage and telescopes the space and time between herself and her African parents:

I am Brown
I am a child of the third world
  my hair black n long
    my soul slavetraded n nappy
yellow brown-Safronia
in this world, illegitimate seed
mishap of the honkies goodtimes
but I recall the past
I remember the sea n my real home
my mother, a queen from the upper Nile
my father, a Congo boatman
I am Zulu
Xhosa / Masai
many rivers flow into my waters
I am from ages ago. [109]

In "Vive Noir," a joyous, defiant celebration of blackness, Mari Evans transforms herself into an Amazon who "turn[s] rivers / from their courses" and "level[s] mountains / at a word."[110]

Such poems are the bridges between contemporary black women and their powerful foremothers like the Queen of Sheba and Nefertiti. This heritage is particularly meaningful for black woman poets because it confers the sense of individual power and tribal authority which women held in ancient Africa. As the historian John Henrik Clarke has described the status of the Amazons of Dahomey and other African women:

> In ancient Afrika . . . [the African woman] often ruled society
> with unquestioning power. Many Afrikan women were great
> militarists, and on occasion led their armies into battle. The
> Afrikan had produced a civilization where men were secure
> enough to let women advance. . . [111]

The 1920s, too, provided an important source of empowering imagery for black women's poetry, primarily in the vital Afro-American blues tradition. Taking the blues somewhat at face value, that is, as an emblem of the grief and suffering of black people's lives and especially of black women's lives, poet Sonia Sanchez, in "For Our Lady," feistily announces to famed blues singer Billie Holiday that black women are refusing to hold onto sorrow any longer—there is a revolution to attend to!

no mo.
            blues/trains running on this track
                they all been de/railed.

am I blue?
        . . . no. i'm blk
                and ready.[112]

But the traditional blues song, of course, is a far more complex
evocation of pain than Sanchez implies. It was—and is—an expression of self-love and anger, of defiance (Ma Rainey's "Bo-Weevil
Blues" and "Prove It on Me Blues," for example) as well as an act of
self-solacing, the transformation of loneliness and vulnerability
through acknowledging, even itemizing one's troubles (Ma Rainey's
"Counting the Blues").[113] Sherley Anne Williams' Bessie Smith
poems address the importance of the blues for encouraging black
women not to be victims. In "I Want Aretha to Set This to Music,"
Williams implies that pain is not "the sum of all of [Bessie's] knowing":

            . . . I'll
        make book Bessie did
        more than just endure.[114]

She calls the misconception that "the blues ain't nothin / but some
man on yo mind" a version only of "young woman Blues."[115] Williams' Bessie acknowledges and celebrates erotic joy ("it wouldn't be
blues if I didn't trance / mens to my side"), but she also uses the blues
to repudiate male violence, insisting that black women have no reason
to tolerate being battered: "Don' no man jes beat on / me . . . / don'
care who / right who wrong that's the time / he stop bein my man."[116]

Like ancient Africa and the Afro-American blues tradition for Afro-
Americans, earlier historical periods of Native American culture provide images of vision and power for many American Indian writers.
Poetry, like prayers, chants, the telling of dreams, folktales, tribal lore,
or oral history, is an essential part of the spiritual and aesthetic survival
of American Indian people. In a culture whose people are disappearing, art and survival are not mutually exclusive, for language is a way
to pass on tradition, history, tribal memory, literally a way to insure the
survival of the culture. For this reason, American Indian poetry often
takes on a quality of urgency. In an oral tradition, language is both
revered and woven into the fabric of everyday life. Like myth or

folklore, legend or dream, poetry makes the unknowable intelligible. In Native American poetry, as in all these language art forms, access is provided to the mysterious and creative powers of the universe and thus to one's own inner power.

For Native American women poets, history also provides a source of female-based power, a psychological return to a period in their native culture in which women were often respected and revered. As Dexter Fisher has noted:

> The respect accorded women in the Creation Myths has been reflected historically in the position of women within tribal societies. Many tribes are matrilineal, passing both clan names and ownership of property through the female line. Navajos honor women in the construction of their traditional home, the hogan, which is built on four poles representing the four directions. Each pole is named after a female deity, so that the support of the home literally depends on the female. Before reservation life considerably changed traditional roles, women often held positions of importance in tribal government.[117]

Grandmother Spider is one such emblem of female power. Paula Gunn Allen's "Affirmation" is a prayer and acknowledgment to Creator-Figure Grandmother Spider, whose unseen gifts reside within the poet, and whose wisdom makes possible the poet's own. Through access to Grandmother Spider's tribal memory, the poet gathers essential knowledge, learns that

> small things count after all:
> each leaf a tale
> each journey retracing some ancient myth . . .
> the power of spider thoughts
> so small
> mount, thread by thread.[118]

Similarly, in "Skeleton of Winter," Joy Harjo responds as shaman to a season of barrenness, forgotten dreams, a time "almost too dark / for vision."[119] Through the transformational power of "Memory / the other-sight," a memory tribal as well as individual, a sensory and verbal knowledge, mythic as well as historic, both the poet's and the earth's power are returned to them. The poet insists on the possibility of memory as it is transfigured in language to give birth to life, to enable those who apprehend it to become one with the earth:

I am memory alive
                    not just a name
but an intricate part
of this web of motion,
meaning: earth, sky, stars circling
my heart

            centrifugal. [120]

This sequence of memory to language to connection with the natural world is not fixed but circular. In Linda Hogan's "Potatoes," nature is the catalyst to memory; in digging for potatoes, the poet and her daughter reconnect with their reverence for the earth and thus with their tribal culture, which instills in them that reverence:

In one day of digging the earth
there is communion
of things we remember
and forget.
We taste starch
turn to sugar in our mouths. [121]

Like Charlotte De Clue's "To the Spirit of Monahsetah," in which the poet repeats as shamanic prescription the refrain "touch earth" after each listing of possible spiritual or geographic displacement, or Celie's observation of the oneness of the human and natural worlds in *The Color Purple* (". . . that feeling of being part of everything, not separate at all. I knew that if I cut a tree, my arm would bleed"), Linda Hogan depicts a world in which "even the trees with their rings / have kept track / of the crimes that live within / and against us," and oceans are "tongues of water / . . . sing[ing] the earth open." [122] Hogan's "To Light" celebrates the reclaiming of spirit-based memory and affinity with the natural world as necessary and essential components not only of Native American culture but of human speech, of poetry, of life:

noisy tongues that once were silenced,
all the oceans we contain
coming to light. [123]

Joy Harjo's "Remember," like Linda Hogan's "To Light," insists on the importance not only of memory and affinity with the natural world but of language as one crucial way in which memory is continued, carried on. The poem is an incantation whose cadence is startlingly similar to Donna Allegra's "When People Ask." In Allegra's poem, Africa is the source of a people's identity and confirmation; in Harjo's poem, that source is the natural universe, "the star's stories," "the sun's birth at dawn," "the earth whose skin you are."[124] These memories, these precious stories of the earth's life, will be lost if they are not remembered through language. Thus, the poet prays that the reader will

> Remember that all is in motion, is growing, is you.
> Remember that language comes from this.
> Remember the dance that language is, that life is.
> Remember.[125]

The invocation to remember the stories passed on by ancestors culminates with the express admonition of the necessity of tradition for survival in Carol Lee Sanchez's "Corn Children," a poem which ends with the magical, nonlinear logic: "you must remember your ancestors so they / will remember you."[126]

In Joy Harjo's "Explosion," the imagined "violent birth of horses" becomes another kind of birth: the poet's explosion into language out of speechlessness.[127] Each has a wild, astonishing beauty to it, volcanic and galvanizing. The poet and the horses "bursting out of the crazy earth" are one, their unwillingness to be tamed, contained, hers. Their urgency, wisdom, and magic, hers as well. She sees the horses through an act of volition, a willingness to apprehend, to be alive to all that is. She knows that like the poem itself, and the vision of transformation, articulation, and power which it represents, the horses which she sees will be invisible to some. But she writes for those who, in reading her words, will be able to

> . . . see the horses with their hearts of sleeping volcanoes
> and . . . be rocked awake
> past their bodies
> to see who they have become.[128]

In another poem from *She Had Some Horses*, Harjo accesses the power of language to make sense out of an often brutally senseless world. In "Rain," a young man loses his life in a truck accident. What remains—for the poet and for the reader—is not the violence of his death but rather the poet's healing and transfiguring vision of "a light in the river / folding open and open / blood, heart and stones / shimmering like the Milky Way."[129] Through language, the scene of Bobby's death is recreated and given its meaning by the poet, not by the outside world.

Finding metaphors that reconcile spirit-based knowledge and perspectives with materialist or political ones is the task of a poet who stands at the center of two worlds and who must unify diverse and conflicting experience, a frequent theme of Paula Gunn Allen's work. Allen writes of the necessity for other reconciliations as well: ceremonial with industrial understandings, psychological with mechanical time, individual with group-shared understandings of public and private events. In her poem "The Blessing," individual memory becomes communal and provides access to shared experiences, perceptions, and understandings, to an ancestral past, to the world of tribal meanings. Memory restores us to ourselves, transforms the present material world to one far more expansive and empowered:

> The circles, however large their arcs,
> close at last,
> reminding us of what we've seen
> and why we come round again.
> And so memory, that
> undying arabesque,
> that blue and silver air of being
> we helpless ride
> forever circles the eternal pueblos
> of our lives, restores the ruined
> and faded kivas of our dreams.[130]

Wendy Rose, Paula Gunn Allen, Leslie Silko, Carol Lee Sanchez, Linda Hogan, and others have referred in their poems to the healing power of ritual, the transformative power of Native American shamanism for its poets. The poet and the Native American storyteller also perform similar roles within the culture: both relate the wisdom of the tribe and are part medicine-woman and part priestess. Harriet Desmoines describes the basis of Native American religion as a poet's vision, as a

> . . . spirit quest, which is essentially a search for balance, a
> dangerous journey undertaken alone, but with the blessings of

the tribe, toward wholeness, toward the moment when inner
and outer forces merge . . . the Native American healer-singer-
poet could draw on hundreds of years of unbroken tradition to
effect her cures. She was a woman equipped to deal with her
fate and the fate of those she cared for. [131]

In a poem of profound beauty, Wendy Rose's "Walking on the
Prayerstick" celebrates the spirit-based lives of Indian people, the
power of tradition and memory, the transformation of pain into song,
song into joy, self-love into radical healing:

When we go to the fields
we always sing; we walk
each of us at different times
on the world held
like a feathered and fetished prayerstick.
We map our lives this way: trace our lineage
by the corn, find our words in the flute,
touch the shapes that feed us with dry seed.
We grow as shrines grow from human belief;
we sing a penetration through our pottery bodies.
Nothing is old
about us yet;
we are
still waiting.

Imagine you float
to those white scar marks
on the granite where water
drains breaking open the rocks
below, turning to ice
and raining on in.
This is where
we first learned to sing
on ancient mornings
because our skin was
red sand, because our eyes
floated in flashflood water,
because our pain was made
of burdens bound in cornhusk,
because our joy flowed
over the land,

> because touching ourselves
> we touched everything.[132]

Linda Hogan reveals a similar legacy of strength, a similar commitment to the future, in "Watch Me," a transcendentally beautiful litany
to survival and joy. The speaker, whose "heart never believed / the end
of anything," summons the majesty of her own indomitable and compassionate spirit to offer words that are both a vow and a prayer.[133] For
all the women of her mother's generation and of her own whose lives
have been bent by sorrow, whose bones have been too burdened to
dance, Hogan promises to "dance the story of life . . . / [of] all our
lives."

In a voice both individual and collective, she speaks for the transformational, tenacious, and empowered vision of all the poets whose
work is discussed here when she announces to the reader, and to the
world:

> I am done with weeping.
> The bones of this body say, dance.[134]

Notes

1. Margaret Atwood, *Survival: A Thematic Guide to Canadian Literature* (Toron-
to: Anansi, 1972); Barbara Charlesworth Gelpi, "A Common Language: The
American Woman Poet," in *Shakespeare's Sisters: Feminist Essays on Women
Poets*, ed. Sandra M. Gilbert and Susan Gubar (Bloomington: Indiana University Press, 1979), pp. 269–279. See also these lines from Robin Morgan's "Mon-
ster" (New York: Vintage/Random House, 1972), pp. 81–86:

   > No colonized people so isolated one from the other
   > for so long as women.
   > None cramped with compassion for the oppressor
   > who breathes on the next pillow each night.
   > No people so old, who, having, we now discover, invented
   > agriculture, weaving, pottery, language, cooking
   > with fire, and healing medicine, must now invent a revolution
   > so total as to destroy maleness, femaleness, death.

2. June Jordan, "Poem about Police Violence," in *Passion: New Poems 1977–1980*
(Boston: Beacon Press, 1980), pp. 34–35.
3. Safiya Henderson, "harlem/soweto," in *Confirmation: An Anthology of African*

American Women, ed. Amiri Baraka (Le Roi Jones) and Amina Baraka (New York: Quill, 1983), pp. 134–135.

4. Audre Lorde, "Power," in *The Black Unicorn* (New York: W. W. Norton, 1978), pp. 108–109.

5. Audre Lorde, "Uses of the Erotic: The Erotic as Power," in *Chrysalis* 9 (Fall 1979): 29–31.

6. Audre Lorde, "For Each of You," in *From a Land Where Other People Live* (Detroit: Broadside Press, 1973), pp. 7–8.

7. Gwendolyn Brooks, "The Boy Died in My Alley," in *To Disembark* (Chicago: Third World Press, 1981), pp. 49–53.

8. Lucille Clifton, "Miss Rosie," in *Good Times* (New York: Random House, 1969), p. 5.

9. Chinosole, "Audre Lorde and Matrilineal Diaspora: Moving History beyond Nightmare into Structures for the Future," unpublished paper, part of a forthcoming Ph.D. dissertation, the University of Oregon, 1986, p. 1.

10. Lucille Clifton, "For de Lawd," in *Good Times* (New York: Vintage Books, 1970), p. 18.

11. Joy Harjo, "Anchorage," in *She Had Some Horses* (New York: Thunder's Mouth Press, 1983), pp. 14–15.

12. Ibid.

13. Audre Lorde, "A Litany for Survival," in *The Black Unicorn* (New York: W. W. Norton and Co., 1978), pp. 31–32.

14. Ntozake Shange, "with no immediate cause," *Nappy Edges* (New York: St. Martin's Press, 1978), pp. 114–117.

15. Audre Lorde, "Feminism and Black Liberation: The Great American Disease," in *The Black Scholar* 10, no. 8/9 (May/June 1979): 17–18. See also her article "Scratching the Surface: Some Notes on Barriers to Women and Loving," in *The Black Scholar* 9, no. 7 (April 1978): 31–35: "Black women and black men who recognize that the development of their particular strengths and interests does not diminish the other, do not diffuse their energies fighting for control over each other. We focus our attentions against the real economic, political and social forces at the heart of this society which are ripping ourselves and our children and our worlds apart."

16. Barbara Smith, "Notes for Yet Another Paper on Black Feminism, or Will the Real Enemy Please Stand Up?" *Conditions: Five* (The Black Women's Issue, ed. Lorraine Bethel and Barbara Smith) 2, no. 2 (Autumn 1979): 124.

17. Paula Gunn Allen, "Riding the Thunder," in *Shadow Country* (Los Angeles: American Indian Studies Center, UCLA, 1982), pp. 31–33.

18. Terri Meyette, "Celebration 1982," in *A Gathering of Spirit*, ed. Beth Brant (North American Indian Women's Issue of *Sinister Wisdom*), nos. 22–23 (1983): 50.

19. Lydia Yellowbird, untitled poem, in *The Third Woman: Minority Women Writers of the United States*, ed. Dexter Fisher (Boston: Houghton Mifflin, 1980), p. 15.

20. Carolyn Merchant, *The Death of Nature: Women, Ecology, and the Scientific Revolution* (San Francisco: Harper and Row, 1980), p. 28.
21. Wendy Rose, "Long Division: A Tribal History," in *Lost Copper* (Banning, Calif.: Malki Museum Press, 1980), p. 10.
22. Ibid.
23. Wendy Rose, "I expected my skin and my blood to ripen," in *Lost Copper*, pp. 14–15.
24. Brant, *A Gathering of Spirit*, p. 95.
25. Chrystos, "I Walk in the History of My People," in *This Bridge Called My Back: Writings by Radical Women of Color*, ed. Cherríe Moraga and Gloria Anzaldúa (Watertown, Mass.: Persephone Press, 1981), p. 57.
26. Cherríe Moraga, "The Welder," in *This Bridge Called My Back*, pp. 219–220.
27. Ibid.
28. Ibid.
29. Audre Lorde, *Between Our Selves* (Point Reyes: Eidolon Editions, 1976). Also in *The Black Unicorn*, pp. 112–114.
30. Audre Lorde, "Outside," in *Between Our Selves*, pp. 18–20. The poem is reprinted in *The Black Unicorn*, pp. 61–62.
31. Wendy Rose, "Epilog," in *Lost Copper*, p. 129. While many Third World feminists write about themselves as powerful women, there are real obstacles and contradictions implicit in moving past romanticized stereotypes of Third World women's strength. Gloria Anzaldúa discusses this issue in an autobiographical essay entitled "La Prieta," in *This Bridge Called My Back*, p. 204:

> I am always surprised by the image that my white and non-Chicano friends have of me, surprised at how much they *do not* know me, at how I do not allow them to know me. They have substituted the negative picture the white culture has painted of my race with a highly romanticized, idealized image. "You're strong," my friends said, "a mountain of strength."
> Though the power may be real, the mythic qualities attached to it keep others from dealing with me as a person and rob me of my being able to act out my other selves. Having this "power" doesn't exempt me from being prey in the streets nor does it make my scrambling to survive, to feed myself, easier. To cope with hurt and control my fears, I grew a thick skin. Oh, the many names of power—pride, arrogance, control. I am not the frozen snow queen but a flesh and blood woman with perhaps too loving a heart, one easily hurt.
> *I'm not invincible, I tell you. My skin's as fragile as a baby's. I'm brittle bones and human, I tell you. I'm a broken arm.*
> *You're a razor's edge, you tell me. Shock them shitless. Be the holocaust. Be the black Kali. Spit in their eye and never cry. Oh broken angel, throw away your cast, mend your wing. Be not a rock but a razor's edge and burn with falling.*

32. Alice Walker, in *The Monthly* (Berkeley), July 1980, p. 43. Delivered to the

testimonial dinner to honor Rosa Parks, Septima Clark, and the Highlander School on May 1, 1980.

33. Jordan, *Passion*, p. xxiv.
34. Alice Walker, "In Search of Our Mothers' Gardens," in *In Search of Our Mothers' Gardens* (New York: Harcourt, Brace, Jovanovich, 1983), p. 234.
35. Alice Walker, *Meridian* (New York: Washington Square Press, 1977), p. 44.
36. Sherley Anne Williams (Shirley Williams), "I Sing This Song for Our Mothers," in *The Peacock Poems* (Middletown, Conn.: Wesleyan University Press, 1975), pp. 79–83.
37. Ibid.
38. Zora Neale Hurston was the first American novelist, black or white, to write an entire novel in black folk idiom and to do so without caricaturing, condescending, or apologizing for it. Hurston's impact on black language can be seen in a poet like June Jordan, who in *Civil Wars* makes an impassioned and eloquent plea for the survival of black English as a cultural and poetic necessity:

> . . . A young friend of mine went through some scarifying times, leaving her homeless. During this period of intense, relentless dread and abuse, she wrote poems, trying to cope. Here are two lines from her poetry: "What have life meaned to me" and, "You are forgotten you use to existed." There are no adequate, standard English translations possible for either expression of her spirit. They are intrinsically black language cries of extreme pain so telling that even the possibilities of meaning and existence have been formulated in a past tense that is empathic, severe. I deeply hope that more of us will want to learn and protect black language. If we lose our fluency in our language, we may irreversibly forsake elements of the spirit that have provided for our survival.

(June Jordan, "White English/Black English: The Politics of Translation," in *Civil Wars* [Boston: Beacon Press, 1981], pp. 72–73). For a fuller discussion of slave narrative as a genre, see Frances Smith Foster, *Witnessing Slavery: The Development of Antebellum Slave Narratives* (Westport, Conn.: Greenwood Press, 1980), p. 122. Darwin T. Turner, in *The Art of Slave Narrative* (Western Illinois University, 1982, p. 134) makes a similar claim for the structural relationship between slave narrative and more contemporary Afro-American work. For a fuller discussion of *Their Eyes Were Watching God* and the use of slave narrative as sources for Sherley Anne Williams, see Lynda Koolish, "Freedom, Selfhood and Language: The Slave Narrative in the Work of Zora Neale Hurston, Alice Walker and Sherley Anne Williams," a paper presented to the Afro-American Literature section of the Philological Association of the Pacific Coast, Santa Cruz, California, November 1985.

39. Sherley Anne Williams, untitled poem, dated February 7, 1868, in "Letters from a New England Negro" section of *Some One Sweet Angel Chile*, p. 32.
40. Ibid. (dated December 15, 1867), p. 25.

41. Sherley Anne Williams, "fragments," in *Some One Sweet Angel Chile*, p. 63.
42. Sherley Anne Williams, "WITNESS," in *Some One Sweet Angel Chile*, p. 69.
43. Kathy Elaine Anderson, "Keep a Weathered Eye Lifting," in *Sunbury* 10 (1981): 53–54.
44. Mari Evans, "The 7:25 Trolley," in *Sturdy Black Bridges: Visions of Black Women in Literature*, ed. Roseann P. Bell, Bettye J. Parker, and Beverly Guy-Sheftall (New York: Doubleday/Anchor, 1979), p. 338.
45. In *The Third Woman*, p. 439.
46. Diana Chang, "Allegory," in *The Third Woman*, p. 430.
47. Nellie Wong, "How a Girl Got Her Chinese Name," in *Dreams in Harrison Railroad Park* (Berkeley, Calif.: Kelsey St. Press, 1977), pp. 8–9.
48. Tina Koyama, "Next," in *Breaking Silence: An Anthology of Contemporary Asian-American Poetry*, ed. Joseph Bruchac (Greenfield Center, N.Y.: Greenfield Review Press, 1983), p. 119.
49. Fay Chiang, *In the City of Contradictions* (New York: Sunbury Press, 1979), p. vi.
50. Audre Lorde, "Prologue," in *From a Land Where Other People Live*, pp. 43–46.
51. Audre Lorde, "Pathways: From Mother to Mother," in *The Black Unicorn*, pp. 71–72.
52. Audre Lorde, "Outside" in *The Black Unicorn*, pp. 61–62. See also Nellie Wong, "When I Was Growing Up," in *This Bridge Called My Back*, pp. 7–8. Gloria Anzaldúa, "La Prieta," in *This Bridge Called My Back*, pp. 198–209.
53. Janice Mirikitani, "Lullabye," in *Third World Women* (San Francisco: Third World Communications, 1972), pp. 164–165.
54. Mary Daly, *Gyn/Ecology* (Boston: Beacon Press, 1978).
55. Cherríe Moraga, "La Güera," in *This Bridge Called My Back*, p. 31.
56. Cherríe Moraga, "For the Color of My Mother," in *This Bridge Called My Back*, pp. 12–13.
57. Aurora Levins Morales, "'. . . And Even Fidel Can't Change That!'" in *This Bridge Called My Back*, p. 53.
58. Cherríe Moraga, "For the Color of My Mother," in *This Bridge Called My Back*, pp. 12–13.
59. Ibid.
60. Wendy Rose, "Sideshow: Julia the Lion Woman/The Ugliest Woman in the World," in *A Gathering of Spirit*, pp. 88–89.
61. Sherley Anne Williams, untitled poem from "Letters from a New England Negro" section, dated November 24, 1867, in *Some One Sweet Angel Chile*, pp. 23–24.
62. Sherley Anne Williams, ". . . a rowboat out on the stormy seas . . . ," in *Some One Sweet Angel Chile*, p. 48.
63. Lucha Corpi, "Como la semilla en espera/Like the seed that waits," in *Palabras de Mediodia/Noon Words*, trans. Catherine Rodriguez-Nieto (Berkeley, Calif.: El Fuego de Aztlán Publications, 1980), pp. 2–3.
64. Chirlane McCray, "I Used to Think," in *Conditions: Five* 2, no. 2 (Autumn 1979): 29.

65. Audre Lorde, "Coal," in *Coal* (New York: W. W. Norton and Co., 1976), p. 6.
66. Audre Lorde, "Black Mother Woman," in *From a Land Where Other People Live*, p. 16.
67. Audre Lorde, "For Each of You," in *From a Land Where Other People Live*, pp. 7–8.
68. Audre Lorde, "From the House of Yemanja," in *The Black Unicorn*, pp. 6–7.
69. Audre Lorde, "For Each of You," in *From a Land Where Other People Live*, pp. 7–8.
70. Lucille Clifton, "The Way It Was," in *Good News about the Earth* (New York: Random House, 1972), p. 3.
71. Lucille Clifton, "homage to my hips," in *Two-Headed Woman* (Amherst: University of Massachusetts Press, 1980), p. 6.
72. Lucille Clifton, "homage to my hair," in *Two-Headed Woman*, p. 5.
73. Ibid.
74. Lucille Clifton, "what the mirror said," in *Two-Headed Woman*, p. 7.
75. Adrienne Rich, "Tear Gas," in *Poems Selected and New, 1950–1974* (New York: W. W. Norton, 1975), p. 140.
76. Audre Lorde, "Uses of the Erotic: The Erotic as Power," *Chrysalis* 9 (Fall 1979): 29–31. See also *Heresies: A Feminist Publication on Arts and Politics* 3, no. 4, and Laura Lederer, ed., *Take Back the Night: Women on Pornography* (New York: William Morrow, 1980) for articles on this subject.
77. Aurora Levins Morales, "'. . . And Even Fidel Can't Change That!'" in *This Bridge Called My Back*, p. 56.
78. Audre Lorde, "The Erotic as Power," *Chrysalis* 9 (Fall 1979): 30–31.
79. Ntozake Shange, "okra to greens/again! special delivery," in *From okra to greens* (St. Paul, Minn.: Coffee House Press, 1984), n.p.
80. Ntozake Shange, "okra to greens/an aside on amsterdam avenue," in *From okra to greens*, n.p.
81. Nikki Giovanni, "Beautiful Black Men," in *No More Masks! An Anthology of Poems by Women*, ed. Florence Howe and Ellen Bass (Garden City, N.Y.: Anchor/Doubleday, 1973), p. 304.
82. June Jordan, "Notes toward a Black Balancing of Love and Hatred (1974)," in *Civil Wars* (Boston: Beacon Press, 1981), p. 87.
83. Ai, quoted in *The Third Woman*, p. 543.
84. Ai, "Before You Leave," in *Cruelty* (Boston: Houghton-Mifflin, 1973), p. 45.
85. Ai, "Twenty Year Marriage," in *Cruelty*, p. 1.
86. Cyn Zarco, "Saxophonetyx," in *Breaking Silence: An Anthology of Asian-American Poetry*, p. 294.
87. Linda Hogan, "Wall Songs," in *Seeing through the Sun* (Amherst: University of Massachusetts Press, 1985), pp. 67–68.
88. Daly, *Gyn/Ecology*, p. 373.
89. June Jordan, "Where Is the Love?" in *In the Memory and Spirit of Frances, Zora, and Lorraine: Essays and Interviews on Black Women and Writing*, ed. Juliette Bowles (Washington, D.C.: Institute for the Arts and the Humanities, Howard University, 1979), p. 31.

90. June Jordan, "Things That I Do in the Dark," in *Things That I Do in the Dark* (New York: Random House, 1977), frontispoem.
91. Ibid.
92. Cheryl Clarke, "Lesbianism: An Act of Resistance," in *This Bridge Called My Back*, pp. 134, 128.
93. Cheryl Clarke, "Of Althea and Flaxie," in NARRATIVES: *Poems in the tradition of black women* (New York: Kitchen Table, Women of Color Press, 1982), pp. 15–16.
94. Ibid.
95. Joan Nestle, "Butch-Fem Relationships: Sexual Courage in the 1950's," in *Heresies* 12 (1981): 21.
96. Judy Grahn, untitled poem from the section *Confrontations with the Devil in the Form of Love*, in *The Work of a Common Woman* (Trumansburg, N.Y.: Crossing Press Feminist Series, 1980), pp. 157–158.
97. Audre Lorde, "Meet," in *The Black Unicorn*, pp. 33–34.
98. Harriet Desmoines, "Sweet Medicine: A Review of *The Black Unicorn*, by Audre Lorde," *Sinister Wisdom* 13 (Spring 1980): 60–61.
99. In "Woman," Lorde uses an equally powerful metaphor for the healing between black and white women; she dreams of a time when the "commonest rock / is moonstone and ebony opal. (*The Black Unicorn*, p. 82).
100. Donna Allegra, "When People Ask," in *Lesbian Poetry: An Anthology*, ed. Elly Bulkin and Joan Larkin (Watertown, Mass.: Persephone Press, 1981), pp. 257–259. The text of Giovanni's claim in "They Clapped" that American blacks found the freedom to be themselves when they returned to Africa only to discover that they had romanticized Africa and their relationship to it is as follows:

> . . . they shook their heads when they understood there was no
> difference between the french and the english and the
>   americans
> and the afro-americans or the tribe next door or the country
> across the border
> they were exasperated when they heard sly and the family
>   stone
> in francophone africa and they finally smiled when little
>   boys
> who spoke no western tongue said "james brown" with
>   reverence
> they brought out their cameras and bought out africa's
>   drums
> when they finally realized they are strangers all over
> and love is only and always about the lover not the beloved
> they marveled at the beauty of the people and the richness
> of the land knowing they could never possess either
>
> they clapped when they took off
> for home despite the dead
> dream they saw a free future.

(Nikki Giovanni, "They Clapped," in *My House* [New York: William Morrow, 1972], pp. 51–52).

101. Harriet Desmoines, "Sweet Medicine," *Sinister Wisdom* 13 (Spring 1980): 61.
102. Ibid.
103. Audre Lorde, "125th Street and Abomey," in *The Black Unicorn*, p. 13.
104. Audre Lorde, "Dahomey," in *The Black Unicorn*, p. 11.
105. Audre Lorde, "A Woman Speaks," in *The Black Unicorn*, p. 4.
106. Audre Lorde, "Harriet," in *The Black Unicorn*, p. 21.
107. Kay Boyle, "For James Baldwin," in *No More Masks! An Anthology of Poems by Women*, pp. 81–82.
108. Mari Evans, "I Am a Black Woman," in *I Am a Black Woman*, pp. 11–12. I am reminded of the contrast between Mari Evans' towering cypress tree and Marge Piercy's dwarfed bonsai tree in "A Work of Artifice," in *To Be of Use* (New York: Doubleday, 1973), p. 3.
109. Thulani (Nkabinde) Davis, untitled poem, in *Third World Women*, p. 50.
110. Mari Evans, "Vive Noir!" in *I Am a Black Woman*, pp. 70–73.
111. John Henrik Clarke, "The Black Woman: A Figure in World History," *Essence* (May 1971): 28. I will refrain from commenting at length here on Clarke's sexism in assuming that women only advanced because men were secure enough to *allow* them to.
112. Sonia Sanchez, "For Our Lady," in *We a BaaddDD People* (Detroit: Broadside Press, 1970), p. 41.
113. For a discussion of the blues and these lyrics in particular, see Sandra Lieb, *Mother of the Blues: A Study of Ma Rainey* (Amherst: University of Massachusetts Press, 1981).
114. Sherley Anne Williams, "I Want Aretha to Set This to Music," in *Some One Sweet Angel Chile*, p. 53.
115. Sherley Anne Williams, "the blues ain't nothin," in *Some One Sweet Angel Chile*, p. 44.
116. Sherley Anne Williams, "port arthur," in *Some One Sweet Angel Chile*, pp. 41–42.
117. Dexter Fisher, *The Third Woman*, p. 11.
118. Paula Gunn Allen, "Affirmation," in *Coyote's Daylight Trip* (Albuquerque, N.M.: La Confluencia, 1978).
119. Joy Harjo, "Skeleton of Winter," in *She Had Some Horses*, pp. 30–31.
120. Ibid.
121. Linda Hogan, "Potatoes," in *Seeing through the Sun*, p. 51.
122. Charlotte De Clue, "To the Spirit of Monahsetah," in *A Gathering of Spirit*, pp. 42–44; Alice Walker, *The Color Purple* (New York: Harcourt, Brace, Jovanovich, 1982), p. 167; Linda Hogan, "To Light," in *Seeing through the Sun*, p. 35.
123. Ibid.
124. Joy Harjo, "Remember," in *She Had Some Horses*, p. 40.
125. Ibid.
126. Carol Lee Sanchez, "Corn Children," in *excerpts from A Mountain Climber's Handbook: Selected Poems, 1971–1984* (Santa Margarita, Calif.: Taurean Horn Press/Out West Limited, 1985), pp. 58–60.

127. Joy Harjo, "Explosion," in *She Had Some Horses*, pp. 68–69.
128. Ibid.
129. Joy Harjo, "Rain," in *She Had Some Horses*, p. 17.
130. Paula Gunn Allen, "The Blessing," in *Shadow Country*, pp. 9–10.
131. Harriet Desmoines, "Sweet Medicine," *Sinister Wisdom* 13 (Spring 1980). 59.
132. Wendy Rose, "Walking on the Prayerstick," in *Lost Copper*, p. 4.
133. Linda Hogan, "Watch Me," in *Seeing through the Sun*, p. 34.
134. Ibid.

Caste, Class, and Canon

I want to consider two problems in this essay, problems
which, as I shall try to show, are closely related, although they may not
at first glimpse appear to be. One problem, as my title suggests, involves the "canon" of literature, that is, the works from the past that we
continue to read, teach, and write about. I am less concerned here
with describing the history or features of a canon or proposing alter-
natives to the canons we have inherited than in exploring some of the
factors which have continued to shape it.[1] In particular, I want to
consider how "class" and "caste," especially as they emerge in the work
of literary analysis, shape canon. Examining the relationships of class,
caste, and canon will, I believe, aid in understanding what we might
mean by "feminist criticism," the second problem I wish to address. To
frame that problem somewhat differently, how does—does?—the project of feminist criticism differ from others forms of literary analysis,
and especially the formalisms rooted in the work of the New Critics?
Can the question of the canon serve as a lens to help focus the project
of feminist criticism?

I want to begin with an experience I had at the 1980 National Wom-
en's Studies Association convention during a session on the practice of
feminist literary criticism. A group of young critics, all women, described to the audience how they met regularly at a library centrally
located in their city, how they prepared and discussed various texts,
and how they aided each other in developing their critical skills and

range. They then handed out a poem and read it aloud, each one taking one section, and began discussing it by having each member of the group present a short statement about it. Then the audience was invited to join in the discussion. It seems like a reasonable process, and I am sure that—especially for those living in relatively isolated areas— it felt like the rushing of waterfalls in the desert. But as the session wore on I found myself getting more and more restive, indeed rather irritated.

I tried to trace my growing anger. It seemed to derive from the dynamic of the panel itself; it had, I thought, to do with the *form* of criticism, almost all close analysis of text. I found myself, reluctantly, painfully, being drawn back into the tortured style of graduate school competition: "Can you top this?" As much macho as mind filled the room. Was this feminist criticism? I began to wonder: is the *form* of criticism value-free? Is critical technique simply a tool, like trigonometry? Well, is trigonometry value-free?

There was a second problem, the poem under consideration. As might be guessed, the poem was one from Adrienne Rich's *The Dream of a Common Language*. I want to be very clear about my comment here: I respect Adrienne Rich's poetry very much, and I particularly like that book. I think the poem that was under discussion quite a good poem indeed. But I remembered Deborah Hilty's questioning such a focus in a paper she prepared for a Midwest Modern Language Association conference. Why was it, she asked, that such panels always seem to take up poems by Adrienne Rich? Why not Judy Grahn or Susan Griffin? Or Vera Hall? Or Malvina Reynolds? Or Gwendolyn Brooks? Adrienne Rich, by the way, was among the first to ask precisely that question.

Those two questions—about the technique of criticism and the subject for analysis—led, in turn, to a third question: what connection existed between the selection of the poem and the kind of criticism, really the kind of response, being undertaken? Or, to put it another way, how is canon—that is, selection—related to, indeed a function of, critical technique? That is the fundamental question I want to consider here—the relationship of style in criticism to the canon of literature. But before I address that question specifically, I want simply to outline the nest of questions implicit in the central one:

—Can the canon significantly change if we retain essentially the same critical techniques and priorities?

—Where do the techniques of criticism come from? Do they fall from the sky? Or do they arise out of social practice? And if the latter, from what social practice?

—Out of what social practice, from what values, did close analysis of complex texts arise?

—Do we perpetuate those values in pursuing the critical practice derived from them?

—Does such critical practice effectively screen from our appreciation, even our scrutiny, other worlds of art?

—Are there other worlds of art out there whose nature, dynamics, values we fail to appreciate because we ask the wrong questions or don't know what questions to ask? Or maybe shouldn't simply be asking questions?

Such questions clearly enough reveal the drift of my argument. But to summarize it: I think the literary canon as we have known it is a product in significant measure of our training in a male, white, bourgeois cultural tradition, including in particular the formal techniques of literary analysis. And further, that other cultural traditions provide alternate views about the nature and function of art and of approaches to it. Indeed, if our concern is to change the canon "radically"—that is, at its roots—as distinct from grafting on to it a few odd branches, we must look at the full range of these alternate traditions. This argument holds, I believe, whether one is concerned with working-class art, the art of minority groups, or much of the art of women. For in significant ways all "marginalized" groups have experiences and traditions distinct from those of the dominant majority. In this paper I focus initially on working-class and black traditions, both for their inherent interest and also because they provide us with revealing perspectives on women's art as well as on feminist criticism.

Raymond Williams' distinction between "working-class" and "bourgeois" culture provides a useful starting point:

> . . . a culture is not only a body of intellectual and imaginative work; it is also and essentially a whole way of life. The basis of a distinction between bourgeois and working-class culture is only secondarily in the field of intellectual and imaginative work. . . . The crucial distinguishing element in English life since the Industrial Revolution is not language, not dress, not leisure—for these indeed will tend to uniformity. The crucial

distinction is between alternative ideas of the nature of social relationship.

> "Bourgeois" is a significant term because it marks that version of social relationship which we usually call individualism: that is to say, an idea of society as a neutral area within which each individual is free to pursue his own development and his own advantage as a natural right. . . . [Both] this idea [of service] and the individualistic idea can be sharply contrasted with the idea that we properly associate with the working class: an idea which, whether it is called communism, socialism, or cooperation regards society neither as neutral nor as protective, but as the positive means for all kinds of development, including individual development.[2]

Writing from a British perspective, Williams perhaps underestimates the significance of works of imagination in defining "working-class culture": "It is not proletarian art, or council houses, or a particular use of languages; it is, rather, the basic collective idea, and the institutions, manners, habits of thought and intentions which proceed from this."[3] But his fundamental point is critical to understand: while broad areas of the culture are common to the working class and the bourgeoisie, there remains a "crucial distinction . . . between alternative ideas of the nature of social relationship." This distinction significantly explains differing "institutions, manners, habits of thought and intentions." Distinct cultures also help shape ideas about the nature of art, its functions, the processes of its creation, the nature of the artist and of the artist's social role.

There is nothing very mysterious about this: people whose experiences of the world significantly differ, whose material conditions of life, whose formal and informal training, whose traditions, sometimes even whose language differ, and especially people whose understanding of their own life-chances and opportunities, their "place" differs will think about things differently, will talk about things differently, will value at least some things differently, will express themselves *to* different people *in* different ways and *about* different experiences, at least in some measure.

But that is all very abstract. We need to be somewhat more specific about differences between working-class and bourgeois art and literature. Unfortunately, there are relatively few cultural, and particularly literary, analyses of working-class materials (at least in Western practice). Martha Vicinus' *The Industrial Muse*[4] is a unique full-length study but confined to Great Britain; Dan Tannacito examines the poetry of Colorado miners around the turn of this century;[5] an article of mine provides bibliographical and some theoretical approaches to working-class women's literature;[6] Lawrence Levine brilliantly explores the historical relationships between black culture and consciousness.[7] Even from this limited number of analyses certain features of working-class or "popular"[8] art emerge clearly. First, working-class art often is produced in group situations rather than in the privacy of a study (or garret) and it is similarly experienced in the hall, the church, the work-site, the quilting bee, the picket line. It thus emerges from the experiences of a particular group of people facing particular problems in a particular time. Much of it is therefore not conceived as timeless and transcendent; rather, it might be called "instrumental." As Tannacito puts it, "the value of the Colorado miners' poetry derived exclusively from the use made of the poems by their audience. The audience was an immediate one. The objective [in writing] was inseparable from those goals" toward which the workers' lives directed them. Vicinus points out that working-class artists, themselves persuaded of the power of literature to "influence people's behavior," aimed to "persuade readers to adopt particular beliefs." Some recommended the bourgeois values embodied in the culture of what they thought of as their "betters." Others, despairing of social and political change, devoted their work to reassuring readers that their lives, debased as they might have become, still had value and to providing at least some entertainment and consolation in an oppressive world. Many wrote to help change the status quo. Their work, Vicinus says, aimed "to arouse and focus social tension in order to channel it toward specific political actions." By "clarifying" or making vivid economic, social, and political relationships between working people and those who held power, they helped to "shape individual and class consciousness" and to "imbue a sense of class solidarity that encouraged working people to fight for social and political equality."

Tannacito provides a number of instances of the ways in which the miner poets tried to accomplish such goals. Poems of "praise," for example, explicitly tried to link heroic deeds of the past with the contemporary workers' community. Other poems sought to inspire specific forms of struggle, job actions, voting, boycotts. Miner poets, like working-class artists generally, wrote about the world they and their readers shared: the job, oppression by bosses, the militia and the scabs, a heritage of common struggle. They saw art not as a means for removing people from the world in which they lived—however desirable that might seem—nor as a device for producing "catharsis" or "stasis." Rather, art aimed to inspire consciousness about and actions within the world, to make living in that world more bearable, to extend experiences of that world, indeed to enlarge the world working people could experience. Thus, even as sophisticated an example of working-class fiction as Tillie Olsen's "Tell Me a Riddle" centrally concerns the problem of inspiring a new generation with the values, hopes, and images that directed the actions and aspirations of an earlier generation and that lie buried under the grit produced by forty years of daily life. Or consider how Morris Rosenfeld renders the experience of time-discipline in his work as a pants presser:

> The Clock in the workshop,—it rests not a moment;
> It points on, and ticks on: eternity—time;
> Once someone told me the clock had a meaning,—
> In pointing and ticking had reason and rhyme. . . .
> At times, when I listen, I hear the clock plainly;—
> The reason of old—the old meaning—is gone!
> The maddening pendulum urges me forward
> To labor and still labor on.
> The tick of the clock is the boss in his anger.
> The face of the clock has the eyes of the foe.
> The clock—I shudder—Dost hear how it draws me?
> It calls me "Machine" and it cries [to] me "Sew!"[9]

Rosenfeld is concerned to capture, and to mourn, the passing in a particular historical moment of an older, less time-disciplined order of work as well as the degradation of the worker to the status of machine. The poem gives names and pictures to the experiences that Rosenfeld and his fellow workers encountered in moving from the shtetl to the sweatshops of the new world.

Working-class art thus functions to focus consciousness and to develop ideology, but it can also play a variety of other roles. Songs were used, especially by black slaves and nominally free laborers, to set the pace of work in a group and, at the same time, to relieve the tension and pent-up feelings born of oppressive labor. Leaders lined out a rhythm for hoeing, chopping, lifting bales, rowing boats. At the same time, the songs spoke realistically about the shared labor, and more covertly, perhaps, about those exacting it.[10] Similarly, sorrow songs or spirituals served not only to express grief and to sustain hope in slavery, but they were also used as signals to prepare for escapes from it.[11] Similarly, during the Civil Rights movement of the 1950s and 1960s, what were originally church hymns underwent conversion to marching songs and sometimes means for triumphing over one's jailers.

Clearly, the conception of the functions of art are here very different from those propounded, say, by Aristotle, or Milton, or Coleridge—or formalist criticism, as I shall indicate in a moment. It is not, however, only conception or function which differs, but also form and technique and even the manner of creation of much working-class art. In characterizing the distinctive qualities of the song styles of black slaves, Levine emphasizes "its overriding antiphony, its group nature, its pervasive functionality, its improvisational character, its strong relationship in performance to dance and bodily movements and expression. . . ."[12] Some of these qualities are peculiar to styles derived from West African roots, but some are characteristic of other working-class cultures. New songs are often based upon old ones, and there is less concern with the unique qualities of art than with building variations upon tunes, themes, and texts well known in the community. For example, songs like "Hold the Fort" and "We Are Building a Strong Union," which began as gospel hymns, went through a series of metamorphoses in order to serve the needs of a diverse sequence of workers' organizations—in the case of the former, including the British transport workers, the Knights of Labor, and the Industrial Workers of the World. The Wobbly poet Joe Hill constructed some of his best-known songs as take-offs on Salvation Army hymns. The spiritual "Oh, Freedom" became one of the most popular songs of the Civil Rights movement; as the movement's militance increased, many singers changed the song's refrain from "Before I be a slave / I be buried in my grave / And go home to my Lord / And be free" to "Before . . . grave / And I'll fight for my right / To be free."

In many ways, working-class art, like other elements in working-class life, is highly traditional; certainly innovative form is not a primary consideration and "make it new" a slogan which would be viewed with some suspicion. Similarly, working-class poetry and song especially, but also tales and stories, are often built around repeated elements—refrains, formulae, commonly accepted assumptions about characters. Language, too, is often simpler, sometimes commonplace, certainly less "heightened" than that of "high culture" verse. Many of these characteristics are common to literary forms rooted in oral art, made necessary by the exigencies of memory and improvisation. Some may arise from the artist's desire to avoid a fancy vocabulary unfamiliar to the audience or esoteric images and allusions. Thus, a poem like Rosenfeld's carefully works with materials as familiar to his readers as gaberdine was to him.

In some respects as well these characteristics are derived from the communal character of the creation of certain working-class art forms. One old former slave describes the creation of a "spiritual" in a pre–Civil War religious meeting in these words:

> I'd jump up dar and den and hollar and shout and sing and pat, and dey would all cotch de words and I'd sing it to some old shout song I'd heard 'em sing from Africa, and dey'd all take it up and keep at it, and keep a-addin' to it, and den it would be a spiritual.[13]

In such situations, the individual creator is generally less significant than the group; or, rather, to the extent that individuals are creators, they shape a common stock to new group purposes without diminishing or expropriating that common stock. The song leader in church is not asked to provide new hymns (much less copyright old ones) and would be looked at with suspicion if she did so. She is asked to reinvigorate a hymn that is known, perhaps to add something especially appropriate for the occasion.[14] The jazz musician may be admired for a new melody, but probably more important—at least until recently—is the ability to ring variations on melodies the listeners know and follow. I am emphasizing here the "folk," communal elements of working-class art, in some degree at the expense of art produced by self-conscious individual working-class artists. I do so because an approach through people's culture helps to focus certain distinctive qualities of working-class art, certain "centers of gravity," not so easily seen if one concentrates on the productions of separate artists. Yet, obviously, a continuum exists between songs, poems, and tales which are, so to speak, common property and works created primarily by individual imaginations.

But what is critical here is precisely the relationship between individual and community. Levine, for example, directly connects the *form* of the spiritual with the underlying social reality of black slave life:

> Just as the process by which the spirituals were created allowed for simultaneous individual and communal creativity, so their very structure provided simultaneous outlets for individual and communal expression. The overriding antiphonal structure of the spirituals—the call and response pattern which Negroes brought with them from Africa and which was reinforced in America by the practice of lining out hymns—placed the individual in continual dialogue with his community, allowing him at one and the same time to preserve his voice as a distinct entity and to blend it with those of his fellows.[15]

I would carry the argument in a slightly different direction by suggesting that one center of gravity of working-class art is its high level of integration of creator and audience. Works often have their origin, as well as their being, in situations which do not absolutely distinguish active performer/artist from passive audience. Or when the distinction is relatively clearer, the artist's "product" is offered not primarily for its exchange value (money for that song or painting), but for its use in the lives of the people to whom it is directed. A moving example is provided by the Kentucky mountain songs sung at the funeral of "Jock" Yablonski and recorded with great majesty in the film *Harlan County, U.S.A.*

In a larger sense, all working-class art (perhaps all art)[16] must be explored precisely in terms of its use. Partly that is a function of marginality itself: the struggle for existence and dignity necessarily involves all available resources, including art. But partly, I think, this phenomenon is explained by the fundamental character of working-class culture, what Williams called "solidarity." It is not simply a slogan or an abstraction that happens to appeal to many people who work. It is, rather, a way of describing the culture of people who have been pushed together into workplaces and communities where survival and growth enforce interdependence. In this context, the work of the artist—while it may in some respects be expressive and private—remains overwhelmingly functional in his or her community. And an approach to it cannot strip it of this context without ripping away its substance.

My argument began from the premise that the conditions of life of working-class people have produced ideas about social relationships crucially distinct from those of the bourgeoisie. This distinction shaped differing institutions, manners, ideas about culture and art. In order to approach working-class culture, then, we must begin not with presuppositions about what literature is and is not, or what is valuable in it or not, but rather by asking in what forms, on what themes, in what circumstances, and to what ends do working people speak and sing and write and signify to each other. We must, in other words, discover the distinctive rules and measures of working-class art and thus the critical strategies and tools appropriate to them.

"Are you saying," someone might object, "that the rules and measures—the critical tools—we now possess are invalid, somehow biased or irrelevant?" Here, indeed, is the nub of the matter. For we do approach culture with certain presuppositions, frameworks, touchstones which we learn and which we learn to valorize. I have tried here to state as neutrally as I can certain of the qualities and origins of working-class art. I have not tried to lay a spiritual like "Roll, Jordan" or a poem like Rosenfeld's alongside, say, Donne's "A Valediction: forbidding mourning" in order to evaluate one in relation to another or all against some "universal" standard of measurement. For the central issue is not which is "better," but what we mean by "better." And I am sure it is clear by now that I believe such standards of judgment, which shape the canon, to be rooted in assumptions derived from class and caste about the techniques, qualities, and especially the functions of art.

I do not want to be misleading here: I do not believe that somewhere out there is a working-class poet, ignored through bourgeois prejudice, who actually wrote better metaphysical poems than Donne or more singular ones than Shelley. No more do I think that a factory organized along truly socialist lines will be more "efficient" and "productive" than a capitalist factory; capitalists often find means to do rather well what it is they want to do—in this case to squeeze as much profit from workers as they can. But that does not necessarily make for a humane, safe, creative, or socially responsible workplace. The goals are different; the values and thus the priorities different. On the other hand, it has been demonstrated that there are forgotten black and white women writers who wrote fiction as good in traditional terms as that of many of the white men with whom we are familiar. As Williams pointed out, there are vast shared areas of culture. My main point, however, is that if there probably are no working-class metaphysical poets, neither did Donne write verses for "Roll, Jordan." And if "Roll, Jordan" does not demonstrate the fine elaboration of complex language to be found in "A Valediction," it is also the fact that none of Donne's poems—not all of them together, I dare say—has served to sustain and inspire so many thousands of oppressed people. What, finally, is art about?

Mr. Allen Tate had an answer for us. "Good poetry," he writes in "Tension in Poetry," "is a unity of all the meanings from the furthest extremes of intension and extension . . . . the meaning of poetry is its 'tension,' the full organized body of all the extension and intension that we can find in it."[17] In the same essay he attacks Edna St. Vincent Millay's "Justice Denied in Massachusetts," a poem written in gloomy reaction to the execution of Sacco and Vanzetti.

> Let us abandon then our gardens and go home
> And sit in the sitting-room.
> Shall the larkspur blossom or the corn grow under this cloud?
> Sour to the fruitful seed
> Is the cold earth under this cloud,
> Fostering quack and weed, we have marched upon but cannot
>   conquer;
> We have bent the blades of our hoes against the stalks of them.
>
> Let us go home, and sit in the sitting-room.
> Not in our day
> Shall the cloud go over and the sun rise as before,
> Beneficent upon us
> Out of the glittering bay,
> And the warm winds be blown inward from the sea
> Moving the blades of corn
> With a peaceful sound.

"These lines," Tate claims, "are mass language: they arouse an affective state in one set of terms, and suddenly an object quite unrelated to those terms gets the benefit of it." The Millay poem, he continues,

> is no doubt still admired, by persons to whom it communicates
> certain feelings about social justice, by persons for whom the

lines are the occasion of feelings shared by them and the poet. But if you do not share those feelings, as I happen not to share them in the images of dessicated nature, the lines and even the entire poem are impenetrably obscure.[18]

It once occurred to me that Tate might be using "obscure" in a Pickwickian sense, for whatever one might think of the Millay poem it seems rather less obscure than Tate's critique. But then, from his point of view, "communication in poetry" is a fallacy. The poet is "not responsible to society for a version of what it thinks it is or what it wants." The poet is responsible to his conscience. And he (the pronoun remains Tate's) is responsible "for the virtue proper to him as poet, for his special *arête*: for the mastery of a disciplined language which will not shun the full report of reality conveyed to him by his awareness: he must hold, in Yeats' great phrase, 'reality and justice in a single thought.'"[19] Elsewhere Tate approvingly quotes I. A. Richards to the effect that poetry is "complete knowledge": "The order of completeness that it achieves in the great works of the imagination is not the order of experimental completeness aimed at by the positivist sciences. . . . For the completeness of *Hamlet* is not of the experimental order, but of the experienced order; it is, in short, of the mythical order."[20]

Given this self-contained idea of poetry, it is not surprising that formalist critics like Tate should develop techniques emphasizing intense analysis of a poem's language and its "tensions," or that they should conceive the primary task of the "man of letters" as preserving "the integrity, the purity, and the reality of language wherever and for whatever purpose it may be used." "He must," Tate goes on to explain, approach this task "through the letter—the letter of the poem, the letter of the politician's speech, the letter of the law; for the use of the letter is in the long run our one indispensable test of the actuality of our experience."[21] How different this conservative, monitory role from that staked out for the American Scholar by Emerson. Besides, is it really necessary to talk about the taste of rotting fruit to test its actuality? However that might be, Tate's ultimate vision of the "man of letters" asserts an even weightier function: ". . . the duty of the man of letters is to supervise the culture of language, to which the rest of culture is subordinate, and to warn us when our language is ceasing to forward the ends proper to man. The end of social man is communion in time through love, which is beyond time."[22] The man of letters thus stands a priest of language, linking society and culture with the transcendent.

But why devote such attention to these ideas, or once again pillory an often-abused guru of the New Criticism? Has not criticism passed beyond the exegetical stage? In theory, it has. In practice, however, and especially in the common practice of the classroom, the dominant mode of procedure remains exploring the "furthest extremes of intension and extension" we may find in a text. And the texts we prefer are, on the whole, those which invite such explication. One or another version of formalism remains, in short, the meat and potatoes of what men—and women—of letters stir up for our students and readers. And while Tate's ecclesiastical trappings may have been doffed as rather too quaint and burdensome, something of the incense lingers in the justifications for what we do. Thus, it seems to me important to ask what social and political values generate the forms of criticism and its jusifications we find in Tate and his fellows.

There is a second, perhaps more fundamental reason for examining Tate's ideas. He and his New Critical peers were the first generation to pose what became, and still is, the dominant paradigm of academic criticism. I want to suggest that, regardless of form, academic criticism in the past half-century has retained a common set of social and political roots and a consistent function. An image may help flesh this assertion. In *Invisible Man* Ellison pictures a statue of the "Founder," his hands holding the edges of a veil which covers the face of the black youth kneeling before him. The speaker of the book comments that it is never clear whether the Founder is lifting the veil from the boy's face or holding it ever more firmly in its place. That ambiguous image may stand for the academic critic; is he (I want to retain the overwhelmingly appropriate pronoun) offering enlightenment by lifting the veil or holding the student in a kind of darkness?

In feminist pedagogy a distinction has developed between two forms of teaching: one, which often involves the display of a specialized vocabulary, has the tendency to overwhelm students, paralyzing them before the erudition of the teacher; another, seen as developing from the equalitarian ideals of feminism, tries to legitimize the student's own responses to a text, to history, to experience as the starting points for analysis and thus understanding. To be sure, it has often been easy to overstate this distinction between—in crude shorthand—lecturer as authority and discussion leader as participant, to convert pedagogical tendencies into behavioral absolutes; indeed, to elevate difference in style into fiercely held educational principles. For all that rhetoric has burdened us with inflation of difference, the differences remain, more perhaps as foci or what I have called "centers of gravity" than as differences in kind. Analogous "centers of gravity" can, I think, be charted in criticism. Is the objective result of criticism to help readers formulate, understand, and develop their own responses? To open a text to a common reader? Or is it to make the reader feel excluded from the critical enterprise, sense his or her own responses to a work as essentially irrelevant to the process of its exploration? The latter result has, it seems to me, the concomitant effect—or, perhaps I should say, underlying motive—of confirming the position, the cultural power of the critic himself, even while, as was historically the case in the 1920s and 1930s, the real social authority of the class from which "men of letters" were drawn was being eroded. In fact, I want to argue, the major project of criticism as it developed from patriarchs like Tate was the confirmation of the authoritative position, at least with respect to culture, of the Man of Letters and his caste. And while the *forms* of criticism have changed—from New Criticism to Structuralism to Post-Structuralism—the *functions* of academic criticism seem to me to have remained constant, related primarily to the status, power, and careers of critics.[23]

There is, furthermore, an awful logic to the changes in form that derives precisely from the persistence of function. At the beginning, formal analysis did—as it still can—help illuminate texts. And as differing kind of analyses developed, these too added to the illumination, albeit with increasing marginality. But a law of diminishing returns necessarily begins to operate with the thirtieth explication of "A Valediction" or the eighteenth lick of ice-cream, and the eye of the beholder starts to shift from the qualities of the text to the qualities of the comment, from the poet to the critic; with the exhaustion of the ways of looking at a pigeon, we begin to observe the antics of the pigeon-watchers. And thus emerges a speculative criticism claiming equality with the literary texts (once the objects to be illuminated) and framed a language increasingly impenetrable to the common reader. The project of such criticism *is* its politics.

This is not to say that academic critics are by character and inclination conscious elitists; my point is not, in any case, characterological.

The very momentum, not to say corpulence, of academic criticism hides its political origins. But in sad fact, cultural institutions move in the directions established by their initial political impetus unless or until they are redirected by the intervention of a new political force— like the social and cultural movements of the 1960s and 1970s. Thus, to understand contemporary academic criticism we must examine its roots and its values as these appear in their rudimentary form.

These values emerge into severe profile from Tate's account of the limitations of Southern literature:

> But the abolition of slavery did not make for a distinctively Southern literature. We must seek the cause of our limitations elsewhere. It is worth remarking, for the sake of argument, that chattel slavery is not demonstrably a worse form of slavery than any other upon which an aristocracy may base its power and wealth. That *African* chattel slavery was the worst groundwork conceivable for the growth of a great culture of European pattern, is scarcely at this day arguable. . . . The distance between white master and black slave was unalterably greater than that between white master and white serf after the destruction of feudalism. The peasant *is* the soil. The negro slave was a barrier between the ruling class and the soil. If we look at aristocracies in Europe, say in eighteenth-century England, we find at least genuine social classes, each carrying on a different level of the common culture. But in the Old South, and under the worse form of slavery that afflicts both races today, genuine social classes do not exist. The enormous "difference" of the Negro doomed him from the beginning to an economic status purely: he has had much the same thinning influence upon the class above him as the anonymous city proletariat has had upon the culture of industrial capitalism. . . .
>
> The white man got nothing from the Negro, no profound image of himself in terms of the soil. . . . But the Negro, who has long been described as a responsibility, got everything from the white man. The history of French culture, I suppose, has been quite different. The high arts have been grafted upon the peasant stock. We could graft no new life upon the Negro; he was too different, too alien.[24]

It is not my intent to comment upon the less than genteel racism, the abysmal cultural chauvinism, or even the simple historical ignorance of this passage. But it does make amply clear the elitist soil in which Tate's formalist ideas of poetry and the "man of letters" are rooted. The New Criticism is the fruit—strange fruit—of such plants. But that metaphor is rather too easy. In plain fact, criticism which makes all important the special languages that specially trained critics share with specially cultivated poets is finally a means for defending special privilege. It is a version of what Raymond Williams calls the "dominative" use of language.

Meridel LeSueur, who studied with Tate and others at the University of Minnesota, has a different way of drawing the connection between the politics and the critical style of these men of letters: "It was just like being bitten every morning by a black spider   paralysis set in. They taught the structure of the short story this way: you run around Robin Hood's barn, have two or three conclusions, and then come to a kind of paralysis. Ambiguity is a very seductive idea."[25] The paralysis of ambiguity in a world crying for change fits well with *Reactionary Essays on Poetry and Ideas*.

I am not suggesting that formalist critics are necessarily racists or political reactionaries in their personal outlooks or that every formalist move necessarily builds higher the bulwarks of bourgeois culture. But it seems to me natural to suspect a project with such roots and thus (returning at last to the nest of questions I raised many pages back) to propose that, indeed, critical tactics carry with them rather more ideological baggage than we might at first have suspected.

In the opening section of *Stealing the Language: The Emergence of Women's Poetry in America* (1986), Alicia Ostriker has analyzed how that ideology operated to marginalize women poets. She cites, among other documents, John Crowe Ransom's essay on Millay,[26] which nicely illustrates how the formalist aesthetic principles Ransom shared with Tate worked in practice. Ransom writes:

> Man distinguishes himself from woman by intellect, but he should keep it feminized. He knows he should not abandon sensibility and tenderness, though perhaps he has generally done so. . . . But the problem does not arise for a woman. Less pliant, safer as a biological organism, she remains fixed in her famous attitudes, and is indifferent to intellectuality. I mean, of course, comparatively indifferent; more so than a man. (P. 78)

Thus, from Ransom's point of view, Millay's is a lesser "vein of poetry," "spontaneous, straightforward in diction," with "transparently simple" structures and "immediate" effects (pp. 103–105). Indeed, a good deal of Ransom's essay is devoted to showing how, in effect, Millay's "excitingly womanlike" poems display little analyzable "intention" or "extension" and thus are not intellectually challenging. It seems to me clear how patriarchy and racism emerge into critical categories and a methodology that helped place the work of most white women and black writers behind the veil.

By this long and perhaps burdensome route we return to that room in Lawrence, Kansas, that panel on feminist criticism, and maybe even my growing anger. For I came to that panel with the ideas I've outlined. It seemed to me that while there are broad shared areas, the social experiences and the cultures of women and men diverge at significant points. I do not have ready terms, like "individualism" and "solidarity," to characterize the distinct organizing principles, but it seemed quite plain that significantly diverse experiences will produce significantly diverse cultural forms among men and women, just as among blacks and whites, working people and bourgeoisie. And that, therefore, the application to women's art of principles and standards derived almost exclusively from the study of men's art will tend to obscure, even hide, and certainly undervalue what women have created. Indeed, the application of critical standards and tactics derived from white, male—not to say racist and elitist—culture not only obscures female accomplishment, on the one side, but reinforces the validity of those critical standards and what they represent, on the other. Thus, I thought that panel's project was grafting Adrienne Rich's poem onto Allen Tate's stock—to borrow a Tate metaphor—rather than joining the dialogue in which *The Dream of a Common Language* and *The Common Woman* poems both participate. It is not that the panelists shared Tate's and Ransom's values; rather, in pursuing their techniques, the panel seemed to me to reinforce the structures of academic elitism.

I hope this will not be misconstrued into an odd shorthand report like "Lauter says there's a peculiar female sensibility and that criticism is male, so feminists should be doing something else, as yet unspecified." I do *not* know if there is such a thing as a female sensibility. "Sensibility" is a psychological category and is approachable, I think, only through individuals. I am talking not of sensibility but of *culture*, which is a social category. It cannot be used to predict individual behavior, but it is critical to understanding how we perceive, indeed what we look at, as well as how we conceive the structures of language we call works of art.

Formalist critics, I am suggesting, are trapped within their culture, restricted in what they look at and by who looks. Why? First, because they have derived much of their cultural data from a narrow base, largely art composed by white Western men (as Tate's comment on Southern culture reveals). They have not adequately considered art from outside that tradition, except, as it were, after the fact, after they had donned their theoretical spectacles. Also, these spectacles have been ground by the social and economic pressures which characteristically mold the residents of academe. For criticism is not solely a pure activity of mind, an expression of altruism directed toward revealing truth, or even the play of intellect upon the surfaces of language. It may upon occasion be these. It will also in some measure be an ideology constructed in order to insure and enhance the social and economic position of the critic and his class—even occasionally, now, "her" class. To put it another way, the connection we have seen of New Critical methodology with reactionary politics is no accident, nor is the obscurity, of, say *Diacritics*. An adequate theory of criticism can only be developed by fully considering the art produced by women, by working people, and by national minorities; further, such art needs to be understood in light of its own principles, not simply in terms and categories derived from so-called high culture or on the basis of the imperatives imposed by careerism or reigning institutional priorities.

Thus, the first task in the project of feminist criticism seems to me the recovery of lost works by women and the restoration of the value of disdained genres. In part a restorative literary history is required simply for the sake of intellectual honesty. But more important, as I have suggested, is the imperative for broadening the "text milieu" from which we derive critical and historical propositions. Now this task has considerably been advanced in the last decade, as witness, on the one hand, the publications of feminist and university presses and, on the other, the recent issuance of Gilbert and Gubar's *Norton Anthology of*

Literature by Women. But the work is by no means complete or, for a number of reasons, is it likely soon to be. For example, women writers of early and mid nineteenth-century America are known to most readers, even most academics, mainly secondhand, through such useful studies as Nina Baym's.[27] In fact, writers of substance like Caroline Kirkland, Lydia Maria Child, Alice Cary are seldom read, in part because their books have not been reissued for over a hundred years,[28] in part because they have not been given the legitimation of academic study even to the degree that someone as marginal as William Gilmore Simms has been. Most important, the modern outlook, and particularly modern criticism, has been out of sympathy with the sensibilities displayed in the work of such authors. I shall have more to say about that in a moment. Suffice it here to say it is unlikely that the deep obscurity in which women writers from Sherwood Bonner to Zitkala-Sa are hidden is peculiarly an American phenomenon; thus, I doubt whether we are close to the end of the process of rediscovery.

More certainly, even, we are far from establishing the distinctive qualities of the art of these and many better-known women writers. This seems to me the second major task of feminist criticism. Studies like Baym's, Barbara Christian's, Elaine Showalter's, and Sandra Gilbert's and Susan Gubar's[29] are only among some of the better-known works devoted to establishing thematic and formal connections among women writers. A parallel task is defining the distinctive thematic and formal characteristics of particular women writers. Elizabeth Ammons' examination of the structure of Jewett's *The Country of the Pointed Firs*[30] provides an especially useful example because it implicitly questions received norms about the structure of short fictions and suggests that Jewett used a distinct and perhaps gender-linked form.

There is, of course, a certain dialectic between the rediscovery of works and an adequate account of characteristics that link them to other texts. In reevaluating the writing of Caroline Kirkland, Judith Fetterley has suggested that *A New Home, Who'll Follow* is in essence a series of elaborated letters and that the letter form represented for women a literary halfway house between the privacy of correspondence and the public act of authorship, an act seen by many in the early nineteenth century as unseemly for women. That suggestion took on for me powerful implications as I recently reread Sarah Grimke's

Letters on the Equality of the Sexes and Lydia Maria Child's *Letters from New York*, thought about the letter form adopted by Margaret Fuller in the last years of her life, and finally focused (thanks particularly to one of my students, Ellen Louise Hart) on the implications of such precedents on the major form of Emily Dickinson's (self-)"publication"—letters:

> This is my letter to the World
> That never wrote to Me . . .

It would at this point claim too much to propose correspondence as constituting a fundamental model for many American nineteenth-century women of letters, but as we come to know more about these writers that may, indeed, be our conclusion. I pose this hypothesis as a minor illustration of how the dialectic between rediscovery and definition of characteristic themes and forms operates. It also leads us toward two additional objectives in the project of feminist criticism.

These I would describe as decentering male texts, on the one hand, and moving female texts from the margins of culture to the core. Decentering male texts (including phallocentric criticism) was in many respects the initial concern of the earliest feminist critics. It took two forms: study of the images of women, often absurd or vile, projected in widely respected work by male writers. Second, and in these days of theoretical sophistication too often condescended to, were works like Kate Millett's pioneering and courageous *Sexual Politics* (1970). It need hardly be said that the work of decentering phallocentric culture as it is expressed in language, syntax, form, and institutional configuration remains a major concern of current feminist criticism. Indeed, the major contribution of contemporary French feminist writing may be in this area. What is surprising, perhaps, is how persistent phallocentric historical models have remained despite the accumulated weight of contrary evidence.

A vivid illustration of how phallocentric literary history continues to obscure the work of women writers was provided by Leslie Fiedler in an essay called "Literature and Lucre" and features in the *New York Times Book Review* (May 31, 1981). Fiedler pictures the history of the novel in America as a struggle between "high Art and low," between "those writers among us who aspire to critical acclaim and an eternal place in libraries" and "the authors of 'best sellers.'" The former, "sophisticated novelists," include Charles Brockden Brown, Poe, Hawthorne, and Melville—all male, as Fiedler points out. The latter tradition, "a series of deeply moving though stylistically undistinguished fictions . . . begins with Susanna Rowson's *Charlotte Temple*, reaches a 19th-century high point with Harriet Beecher Stowe's *Uncle Tom's Cabin* and a 20th-century climax with Margaret Mitchell's *Gone with the Wind*."

This spurious battle of the sexes and the image of the failed artist which supposedly emerges from it can be sustained only by ignoring huge parts of American literary history. For example, Fiedler proclaims that "only in the last decade of this century did it become possible, first in fact, then in fiction, for a novelist highly regarded by critics (Norman Mailer is an example) to become wealthy long before his death." This is patrifocal history with a vengeance, since it altogether ignores Edith Wharton, Willa Cather, and Ellen Glasgow, not to speak of Stowe, E. D. E. N. Southworth (who was much praised by contemporary critics), Jewett, Mary Austin, and even William Dean Howells. Most of these women novelists, among others, were and still are "highly regarded by critics" and did very well from their writing. But more to the point, bringing them up altogether explodes the theory, or perhaps myth, Fiedler wishes to float, that in America writers have either been (until our generation) successful *or* artistic: "both primary and secondary literature in the United States, the novels and poems of which we are most proud and the critical autobiographical [*sic*] works written on them, reflect the myth of the 'serious' writer as an alienated male, condemned to neglect and poverty by a culture simultaneously commercialized and feminized." Since the women novelists don't fit this nice theory, "we" need to ignore them. And also ignore the fact that writers like Melville and Hawthorne indeed aspired to popularity and were enraged by what they took to be the failure of their audience to appreciate them.

Nor is it at all clear, as Fiedler makes out, that Stowe, for example, was not artistic as well as successful. On the contrary, recent studies have documented her artistry. In linking her to Rowson and Mitchell, Fiedler is trying to stigmatize her with the unstated labels, familiar from critics like Tate, of "sentimental" and "mass market." "Sentimental" and "mass" are terms, like "regional," "popular," "minor," which have been undergoing reexamination[31] since it became clear they were used to bury much of value on specious assumptions, like the proposition that the suppression of feelings, even tears, is a more legitimate basis for fiction than their display. [32] In short, the problem with Fiedler's theory is that it begins with a truncated set of data, examines them from a dazzlingly parochial angle of vision, and, not surprisingly, concludes by reinforcing the artistic centrality of the traditional male texts which have constituted the canon.

Moreover, the myth of the unappreciated artist itself requires a differing analysis. Myths constitute metaphorical ideologies. Here, the problem for American male writers is construed as the frailty of his audience. It might equally well be posed as the obstinate refusal of many male novelists to take that dominantly female audience seriously. In concluding her second series of stories entitled *Clovernook* (1853), Alice Cary deftly questions the motives of those who, as Fiedler puts it, aspire to "an eternal place in libraries":

> In our country, though all men are not "created equal," such
> is the influence of the sentiment of liberty and political equality,
> that:
> "All thoughts, all passions, all delights,
> Whatever stirs this mortal frame,"
> may with as much probability be supposed to affect conduct and
> expectation in the log cabin as in the marble mansion; and to
> illustrate this truth, to dispel that erroneous belief of the neces-
> sary baseness of the "common people" which the great masters
> in literature have in all ages labored to create, is a purpose and
> an object in our nationality to which the finest and highest
> genius may wisely be devoted; but which may be effected in a
> degree by writings as unpretending as these reminiscences of
> what occurred in and about the little village where I from child-
> hood watched the pulsations of surrounding hearts. [33]

Cary's comment not only raises questions about the values of the literary "masters," but suggests the importance of an alternative standard embodied in the "unpretending . . . reminiscences" of her village which she—and, indeed, many American women writers—presents.

And that comment brings me to the last part of the project of feminist criticism upon which I wish to touch: the effort to move the work of women from the margins toward the center of culture. Here the work of criticism and of political action most fully converge. For in the first instance it was not the work of critics that refocused attention on the distinctive concerns of women writers any more than black aestheticians initially established the conditions for recognizing the traditions of African-American composition. On the contrary, it was the movements for social, economic, and political change of the 1960s and 1970s that challenged long-held assumptions about what was significant as subject matter for literary art by challenging the assumptions about what was significant for *people*. Meridel LeSueur once described how her story "Annunciation," which deals with pregnancy, was turned down by editors demanding conflict and action. That may stand as a symbol of my point here: it will *not* be on the basis solely of "literary" criteria that the days and works of women—any more than of other marginalized groups—will be established at the center of cultural concern.

In California, the school system in cooperation with certain universities has launched an ambitious "literature project" designed to reinvigorate the teaching of English at the secondary level. Part of that effort has involved the creation of model curricula, including what are called "core" and "extended" readings. One model thematic unit is titled "Journey to Personal Fulfillment." The "core" readings are these: Dickens, *Great Expectations*; Twain, *Huckleberry Finn* and *Life on the Mississippi*; Shaw, *Pygmalion*; Cather, "Paul's Case"; Kafka, "The Hunger Artist"; Auden, "The Unknown Citizen"; Eliot, "The Hollow Men"; and Whitman, "The Ox-Tamer." These selections suggest that an old canard still lives: "Choose works that interest the boys; the girls will read anything." That reflection is reinforced by considering that among the "extended readings" are *Jane Eyre*, *Wuthering Heights*, E. B. Browning's *Sonnets from the Portuguese*, the autobiographies of Mme. Curie and Helen Keller, and Alice Walker's "African Images." Further, one might wonder, in a state in which Latinos, Asian Americans, American Indians, and blacks will shortly constitute a majority, whether all of these works together constitute any adequate portrait of journeys to "personal fulfillment." I do not cite this instance to mock the very concerned people working in this important project. On the contrary, I think we need to admire and support their efforts even as we criticize them. But it will not be critical practice alone that will shift what is perceived and treated as "core." To be sure, as literary people we need to reexamine hierarchies of taste as expressed in subject matter, genre, language, and imagery as well as in conceptions of literary function and audience.[34] Still, there is little more that can be done to establish the *literary* equality of the work of the Brontës and Twain. It will be our work as political people—rather, as citizens of real communities—that will be critical to achieving the axial transformation to which we aspire. Revolution is not, finally, in and of the word alone.

Nor should this come as a surprise. It is a commonplace of scholarship informed by a working-class perspective—often honored, I must admit, in the breach—that the point is not to describe the world but to change it. So it must be, I think, with feminist criticism: it cannot be neutral, simply analytic, formal. It needs always to be asking how its project is changing the world, reconstructing history as well as consciousness, so that the accomplishments of women can be fully valued and, more important, so that the lives of women and men can more fully be lived.

Notes

1. I have examined the history of the American literary canon in "Race and Gender in the Shaping of the American Literary Canon: A Case Study from the Twenties," *Feminist Studies* 9 (Fall 1983): 435–463, and have posed some alternative frameworks to the existing canon in the introduction to *Reconstructing American Literature* (Old Westbury: Feminist Press, 1983), pp. xi–xxv.
2. Raymond Williams, *Culture and Society, 1780–1950* (New York: Harper Torchbooks, 1966), pp. 325–326.
3. Ibid., p. 327.
4. Martha Vicinus, *The Industrial Muse* (New York: Barnes and Noble, 1974), see especially pp. 1–3.
5. Dan Tannacito, "Poetry of the Colorado Miners: 1903–1906," *Radical Teacher* 15 (March 1980): 1–8. Appended to Tannacito's article is a small anthology of miners' poetry.
6. Paul Lauter, "Working-Class Women's Literature—An Introduction to Study," *Women in Print, I*, ed. Ellen Messer-Davidow and Joan Hartman (New York: Modern Language Association, 1982), pp. 109–134.
7. Lawrence Levine, *Black Culture and Black Consciousness: Afro-American Folk Thought from Slavery to Freedom* (New York: Oxford University Press, 1977).
8. I am distinguishing between "working-class," "folk," or "popular" (peoples') culture and what Dwight MacDonald characterized as "mass culture." Popular culture, what people who share class (or ethnicity and race) produce in communicating with one another, can be separated from what is produced as a commodity, generally at the lowest common denominator, for consumption by

masses of people. To be sure, the distinction is not always clear-cut, but it is worth seeking.

9. Quoted by Herbert G. Gutman, *Work, Culture, and Society in Industrializing America* (New York: Knopf, 1976), pp. 23–24, from Melech Epstein, *Jewish Labor in the United States* (New York, 1950), pp. 290–291.

10. See John W. Blassingame, *The Slave Community* (New York: Oxford, 1972), pp. 49–59.

11. See Levine, *Black Culture and Black Consciousness*, pp. 30–31.

12. Ibid., p. 6.

13. Jeanette R. Murphy, "The Survival of African Music in America," *Popular Science Monthly* 55 (September 1899): 662; quoted by Blassingame, *The Slave Community*, pp. 27–28.

14. See "The Burning Struggle: The Civil Rights Movement," an interview with Bernice Johnson Reagon, *Radical America* 12 (November–December 1978): 18–20.

15. Levine, *Black Culture and Black Consciousness*, p. 33; cf. p. 207.

16. The usual distinctions between "poetry" and "propaganda," or between "fine arts" and "crafts" hinge on the issue of function. Modern critics have, in one form or another, generally assumed that "poetry is its own excuse for being" and that a poem should "not mean, but be." This is not the place to argue such claims. I don't find them particularly convincing, though it is obvious enough that art can have differing functions in different cultures. Let it suffice here to assert that viewing working-class culture from the standpoint of such assumptions will fatally mislead the critic.

17. Allen Tate, "Tension in Poetry," in *Essays of Four Decades* (Chicago: Swallow Press, 1968), pp. 64, 65.

18. Ibid., p. 58.

19. "To Whom Is the Poet Responsible?" in *Essays of Four Decades*, p. 27.

20. "Literature as Knowledge," in *Essays of Four Decades*, p. 104.

21. "The Man of Letters in the Modern World," in *Essays of Four Decades*, p. 14.

22. Ibid., p. 16.

23. In rereading this, it seems to me that I have made it sound like all academic critics are centers of independent power. Clearly, people in academe respond to institutional priorities, corporate definitions of appropriate career tracks. Indeed, most teachers and literary scholars are the victims of established modes of performance rather than their creators. It is not my intention to blame the victims but rather to make clear the source of that victimization.

24. Allen Tate, *Reactionary Essays on Poetry and Ideas* (Freeport, N.Y.: Books for Libraries, 1968), pp. 154–157.

25. The comment was quoted in a press release connected with the publication of her collection *Ripening* (Old Westbury, N.Y.: Feminist Press, 1982).

26. "The Poet as Woman," *The World's Body* (New York: Scribner's, 1938).

27. *Women's Fiction: A Guide to Novels by and about Women in America, 1820–1870* (Ithaca: Cornell University Press, 1978).

28. Steps toward changing the absolute unavailability of texts were taken when Indiana University Press issued Judith Fetterley's collection of early and mid-nineteenth-century American women writers and Rutgers University Press began to issue its series of reprints of the work of writers like Child, Susan Warner, and Cary. But these are only beginning steps. To illustrate the problem: none of the work of Catherine Maria Sedgewick, considered in her day the equal of Cooper and Irving, is easily available. Little of Child, Fanny Fern, or Sarah Josepha Hale is accessible. Only one work by Rebecca Harding Davis is available, "Life in the Iron Mills," first restored in an edition from the Feminist Press and now enshrined in the Norton anthology of American literature. Only within the last two years have two works by Elizabeth Stuart Phelps become available: *The Silent Partner* (Feminist Press) and *The Story of Avis* (Rutgers). Even some of H. B. Stowe's texts are unavailable in paperback. Nor is there any edition of the work of the most widely published black woman writer of the nineteenth century, Frances Ellen Watkins Harper.

29. Barbara Christian, *Black Women Novelists: The Development of a Tradition, 1892–1976* (Westport, Conn.: Greenwood Press, 1980); Elaine Showalter, *A Literature of Their Own: British Women Novelists from Brontë to Lessing* (Princeton: Princeton University Press, 1977); Sandra M. Gilbert and Susan Gubar, *The Madwoman in the Attic: The Woman Writer and the Nineteenth-Century Literary Imagination* (New Haven: Yale University Press, 1979).

30. "Going in Circles: The Female Geography of Jewett's *Country of the Pointed Firs,*" *Studies in the Literary Imagination* 16 (Fall 1983); especially 85–89.

31. See, for example, Jane Tompkins, "Sentimental Power," *Glyph* (1981).

32. See, for example, Baym, *Women's Fiction*, pp. 25, 144.

33. Alice Cary, *Clovernook, or Recollections of Our Neighborhood in the West, Second Series* (New York: Redfield, 1853), pp. 363–64.

34. I have taken some steps in this area in a paper entitled "The Literatures of America—A Comparative Discipline," prepared for a Soviet-American conference on minority literatures in the United States, University of Pennsylvania, July 1985.

Adrian Oktenberg

⟩⟩ From the Bottom Up:
Three Radicals of the Thirties

Those of us who came to maturity in the sixties would do well to remember the thirties. From a certain perspective, the two decades are not so far apart. In fact, they overlap. Nor is it only that the differences between the Old Left and the New, in hindsight, seem more apparent than real. In both periods the separate worlds of art and politics interlocked. Briefly, the classic alienation of intellectuals from the masses of ordinary people was dissipated; boundaries between high culture and low seemed dissolved; those who thought and those who acted were one and the same; those who created culture and those who made history were one. For makers of poetry it was a time when poetry meant politics. And whether they were artists or not, people who lived through the experience were afterward profoundly marked by it.

When we think of the poetry of the thirties, we are apt to think of Auden, Spender, and Day Lewis. They were English, and as poets they have not been neglected.[1] I have omitted discussion of them here. Turning to the American scene, it is apparent that the signal works and names of the decade are clustered in areas that are also beyond the scope of this essay. The thirties were rich in reportage,[2] polemic, and criticism—Agnes Smedley, Josephine Herbst, Meridel LeSueur, and Dorothy Thompson gave first-hand reports from the various fronts, Joseph North, Mike Gold, and Granville Hicks argued current issues, and Edmund Wilson, Kenneth Burke, and V. F. Calverton played the role of engagé critic. As an extension of many of the same concerns,

83

much of the literature of the period, especially that which is remembered now, takes the form of fiction or drama. In the short story, there were Tillie Olsen, Tess Slesinger, and Dorothy Parker. In the novel, John Dos Passos, James T. Farrell, and Jack Conroy. In drama, Lillian Hellman and Clifford Odets and the Group Theatre.[3]

Who, then were the American poets of the thirties, and why are they so little thought of now? If they were writing proletarian poetry, poetry "from the bottom up," what was it and how has it survived the years? In a time when literature and politics met, what was the result, and were the aims of each so irreconcilable that one extinguished the other?

First and always, when speaking of proletarian poetry or art we must keep in mind what Big Bill Haywood said to the members of Mabel Dodge's salon (as described in Max Eastman's novel *Venture* [1927]):

> "Not only is art impossible to such a man [a Pittsburgh steelworker]," he said, "but life is impossible. He does not live. He just works. He does the work that enables you to live. He does the work that enables you to enjoy art, and to make it, and to have a nice meeting like this and talk it over. . .
>
> "The only problem, then, about proletarian art," he continued, "is how to make it possible, how to make life possible to the proletariat. In solving that problem we should be glad of your understanding, but we don't ask your help. We are going to solve it at your expense. Since you have got life, and we have got nothing but work, we are going to take our share of life away from you, and put you to work.
>
> "I suppose you will want to know what my ideal of proletarian art is," he continued, "what I think it will be like, when a revolution brings it into existence. I think it will be very much kindlier than your art. There will be a social spirit in it. Not so much boasting about personality. Artists won't be so egotistical. The highest ideal of an artist will be to write a song which the workers sing, to compose a drama which great throngs of workers can perform out of doors. When we stop fighting each other—for wages of existence on one side, and for unnecessary luxury on the other—then perhaps we shall all become human beings and surprise ourselves with the beautiful things we do and make on the earth. Then perhaps there will be civilization and civilized art. But there is no use putting up pretenses now. The

important thing . . . is that our side, the workers, should fight
without mercy and win. There is no hope for humanity anywhere else."[4]

In other words, there is a great silence where proletarian art, art created
by the common people, ought to be. Our task is, first, to attend to the
reasons for that silence and, second, to end it. Another task is to be
aware of the system of valuation implicit in the definition of art and to
resist it.[5] Art created by and for common people, "folk art," and that
created by those who are considered "outsiders" to mainstream culture
(whose work for one reason or another is alien to what Fanon called
"Mediterranean values"), has not been seen as worthy of the accolades
"masterpiece" or "classic."

Whatever its origin, art has always been made against the odds. For
artists of proletarian origin, the odds against them have been greater.
Not only economic, but also social and racial oppression have added
weight to the silence.[6] Despite the odds, American proletarians—Colorado miners, Pittsburgh steelworkers, New York "Jews without money"
—did make art. Some of it is unjustly neglected.[7] And, what is probably true with respect to any given current or undercurrent in art, much
of it does not bear sustained attention.[8]

The movement for proletarian poetry in the thirties was a political as
well as a literary movement.[9] Its partisans were not limited to those of
strictly proletarian origin or to those who earned their living in literary
vineyards. Despite the publication of manifestos, petitions, and calls
for writers' congresses, there was never a cohesive or organized group
called "proletarian poets" or anything like one. The partisans of the
movement were not all communists, fellow travelers, sympathizers
with the American or Russian Communist parties, with the Comin-
tern, or with other organized groups for political action. Few writers of
the time ever were, being writers. About as far as many went was to
join one of the John Reed Clubs, an early (and very loose) effort by the
American Communist party to organize writers. By nature, writers are
great signers of petitions and open letters but not great actors on the
stage of history.

The battles for proletarian poetry and the barricades that were set up
against it for the most part took the form of debates and publications.
Just as communism and fascism were the great ideas of the decade,

posed in dialectical opposition, there were similarly opposed doctrines in poetry. Proletarian poets took their places on the left, with "art as a weapon" as their slogan. On the right were the fighters for "art for art's sake."

I take the *Partisan Review* of 1934 to 1936 to be the most vocal exemplar of the right wing "art for art's sake" position, although many may differ with my opinion; such a choice only shows how narrow was the spectrum of opinion. It was originally founded as the literary organ of the New York City John Reed Club and its editors (William Phillips and Philip Rahv) were Trotskyists. Ostensibly "left," it supported such fundamentally bourgeois tenets as the individualism of the artist and the uniqueness of the artist of genius. But those who believed in "art for art's sake" were essentially anarchist at heart. They believed that art has its own imperatives which must be respected; that artists can subscribe to no given line or position but must remain individualist, solitary, and free; that art transcends the dictates of party, organization, government, and nation. At one time or another its partisans included some Southern agrarians, certain New Critics, and, most important, the modernist faction whose names (Pound, Eliot, Williams, Stevens, Moore, Crane) have become icons.

On the left were the revolutionary proletarian poets who saw "art as a weapon." They believed that literature above all else is communication, and that communication from one ivory tower to another is as valuable as that kind of law which "forbids the rich as well as the poor from sleeping under bridges." Far from existing in a world apart, literature for them was part of the forward motion of history; they saw the literary transmutation of ideas into art as part and parcel of that historical context.[10] Since a Marxist view of history foretold the collapse of capitalism and the eventual triumph of the working class, they believed that the purpose of art must be to raise and sharpen the consciousness of that class which alone could make, or remake, history. They strove to make of the working class a class not "of itself" but "for itself" so as to hasten the revolution which was inevitable anyway. Accordingly, they tried to write not for the intellectuals but for the people. If they were not themselves of proletarian origin they tried to write for proletarians, to make their silence articulate. They wanted to address the basic concerns of ordinary people in language and forms that would be accessible and intelligible to them. For if once the people awakened and united moved, the earth would be moved also and history transformed.

If the substance of this debate (which I have only outlined, so that it lacks texture) sounds naive or simplistic to modern readers, I must point out that any epoch, but particularly the thirties, must be understood in its own context.

Let us think for a moment about the year 1932.

After the stock market crash in 1929, the twenties had come to a precipitous end. The Jazz Age, the heyday of the flapper and bootleg liquor, the "new woman" amidst the bohemianism of Greenwich Village, the energy and spirit of the Harlem Renaissance—all must have seemed as irrevocable as one's youth. The policies of Hoover had been declared bankrupt and Roosevelt was elected for the first time that year. It was the depth of the Depression, and by the end of the year fifteen million Americans were out of work.[11] National income had dropped from $81 billion in 1929 to $42 billion, and bank "holidays" had become epidemic. That summer thousands of Bonus Marchers (veterans of World War I who had petitioned the government for immediate payment of their army bonuses) had been driven from Washington, D.C., by General (then Captain) MacArthur's troops. Evicted and jobless people camped out in "Hoovervilles" and many took to the roads and trains in a vast migration of people seeking work. There was no welfare to speak of, no unemployment insurance, no Social Security pensions (those were the result of later New Deal reforms). Roosevelt's inauguration speech the following spring, in which he declared that "we have nothing to fear but fear itself," must have been brave indeed, since he had hardly a clue as to what policies might augur recovery.

An upheaval in political attitudes had also occurred. Back in 1916, Max Eastman had commented that the word *bourgeoisie* was one "we didn't even know how to spell in America," and another reporter had translated a banner in Petrograd as "Proletarians of every country, join yourselves together!"[12] By now the phrases of radicalism came fluently from many tongues and not exclusively in the accents of the foreign born. Not only the Democratic and Republican but also the Communist, Socialist Labor, and Farm Labor parties were active, while the Prohibition party still lingered. Bloody Harlan County in Kentucky and other areas had become battlegrounds between the forces of capital and labor. Domestic demagogues like Huey Long ("Every man a king") in Louisiana and Father Coughlin of Michigan, a "radio priest," attracted considerable followings. Sacco and Vanzetti had been executed in 1927; the Scottsboro Boys, after a circuslike trial in 1931, would spend years in jail. Lynching of blacks was still a common outrage in the South and would continue into the forties; "Jim Crow," the color line, was still a way of life there. The Klan was both powerful and active and not just in the South; one of its strongholds was red-neck Oregon and Washington.

The forces of progress and reaction battled also on foreign fronts. After the Reichstag fire, Hitler came to power in Germany. The anti-Semitic attitudes of his Brown Shirts were already well known and Jews were emigrating or being expelled from Germany; Einstein among others came to the United States the following year. Mussolini had been in power in Italy for years and would invade Ethiopia within a few more. Léon Blum, who with Britain and the United States would pursue a rigid "noninterventionist" policy with regard to Spain after Franco's coup there in 1936, headed the government of France. The single word Spain would thereafter become the catalyst for a generation. In Asia, the Chinese Communists had been betrayed and massacred by Chiang Kaishek and the Kuomintang in 1926–27, and the two groups were engaged in a bloody civil war in the midst of invasion, for imperialist Japanese forces had invaded Manchuria in 1931 and occupied Shanghai in 1932. In Latin America, Cuba and Haiti were both under brutal dictatorships. The Mexican Revolution, which had been vividly reported by John Reed, was long dead, and U.S. Marines would shortly put the Somozas in power in Nicaragua.

In the view of many in the United States it seemed that capitalism was on the point of self-destruction and the American "way of life" had lost its promise. Many eyes turned to the Soviet Union, where Stalin was at the helm. He had already murdered millions of peasants in the drive for collectivization and purges were well under way, but much of this was not yet widely known. The show trials were yet to come (1936 to 1938), followed by secret ones, to be followed by later and fuller accounts of atrocities and the camps. What American intellectuals knew was that the Russian Revolution of 1917 had been the only successful Marxist revolution in history and that the Soviet Union was the only existing socialist state. To be sure, there was famine in Russia in

1932 and widespread poverty and illiteracy, but it was felt that hardships were shared equally; the country was on a crash program of modernization. While many objected to the lack of freedom of speech and other fundamental democratic rights in the Soviet Union, others were satisfied that these were temporary necessities in a country which was still very much in the process of defending the revolution and building socialism. But most important, *everyone in the Soviet Union was employed.* At a time when having any kind of job, not a "good" job but any kind at all, literally meant survival, this seemed the economic equivalent of nirvana.

Moreover, many American intellectuals were aware of and admired the new Russian art. Experiments in Constructivism and Futurism were indicated if not yet clearly delineated. The work of Meyerhold in theater, Eisenstein and others in films, was known and admired. Mayakovsky, Pasternak, Pilnyak, and Babel had been translated into English; there were various anthologies of Russian revolutionary writing in circulation, and enthusiastic criticism of it was written by various hands. To many on American shores (and not just ideologues), the contrast between the apparent forward mobility of the Soviet Union and the obvious decline of the United States led to a striking conclusion. In Arthur Koestler's words: "They are the future—we, the past."[13]

Proletarian literature, its forms, language, and attitude, was largely imported to this country from another; partly for that reason, it never gained a strong hold on American literary minds. And political disillusion came fast, so the proletarian movement in American literature was a short one. But it was revived again in the sixties, under different conditions, with new young faces (many more of them black and female), and with a new style. And again it was eclipsed. But it remains true today that many more of us are poor than rich, many more are shut out than let in, and for these among other reasons I expect it to come round again.

Although their political attitudes and publication dates vary, the writers I have chosen to discuss—Carl Sandburg, Langston Hughes, Meridel LeSueur—were part of the proletarian movement in literature in the thirties.[14] Their sympathy for and identification with the common people was basic to their work, coupled with an expressed desire for radical change in the interests of greater equality and justice.

Carl Sandburg, Roughneck Singer

Carl Sandburg is almost unread today, when he is not a laughingstock, among those who still read poetry. The charges against him are severe, and of many of them his poetry stands convicted. Yet there are many other poets, poets who *are* read (or at least taught) and whose reputations are higher, who are equally guilty. During his life-time, Sandburg's work was taken seriously by many whose business it is to take poetry seriously. And—what is not true of others—Sandburg was one of the most genuinely popular American poets of this century.

In some ways it is difficult to write about Sandburg without sound-ing an apologia. It may be true that his intellectual capacity was slight and his capacity for sentimentality great. His imagery is jejune, his philosophizing worse. His poetry is far too dependent on nouns and adjectives and not enough on verbs. It contains copious description and yet little imagery. His lyrics are not lovely, his narratives have no dramatic tension, his meditations lack depth. His longer poems are almost entirely shapeless, and he has a tin ear.

All this and more is readily conceded. But it was Whitman who wrote, "The words of my book nothing, the drift of it everything." However much he liked to affect the lingo of a bumpkin, Sandburg was not ignorant of the rules. He broke them deliberately in the in-terests of a larger intention, something poets have done since poetry was named. For Sandburg, this most Whit/manic of poets, the drift was everything. It carried him far.

But where? Toward the creation of an American myth. Stubborn as a Swede (and he was fond of ethnic characterizations), Sandburg had one subject: America, meaning the United States, and one politic: radical democracy. Beyond that, his policy like Lincoln's was "not to have a policy." Accordingly, he took everything that came in his line of vision or experience—a great grab bag of people, ideas, objects, land-scapes—and tried to make of it a mythic expression of America and its people.

Myth is an expression of "primitive" people, people in the process of making what we call civilization, and its purpose is to explain and support them against the darkness. Sandburg took the long view, saw the country as young, its people still in the process of forging an iden-tity, of testing and examining the possibilities of who they might become. The time in his poetry is therefore the present—and the future. Even in his historical poems he does not dwell on the past but uses it as an exploration of what might come next.

Myth is also a counter against mortality in a world in which life is "solitary, nasty, poor, brutish, and short." Death is a constant presence in Sandburg's poems, and this is significant in a poet who has been read as an optimist. Nor does he emphasize only human frailty on an individual scale, but also constant is the consciousness of death of whole peoples, nations, civilizations. Sandburg's emphasis on the solitude, brevity, and transitoriness of all things human is almost Greek in its proportions.

Myths are also composed—if they are "composed" and not built by accretion, like deltas—by anonymous authors. It would never occur to us to wonder, for example, who wrote the one about Demeter and Persephone. Nobody wrote it. Everybody did. It doesn't matter.

And herein we begin to define the difference between Whitman and Sandburg. A century apart, each chose the same subjects and many of the same attitudes and methods—traveled the same ground, as it were. It was even the same act of optimism or faith for each to publish his major work when he did. *Leaves of Grass* first appeared in 1855, when the country was rushing toward civil war and possible dissolution. Sandburg brought out *The People, Yes* in 1936, when it was by no means clear that the country would survive as an economic or political entity. An American myth—yes. Democracy—yes.

But the voice through which Whitman's oracle spoke was not anonymous, unknowable, terrifying, like the oracle at Delphi. *Leaves of Grass* had a distinctive voice, highly idiosyncratic and personal (difficult and contradictory as that was), and it was Whitman's own. Its hero was The Poet, the visionary and seer who could prophesy the promised land. Sandburg's voice is altogether different from this; it strives to melt into the anonymous voices of the people; its ideal is not the particular but the general—or the universal, if you will. Lincoln was Sandburg's personal hero, but Sandburg's poetry is distinguished largely by Lincoln's absence. The hero of Sandburg's work is not Lincoln but the people, "democracy en masse." Hence, it lacks the concern, so striking in Whitman, for the self, the I, the ego, the personality. In this sense, at least, Sandburg's voice was more essentially mythic than Whitman's. Thus, Sandburg is not a later and weaker clone of Whitman.

Rather, he is more like Allen Ginsberg—a new hybrid grafted from the original tree.

In general, Sandburg's best poems are also his best-known poems: "Chicago," "Slabs of the Sunburnt West," "Good Morning America," and "The People, Yes."[15] All are long versions of incantations, invocations, and chants (primitive prayers) written in favor of ancient verities and sometimes flung into the void of an indifferent universe. Their language is a peculiar mix of the slangy lingo of a low-down cuss combined with the intonation of a preacher or priest; half of it is reminiscent of the speech of "Waiting for Lefty" while the other half is derived from ancient texts like the Bible. Choosing at random a few lines from a Sandburg poem, the first half might look like this: "Go to it" and "independent as a hog on ice." An example of the second half is this: "Remember this city" and "fished from its depths" and "a text." Combined as Sandburg wrote them in "The Windy City," the lines are these:

> Go to it and remember this city fished from its
> depths a text: "independent as a hog on ice."[16]

The poems are constructed like ancient religious rituals: slow, deliberately repetitious, the main chant-line changing slightly each time it is brought around again, sparks from the bonfire shooting occasionally into the circle of celebrants, the climax building, reached, then released in a final coda. The whole appears loose enough to permit spontaneity and also varying lengths, depending on the needs of each performance (though on the page the poems are presented in full).

I have no doubt that Sandburg consciously strove to recall and reclaim *in an utterly American context* both the lyric and epic voices of the ancient Greeks. "Good Morning, America" is an example.[17] It is crammed with American folk tales, tall tales, and legends, from Paul Bunyan to Sleepy Hollow, used in various versions, with proverbs, aphorisms, epigrams, and fables, commercials, slogans, pamphleteering, huckstering, folk songs, and hymns. It utilizes almost everything that Sandburg can find or think of which can be placed or identified as in some way American. Yet its central trope plays on the theme of mutability and its closing section is a kind of hymn to the earth.[18]

A myth is not made by a single voice but by a chorus of voices over time; it also requires a community, a system of shared values which we as Americans may not have. It may also be the product of a more finite world than the one in which we live. Or Sandburg's failure, truth be told, may simply be the result of his own shortcomings as a poet.

But his popularity in his lifetime seems to me indicative of something—that Sandburg, like Will Rogers, Charlie Chaplin, and a few others, touched a deep and responsive chord in common people, in common American people, to whom all his work was dedicated. Sandburg tried to speak to them and for them in their own various and anonymous voices, for he believed that art as well as American politics was a radical experiment in democracy. His poetry was intended as a modest contribution to that experiment.

Langston Hughes, Comrade Singer

As a young poet, Langston Hughes was influenced by the poetry of Sandburg for reasons which go beyond the fact that both grew up in the Midwest.[19] Through Sandburg, Hughes first began to study the art of unrhymed free verse; through Paul Laurence Dunbar, Negro dialect poems. But Hughes shortly went beyond both, and in one of his first major poems, "The Negro Speaks of Rivers,"[20] found his true subject from which his politics developed. This was negritude, or soul.

Hughes is called "the poet laureate of the Negro people" and as such his work has not been neglected. But his work is generally discussed in the context of something called "folk poetry," a term I confess I fail to understand.

Almost all poetry I can think of was originally derived from an oral tradition of chants, songs, and storytelling—from a folk tradition based on a kind of collective or racial memory; that is, it was preliterate. It seems immaterial to me whether the particular "folk" involved were Homeric or Scottish as opposed to African, Caribbean, or Asian. What they made was poetry. And everything we are now accustomed to call poetry was once, in an earlier incarnation, folk poetry.

The fact that a literate tradition (written as opposed to oral literature, and literature based on other literature) later developed in the West, and that this *kind* of literature became the sum of what we know and recognize *as* literature, is to me a historical development which is most relevant.[21] For in the course of that development certain unspoken judgments were made. Folk art was not only differentiated from other kinds of art, it was also differentiated in terms of what was seen as its quality. Not only the artifacts of a particular culture but also whole cultures came to be stratified in terms of "high" and "low," "advanced" and "backward."[22] The evaluation of literature became similarly stratified: literature itself was defined as that which was within the literate tradition (the *Western* literate tradition at that), and this kind of literature was seen as worthy of the attention of educated, that is, "civilized," people. Literature based on an oral or folk tradition was acknowledged as something, but not-quite-yet literature, not deemed worthy of serious or extended critical attention. It was reserved for "primitive" or "developing" peoples, and folk poetry was relegated to a subgenre.

Since I do not subscribe to those kinds of critical judgments I do not distinguish between folk poetry and other kinds of poetry. Distinctions must continue to be made in terms of the epoch or cultural milieu in which a particular work was produced—poems must be read in their own context. A poem produced by a black American slave in the year 1619 (if we knew one) would certainly be different from a sonnet composed by Shakespeare in the same year. But I am not willing to say that one is poetry and the other is not, or that one is better poetry than the other. Who is to do the saying? The kind of reader who would choose Shakespeare is one who is trained to appreciate Shakespeare; that is, is familiar with Spenser or Petrarch or—again—a certain literary tradition. The community in which that slave lived might feel that he is the Shakespeare of *his* tradition.

So I am willing to acknowledge Langston Hughes as the Shakespeare or master of his tradition, because black readers (who ought to know) believe him to be one,[23] but I am not so willing to categorize him as a "folk poet," because the category itself is fraught with difficulty. To be sure, his poetry is infused with jazz, blues, spirituals (forms of black music which are also outside the canonical tradition), and the argot of the urban ghetto. Those things are elements of black culture, and if he hadn't drawn on that culture for his poetry, I would like to know what culture we would have expected him to draw on, or what he might have written. I feel sure that he would not have become a poet laureate of anything in particular. He would have been a poet in exile from his sources, in limbo; being himself, he might have made great poetry out of *that*, but it would have been poetry of an altered kind. To call Langston Hughes the "poet laureate of the Negro people" in nearly the same breath as calling him a "folk poet" seems to me to equate black culture with primitive culture, and this is misleading, to say the least.

If Langston Hughes is a folk poet, it means only that he wrote out of a certain time and place from the perspective of a minority people,[24] much as Wordsworth did when he wrote "Michael," or Allen Ginsberg when he wrote "Kaddish." Which is not to suggest an argument for the so-called universality of poetry, for I do not believe in one. The *particular* time and place, the *particular* people, are facts not to be ignored or glossed over in the interests of an easy identification by those who are different, who live by different assumptions. Adrienne Rich's "Twenty-one Love Poems," written by a woman to a woman, are violated by heterosexual lovers who read them aloud to each other, gazing with liquid eyes.[25] Rather, the reader must do the additional work necessary to identify the particular time and place, the particular perspective, from which the poems came, to become familiar with their context, and therby begin to understand the poems on their own terms.

The identification of Hughes as a folk poet obscures the fact that he is a brilliant poet of ideas, and radical ideas at that. The concepts of negritude and soul, the politics of Black Power, the psychology of black rage, are so familiar to children of the sixties that it comes almost as a shock to realize that Hughes was presenting articulate and concrete images of them in his poetry in the twenties and thirties. While these ideas did not originate with him,[26] he embodied them in verse of such fluency and power that it seems undated half a century later. Moreover, he consistently combined them with the basic premises of revolutionary socialism,[27] and this sympathy is evident—hard to miss—in his work not only of the thirties but to the end of his life.

"The Negro Speaks of Rivers,"[28] then, is only the beginning of a long chain of poems by Hughes which confront, distill, extend, and transform the historical experience of black people into an art both limpid and programmatic. As in all of Hughes' hallmark poems, its distillation is as extreme as any in Issa's haiku. The "I" of the poem is not that of "a" Negro but "the" Negro, suggesting the whole of the people and their history. Most of the consonants—*d*'s, *n*'s, *l*'s, *s*'s—are soft, and of the vowels, long *o*'s reoccur, contributing by sound the effect of an ancient voice. The tone of the repeated declarative sentences is muted, lulling. Every element of the poem combines to suggest that when the Negro speaks of rivers it is with the accumulated wisdom of a sage. The function of a sage is to impart the sometimes secret but long accumulated history of a people to its younger members so that they might make the lessons of the past active in the future. This impartation occurs in the central stanza of the poem:

> I bathed in the Euphrates when dawns were young.
> I built my hut near the Congo and it lulled me to sleep.
> I looked upon the Nile and raised the pyramids above it.
> I heard the singing of the Mississippi when Abe Lincoln
>   went down to New Orleans, and I've seen its muddy
>   bosom turn all golden in the sunset.

Moving by suggestion, by naming particular rivers and particular activities performed nearby, the poem implicates the whole history of African and American slavery without ever articulating the word. "I bathed in the Euphrates" and "I built my hut near the Congo" are the normal activities of natural man performed in his natural habitat. That may be an unnecessarily anthropological way of putting it, but the lines are the equivalent of the speaker having said, "I made my life undisturbed in the place where I lived." The shift—and the lesson—occurs in the next two lines. Raising the pyramids above the Nile was the act of slaves, and if ever "Abe Lincoln went down to New Orleans,"[29] it would have been in the context of American slavery and the Civil War. Implicit in the history of a people who had first been free and then enslaved is the vision of freedom regained, and therein lies the program. The final line of the poem, "My soul has grown deep like the rivers," suggests wisdom in the word "deep." The wisdom imparted by the poem, beyond the memory of the suffering of slavery, includes a more deeply embedded memory of freedom. This is perhaps the more powerful memory, or the more sustaining one, and even if deferred,[30] will reemerge in one form or another.

But now I will skim over Hughes' other great poems of soul, which are well known, in order to concentrate on his less well known poems of political action. The two themes are inextricably twined in his work, but the specific radical content of the latter has often been ignored.

While Hughes was never a member of the Communist party,[31] he was more sympathetic with its ideals than is usually acknowledged.[32] Reading him solely as a folk poet or making him into a kind of (passive) black saint is an error partly because it obscures or diminishes the very important part played by political activisim in his work.

"Good Morning, Revolution"[33] is one of the most emblematic poems of Hughes' radical work. Significantly, it is not included in Hughes' *Selected Poems*.[34] Its opening greetings sets the tone:

> Good morning, Revolution:
>   You're the very best friend
>   I ever had.

Never a friend of organized Christianity, which Hughes saw as an agent of oppression, contributing to the ignorance and passivity of the people,[35] the "great day in the morning" for Hughes was not the Second Coming but the coming of the revolution.

> Listen, Revolution,
>   We're buddies, see—
> Together,
> We can make everything. . . .

The poem makes it crystal clear that worker "buddies" will wrest "all the tools of production" from "the boss" who has "got all he needs, certainly. . . ."

> And turn 'em over to the people who work.
> Rule and run 'em for us people who work.

As always for Hughes, whose vision is consistently international, intercultural, and interracial,[36] whose poems always begin with the familiar gritty texture of home but expand therefrom into wider realms, the revolution will spread around the world:

> Greetings to the Socialist Soviet Republics
> Hey you rising workers everywhere greetings
>   And we'll sign it: Germany
>   Sign it: China
>   Sign it: Africa
>   Sign it: Poland
>   Sign it: Italy

> Sign it: America
> On that day when no one will be hungry, cold, oppressed,
> Anywhere in the world again.
>
>   That's our job!
>   . . . . .
>   Let's go, Revolution!

When it is quoted in pieces, as I have been forced to quote it for reasons of space, the poem gives the impression of agitprop. But anyone who reads it in full, especially if he is familiar with the leaden lines of some political poetry, will greet the poem as a breath of light, stunning air. Hughes uses blueslike repetitions and, in the partial last stanza I have quoted above, the call-and-response pattern of gospel preaching and song to inject energy into emblematic lines. This poem, as in Hughes' most characteristic political work, distills complex ideas into images which are powerful in themselves and at the same time comprehensible to ordinary, "unlettered" people, those who are "just folks." To anyone who has tried to put statement into poetry, the apparent ease of Hughes' achievement is extraordinary.

Hughes' political party is successful as poetry because, in this as in his other work, he retained his own poetic voice and his individual political integrity. When he wrote poems in defense of the African, Chinese, Cuban, Russian, or Spanish peoples, as he did at various crucial historical moments, he continued to write in the voice of your average "Joe" or "Simple" which could nevertheless reach eloquence.[37] His integrity is also evident where, in his political poems, he frankly refuses to endorse the orthodox or "correct" political line. In "Good Morning, Revolution" he acknowledges the fact that, in "democratic" America and despite its own origins, the country at large (including perhaps much of his audience) did not view revolution as a friend:

> He wrote a long letter to the papers about you:
> Said you was a trouble maker, a alien-enemy,
> In other words a son-of-a-bitch. . . .[38]

In "Final Call," a call for heroes in a time of trouble, some of the heroes called upon would in certain circles be considered outrageous choices. These include Jesus *and* Robespierre, Lenin *and* Trotsky, Malcolm X *and* Adam Powell.[39] In "Black Panther" Hughes sees that revolutionary group as righteously mistaken. [40] While he wrote much topical poetry on minor and major political issues, Hughes retained his integrity by remembering who he was and by keeping his personal priorities straight.

It seems to me significant that Hughes' radical influence has been largely ignored in this country while it has been great abroad, especially in the Third World. [41] Poets take what they need from wherever they find it, without regard to conventional critical categories or interpretations. The poets of Africa and Latin America have long recognized Hughes as a master of political poetry and used his voice as a model for their own. [42] It is past time for us in the United States to repair a myopic critical vision and, perhaps for the first time, read the work of Langston Hughes whole.

Meridel LeSueur, Mother Singer

The work of Meridel LeSueur is worse than neglected; it is part of that great body of work by women which has been "hidden from history." In the thirties she was part of a group of radical writers which included Tillie Olsen, Agnes Smedley, Grace Lumpkin, Tess Slesinger, Genevieve Taggard, Josephine Herbst, and Margery Latimer; most of this work is still largely unknown or only recently rediscovered. "Every woman who writes is a survivor," Tillie Olsen has said, and LeSueur added, "Survival is a form of resistance." As survivor and resister, LeSueur has turned out to be one of the hardiest of all. [43]

LeSueur was born in Murray, Iowa, in 1900, and throughout a life of "migrations" (a key word for her) has remained a creature of the Midwest. Her father was the first socialist mayor of Minot, North Dakota, and her mother overcame shyness and the most straitlaced of small town backgrounds to become an activist on behalf of women's and workers' rights. LeSueur grew up in a home steeped in political radicalism, and it remained a commitment which shaped all her work. By her own account she joined the Communist party as early as 1924; lived in various communes in New York and the Midwest; participated in numerous political actions, including the Minneapolis truckers' strike in 1934 through the Poor People's March on Washington in 1968; was blacklisted in the forties and fifties and rediscovered with the reemergence of the women's movement in the sixties and seventies. Her life has been marked by rootlessness, poverty, and struggle, and her work, especially of the thirties, reflects these experiences to an agonizing degree. But she considers that her life has been a long "ripening" and her recently published work, especially her poetry, constitutes an affirmation of life that only the most visionary poetry achieves.[44]

Unlike Sandburg's optimistic vision, LeSueur's America is a scene of a civilization dead and dying. The words and images which reoccur in LeSueur's writing of the thirties are of devastation, ruin, wreckage, violence and ravishment, suffering, desperation, and terror. "When you look at the unemployed women and girls you think instantly that there must be some kind of war,"[45] and she thought the Depression was "worse than a war." Her fiction and reportage of the time is an extended investigation into the causes and effects of that destruction, destruction which extended to all strata of society and culture. In her work, LeSueur shows how the mechanisms of developing capitalism had destroyed the dignity of human labor;[46] its cyclical failures destroyed any possibility of "upward mobility" for working people;[47] its requirements for wider markets meant abuse of the land as a means of production;[48] and in the process the people who created value were destroyed, denied, abused.[49] If LeSueur's work of this time were limited to a detailed catalog of such destruction it would be almost too painful to read and might have value as journalism or history but not as art.

That is not the case, however, because LeSueur's work is informed at the same time with a call for reconstruction, restoration, recreation, and rebirth.

> Capitalism is a world of ruins really, junk piles of machines, men, women, bowls of dust, floods, erosions, masks to cover rapacity and in this sling and wound the people carry their young, in the shades of their grief, in the thin shadow of their hunger, hope and crops in their hands, in the dark of the machine, only they have the future in their hands.
> Only they.[50]

The Communist critic in the thirties who called the emphasis on human suffering in LeSueur's work "defeatist" and symptomatic of a "nonrevolutionary spirit" missed the point.[51] LeSueur was anything but defeatist in her emphasis on a vision of the future based on what she called "communal solidarity."[52] For only when people were linked fully and consciously together across the divisions of sex, class, and generation would reconstruction be possible.

LeSueur's vision of recreation and rebirth amid the ruins may also have been missed or misunderstood because she so often expressed it in terms of women and the earth. These above all were the mnemonic sources of her generative re-vision, and she returns to them again and again. Women had historically been identified with the earth as givers and nurturers of life, and LeSueur returned to this ancient and mystical identification as a means through which a new culture could be created.

Of her contemporaries, LeSueur was a pioneer in her exploration of women as a central subject for her work, and specifically of what has been called the "biological reality" of women.[53] Few others made the subject so central an inspiration or approached it in a similar way. LeSueur's closest peers in this regard would have been Gabriela Mistral, the Chilean poet, and Georgia O'Keeffe, the American painter. Waldo Frank, writing in *The Nation*, called Mistral "the bard of mothers and children" and "the laureate of her vast American earth,"[54] and by the thirties she was almost revered as a kind of Latin American Demeter. Her influence during those years was very great, culminating in the award of the Nobel Prize for Literature in 1945, but her reputation has since declined. While Mistral's work was not translated into English until 1957, it is likely that LeSueur was aware at least of its basic themes. There is no doubt that she knew O'Keeffe's; the two women were friends, and LeSueur later said that she could not have written without O'Keeffe's encouragement and example.[55] She pronounced O'Keeffe "probably nearer to the inner dream of women who want to see as women. . . ."[56] "At last, a woman on paper!" is what Stieglitz is supposed to have said on first looking into a sheaf of O'Keeffe's drawings.[57] Indeed, O'Keeffe's imagery, particularly of pubiclike mounds, breastlike hills, flowers blooming in skulls, and many of the Native American motifs of her later work, is similar to the imagery used in LeSueur's poems.

It is in her poems, published as a group only late in her life, that LeSueur's generative re-vision of women and earth begins to come clear. "I returned to the haven of woman, land, the great beloved woman of my country," LeSueur had written, [58] and her poems take up this theme with mystical intensity. In her eighties, LeSueur said, "I think I am daring to write as crazily excessive abundant absolutely in extremity . . . on the far edge of the circle."[59] The poems are written with that intensity, almost seeming to emerge out of the earth's surface like lava under pressure, out of a generations-long conflict of struggle and suffering. They are written not in an individual or private voice, but in the voice of LeSueur's own "continuous woman": "the woman linked to other generations of women both biologically, through the body, and historically and spiritually, through the reality of struggle and survival."[60]

Most of the poems in LeSueur's book *Rites of Ancient Ripening*[61] draw on Native American sources for their imagery and symbolism. These are used to express LeSueur's Demeter-like identification with the natural cycle of birth/death/rebirth, that repetition which has no beginning or end. In the title poem an old woman faces her death, which is envisioned as an ultimate reopening into new life. As in the mystical poems of Saint John of the Cross or of Sor Juana Inés de la Cruz, death is longed for, not (as in their poetry) as a deliverance unto God, but (in LeSueur's) as a union with earth. As in their poetry also, the language is heavily oxymoronic.

> I am luminous with age
> In my lap I hold the valley.
>
> .   .   .   .
>
> The corn kernels cry to me in the fields
>   Take us home.
>
>   .   .   .   .   .
>
> I fall and burst beneath the sacred human tree.
> Release my seed and let me fall.
> Toward the shadow of the great earth
>   let me fall.
>
>   .   .   .   .
>
> Pound me death
>   stretch and tan me death
> Hang me up, ancestral shield
>   against the dark.

Burn and bright and take me quick.
Pod and light me into dark.
.   .   .   .
The little seeds of my children
                with faces of mothers and fathers
Fold in my flesh
                        in future summers.
                .   .   .   .   .   .
All was ground in the bodies bowl
            corn died to bread
                woman to child
                        deer to the hunters.
                        .   .   .   .   .   .
The rites of ancient ripening
Make my flesh plume
And summer winds stir in my smoked bowl.
Do not look for me till I return
                        rot of greater summers
Struck from fire and dark,
Mother struck to future child.
Unbud me now
Unfurl me now
Flesh and fire
            burn
                requicken
                    Death.[62]

The dying woman is not faded with age but luminous as a ripening bud. Her death is not the end of her life but a merging with past and future generations of human life, with the entire life cycle both natural and human, and this is not a terrifying event but one both solemn and ecstatic. As in Keats' "Autumn" ode, the end of the life cycle is not a weakening fade into oblivion but a culmination of great richness and beauty.

And of course it is a culmination drenched in sensuality. In this respect, LeSueur's poems draw less on Native American sensibility than on the tradition of ecstatic mystical poetry already mentioned and on her own constant reworking of the Demeter-Persephone myth. "Green Unfurl Me," "Lost Mother Lode," "I Light Your Streets," and others are poems in which the Persephone figure cries out her violation; "I Hear You Singing in the Barley Ripe," "Behold This and Always Love It," and "Budded with Child" are written in the voice of the Demeter figure.[63] In these poems LeSueur uses mythic figures to suggest a primal connection, beginning with mother and daughter but extending to all generations of women, between women *as* women, and to make what she called "a great song" rising out of their suffering. LeSueur acknowledged D. H. Lawrence as the writer who first freed her into sensuality in her writing,[64] and one of the limitations of that influence is that heterosexuality is emphasized but homosexuality is largely unacknowledged. Some of the influence of Sappho might be beneficial here. But it has always been a characteristic of LeSueur's work, in fiction as well as poetry, to delineate a knifelike edge of violence in male sexuality, and this often appears prominently in the midst of mutual heterosexual passion.[65]

In LeSueur's poetry generations of women are drawn together across boundaries of nation, culture, class to form in a single stream one "continuous woman." In *"Corridos* of Love,"[66] a hemisphere-to-hemisphere dialogue takes place between a white North American woman and a brown woman "below the border." The brown woman speaks first of her suffering and in an accusatory voice asks the other, "Didn't you hear my crying? . . . / Didn't you hear me plowing with my fingernails? / Or the sound of the spades of a million small graves? / Did our pain rise above the border you stole? / Was your sky darkened with our darkness? / Did you pay duty at the border of pain? / Have you a visa to permit you to feel it?"[67] The white woman replies by acknowledging the other's suffering, then describes her own, at every point emphasizing the similarity of oppression between the two women, and ends by seeking alliance with the other.

> Amidst lamentations, wounds, separations and lesions,
> continuously and massively bruised under the hooves of
>   conquerors,
> we have loomed our lives,
> with the same passion as high corn,
> for the velocity of pollen spreading to all days.
> As an ally I take you to my village.
> In the diurnal green
> the leaves forgive the root and raise the fruit!

> I'm seeking you among the ancient stone!
> In the dusty faces,
> In the raised fist,
> In the resurrected heart![68]

The hope of the poem is in solidarity based on shared suffering, shared understanding of the ways in which history has dealt with them similarly (while recognizing genuine difference), shared life dependent on each other and on the earth, and, finally, shared action ("in the raised fist") to achieve resurrection of the human heart. The poem is Job-like in its voices but not at all in its resolution. This is also true of "Dòan Kêt," a long poem addressed to Vietnamese women (the title means "solidarity" in Vietnamese), which expresses the mutuality of suffering between women, a prescient sense of ecology and the interdependence of peoples on earth, and which also ends with a guerrilla fighter's song of love and cry for action.[69]

So, in her recent poetry as well as in her fiction and reportage of the thirties, LeSueur begins to close the circle at the point where she commenced: with frankly radical political work based on the shared consciousness of women as women. The portrait she has drawn is of the "continuous woman" rooted in the continuous earth. She began with a vision of civilization dead and dying from which she developed a vision of recreation and rebirth.

Conclusion

Carl Sandburg, Langston Hughes, and Meridel LeSueur were all radicals who lived in an epoch distinguished even more than most by physical suffering and human terror. It cannot be surprising if some of their solutions were radical or if their responses during the thirties now seem to us naive, narrow, or arcane. They were honest writers who did honest work, and all of them did a great deal of it. They shared an activist view of their art, one which is now out of fashion. They tried to address the pressing issues of their time in ways which most people would understand and appreciate. They wrote their poetry "from the bottom up," simply enough, because the world as we know it was made the same way. Their work may have been neglected outright, misinterpreted, or put to uses they would never have intended or approved, but it should not be ignored.

Notes

The title is taken from historian Jesse Lemisch, who called for "a revolution in historiographical attitudes, a rejection of elite history: a history 'from the bottom up' will be more nearly objectively valid than has been the attempt to understand the past through the eyes of the few at the top." Quoted by Barton J. Bernstein, ed., in his introduction to *Towards a New Past: Dissenting Essays in American History* (New York: Random House, 1968), pp. xi–xii. The poets I will discuss tried to write from this point of view, and I believe their work, and poetry in general, should be written and read in this way.

This essay is dedicated to Amy Kesselman, who first introduced me to radical history, and, for her sustained love and work, to Ruth Gundle.

1. See, e.g., Samuel Hynes, *The Auden Generation: Literature and Politics in England in the 1930's* (New York: Viking, 1977).
2. Radical reportage in the thirties was somewhat different from mainstream journalism and was more or less a precursor of the "New Journalism" of the sixties. Writers injected fictional elements and personal narrative into their accounts in an effort to bring the reader more fully into the action. One source for this method was probably John Reed, and Mencken may also have been an influence.
3. Two useful anthologies are the following: Granville Hicks et al., eds., *Proletarian Literature in the United States* (New York: International Pub., 1935), and Joseph North, ed., *New Masses: An Anthology of the Rebel Thirties* (New York: International Pub., 1969). My list is obviously partial. Such luminaries as Fitzgerald and Hemingway have been omitted because they believed that living well, as opposed to doing much, is the best revenge.
4. Quoted by Daniel Aaron in *Writers on the Left* (New York: Avon, 1961), p. 34; this book is a valuable guide to the entire period. Haywood's was a Wobbly view and characteristically appealing and romantic; Communist party views were more rigid and doctrinaire.
5. The work of my friend Barbara Herrnstein Smith is instructive on the point. See "Contingencies of Value," in *Critical Inquiry* 10, no. 1 (September 1983).
6. On the silence of women writers, see Tillie Olsen, *Silences* (New York: Delacorte, 1978); the difficulties of black writers are amply documented in C. W. E. Bigsby, ed., *The Black American Writer, Vol. I: Fiction, Vol. II: Drama and Poetry* (Baltimore, Md.: Penguin, 1969).
7. For example, see the poetry of Kenneth Fearing in *Proletarian Literature in the United States*; see also Dan Tannacito, "Poetry of the Colorado Miners: 1903–1906," followed by an anthology, and Paul Lauter, "Working Class Women's Literature—An Introduction to Study," followed by a bibliography in *The Radical Teacher* 15 (December 1979).

8. A phenomenon which appears to be peculiar to poetry, as opposed to the other literary arts, is that many are attracted to it who would be better off elsewhere. The poetry of Mike Gold is a case in point. He was a kid from the New York slums who grew up to be a skilled organizer, a sensitive reporter, and a fiery polemicist (although in 1930 he did manage to lose a debate with that famous orator Georgia O'Keeffe). But he was not a poet. "A Strange Funeral in Braddock," reprinted in *Proletarian Literature in the United States*, p. 158, must be one of the slowest dirges ever written.

9. For the sketchy account that follows I rely heavily on *Writers on the Left*; see also Daniel Aaron and Robert Bendiner, eds., *The Strenuous Decade: A Social and Intellectual Record of the 1930's* (New York: Anchor, 1970); Christopher Lasch, *The New Radicalism in America 1889–1963: The Intellectual as a Social Type* (New York: Knopf, 1965); Wilson Record, *Race and Radicalism, the NAACP and the Communist Party in Conflict* (Ithaca, N.Y.: Cornell, 1964); William L. O'Neill, *Everyone Was Brave, a History of Feminism in America* (Chicago: Quadrangle, 1969). Numerous memoirs of the period, many of them well known, have been intuitively relied on but are not cited here.

10. Carl Sandburg saw that the consequences of an "ivory tower" view of art would be the writer's silence on living issues, and that "a writer's silence on living issues can in itself constitute a *propaganda of conduct* leading toward the deterioration or death of freedom" (emphasis added). From "Notes for a Preface," in *The Complete Poems of Carl Sandburg, Revised and Expanded Edition* (New York: Harcourt, Brace, 1969), p. xxvi.

11. The population reported in the 1930 census was 122,775,046. Much of this account is drawn from Irving S. Kull and Nell M. Kull, *A Chronological Encyclopedia of American History* (New York: Popular Library, 1952).

12. Quoted in *Writers on the Left*, p. 60.

13. From *Arrow in the Blue*, quoted in *Writers on the Left*, p. 169.

14. Other poets who were at one time or another part of the movement included Muriel Rukeyser, Kenneth Patchen, Horace Gregory, Archibald MacLeish, Claude McKay, James Agee, Stanley Burnshaw—all of whom came to be widely known in other contexts or admired for other kinds of work.

15. From *The Complete Poems of Carl Sandburg*, found respectively at pp. 3, 307, 320, 439. This list is meant to be more indicative than definitive. "Fog," while well known, is omitted from the list. It is one of Sandburg's better lyrics, principally because he resisted the temptation to add what would have been a more characteristic last line, something like "So the fog comes." In general, I think Sandburg's better poems are the longer ones.

16. From *The Complete Poems of Carl Sandburg*, p. 271.

17. Ibid., p. 320.

18. "The People, Yes" is omitted from this discussion because it is a book-length poem and I cannot hope to do justice to it here. The points I would make about it parallel those I have made about "Good Morning, America," and I note that its ending, almost in recognition of the myth-making process, is open. (ibid., p. 617)

> In the darkness with a great bundle of grief
>   the people march.
> In the night, and overhead a shovel of stars
>   for keeps, the people march:
>   "Where to? What Next?"

19. Langston Hughes, *The Big Sea, an Autobiography* (New York: Hill and Wang, 1940), p. 28. His second autobiographical volume was *I Wonder as I Wander*.
20. From Langston Hughes, *Selected Poems* (New York: Knopf, 1959), p. 4.
21. See B. H. Smith, "Contingencies of Value."
22. I see this stratification as a consequence of white and patriarchal cultural hegemony and the whole course of it connected with the eventual development of capitalism. But this is an essay, not a history of the world.
23. I put the sentence this way because I believe that when a white reader (like myself) reads the work of a black poet (when a woman like myself reads the work of a man, and so on), she or he must be conscious of performing an act of translation. As in any translation, much is lost, and much of which the reader might not even be aware.
24. People of color, of course, are hardly "a minority" in the world at large. I speak of them as a minority in terms of the perspective of the United States, and also as makers of minority cultures, as seen from the perspective of the prismatic Western tradition which I have been criticizing.
25. See my essay, "Disloyal to Civilization: The Twenty-one Love Poems," in Jane Roberta Cooper, ed., *Reading Adrienne Rich: Reviews and Re-Visions 1951– 1981* (Ann Arbor: University of Michigan Press, 1984).
26. The themes of rebellion and revolt and black solidarity and pride had been an integral part of black history and literature from the beginning of the colonialist era. Hughes was intimately familiar with this history and much of his work constitutes the teaching of it. Also, the thirties in Africa was a pivotal decade in the development of negritude and I am sure its influence on Hughes was great. "A new era, combining modern scholarship, militancy, and the authentic voice of African humanism, began in the 1930's. This was a most productive period, culminating in 1938 with the publication of Jomo Kenyatta's *Facing Mount Kenya*. During the previous year Nnamdi Azikiwe brought out his *Renascent Africa*, and Leon G. Damas's *Pigments* appeared in Paris. The following year Aime Cesaire's *Cahier d'un retour au pays natal* and Senghor's 'Ce que l'homme noir apporte' were published. These were the years when négritude was discovered in Paris by French-speaking African students, led by Senghor of Senegal, Cesaire of Martinique, and Damas of French Guiana." Mercer Cook, "African Voices of Protest," in Mercer Cook and Stephen E. Henderson, *The Militant Black Writer in Africa and the United States* (Madison: University of Wisconsin Press, 1969), p. 11. Hughes knew French, was widely traveled in both Europe and Africa, and would have been moved by these currents.
27. A valuable (but out of print) collection which makes this point indisputably is Langston Hughes, *Good Morning, Revolution: Uncollected Writings of Social*

Protest, ed. Faith Berry (New York and Westport, Conn.: Lawrence Hill and Co., 1973).

28. From *Selected Poems*, p. 4. The poem, if the author's account is to be credited, was written before Hughes was out of high school. See *The Big Sea*, pp. 55–56.
29. I cannot confirm that Lincoln ever made such a trip, and I doubt it. But the uses of the idea as metaphor are obvious: the Great Emancipator of the slaves sailing past Cairo, Memphis, Vicksburg, and Port Hudson, battlefields all, to one of the commercial and political strongholds of the Confederacy is a powerful image.
30. I am thinking of course of "Harlem," which begins, "What happens to a dream deferred?" See *Selected Poems*, p. 268.
31. While Richard Wright, Claude McKay, and others were. But for various reasons they have been excluded from this discussion.
32. It is probably fair to describe Hughes as a fellow traveler of the party until the Nazi-Soviet Pact in 1939. While this was a point of massive defection from the party, in the context of the thirties it is rather late. It is true that Hughes differed with many important policies of both the American and Russian Communist parties and said so. He never followed the American party's call for a separate black "nation" to be carved out in the South; he objected publicly (though not, I think, while he was there) to the limitations on freedom of speech of writers and others in the Soviet Union. However, he was extremely active in Communist and (what McCarthyites would call) Communist-front activities for many years. To wit: (*a*) He went to the Soviet Union in 1932 as part of a group of black Americans who were engaged to work with the Russians on a film called *Black and White*. When the film project fell apart, most of the others in his group returned to the United States; Hughes stayed for a year and wrote numerous articles and poems in support of the revolution and the regime. (*b*) He was a U.S. delegate to the Second International Writers Congress, held in Paris in 1937. (*c*) Also in 1937 he spent six months in Spain as a correspondent for *The Afro-American Newspapers*; during that time he wrote numerous articles and poems in support of the Loyalist cause. (*d*) He was elected a vice-president of the League of American Writers in 1937 and remained one of its most active supporters until it was dissolved in 1942. (*e*) In 1949 and later he wrote a number of articles and poems in support of the Chinese Revolution. (*f*) He gave militant speeches at two of the four American Writers Congresses in 1935 and 1939. (*g*) In the late forties and early fifties some of his books were banned by certain agencies of the U.S. government and he was blacklisted in some quarters. He was called before (McCarthy's) Senate Committee on Government Operations in March 1953, and his statement to that group is a model of skillful evasion; it is neither apologetics nor lies. All this is described and documented in *Good Morning, Revolution*.
33. From *Good Morning, Revolution*, p. 3; first printed in *New Masses*, September 1932.
34. The accounts of Saunders Redding and Faith Berry in *Good Morning, Revolution* make clear that Hughes was often reluctant to read publicly or allow to be widely printed (in anthologies) his most radical work. He had been wounded by

right-wing attacks on his work, notably a campaign that had been conducted against "Goodbye, Christ." Berry attributes Hughes' nervousness not to any change in his political commitments but to the fundamentals of bread and butter: Hughes made his living by giving readings and lectures and by writing books. It is not hard to imagine what Hughes' circumstances might have become it such poems as the "Ode to Lenin" or "Roar China!" were more widely known.

35. See "To Certain 'Brothers,'" "God to Hungry Child," "A Christian Country," "Goodbye, Christ," pp. 35–36, and "Concerning 'Goodbye, Christ,'" pp. 133–135, in *Good Morning, Revolution*; cf. James A. Emanuel, "Christ in Alabama: Religion in the Poetry of Langston Hughes," in Donald B. Gibson, ed., *Modern Black Poets, A Collection of Critical Essays* (Englewood Cliffs, N.J.: Prentice-Hall, 1973), p. 57.

36. *And* anti-anti-Semitic *and* anti-sexist.

37. Simple is the hilariously wise antihero of several Hughes stories: *Simple Speaks His Mind, Simple Takes a Wife, Simple Stakes a Claim*.

38. From *Good Morning, Revolution*, p. 4.

39. From Langston Hughes, *The Panther and the Lash, Poems of Our Times* (New York: Knopf, 1967), p. 20.

40. From *The Panther and the Lash*, p. 19.

41. With the crucial exception of American *black* radical poets, especially those of the sixties (Baraka, Lee, Sanchez, Giovanni, and others). They have themselves been largely ignored by the establishment.

42. See *The Militant Black Writer in Africa and the United States*, pp. 12, 102–103. Hughes edited a volume, *Poems from Black Africa*, and translated the work of Gabriela Mistral, Nicolás Guillén, and others; such attention was repaid.

43. Of the writers under discussion, she is the only one still living.

44. The biographical information here is taken from Elaine Hedges' introduction to Meridel LeSueur, *Ripening: Selected Work, 1927–1980* (Old Westbury, N.Y.: Feminist Press, 1982), edited by Hedges.

45. From "Women Are Hungry," in *Ripening*, p. 44.

46. See "Harvest," in Meridel LeSueur, *Harvest* (Cambridge, Mass.: West End Press, 1977), p. 29, a story in which a farm wife resists her husband's "lust" for a threshing machine.

47. See "The Return of Lazarus," in Meridel LeSueur, *Song for My Time* (Cambridge, Mass.: West End Press, 1977), p. 59, a story in which an old man's refrain, "the mortgage, the mortgage," becomes a lament for a needlessly wasted life.

48. See "Eroded Woman," in *Song for My Time*, p. 19, a story about a struggling family in an abandoned mining town, "a wasteland of ruined earth and human refuse."

49. See "Annunciation," in *Ripening*, p. 124, a story in which a young husband tries to talk his wife into ending her pregnancy because he cannot afford another mouth to feed. These examples are used by way of shorthand illustration only and can be multiplied throughout LeSueur's work.

50. From "The Dark of the Time," in *Ripening*, p. 239.

51. Quoted by Hedges in *Ripening*, p. 11.
52. From "The Fetish of Being Outside," quoted by Hedges in *Ripening*, p. 15. What LeSueur meant is dramatized in her famous story "I Was Marching," in *Ripening*, p. 158.
53. The phrase is taken out of context from Robert Duncan, *The H. D. Book*, quoted in Jerome Rothenberg and George Quasha, eds., *America a Prophecy, a New Reading of American Poetry from Pre-Columbian Times to the Present* (New York: Vintage, 1973), p. 543. In my view, H. D. was too much a disciple of Pound and Freud to have had a very articulate vision of the "communal sensibility" of women, although there are striking glimpses of it in her work.
54. Quoted on the jacket of *The Selected Poems of Gabriela Mistral*, trans. Langston Hughes (Bloomington: Indiana University Press, 1957).
55. See Laurie Lisle, *Portrait of an Artist: A Biography of Georgia O'Keeffe* (New York: Seaview Books, 1980), pp. 164–165.
56. Ibid., p. 430.
57. Ibid., p. 85.
58. From "The Dark of the Time," in *Ripening*, p. 232.
59. Quoted by Hedges in *Ripening*, pp. 18–19.
60. See Hedges in *Ripening*, p. 19.
61. Meridel LeSueur, *Rites of Ancient Ripening* (Minneapolis, Minn.: Vanilla Press, 1975).
62. From *Rites of Ancient Ripening*, pp. 24–27.
63. Ibid., pp. 12, 8, 4, 35, 22, 20.
64. See Hedges, in *Ripening*, p. 6.
65. See, e.g., "O Prairie Girl, Be Lonely," in *Ripening*, p. 175; "Summer Idyl, 1949," in *Song for My Time*, p. 26; "Fudge," in *Harvest*, p. 40; "Autumnal Village," in *Harvest*, p. 52; in the poems, see "Lost Mother Lode," in *Rites of Ancient Ripening*, p. 8; "Green Unfurl Me," p. 12; "Corridos of Love," p. 47.
66. From *Rites of Ancient Ripening*, p. 47.
67. Ibid., p. 48.
68. Ibid., pp. 49–50.
69. Ibid., p. 51.

Annette Kolodny

The Influence of Anxiety
Prolegomena to a Study of the Production of Poetry by Women

A sister's hand may wrest a female pen,
From the bold outrage of imperious men.

Mercy Otis Warren, "To Mrs. Montague" (1790)

In 1973, in *The Anxiety of Influence: A Theory of Poetry*, Yale critic Harold Bloom first propounded his theory that those whom he termed "strong poets"—like Blake, Keats, and Wordsworth—were successful combatants in a defensive battle for psychic survival. Compounded from various sources, including Freud, the books of the Kabbalah, Vico, and Valéry, Bloom's thesis rests on the central assumption that there exists in every poet's creative imagination a constellation of beings within which he reenacts a psychological drama not unlike that which Freud attributed to the biological nuclear family. Before a rich and overwhelming tradition in which prior poets—or precursors—appear to have exhausted the very resources which the aspiring poet would claim for himself, Bloom's poet-ephebe becomes "not so much a man speaking to men as a man rebelling against being spoken to by a dead man (the precursor) outrageously more alive than himself."[1] Seeking to overcome "the dread that there will be not enough for oneself . . . the fear of there not being enough left to do"[2] (which Bloom terms an anxious sense of "belatedness"), the would-be poet attempts to rewrite, correct, or even appropriate a precursor's poetic vision as his own. As Bloom explained in *A Map of Misreading* (1975),

112

in order "to live, the poet must *misinterpret* the father, by the crucial act of misprision, which is the re-writing of the father" (AMOM, p. 19). If the poet-ephebe is successful in this he emerges as a "strong poet," having performed an imaginative act of displacement that closely approximates the Freudian schema of the son doing battle with the father who had sired him. Blake thus confronts Milton as did Oedipus and Laius at the crossroads.

The result is a theory of poetic influence which does away with our more usual notions of generic evolution or creative borrowings. Instead, Bloom posits a dialectical poetic history which *"always proceeds by a misreading of the prior poet, an act of creative correction that is actually and necessarily a misinterpretation."*[3] For Harold Bloom, in other words, "mis-reading or misinterpretation" constitutes "the commonal or normal mode of poetic history."[4]

To be sure, Bloom has repeatedly insisted that it was never his aim "so to apply Freud (or even revise Freud) as to arrive at an Oedipal interpretation of poetic history."[5] Bloom's version of the family drama places "the emphasis less upon phallic fatherhood, and more upon *priority*" (TAOI, p. 56), and his notion of the precursor/father is flexible enough to incorporate the possibility of several personages compounded and experienced as one or, theoretically, all of poetic history itself (though his examples tend toward individual precursor figures) (TAOI, p. 11). Even so, Bloom's iteration of "intra-poetic relationships as parallels of family romance" (TAOI, p. 8) did not long remain in the realm of parallels or extravagant models. Less than two years after the appearance of *The Anxiety of Influence*, Bloom laid claim to "latent principles, principles that can be uncovered and then taught systematically."[6] The new language clearly imputes cognitive import, tacitly signalling Bloom's belief that his revisionist family romance, to use Paul Ricoeur's phrasing, "suggests, reveals, unconceals . . . the deep structures of reality."[7] And, in fact, repeated through five books and innumerable articles, Bloom's metaphoric psychodrama so galvanized attention and so focused the shape of subsequent inquiry that it ceased to serve as merely analogue or parallel and became, instead, a cognitive solution to the question of poetic influence.

"Ironically," then, noted the *New York Times* book reviewer, when a major new study of women's intrapoetic relationships appeared in 1979, it too found itself "indebted to that most patriarchal of critics,

Harold Bloom"[8] The irony, of course, lay in the fact that a feminist analysis had accepted as its inspiriting authority a male critic who, with only the rarest exceptions, ignores the fact of women's poetic production and accepted as its paradigmatic model a version of literary history in which the female symbolizes only threat or harlotry. For, in Bloom's version of the family romance, Lilith (Adam's first wife and "the Adversary Female of Kabbalah") reminds the poet of his belatedness (FOCI, pp. 264–267), while the more conventional Muse "is mother and harlot at once" (TAOI, p. 63)—incestuously embracing her lover/son so that he may beget himself upon her (TAOI, p. 37) but reminding him always that she has "whored with many before him" (TAOI, p. 61). Not only are the images of the female here decidedly unappealing, but nowhere does Bloom consider how the psychology of the flesh-and-blood woman might participate in this particular dynamic of literary engendering.

The irony notwithstanding, it was precisely to answer this last question—and to compensate for Bloom's omissions—that Sandra Gilbert and Susan Gubar attempted their 1979 construction of a feminist poetics. As they explained in the preface to *The Madwoman in the Attic: The Woman Writer and the Nineteenth-Century Literary Imagination*, their aim—as that of so many other feminist critics—was to "recover not only a major (and neglected) female literature but a whole (neglected) female history."[9] In this, they followed Joanne Feit-Diehl, who had argued in an earlier article that "any theory of influence must" take into account the sex of the poet because, inescapably, "the constellation of the 'family romance' alters when the poet is a woman."[10] Concurring with Feit-Diehl in "the Bloomian premise that literary history consists of strong action and inevitable reaction" (MA, p. xiii) and accepting as well Bloom's version of literary history as male, Gilbert and Gubar—like Feit-Diehl before them—sought to understand "the dynamics of female literary response to male literary assertion and coercion" (MA, p. xii). They took seriously, in short (as Bloom never does), the peculiar dilemma of the woman poet who must acknowledge, along with Adrienne Rich, "that my style was formed first by male poets."[11]

Gilbert and Gubar's study of the stratagems by which (mainly) nineteenth-century English women novelists struggled both with male literary priority and with male literary versions of the female may have yielded what another feminist critic termed only "a schematized and essentialist view of the relation between women and writing."[12] But that is beside the point. For, in addition to exhilarating readings of individual texts, *The Madwoman in the Attic* initiated two vital swerves in current critical thinking. First, it opened what had been Bloom's controlling metaphor to discussion and dissection. And, second, it insisted that Bloom's (and others') relative silence concerning poetry by women could not be accepted as tacit evidence that would-be women poets had failed to successfully overcome some father/ precursor. Instead, Gilbert and Gubar offered the humbling notion that, in our ignorance of the processes governing the production of poetry by women, we may stand—along with Bloom—simply and sadly unable to recognize a strong woman when we read her.

> **When to her lute Corinna sings**
> **neither words nor music are her own . . .**
>
> Adrienne Rich, "Snapshots of a Daughter-in-Law" (1963)

In a strikingly compassionate passage in *Figures of Capable Imagination* (1976), Bloom sympathizes with the Jewish poets of his generation as he considers what it meant for them, as in a Charles Reznikoff poem, to have " 'married the speech of strangers' " (FOCI, p. 252). Never, however, does Bloom contemplate any analogous "peculiarly internalized disadvantage" (FOCI, p. 156) for women poets who, in their own way, might also be said to have been forced to marry the speech of strangers. That Bloom did not make this connection is surprising in light of the fact that, just a year earlier, in *A Map of Misreading*, he had at least hinted at the possibility that Homer might have sired daughters as well as sons: "Everyone who now reads and writes in the West, of whatever racial background, sex or ideological camp, is still a son or daughter of Homer" (AMOM, p. 33). But in keeping with his model of male competition, the emphasis Bloom derives from this passage is on Homer as the primary father/precursor for all subsequent male poets. In Bloom's schema, Sappho enjoys no similar priority. (She simply does not exist.) Nor do Homer's potential daughters— whether as readers or as writers—attract more than this passing notice. Unfailingly, Bloom inscribes the gendered assumptions of what Tillie

Olsen has called the sheer "saturation—the never-ceasing, life-long saturation" of "The poet: he (his). The writer: he (his)."[13]

To consider for a change *The poet: she (hers)* is to question whether that sense of "belatedness," which Bloom asserts as "probably the largest component in the anxiety-of-influence" (FOCI, p. xi), encompasses the same meaning for the daughters of Homer as he says it does for the sons. After all, given Bloom's view of literary history as overwhelmingly male, a woman's perception of her late-coming may have little to do with any fear that a rich tradition of gifted precursors had exhausted her potential resources and materials. Rather, as Emma Lazarus suggests in "Echoes" (1880), a woman's sense of belatedness may derive from the anxiety that *her* unique resources have yet to find a place in poetic discourse:

> Late-born and woman-souled I dare not hope
> The freshness of the elder lays, the might
> Of manly, modern passion shall alight
> Upon my Muse's lips, nor may I cope
> (Who veiled and screened by womanhood must grope)
> With the world's strong-armed warriors and recite
> The dangers, wounds, and triumphs of the fight;
> Twanging the full-stringed lyre through all its scope.

Taking her cue from the misfortunes of the nymph whose name titles the sonnet,[14] Lazarus poses in the opening octave the problem of being deprived of authentic expression. The speaker's late-coming onto the stage of poetic history deprives her of the ability to sing with "the freshness of the elder lays." But—and this is given the greater emphasis—the fact of her being "woman-souled" deprives her of access to the very drama and subject matter that appear to constitute the "scope" of that history.

The "act of creative correction that is actually and necessarily a misinterpretation," to which Bloom attributes the dialectical continuity of "the main tradition of Western poetry since the Renaissance" (TAOI, p. 30), is unavailable to the speaking voice of "Echoes." "Veiled and screened by womanhood," she can neither experience directly "the might / of manly, modern passion" nor "cope . . . With the world's strong-armed warriors" to "recite / The dangers, wounds, and triumphs" to which such passions give rise. Deprived thus by both chronology and sex from direct and authentic participation in the well-springs of that tradition, unable ever to twang "the full-stringed lyre through all its scope," let alone contribute her own corrective refrain, she resolves the problem by resigning herself to the only possibility that remains: an echoing retreat.

> But if thou ever in some lake-floored cave
> O'erbrowed by rocks, a wild voice wooed and heard,
> Answering at once from heaven and earth and wave,
> Lending elf-music to thy harshest word,
> Misprize thou not these echoes that belong
> To one in love with solitude and song.[15]

Given the generic options within which Lazarus places her speaker's dilemma, the conventional alternative to the epic of martial strife is the lyric (or song) of pastoral solitude. Here, though, the significance of the song that issues from that solitude is rendered ambiguous by its clear association with the plight of Echo. Able to plead her love for Narcissus only by repeating fragments from his speech and failing in her attempt to woo him, it is variously reported that Echo pined away, leaving merely her voice behind, or, as in Ovid, that she was changed into a stone which still retained the power of echoing human speech. The voice in the poem appears caught between the continuing attempt to engage the very tradition which has excluded her and, at the same time, the acknowledgment that, at best, she can respond to it only with what are to be the "misprized" and muted echoes of its "harshest word." Wanting to be "wooed and heard," she is nonetheless incapable of independent action or expression; and even if her voice be that of nature itself, it is no more than passively responsive, "*Answering* at once from heaven and earth and wave."

Echo's story thus provides Emma Lazarus the poignant paradigm for the recurrent dilemma of the woman seeking to create poetry within the Western literary tradition as Bloom describes it; that is, the woman for whom Homer figures as the inevitable and inescapable precursor. The speaking voice's inability either to share in or to disavow "the elder lays"—as Echo could neither consummate nor evade her love for Narcissus—accounts for the juxtaposition of the octave's frustrated yearning to twang "the full-stringed lyre" with the sestet's resignation to total dispossession. The sonnet's profferred consolation in pastoral withdrawal is undercut by the fact that the songs produced are only the fleeting echoes of "elf-music" contrasts, and the "solitude," for Echo, is not so much chosen as imposed. At best, to use Bloom's terminology, the speaker may woo the "strong-armed warrior"/precursors by forever echoing back to them fragments of their own songs; but, even so, whether "veiled and screened" or "o'erbrowed by rocks," she will still remain hidden and unseen where the act of making (or simply repeating) poetry is concerned.

In composing this chilling study of women's accommodation to their exclusion from the main tradition of Western poetry, Lazarus succeeded not only in exposing that tradition's inherently self-regarding narcissism but, as well, she tacitly invoked a precursor other than Homer. In this sense, the poem is itself a solution to the dilemma it poses. The speaker's preference for "solitude and song," articulated within a sonnet, aligns the work not with celebrations of "the world's strong-armed warriors"—whose reciters, after all, "misprize" the speaker—but rather with the singers of lyric, said to trace *their* lineage from Sappho. If that reading is permitted, then to refuse Echo's invisibility, to assert a voice that is more than echo, means that a woman need not (to use Bloom's phrase) creatively rewrite the father/ precursors. Instead, she must refuse that heritage altogether, and with it the dialectic that is for Bloom the history of poetic influence.

In its most familiar rendering, the refusal takes a defensive or an apologetic posture—or some combination of the two. Antedating Lazarus by two hundred years, Anne Bradstreet obviously felt some need to explain the absence in her work "of wars, of captains, and of kings, / Of cities founded, commonwealths begun." Composed as a formal prologue to the first major body of English poetry written by a woman in America (1650), Bradstreet's lines adapt the conventional "apologia" in such a way as to anticipate both those who would say "my hand a needle better fits" and, as well, those who would find in her *lack* of martial and epic sweep evidence of a "foolish, broken, blemished Muse." Her tack was to charm her potential adversaries into silence by using their arguments against her as a protective shield. Insisting that she will attempt only what she can, "according to my skill," she wonders why any tongue should carp when her admittedly limited lines must surely serve, by comparison, to reflect back the superior worth of more established traditions:

And oh ye high flown quills that soar the skies,
And ever with your prey still catch your praise,
If e'er you deign these lowly lines your eyes,
Give thyme or parsley wreath, I ask no bays;
This mean and unrefined ore of mine
Will make your glist'ring gold but more to shine.[16]

It is a stratagem that many a woman poet has been forced to employ, in one form or another, at some time during her career in order to be able to assert for herself her right to a craft which had, since Homer, been expropriated from *human*kind to *man*kind. (Sappho, we recall, comes down to us only in fragments.)

In the process of taking up that challenge, it appears that most women writers experience some aspect of Echo's plight. For the strong woman poet (by which I intend the poet who will essay an authentic voice despite the absence of audible or available female precursors and in the presence of a dominant male tradition in which she is either silenced or excluded), for *this* poet, at some point in her development, there comes the recognition that, as Tillie Olsen put it, she had previously been "writing in dominant male forms, style, although what seeks to be expressed might ask otherwise."[17] The characteristic response is a shocked, angry, bitter, or even ironic outcry against oneself for having so loved Narcissus as to falsify one's art. Almost confessional, asking forgiveness for the fraud, but newly empowered by "memory" that gives access to the authentic event which her adherence to formulae from the male literary tradition had obscured, Muriel Rukeyser's "The Poem as Mask" (1960) marks precisely this turning point:

When I wrote of the women in their dances and wildness, it was
  a mask
on their mountain, god-hunting, singing, in orgy,
it was a mask, when I wrote of the god,
fragmented, exiled from himself, his life, the love gone down
  with song,
it was myself, split open, unable to speak, in exile from myself.

There is no mountain, there is no god, there is memory
of my torn life, myself split open in sleep, the rescued child
beside me among the doctors, and a word
of rescue from the great eyes.

Punning on the multiple meanings of *mask* and *masque*, the first stanza owns up to the fact that, in an earlier work (her long poem, "Orpheus" [1949], which was itself composed as a masque), the poet had employed forms of disguise, masking both experience and identity, and had thereby diminished true Orphic power. The disguise, in short, produced only an elaborate entertainment, akin to the ornate but essentially trivial court masques of the seventeenth century. The maenads tearing Orpheus to pieces is a physical sensation *she* knows through childbirth; but what she successfully rescued from death, through her own body, was a child rather than a lover. The storehouse of symbolic structures which we call our literary heritage, however, offered neither models nor validation for the importance of *that* kind of tearing and rescue; only "memory" had preserved the masked truth of the event intact.

Quite literally, then, the first stanza becomes itself a mask, at once exposing the earlier poem's *masque*rade and, with that, serving as prelude to the significant action which is to follow; that is, the second stanza's fuller explanation of the deception and the consequent revelation of the poet's (painful) ecstasy in childbirth. The myth's assertion of the Orphic power that comes only through the ecstasy of dying is here displaced by Rukeyser's assertion of the ecstasy of bringing forth life. And, as the closing lines indicate, this ecstasy, this "aggressive act of truth-telling,"[18] also renders Orphic power, as life replaces death and fragments become whole:

> No more masks! No more mythologies!
>
> Now, for the first time, the god lifts his hand,
> the fragments join in me and with their own music.[19]

Repossessing the significance of the "memory / of my torn life," Rukeyser is liberated from a sense of "exile from myself." No longer "unable to speak," capable now of renewed—but also different—music, Echo is returned to speech.

> "Mother, I'm pregnant with a baby girl and. . . She
> wants to know who else is coming."
> "Tell her Mother Margaret is coming, Mother Louisa is
> coming, Mother Emily is coming, Mother Rosa is coming,
> Mother Doris is coming, Mother Charlotte. . ."
> "Then she has many friends."
>
> Esther Broner, *Her Mothers* (1975)

In many ways, Amy Lowell anticipated the recent feminist critique of Bloomian poetics when, in 1925, she applied his question "For why do men write poems?" (TAOI, p. 22) to "we women who write poetry":

> Taking us by and large, we're a queer lot
> We women who write poetry. And when you think
> How few of us there've been, it's queerer still.
> I wonder what it is that makes us do it.

She explains why there have been so few women poets by noting that women are "mother-creatures, double-bearing, / With matrices in body and in brain." "There is just the reason" for their relative scarcity, she avers, for in the societal trappings of female procreativity, "The strength of forty thousand Atlases / Is needed for our every-day concerns." As to "what . . . makes us do it," in spite of all, she consults a precursor/sisterhood that includes Sappho, Elizabeth Barrett Browning, and Emily Dickinson. What she discovers, to her dismay, is "how extraordinarily unlike / Each is to me." "For older sisters are very sobering things," to be sure, but they cannot tell Lowell "which way shall I go" or answer for her "What it is that makes us do it." What her imagined afternoon visit to "these my spiritual relations" offers instead is both a recognition of just how little of that tradition begun by Sappho remains to "tell / The reasons, as she possibly conceived them" and, as a result, a heightened experience of participating in "a strange, isolated little family": "For we are such a little family / Of singing sisters."

The frailty which such an image conjures up denies the need for any Bloomian battle for "breathing space" (KC, p. 84) because, clearly, the speaking voice here—presumably Lowell herself—does not regard Sappho, Browning, or Dickinson as having usurped her poetic possibilities by their priority. And so, in place of the Bloomian combat for psychic survival she can assert a sisterly intimacy:

> I understand you all, for in myself—
> Is that presumption? Yet indeed it's true—
> We are one family.

At the same time, she accepts the inadequacy of that sisterhood to provide either solace or direction:

> Good-bye, my sisters, all of you are great,
> And all of you are marvellously strange,
> And none of you has any word for me. [20]

By thus invoking a female literary history modelled on sisterhood, Lowell not only does away with the Freudian romance of murderous competition; she also renders misprision—that is, the rewriting of the precursor—unnecessary to a dynamic of literary influence. The poem *is* composed, after all, though it corrects nothing that her precursor/sisters have written. On the darker side of Lowell's constellation, however, stands the tacit admission that sisters, unlike parent/progenitors, are somehow inadequate or insufficient: "And none of you has any word for me." The fact of their priority has helped Lowell ward off her anxious sense of isolation and aberrance, but she credits it neither with nurturing nor engendering her own poetic efforts. And, in the end, the imagined afternoon visit has still failed to answer for her "what it is that makes us do it."

At least in part, "what it is that makes us do it," and what it is women often do when they write, is precisely what Lowell's "The Sisters" is all about; that is, the woman poet's repeated need to assert for herself some validating female tradition and to repossess its voices for her own needs. In the continental United States, at least, this is the stance with which women's poetry begins. In the eighteenth century, Annis Boudinot Stockton (1736–1801) nominated herself "a sister muse" to the Philadelphia poet Elizabeth Graeme Fergusson (1737–1801), declaring that Fergusson's work had

> ". . . rais'd ambition in my breast," but
> Not such as envious souls possess,
> Who hate another's praise. [21]

Judith Sargent Murray (1751–1820) looked to the English playwright

Hannah Cowley to celebrate a woman writer whose work "inspires, / Wraps my glad soul, and all my fancy fires,"[22] while Mercy Otis Warren (1728–1814) felt that she could "take my stand by fam'd Parnassus' side, / And for the moment feel a poet's pride" if only the English critic of Shakespeare, Elizabeth Robinson Montague, might "across the Atlantic stretch her eye" and cast an approving glance on Warren's work.[23] When a sisterhood of contemporaneous writers on both sides of the Atlantic would not suffice, the earliest women poets of America turned to the originating precursor they recognized as their own. Invoking inspiration from her Muse in 1725, Jane Colman Turell (1708–1735) pleaded, "O let me burn with Sappho's noble fire."[24]

Misogynist pundits like the anonymous author of "To a Poeticall Lady" in the *Boston Weekly Magazine* for March 2, 1743, might try to discourage—"Yet still, to rule her house aright / Would better far become her, / Then to surpass the noblest flight / In Milton or in Homer"[25]—but such verses fell wide of the mark. The women privileged to have the education and the leisure to compose poetry in eighteenth-century America continued to publish, to dedicate their work to one another, and to circulate their manuscripts among themselves. Milton and Homer, moreover, were not the only models to whom they looked. (And Lowell's "little family / Of singing sisters" was larger than she knew.)

But the very fact that in 1925 Amy Lowell could read Sappho only in fragments and find only bowdlerized and highly selected editions of Emily Dickinson and that she seemed unaware, as well, of two prior centuries of women's poetry on this continent denotes not so much absence (as Lowell implied) but loss. There *was* a history, after all, but it had never *carried over,* so to speak. In the first major attempt to compose a literary history of early America, for example, only two women received recognition. Moses Coit Tyler's two-volume *A History of American Literature, 1607–1765* (1878) offers a respectful discussion of Anne Bradstreet, while Jane Colman Turell merits merely brief mention and a footnote as a "verse-writer."[26] Relatively prolific poets like Phillis Wheatley, Mercy Otis Warren, Ann Eliza Bleecker, or the scores of women whose poetry peppered the pages of eighteenth-century magazines find no mention in Tyler's literary history. Indeed, so little of what eighteenth-century women had accomplished remained available to their nineteenth-century daughters that

women themselves began to internalize that loss as absence and restriction. In consequence, as early as 1829 Sarah Josepha Hale (who
later became editor of the influential *Godey's Lady's Book*) predicted
precisely the problem with which Emma Lazarus would grapple at the
end of the century. As Hale told readers of the *Ladies' Magazine*, "the
path of poetry, like every other path in life, is to the tread of woman,
exceedingly circumscribed. She may not revel in the luxuriance of
fancies, images and thoughts, or indulge in the license of choosing
themes at will, like the Lords of creation."[27]

Despite such prescriptions, the nineteenth century—like the eighteenth—saw an outpouring of creative and experimental poetry by
women as diverse as Margaret Fuller in New England and sisters Alice
and Phoebe Cary in the Ohio Valley. But these, again, did not *carry
over*. And so, harking back to the only validating precursor upon whom
they might securely call, nineteenth-century American women began
to articulate the anxiety which now beset them, the anxiety that despite
present popularity and critical acclaim their voices would soon enough
be lost.

At mid-century, Mary E. Hewitt covertly inscribed in "Sappho to
the Sibyl" (1853) her fear that, like Sappho's, her work too would go
unheard or even disappear from literary history. Casting herself in the
voice "of a popular poet whose lover has perhaps never listened to her
song," Hewitt's irony, as critic Emily Stipes Watts has noted, was palpa-
ble.[28] For, in the face of the growing circulation of a number of
women poets and despite her own critical success among the New York
literati in the 1840s and 1850s, Hewitt nonetheless announced in
"Sappho to the Sibyl" not the power of women's poetry but rather its
powerlessness before a recalcitrant male audience:

> Beyond the hills, where flows the Egean wave,
>   I sweep the lyre amid the applauding throng—
> Tell me, dread sibyl of this mountain cave,
>   Has he I lov'd e'er listened to my song?[29]

Following what was then the common misconception that Sappho had
exhausted both her life and her talent in unrequited love, the poem's
concluding stanzas strongly hint that the answer to the speaker's question will continue to be *no*. Thus, in the nineteenth century, the historic Sappho took on some of the characteristics of the mythic Echo.
And, as a precursor, Sappho came to stand not only as a figure of

validating priority but as an emblem of women's literary history, past and present.

Hewitt's poem was prophetic. Along with all but one of her female contemporaries—Emily Dickinson—her work was forgotten soon after her death and thereby denied the status of "influence that extends past one generation." She could not, in other words, participate in that "carrying-over of influence" that for Harold Bloom constitutes the essence of an ongoing "tradition" (AMOM, p. 32). The only tradition Bloom recognizes, however, is that in which "the covert subject of most poetry . . . has been the anxiety of influence, each poet's fear that no proper work remains for him to perform" (TAOI, p. 148). But the poetry of women like Hewitt suggests another "covert subject" altogether: the fear that, like Sappho, her works will be lost or, like Echo, her words go unheeded. This hardly suggests any Bloomian anxiety of influence but, rather, *the influence of anxiety*. It is women poets' peculiar anxiety, as Muriel Rukeyser framed it in our own century, lest they join the ranks of "the wasted ones, lost as surely as soldiers . . . / gone down under centuries / Of the starved spirit."[30]

> I want to remember this season in layers
> of colors   the year I was ten
> and discovered pointillism
> red blue green gold silver
> spreading slow hot points
> on the tree
> because my mother started up in us this urge
> for more
>
> Kathleen Fraser, "Dear Laura, in December" (1978)

Joanne Feit-Diehl, in her essay "'Come Slowly—Eden': An Exploration of Women Poets and Their Muse," and Sandra Gilbert and Susan Gubar, in *The Madwoman in the Attic*, concluded that Bloom's adaptation of the Freudian family romance must undergo nothing less than radical revision if it is ever to account for the pathways of literary influence affecting women. Any theory of poetic influence which claims completeness, they argue, would have to begin by distinguishing between the male poet's need to make a place for himself in a tradition already overcrowded with (male) greatness and the female's discovery of her exclusion from or veiled presence within that same tradition. Their emphasis, therefore, is on a psychodrama for women that emerges amid a pantheon of precursors which, from Homer on, offered narcissistic fathers/lovers but precious few nurturing mothers or audible precursor/sisters.

Following Bloom's family model rather closely but altering his basic question so as to ask "how . . . women poets perceive their relation to a male-dominated tradition," Joanne Feit-Diehl discovered in the work of Elizabeth Barrett Browning, Christina Rossetti, and Emily Dickinson an essential and dramatic engagement with a variety of male persona and, in Emily Dickinson's work especially, "overwhelming proof of the taut balance she strives to maintain between independence and the power of the Precursor/father."[31] Similarly, in examining women's responses "to male literary assertion and coercion," Gilbert and Gubar revealed their authors' strategies for subverting male-made forms and image patterns to female use. Redefining Bloom's notions of "revision" and "misprision," Gilbert and Gubar insists that the strong woman writer's "battle . . . is not against her (male) precursor's reading of the world but against his reading of *her*." As a result, their theoretical chapters survey the means by which eighteenth- and nineteenth-century women were able to conceive "fictional worlds in which patriarchal images and conventions were severely, radically revised" while their readings of specific texts and authors examine women's special "concern with assaulting and revising, deconstructing and reconstructing those images of women inherited from male literature" (MA, pp. 49, 44, 76).

Taken together, these studies declare that the would-be woman writer inevitably and irrevocably enters literary history subdued, intimidated, and alienated. Her work invokes a mythology of madwomen and fractured psyches, the daughters relentlessly given over to the fathers' imperatives. After all, the law that declares that "culture is by definition both patriarchal and phallocentric" must, as Sandra Gilbert acknowledged, always and only "transmit the empty pack of disinheritance to every daughter."[32] Compelling as their readings are, it may be that these critics err in acceding too easily to the "essentially male literary history Bloom describes" (MA, p. 48). "No song or poem will bear my mother's name," writes Alice Walker, "yet so many of the stories that I write . . . are my mother's stories."[33] For pathways of literary influence such as this, Bloom's controlling metaphor leaves no room. Thus cognitively fixing the limits of discourse, he prevents us from seeing whether, side by side with a poetics forged in the face of female absence and male priority, women writers have been enabled by another, alternative linkage: a poetics that rescues female priority.

In pursuit of this possibility, Bloom's "radical analogue between human and poetic birth" and, with that, "between biological and creative anxiety" (TAOI, p. 58) leads to a renewed appreciation of Virginia Woolf's insight in A Room of One's Own (1929): "we think back through our mothers if we are women."[34] "If not to have conceived oneself" stands as the burden which translates, for the strong male poet, into that "more hidden burden: not to have brought oneself forth" (and thereby initiates the ephebe's anxiety of influence [AMOM, pp. 15–17]), it is hardly a burden generated by the psychodynamics of women's relationships in the world. Although, as in Bloom's paradigm, men "must enter by force, drawn back like Jonah / into their fleshy mothers," Anne Sexton discerned that "A woman is her mother. / That's the main thing."[35] Nowhere are the creative implications of that more clear than in the career of the second Elizabeth Stuart Phelps.

Written when she was in her fifties, Phelps' autobiography Chapters from a Life (1896) opens by recounting the writing talents and successes of the pious New England ministers who were her forebears. Distinguishing writers from other sorts of people by their greater tendency to be "either rebels to, or subjects of, their ancestry," she locates the beginning of her vocation "a good while before" her birth and announces herself "one whose literary abilities all belong to one's ancestors."[36] It is a matter of wonder for her to consider "the beautiful and terrible law by which the dead man and women whose blood bounds in our being control our destinies" (CFAL, p. 4). Her autobiography thus opens with a statement of both biological and creative belatedness. But as it progresses, the story swerves from engagement with male ancestors and reveals instead the daughter's lifelong impulse "to extend, reveal, and elaborate her mother's . . . thwarted talents." As Rachel Blau DuPlessis has phrased it, "the younger artist's future project as a creator lies" not in competing with but "in completing the fragmentary and potential work of the mother."[37]

Having touted the publishing successes and the longevity of her grandfathers and great-grandfathers, Phelps leaves off the men, turns abruptly to her most obvious progenitor, her successful writer-mother, the elder Elizabeth Stuart Phelps, and introduces, first thing, the fact "of her death . . . at the first blossom of her very positive and widely-promising success" (CFAL, pp. 12–13). Whether intended or not, the contrast between the male ancestors' longevity and the mother's early death is obvious and pointed—as obvious and pointed as the young girl's decision then to take on her mother's name and craft. Only eight years old at the time of her mother's death, she admits in her auto-biography to a lifelong inability to clearly "distinguish between the effect produced upon me by her literary success as I have since under-stood it, and that left by her own truly extraordinary personality upon the annals of the nursery" (CFAL, p. 11). What does emerge—perhaps because of this very confusion—is the daughter's early awareness of the price exacted by her mother's "difficult reconciliation between genius and domestic life" (CFAL, p. 12). Not until her mid-thirties had her mother begun to find time for her writing, but even then, as the daughter recalled, there was never "one hour in which her children needed her and did not find her" (CFAL, p. 13). Her energies ex-hausted by domestic toil and loving obligations, her precious free hours "torn by the civil war of the dual nature which can be given to women only" (CFAL, p. 12), the mother came to personify for her daughter the woman caught between her duty to her family and her duty to her own talents and interests, a conflict depicted in the moth-er's finest short story, "The Angel over the Right Shoulder." Themes from that story, in fact, resonate throughout the daughter's cameo of her mother:

> Now she sits correcting proof-sheets, and now she is painting apostles for the baby's first Bible lesson. Now she is writing her new book, and now she is dyeing things canary-yellow in the white-oak dye—for the professor's salary is small, and a crushing economy was [required]. . . . Now she is a popular writer, in-credulous of her first success, with her future flashing before her; and now she is a tired, tender mother, crooning to a sick child while the MS. lies unprinted on the table. . . . (CFAL, p. 14)

Repeatedly, as she dredges up these memories, the mature woman lashes out at the cause of her mother's death: "Her last book and her last baby came together, and killed her." And, again, three pages later: "The struggle killed her" (CFAL, pp. 12, 15).

"Impossible to be her daughter and not to write," she concludes (CFAL, p. 15), her pages hinting all the while that the daughter of the woman who had composed the phenomenally successful *The Sunny Side; or, The Country Minister's Wife*[38] might, in her own time, deal instead with the shadows. The rest of her life essentially given over to answering "what would have been the fate . . . of my mother, had she lived to work her power to its bloom" (CFAL, p. 133), Elizabeth Stuart Phelps began to write in earnest at an early age, first finding her way into print at thirteen (with a short story in *The Youth's Companion*). Confirmed in her chosen vocation by reading Elizabeth Barrett Browning's *Aurora Leigh* at age sixteen (CFAL, pp. 65–66), comforted, perhaps, by discovering there the story of another poet who, as a girl, had longed to recover the memory of her own dead mother, Phelps toiled diligently for the next few years at the moral and moralizing juvenile fiction which she called her "safe and respectable . . . dozen Sunday-school books" (CFAL, p. 106). But she nonetheless found herself, by 1864, at age twenty, ominously repeating her mother's struggle: resentful of her household chores, called to attend an increasingly invalided father, and unable, amid the playful noise of the children of his third marriage, to secure the peace and quite required for her writing, she set about, in spite of all, on what she "distinctly" understood to be "a venture totally dissimilar" to anything she'd done before (CFAL, p. 106). Wrapping herself in an old fur cape of her mother's, she resorted, when she could, to her unheated bedroom or to the attic and that year began *The Gates Ajar*,[39] the novel which was to bring her immediate acclaim and, a little later, the funds with which to refurbish as her own the summer house which had once served as her mother's study (CFAL, pp. 114–115). Published in 1868, *The Gates Ajar* "became the century's second best-selling book by a female author." As Christine Stansell reminds us, "only *Uncle Tom's Cabin* surpassed it in fame and sales."[40]

"Impossible to remember how or when the idea of the book first visited me," Phelps would later write of *The Gates Ajar*: "The angel said unto me 'Write!' and I wrote" (CFAL, p. 95). Though surely never consciously intended as such, the statement links this, her first serious literary effort, with her mother's short story "The Angel over the Right

Shoulder" (1852). In that story, a dream sequence records a kind of internal debate between two competing obligations in a woman's mind: while the angel over the right shoulder keeps track of Mrs. James' devotion to maternal duties and household chores, the fearsome angel over her left shoulder enters into God's Ledger Book every moment withheld from the children for herself, every fragment of time given over (however guiltily) to the cultivation of her own mind and heart. By the end of the dream, the angel over the right shoulder has taken precedence, and the best that Mrs. James can hope for, as she croons over her infant daughter's cradle, is that she may pass on to her child a life "all mended by her own experience. It would have been a comfort to have felt that, in fighting the battle, she had fought for both."[41] We may speculate from her autobiography that when the younger Elizabeth Stuart Phelps embarked upon *The Gates Ajar*, she did so—at least in part—in order to enter the debate posed by her mother's story. Only *her* purpose was to give the fearsome angel its due, as her mother and her mother's protagonist could not.

To give the angel its due, she had to reckon with her mother's major literary legacy, the best-selling quasiautobiographical novel about the domestic life of a country minister's wife. Filled with graphic details about the daily round of activities such a woman would take on, even in the face of hardship and poverty, *The Sunny Side; or, The Country Minister's Wife* not only utilized its author's experiences as the wife of the Andover, Massachusetts, professor of theology, Austin Phelps, but, as well, served as a memorial to the older Phelps' mother, Abigail Clark Stuart, who had herself raised seven children while shouldering the burdens of a country minister's wife. Little wonder that Elizabeth Stuart Phelps the daughter said of *The Gates Ajar* that it "grew so naturally, it was . . . inevitable" (CFAL, p. 95). It had been inevitable for three generations. It was the opening salvo in what Carol Farley Kessler has called the "daughter's quarrel with the world on her mother's behalf"[42]—just as *The Sunny Side* had been, in its way, a muted protest against the self-effacement required in the life of the elder Elizabeth Stuart Phelps and in that of her mother's before her. But where the elder Phelps tried to show a heroine capable of sustaining the superhuman demands upon her, her daughter would identify the only appropriate realm for such domestic fantasies.

Long dismissed for its lachrymose sentimentality and for its covert tendency toward "spiritualism," repeatedly relegated to the sorry status of "the apotheosis of the consolation literature of the day,"[43] *The Gates Ajar* has too often been treated merely as a vision of heaven which provided ready consolation to the bereaved mothers, widows, and sisters of the Civil War dead. Indeed, "so far as I can remember having had any 'object' at all in its creation," Phelps recorded in her autobiography, "I wished to say something that would comfort some few . . . of the women whose misery crowded the land" (CFAL, p. 96). And the novel does, in fact, revolve around conflicting attempts, by friends and relatives, to offer solace to young Mary, whose brother Roy has been lost in the war.

Until the recent rereadings by Christine Stansell and Carol Farley Kessler, however, what had generally escaped critical notice was the fact that the novel derives its power from depicting heaven as a comfortably middle-class order of existence in which the domesticity that, in real life, brought only drudgery and self-denial could, in fact, offer women peace of mind, affection, and leisure—even time to play the piano. In Carol Farley Kessler's words, the novel transmitted "a view of Heaven as compensation for earthly ills."[44] Mary's aunt's vaunted vision of heaven, moreover, closely resembles in its details the fictionalized township of Weston in *The Sunny Side*. It is what Bloom would call "misprision" of a high order—but with a difference. For, in thus restoring her mother's fictionalized Weston as her own fictionalized heaven, Phelps rewrote or, better still, elaborated her mother's muted protest by displacing the blissful elements in the elder Phelps' domestic scene to what the daughter regarded as its proper domain: the imaginative and, in this world, unattainable. In so doing, she tacitly commented upon her mother's fictionalized and overly optimistic delusions while, at the same time, she made of heaven not so much "a consolation prize," as Ann Douglas put it,[45] but an acceptably pious emotional abstraction, granted sufficiently graphic visual detail, so as to bear critical witness to the deficiencies and unfulfilled promises of a disappointing present reality.

The success of *The Gates Ajar* empowered the young author to assert a voice of her own. Rejecting Austin Phelps' adamant (and, later, published) opposition to women's suffrage, his daughter declared "that she should forthwith approve and further the enfranchisement and elevation of her own sex" (CFAL, p. 250). To that end, in a variety of subsequent sketches and novels—including two sequels to *The Gates Ajar* (*Beyond the Gates*, published in 1883, and *The Gates Between*, published in 1887)—Phelps continued to explore the full implications of women's frustrating struggle to lead fulfilling lives in the face of an impoverished set of life choices. Rescuing in that process her mother's muted voice and name in the wide circulation of her own uncompromising protests, the adult Elizabeth Stuart Phelps was at last consoled for the eight-year-old's loss. And in *The Story of Avis*, undoubtedly her strongest novel, her mother's failed blooming was at last made good as the daughter anatomized her own hard-won understanding of the struggle that had destroyed her parent.

If the elder Elizabeth Stuart Phelps had intended *The Sunny Side* both as fictionalized autobiography and as a memorial to her own mother, so too may her daughter have intended *The Story of Avis* (1877). Avis Dobell, the central character in that novel, reads Elizabeth Barrett Browning's "Aurora Leigh" when she is sixteen—as had Elizabeth Stuart Phelps—and for the same reasons. Like the author, Avis Dobell has lost her mother at an early age. A father who does not encourage his daughter's early strivings (as Austin Phelps had never nurtured *his* daughter's abilities) causes the girl to long for maternal support, hoping for "a soul which loved her so, that it could not *help* believing in her."[46] Again, like Phelps, Avis' mother had also been an aspiring artist (an actress) but had been forced to waste her energies in domestic duties.

These autobiographical resonances notwithstanding, other elements in the novel point back toward the author's mother as the model for Avis. The fact that Avis is an artist of some talent suggests Phelps' belated homage to her mother's potential in that area. As an adult remembering her mother's illustrations for the stories she wrote for her children, Phelps judged her "gift" as "original" and surmised that "had she not been a writer she must have achieved something as an artist" (CFAL, p. 13). Beyond this is the fact that the structure of *The Story of Avis* takes up the debate which was at the heart of the mother's story "The Angel over the Right Shoulder." And crucial elements from that story echo within the lines of *Avis*.

Countering the habit of popular romantic novels and stage comedies to end with the marriage of the heroine, Phelps makes it the major concern of her novel's second half. She examines what happens to the talented young painter Avis Dobell when she "surrenders" to the urgings of the man who loves her and permits her engagement to become a marriage. The change brings with it neither obvious bondage nor even, at first, the harsh cruelties of a demanding husband; instead, it entangles her by love. The result is a recapitulation of Phelps' mother's dilemma as the novel offers a heartbreakingly detailed study of the impossibility of reconciling artistic aspirations with a woman's domestic duties. Although the text does not end with the physical death of the would-be artist, it does nonetheless signal an analogous failure of talent to come to fruition:

> The year ran fleetly. Van [her young son] was ailing a great deal that spring; and in the summer her father was ill. Thus, in the old, sad, subtle ways, Avis was exiled from the studio. She could not abandon herself to it without a feminine sense of guilt. . . . She was stunned to find how her aspiration had emaciated during her married life. Household care had fed upon it like a disease. . . . She wished, with all the wild, hot protest of her nature, that the spirit of this gift with which God had created her—in a mood of awful infinite irony, it seemed—would return to Him who gave it, that the dust of her days might descend to the dust in peace. She wished she were like other women,—content to stitch and sing, to sweep and smile. She bowed her face on the soft hair of her children; but she could not forget that they had been bought with a great price. She thought of the husband whose love she had mislaid, and counted the cost of her marriage in the blood of her soul.

In the elder Phelps' short story, the angel over the right shoulder—the angel who records the woman's conventional domestic responsibilities—proves victor in Mrs. James' psychomachy. Even so, the author's sympathies—and ours, as readers—remain with Mrs. James' thwarted attempts to preserve some space for herself amid the daily grind of household chores. In compensation for what has been given up, the story closes with Mrs. James hoping to pass on to her infant daughter a life "all mended by her own experience." In fact, the story offers no tangible evidence that Mrs. James' efforts have in any way altered the limitations on women that her daughter, too, will ultimately inherit. And so the story ends on an ambiguous note with the conditional "it would have been" signaling a consuming doubt: "It would have been a comfort to have felt that, in fighting the battle, she had fought for both." The assurance of that comfort, though, is grammatically withheld.

What the elder Phelps could not prophesy the daughter would. In the closing pages of *The Story of Avis*, Avis reflects, "It would be easier for her daughter to be alive, and be a woman, than it had been for her; so much as this, she understood." The grammatical assurance withheld by the writer-mother is offered by the daughter. But so too does the second Elizabeth Stuart Phelps repeat her mother's consuming doubts.

Visiting with her friend Coy in the neighboring parsonage (Coy is married to a minister), Avis questions how Coy " 'seem[s] to keep pretty well, . . . with all your care.' " Coy answers with a catalog of family trials and domestic tribulations, only to conclude with a single complaint: " 'There is one thing I must admit: I do *not* like to ask John for money. There! But that is all, Avis.' " "Was it all indeed!" wonders Avis, deciding to herself that "it was a peaceful, pleasant story." The suggestion, of course, is of amelioration—not truth—in this "pleasant story." Just a few paragraphs later, as the novel closes, we are confronted again with a story that teases assent. It is the tale of Galahad's successful quest for the grail following upon the failure of his father, Lancelot. Avis' little daughter has asked her mother to read it to her. In the view of Rachel Blau DuPlessis, this ending symbolizes "generational displacement": "The mother reads her child the story of the Quest for the Holy Grail, and we understand that while the first generation (Sir Lancelot) failed, the second, purer generation of seekers will achieve the quest."[47] The child, in other words, will accomplish what the mother could not. But with Coy's "pleasant story" still fresh in the reader's mind, it may be that a different kind of displacement is occurring: Avis' earlier certainty that "it would be easier for her daughter to be alive, and be a woman" has now been identified with yet another amelioration. Like Coy's obfuscations, the stories of the Round Table are indeed pleasant, but they are also full of romantic delusions. The ending is, at best, ambiguous. In the finest of her works, then, Elizabeth Stuart Phelps engaged the central theme of her mother's life and work. Not in the Bloomian sense to rewrite either, but to write both again.

Rather than any "fear that no proper work remains," Phelps' fiction thus reveals the daughter's painful perception of just how much her mother—as both precursor and Muse—had left unsaid and, as well, her perception of how much of what her mother *had* said needed to be said again. Baptized Mary Gray Phelps and later married to Herbert Dickinson Ward, Elizabeth Stuart Phelps early took on her mother's name and continued to publish under it for the rest of her life. Attempting thereby to resurrect her mother's unused talents, the daughter devoted her entire career to keeping at bay her anxiety that not only would her own talents go unused but that they would go unused as had her mother's before her. This hardly constitutes the murderous engagement of Laius and Oedipus at the crossroads.

It may be objected here that I have altered the terms of the argument by switching from poetry to prose, using for my example only a second-rate novelist and, with that, made of Bloom's "radical analogue" a case history. To which I answer: Bloom himself does not intend "by 'poet' . . . only verse-writer," including, as he does, Emerson, Nietzsche, and Freud under that rubric.[48] Further, it is Bloom's failure to investigate the pathways of literary influence for women which forces me to seek out, wherever I can discover it, the illuminating case history that comes from life *as women know it*. It is, moreover, a case history whose resonances are to be found throughout women's poetry, beginning perhaps with Sarah Wentworth Morton in the United States. When preparing *My Mind and Its Thoughts* (Boston: 1823) for the printer, she incorporated her mother's name (Sarah Wentworth) into her own on the title page and for the first time signed her name to her published work.[49] Such instances recommend the potential applicability of the mother-daughter relationship as both descriptive model and interpretive paradigm. And finally, as we learn better how to read an author like Elizabeth Stuart Phelps we may discover that she is not, after all, anything less than the strong woman writer whom Bloom and others simply could not properly value.

And no one comes to cradle cold Narcissus. . .

Maxine Kumin, "Nightmare" (ca. 1958)

In our own time, as feminist scholars excavate a rich history of "singing sisters," the singular mother/daughter relationship of the two Elizabeth Stuart Phelpses is fast being replaced by generations of

women poets who can remember their nonbiological mother/pro-
genitors. "And when I think of them," declared Alice Walker at a college convocation in 1972, "I understand that each woman is capable of
truly bringing another into the world." When women do it, that hark
ing back to literary forebears entails neither psychic competition nor
any antiquarian dwelling on the past for its own sake. Rather, what
women redeem from the past is a renewed capacity to know and
thereby express their present selves because of the secure context offered by a rich and ongoing cultural accretion. For the would-be white
woman poet as for the black, as Alice Walker put it, "there is not
simply a new world to be gained, there is an old world that must be
reclaimed. There are countless vanished and forgotten women who are
nonetheless eager to speak" to the woman who would take up the pen
today. [50]

In thus reconstituting what Adrienne Rich has termed "an interconnectedness which . . . would give me back myself,"[51] however, lies
both the promise and the threat of what women writers now attempt.
Consider: In the process of "becoming her own midwife, creating herself anew"[52] and enacting thereby the successful female analogue to
Bloom's frustrated poet/son who would (but cannot) be self-begotten,
the woman poet is essentially declaring her independence of male poetry and masculinist poetic theory alike. With Adrienne Rich, she advances "a whole new poetry beginning here."[53] And she follows Alice
Walker's "sisterly advice" to "be nobody's darling":

> Make a merry gathering
> On the bank
> Where thousands perished
> For brave hurt words
> They said.
>
> Be nobody's darling;
> Be an outcast.
> Qualified to live
> Among your dead. [54]

Precisely these declarations of poetic independence may explain the
peculiar anxiety that permeates the work of a critic like Harold Bloom.
Delcaring the "Muses, nymphs who *know*, . . . are now departing,"
Bloom ominously prophesies that "the first true break with literary

continuity will be brought about in generations to come, if the burgeoning religion of Liberated Women spreads from its clusters of enthusiasts to dominate the West. Homer will cease to be the inevitable precursor, and the rhetoric and forms of our literature then may break at last from tradition" (AMOM, p. 33). To be fair to him, Bloom acknowledges some ambivalence about The Great Western Literary Tradition—an ambivalence stemming from his preference for "the morality of the Hebrew Bible to that of Homer" (AMOM, p. 33). But the possibility that the "burgeoning religion of Liberated Women" might free him from the strictures of that tradition seems only a threat, never a promise, to Bloom.

Given the psychology of his theory of literary influence, his anxiety is understandable. If "all men are belated in their stance towards all woman," as Bloom asserts (FOCI, p. 273), and then, as ephebe, the poet also knows himself cuckolded by a whoring mother/Muse, it would be psychological suicide for him to face as well the power of a real flesh-and-blood female poetic precursor. As Bloom reads Freud, in other words, the male poet-ephebe could not survive meeting Jocasta at the crossroads.

It is not clear, however, that even if it emerges "a whole new poetry" by women would necessarily entail the total break with "the rhetoric and forms of our literature" that Bloom predicts. For, as Gilbert and Gubar have demonstrated, what eighteenth- and nineteenth-century women bequeathed their twentieth-century successors were increasingly more effective defensive strategies by which to resist Homer's priority; and insofar as twentieth-century women utilize and elaborate those strategies, then their poetry, too, must inevitably betray its origins in the forms of that resistance. Thus, Bloom's prophecy will have to be modified: still trained by mostly male teachers to read mostly male texts, forced, in effect, from a very early age to "marry the speech of strangers," even those women who would seek to locate themselves in an exclusively female tradition will necessarily turn to precursors who, in part, learned their own evasions by resisting male texts. In the face of an educational establishment that continues to accord women and women's creations only second-class citizenship, and in the face of the irremediable loss of a coherent history of women's writing commencing with Sappho, even the increased access to the last three hundred years of women's poetry will not soon displace Homer as an inevitable precursor; but, as Bloom surmises, it may help to render him eventually no longer *the* inevitable precursor.

That said, Bloom's anxiety is not unjustified. The Muses *are* departing—at least from *his* version of literary history. Women's poetry today announces, as it never has before, that women "can no longer be primarily mothers and muses for men." Discovering, with Adrienne Rich, that "we have our own work cut out for us,"[55] women now call back the Muses as their own, revel in their shared misprisions and revisions of the whole of poetic history, and, like choruses of Echoes all declaring their independence, attempt the restitution of so much that our literary tradition had previously misprized, discarded, or ignored:

> I have written so many words
> wanting to live inside you
> to be of use to you
> Now I must write for myself   for this blind
> woman scratching the pavement   with her wand of thought
> this slippered crone   inching on icy streets
> reaching into wire trashbaskets   pulling out
> what was thrown away   and infinitely precious[56]

No, "the nymphs who *know*" are not "departing" altogether. But until such time as male poets and otherwise sensitive and astute critics like Harold Bloom will look up from their reflecting pools, they will fail to understand that the nymphs have become crones who will no longer woo Narcissus.

Notes

1. Harold Bloom, *A Map of Misreading* (New York: Oxford University Press, 1975), p. 19; henceforth cited in the text as AMOM.
2. Harold Bloom, *Figures of Capable Imagination* (New York: Seabury Press, 1976), p. xi; henceforth cited in the text as FOCI.
3. Harold Bloom, *The Anxiety of Influence: A Theory of Poetry* (New York: Oxford University Press, 1973), p. 30; henceforth cited in the text as TAOI.
4. Harold Bloom, *Kabbalah and Criticism* (New York: Seabury Press, 1975), p. 107; henceforth cited in the text as KC.
5. Harold Bloom, "Poetry, Revisionism, Repression," *Critical Inquiry* 2, no. 2 (Winter 1975): 250; see also his *Poetry and Repression: Revisionism from Blake to Stevens* (New Haven: Yale University Press, 1976), p. 25.
6. Ibid.

7. Paul Ricoeur, "The Metaphorical Process as Cognition, Imagination, and Feeling," *Critical Inquiry* 5, no. 1 (Autumn 1978): 153.

8. Le Anne Schreiber, "I'm Nobody. Who Are You?" *The New York Times Book Review*, December 9, 1979, p. 11.

9. Sandra M. Gilbert and Susan Gubar, *The Madwoman in the Attic: The Woman Writer and the Nineteenth-Century Literary Imagination* (New Haven: Yale University Press, 1979), p. xii; henceforth cited in the text as MA.

10. Joanne Feit-Diehl, "'Come Slowly—Eden': An Exploration of Women Poets and Their Muse," *Signs* 3, no. 3 (Spring 1978): 586.

11. Adrienne Rich, "When We Dead Awaken: Writing as Re-Vision" (1972), repr. in *Adrienne Rich's Poetry*, ed. Barbara Charlesworth Gelpi and Albert Gelpi (New York: W. W. Norton, 1975), p. 94.

12. Mary Jacobus, review of *The Madwoman in the Attic*, *Signs* 6. no. 3 (Spring 1981): 521.

13. Tillie Olsen, *Silences* (New York: Delacorte Press/Seymour Lawrence, 1978), p. 239.

14. According to Ovid's *Metamorphosis*, Hera, angered that Echo's chatter prevented her from detecting Zeus' illicit liaisons, deprived the nymph of normal speech, allowing her the power only to repeat what others had said. When Echo later fell in love with Narcissus, she could woo him only by repeating fragments from his own (self-adoring) speech.

15. Emma Lazarus, "Echoes," a manuscript sonnet dated October 10, 1880, but unpublished until the posthumous collection edited by her sisters, *The Poems of Emma Lazarus*, 2 vols. (Boston: Houghton, Mifflin and Co., 1889), vol. 1, p. 201. See Dan Vogel, *Emma Lazarus* (Boston: Twayne Publishers, G. K. Hall, 1980), p. 95.

16. Anne Bradstreet, prologue to *The Tenth Muse Lately Sprung Up in America* (London: 1650), pp. 3–4.

17. Olsen, *Silences*, p. 250.

18. See Rachel Blau DuPlessis, "The Critique of Consciousness and Myth in Levertov, Rich, and Rukeyser," *Feminist Studies* 3, nos. 1–2 (Fall 1975): 203.

19. Muriel Rukeyser, "The Poem as Mask," in *The Speed of Darkness* (New York: Random House, 1960; repr. 1968), p. 3.

20. Amy Lowell, "The Sisters" (1925), repr. in *No More Masks! An Anthology of Poems by Women*, ed. Florence Howe and Ellen Bass (Garden City, N.Y.: Anchor/Doubleday, 1973), pp. 40–44.

21. Annis Boudinot Stockton, "To Laura," in Pattie Cowell, *Women Poets in Pre-Revolutionary America, 1650–1775: An Anthology* (Troy, N.Y.: Whitston, 1981), pp. 95–96.

22. Judith Sargent Murray, "Valedictory Epilogue to 'Who's the Dupe,' a Farce which Is the Production of the Elegant Pen of Mrs. Cowley. . . Written by Constantia, in the Spring of 1790, and Spoken by Mr. Allen," in Cowell, *Women Poets*, pp. 131–133.

23. Mercy Otis Warren, "To Mrs. Montague, Author of 'Observations on the Genius and Writings of Shakespeare'" (1790), in Cowell, *Women Poets*, p. 86.

24. Jane Colman Turell, "To My Muse, December 29, 1725," in Cowell, *Women Poets*, pp. 48–49.

25. Quoted in Cowell, *Women Poets*, p. 9.

26. See Moses Coit Tyler, *A History of American Literature, 1607–1765*, 2 vols. (New York: G. P. Putnam's Sons, 1878), vol. 1, pp. 277–292 and vol. 2, p. 133, n. 1.

27. Quoted in Susan Phinney Conrad, *Perish the Thought: Intellectual Women in Romantic America, 1830–1860* (New York: Oxford University Press, 1976), p. 47.

28. Emily Stipes Watts, *The Poetry of American Women from 1632 to 1943* (Austin: University of Texas Press, 1977), p. 81.

29. Mary E. Hewitt, "Sappho to the Sibyl" (1853), quoted in Watts, *Poetry of American Women*, p. 81.

30. Muriel Rukeyser, "Letters to the Front," from *Beast in View* (Garden City, N.Y.: Doubleday, Doran and Co., 1944), p. 37.

31. Feit-Diehl, " 'Come Slowly—Eden,' " pp. 573, 586.

32. Sandra M. Gilbert, "Life's Empty Pack: Notes toward a Literary Daughteronomy," *Critical Inquiry* 11, no. 3 (March 1985): 358.

33. Alice Walker, "In Search of Our Mothers' Gardens" (1974), in *In Search of Our Mothers' Gardens: Womanist Prose* (New York: Harvest/Harcourt Brace Jovanovich, 1984), p. 240.

34. Virginia Woolf, *A Room of One's Own* (1929) (repr. Middlesex, England: Penguin, 1945, 1972), p. 76.

35. Anne Sexton, "Housewife," in *All My Pretty Ones* (Boston: Houghton Mifflin, 1961), p. 48.

36. Elizabeth Stuart Phelps, *Chapters from a Life* (Cambridge, Mass.: Riverside Press/Houghton Mifflin, 1896), pp. 3–4; henceforth cited in the text as CFAL.

37. Rachel Blau DuPlessis, *Writing beyond the Ending: Narrative Strategies of Twentieth-Century Women Writers* (Bloomington: Indiana University Press, 1985), pp. 93–94.

38. H. Trusta [Elizabeth Stuart Phelps], *The Sunny Side; or, The Country Minister's Wife* (Philadelphia: American Sunday-School Union, 1851).

39. Elizabeth Stuart Phelps, *The Gates Ajar* (Cambridge, Mass.: Riverside Press/Houghton Mifflin, 1868).

40. Christine Stansell, "Elizabeth Stuart Phelps: A Study in Female Rebellion," *The Massachusetts Review* 13, nos. 1–2 (Winter–Spring 1972): 239, n. 1.

41. Elizabeth Stuart Phelps, *The Angel over the Right Shoulder; or, The Beginning of a New Year* (Andover, Mass.: Draper, 1852).

42. Carol Farley Kessler, "A Literary Legacy," *Frontiers* 5, no. 3 (1981): 29.

43. See Ann Douglas, *The Feminization of American Culture* (New York: Alfred A. Knopf, 1977), p. 224.

44. Carol Farley Kessler, "The Heavenly Utopia of Elizabeth Stuart Phelps," in *Women and Utopia: Critical Interpretations*, ed. Marleen Barr and Nicholas D. Smith (Lanham, Md.: University Press of America, 1983), p. 89.

45. Douglas, *Feminization*, p. 224.
46. Elizabeth Stuart Phelps, *The Story of Avis* (1877), ed. Carol Farley Kessler (New Brunswick, N.J.: Rutgers University Press, 1985). All quotations from the novel are from this reissue.
47. DuPlessis, *Writing beyond the Ending*, p. 90.
48. See Bloom, *Poetry and Repression*, p. 2.
49. See Cowell, *Women Poets*, p. 181.
50. Walker, "A Talk: Convocation 1972," in *In Search of Our Mothers' Gardens*, pp. 39, 36.
51. Rich, "When We Dead Awaken," p. 97.
52. Ibid., p. 98.
53. Adrienne Rich, "Transcendental Etude" (1977), in *The Dream of a Common Language: Poems 1974–1977* (New York: W. W. Norton, 1978), p. 76.
54. Walker, "Be Nobody's Darling," in *In Search of Our Mothers' Gardens*, pp. 39–40.
55. Rich, "When We Dead Awaken," p. 98.
56. Rich, "Upper Broadway" (1975), in *The Dream of a Common Language*, p. 41.

Raymond R. Patterson

What's Happening in Black Poetry?

"We are almost a nation of dancers, musicians, and poets," declares Olaudah Equiano in *The Interesting Narrative of the Life of Olaudah Equiano, or Gustavus Vassa, the African,* first published in London in 1789. "Thus every great event [in Igbo life] . . . such as a triumphant return from battle or other cause of public rejoicing is celebrated in public dances, which are accompanied with songs and music suited to the occasion." Almost two centuries later, assessing "What Black Writers Owe to Music," the *New York Times* of October 4, 1985, announced that "spirituals, jazz and the blues have influenced the style and content of Black writers from Langston Hughes to Alice Walker."

The *Times* article, occasioned by the Broadway production of August Wilson's *Ma Rainey's Black Bottom,* a play concerning blues singer Gertrude ("Ma") Rainey (1886–1939), identifies a number of contemporary black playwrights, novelists, and poets—Ralph Ellison, Amiri Baraka, Charles Fuller, and Michael S. Harper, among others—whose work reflects the influence of Afro-American music. Significantly, what the article suggests is how consistently the New World descendants of Olaudah Equiano have worked within a tradition, an Afro-American literary tradition rooted in Africa but growing from the first utterances of African slaves on American shores through their songs and shouts, their stories, their patterns of expression, to become a recognizable, formal literary tradition by the middle of the eigh-

142

teenth century, as seen in the writings of slave poets Phillis Wheatley, Jupiter Hammon, and, later, George Moses Horton and Frances Ellen Harper.

To understand what is happening in black poetry today, one must first consider the literary tradition out of which black poets write, a tradition in which music plays an important part along with a number of other distinguishing elements—a tradition that allows for a continuity rich in variety and promise.

Former University of Grenoble professor of American Studies Jean Wagner (1919–1984), in his *Black Poets of the United States*,[1] published in English in 1973 and hailed as the first full-length study of black poetry, develops the central thesis that two interdependent themes exist in Afro-American poetry—the racial and the religious, both resulting from the Afro-American experience with the contradictions of slavery in a Christian society. For example, Wagner identifies Harlem Renaissance poets like James Weldon Johnson, Langston Hughes, and Sterling A. Brown as poets in whose work the racial theme predominates. These poets, for the most part, rejected Christianity and took their poetic inspiration from the race, the folk tradition: its folk sermons, work and prison songs, ballads, blues, and jazz. Wagner identifies Harlem Renaissance poets like Claude McKay, Jean Toomer, and Countee Cullen as "spiritualists" in their emphasis on religious (Christian) themes. Afro-American poets prior to the 1920s (poets from Phillis Wheatley to Paul Laurence Dunbar), Wagner argues, concentrated on religious themes, Dunbar being a transitional poet who moved Afro-American poetry away from the spiritual realm into the secular with his use of dialect and his depiction of the folk aspects of plantation life.

Wagner's study stops short of a discussion of poets like Gwendolyn Brooks, Margaret Walker, Robert Hayden, Owen Dodson, and those who began publishing in the 1960s and makes too sharp a distinction between the racial and the spiritual, the folk and the literary, as Professor Eugene B. Redmond points out in *Drumvoices*,[2] his critical history of Afro-American poetry, but Wagner does perform an important service in identifying race and religion as two important themes in Afro-American poetry, and he approaches his subject with an absence of condescension still rare in the criticism of black poetry by scholars who are not black.

Stephen Henderson's *Understanding the New Black Poetry,*[3] in contrast to Wagner's work, is an anthology with an extended introduction that focuses on poetry written in the 1960s by poets most of whom are still writing today: Amiri Baraka, James Emanuel, Gerald Barrax, Mari Evans, Sonia Sanchez, Audre Lorde, Jay Wright, Etheridge Knight, Haki Madhubuti (Don L. Lee), Michael S. Harper, Eugene B. Redmond, Dudley Randall, Ted Joans, Carolyn Rogers, Nikki Giovanni, and others, as well as Margaret Walker and Gwendolyn Brooks—poets of what Professor Henderson terms "The New Black Consciousness," a consciousness that "shifted from Civil Rights to Black Power to Black Nationalism to Revolutionary Pan-Africanism." On the basis of his investigations, Professor Henderson concludes that there are two overlapping and intersecting traditions in black poetry, the folk and the formal, and that there exist clusters of themes around the idea of Liberation/Freedom—an idea which, he says, is energized by the oral tradition, where one finds "the dogged determination of the work songs, the tough-minded power of the blues, the inventive energy of jazz, and the transcendent vision of God in the spirituals and sermons." Professor Henderson, who is director of the Institute for Arts and Humanities at Howard University, observes that the best poets of the 1960s, although influenced by those of the Harlem Renaissance, moved beyond them in challenging their community to view itself "in the larger political and spiritual context of Blackness." Much better informed about their African heritage and no longer interested in writing protest poetry or proving their humanity through their performance in the arts, the poets of the 1960s attempted to speak directly, if not exclusively, "*to* Black people *about themselves* in order to move them toward self-knowledge and collective freedom." This concern of black poets for the welfare of the community is, Professor Henderson implies, an essential feature of the Afro-American literary tradition.

Crucial to an understanding of this new black poetry, Henderson points out, is an appreciation of the importance of black speech and black music as "poetic references." In black speech Henderson finds "a complex and rich and powerful and subtle linguistic heritage whose resources have scarcely been touched that [black poets] draw upon." This "black linguistic elegance," as he terms it, can be seen in naming and enumerating techniques; "jazzy rhythmic effects" (often lost unless the poem is read aloud by the poet); hyperbolic imagery common to black vernacular speech and church sermons; understatement; compressed and cryptic imagery; and "worrying the line," an expression for "changes in word order, repetitions of phrases within the line itself, and the wordless blues cries that often punctuate the performances of . . . songs" (as defined by poet Sherley A. Williams in her essay "The Blues Roots of Contemporary Afro-American Poetry").[4] Henderson also sees in black poetry a typical bluntness of language and the use of "mascons," words containing "a massive concentration of Black experiential energy"—what Sherley A. Williams refers to as "Afro-American archetypes." All of these techniques and concepts can be found in the folk forms—street rhymes, church sermons, toasts and boasts, the blues, jazz, and spirituals.

Henderson locates instances of the use of music as a poetic reference in the frequent selection by black poets of musicians and songs as subjects for poems; the inclusion of song titles and lines from songs in poems; the use of musical forms such as the blues, spirituals, gospel, and jazz; the treatment of the written poem as a performance score or chart—a technique applied with notable success in the poetry of Askia Muhammad Toure, the late Larry Neal, the ensemble presentations of The Last Poets and the performance poetry of Nikki Giovanni, Sonia Sanchez, Jayne Cortez, Ntozake Shange, and Amiri Baraka, whose poem "Reggae or Not" is subtitled "A Piece to be read with Reggae accompaniment." These poets "play the air like a drum," as poet Camille Yarborough describes the technique in her manuscript on the spiritual.

Stephen Henderson emphasizes what he sees as the political commitment of poets of "the New Black Consciousness" and takes the position that black people are best qualified to judge black poetry because only they understand its ethnic roots. Nevertheless, *Understanding the New Black Poetry*, through its development of a vocabulary and a context (although it overlooks important poets like Ed Roberson, Isaac J. Black, and Primus St. John), serves to move the discussion of poetry by black writers beyond the limits of psychological or sociological analysis.

A more recent contribution to an understanding of what is happening in black poetry today is a group of essays, *Black Literature and Literary Theory*, edited by Cornell University professor Henry Louis Gates, Jr.[5] Concerned with the question of the formal relation between black literatures and Western literatures, these scholars attempt to consider how applicable is contemporary literary theory—"Anglo-American and French structuralist, feminist and post-structuralist criticism"—to the reading of the African, Caribbean, and Afro-American literary traditions by analyzing significant black literary works.

In his provocative introduction, which is followed by essays from writers and scholars such as Wole Soyinka, Robert Stepto, Mary Helen Washington, and Houston C. Baker, Gates argues that every great work in the black literary tradition, which consists of interrelated formal and vernacular traditions, is "double-voiced"—possessed of what W. E. B. DuBois in *The Souls of Black Folk* identifies as "double consciousness," the consciousness of being both American and black. Gates also asserts that there exists in the black literary tradition identifiable "black" uses of figurative language. "Black people," he says, "have always been masters of the figurative: saying one thing to mean something quite other has been basic to black survival in oppressive Western cultures."

Professor James A. Snead, in his essay "Repetition as a Figure of Black Culture," discusses the relationship between the uses of repetition and improvisation and offers insights essential to a full appreciation of contemporary Afro-American performance poetry. Identifying what he sees as African-derived patterns of repetition and recurrence, which "find their most characteristic shape in performance: rhythm in music, dance and language," the Yale scholar notes that "without an organizing principle of repetition, true improvisation [a major feature of black creative expression, found notably in jazz and the blues] would be impossible."

Professor Barbara E. Bowen of Wellesley College gives additional insight into the blues form through her "Untroubled Voice: Call and Response in *Cane*," an analysis of Jean Toomer's classic. She writes: "The statement-variation-response sequence which is the essence of the blues is a development of the call-and-response pattern of collective work-songs and spirituals. For the blues singer, the importance of the call-and-response pattern is its continual affirmation of collective voice." This "affirmation of collective voice" is no doubt what Walt Whitman had in mind when he said, "To have great poets there must be great audiences too."

Clearly at odds with the exclusively black critical orientation of Henderson's *Understanding the New Black Poetry* and more concerned with literary theory and the close reading of black texts than Wagner's *Black Poets of the United States,* Gates' *Black Literature and Literary Theory* presents useful models for discussing the work of Afro-American, African, and Caribbean poets—perhaps one day permitting us to see them as part of a single, broad tradition.

What I have tried to suggest by identifying these three approaches to black poetry is that not only are its features being thoughtfully defined—and one has only to read journals such as *Callaloo, Obsidian, Black American Literature Forum, Black Scholar,* and old issues of *Black World* and become familiar with the work of poet-scholars Sherley A. Williams, Eugene B. Redmond, Melvin Dixon, and Lorenzo Thomas to see the wealth of discussion that exists—but that certain features identifying a black poetic tradition can be observed in what poets are writing today. A few of these features are: (1) an extensive use of black music and speech as poetic references; (2) an interplay of the folk (vernacular) and formal traditions; (3) an impulse toward racial and spiritual themes; (4) a double-consciousness operating in structure and language; and (5) a social and political awareness that relates to a sense of community responsibility.

The rich variety that an Afro-American poetic tradition allows is nowhere more strikingly illustrated than in the uses contemporary poets make of the blues, with its classic three-line stanza (the first line making a statement; the second line repeating it, with or without variation; and the third line providing a rhymed response or resolution, often in strict iambic pentameter), its attitude of stoicism, its tough humor, its themes of love, work, travel, pain, death, and transcendence. From Ma Rainey's "Countin' the Blues":[6]

> Layin' in my bed with my face turned to the wall,
> Lord, layin' in my bed with my face turned to the wall,
> Tryin' to count these blues so I could sing them all

through Langston Hughes' "Midwinter Blues":[7]

> I'm gonna buy me a rose bud
> An' plant it at my back door,
> Buy me a rose bud,
> Plant it at my back door,
> So when I'm dead they won't need
> No flowers from the store

and "The Backlash Blues":[8]

> Mister Backlash, Mister Backlash,
> Just who do you think I am?
> Tell me, Mister Backlash,
> Who do you think I am?
> You raise my taxes, freeze my wages,
> Send my son to Vietnam

and Sterling A. Brown's "Tin Roof Blues":[9]

> I'm goin' where de Southern crosses top de C. & O.
> I'm goin' where de Southern crosses top de C. & O.
> I'm goin' down de country cause I can't stay here no mo'

contemporary poets have received an inheritance to which they frequently turn.

Mari Evans, in her "Cellblock Blues,"[10] uses the classic blues structure and traditional subject matter while exploiting the orthographic possibilities of words to effectively convey the class and emotional condition of the speaker, "Layen" and "Layin" providing a fine example of the repetition/improvisation feature associated with the blues:

> Layen in the joint wonderin
> when ah mona raise
> Layin in the joint wonderin
> when ah mona raise
>> Doin black/time by the hour
>> don eeeven be about no days

In "Transformation,"[11] Quincy Troupe abandons the classic structure to address the ironic mingling of joy and pain found in the blues, its transformational capabilities, its oral ("rap") qualities, the poem echoing Ralph Ellison's definition in *Shadow and Act*:[12] "The blues is an impulse to keep the painful details and episodes of a brutal experience alive in one's aching consciousness, to finger its jagged grain, and to transcend it, not by the consolation of philosophy, but by squeezing from it a near-tragic, near-comic lyricism." Quincy Troupe writes:

> catch the blues song
> of wind in your bleeding
> black hand, (w)rap it around
> your strong bony fingers
> then turn it into a soft-nosed pen

> & sit down & write the love
> poem of your life

Contemporary poets working within the blues tradition seem to draw more frequently upon the subject matter than upon the classic form. Nevertheless, simply to call a poem a "blues"—a "mascon" word of tremendous power—can place it and the tradition in resonant relationship. Sonia Sanchez's "Blues" presents a nightmare:[13]

> i see walls dripping screams up
> and down the halls
>   won't someone open
> the door for me? won't some
> one schedule my sleep

from which the speaker finds release remembering a moment of sexual fulfillment, the emotion's objective correlative represented by images in a Bessie Smith song:

> Yeah, bessie he put in the bacon
> and overflowed the pot.

Al Young's "What Is the Blues?"[14] gives a hard, direct look at the human condition. Its three stanzas play against the three-line stanza of the classic blues and capture the style and attitude of the quintessential blues singer who, though drowning in the blues, keeps

>   coming up for air: my
> tiny fair share of cool fulfillment.
>
> And to vanish wouldn't be so bad.
> Look at the visible, behold it slowly
> and closely with unreddened eyes.
> Without the stirrings of the heart
> swimming in borrowed light, what could
> we ever possibly lie down and see?

Calvin Hernton's "D Blues"[15] answers Al Young's question by stripping the language to its essentials, the idea to its concrete representation, undercutting the agony of utter loneliness with the language of the minstrel show:

> De blues
> What you woke up wit
> Dhis mourning

What you toss and turn
All night in your bed wit

From a sharecropper's battle with floods and boll weevils to John Henry's legendary confrontation with a steam drill, conflicts with nature and machines have always provided materials for blues poets. Where man is the measure of all things earthly, technology (even The Bomb) comes under wry scrutiny. Raymond R. Patterson's "Computer Blues" complains:[16]

> I put my troubles in the computer
> To find out what's troubling me.
> I say I put my troubles in the computer
> To see what's the matter with me.
> My card had so many holes,
> Holes was all that I could see.

The pain of the blues, unrelieved by humor but transformed through craft, is captured in Michael S. Harper's "Village Blues."[17] The poem transplants the "strange fruit" of Billie Holiday's American South (perhaps to South America) to render a monstrous image (suicide or lynching?) familiar by virtue of the poem's double consciousness and its ironic allusions not only to Christian ideas of resurrection but also to black texts such as "Christ in Alabama" by Langston Hughes:

> The birds flit
> in the blue palms,
> the cane workers wait.
> the man hangs
> twenty feet above;
> he must come down;
> they wait for the priest.
> The flies ride on the carcass

Great female blues singers Ma Rainey, Bessie Smith, Big Mama Thornton, Billie Holiday, and Dinah Washington, along with their songs of lost love and abuse at the hands of some "no-good man," also sang of assertive women who celebrate their strength and independence. Two contemporary blues poems in that tradition are Mariah Britton's "reports"[18] and Lucille Clifton's "Miss Rosie."[19] Landlords, store owners, and racism, not lovers, are the source of trouble for Mariah

Britton's "woman / with a mountain / of stones / she didn't / throw. . . . lately though," she says, "i hear / reports of / broken glass." In Lucille Clifton's poem, the strength of women who survive the ravages of time and circumstance is evoked through the archetypal Miss Rosie. "When I watch you," the poet declares, "I stand up / through your destruction / I stand up."

Contemporary black poets writing out of an Afro-American literary tradition have not limited themselves to lyric poems but have produced examples of epic poetry deserving attention. A connection between contemporary Afro-American epic poetry and traditional African epic poetry awaits explication, but African epic features no doubt survived in the narratives of early slave poets, those "black and unknown bards of long ago" immortalized by James Weldon Johnson. The Afro-American literary epic, however, finds its earliest formal expression in the nineteenth century in Albery A. Whitman's *The Rape of Florida* (concerning the Seminole Indian Wars) and *Not a Man and Yet a Man* (chronicling an individual's quest for freedom). Nevertheless, characteristics of the genre can be seen in the poetry of Phillis Wheatley, and certainly the twentieth century contains fine examples in Melvin B. Tolson's *Libretto for the Republic of Liberia* and *Harlem Gallery*, Calvin Hernton's *The Coming of Chronos to the House of Nightsong*, and *Black Anima* by N. J. Loftis. If one thinks of the urge to write the epic as an urge to establish a sense of community, to delineate an ethos, it is not surprising that black poets move in that direction. Twentieth-century contributions to the poetic sequence, in its various modes including the epic, are numerous and can be seen in the work of Jean Toomer, James Weldon Johnson, Countee Cullen, Langston Hughes, Robert Hayden, and Gwendolyn Brooks and in the work of younger poets such as Michael S. Harper, Sonia Sanchez, Ishmael Reed, June Jordan, Ai, Sherley A. Williams, and Caribbean poets Edward Brathwaite, Derek Walcott, and Wilfred Cartey.

Two recent attempts at the epic by black poets are *The Double Invention of Komo*[20] by Jay Wright and *Iwilla/Soil* by Yvonne.[21] *The Double Invention of Komo*, the author tells us in his afterword, is a poem of initiation given shape by a study of African, Mexican, and South American cosmologies with elements of Western culture, using the rituals of the Bambara Komo initiation rite to open an exploration of history as a way toward self-knowledge. The poem's voices are African, European, and American. In the poet's words, the poem seeks to redeem and to discover social, historical cultural, intellectual, and emotional dimensions now obscure in the African and Afro-American worlds and to make these dimensions available for creative use in the necessary transformation of an enhanced world of intransigent act.

Ambitious and complex, the poem owes allegiance to a variety of literary ancestors and does not readily reveal itself through excerpts; however, one theme, that of double consciousness operating in structure, language, and idea, is unmistakably sounded as only a true son of Olaudah Equiano would:

> I know my double exile in song,
> and the way the heel comes down,
> remembering a dance,
> on unfamiliar ground.

Yvonne's *Iwilla/Soil*, a poetic sequence of epic sweep, combines African, Native American, and Judeo-Christian ritual in a New World setting. Book 1 of a projected trilogy, it is structured as an arrangement of voices telling the story of Iwilla, "the first American Mother of my family," and the daughters who came from her. Aunt Ida (1881–1971) operates a hair-dressing parlor. This fragment of her life captures the sad eloquence of the blues:

> Radiant
> glorified
> effervescent
> they scatter from beneath Aunt Ida's hands
> the Negro women of this shambling town
> a shattering of raven wings
> chatoyant
> falling stars

The long and well-established tradition of social and political awareness in Afro-American poetry extends back to the earliest recorded poem by an Afro-American, "Bars Fight" by Lucy Terry, which concerns an Indian attack in Deerfield, Massachusetts, in 1746. Phillis Wheatley's lines to Britain's Lord Dartmouth[22]—"Should you, my lord, while you peruse my song, / Wonder from whence my love of Freedom sprung"—are also of that tradition, as are the slave spirituals, the abolitionist verse of the nineteenth century, the protest po-

etry of the early decades of the twentieth century, and the revolutionary
poetry of the 1960s and 1970s. Such poems continue to be written by
black poets. Jayne Cortez reminds us in the opening lines of "For the
Brave Young Students in Soweto":[23]

Soweto
when i hear your name
i think of you
like the fifth ward in Houston Texas
one roof of crushed oil drums on the other
two black hunters in buckets of blood
walking into the fire of Sharpeville
into the sweat and stink of gold mines
into your children's eyes suffer from malnutrition
while pellets of uranium are loaded into boats
headed for France for Israel for Japan
away from the river so full of skulls
and Robben Island so swollen with warriors
and the townships that used to overflow
with such apathy and dreams

And so it would appear that many black poets today work out of a
tradition that can best be understood as distinctly Afro-American, the
African element proclaimed long ago by Olaudah Equiano; the American element only partially understood by Stephen Vincent Benét in
1928, when in *John Brown's Body*[24] he envisioned the yet unwritten
"black-skinned epic, epic with the black spear," with its "Deep mellow
of the husky, golden voice / Crying dark heaven through the spirituals, / Soft mellow of the levee roustabouts, / Singing at night
against the banjo-moon"—Afro-American poetry is all of that, yet
much more.

Notes

1. Champaign: University of Illinois Press, 1973.
2. Anchor Press, 1976.
3. New York: William Morrow and Co., 1973.
4. *Massachusetts Review* (Autumn 1977).
5. New York: Methuen, 1984.
6. In *Woke Up This Morning* (New York: Bantam, 1973).
7. In *Selected Poems* (New York: Alfred A. Knopf, 1975).

8. In *The Panther and the Lash* (New York: Alfred A. Knopf, 1967).

9. In *The Collected Poems* (New York: Harper and Row, 1980).

10. In *Nightstar* (Los Angeles: UCLA Publications, 1981).

11. In *Snake-Back Solos* (Danbury, N.H.: Reed Books, 1978).

12. New York: Random House, 1964.

13. In *I've Been a Woman* (Black Scholar Press, 1978).

14. *Hambone* 2 (Fall 1982).

15. In *Medicine Man* (New York: Reed, Cannon and Johnson, 1976).

16. In *Elemental Blues* (New York: Cross-Cultural Communications, 1983).

17. In *Images of Kin* (Champaign: University of Illinois Press, 1977).

18. In *With Fire* (New York: Meta Press, 1982).

19. In *Good Times* (New York: Random House, 1969).

20. Austin: University of Texas Press, 1980.

21. New York: Chameleon Productions, 1985.

22. In *The Poems and Letters of Phillis Wheatley* (Mnemosyne Publishing, 1969).

23. In *Coagulations: New and Selected Poems* (Thunder's Mouth Press, 1984).

24. New York: Holt, Rinehart and Winston, 1928.

John F. Crawford

Notes toward a New Multicultural Criticism

Three Works by Women of Color

I wish to examine works of three women poets from distinct cultural traditions—Joy Harjo, Creek Indian; Lorna Dee Cervantes, Chicana; and Janice Mirikitani, Japanese American. Harjo and Cervantes were born in the early 1950s, Mirikitani near the end of the Second World War. Each represents a broader culture—American Indian, Hispanic, Asian American—which has produced a significant new literature within the author's lifetime. In sections to follow I will treat the specific project of each of these writers; here I wish to examine what they have in common.

All three are members of oppressed minorities in the United States. The ancestors of present-day American Indians were subdued by military conquest by their Euro-American invaders and placed on reservations. The Southwestern ancestors of the Chicanos, themselves descendants of Hispanic and indigenous peoples, were subjugated politically and sometimes militarily by the same Euro-Americans. They were followed to the United States by waves of poor Mexican immigrants, especially after the Mexican Revolution. The immigrants from Japan, China, and the Philippines came seeking employment and were subjected to systematic legal repression governing their entry, the nature of their employment, and their segregation from the dominant society. In addition, Japanese Americans like Mirikitani suffered internment in military prison camps during the Second World War as suspected agents of a hostile foreign power. Members of all these

155

groups have also been subject to acts of racial prejudice (including racial murders and lynchings) and have been punished economically, in the job market, and by restriction of access to homes and other material benefits. This may be said to be stating the obvious. But it is important to realize that the women poets represented here are emergent writers who have struggled to gain a new voice, not simply "multi-ethnic" writers exercising the privilege of self-expression in an American "melting pot."

All three writers have witnessed and participated in the increasing politicization in their cultures in the decades since the Second World War. The contrast between the boom period enjoyed by the white majority population in the 1960s and the situation on the reservations and in the barrios and ghettos gave oppressed peoples substantial cause for organized defiance and revolt. In the case of Native American tribes, earlier attempts by the U.S. government to terminate some and relocate others into city slums led to political and cultural resistance. The young "City Indians" of the 1960s and 1970s sought to fight ghetto conditions and at the same time to reconnect with their tribal pasts. Chicanos, politically active since the end of World War II, paid special heed in the 1950s and 1960s to the condition of migratory farm workers in California; many other people in the nation supported them in this effort. Asian Americans developed a keen sense of community organizing in such cities as San Francisco and New York while undertaking a close study of their past. They concluded that the dominant culture in America, working "under legislative racism and euphemized white racist love," had "left today's Asian Americans in a state of self-contempt, self-rejection, and disintegration,"[1] and they banded together to fight these conditions.

The Modern Language Association took note of the emerging literatures of these groups in the 1970s. Its Commission on Minority Groups and the Study of Language and Literature sponsored a national symposium on minority literature in New York in 1976, some of the proceedings of which were published the following year.[2] The literature of American Indians, Chicanos, and Asian Americans was specifically treated in another volume, *Three American Literatures*, gathered in the 1970s and published in 1982.[3] Perhaps the most significant result of the MLA project was an anthology, *The Third Woman: Minority Women Writers of the United States*, edited by Dexter Fisher in her capacity as director of English Programs for the MLA and published in 1980.[4] Copiously documented, annotated, and footnoted, it provided essential texts of American Indian, black, Chicana, and Asian American women writers of the 1960s and 1970s for later editors to follow.[5] Harjo, Cervantes, and Mirikitani were all included in this volume.

Perhaps half a dozen major works of scholarship have been written or compiled in the three literatures up to the present time. Of these, three major works have been produced by women scholars: *Studies in American Indian Literature*, an MLA critical reader and handbook edited by Paula Gunn Allen; *Contemporary Chicana Poetry*, a critical study by Marta Ester Sanchez; and *Asian American Literature* by Elaine H. Kim. I will make use of these works in the pages to follow.[6] I will rely first on the testimony of critics before me (especially women within each poet's own culture), then give close textual readings based on the standard methods of current criticism, and argue finally for the consideration of these works as part of a revised canon of American literature.[7]

She Had Some Horses by Joy Harjo

> The ceremonies as they had been performed were enough for the way the world was then . . . elements in this world began to shift, and it became necessary to create new ceremonies.

Leslie Marmon Silko, *Ceremony*[8]

The essential focus of modern-day American Indian literature from the time of its emergence after World War II has been survival. The survival of many peoples under material and spiritual attack has been the theme of its great novels, from N. Scott Momaday's *House Made of Dawn* (1969) to Leslie Marmon Silko's *Ceremony* (1977) to Louise Erdrich's *Love Medicine* (1984). The use of ceremonial devices in the stories to suggest or promote psychological or social healing (they are the whole subject of Silko's *Ceremony*) has generated critical interest.[9] What has not been so often remarked is that the theme of survival and the techniques of ceremony have also permeated the poetry, most apparently in the women poets such as Wendy Rose, Leslie Marmon Silko, and Joy Harjo.

Paula Gunn Allen has remarked that American Indian literature calls for a "functional" definition of genre into "ceremonial and popular, as opposed to the Western prose and poetry distinction."[10] Ceremonial literature "includes all literature that is accompanied by ritual actions and music and that produces mythic (metaphysical) states of consciousness and/or conditions" and thus is invested with "an intangible but very real power or force." Using "language of its own," it may include "songs for many occasions," such as healing, harvesting, blessing new undertakings, personal power songs, and vision seeking. "Each serves to hold the society together, create harmony . . . [and] ensure prosperity and unity."[11] Allen takes pains to distinguish sacred Indian ceremony, which is wholly or partly secret to the tribe, from the literary use of ceremonial devices. But it is clear that aspects of ceremonial understanding have entered literature. These include ritual elements such as opening and closing prayers, references to and actual use of "old stories," uses of natural symbolism and symbolic persons, and certain narrative devices such as telling a story on several levels and alluding to things forbidden to be spoken.

Indian symbols are never counters for other things which they are not; they are natural entities subject to transformation through ritual. Allen describes this use of "magic":

> The tribal person perceives things, not as inert, but as viable and alive, and he or she knows that living things are subject to processes of growth and change as a necessary component of their aliveness. Since all that exists is alive, and since all that is alive must grow and change, all existence can be manipulated under certain conditions and according to certain laws.[12]

The inseparability of symbols and the world of which they are a part, and their availability for interpretation, are movingly described by Lame Deer, quoted by Allen:

> We Indians live in a world of symbols and images where the spiritual and the commonplace are one. To you, symbols are just words, spoken or written in a book. To us they are a part of nature, part of ourselves, even little insects like ants and grasshoppers. We try to understand them not with the head but

with the heart, and we need no more than a hint to give us meaning. [13]

Can we speak of the "role of the poet" in American Indian culture? Only in guarded and qualified ways. What we seem to find are writers privileged to take on poetic roles as witnesses to the dangers of the time. These writers are to be seen as representative members of a social group, all of whom enjoy a personal relationship with nature. But if the writer is both an observer and a manipulator of symbols, the work is likely to be polysemous in "story lines," with literal and symbolic levels of interpretation. Allen has remarked of writers such as Momaday and Silko that they share an "achronicity":

> These people can actually think four stories at the same time. And they can do it simultaneously in their brain, which is analogous to the sort of universe the [modern] physicists are describing. That's one of the marks of an Indian person. They do it automatically. [14]

One reason for the complication of the stories is that one level at least—the most occult kind of knowledge—is only alluded to. This may be the level of witchery or of other ceremonial secrets. Often this level awaits the unraveling of the other levels of the story in order to be fully understood. Such would appear to be the case with *She Had Some Horses* by Joy Harjo.

In her early writing, Joy Harjo already addressed themes of land and people, fear and healing. Speaking of her native landscape, she remarked:

> What is breathing here is some sort of dangerous anger that rises up out of the Oklahoma landscape. The earth is alive with emotions, and will take action on what is being felt. This way of seeing is characteristic of most native poets and writers of Oklahoma. That which has happened to the earth, has happened to all of us as part of the earth. . . .
>
> What Oklahoma becomes, in a sense, is a dream, an alive and real dream that takes place inside and outside of the writer. . . . Our words begin inside of the dream and become a way of revealing ourselves within this landscape that is called Oklahoma. Language becomes all of the people that we are. Living voices surround us and speak from the diverse and many

histories we have been, the ones we have become, and most of all, how we will continue. There are those voices among us who will assume the cadence of an ancient and living chant.[15]

Nothing in Harjo's early work quite prepares the reader for the overall arrangement—a plot structure operating on several levels—of *She Had Some Horses,* her third book, published in 1983.[16] The book begins by confessing the poet's fear. It then describes the fate of other "survivors" like herself who have had to deal with such fear. It introduces intermediary figures—human and symbolic—who negotiate between the poet and her fear. It tells a story of the breakup of the poet's relationship with a man and her discovery of the love of a woman. It ends with the freeing of the horses, who are the symbols of her frightened spirit, and the freeing of the poet from old, repressive images to live her own life. The end is a ritual prayer, closing off the matter begun with the first poem.

The first poem, "Call It Fear," introduces most of the thematic material in the book.

> There is this edge where shadows
> and bones of some of us walk
> > backwards.
> Talk backwards. There is this edge
> call it an ocean of fear of the dark. Or
> name it with other songs. Under our ribs
> our hearts are bloody stars. Shine on
> shine on, and horses in their galloping flight
> strike the curve of ribs.
>
> . . . .
> There is this edge within me
> > I saw it once
> an August Sunday morning when the heat hadn't
> left this earth. And Goodluck
> sat sleeping next to me in the truck.
> We had never broken through the edge of the
> singing at four a.m.
>
> . . . .
> > And there was this edge—
> not the drop of sandy rock cliff
> bones of volcanic earth into
> > Albuquerque.

Not that,
          but a string of shadow horses kicking
and pulling me out of my belly,
               not into the Rio Grande but into the music
barely coming through
                    Sunday church singing
from the radio. Battery worn-down but the voices
talking backwards.

The "edge" of fear is the subject of the book. The fear is protean, taking many shapes: notably the backwards-talking Holy Rollers on the radio and the nightmare of the horses pulling the poet's entrails out of her belly ("Or name it with other songs"). The people of Harjo's acquaintance sit by the volcanic cliffs outside Albuquerque trying to propitiate this fear ritually by talking and singing and "walking backwards." Still it persists ("Under our ribs / our hearts are bloody stars"). Someone who might stand as an intermediary between the poet and her fear, Goodluck, her friend and a symbolic figure, has been unable like her to "[break] through the edge of the singing at four a.m."

Succeeding poems speak of those who survive even in a hostile environment. The poet quickly establishes her sense of identity with people of color in America in her poem to Audre Lorde, "Anchorage":

And I think of the 6th Avenue jail, of mostly Native
and Black men, where Henry told about being shot at
eight times outside a liquor store in L.A., but when
the car sped away he was surprised he was alive,
no bullet holes, man, and eight cartridges strewn
on the sidewalk
          all around him.

Everyone laughed at the impossibility of it,
but also the truth. Because who would believe
the fantastic and terrible story of all of our survival
those who were never meant
                    to survive?

The survivors take many forms, but perhaps the most stirring image in these poems is the relationship of women to the earth. It begins in the poem "For Alva Benson, and for Those Who Have Learned to Speak":

> And the ground spoke when she was born.
> Her mother heard it. In Navajo she answered
> as she squatted down against the earth
> to give birth. It was now when it happened,
> now giving birth to itself again and again
> between the legs of women.

The image is heightened in a later stanza, the action of which makes a completed circle, with Mt. St. Helens the governing symbol:

> The child now hears names in her sleep.
> They change into other names, and into others.
> It is the ground murmuring, and Mt. St. Helens
> erupts as the harmonic motion of a child turning
> inside her mother's belly waiting to be born
> to begin another time.

Contrasting to this woman-image of cyclic restoration is the tragic image of the man, drinking and out of control, which repeats itself in several poems. In "Night Out" it is a man in a barroom on New Year's Eve:

> Your voice screamed out from somewhere in the
> darkness
> another shot, anything to celebrate this deadly
> thing called living. And Joe John called out to bring
> another round, to have another smoke, to dance dance it good
> because tomorrow night is another year—
> in your voice.
> I have heard you in my ownself.
> And have seen you in my own past vision.

The poet takes pains to universalize and understand the figure:

> It doesn't end
> For you are multiplied by drinkers, by tables, by jukeboxes
> by bars.
> You fight to get out of the sharpest valleys cut down into
> the history of living bone.
> And you fight to get in.
> You are the circle of lost ones
> our relatives.

> You have paid the cover charge thousands of times over
> with your lives
> > and now you are afraid
>
> > > you can never get out.

These poems show separate ways of knowing: a man's way, harsh and fatalistic, of meaningless rebellion, or a woman's way, embracing the history of the whole earth of which one is a part. It is the second way the poet will choose to follow as the book develops.

The figure of Noni Daylight appears in three poems near the end of the first section. Old and shrunken, the mother of many children by as many fathers, she is first cited as the woman who stayed where she was to raise her family:

> > Because she knew
> that each star rang with separate
> colored hue, as bands of horses
> and wild
> > like the spirit in her
> that flew, at each train whistle.
> > > ("Kansas City")

In the next poem where she is mentioned, Noni is afraid of familiar voices.

> > She talks softly
> > > softly
> To the voice on the radio. All night she drives.

Finally she perceives how she will free herself.

> > It is not the moon, or the pistol in her lap
> but a fierce anger
> > that will free her.
> > > ("Heartbeat")

In the third poem in which she appears, Noni reveals her true character to the poet and proposes the key to the poet's rescue.

> "We are closer than
> blood," Noni Daylight
> tells her. "It isn't
> Oklahoma or the tribal

blood but something more
that we speak."

She speaks directly to the poet of her "cure" and reveals herself as a spiritual intermediary.

"Should I dream you afraid
so that you are forced to save
yourself?

Or should you ride colored horses
into the cutting edge of the sky
to know

that we're alive
we are alive."
("She Remembers the Future")

The poet must now seize the initiative.

The second section, "What I Should Have Said," focuses on the poet's changing of her relationship from a man to a woman lover and the confusion, disruption, and difficulty she has in "commuting" (literally from Albuquerque to Santa Fe and back again) to teach, care for her children, and be with her new lover. The moon becomes the symbol of her new consciousness, but also her new fate:

She is moon.
Her eyes slit and yellow she is the last
one out of a dingy bar in Albuquerque—
Fourth Street, or from similar avenues
in Hong Kong. Where someone else has also
awakened, the night thrown back and asked,
"Where is the moon, my lover?"
And from here I always answer in my dreaming,
"The last time I saw her was in the arms
of another sky."
("Moonlight")

In her acceptance of the promiscuity of the moon, the poet affirms a new existence, one which Noni Daylight unlocked when she told her she must "know / that we're alive / we are alive." In a new poem, written while driving between her lover and home, the poet begins to explore the meaning of this.

Alive. This music rocks
me. I drive the interstate,
watch faces come and go on either
side. I am free to be sung to;
I am free to sing. This woman
can cross any line.

            ("Alive")

The horses which figured in the first poem in the book return in the third section, bursting forth in a terrible and wonderful emergence.

The title poem of the section "She Had Some Horses" is an extended catalog of "horses"—personal traits, poetic images, manifestations of fear and anxiety or danger from external forces—known to the poet. She writes it with bare logical connection, in the manner of Christopher Smart's "For I Will Consider My Cat Jeffrey." The ending of the poem gives some of its most important elements, threats from within and without and what they actually have amounted to.

She had horses who whispered in the dark, who were afraid to
   speak.
She had horses who screamed out of fear of the silence, who
carried knives to protect themselves from ghosts.
She had horses who waited for destruction.
She had horses who waited for resurrection.

She had some horses.

She had horses who got down on their knees for any saviour.
She had horses who thought their high price had saved them.
She had horses who tried to save her, who climbed in her
bed at night and prayed as they raped her.

She had some horses.

She had some horses she loved.
She had some horses she hated.

These were the same horses.

Several more poems treat horses in their different aspects. In the fifth poem, the remarkable "Explosion," all the horses are set free—those belonging to others and to the poet herself.

The explosion—on a highway—takes place in the poet's home country. (We may recall what Harjo saw elsewhere as "some sort of dangerous anger that rises up out of the Oklahoma landscape.") She first tries to associate it with an apocalyptic future event of significance to her people. Finally she sees what has happened.

> But maybe the explosion was horses,
>   bursting out of the crazy earth
> near Okemah. They were a violent birth,
> flew from the ground into trees
>   to wait for evening night
> mares to come after them . . .
> .   .   .   .
> Some will not see them.

> But some will see the horses with their hearts of sleeping
>   volcanoes
> and will be rocked awake
>   past their bodies
>
>   to see who they have become.

It is important to view the horse poems not as simply a hodgepodge of loosely related material but as ceremonial shapes, from the naming of the horses to their freeing, which make it possible for the poet and others who believe her to look to the future with hope and to "see who they have become" (the "they" of the last line is, I believe, purposely ambiguous). This freeing is the climax of the book, leading to the concluding poem, which echoes the beginning.

"I Give You Back" works at many levels. The first level is the ritual release of the fear that was expressed in the beginning.

> I release you, my beautiful and terrible
> fear. I release you. You were my beloved
> and hated twin, but now, I don't know you
> as myself. . . .
> You are not my blood anymore.

Also released are paralyzing memories of genocide and the poet's susceptibility to future harm at the hands of the oppressor.

> I give you back to the white soldiers
> who burned down my home, beheaded my children,
> raped and sodomized my brothers and sisters.
> .   .   .   .

> I release you, fear, so that you can no longer
> keep me naked and frozen in the winter,
> or smothered under blankets in the summer.

There follows a sequence in ritual repetition, first declaring simply, "I release you" and then itemizing what the poet is "not afraid to be." Then the poet admits her own past complicity in her fear:

> Oh, you have choked me, but I gave you the leash.
> You have gutted me but I gave you the knife.
> You have devoured me, but I laid myself across the fire.
> You held my mother down and raped her,
>   but I gave you the heated thing.

After another sequence announcing her separation from her fear, the poet ends with a passionate inversion, showing the formerly weak element to now be the strong and the strong the weak. It is a note of triumph and even of compassion for the enemy.

> But come here, fear
> I am alive and you are so afraid
>   of dying.

Harjo's indebtedness to traditional storytelling devices, such as her use of ceremonial elements at the beginning and end of the poem, her use of symbols like the horses, the moon, and the spiritual guide Noni Daylight, and her use of multilevel narrative are integral to the structure of the poem: they establish the naming of the fear at the beginning, the intervention of Noni Daylight in the middle, and the freeing of the horses at the end. Two levels of the narrative are literal: the story of the author's changes in lovers and the historical thread running through the book, reminding the reader of the history of white oppression. In both these cases it is important to notice the author's point of view. When she says, "You have gutted me but I gave you the knife," she is making a point both personal and political. Both she and her people, as she has come to understand them, are learning not to be victims.

Optimism is conveyed at the end of *She Had Some Horses* through the notion brought first by Noni Daylight, "We are alive." The poet pronounces this for herself in the course of the discovery of her new love while driving between Alburquerque and Santa Fe one day. Armed with the knowledge, she banishes fear: "I am alive and you are so afraid / of dying." We should recall again what Paula Gunn Allen describes as the "magic" involved in the enactment of ceremony. "Since all that exists is alive and since all that is alive must grow and change, all existence can be manipulated . . . according to certain laws." We may conclude that the method and content of Harjo's book are the same.

Emplumada by Lorna Dee Cervantes

Although Chicano literature has emerged only since the 1960s, it has a remarkable consciousness of its own origins. An early textbook, *Literatura chicana: Texto y contexto* (1972), could already state that it was "composed with the Chicano reader in mind" and trace a cultural heritage including "antecedent Mexican texts [and] pre-Hispanic selections."[17] By 1980, the critic Bruce-Novoa had proposed a paradigm of Chicano poetry as a response to the overall problematic of Chicano history. Such a poetry contained

> a nostalgia for a prior unity, either lost, forgotten, or in the
> process of disappearing; a lamenting of alienating oppression in
> the present, a situation which must be corrected lest Chicano
> culture disappear; and a hope for a future regrouping in a home-
> land (Aztlan) reclaimed from the United States, and around
> cultural/historical traditions—a recuperation of the lost unity.[18]

Bruce-Novoa's critical work *Chicano Poetry* (1982) treats eleven men and one woman. In the decade since 1975, however, women have emerged as major voices, a "second generation" of poets marked by different concerns from their male counterparts. Marta Ester Sanchez, in her book *Contemporary Chicana Poetry* (1985), has typified these concerns as ones of gender and ethnic identification, joined by common identity as a poet, and sees the major distinctions among women writers to come from which element of this "triad" they emphasize.[19] Naomi Quiñonez, Los Angeles poet and teacher, has been perhaps more helpful in this connection by viewing the emergence of the Chicana in a concrete perspective:

> In the process of writing, for the Third World woman, several
> things are happening. The connection with a past, with a

culture, is the motivating force; so you see many women who
will bring back the images of our ancestral past, give them new
light, put them in a new context, recreating symbols and images
that have been given to us effectively from our own culture.
Also, we are redefining the images and symbols that have been
given to us by the dominant society, putting those in a new
context. Finally, we are creating new symbols, new images, and
synthesizing all those aspects into new myths sometimes, using a
combination of what our past is and what has been imposed on
us, giving us something relevant to really be a part of.[20]

Born in 1954 in San Jose, California, Lorna Dee Cervantes is an
inheritor of the Chicano tradition that was being thematically established as she was growing up. She had access as a beginning writer to
the works of the "first generation" of politically active, primarily male
Chicano writers. She began writing the poems that would make up her
book *Emplumada* in 1974 and spent seven years arranging the manuscript. While she herself speaks of the "different styles" and "poems
dealing with different issues" in the book, she also makes it clear that
the arrangement of materials is deliberate: "The book is meant to be
read in one sitting. It's meant to be read from beginning to end."[21]

The particular challenge that Naomi Quiñonez sees confronting the
first generation Chicana artist is that of combining the materials she
found in books with the experience of her own life to produce new
poems. There is in this a strong sense of historical process. The *Chicanismo* of the first generation of male poets, especially their search for
the "lost unity" of Aztlan, is a gender-influenced myth of heroic discovery.[22] The emergence of *La Chicana* as poet, on the other hand,
brings other "images of our ancestral past"—the figures of the grandmother and the mother as nurturing and sustaining forces, the home
as the center of the world, and the artist as the synthesizer "using a
combination of what our past is and what has been imposed on us,
giving us something relevant to really be a part of." According to this
view, Cervantes is not so much the seat of conflicting impulses as she is
the synthesis of two generations of poetic effort.[23]

Bruce-Novoa observed, in his work *Chicano Poetry*, that Chicano
poets in their work follow "basic antimonies of thought" such as those
found in the structures of myth. "A system of primitive irreconcilable
tensions struggling for resolution, they are manifested in a text in the

form of binary oppositions such as life vs. death, individual vs. group, freedom vs. necessity."[24] Cervantes, in *Emplumada*, divides the work according to pairings of binary opposition, in which each new stage of dialectical development leads to new propositions awaiting similar testing in the future.

Cervantes is a great definer of terms. At the very beginning of *Emplumada*, she devotes a whole page to defining her title, according to a binary opposition.

> em-plu-ma-do [adj.] m., feathered; in plumage, as in after
>   molting
> plu-ma-da n.f., pen flourish[25]

My reading of this pairing is that the act of writing has to do with coming into one's own, being empowered for flight (the colorful image of plumage is linked to the Chicano heritage).

The book is divided into three sections. Each has a headnote or short title. Each of these consists of two terms, either stated or understood. The headnote of the first section is ominous: "Consider the power of wrestling your ally. His will is to kill you. He has nothing against you." The pairing around the image of "ally" introduces the contradiction of malign will versus moral indifference. The second section, with the headnote "This world understands nothing but words and you have come into it with almost none," concerns the acquisition of a language necessary to survive in the world. Language has now become the ally with which one must wrestle in order to succeed. The third section is titled simply "Emplumada," referring us back to the pairing "feathered; in plumage" and "pen flourish." This would appear to speak of some synthesis, where the dangers of the world are confronted by a language appropriate to their expression, resulting in the freeing of the writer for an as yet unspecified task.

As the binary terms of each section of *Emplumada* suggest, the book is always in a state of development. The first section, governed by the image of "wrestling your ally," treats the poet growing up in her single-parent household of mother and grandmother, mediating images of "hardness" and "softness" to understand how she will confront the world. The image of the "Ally," along with other imagery of initiation, is borrowed from Carlos Castaneda's *The Teachings of Don Juan*;[26] much of the incidental lore of the first section treats drugs and intimates of the art of the *bruja* or sorcerer. The second section, governed by the problem of language, shows the poet cast out into the world, unable to recover her Mexican heritage and seriously challenged by the harsh world of the Anglo dominant culture. The third section attempts a reconciliation of tradition and modernity. The persona of the poet develops in each case. In the first section a myth of the past is brought into place, showing formative influences on the girl growing up in the barrio. The second section shows the poet in transaction with Mexican and Anglo culture. In the third section she speaks in her own voice. The identity of the poet Lorna Dee Cervantes and the persona of the book become more marked as the book progresses.

In the first poem, "Uncle's First Rabbit," the persona's uncle encounters the world and finds it full of dangerous knowledge. The uncle, while still a boy, kills a rabbit, thinking it a part of his initiation into manhood. Immediately after the killing the boy dreams of escape.

> He was a good boy
> making his way through
> the Santa Barbara pines,
> sighting the blast of fluff
> as he leveled the rifle,
> and the terrible singing began.
> He was ten years old,
> hunting my grandpa's supper.
> He had dreamed of running,
> shouldering the rifle to town,
> selling it, and taking the next
> train out.

The "terrible singing" is his memory of the crying of his baby sister, "pushed . . . into birth" by "his father's drunken kicking," her voice "going faint at its end"—a sound that blends with the cry of the rabbit he bludgeons to death. But killing the rabbit has not only brought the terrible memory back to life, it has passed the crime of the father onto the son. Instead of leaving his brutal and abusive father behind, the boy becomes him. When a young man he goes off to war; he returns to brutalize his own wife; and, as the poem moves to the present, is seen waiting in empty triumph for her to die, still hearing the accusatory singing in his head. The poem ends with the uncle's childhood fantasy still haunting him:

> . . . how he'd
> take the new pickup to town, sell it,
> and get the next train out.

The next poem is also full of hard knowledge, but of another type. In "Cannery Town in August" the poet describes the numbing effects of factory labor.

> . . . Women
> who smell of whiskey and tomatoes,
> peach fuzz reddening their lips and eyes—
> I imagine them not speaking, dumbed
> by the can's clamor and drop
> to the trucks that wait, grunting
> in their headlights below.
> They spotlight those who walk
> like a dream, with no one
> waiting in the shadows
> to palm them back to living.

It appears that in these first two poems the "ally," whose "will is to kill you" though "he has nothing against you," has conquered.

But in the poem actually titled "The Ally," the first of two linked rape poems, Cervantes uses the symbol of "wrestling with your ally" to a different end. While the rapist of this poem is real enough and the stage is set for total defeat and subjugation, the very danger of the event provokes the girl's heroic attempt at defiance.

> But it was the glint
> of steel at her throat
> that cut through
> to her voice.
> She would not be
> silent and still.
> She would live,
> arrogantly,
> having wrestled
> her death
> and won.

The role of this "ally" in bringing the girl to voice is reemphasized, in more bitter detail, in the second poem in the series.

> I picked myself up   ignoring
> whoever I was   slowly
> noticing for the first time my body's stench
> I made a list in my head
> of all the names who could help me
> and then   meticulously   I scratched
> each one
> > *they won't hear me burning*
> > *inside of myself*
> my used skin glistened
> my first diamond
>
> > ("Herself")

In a subsequent poem, "Meeting Mescalito at Oak Hill Cemetery," the poet intermingles themes of "hard" and "soft" while keeping to the subject matter of initiation. She is sixteen, sitting "crooked with drug" in the cemetery. The gravestones appear "soft and harmless." Here, in a safe world, the drug has triumphed.

> I knelt to a lizard with my hands
> on the earth, lifted him and held him
> in my palm—Mescalito
> was a true god.

At night, although "nothing had changed" (Mama sleeps on the sofa and the poet locks her bedroom door "against the stepfather"), as she goes to sleep she sucks "the last of the sweet fruit" and thinks "nothing of death."

("Meeting Mescalito at Oak Hill Cemetery" is a deceptively simple poem. The iconography of much that is within it—"Mescalito," the lizard—comes from *The Teachings of Don Juan*. Lizards are an aid to divination; "Mescalito" (which is Don Juan's favorite name for the peyote plant) is a strenuous endeavor requiring courage on the part of the taker. Perhaps most interestingly in this poem, the apricot pits which the poet sucks while thinking "nothing of death" contain deadly cyanide. It would appear that the poet is gaining in both innocence and experience at the same time and has come closer to death than the surface of the poem makes clear.[27])

Cervantes traces the themes of "hard" and "soft" with delicacy and irony in "Beneath the Shadow of the Freeway" and subsequent poems in the first section. The trusting little girl of that poem ("But Mama, if you're good to them / they'll be good to you back") is echoed in some of the characters she meets in succeeding poems. "For Edward Long" is a poem to an itinerant ditchdigger who "stayed / long enough to give me my voice" and "knew a key so secret / they locked it away." The gentleness of this Anglo man most strikes the poet:

> Pardner, Doctor, crazy
> mathematician and sometimes
> wizard to the child I still am,
> I still believe you.

The last poem in this section tests the poet-persona's "softness" in the same way. Her friend the "Caribou Girl" is the neighborhood character who claims to receive poems and lovenotes from the crows and dances with a peculiar arch of her back, spinning down the street. This figure "spoke the cadence / of her own mythology" and is beloved for this by the poet. But in a final scene, Caribou Girl is seen in a dreamstate slipping from the rocks above into the water, "a thin crazed girl / . . . / and I know she will drown." The author descends a little way with her, but preserves her own safety:

> . . . I'm going
> to leave her
> for another breath
> before I plunge
> with her again.

This section transforms the images of disaster in the opening poems into images of resistance to adversity, finally coming to a clarity about how far one may go in weaving a personal mythology with which to meet the world. Praising the mad girl but not drowning with her, the poet/persona has learned something about survival. But at the same time the transactions described in this section have taken place only at the level of the poet's own protected world of childhood in the barrio. She has yet to confront the dominant culture.

The beginning quotation of the second section, "This world understands nothing but words and you have come into it with almost none," may be confusing at first; surely this poet has already found a voice, and a measure of confidence, in the world described by the poems in the first section. But the new poems of the second section disturb that confidence and threaten to still that voice. Their message is that we are helpless before imponderables. The four-sectioned poem "Four Portraits of Fire" begins with an abstract vision of fire in the mountains; passes to the death of baby birds, fallen from their nest; then relates the tale of a Chicano family burned to death at Christmas while trying to stay warm with a heater improvised from a cannister of oil. Taking in these events, the poet concludes that she can find no charm or magic in her repertoire to provide comfort or security in such cases:

> I am away from the knowledge
> of animal mystics,
> brujas and sorcerers
> or the nudging chants
> of a Tlingit Kachina.
> I am frightened by regions
> with wills of their own,
> but when my people
> die in the snow
> I wonder
> did the depths billow up
> to reach them?

Some of Cervantes' most artful lyrics are in this section. "Starfish" and "Spiders," for instance, bring the poet/persona to consider the transcendence of form over death (in the case of the starfish) and over ugliness (in the case of the spiders) in terms which challenge human comprehension. But that is exactly the problem. The poet's peculiar frustration—at having to discard her poetic language in order to deal with situations it cannot control—surfaces in a poem relating the world of nature to the world of man.

> We watch seabirds flock the tour boat.
> They feed from the tourist hand.
>
> We who have learned the language
> they speak as they beg
>
> understand what they really say
> as they lower and bite.
> ("From Where We Sit:
> Corpus Christi")

In this literal picture of tourists feeding birds in the Texas gulf, a plainer language is being spoken than before—the language of the oppressed. It is used again in the ironically titled "Poem for a Young Man Who Asked Me How I, an Intelligent Well Read Person, Could Believe in the War between Races." From its beginning, this poem offers a contrasting duality—the poet's "land" of wished-for harmony versus the real world where "there is war." The poet angrily confesses that the land of her fantasy is impossible. It is described in terms of an unrealizable future:

> In my land there are no distinctions.
> The barbed wire politics of oppression
> have been torn down long ago.

Or it is depicted in childish terms, easily seen through and even mocked by the poet:

> In my land
> people write poems about love,
> full of nothing but contented childlike syllables.
> Everyone reads Russian short stories and weeps.

The poet stands between this fantasy creation and the real world pressing in on her. She personally embraces the contradiction:

> I am not a revolutionary.
> I don't even like political poems.
> .   .   .   .
> I believe in revolution
> because everywhere the crosses are burning.

In this poem, Cervantes adds important information to the emerging portrayal of her search for a new language with which to deal with oppression. The forces of the dominant culture have damaged her ability to express herself—in effect, stolen her language.

> Let me show you my wounds: my stumbling mind, my
> "excuse me" tongue, and this
> nagging preoccupation
> with the feeling of not being good enough.

In subsequent poems, Cervantes addresses—as have other Chicano and Chicana poets—the problem of being separated from one's original culture and language.

> Mama raised me without language.
> I'm orphaned from my Spanish name.
> The words are foreign, stumbling
> on my tongue. I see in the mirror
> my reflection; bronzed skin, black hair.
>
> I feel I am a captive
> aboard the refugee ship.
> The ship that will never dock.
> *El barco que nunca atraca.*
> ("Refugee Ship")

In another poem, a vacation in Mexico does not provide a sense of cultural recovery but only further realization of the distance the poet has traveled:

> Mexico,
> I look for you all day in the streets of Oaxaca.
> The children run to me, laughing,
> spinning me blind and silly.
> They call to me in words of another language.
> ("Oaxaca, 1974")

It is only possible for this poet to reconcile her relationship to the two cultures and the two languages when she is faced again with the raw edge of the contradiction between them: oppression. This confrontation takes place in the last poem of the section, "Visions of Mexico while at a Writing Symposium in Port Townsend, Washington."

In the first part of the poem "Mexico," the poet again confronts her own awkwardness in Spanish and concludes something about the Chicano heritage: the culture runs far deeper than language alone.

> I don't want to pretend I know more
> and can speak all the names. I can't.
> My sense of this land can only ripple through my veins
> like the chant of an epic corrido.
> I come from a long line of eloquent illiterates
> whose history reveals what words don't say.
> Our anger is our way of speaking,
> the gesture is an utterance more pure than word.

Back "home," at a writer's conference at the Northwestern corner of the United States, Cervantes observes in a tavern a particularly racist tableau depicting Mexicans "drooling in a caricature of machismo" and responds to it by repeating her thoughts, this time determining to act upon them:

> there are songs in my head I could sing you
> songs that could drone away
> all the Mariachi bands you thought you ever heard
> songs that could tell you what I know
> or have learned from my people
> but for that   I need words
> simple black nymphs between white sheets of paper
> obedient words   obligating words   words I steal
> in the dark when no one can hear me

The poet has come to a realization. Stripped of the language of power by the dominant culture, she has come to see that she must steal it back, fashioning her own power out of the words she can recapture. She has returned to the United States precisely to recover her culture:

> as pain sends seabirds south from the cold
> I come north
> to gather my feathers
> for quills.

The double meaning of the book's title is reinforced in the last two lines. The time is ripe for empowerment.

The third section begins at once, almost comically, with the poet's awakening to the possibility of a new language. She dreams she sees "a hundred robins" on her lawn, "telling it their way." She concludes,

> I am driven from this world, alive
> I come to this world, in dreams.
> ("This Morning")

The action of the final section of the book is quite different from that of the first two. Poems in the first two sections tend to be narrative and descriptive, about dilemmas faced by the poet/persona, pointing often to partial resolutions which in turn open up further dilemmas. But these final poems are either love poems set in the present, which also may define aspects of the poet's self, or what I call "process" poems, which describe the act of becoming what one will be.

Much of the love poetry in this section contains self-description.

Whether speaking in a corrective spirit to an intended lover or in the language of love itself to the man to whom she has dedicated this book, Cervantes (hardly distinguishable now from her persona) is at pains to describe herself:

> I'm an ugly woman, weedlike,
> elbowing my way through the perfect
> grass. The best of what I am
> is in the gravel behind the train yard
> where obsidian chips lodge
> in the rocks like beetles.
> I burrow and glow.
>
> ("Beetles")

The last two poems of the book are perhaps the author's final statement on the maturation of her art. "Oranges" pictures an old woman "crossing herself, / her eyes burning winter oranges," and compares this to a painting the poet/persona remembers in her grandmother's room depicting a miracle. Just as two children in the painting are about to be swept away in a flood, a guardian angel appears to save them. So now, in the action of the old woman passing by, the poet and her lover "are guided out / of falling." By transmuting a small, mundane event into a miracle, the poem accumulates some of the uncanny power caught in the lyrics of John Donne.

In the final, title poem, the message is a simple one—ripeness is all. The poet sees this in "flowers / . . . born when the weather was good" and again in "two hummingbirds" seeking "what is / given them to find." She concludes,

> . . . These are warriors
> distancing themselves from history.
> They find peace
> in the way they contain the wind
> and are gone.
>
> ("Emplumada")

Following Quiñonez' observation that Chicana poets are "creating new symbols, new images, and synthesizing all of those aspects into new myths," I would take *Emplumada* as a fabulous narrative of development in which we see simultaneously the autobiographical figure of the young poet, the spiritual figure of the artist taking flight, and the social figure of the Chicana struggling to find a language appropriate to deal with reality. After the crafted "family" poems in the first section come more social pieces where the lessons of the world are treated in a vivid way that still allows for a certain didacticism (you must learn to survive in a place full of danger). The increasingly lyrical and personal poems of the last section appear to announce the poet's emergence in her own voice, no longer looking back to family mythology or the "stage" she has passed through of learning how to deal with the world. Cervantes is portraying her own development in the form of a "portrait of the artist as Chicana." Of necessity, she will return to her origins and her social concerns in subsequent writings, with different strategies and seeking different results in the poetry.[28]

Awake in the River by Janice Mirikitani

In the 1970s, encouraged in particular by the black editors of Yardbird Publishing Company in San Francisco, a group of young male Asian American scholars embarked on heroic undertakings. Frank Chin, Jeffrey Paul Chan, Lawson Fusao Inada, and Shawn Hsu Wong put together a ground-breaking anthology, *Aiiieeeee! An Anthology of Asian-American Writers*, which was published by Howard University Press in 1974. This collection restored to print major works of Asian American literature of earlier decades by writers such as Carlos Bulosan, John Okada, Louis Chu, and Tosuio Mori while also publishing current writers, including Chin and Wong. The same scholars were instrumental in forming the Combined Asian Resources Project which, working through several sympathetic university publishers, published or republished editions by Bulosan, Okada, Chu, Mori, and others, including Ben Santos and Monica Sone.[29]

At the same time, the editors of *Aiiieeeee!*—three Chinese American men and one Japanese American man—took a controversial position regarding the roles of Chinese American women as writers in the early immigrant literature. Noting that the novels of Jade Snow Wong, Pardee Lowe, Virginia Lee, and Betty Lee Sung all had tended to reinforce the stereotypes of the dominant culture in the United States, the editors concluded:

> The white stereotype of the acceptable and unacceptable
> Asian is utterly without manhood. Good or bad, the ster-
> eotypical Asian is nothing as a man. At worst, the Asian-Ameri-
> can is contemptible because he is womanly, effeminate, devoid
> of all the traditional masculine qualities of originality, daring,
> physical courage, and creativity. The mere fact that four out of
> five American-born Chinese-American writers [of the period] are
> women reinforces this aspect of the stereotype. [30]

The implication was left to be drawn that Asian American women writers should step aside until the male writers recovered their literary "manhood." Echoes of this pronouncement have persisted in the literary community over the years, and partly as a result Asian American women have had to struggle for an equal voice in the literature of this movement.

Other organizing efforts touching the Asian American community in the same period were conceived to unite people around common goals. The project started by the San Francisco–based group Third World Communications brought men and women from all the oppressed communities together to produce literary collections and public performances in solidarity against oppression at home and the Vietnam War overseas. Janice Mirikitani was one of the organizers of Third World Communications. Through the work of its Women's Collective, the anthology *Third World Women* was produced in 1972. Mirikitani co-edited another project for Third World Communications, an anthology of Third World men and women writers called *Time to Greez!* in 1975. She then assumed the role of editor for the Japanese American Anthology Committee of *Ayumi: A Japanese American Anthology* in 1980. The "blurb" on the back cover of *Time to Greez!* speaks for the principle of unity in struggle at the heart of these collections.

> The Editors of *Time to Greez!* have come together from the
> respective Third World cultures/races represented in this an-
> thology. We feel it is a many-sided mirror of our lives, reflecting
> the colors, shapes and sounds, tastes, smells, touch of our
> homes, the rhythms of our music, the music of our food, the
> food of our lives. Share in the feast with us, TIME TO
> GREEZ! [31]

Janice Mirikitani is a Sansei (third-generation American) who was incarcerated as a small child in a U.S. detention center in Rohwer, Arkansas. Too young at the time of her internment to recall it clearly, Mirikitani has reconstructed it in her poetry and prose, collected in the volume *Awake in the River.*[32]

The camp experience has been the central trauma of Japanese American history. As literary historian Elaine Kim says, it "propelled to crisis dimensions the conflicts and tensions already existing in the Japanese American family and community."[33] It also provided a way of conceiving history from within one's own racial and cultural perspective. Japanese American writing reached its maturity in the camps: writers such as Toshio Mori, Hisaye Yanamoto, and Mine Okubo worked there, publishing in the camp magazines, and the great novel of the Nisei (second generation Japanese), *No-No Boy* by John Okada, grew out of camp experience.[34] At the same time, the particular sense of history which was a result of camp life—a history of subjugation within the country of one's residence—provided a backdrop against which to see other events in the world: the bombing of Hiroshima and Nagasaki, U.S. imperialism in Southeast Asia, and the effects of the dominant ideology in the United States on people of color globally. Mirikitani—raised in this place of shame and exile—absorbed these painful experiences and turned her sense of history into a weapon which she has used in all her creative work.

In Mirikitani's work I am concerned with the relationship between two ways she conceives events: diachronically ("horizontally," in terms of temporal succession) and synchronically ("vertically," in terms of simultaneous and systematically organized elements). Mirikitani's poetry is dominated by certain vivid and terrible memories, such as the internment camps, Hiroshima, and Vietnam. The poetry plays itself out in time, encountering the recurrent images and responding to their onslaught. The resolutions are, as in the case of Cervantes, dialectical. But events in history—especially the culturally shared atrocities—rule these poems more absolutely than they do in the work of the other two poets I have considered.

Although *Awake in the River* does not organize itself as a whole book to the degree of *She Had Some Horses* or *Emplumada* (it is not, taken from beginning to end, a ceremony of recovery or a symbolic seizing of images to bring the writer to power), its opening poem sets forth many of the problems, conditions, and dominant imagery of the rest of the author's work. "For My Father" presents contradictory images of one man and suggests that the reasons for the contradictions lie in history. We see first a heroic image:

> He came over the ocean
> carrying Mt. Fuji
> on his back/Tule Lake on his chest
> hacked through the brush
> of deserts
> and made them grow
> strawberries.

Counterpointed to this image is the humble situation of the children (as in much of what is to follow, the contradictory images are indented from the main body of type in the poem):

> we stole berries
> from the stem
> we could not afford them
> for breakfast

The father reveals a second side to his character as he reacts to the children.

> his eyes held
> nothing
> as he whipped us
> for stealing.

> the desert had dried up
> his soul.

> wordless
> he sold
> the rich
> full berries
> to hakujines
> whose children
> pointed at our eyes

> > they ate fresh
> > strawberries
> > with cream.

The economic need which has made the father deny his own children a simple pleasure in order to sell every piece of fruit to support the family is also a terrible form of cruelty, imposed to be sure on the father but imposed by him in turn on the children. This human face of oppression is not lost on the poet.

> Father,
> I wanted to scream
> at your silence.
> Your strength
> was a stranger
> I could never touch.
> Iron
> in your eyes
> to shield
> the pain
> to shield desert-like wind
> from patches
> of strawberries
> grown
> from
> tears.

This poem powerfully establishes a context and certain images for the rest of the book. The contrast between the white world, the world of the "hakujines," and the world of the Japanese Americans is between wealth and poverty, control and oppression, owners and outcasts. The contrast is formed by the relocation experience of the Second World War and confirmed in the genocide at Hiroshima and Nagasaki. The desert is a powerful image of the place of origin-in-exile for the people of Mirikitani's generation who struggle to emerge from it into a world of human relationships again. Cruelty has a historical origin in oppression and emerges as its bitter fruit, whether it takes shape in the oppressor or the oppressed. The naked self stands in furious but often silent protest at this stream of images and events, struggling to be born but carrying the scars of history which have been imposed without mercy and beyond understanding.

A poem near the beginning of the book, "August 6," opens up the poet's technique of juxtaposing synchronic events within the flow of the narrative. In vivid passages the poet juxtaposes the memory of Hiroshima and the official hypocrisies surrounding it:

> Yesterday
> a thousand cranes
> were flying.
> Hiroshima,
> your children
> are still dying
>
>   and they said
>
>   it saved many lives

Later, more intensely:

> Yesterday
> a woman
> bore a child
> with fingers
> growing from her neck
> shoulder
> empty
>   and they said
>   the arms race

Mirikitani uses this technique later in the volume with the intent of highlighting materials for our closer study so that we will understand them in their full horror. For example, in "A Certain Kind of Madness" she is watching TV with her daughter:

> When we saw Letelier blown up
> in a car, full screen
> you said he must've done something bad.
>
> I told you
> there are hunters who kill by color.
>   ("A Certain Kind of Madness")

The effect of television—to create a powerful image without a context—is countered by the mother teaching the child the part of the message that is withheld.

Perhaps the most effective use of juxtaposition comes in "Crazy Al-

ice," a poem about "Aunt Alice, who has touched the sun . . . victim
of American Concentration Camps." The figure presented is a familiar
one in recent Japanese American writing: the sufferer of the humilia-
tions and tortures of American incarceration, still present today amid a
generation trying to forget the past and embrace the American present
as loyal citizens of the United States.[35] Alice's appearance at the start
of the poem signals the discomfiture she will bring the wedding party:

> She came to the
> wedding
> in a tattered coat
> called us all by
> the wrong names
>
> Yukio/Mizume/Kyoko
>
> No, crazy Alice
> we died in the camps

Alice fails to recognize the bride, her own daughter. Lost back in the
time "before the war" when "i had a name," Alice by her very presence
forces the speaker in the poem, a wedding guest, to remember her fate
in the postwar era:

> twenty years ago
> she would come to us
> face blue
> eyes like black walnuts
> and down her nose
> blood flowed like tears
>
> battered by husbands
> and lovers
> for hoarding food
> and love
>
> where has love gone?

When the speaker tries to jolt Alice's attention by pointing to her surviving daughter, about to marry, Alice responds, matter-of-factly:

> my child is dead
> my breasts dried
> during the war

and she died
from hunger

And when once again the speaker calls her from her bitter reveries,
desperately seeking to have her join the present celebration,

rejoice
Crazy Alice/your child
has a new name

she is met with a chillingly metaphysical rebuke:

life's so strange
before the war
i was my child
i had a name.

The haunting final remark forcibly recalls the time of her innocence
before the events which changed her life forever. Alice's wounds will
not be silent.

Another kind of juxtaposition comes where the poet encounters
white racist stereotypes. The racist speaker is played off against the
judgment inherent in the poem, whether the poet actually responds or
not:

The woman
did not mean to
offend me,

her blue eyes
blinking
at the glint
of my blade,
as I cut
precisely
like magic
the cucumber in
exact, even,
quick slices.

Do you orientals
do everything
so neatly?
("Salad")

Mirikitani speaks about her own family and the generational differences between grandmother and mother, mother and child, in several poems. The tone is suggested by the overriding intent of the poem in each case. In "The First Generation," subtitled "Elegy to my grandmother," the tone is respectful and grandmother is remembered in her beauty and dignity.

> She grew wisteria
> as a temple
> in her garden
> and there kept her private peace
>
> . . . .
> Her love wore long
> as my sorrow.
> The withered roots
> have given back beauty to the soil.

In "Desert Flowers," Mirikitani sympathetically remembers her mother, daydreaming of a handsome savior while incarcerated in a desert relocation center:

> Mama, did you dream about that
> beau who would take you
> away from it all,
> who would show you
> in his '41 ford
> and tell you how soft
> your hands
> like the silk kimono
> you folded for the wedding?
>   ("Desert Flowers")

But the entire construct is a fantasy, as Mirikitani makes plain at the beginning,

> No flowers grew
> where dust winds blow
> and rain is like
> a dry heave moan.

When Mirikitani remembers her own needs as a child, her judgment of her mother's acquiescence to the military command becomes harsh. In a poem mixing historical detail with comment, Mirikitani juxtaposes her mother's "songs" and her own:

Her song:
shikata ga nai
        it can't be helped

. . . .

My song:

Watashi ga kadomo wa matte eru
    I am a child waiting
            waiting

Watashi no nahaga umareta
    for the birth of my mother.
                ("Lullabye")

This is a book in which knowledge is handed down by generations but not in the traditional sense: it is knowledge of genocide, of pitiful surrender, of betrayal and self-betrayal, or of resistance to the death. Some of the most terrible images have to do with Aunt Alice's life after the war:

and thinking of
invasions
and prison camps
she opened her legs
to the white boss man
        ("Crazy Alice")

and the mother's experience riding to the camps:

She rode on the train
destined for omission
with an older cousin

who died next to her
gagging when her stomach burned out.

Who says you only die once?
            ("Lullabye")

But perhaps the most remarkable creations of all have to do with love-making, juxtaposed against the brutalities of white America intent on war, murder, and atrocity against people of color.

In "Jungle Rot and Open Arms" Mirikitani confesses that her "politically correct" view of Vietnam falls apart when confronted with the anger of a returning veteran, is "nothing / in the wake / of his rage."

The story of love literally torn away from the solider is indented and set apart from the rest of the poem:

> "Her hair was
> long and dark—like yours"
>   he said
> "her eyes held the
> sixth moon
> and when she smiled
> the sky opened
> and I fell through.
>
> I would crawl
> in the tall grasses
> to her village
>
> and sleep the war
> away with her
> like a child on my thighs
>
> I did not know
> of the raid
> and woke
>
> with her arm
> still clasping mine
>
> I could not find
> the rest of her
>
> so I buried her arm
> and marked my grave."

Another soldier, in "Loving from Vietnam to Zimbabwe," describes American atrocities against the Vietnamese, knowing (the poet tells us) "they looked like me." But the shocking thing about this poem is that it describes the couple's lovemaking, sometimes playfully and sometimes painfully, in stanzas parallel to the story of his incursion into the Vietnam jungle.

> you plod weighted by
> days of marching
> nights of terror
> holding this patch of ground
> shaped like a crotch.

> my teeth on your
> shoulder
> hungry to enter your flesh
> as you call me strange names.

The poem powerfully combines the images of life and death, love and pain, which are the great themes of the book:

> I, in the
> heavy hot air
> between us,
> in the crimson room
> that begins to blur
> feel you enter
> my harbor/kiss the lips
> of my soul
>
> Call Me Strange Names
>
> > hanoi
> > bachmai
> > haiphong

It ends with a rare summation made by the poet in her own voice:

> loving in this world
> is the silver splinting
> edge
> is the dare
> in the teeth of the tiger
> the pain of jungle rot
> the horror of flesh unsealed
> the danger of surviving.

In the final piece in the volume, "Awake in the River," Mirikitani discusses camp life in the most vivid and literal detail, emphasizing themes of dignity and survival.

The little child of the piece (the author) compares herself to a tortoise "digging her toes in the sand." But unlike the tortoises, "she could not go beyond the barbed wire." A tortoise crawls through the camp and the children try to hem it in "in the garden the men had grown from stones and succulents. Making beauty from adversity." But the women urge that it be set free: "It is wrong to imprison any living thing." The ending of the story/poem fuses the image of the people waiting for the end of the war and the tortoise seeking its freedom.

> The men kept their war inside. Pulling weeds by roots.
> Figures bent, not broken, wind rounding their backs.
> Grandfather wears his wait like a shell. Sleep in the desert,
> he warned.

> Tortoise, empty,
> worn,
> plunges to the deep.
> In the steady
> pounding of the waves,
> offsprings wake.

> Mother steady singing by the crib.

> Sleep in the desert.
> Awake in the river.
>   ("Awake in the River")

It would be foolish, and futile, to attempt to reconcile the techniques, images, or use of material in the work of Joy Harjo, Lorna Dee Cervantes, and Janice Mirikitani. The common element of their work, after all, is that it is different from the poetry of the dominant Anglo-American culture which represents the aspirations and interests of the majority of the population of the United States (if we are to count the assimilated white ethnic minorities). All then that we can generalize about is the *difference* of this work, which sees its project in diverse ways as one of rescuing images from the dominant culture, restoring a sense of rightness in a threatened social and personal world, and proposing a means of continuing to exist—and to struggle—in the future. The ceremonial long poem of Joy Harjo, the symbolic journey of Lorna Dee Cervantes, and the political and historical enactment of Janice Mirikitani do embody, however, the strength of a literature that is not subjugated, is not silenced, is not bought off. Those of us who care about both literature and political and cultural survival would do well to attend to this work, both for what generalizations about its "difference" we care to draw and for the specific brilliance, passion, and clarity of each author and her project.

Notes

While the conception of this project was my own, I owe a debt to Professor Naomi Quiñonez of the Department of Spanish, California State University College at Northridge, who joined me as co-presenter in a workshop, "Women of Color: New American Writing (1980's)" at a conference, "Our Hidden Heritage of People's Culture," in Kansas City, Missouri, January 26, 1985. I also wish to thank Professor Patricia Clark Smith, Department of English, University of New Mexico, and Constance Coiner, Departments of English and History, University of California at Los Angeles, for reading the manuscript and offering suggestions. The responsibility for the outcome is wholly my own.

1. Frank Chin, Jeffrey Paul Chan, Lawson Fusao Inada, Shawn Hsu Wong, eds., *Aiiieeeee!: An Anthology of Asian-American Writers* (Washington, D.C.: Howard University Press, 1974), p. viii.
2. Dexter Fisher, ed., *Minority Language and Literature* (New York: Modern Language Association, 1977).
3. Houston A. Baker, ed., *Three American Literatures* (New York: Modern Language Association, 1982).
4. Dexter Fisher, ed., *The Third Woman* (Boston: Houghton Mifflin Co., 1980).
5. See, for example, Cherríe Moraga and Gloria Anzaldúa, eds., *This Bridge Called My Back: Writings by Radical Women of Color* (Watertown, Mass.: Persephone Press, 1981); Beth Brant, ed., *A Gathering of Spirit: Writing and Act by North American Indian Women* (Rockland, Maine: Sinister Wisdom Books, 1984); and Rayna Green, ed., *That's What She Said: Contemporary Poetry and Fiction by Native American Women* (Bloomington: Indiana University Press, 1984).
6. Paula Gunn Allen, ed., *Studies in American Indian Literature: Critical Essays and Course Designs* (New York: Modern Language Association, 1983); Marta Ester Sanchez, *Contemporary Chicana Poetry: A Critical Approach to an Emerging Literature* (Berkeley: University of California Press, 1985); and Elaine H. Kim, *Asian American Literature: An Introduction to the Writings and Their Social Context* (Philadelphia: Temple University Press, 1982).
7. For remarks on the importance of reevaluating the canon of American literature, see Paul Lauter, *Reconstructing American Literature* (Old Westbury: Feminist Press, 1983), pp. xi–xxv; and Wayne Charles Miller, "Toward a New Literary History of the United States," *Melus* 11, no. 1 (1984): 5–26.
8. Leslie Marmon Silko, *Ceremony* (New York: New American Library, 1978), pp. 132–133.
9. Paula Gunn Allen, "The Psychological Landscape of *Ceremony*," *American Indian Quarterly* 5 (February 1979): 13–18.
10. Allen, "The Sacred Hoop: A Contemporary Perspective," in Allen, *Studies*, p. 18.
11. Ibid., p. 19.

12. Ibid., p. 15.

13. Ibid., p. 16.

14. Allen, "A Melus Interview," *Melus* 10, no. 2 (1983): 19.

15. Joy Harjo, "Oklahoma: The Prairie of Words," in Hobson, *The Remembered Earth*, pp. 43–44.

16. Harjo, *She Had Some Horses* (New York: Thunder's Mouth Books, 1983). Subsequent citations from poems in this book are identified by title.

17. Antonia Castañeda Shular, Tomas Ybarr-Frausto, and Joseph Sommers, eds., *Literatura chicana: Texto y contexto* (Chicano Literature: Text and Context) (Englewood Cliffs, N.J.: Prentice-Hall, 1972), p. xxi.

18. Juan Bruce-Novoa, *Chicano Authors: Inquiry by Interview* (Austin: University of Texas Press, 1980), pp. 10–11. Bruce-Novoa returned to treat the poetry in detail in *Chicano Poetry: A Response to Chaos* (1982).

19. Sanchez, *Contemporary Chicana Poetry*, pp. 6–7.

20. From a speech, "Women of Color: New American Writing of the '80's," delivered with John Crawford at "Our Hidden Heritage of People's Culture," a conference held in Kansas City, Missouri, on January 25, 1985. Transcribed with editing from tape.

21. Bernadette Monda, "Interview with Lorna Dee Cervantes," *Third Woman* 2, no. 1 (1984): 104.

22. See Annette Kolodny, *The Lay of the Land* (Chapel Hill: University of North Carolina Press, 1975).

23. On Chicana sense of "traditional values," see Tey Diana Rebolledo, "Abuelitas: Mythology and Integration in Chicana Literature," *Revista Chicano-Riqueña* 11, no. 3–4 (1983): 148–158.

24. Bruce-Novoa, *Chicano Poetry*, pp. 4–5.

25. Lorna Dee Cervantes, *Emplumada* (Pittsburgh: University of Pittsburgh Press, 1981), p. viii. Subsequent citations of poems from this book are identified by title.

26. Carlos Castaneda, *The Teachings of Don Juan: A Yaqui Way of Knowledge* (Berkeley: University of California Press, 1968).

27. I am indebted to Professor Patricia Clark Smith of the University of New Mexico for this interpretation.

28. Cervantes may give a hint of what is to come in a recent interview. "I guess I'm real concerned with presenting certain class issues and I think if I'm going to draw the line, that's where it is because I think it's important to document my history." Monda, "Interview," p. 106.

29. The University of Washington Press published new editions of Bulosan's *America Is in the Heart* (1973), Okada's *No-No Boy* (1976), Chu's *Eat a Bowl of Tea* (1979), Sone's *Nisei Daughter* (1979), and a revised edition of stories by Santos, *Scent of Apples* (1979). The Asian American Studies Center at UCLA published two works by Mori, *The Chauvinist and Other Stories* (1979) and a new edition of *Yokohama, California* (1984). See Kim, *Asian American Literature*, p. 175.

30. Chin et al., *Aiiieeeee!*, p. xxx.

31. *Time to Greez!* (San Francisco: Glide Publications, 1975), back cover.
32. Janice Mirikitani, *Awake in the River* (San Francisco: Isthmus Press, 1978), afterword [p. 83]. Subsequent citations from poems in this book are identified by title.
33. Kim, *Asian American Literature*, p. 148.
34. On camp life and literature, see Kim, *Asian American Literature*, pp. 147–156, and Chin et al., *Aiiieeeee!*, pp. xxxiv–xxxvii.
35. See Kim, *Asian American Literature*, pp. 253–255. She notes that the figure of the "crazy woman" of the older generation also appears in other Asian American literatures.

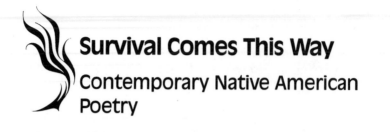

Survival Comes This Way
Contemporary Native American Poetry

Few myths are as deeply ingrained in American literature and the popular consciousness of this nation as those regarding Native Americans. From before Fenimore Cooper, the American Indian's presence in the writing of non-Indian Americans has usually been as one of two opposed yet complementary incarnations: "the murdering redskin" or "the noble savage." These guises, of course, are two sides of the same coin, a currency unfortunately not yet devalued by overuse. As Michael Castro points out in his study of Native Americans in American poetry, *Interpreting the Indian*, the American Indian was either Caliban or Uncas, each stereotype "serving underlying psychic needs of Western culture." Further, whether bloodthirsty beast or nature's nobleman, the Indian continues to be portrayed as one whose culture and bloodlines, for better or worse, are slowly and surely being eroded away by the uncheckable tide of white civilization.

There are notable exceptions, such as John Neihardt's epic poems about the Sioux. By and large, however, American Indian people have been stereotyped, misrepresented, and used as "exotic" characters (a considerable irony when one considers who inhabited this continent to begin with) in the poems of non-Indian Americans past and present. And inaccuracies abound. Longfellow's *Hiawatha*, which presents a noble Indian hero in a misty never-never land, is the most famous example. The deeds Longfellow attributes to Hiawatha were those performed by Manabozho, the great culture hero of the Chippewa. The

196

real Hiawatha was a statesman and political leader of the Iroquois people, one of the founders of the Great Iroquois League of Peace (on
which the structure of the U.S. Constitution appears to have actually
been modelled). It is rather like writing a poem about the exploits of
Paul Bunyan and calling the main character George Washington.
Even America's other "ethnic" writers have fallen prey to stereotyping
the Indian. More than two-hundred years ago, black poet Lucy Terry
described the Indians as "awful creatures" in her poem "Bars Fight,
August 28, 1746" about the Deerfield Massacre.

The still strong tendency on the part of majority American culture
and its poets to see the Native American as "the vanishing (or already
vanished) redman" can be observed in much of the poetry written
about American Indians and "from Indian traditions" by contemporary
non-Indian writers. In the *Annual Reports of the Bureau of American
Ethnology* such diligent field ethnologists as Natalie Curtis, Frances
Densmore, and Washington Matthews published thousands of translations of songs, stories, and oral histories from many American Indian
cultures around the turn of the century. Over the past two decades
innumerable new translations or "reworkings" have been produced and
published by non-Indian writers drawing on those same written
sources, usually without ever talking to a real Indian from any tribe.
The results are that most of those "reworkings" are painfully inaccurate
and much less interesting than the original (and sometimes flawed)
translations from which they were lifted. (I am not referring to the
work being done with living American Indian people now by a few
good ethnologist-poets. Dennis Tedlock, for one, has done such wonderful collaborations with Zuni storytellers as *Finding the Center*,
which records living oral traditions.) In some cases, those non-Indian
translator-reworker-poets have even set themselves up as being "more
Indian" than living Native Americans today whom they seem to see as
a scattered people of uncertain ancestry. The only good Indian poet is
an illiterate dead one.

In 1979, the Twayne World Authors Series contributed to this misconception by publishing *American Indian Poetry* by Helen Addison
Howard. Though dozens of contemporary American Indian poets
were writing and publishing their work by then, the book does not
contain the name of even one living Native American. Instead, it sur-
veys the work of white ethnologists and a few "interpretive" writers who

"made good use of" American Indian oral traditions. "The characteristics of Native American poetry," Howard tells us, "are subjects that are close to the daily lives of a primitive people." Her only reference to the possibility of living American Indian writers is an indirect one: "It is hoped that American poets, including modern Indian ones, will continue to develop this virgin field."

There is no doubt that Native American oral traditions constitute a great literary heritage. If anything, the range and meaning of that heritage has only begun to be appreciated. (One of the better recent publications is Karl Kroeber's *Traditional American Indian Literatures*, published in 1981.) Some aspects of certain Native American oral traditions are, in fact, preserved only in the writings of the ethnologists. However, in many Native American communities today the oral traditions are not only alive but growing. Further, anyone who believes that the transcriptions from past decades of American Indian oral traditions represent the full range of American Indian literature is making a great mistake. There is a new, vitally important generation of contemporary American Indian writers. Drawing on both their Native American cultural heritages and the realities and resources of Western culture, they have remained "Indian" while producing a growing body of significant written literature.

In the last two decades a conscious assault has been made by a growing number of Native Americans from many different tribal traditions on the assumption that the end of the "American Indian race" is inevitable. And their efforts have produced results. One example is Louis Oliver, a Creek poet in his eighties who began writing contemporary verse only within the last decade. His first book of poems, *The Horned Snake*, was published in 1982. When interviewed in his home in Tahlequah, Oklahoma, he said, "We were always taught in the schools that the Indian was doomed to be absorbed into the American melting pot and that all of our old ways were only memories. Before I met some younger American Indian writers I was just like that old ground hog. I had crawled in my hole and just accepted that I was forgotten. Now I know different."

Until mid-century, the common assumption was that the American nation's movement was progressive—tomorrow would be better than today. Today, however, everyone knows that technological miracles have spawned not only the luxuries of electricity and indoor plumbing but also Hiroshima and the nuclear balance of terror, the pollution of air and water, and the seemingly unsolvable social inequities of class and race. Today, as we question Pentagon budgets, drug-ridden class-rooms, the PCB-filled streams, many ask if the secret of surviving might be found not just in the dreams of the future but also in the lessons of the past.

But what is the true American past? How far back does the past go in a "nation of immigrants"? For that answer we might well turn to those "Americans" whose roots are deep as the rocks. As the one group of writers whose ancestors are not recent immigrants, American Indian poets are unusually well equipped to speak of the American past and to draw from it lessons relating to survival.

Their very histories and, in fact, their continued survivals as peoples despite mixed bloodlines, lands sold and stolen, ancient customs out-lawed or made impossible point to the tenacity of what might loosely be called the "Indian Way." That the most recent national census shows a doubling of the numbers of American Indians in only twenty years is an indication of that tenacity. It may also be seen as an indica-tion of a growing pride in affirming one's Indianness. Past censuses may have contained many more Indian people than figures actually showed. "Passing for white" is easily done by many Native American people who have discovered that an Indian, even with a face like Geronimo's, can go unrecognized when he or she dresses and talks like those in the majority culture. "Invisibility" has been a survival tactic for at least four centuries for many Native Americans, including some entire communities.

Survival is one of the major themes in contemporary Native Ameri-can writing—survival of the old ways, survival of Indian nations, per-sonal survival, and, in the long run, the survival of the whole bio-sphere. Acoma Pueblo in New Mexico is the oldest continuously occupied settlement on the North American continent. It is the home-land of Simon Ortiz, whose poem "Survival This Way" exemplifies that theme of continuance as it begins:

> Survival, I know how this way.
> This way, I know.

It rains.
Mountains and canyons and plants
grow.
We travelled this way,
gauged our distance by stories
and loved our children.

Notice how alive that landscape is. Not only the plants but even the mountains and canyons are growing, living presences that respond to the blessing of the rain. His images are rooted in the Southwestern landscape of his childhood and the traditions of his people, yet the message is one which virtually any Native American poet would recognize. I have heard it said, for example, by Iroquois writers from the Northeast that "everything which is, is alive." American Indian people—and their poets—survive through the recognition that they are part of, not apart from, the natural world. The language of the poem is simple, declarative, a bit repetitive in structure—like something from the oral traditions. Yet it is an entirely new poem at the same time that it is a very old one.

When N. Scott Momaday's novel *House Made of Dawn* was published in 1968 and won the Pulitzer Prize in 1969, it opened the eyes of a new generation of Native American writers. They read the novel and heard the deeper message of its powerful writing: a person caught between cultures can, despite the deepest of problems, find a way to survive, a road which circles out of the past, "The House Made of Dawn," and ends in understanding. Hopi/Miwok poet Wendy Rose is one of those in-between people and her work contrasts with that of Simon Ortiz. Her language seems more complex, her themes bleaker. An urban Indian (like a number of other successful contemporary Native American artists), Rose was not raised on or near a reservation but in Berkeley, California. A teacher and anthropologist, some of her poems deal with the dilemma of being a student in a discipline which has treated one's own ancestors as little more than bones to be dug up and labelled. She begins her poem "Indian Anthropologist: Overhanging Sand Dune Story":

They hope, the professors
to keep the keyhole locked
where my mind is pipelined

> to my soul; they block it
> with the shovel and pick
> of the pioneer spirit,
> the very energy that made
> this western earth turn over
> and throw us from her back
> bucking and hollering
> like stars were whipping her . . .

The language and imagery of the poem are markedly different from Ortiz's. Such non-Indian concepts as "professors," "keyhole," "pipe-lined," "shovel and pick," and "pioneer spirit" show the influence of Western civilization. Yet, as in "Survival This Way," the earth itself is alive and showing her displeasure with the arrogance of human beings who've mistreated her by creating earthquakes. The poem returns to a Native vision, especially in the last lines of the poem when Rose says, ". . . I can go on like this / only if I shut my ears / but keep awake in the eyes."

Lance Henson, a southern Cheyenne who is deeply involved in the traditional ceremonies of his people, entitled one of his poems "comanche ghost dance   an impression." It begins "we will return to life . . ." and concludes:

> there will be no distance between our words and the
> banished moon
>
> in all that grows while the winter reaps
> we will live again

In just a few lines we feel the closeness of the natural world, even at a time when the moon has been "banished" (presumably by the harsh lights—both electrical and intellectual—of modern civilization). Just as plants survive under the blanket of winter snow, the ghost dancers—who stand for the survival and renewal of the old American Indian values—persist and their song is for the life of all things.

One of my favorite poems of Henson's is called "at chadwick's bar and grill." Here are the first few lines:

> tu fu and li po have
> forgiven nothing
> not waking drunk under any moon

> or the incessant calling
> of a loon

Henson's evocation of those great T'ang Dynasty poets shows that he feels a kinship with those writers for their love of life, their clarity of image, their unsentimental relationship to the natural world. It illustrates how, though frequently focusing on American Indian concerns, Native American poetry is neither insular nor static. There is a wider world beyond the poet's individual vision, a world which does not depend upon him for validation, as we see in the last lines of the poem:

> the spider catches the fly
> at morning
> whether i am here
> or not

The deliberate lack of punctuation and the use of the lower case "i" is characteristic of a number of Native American poets. Peter Blue Cloud, Karoniaktatie (Alex Jacobs), Norman Russell, and Barney Bush are only a few of those who use this device, viewing capitalization and punctuation as unnatural barriers between themselves and the living creation all around them. As Barney Bush, the Seneca-Cayuga writer put it when I interviewed him, it gives him a feeling of naturalness and freedom. Responding to critics who said that it made his poems harder to read, he said, "What you need to do with people like that is take them out into the country for two or three weeks and get them to take off their shoes and clothes and just run around naked. Then they begin to understand."

Language, for the Native American poet, is power. N. Scott Momaday exemplifies the American Indian view of the ability of words to make things happen in his essay "The Man Made of Words." In his essay he speaks the name of Ko-sahn, an ancient Kiowa woman he knew when he was a small child. As soon as he says her name, he tells us, she appears in front of him, her reality as solid as anything else around him. Then, as she begins to speak with him, Momaday finds his own identity defined by looking into the history of his Kiowa people through the vision of that suddenly materialized, one-eyed old woman. Just as his words made her appear, her words make him.

Another example of how Momaday (and other Native American writers) find themselves and a right relationship through the spirit of words can be seen in these lines from his poem "The Delight Song of Tsoai-Talee." (Tsoai-Talee is Momaday's Kiowa name.)

> You see, I am alive, I am alive
> I stand in good relation to the earth
> I stand in good relation to the gods
> I stand in good relation to all that is beautiful

The shared themes of survival, of the aliveness of all creation, of the necessity for balance, and of the making power of words are some of the concepts which are part of what might be called a "Pan-Indian" consciousness, which might be seen as similar to the Pan-African consciousness that informs so much of the powerful poetry which has come from the African continent in the past five decades. It is also reminiscent of the negritude movement, which proclaimed the beauty of blackness and the richness of the African heritage. The African and Caribbean intellectuals, especially Leopold Sedar Senghor of Senegal, Aimé Césaire of Martinique, and Leon Damas of Guyana, who founded negritude, were schooled in France and still living there when they returned in their poetry to the vitality of ancestral African folkways. Like the negritude poets, American Indian writers are from nations which have been colonized. Like the poets of Africa, Native Americans have, until recently, been taught that their own traditions were, at best, of interest only to ethnologists and secondary to the cultures of those of European origin. Like Damas and Senghor and Césaire, they have been educated in some of the finest schools and lived—in many cases—for a good part of their lives in white cities, yet they have not become "white." Instead, they have come away from their educations with a stronger sense of their ethnic and tribal identities and with the sophisticated knowledge of contemporary literary techniques which enables them to express the enduring values of their Native American identity to both white and Indian alike.

Maurice Kenny is one example. A Mohawk who has lived for decades in New York City, he still speaks of the Akwesasne Reservation along the St. Lawrence River as home. Though he hears the sounds of police sirens out his windows at night, his poems return to the rhythms of Iroquois social dances and old chants. One of his most important works is a book-length cycle of poems called *Black Robe*, which was recently made into an award-winning radio drama. It tells the story of

Isaac Jogues, the Jesuit missionary among the Mohawks, from an Iroquois point of view, pointing out with great precision how Jogues still symbolizes much of the insensitivity and destructiveness which the Native American associates with white civilization.

Louise Erdrich, whose first novel *Love Medicine* won the National Book Critics Circle Award in 1984, is yet another example. Her first book of poems, *Jacklight,* was also published in 1984 while she was living in Concord, New Hampshire, not far from her alma mater, Dartmouth College. She draws pictures of contemporary reservation life which are gritty and powerfully detailed, rich in vision and in a reality different from that of majority culture. We can see this in the following lines from the final poem in that book, "Turtle Mountain Reservation," named for her family's Chippewa homeland in North Dakota:

> Grandpa leans back
> between spoonfuls of canned soup
> and repeats to himself a word
> that belongs to a world
> no one else can remember . . .
>
> He walks from St. Ann's, limp and crazy
> as the loon that calls its children
> across the lake
> in its broke, knowing laughter.
> Hitchhiking home from the Mission, if he sings
> it is a loud rasping wail
> that saws at the spine
> of Ira Comes Last at the wheel . . .

Any list of significant contemporary American Indian poets would have to be a long one. In editing *Songs from This Earth on Turtle's Back,* an anthology of American Indian poetry, in 1983, I ended up with fifty-two writers, most of whom have had at least one book of poetry published. Yet were I to edit that anthology today I can think of at least a dozen more writers I would certainly include. That so many poets should be surfacing from a total Native American population in the United States of less than two million might relate to the fact that a great percentage of Native Americans are artists. Art, whether it is pottery or poetry, seems to come naturally to Native American people, perhaps because the traditionally "permissive" and encouraging methods of child-rearing found among Indian people throughout the continent emphasize self-discovery and leave out corporal punishment. It is quite possible that Native American child-rearing methods do not "kill off" the creative spirit that leads an imaginative child to be an artist as an adult. Whatever the reason, there are too many fine American Indian writers for me to mention them all. In addition to those already mentioned, some of the most important, powerful poets are James Welch, Duane Niatum, Joy Harjo, Ray Young Bear, Roberta Hill Whiteman, and Linda Hogan. From their words, which speak *for* Native American people and *to* us all, we can learn many things—not the least of which is that we may find survival by remembering our place on this living planet.

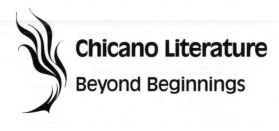

Chicano Literature
Beyond Beginnings

The awarding of the *Premio Casa de las Americas* to Rolando Hinojosa in 1976 for a Chicano novel, *Klail City y sus Alrededores*, shook to awakening the U.S. literary world. The *Premio* is to Latin America what the Pulitzer is to the United States, and this international literary award has never been taken lightly by those at the forefront of world literature. Chicano literature, on the other hand, has frequently been taken lightly in the U.S. literary world, and major language associations have hesitated to accept it as an appropriate area for research and attention.

This disregard did not surprise those who had for years alleged that "world literature" classes in U.S. colleges and universities reviewed to excess the literatures of England, France, and Germany while ignoring the rapid succession of innovations in style and thought surging out of Latin America (and the rest of the Third World and U.S. minorities). Curiously enough, this occurred while literary critics in France and Germany were focusing on modern Latin American masterpieces and begging for more. The entire situation taken into account, it was hardly shocking that U.S. critics argued that Chicano literature was not "quality literature" and that they based this finding more on what they heard than on what they read.

The *Premio*-winning *Klail City* (later released in the United States as *Generaciones y Semblanzas*) was not the first Chicano *obra* (work) of its kind. For years, those in Chicano circles had praised the sensitivity of Rivera's *And the Earth Did Not Part* and the character development of the haunting protagonists of *Bless, Me, Ultima*. For years Chicano writers and readers had admired the dramatic texture of Estela Portillo Trambley's *Rain of Scorpions* and the *mestizaje* (blending) of worlds, languages, and concepts in poetry by Alurista, Lalo Delgado, Ricardo Sanchez, and Angela de Hoyos. The unforgettable poetic figures of *La Jefita* and *El Louie* in the work of José Montoya epitomized cultural realities, and the Chicano reader responded with a fervent "*Los conozco*" ("I know these people"). These early favorites reflected and defined the characters of the barrio, and we could all appreciate and *see* the pachuco-turned-solider-turned-pool-hall-hero, "with all the paradoxes *del soldado raso*-heroism and the stockade."

> And on leave, jump boots
> shainadas and ribbons, cocky
> from the war, strutting to
> early mass on Sunday morning.
>
> "Wow, is that ol' Louie?"
>
> "Mire, comadre, ahí va el hijo
> de Lola!"
>
> Afterward he and Fat Richard
> would hock their Bronze stars
> for pisto en el Jardín Canales. . . .[1]

Often for the first time in their literary lives, Chicano readers would recognize characters from *their* cultural context—not stereotyped humble peasants and Hollywood hoods and revolutionaries, but guys from just down the street who were, after all, just "*el hijo de Lola*" ("Lola's son"), hocking their war medals for something to drink, heroic-tragic figures whose lives fell short of what society asked of them and whose dreams far outreached what society could offer them.

There was extensive reason why U.S. society was slow to recognize these writings. They were not only alien to the mainstream culture and laden with images that activated gut biases among those who knew "Meskins" only as a servant class, a lower class, or a problem class, but the early writings were doused generously with direct criticisms of the very institutions that were "carriers of the word" for literary acceptance—centers of formal education. Prose and poetry were replete with images of school policy that put student needs second to building needs, daily mass friskings at junior highs, and other indictments of American society and its schools.

> stupid america, see that chicano
> with a big knife . . .
>
> .   .   .   .
>
> he doesn't want to knife you
> he wants to . . .
> . . . carve christ figures
> but you won't let him.
> stupid america, hear that chicano
> shouting curses on the street
> he is a poet
> without paper and pencil
> and since he cannot write
> he will explode.
> stupid america, remember that chicanito
> flunking math and english
> he is the picasso
> of your western states
> but he will die
> with one thousand masterpieces
> hanging only from his mind. [2]

Amidst the ever-present criticism that the mixing of English and Spanish reflected a linguistic deficiency (of "culturally deprived" individuals), linguistic masterpieces continued to be woven from the beauties and strengths of both languages. Doubled possibilities for alliteration and double entendre were found in concentrated mélanges of Spanish, English "Texan," black English, even Mayan and Nahuatl word concepts. Imaginations exploded beyond limits, beyond conventions, beyond even our own beginnings.

Regional chauvinists continued to criticize our "Tex-Mex" and to treat it as a "language deficiency" caused by low educational or intellectual levels. And Chicano writers continued to indulge in "language play" (for example, Nephtalí de León's play *Tequila Mockingbird* and Alurista's *Spik in Glyph?*), an inventive and intriguing challenge for linguistic creativity. What had begun with reflections of our own bilingual reality—my own *"me senté allí en la English class"* and Delgado's "chicotazos of history"—turned into the formulation of totally new grammatical styles. Lexical creations sprang from an awareness of our own dually bilingual existence and from the discovery of new worlds of thought and literature—the Mayan, Aztec, Native American, and so forth. Formerly we would, in our daily lives, hispanicize English realities: "I missed" would resurrect in Spanish as "*mistié*," "I flunked" would expand the traditional lexicon with "*flonquié*," and the "big, old thing" ending "*azo*" would turn a party in an English sentence into a *porazo* in a Spanish conversation. Now, those same traditions of interlanguage play would apply to the newly discovered language heritage. Acutely aware of the sounds of English, we would accent our Spanish to a mock-Anglicized "free holes" (for *frijoles*) and then play the reverse by accenting our English with the sounds of Spanish: *pino borra* for "peanut butter." Now, reading through Aztec accounts of *teotl, mitotl, coatl, tomatl,* we exclaimed, instead of the commonplace "*¡Qué loco!*" ("Crazy!"), "*¡Qué locotl!*" And the new *mestizaje* of language yielded concentrated high-impact packs, like the three-word label of the moon by Victoria Moreno—"vanilla, canela crescent."

The juxtaposition in selection of English, Spanish, or a combination of both adds to the power of each word and to the entire verbal context. Some works are, by necessity, in English, utilizing the compact, businesslike high-powered impact of each short jabbing word. The following poem by Sylvia Chacón is an excellent example of this style of writing and of the visual arrangement of the words. The format, together with the words themselves, seems chopped up like little pieces of spaghetti so that the meaning comes out not only from the context of the language but also from the shape and texture of the poem itself. The author compares herself to tangled spaghetti which was not eaten because she

> refused
> to be knifed
> and forked along
> in your eagerness
> to get
> the
> meat.[3]

The eloquence of Reyes Cárdenas' *Poema Sandino* was deliberately woven in an all-Spanish fabric. The profound personal sentiment, the political intent, the entire Spanish-speaking world's contemporary political context add to what is already one of the most powerful statements ever made in Chicano poetry. An excerpt:

estas cosas que nos arrastran por el piso
tenemos que pararlas como un arbol seco de navidad
tenemos que echarle agua hasta que le salgan hojas
hasta que podamos hablar otra vez
hasta que podamos mover al siglo

.   .   .   .

pero nosotros, nosotros tenemos que resistir al tiempo
levantar la pluma aunque sea con huesos
tenemos que ofender a los que cierran los ojos
que hasta páginas vacías ahoguen sus sueños dulces
que despiertan tosiendo buscando aire.[4]

Translation, in poetry, is a dependent and limited form of expression. But, with apologies for this sacrilege, I offer this translation of the segment quoted:

these things that drag us across the floor
we have to stand them up like a dried-up Christmas tree
we have to sprinkle water on them until they sprout leaves
until we can speak again
until we can move the century

.   .   .   .

but we, we have to fight off time
lift the pen, even if it's with our bones
we have to offend those who close their eyes
so that even empty pages drown their sweet dreams
and they wake up coughing searching for air.

Language mixture is an art as surely as any other manipulation of words, as evidenced in the beautiful flow and rich image-laden texture of the first few lines of "*Mis ojos hinchados*" by Alurista.

Mis ojos hinchados
    flooded with lagrimas
de bronce
melting on the cheek bones

of my concern
    razgos indígenas
the scars of history on my face
    and the veins of my body
that aches
    vomito sangre
y lloro libertad . . .[5]

The early stages of Chicano literature were full of identity assertions: "I am Joaquín, lost in a world of confusion," or "I am a Quetzal who wakes up green with wings of gold, and cannot fly," or "I am the Aztec Prince and the Christian Christ," or "I do not ask for freedom—I *am* freedom." But Chicano literature has gone beyond its beginnings. It no longer simply asserts and defines an identity. It now paints its context and carries out its visions. The identities of crazy gypsy, Aztec Angel, Mud Coyote, and Crying Woman of the Night now go beyond their own definitions to live out their lives in the more fully developed mythological and social context of Chicano literature.

The symbols and images have already become familiar—we speak a common mythological language. Critics such as Juan Rodriguez, Max Martinez, and José Flores Peregrino have begun to explain and nourish the literary symbols. Flores Peregrino identifies and substantiates motifs, visions, and symbols such as the mirror (symbol of self-knowledge), the creative serpent (cyclical nature of energy and transformation, rather than a linear definition of progress), *in lak ech* (Mayan principle of behavior) and, of course, the parent earth, *la tierra*, as birther, burier, and healer. With a critical base for study, Chicano literature can no longer be ignored by those unfamiliar with its symbols and settings.

The voice of the Chicana poet and writer, the woman, is a strong one within this stream of expression. The powerful work of Margarita Cota-Cárdenas, Evangelina Vigil, Estela Portillo Trambley, and countless others provides a counterbalancing and whole image of our *entire* culture, not just the male perspective of it. The Chicanas remind us emphatically and eloquently of the healthy duality of indigenous cultures, in which the Creative Spirit is both a Mother God and a Father God, combining these two aspects of its reality in its power and sustaining spirit.

Alma Villanueva reflects this search for wholeness on the personal level, reminding her sons that she has "called on the / girlchild inside of / you—made / you live with / her—with me" and that their journey will struggle to mend them:

> . . . until your
> bodies become pregnant
> with birth—then
> you will really be
> men. Men
> who may love
> the woman outside them, like
> the woman inside them—and
> perhaps each other, the
> earth can't wait forever.[6]

Legendary Mexican figures such as La Llorona, La Virgen de Guadalupe, and La Adelita echo feminine voices of pain, protective power, action, and valor. Real predecessors in Chicana and Mexican history provide strong character bases for modern writers—women soldiers, colonels, and a general in the Mexican Revolution, outspoken female intellectuals and writers, the everyday community roles of women leaders in our barrios who are *curanderas* (healers), political organizers and businesswomen, even our own mothers and grandmothers. These images are reflected in our *obras*.

Yet the writings are not merely covered with roses and adulations. The awareness of sex-role oppression voiced loudly by the poet Sor Juana Inés de la Cruz in the 1600s is carried on by the modern Chicana writer. A strong feminist protest of the treatment of human beings as objects to be bought and sold and owned is evident in the mischievously potent poem *Soliloquio Travieso* (Michievous Soliloquy) by Margarita Cota-Cárdenas, who knowingly epic-izes one woman's life in the not-too-subtle image of a flower.

> mucho trabajo   ser flor
>   a veces
>   solitas
>   y en camino
>   concentramos muy fuerte   así
>   arrugamos la frente

para marchitarnos antes
y al llegar al mercado   ji   ji
    no nos pueden vender

it's a lotta work   being a flower
    sometimes
        all alone
            and on the road
we concentrate real hard   like this
    we wrinkle our foreheads
        so we can wither before we get there
and when we get to the marketplace   hee hee
    they can't sell us[7]

The unconquerable independence of the statement is but one example of the eloquence and expression of power in Chicana literature. The question of power is an important one within Chicano writings and perhaps more crucially within Chicana writings, where oppression and the theft of personal power seem evident in not only the economic and social spheres but even on the most intimate and corporal level, where the ownership of one's body is at question. While numerous writers handle this concept of La Chingada (the raped or screwed one) within the poetic confrontation of such issues as rape, disempowerment, confinement, battering, and degradation, prose writers have also woven messages of autonomy and power into their works. A more expanded personal power is achieved in the victory of the protagonist of the short story "The Paris Gown" by Estela Portillo. Clotilde is the older woman who accounts to a granddaughter her own story of her struggle for freedom and autonomy. As a rebellious young girl, she was scheduled by her father's decision to marry a rich older gentleman who her father felt could tame her. Despite her objections, plans proceed, and she finally agrees to quiet her protests on the condition that she be bought an elegant Paris gown for the engagement party. The conditions are met, the engagement party begins, and the young Clotilde makes her stunning entrance down the stairs clothed in nothing at all.

It was simple after that. My father could not abandon an insane daughter, but he knew that my presence meant constant reminder. He let me come to Paris with sufficient funds . . . and here I made my home.[8]

A solution as creative as that of Cota-Cárdenas' flower results in the acquisition of the basic freedom—autonomy over one's body and, in Clotilde's case, context. The expressions of power found in Chicana literature are often of this most immediate form. The embodiment of power in Chicana writing does not take the form of power as it is defined in White Male Club circles. It is not the power of possession, domination, or exclusion. It is not the power to control others. It is an internal expression, less exclamation than awareness, less containment than context, and less fact than value. Cota-Cárdenas stripped power to its essence, not as control over others but as control (autonomy) over self. Portillo's character embodies her own most naked power not in the visual possession of her body but in the ultimate possession of it. Other Chicana writers also echo this sentiment; this *"no nos pueden vender"* ("they cannot sell us") is only the beginning of a linked chain of "no"s which claim, obstinately, the full extent of the power which one possesses, even if that power is the bare minimum, cleverly created and resurrected from a situation of total repression, of what "You, for all that you can do, cannot do to me." The poem "19 años" is another statement of stubborn survival and the ultimate message that I am still *"dueña de mis propios sentimientos"* ("owner of my own emotions"), as line after line in the writings state *"no me pueden chingar el corazon"* ("19 años"), and "she was taking off those bandages / she carried over those wounds in her heart . . . her laugh rising up to meet the air—natural-like" ("Let the Good Times Come").[9] It is power in its final, most haunting standing-of-ground, naked power, stripped of all accoutrements, stripped of external respect, stripped of even food, but with the inimitable pride that flows from the essence of our humanness, that pride that is its cleanest and kindest when stripped of its nonhuman coverings, that pride that comes from distant eyes and gnarled hands, not rings or robes, that pride of backs that slowly, threateningly, straighten. The following excerpt from "About Emma Tenayuca and the Pecan Shellers" by Teresa Acosta speaks this powerful unfolding of liberty.

> and enter their fight
> sideways/backways
> not always sure which direction is next
> —yet enter their fight—
> knowing that there is a

cleanness
in a workroom empty
of Seligmann's
BIGGEST LITTLE Texas industry

a cleanness
that is empty of his profits in our hunched backs
backs
which have to be stretched
up and right
upright
all
the
time[10]

While some male critics theorize that Chicana writers are more "tense" because of their mission to portray racism and sexism,[11] these writers could be more clearly interpreted as intense; that is, unafraid to speak emotional realities in raw and concentrated form. This taste for directness is evidenced among other minority women writers as well; black writer Alice Walker commented on the tendency to assess her work as "too direct":

> . . . as I write I have a real consciousness of where we are as a people and as a globe in this age of nuclear action and reaction. I don't think that there's a whole lot of time for subtlety, when directness will serve. So I think I'm always moving toward more and more clarity and directness.[12]

This reflects a pattern perhaps typical of women "who handle too much / shit / to use a dust / rag and furniture / polish on it—shovels work just fine."[13]

There is a directness in Chicana literature, there is too much to be said to waste time on conventionalities, too much that is alien not only to the mainstream culture's literature but also to the literature and experience of men. Alma Villanueva handles rape, motherhood, and inhumanity in very physical, immediate terms, not the ethereal "Rape of the Sabines"–type romanticization typical of some male writers. There is no hint of "bleeding poet" myth—sensitive, frail, searching for the dispossessed and the tragic, searching for that suffering from which to feel and hence write.

"We hid our daughters in cellars—
they raped us all, youngest to
old—laughing, grunting
making us suffer more to
watch and hear our children
scream and cry for
Mama, Mama, Mama—I
do not believe these men
were born of women!"

Dark cries.   Dark whispers.

Dark heaving out.   Dark blood.

Jagged entries.   Forced flesh.

Mute skin slicing tongue.

Bound feet.   Bound hands.   Bound womb.[14]

There is a sense of purpose—one that is right in front of our eyes. To call it "tension" is to trivialize the reality of the surroundings. It is more appropriate to see it as the revolutionary *el pésame* of poet Vangie Vigil—a world hard to survive, but in the face of that, amazingly cool strength and sanity, not a tubercular "tension."

A gap in the growing recognition of Chicano writings occurs in the relative absence of quality criticism of Chicana women's writings. What little analysis has been done has often been from the perspective of and in comparison to either white male literature or Chicano male literature. The result is that Chicana literature has often been deemed to have fallen short merely by being different. Again, the symbols and the contexts are misinterpreted or the entire work is sifted through a "biasing filter" which narrows the literary vision of the critic and his expectations of the writer. Male writers are usually assumed to deal with a full gamut of topics; Chicano males are sometimes victims of a critics' debate on "universalism or regionalism" (if they write in Chicano contexts, they are usually accused of nonuniversalism), but even within these accusations they are usually seen as dealing with a variety of topics. For Chicana women writers, the limitation becomes more extreme. The sexual question is forced. Too frequently, the literary interaction of *any* two characters of different gender is assumed to be a "statement" on the existential relationship of men and women. Two

examples of this occur in the critical treatment of the poems "La Malinche" and "La Isabela de Guadalupe y el apache Mio Cid." In the
former, the poet treats the heroic figure of a noted woman in Mexican
history, La Malinche, advisor, interpreter, and lover to Hernan Cortes,
from *her* voice, not that of the Spanish conquerors:

> I saw our world
>   And I saw yours
>   And I saw—
>   another.
> No one else could *see!*
>
> . . . .
> You cried broken tears the night you saw your destruction.
> . . . .
> But Chingada I was not. . . .
>   I saw a dream
>   and I *reached* it.
>   *Another world* . . .
>
>   la raza.
>
>   la raaaaaaaa-zaaaaa . . . [15]

One critical analysis of the poem, however, states that "the poem on
La Malinche poses the main attitude of feminine complaint and rebellion against male predominance."[16] In the second poem, the cultural mélange of the *raza* is juxtaposed in two characters of very different social classes, one male, one female, who manage, by the end of
the poem, to see the overlap between their worlds, and their selves,
and to make love.

> I, as an Indian,
> And you, as a Spaniard,
>   How can we ever make love?
>
> I, by *mecate* tied
>   to a red dirt floor
>   *y una casucha de adobe*
>
> . . . .
> *Y tu,* . . .
>   *Rey en España,*
>   *Hacendado en Mexico*
>   *Y Emplumado Emperador entre los Aztecas.*

Pero yo NUNCA FUI dese tipo!
En España, gitana
En México, criada
Y hasta entre Aztecas,
yo no fuí Azteca, sino obrera,
cara triste,
y calma.[17]

By the end of the poem, the identities merge and the female persona becomes the Spanish queen, the Aztec, the Moor, as he becomes the Apache, the Toltec, the Jew, and "Nosotros la gente y / nosotros / la gente / y / Amamos" ("We the people and we the people and we love"). However, once more the critic forces the narrow limitations of theme on the writer and states, "'La Isabela de Guadalupe y el apache Mío Cid' . . . deals with the subject of La Chingada and represents Chicana women as slaves of men."[18] This "relationship between man and woman"[19] becomes, in too many of the critical writings, the sole statement and sole competence of Chicana women writers. While this is a pattern not absent in the traditional treatment of mainstream women writers, it is further exaggerated in the case of Chicana writers by the narrower, often hollow, societal images of them and complicated by the fact that even their symbols and processes are misunderstood within the existing structure. In short, "they have not met creatures of our ilk in the literary field before"[20] and, hence, there is no given formula on which to judge us, short of using a forced fit to the world of Chicano men or white women. The rich symbolism of Chicana writers is lost in the face of this blindness.

This gap in relevant criticism and acceptance has, while slowing down recognition and hence to some degree facility and publication, not slowed the pace of progress within Chicana writing. Chicana poets and prose writers alike have continued to innovate and to polish with a sense of purpose that ignores, without spiting, the structure of literary criticism. This purpose is a collectively felt direction, as in an Aquarian Conspiracy,[21] and evokes an exciting recognition on the part of those few critics who are less concerned with their own status in the accepted structure of critics than with their excitement at quality literature:

> . . . three fresh, exciting poets who represent the best . . . of
> the hundreds of Chicano writers across the country today who

do not make excuses for being a Chicano writer, who do not
secretly covet the Lamont Poetry prize, who do not seek tenure.
They write with care about and for us, recognizing that beautiful
art can only come from caring pens, from the people who give
us strength to survive the constant barrage of messages that come
to tell us we are indeed not free . . . yet. [22]

Once the initial breaking of accordance with stereotype occurred
(Chicana writers were, after all, not living up to their image as silent
tortilla-makers, bowing humbly to the man's preeminence), all other
barriers and limitations began to be questioned, including those dealing with traditional definitions and analyses of literature. Most of their
works speak not only to the oppression of human beings for reasons of
gender but also for reasons of color, culture, language, accent, and
philosophy. They protest the limitation of human beings' rights to full
autonomy and personal development. It is a natural connection, for all
forms of oppression, behind the masks and labels, are the same—a
limitation of growth, a limitation of life.

Chicano writers, male *and* female, charge forward, building their
own structures and realities, unlimited by the truisms of accepted
modes or encouraged styles. There is indeed a *concientización* in action in Chicano writing, as noted by such Latin American scholars as
Guillermo Hernández, who lists four *tendencias* representative of this
Chicano literary epoch: *concientización* ("an artistic front in the struggle for the interests and well-being of the Chicano . . . a call of
awakening to a new vision of the surrounding reality"), personalism,
aestheticism, and professionalism. [23] The first *tendencia* is epitomized
in such mythical and concrete realities as the RCAF—teasingly
known in Chicano literary circles as "The Royal Chicano Air Force."
This nonaeronautic group of nonmembers began as a community of
artists and writers working on a *causa*, while the sign on the door read
RCAF (Rebel Chicano Art Front). From the first joking reference to a
Royal Chicano Air Force, through the growth of the barrio legend and
the subsequent investigation of this supposedly military group by the
CIA, the community retained its calm and its commitment to an intangible "air force" of artists struggling to win a victory of human
awareness and aesthetic freedom. Artist and writer José Montoya serves
as informal leader, although the tone of *concientización* insists that it is
the elderly janitor who serves as commanding officer of the group.

A parallel development, although more visibly involved in all four *tendencias,* is evidenced in the dramatic literature of Luis Valdez and the Teatro Campesino, where theatrical works were taken to the people and to the streets and expressed in the language of the barrios, continuing from there to a wider acceptance and recognition by theater and film audiences, most notably in the chef d'oeuvre *Zoot Suit.* This Broadway and film success made no apologies for its barrio language mixing, barrio culture, or dual-reality aesthetics as the main character became not a character in the film but the meaning of the film, involved always in opposites, a reflection of himself and of all the others. The conclusion plays out in one way, then another, then another, engulfing all of the realities of different human beings, incorporating audience as actor and actor as audience. It is altogether a new form of media—it is not just a "movie about an event," it is an experience, a philosophy, and ultimately requires the audience to choose the ending.

Such subsequent recognition as the translation of significant Chicano works into German and French and the awarding of other literary markers—a second *Premio Casa de las Americas* for *Tú Nomás, Honey* to poet Jim Sagel; the *Before Columbus America* Book Award for *Thirty an' Seen a Lot,* a collection of poems by Evangelina Vigil; and the 1985 American Book Award for *Living Up the Street,* a collection of short stories by Gary Soto—validated to still others the worth of this genre. Perhaps most significant of all was the tipping of the hat of the literary establishment to a writer who seemed to break all the rules, who explored and transcended all the limits of poetry from form and line to language and content. The author of *Chicano Territory, Anti-Bicicleta Haiku,* and *Survivors of the Chicano Titanic,* co-author of *Get Your Tortillas Together,* this poet also explored the arena of prose in such outrageous, tongue-in-cheek essays as "The Machismo Manifesto" and "Anti-Carnalismo" (which promised a sequel "In Defense of the Vendido [sellout]") and the novel "Los Pachucos y la Flying Saucer." His more experimental poems, including "Agua Jackets," left many critics hesitant to approach him.

> Marxist leanings   ESOS
> o lo que dejan   VATOS
> los last
> amores.

Muevo
mi pata inside
the Gulf of Mexico
con Asor.

Años pasan things change
las cositas
but terror.

Mickey Mouse, your cejas French . . . French . . .
become the tail
de una
yegua that's back again
volando . . . vaseline.

And Italy crumbles
cuando tengo mucho.
Cuando tengo muchas palabras
that never decide like agua jackets. [24]

Among the few who did comment were other innovators such as
Cecilio Garcia-Camarillo, poet-editor-journalist, who also experi-
mented with such forms as "bottle poetry," sound poetry, and trilingual
poetry.

> In *Anti-Bicicleta Haiku* el camarada Reys Cárdenas assaults
> conventional logic in the most outrageous manner since the
> invention of lunacy. Present also . . . is Reyes' flippant parox-
> ysms, his now famous rubberization of time, his sexual calen-
> turas, his surgically precise imagery, and that notoriously
> Chicano gusto for language. For the first time Reyes also messes
> around with a kind of double/parallel stanza for sound effect and
> extension of meaning. [25]

Long neglected because his writings were not "understood," in 1985
Reyes Cárdenas received the Austin Book Award for *I Was Never a
Militant Chicano*, a title hardly descriptive of the soft-spoken, black-
and-white-haired shaman with unsinkable humor and unshaken seriousness of purpose. In the title poem of the book, he negates confinement in any of the mythological, literary, or historical categories into
which we are stereotyped and states, with an unvarnished honesty, his
underlying purpose.

I was never like a Louie
and I'm not like Joaquin
* * *

I was never
really a pachuco
but I saw then
what I still
see now—
that we're
getting nowhere
that things
are worse
than they were
in the 40's
and 50's
I was never
the Ché Guevara type
but there's
nothing wrong
with revolution
Everybody says
it can't happen here
but hell
it can happen anywhere
I was never
a militant
Chicano
but only because
I've always wanted
more than a revolution
can provide. [26]

The works which have appeared do not complete the story, they simply lead to new frontiers. The work in progress by Chicano writers at present holds promise for even greater innovation. The sensitivity and depth of Rudolfo Anaya's novel-in-progress *Albuquerque* speaks a layered spirituality which superimposes reality on reality as the GI in Vietnam stalks the old man in the village with all the respect and spiritual awe that he used in the hunt of the deer in the mountains of New Mexico. Both men survive, not only physically but spiritually, as the Indian GI and the Vietnamese old man give their communication, their prayersong, and their life to each other without words and without foreignness. The boundaries between the two worlds have melted and the worlds become one. The ongoing power of the works of poets like José Flores Peregrino and Isidro Ortega and the haunting massiveness of impact of prose works by Max Martínez and Helena María Viramontes are simply steps in an *onda* of artists whose styles have come of age.

Chicano literature is not where it began. Tomás Rivera—the late writer and academician best known perhaps for his novel . . . *y no se lo tragó la tierra/. . . and the earth did not part*, which won the first Premio Quinto Sol, a national Chicano literary award, at a time when Chicanos had to build their own publishing houses, critical structures, and awards for lack of other outlets—identified three stages in Chicano literature: (1) a stage of socioanthropological documentation—the preservation of deeds and people in a manner not incongruous with that of folk and oral literature, (2) one of rebellion and conflict, a statement of protest, and (3) a stage of invention and creation.[27] There is ample evidence that the third stage has come to a precocious maturity. Not only can Chicano writers authentically and effectively utilize non-Chicano personas, but non-Chicano writers can effectively utilize Chicano personas and styles and hence participate in a movement of Chicano literature.[28]

And while many local critics, still heavily imbued with a prejudice against language mixing, regional dialects, and ethnic identifiability in literature (when these apply to things Chicano), argue about the relative worth of Chicano writers according to their "freedom" from Chicano themes or universality, Chicano literature continues, recognizing that that which is most characteristic of a human individual, be it in a Chicano cultural context, a coastal fisherman's, or a Steinbeckian Okie's, is that which is most characteristic of humanness itself and is linked by an undercurrent of emotion and intuition, a collective unconscious, to all forms. Rather than trying to write "like a New Yorker" or imitating the current trend in acclaim, the bulk of Chicano literature is moving as it has in the past—with an unswerving awareness of artistry, of self, and of the community in *desarollo*, the human community.

In short, Chicano literature has gone beyond beginnings in many respects—it has gone beyond a definition of our cultural origins, it has gone beyond the beginning stages of myth creation and symbol kinship, it has gone beyond its own awareness of the literary action itself, and, perhaps most significantly to those who struggled for years to be read and to read, it has gone beyond the beginnings of its acceptance and recognition by the literary world as a whole.

Notes

This article was based on a briefer commentary by the same title published in *Southern Exposure* 9, no. 2 (1981).

1. José Montoya, "El Louie," in *Chicano Literature: Text and Context*, ed. Antonia Castañeda Shular, Tomas Ybarr-Frausto, and Joseph Sommers (Englewood Cliffs, N.J.: Prentice-Hall, 1972), p. 173.
2. Abelardo, "stupid america," in *Chicano: 25 Pieces of Chicano Mind* (El Paso: Barrio Publications, 1972), p. 32.
3. Sylvia Chacón, "I am the jealously entangled," *Tejidos* 3, no. 4 (1976): 7.
4. Reyes Cárdenas, "Poema Sandino," in *Survivors of the Chicano Titanic* (Austin: Place of Herons Press, 1981), p. 44.
5. Alurista, "mis ojos hinchados," in *El Espejo/The Mirror*, ed. Octavio Ignacio Romano and Herminio Rios (Berkeley: Quinto Sol Publications, 1969), p. 268.
6. Alma Villanueva, "La Chingada," in *Five Poets of Aztlán*, ed. Santiago Daydí-Tolson (Binghamton, N.Y.: Bilingual Press/Editorial Bilingue, 1985), pp. 151–153.
7. Margarita Cota-Cárdenas, "Soliloquio Travieso," in *Noches despertando en conciencias* (Tucson, Ariz.: Scorpion Press, 1975), n.p.
8. Estela Portillo Trambley, *Rain of Scorpions* (Berkeley: Tonatiuh International, 1975), p. 8.
9. Carmen Tafolla, "19 años," in *Canto al Pueblo*, ed. Leonardo Carrillo et al. (San Antonio: Penca Books, 1978), pp. 61–62; Teresa Palomo Acosta, "Let the Good Times Come," personal papers, 1984.
10. Teresa Palomo Acosta, "About Emma Tenayuca and the Pecan Shellers," in *Passing Time* (Austin: Chapbook, 1984), p. 7.
11. Santiago Daydí-Tolson, introduction to Daydí-Tolson, *Five Poets of Aztlán*, p. 46.
12. Alice Walker, "Writing to Survive," *Southern Exposure* 9, no. 2 (1981): 15.
13. Carmen Tafolla, "Porfiria," personal papers, 1985.
14. Vallanueva, in Daydí-Tolson, *Five Poets of Aztlán*, p. 157.
15. Tafolla, in Carrillo et al., *Canto al Pueblo*, p. 39.
16. Daydí-Tolson, *Five Poets of Aztlán*, p. 51.
17. Tafolla, in Daydí-Tolson, *Five Poets of Aztlán*, p. 10. Translation: "I, by country rope tied / to a red dirt floor / and a small adobe hut / And you / King in Spain / Big rancher in Mexico / And Plumed Emperor among the Aztecs / But I never

was that type! / In Spain, a gypsy / In Mexico, a maid / And even among Aztecs, / I wasn't an Aztec, but a worker / face sad / and calm."

18. Daydí-Tolson, *Five Poets of Aztlán*, p. 51.
19. Ibid.
20. Martha P. Cotera, personal correspondence, Austin, Texas, December 12, 1981.
21. See Marilyn Ferguson, *The Aquarian Conspiracy: Personal and Social Transformation in the 1980's* (Los Angeles: J. P. Tarcher, 1980), for a discussion of the physical and spiritual transformation of the collective unconscious and the informal network or "conspiracy" of individuals of widely varying views and backgrounds who move educational, political, scientific, and social spheres to a new level of community and self-definitions.
22. Juan Rodriguez, introduction to Mary Sue Galindo, María Limón, and Jesse Johnson, *Merienda Tejana*, ed. Juan Rodríguez and Petra Rodríguez (Austin, Tex.: Relámpago Books Press, 1985), p. vii.
23. Guillermo E. Hernández, "El México de fuera: Notas para su historia cultural," *Cuadernos Americanos* 44, no. 259 (1985): 115–119. Trans. C. Tafolla. From pp. 115–117: "Son cuatro las tendencias que ha seguido la literatura en esta epoca y que denomino respectivamente: concientización, personalismo, esteticismo, y profesionalismo. . . . las corrientes son representativas de la época y por lo tanto no todos sus autores y obras exhiben nítida y exclusavamente estos rasgos. . . . En esta época (concientización) se publican una serie de periódicos y revistas y se celebran festivales poéticos, constituyendo todos estos esfuerzos un frente artístico en la labor en pro do los intereses y bienestar del chicano . . . un llamamiento al despertar a una nueva visión de la realidad circundante."
24. Reyes Cárdenas, "Agua Jackets," in *Anti-Bicicleta Haiku* (Chapbook, 1976).
25. Cecilio Garcia-Camarillo, jacket commentary to *Anti-Bicicleta Haiku*.
26. Reyes Cárdenas, "I Was Never a Militant Chicano," in *I Was Never a Militant Chicano* (Austin: Relámpago Books Press, 1985).
27. Tomás Rivera, "Remembering Discovery and Volition in the Literary Imaginative Process," *Atisbos* (Summer 1975): 66–77.
28. Jim Sagel and Amado Muro are among the non-Chicanos who have convincingly and profoundly perfected works which are, in every respect, part of the body of Chicano literature. "Chistizos" (or the "New Mestizo," half Anglo, half Chicano) are also significantly involved in producing works which reflect this bicultural reality, as evidenced by the effective voices of El Huitlacoche (Gary Keller) and Teresa Anderson—bloodline is irrelevant, but the spirit of a Chicano literary reality is not.

Chicano Poetry
An Overview

Attempts to set a point zero somewhere in history for the beginning of Chicano literature are varied and indecisive. Each opinion reflects aesthetic, regional, and ideological concerns which limited space does not permit me to explain fully here. For the purpose of this essay, I shall repeat my position: Chicano literature is a recent phenomenon that coincides with the civil rights struggle known as the Chicano Movement and the awakening and expression of a cultural consciousness which that movement produced.[1] I also should repeat that for me, Chicanos are all those people of Mexican heritage residing permanently in the United States, call themselves what they may; hence, Chicano poetry is all poetic expression by writers who fit the above definition. However, this does not mean that Chicano literature, and most specifically the poetry, lacks roots predating the Chicano Movement, because there exists a wealth of cultural production upon which it legitimately draws, a precursor body of poetry that is slowly growing with each research project on the communities of Mexicans who lived in the territory of the United States before the contemporary period. To understand Chicano poetry it is necessary at least to review the historical context. Only in this way can one appreciate the poetry of the last decades.

Before beginning permit me to set some parameters. There will be no attempt to list every poet of significance, or every poem or book of merit. Those works and authors discussed here have been chosen for their exemplary value or their essential role in what we now call Chicano poetry. Omissions should not be read as negative critical judgments or as recommendations to readers to exclude a text from their own exploration of the literature; no general essay could claim to accommodate all the writers without becoming a simple enumeration, a bibliography at best.

Background

Considering the strength of the oral tradition in all of the European countries during the period of the discovery and exploration of the Americas, we could speculate that Spanish oral poetry made its appearance in what is now the United States with the very first explorers in the sixteenth century. It should be remembered that those ventures of discovery and exploration ranged far beyond the southwestern region of what is now the United States to encompass the entire coast of what only much later came to be known as New England. And if naming one's surroundings can be considered the most basic act of poetry, then Spanish poetry predates English poetry even on the northeast coast. Recently William Boelhower has speculated about interesting correlations among cartography, cultural identity, and national expansionism.[2] The act of tracing a map and naming zones in relation to one's own center is a rhetorical act of possession often followed by actual incorporation of those zones into the territory of the nation. In this sense the naming of the northeast coast of North America, first by the Spanish and then by the English (not to mention previous Native American namings and other European ones), was rhetorical warfare, a precursor of the very real war between Hispanic and Anglo cultures that ensued and is still with us. Since the earliest colonial period, the history of North America has been one of cross-cultural conflict that included a battle of rhetorics, of words, of images—a true war of and for poetic dominance.

In a more specific literary sense, we know that the Oñate expedition to colonize New Mexico (1598) celebrated its crossing of the Rio Grande with a Catholic Mass and a play in the style of the Spanish Golden Age, and since the drama of the times was almost exclusively in verse it would be more than probable that at least part of this work was poetry. Moreover, accompanying the expedition came one Gaspar Pérez de Villagrá, a poet who chronicled Oñate's efforts in an epic poem published in Spain in 1610.[3] Of course we should not overlook the fact that Native Americans also had forms of poetry and song, although to date no study has explored their possible influence on the roots of Chicano poetry. Yet all of the oral expressions are roots, as valid as the early works by the New England Puritans are for the literature of more recent English-writing U.S. authors. However, those early expressions were not yet products of the synthesis of Mexican and Anglo-American cultures, as Chicano expression is, though they certainly are the record of the Spanish and Native American cultures coping with the geographical space we now consider the home ground of Chicanos, and therefore somehow they are precursors.

If we move forward two centuries we find, in records and studies, that the Hispanic inhabitants of what is now U.S. territory had a varied oral tradition as well as some limited access to printed literature. Spanish verse forms survived—and still do—such as the *villancicos, décimas,* and the Mexican adaptation of the European romance, narrative ballads in Mexico called *corridos.* At the same time this society continued to center itself around the Catholic church, with much of its cultural production tied to rituals and feast days. The Catholic church employed music and song for services as well as theater for didactic instruction and reinforcement. We know from sources like the *Tratado de Pablo Tac* that Native Americans were taught to memorize songs for religious services in the California missions in the 1830s.[4] From the same source we also learn that these indigenous mission dwellers maintained their traditional songs and dances and that at least one type resembled what Pablo Tac called the Spanish style of dance. Most likely cross-culturalization was taking place at a popular-culture level that went unrecorded, having come down to us only as oral tradition and music. Prestigious Mexican writers like Sor Juana Inés de la Cruz and Sigüenza y Góngora had introduced indigenous elements into the level of high-culture writings in the seventeenth century. We can assume that some form of this process began to occur all along the cultural borderland in communities throughout the areas Chicanos now inhabit.

Written materials had to be imported into the region during the colonial period and were scarce. The printing press was absent until

1834, when the territories we are concerned with had become part of the newly independent Mexican nation. The first press opened for business in Santa Fe, New Mexico, with a second following shortly after in Monterey, California.[5] But with more pressing needs—political, religious, and social—to occupy the printers, no books of poetry were among their first products.

The first book in Spanish published in the Southwest, *Cuaderno de ortografía* (Santa Fe: 1834), can serve, however, to illustrate a significant characteristic of one predominant trend in Chicano poetry; namely, its didactic purpose. In section 2 of the *Cuaderno*, within a discussion of capital letters, the anonymous author—thought to have been Father Martínez, the Catholic patriarch of New Mexico—resorts to verse for emphasis:

> La doctrina que te doy
> Para que correcto escribas,
> Como atento la percivas
> A tu honor; y fama estoy
>
> . . . .
>
> atiende á las letras,
> y escrituras de los hombres que
> cuerdo congeturas.

> The doctrine that I give you
> So that you might write correctly
> If you perceive it carefully
> Will honor and fame serve you.
>
> . . . .
>
> pay attention to the letters,
> and writings of those men whom
> you imagine reasonable.

This venerable method of teaching children their first lessons can be found in any culture which retains some vestiges of oral tradition. The point is that just as New Mexicans utilized poetry to teach in this first Spanish text printed in the Mexican Northern Territories, those same people, trapped in the U.S. Southwest by the shifting border in 1848, as well as the later immigrants and much later the Chicanos, continued to use poetry for didactic purposes.

With the Treaty of Guadalupe-Hidalgo (1848), the United States annexed its present Southwestern states. The influx of foreigners that had begun twenty years earlier steadily increased after the treaty until the Hispanics were outnumbered. In the case of Texas, Mexicans were at a four-to-one disadvantage already before its independence in 1836. The discovery of gold deluged California with newcomers in 1848. During this period Anglo-Mexican interculturization began intensely, with results varying depending on the regional composition of the population. Ironically, while literature could not avoid documenting the process, it also became a means of preserving a Hispanic culture; this dual character prefigures that of Chicano literature.

Since the U.S. occupation of the Southwest, the Hispanic communities have never stopped producing both oral and written poetry. In California, poems and songs chronicled the exploits of the resistance fighter Joaquín Murrieta, although recently Luis Leal has discovered that the poem most often quoted as the original version of the Murrieta story was an adaptation of a *corrido* from Mexico, casting doubt on all of the assumptions of historical reliability claimed for the *corridos*. Américo Paredes' classic study of the *corrido* form demonstrated the workings of the oral process in full strength, its ability to document the story of communal heroes.[6] Yet the Leal discovery reminds us that ballads, like the epic itself, are not concerned as much with historical accuracy as with creating, within traditionally dictated patterns, entertaining narratives. This lesson should not be lost on readers of contemporary Chicano poetry who at times read a poem as a prose statement of fact instead of a fictive creation of literary reality.

As for written poetry, Doris Meyer's studies of New Mexican newspapers from 1880 to 1900 reveal that popular verses were being printed.[7] Predictably, content was usually political; form, narrative. Yet one author, who signed only XXX, published Spanish translations of Byron, Shelley, and Bryant. Thus, in Spanish-language publications at the turn of the century there was already, if not the cross-fertilization of oral and written material and Spanish and English sources, at least the juxtaposition of these texts in the printed matter considered source material for the Chicano community.

Recent research on two major newspapers, *La Prensa* in San Antonio, Texas, and *La Opinión* in Los Angeles, California, initiated during the Mexican Revolution, has found more significant facts. Both publications provided Chicano readers with a steady diet of the best

Latin American poetry. Leading poets from Mexico and other Latin American countries were published almost daily. The ramifications of this discovery are not yet clear, but it indicates necessary revision of scholarship on the backgrounds of Chicano literature. Most likely we will not uncover a great wealth of Chicano poetry from this period written in Spanish according to Latin American models. A more significant question arises, however: why were/are Chicano writers not more influenced by Spanish-language poets? What we can state without reservation is that this poetry was available in the major Chicano communities in a format readily accessible to the average public.

In "Chicano Poetry: Roots and Writers," Philip Ortego gave examples of Mexican American poetry published in the first half of this century.[8] In 1916 Vicente Bernal's *Las primicias* appeared, a collection of banal love poetry in standard English. From the *LULAC News*, 1939, Ortego cites Robert Felix Salazar's "The Other Pioneers," a poem designed to remind both Mexican Americans and Anglos that the first Europeans in the Southwest had Spanish names, as their descendants, now U.S. citizens, still do. The outstanding poet of this period, however, was Fray Angélico Chávez. His *Eleven Lady-Lyrics and Other Poems* (1945) are well-written lyric prayers of praise to Mary the Mother of God in her many forms. The language is standard English; the form and content are universal. Although a native New Mexican who has explored his Hispanic heritage in several publications, in his poetry Chávez seems to be the epitome of the assimilated writer. However, one must recognize that his poetry represents as well a considerable portion of the Chicano community which is still conservative, Catholic, and open to assimilation. To deny this, as was often done in the 1960s and 1970s, is to indulge in utopian fantasies about ourselves.

In the same period that Chávez was writing, however, another New Mexican, Arturo Campa, university professor and eminent folklorist, was interviewing old storytellers and singers of *corridos*, recording the traditional voice of the people. Campa found, for example, Arculiano Barela, who in 1914—two years before *Las primicias*—had composed "El estraique de 1910" (The 1910 Strike) about the Ludlow massacre of unionized miners in southern Colorado.[9] The Barela poem is significant for several reasons. First, it proves that while some writers were moving toward an Americanized form of expression, the oral tradition was alive and well among the people. Also, it documents that later Chicano poems about unionism and strikes are continuations of a tradition of expression of solidarity with the working class. Moreover, the title demonstrates that interlingualism, the combining of two or more languages to form a new synthesis, is not an innovation by contemporary Chicano poets, as some people claim, but that it was already an accepted practice as early as 1914. Finally, Campa's research, his preservation of the oral tradition, prefigures the preoccupation with the oral tradition that marks the study of Chicano literature as well as so much of the poetry itself, where the oral tradition is a theme as much, if not more so, than a process of creation.

In summary, by the time the Chicano Movement took place, producing interest, outlets, and audiences for more intensified literary activity, there existed a poetic process, both oral and written, in the Chicano community. The features of that poetry were a tendency toward didactic purpose and the use of narrative form; an acceptance of both folk-oral and written forms but with a clear preference for the former as a more authentic community expression; a minority of writers seeking to develop a poetry more in tune with the written models of either Mexican, Spanish, or Anglo poets; close links between writing and political activism; the use of poetry to rescue communal history and heroes from oblivion.

Chicano Movement

As the 1960s Civil Rights movement stirred interest in non-black minority groups, Chicanos also organized around a number of regional projects. Each locally based organization utilized print media to propagandize its cause. Tomás Ybarra-Frausto has documented that the major political groups from that early period produced publications in which poetry was included.[10] While the United Farm Workers had *El Malcriado*, Reies López Tijerina's Alianza Federal de Mercedes (Federal Alliance of Land Grants) in New Mexico had *El Grito del Norte*. Both published traditional popular poetry, closer to oral verse than to written forms and almost exclusively propagandistic. These publications allowed the unheard voices of agrarian workers to enter the printed realm. This invasion of the print media by the oral tradition on behalf of the silent, marginal peoples of the United States is one of the principal concerns and themes of Chicano writing present from the start. We must, however, observe that these early publications are the highwater mark of the availability of the unmediated worker's voice. Since then the expression is less from workers and more about workers (albeit poetry written by writers who once shared the workers' background or whose parents belong to that class), yet they have often moved beyond that status. This does not make the poetry of the latter writers better or worse per se, just less a direct expression of those groups usually excluded from print.

If those two political groups preferred a newspaper format open to participation by many writers, the other two major political centers were headed by individuals who also wrote poetry. José Angel Gutiérrez, leader of La Raza Unida, a third-party political movement in South Texas, wrote an autobiographical narrative in verse about his disillusionment with the assimilationist ideal so prevalent in Texas. "22 Miles" is a good example of a mediocre poem from the start of the Chicano Movement much anthologized in the early 1970s, selected more because of the author's political importance than for its value as a poem.[11] However, it does represent much of the expression of those first years, as well as the type of political doggerel that editors from the mainstream wanted to find among minority writers: it is prosaic, simplistic, cliché ridden, predictable. As José Montoya, the master Chicano poet, has said about this period, there were a lot of bad songs.

The poetic production that emerged from the other center of political action, the Denver-based Crusade for Justice, on the other hand, is far from mediocre. Rodolfe Corky Gonzales' poem *I Am Joaquin* (1967)[12] may be simple, but it is not simplistic; it may depend on popular-culture clichés, but it uses them to their and the poem's advantage as in-group signs and historical symbols; it may create a narrative line based on Mexican-Chicano history, but it also utilizes the proven techniques of oral poetry. While "22 Miles" is a personal confession of assimilation and disillusionment, *I Am Joaquin* is the voice of the community rejecting assimilation in favor of its vast history of struggle. Finally, while "22 Miles" is mediocre as a literary creation, *I Am Joaquin* is, within its own limits and goals, an exceptionally well realized piece of writing. Of the two, only the latter survives today as a poem.

I Am Joaquin probably would have had good distribution and been anthologized strictly because of Gonzales' position as a political leader even had its merits as a poem been poor, but its success, its enormous appeal for Chicanos from the start, and the admiration it provokes from non-Chicanos stem from its intrinsic power as a synthesis of political manifesto and well-planned, carefully structured poem. In fact, it probably has become more important among Chicanos than the author. Enthusiasm for political involvement has ebbed in recent years, but Gonzales' poem is still the best-known and most-read piece of Chicano poetry. More than merely summarizing a historical quest and an identity for Chicanos, *I Am Joaquin* created a way of seeing the present through our history to be able to then move forward, united, toward a common goal. That the actual praxis of goal-achievement never has lived up to the poem's promise is a political problem. Yet at the point when the Chicano Movement reached its zenith this poem best defined it. For that reason we should give it close attention.

Joaquin, the Chicano Everyman, finds himself in a cultural diaspora, besieged by an alien world that threatens to tear him to pieces. So many Chicano works begin in this fashion that *I Am Joaquin* can be seen as the prototype. Joaquin's retreat from society back into his community and its history are also prototypical. Joaquin reviews history from the protection of his communal circle; with the peace which this circle provides him, Joaquin can study the past, formulate a logical version of history (a usable past), and discover why and how he has come to be almost destroyed. His review of Mexican history, from pre-Columbian times to the Mexican Revolution, reveals a process of miscegenation based on bloodletting by and of both master and slave. Equality, in spite of social injustice, sprang from common land ownership, religious ideals of equality before God, and a mutual sharing of death. This evocation of a lost golden age, when Chicanos or their ancestors lived in harmony or peace or balance or whatever, is also common to most Chicano poetry of the early period. Joaquin's review of history on the U.S. side of the border reveals that the Anglo-American has refused to enter into any mixture of blood despite the opportunities offered by Chicanos; hence, the Anglo-American has excluded his group from participation in the human history of the region. Chicanos cannot expect to mix with Anglos and so they must accept that their blood has reached definition and is now "pure"; that is, all the blending of different bloods has produced the Chicano and no more admixture will be tolerated. Armed with a historical perspective and a group identity, the people can now rise up and reclaim their rights—land and a separate nationhood. This appeal to land rights and nationalism, with variations, was also common to many early poems.

I Am Joaquin's style is oral—it functions more with cliché and metonymy than with original tropes and metaphors. Its uncomplicated, short verses flow well with the natural voice and breath. Yet, in spite of its glorification of *corridos* as the source of Chicano history, the poem does not employ the *corrido* form of versification and rhyme but rather a typically American English style of free verse. This is cultural synthesis at work—again, a contradiction of the poem's explicit rejection of any miscegenation with the Anglo-American. Yet this synthesis of cultural sources is, too, a Chicano trait, reappearing in work after work.

Political ideology aside, *I Am Joaquin* is well structured. Framed between two images of opposing giants (the menacing one of Anglo progress and the newly evoked one of the Chicano Movement), a series of historical resumés provide a catalog of facts and images as well as a dynamic process that expands with each venture into the past. Inversely, each resumé can be shorter because previous ones have built up knowledge in the reader which can now be recalled as a vital context for the new material. The poem accelerates as it reaches the final explosion back out from the circle and into the battle with the enemy. This emergence is marked by the prophecy of a future for the pluralistic but unitary Chicano race—a utopian declaration found in many Chicano works. This skillful writing makes the poem an admirable work of art if not always politically or ideologically pleasing.

While it is important that Chicano poetry has often been linked to political groups, it is equally significant to note that most of it has been published by small presses independent from specific political organizations. Abelardo Delgado has been publishing his own work since 1969 through his Barrio Publications—often mimeographed or xeroxed pamphlets.[13] Ricardo Sánchez founded Mictla Publications to print his poetry.[14] Both poets expressed the belief that the necessary social transformation of U.S. society would be achieved, in part, through a takeover of the printed word by Chicanos. In "Chicano Manifesto" Abelardo seemed to think that both Anglos and Chicanos were anxiously thirsting for his words. His "Stupid America" centers the Chicano poet as the future artist of the Americas, the synthesis of all Hispanic tradition from the New Mexican *santeros* to internationally acclaimed Picasso. To this poet falls the obligation of saving the United States from racial warfare. Abelardo metaphorically speaks of the Chicano community itself, but, as is typical of many Chicano poets, he exalts the role of the poet and the printed word in the struggle for equality. In "Homing" Sánchez claims for his press the ability to change stereotypes and free Chicanos from oppression.[15] This faith is explicit in the title of his first book, *Canto y grito mi liberación*: poetry achieves liberation. Many Chicano poets expressed these ideals, but now, far from the heady enthusiasms of the early movement, they seem naive and hyperbolic. Clearly literature's power to transform reality was overestimated, as was poetry's appeal to audiences more conditioned to mass media than to the recitation of verse. Yet at the time the faith and its expression were sincere.

All of the early works were regionally based, even *I Am Joaquin*. This reflected the political movements of the period, which were never firmly united. What appeared on the scene to bring a semblance of unity at an interstate level, if not a national scale, was the student movement in 1968–69. And it, too, had poetry.

At first the activity related to learning centers came from Chicano academics at Berkeley who came together to publish *El Grito* (1969), a journal, and later *El Espejo/The Mirror* (1969), the first anthology of Chicano literature.[16] *El Grito* introduced to a wide reading public poets such as Alurista and José Montoya.

The students began their own movement in 1968 by walking out of schools—first the high schools, later the universities—in protest against the lack of sensitivity of Chicano culture. They demanded Chicano courses; they founded school newspapers and magazines. Thus, on two fronts they opened doors for literary expression. The creation of Chicano literature classes produced consumers for which materials were needed, thus providing a market for Chicano presses. The school publications became an outlet for Chicano poets as well as a training ground for those who aspired to the title. While the school publications have been decimated by economic recession and the rising apathy among Chicano students during the last decade and a half, we can still safely say that the academic audience, although itself dwindling, still accounts for most of the sales of Chicano poetry.

One poet more than any other personified the student spirit: Alurista. He was the first major poet to arise from the student ranks and perhaps for that reason expressed more closely their concerns, and he did so in their language. Yet he was far from a simple barrio poet. We would be better served by thinking of a Bob Dylan figure, a combination of popular forms with highly intellectualized material. His *Floricanto en Aztlán* drew from academic sources such as pre-Columbian mythology and Existentialism and from pop-culture fads like Carlos Castaneda, as well as barrio-life images. [17] His mixture of Spanish and English and a variety of sublanguages like black and Chicano slangs reflected the way students, especially in California, spoke. But his most significant accomplishment was the promulgation of the concept of Aztlán. Alurista is credited with inventing the Chicano version of a homeland myth: Aztlán was the original homeland of the Aztecs. Accordingly, Chicanos were transformed into the heirs of the glorious Aztec tradition and became the seekers of a lost homeland, located by Alurista and others in the Southwest of the United States. However, Alurista was never a cultural nationalist in the limited sense of Rodolfo Gonzales; he always favored a third-worldist vision of the future in pluralistic terms, each race and each ethnic group retaining its uniqueness within a social blending of free choice. This egalitarian pluralism helps explain Alurista's anticapitalism and the subsequent radicalization of his Marxist leanings. His ideal order cannot exist in a society divided into classes. He must call for the radical decapitalization of the state and a return to communal values and traditions. Alurista was in close harmony with the student movements of the 1960s, although perhaps we can now say that those students who actually held sophisticated ideological views were the extreme minority.

The other major poet to emerge from *El Grito* was neither young nor a student but an older teacher—José Montoya. Although a tireless writer, his publications seem few: poems scattered in magazines and one book, *El sol y los de abajo*. [18] His fame, however, rests on even less, one poem: "El Louie." This masterpiece is the epitome of the Chicano literary enterprise, a true prototype. Its language is interlingual, as is much of Alurista's, but with the difference that in

Montoya the languages flow so smoothly that they seem to blend instead of clash.

> Hoy enterraron al Louie
> And San Pedro o sanpinche
> are in for it. And those
> times of the forties
> and early fifties
> lost un vato de atolle.
>
> .   .   .   .
>
> 48 Fleetline, two-tone—
> buenas garras and always
> rucas—como la Mary y
> la Helen . . . siempre con
> liras bien afinadas.[19]

The theme of the poem is the loss of a cultural signifier for group
cohesion, in this case the leader of a pachuco gang. This loss threatens
to deprive the poem's persona's group of its life. The poem recalls the
figure in its context, thus restoring structure and significance to the
world. It is the poem itself which, in the final analysis, becomes the
space of signification as well as the protagonist of the signifying act,
replacing the dead pachuco as the centralizing cultural force. This
process, which I first discussed in "The Space of Chicano Literature,"[20] is the basis for the first book on Chicano poetry: *Chicano
Poetry: A Response to Chaos.*[21]

Louie, a pachuco leader, dies. The poem recalls his image, which
in turn brings his extended family, the immediate society, and their
relationship to the world in ever-expanding circles. At the end of the
poem, when the persona is forced to face the fact of the death of Louie,
the poem has its own presence, an alternative body to replace Louie's
buried one, and thus can ensure the stability of the threatened cultural
unit. Chaos is forestalled, cosmos affirmed through the poetic substitution of poem for dead leader. This process is, of course, similar to—if
not the same as—that of religious sacred rituals that call a divine but
distant presence back from the beyond to commune with the faithful,
who would fall into despair without some means of touching the signifying center of their cosmos. We should not overlook the presence of
this sense of poetry as sacred act which is strong among some Chi-

canos. It is this that links them, even more than subject matter, to the Native American tradition.

Following the same pattern, Raul Salinas did for the barrio what Montoya did for pachucos. In "Trip through the Mind Jail,"[22] Salinas resists chaos by restoring to the world the images of his destroyed barrio. The signifying space becomes the setting for the recalled history of the persona's peer group, from street urchins to school mates to pachuco gang members to prison immates. In the end the barrio has been recalled from oblivion, given a new space in that which the poem opens in the world. The poem itself is the new barrio, the space of life-giving significance. Its existence grants the author and his readers a sense of orientation in life, a place in the world. The poem creates cosmos out of menacing chaos.

The poems of Montoya, Salinas, Gonzales, and Alurista spawned countless imitators. Student and community publications were full of sincere but forgettable parodies of major works. Most of them spoke in the fad interlingual patterns, repeating the new images of Chicanismo until they became dull clichés. And when the models themselves used techniques and images often bordering dangerously on cliché, then the imitators were on the shakiest of ground. The Chicano doggerel writers were highly visible because they provided the facile political slogans utilized by the movement. But what the imitators failed to capture was the art of these writers. The models make careful use of detail and selected use of traditional symbols and place them within a harmonious structure, leaving the reader with a sense of totality, of the necessity of each part in the whole. Most important, the model poems, even when utilizing popular clichés, make the images emerge from a logic essential to the poem; the imitations betray the arbitrariness of usage, the sense of superfluousness, of empty repetition. From the start Chicano poetry has been plagued with well-meaning formula writers—but then most poetic movements have the same problem. Time usually filters them out.

Montoya and Salinas are also interesting as examples of the synthesis of Mexican and U.S. sources that characterizes Chicanos. Like the pachucos they write about, these poets come from a Mexican environment; it is in their language and images. Both, however, are well aware of U.S. poetry, especially that of the Beat poets. Neither employs the traditional verse and rhyme forms of Mexican popular verse. They create narrative-style poetry more like U.S. models, free of set meter, leery of simple rhyme. Both play with U.S. popular and even pop lore such as movies, cars, music, or junk food. Alurista is similar, adding to this mixture a delight in classical and rock music. Montoya and Alurista both draw on philosophical concepts from academic readings. All three are within the Whitmanesque tradition. Yet this should not surprise us. It is the space of Chicano culture, the intercultural free play of influences open to experimentation. Chicano authors draw eclectically from Mexican and U.S. sources, which in turn open to them a wealth of further international references. Authors can pick and choose, but the essential situation of creating from at least two major cultural sources is a defining characteristic of Chicano literature.

Examples of varying blends can be found in other major poets. Tino Villanueva is a prime example.[23] He writes sonnets in English or Spanish. He pays tribute to Dylan Thomas and creates intertextual references to Borges and Octavio Paz. Yet he also produces interlingual poems about farm workers, pachucos, and political ideology. In his critical writing he insists that Chicanos have "bisensibility," meaning that they experience the world from two points of reference, one Chicano, the other Anglo-American. Theory aside, Villanueva demonstrates in his poetry an ability to slide along the spectrum of interlingualism from standard English to standard Spanish, a remarkable range of tones and registers that few poets can match.

Most Chicano poets definitely favor one or the other pole of reference. Ricardo García, for example, stays much closer to the U.S.-inspired style, with a strong dose of surrealism.[24] Sergio Elizondo swings us back to the Mexican popular tradition in his language and imagery.[25] For him the Anglo-American pole of society is a negative catalyst for Chicano action, a source of Chicano action leading to self-destruction. Elizondo locates his work in the Mexican tradition as a political and cultural statement of resistance to assimilation. Miguel Méndez creates difficult poetry of highly cultured language and intricate symbolism. His long poems develop through permutating images and leitmotifs—he is the expert at mixed metaphors. *Los criaderos humanos (épica de los desamparados) y sahuaros* is a devastating satirical allegory of capitalism and at once an *ars poetica* of commitment to cultural revival through literature.[26] All of these poets, so different in styles, language, and content, share the search for original expression, for a poetic voice. They represent the evolution of that group of writers who sought to create a written tradition of poetry for the Chicano people, in spite of the fact that each of them expresses a concern for the loss of oral culture. Apparently, they believe that the content of oral tradition can only be preserved through written media.

Coexisting with the written poetry, there are oral tradition–style pieces. The authors attempt to publish works modeled on performance poetry. These usually remain at the level of cliché, simple rhyme, blatant expository statement, and trite emotionalism. Their best moments are when they indulge in humor, especially ethnic humor, which produces in audiences a sense of unity. This poetry must be experienced to understand its closeness to ritual. The message is less important than its function as shared act, as communion. The master of this style is José Antonio Burciaga, although others indulge in it at times.[27] Alurista's latest word-play poetry falls somewhat into this category. This poetry is unlikely to please the reader of modern poetry because it indulges in banal prose and lacks original expression. Yet it can be very successful with audiences who have no training in academic poetry.

Recent Trends

A decade after the publication of *I Am Joaquin* the vitality of the early poetry was wearing thin. Readers were tiring of the same clichés. As the political movement lost impetus, the committed poetry lost its contextual support. In 1976 Alurista's third book, *Timespace Huracán*,[28] and Ricardo Sánchez's second, *HechizoSpells*, appeared. Both books are notable in that they disappointed readers. They had the feeling of a spent wave. Alurista was beginning his drift into esoteric and somewhat superficial word games, a tendency he later would intensify in *Spik in Glyph*.[29] Sánchez managed to give us his masterpiece, "Homing," but this poem, which ranks with "El Louie" and "Trip through the Mind Jail," got lost in the shuffle of page after page of circumstantial chatter. The oversized manuscript could have easily been cut to the best pieces and remained a respectable volume. Both poets could have used a good editor at that point. Their plight reflected well the general tendency among minor poets who were bogging down in clichés and incestual inreading (*sic*). Luckily, something else was beginning to happen.

The first, and perhaps the most significant change, was that women began to publish book-length works. Not that Chicanas had not been writing earlier, they had. However, their manuscripts had not been received well by Chicano presses. The major anthologies of Chicano literature, most of which were published before 1976, were edited by men who seemed to be unaware of women writers or not pleased by what they knew about them.[30] Chicanas were often forced to publish their own books, just as Chicanos had published theirs, the difference being that Chicanas felt excluded by the same Chicanos who had engaged in the rhetoric of liberation just a few years earlier. In 1975 Margarita Cota-Cárdenas (*Noches despertando inconciencias*),[31] Angela de Hoyos (*Arise, Chicano* and *Chicano Poems for the Barrio*),[32] and Dorinda Moreno (*La mujer es la tierra*)[33] published significant books. They confirmed what readers of magazines had suspected all along: Chicana writers had a wealth of material just waiting for publishers to discover. Also, it was immediately obvious that the women's self-image was not the same as the one men had imposed on them. From this moment on Chicanas have enriched the space of Chicano literature in ways that would have been impossible for Chicanos alone to achieve.

Bernice Zamora's *Restless Serpents* appeared a year later.[34] It put her among the leading figures in Chicano literature. No one could ignore the tight control of language, the panoramic knowledge of poetic techniques and forms, the uninhibited intertextual plays with major poets, the carefully planned structure of the book. And all of this to convey a Chicano message with a definitely feminist bent. At the heart of the text were two inseparable themes: first, the characteristic Chicano concern for recovering traditions that have centered the Chicano community, once again the response to the threat of chaos, and second, the insistence on women's right to share equally in the exercise of any and all cultural rituals, a mirroring of Chicanos' demand with respect to Anglo-American society. That same year Miriam Bornstein-Somoza published *Bajo cubierta*, a fine collection in Spanish.[35] Not as ambitious as Zamora's book, it is nonetheless remarkable for its craft and the skill at Spanish language usage. Together they demonstrated that even when individual poets are not openly interlingual, the space itself of Chicano poetry is—these two poets co-exist, and their dialogue creates that space. Obviously they also co-exist with the larger group of Chicano poets, and it is with them that the women forced a dialogue that opened that space to an ignored minority. If Chicano poetry had begun with a focus on the man's responsibility to regenerate his culture while the woman stood faithfully and lovingly and silently by, a passive witness and storehouse of tradition, within ten years woman had come to demand a vocal and active role in the creation of whatever Chicano culture was to become. This demand and its poetic expression changed Chicano poetry, marking profoundly its recent products and reshaping its configuration.

Another sign of renewal appeared in the mid 1970s with the publication of texts by poets who openly declared the need for better craftsmanship. First among them was the above-mentioned Bernice Zamora. *Restless Serpents* arises and never drifts far from identifiable Chicano concerns and social reality, but it is anything but trite or careless. Zamora's years of dedication to the manuscript and the study of poetry show in the polished product. Second, a group of young poets began publishing small magazines with a markedly different tone. On the east coast, Orlando Ramírez and José Saldívar collaborated on *Cambios/Phideo*. Ramírez would go on to win the Irvine Prize for poetry in 1979 with *Speedway;*[36] Saldívar has become one of the most promising young literary critics in the new generation of Chicano academics. *Mango's* editor was Lorna Dee Cervantes, who would go on to win a Pittsburgh Press Award for her first book of verse, *Emplumada.*[37] The three of them came together in the late 1970s to work at *Mango* along with Gary Soto, whose *The Elements of San Joaquin* preceded Cervantes as a Pittsburgh Award winner by several years.[38] These young poets worked with some of the established writers of the earlier generation to produce a series of publications that for the most part demanded craft before message. The magazine and its chapbook series did not ignore social poetry or limit itself to any one style of writing, but with few exceptions the material published displayed attention to technique. And in the context of the first ten years of movement poetry this change was significant.

The case of Gary Soto has attracted much attention. From the very start his success at publishing in mainstream, prestigious magazines like *The New Yorker* and winning the United States Award of the International Poetry Forum (1976) with *The Elements of San Joaquin* provoked mixed reactions. Some saw him as the awaited breakthrough author, capable of communicating with Anglo-American readers in the language of contemporary U.S. poetry. Others saw him as the feared assimilationist, the Chicano who won awards because he wrote the way the mainstream demanded and without ethnic concerns. No one could deny his craft—he composes tight poems based more on image and metaphor than on narrative anecdote. There is no superfluous verbiage or ethnic clichés. He has published a series of books at the rate of about one a year and continues to garner praise from mainstream critics. Yet slowly Chicanos have come to recognize his work as one more facet of their cultural production. Of course, in his subsequent publications his Chicano culture has shown through in more obvious fashion. Perhaps audience and writer have drawn each other to a middle ground. Whatever may be thought of his handling of ethnic content (personally I read him as Chicano from the very essence),[39] the quality of his work has set a standard that continues to serve others as a benchmark.

Craftsmanship, quality, and dedication to a personal vision, however, are not limited to Soto or to those who follow the mainstream line. In 1978 Leo Romero published *During the Growing Season*.[40] He attracted none of the national attention that Soto received, but then he had not studied with a major mainstream poet (Philip Levine) as Soto had, so prestigious reviewers were not alerted. Also, the context and region that Romero transposes into poetry, New Mexico, are far from the more familiar backroads of Soto's California. Romero is more in tune with the narrative style of most Chicano writers and, thus, further from the mainstream techniques which most critics favor. Yet in his series of books he too displays a dedication to craft and an avoidance of the facile Chicano cliché. His world is that of the oral tradition, full of magic and folktales conveyed often through the persona of Celso, an aged Chicano free spirit. Alberto Ríos, whose *Whispering to Fool the Wind* won the Walt Whitman Award in 1981, is another young craftsman with a similar obsession for the magical nuances lying just beneath the surface of rural life, this time in Arizona.[41] Then there is Lorna Dee Cervantes, mentioned above, who works her poems over and over until each word fits perfectly. She too falls comfortably into the narrative anecdote, although within that context she displays some brilliant images. Her *Emplumada* (1980) is a purposefully structured voyage of the developing artist from child to commited writer to master poet, an eloquent personal statement among the best in Chicano literature. 1980 also brought us *Palabras de mediodía / Noon Words,* an excellent first book in Spanish by Lucha Corpi, published bilingually in facing translations.[42] Once again the interlingual space renewed itself. And the list could go on and on.

It would be misleading to leave the impression that the poets from the early years have disappeared or receded en masse into mediocrity. First, we must admit that, in most academic courses on the subject of Chicano poetry, it is still the early period that is taught. Therefore, for Chicano students the early poets and works are experienced as the main corpus of our poetry. The best endures while the doggerel assumes the character of historical document, in need of ever more external support for its justification. Second, some of those poets have produced recently some notable additions to their bibliography. Omar Salinas, known for his much anthologized "Aztec Angel" from his now collectors-item book *Crazy Gypsy* (1970),[43] returned to the scene to win the Stanley Kunitz Poetry Prize a full decade later with *Afternoons of the Unreal.*[44] A section of new poems by Alurista in *Return* (1983) shows signs of renewal, especially along the lines of a personal, more intimate voice.[45] Tino Villanueva's long awaited second book finally appeared in 1984, appropriately titled *Shaking Off the Dark.*[46] Villanueva has lost none of his precision; the poems are both personally moving and communally relevant. Villanueva at the same time has initiated a quality international poetry journal, *Imagine,* to serve as a format for Chicano poets to dialogue with their counterparts from all cultures. In 1980 he had edited *Chicanos: antología histórica y literaria,* the best collection of recent poetry by Chicanos, in which the established writers are presented through new poems instead of the standard, well-worn pieces.[47] And the old master, José Montoya, has combined his writing talents with music to collaborate in the long play album *Casindio, Chicano Music All Day.*[48] The older generation is by no means stagnant.

Since the mid 1970s there has been an explosion of poetry by both men and women. The problem for the critic with respect to any ethnic group is trying to define what makes it ethnic. In the first years of contemporary Chicano poetry it was not that difficult, but now the scene is radically different. Chicano poets are less concerned with ideology and more with craft; they explore the personal voice in any register and through any technique. Most still reflect a regional social context and strong ties to their community, notable particularly through the use of regional speech, the details of landscape, and a fascination for popular lore. While many of them still feel the need to rescue a Chicano past from marginal status and to instruct their community about themselves and the world, they no longer feel the need to speak as political prophets. During the 1970s we came to accept what should have been apparent from the beginning, that the Chicano community is far from homogeneous. We cannot expect its poets to speak a monolithic language when there is no monolith to speak for; we cannot expect writers to voice one political ideology when their community has not yet forged that ideological unity and in many cases seems to have rejected the militancy of the 1960s. This makes the recent poetry much harder to study and categorize, much harder to reduce for the sake of students and dabblers from other cultural milieu—but for that very reason much more dynamic, healthy, and interesting.

Notes

1. Bruce-Novoa, *Chicano Authors, Inquiry by Interview* (Austin: University of Texas Press, 1980), pp. 2–10.
2. William Boelhower, *Through a Glass Darkly: Ethnic Semiosic in American Literature* (Venezia: Edizioni Helvetia, 1984).
3. Gaspar Pérez de Villagrá, *Historia de la Nueva México* (Alcalá, 1610).
4. José de Onís, *Las misiones españolas en los Estados Unidos* (New York: 1958).
5. Bruce-Novoa, "*El Crepúsculo* and *Cuaderno*, Oldest Newspaper and Book in the Southwest," *La Luz* (October 1973): 12–14.
6. Américo Paredes, *With His Pistol in His Hand: A Border Ballad and Its Hero* (Austin: University of Texas Press, 1958).
7. Doris Meyer, "Anonymous Poetry in Spanish-Language New Mexico Newspapers (1880–1900)," *Bilingual Review* 2, no. 3 (1975): 259–275.
8. Philip Ortego, "Chicano Poetry: Roots and Writers," *Southwestern American Literature* 2, no. 1 (Spring 1972): 8–24.
9. Arthur L. Campa, "Spanish Folksongs in Metropolitan Denver," *Southern Folklore Quarterly* 24, no. 3 (September 1960): 185.

10. Tomás Ybarra-Frausto, "The Chicano Movement and the Emergence of a Chicano Poetic Consciousness," *New Scholar* 7 (1977): 81–109.
11. In *Aztlán: An Anthology of Mexican American Literature*, ed. Stan Steiner and Luis Valdez (New York: Random House, 1972), pp. 328–330.
12. Rodolfo Gonzales, *I Am Joaquín/Yo soy Joaquín* (New York: Bantam, 1972).
13. Abelardo Delgado, *Chicano: 25 Pieces of a Chicano Mind* (Denver: Barrio Publications, 1969).
14. Ricardo Sánchez, *Canto y grito mi liberación* (El Paso: Mictla Publications, 1971).
15. Ricardo Sánchez, *HechizoSpells* (Los Angeles: Chicano Studies Center, UCLA, 1976), pp. 144–148.
16. *El espejo/The Mirror*, ed. Octavio Romano (Berkeley: Quinto Sol, 1969).
17. Alurista, *Floricanto en Aztlán* (Los Angeles: Chicano Studies Center, UCLA, 1971).
18. José Montoya, *El sol y los de abajo* (San Francisco: Ediciones Pocho-Che, 1972).
19. José Montoya, "El Louie," in *Aztlán*, p. 333.
20. Bruce-Novoa, "The Space of Chicano Literature," *De Colores* 1, no. 4 (1975): 22–42.
21. Bruce-Novoa, *Chicano Poetry: A Response to Chaos* (Austin: University of Texas Press, 1982).
22. José Montoya, "Trip through the Mind Jail," in *Aztlán*, pp. 339–344.
23. Tino Villaneuva, ed., *Hay otra voz Poems* (Staten Island: Editorial Mensaje, 1972).
24. Ricardo García, *Selected Poetry* (Berkeley: Quinto Sol, 1973).
25. Sergio Elizondo, *Perros y antiperros* (Berkeley: Quinto Sol, 1972).
26. Miguel Méndez, *Los criaderos humanos (épica de los desamparados) y Sahuaros* (Tucscon: Peregrinos, 1975).
27. José Antonio Burciaga, *Restless Serpents* (Menlo Park: Diseños Literarios, 1976).
28. Alurista, *Timespace Huracán* (Albuquerque: Pajarito, 1976).
29. Alurista, *Spik in Gylph* (Houston: Arte Público Press, 1981).
30. Miriam Bornstein-Somoza, "The Voice of the Chicana," *Denver Quarterly* 16, no. 3 (Fall 1981): 32–33.
31. Margarita Cota-Cárdenas, *Noches despertando inconciencias* (Tucson: Scorpion Press, 1975).
32. Angela de Hoyos, *Arise, Chicano* (Bloomington Books, 1975) and *Chicano Poems for the Barrio* (Bloomington Books, 1975).
33. Dorinda Moreno, *La mujer es la tierra* (Berkeley: Casa Editorial, 1975).
34. Bernice Zamora, *Restless Serpents* (Menlo Park: Diseños Literarios, 1976).
35. Miriam Bornstein-Somoza, *Bajo cubierta* (Tucson: Scorpion Press, 1976).
36. Orlando Ramírez, *Speedway* (San Jose: Mango úress, 1979).
37. Lorna Dee Cervantes, *Emplumada* (Pittsburgh: Pittsburgh Press, 1980).
38. Gary Soto, *The Elements of San Joaquin* (Pittsburgh: Pittsburgh Press, 1977).
39. Bruce-Novoa, *Chicano Poetry*, pp. 185–211.
40. Leo Romero, *During the Growing Season* (Tucson: Maguey Press, 1978).

41. Alberto Ríos, *Whispering to Fool the Wind* (New York: Sheep Meadow Press, 1982).
42. Lucha Corpi, *Palabras de mediodía/Noon Words* (Berkeley: El Fuego de Aztlán, 1980).
43. Luis Omar Salinas, *Crazy Gypsy* (Fresno: Orígenes Publications, 1970).
44. Luis Omar Salinas, *Afternoons of the Unreal* (Fresno: Abramas Publications, 1980).
45. Alurista, *Return* (Epsilanti: Bilingual Press, 1983).
46. Tino Villanueva, *Shaking Off the Dark* (Houston: Arte Público, 1984).
47. Tino Villanueva, ed., *Chicanos: Antología histórica y literaria* (Mexico City: Fondo de Cultura Económica, 1980).
48. José Montoya, Esteban Villa, and R. Carrillo, *Casindio, Chicano Music All Day* (Sacramento: Centro de Artistas Chicanos, 1985).

Ayumi
"To Sing Our Connections"

While the influence of Japanese poetry has had a profound impact upon American poetry in this century (witness the work of Pound, Rexroth, and Snyder), Japanese American poetry has gained little critical recognition or acceptance into the American canon. This is not so surprising when one considers that with the exception of Lawson Fusao Inada, whose volume *Before the War*[1] was the first book of poems published by a Japanese American, no Japanese American poets have had books published by major publishing houses. And in fact, Inada's book was ignored or attacked by critics such as Allen Beekman, reviewer for the *Pacific Citizen*, who called it "outhouse poetry." When *Yokohama, California*, the short story collection by Toshio Mori, was published in 1949, William Saroyan took time out from his introduction to chastize Mori's "bad grammar." Until recently, then, writing by Japanese Americans has either been ignored or been found wanting by critics who judged it not on its own terms but according to the conventions of standard English.

But as the editors of *Aiiieeeee! An Anthology of Asian American Writers* observe in their introduction, "The universality of the belief that correct English is the only language of American truth has made language an instrument of cultural imperialism. The minority experience does not yield itself to accurate or complete expression in the white man's language." Instead, the task of the Asian American writer is "to legitimize the language of his people's experience, to codify the experiences common to his people into symbols, clichés, linguistic mannerisms, and a sense of humor that emerges from an organic familiarity with the experience."[2]

A literary tradition has long existed in our community, but the work of our writers has largely been confined to the world of small presses, community newspapers, and, most recently, Asian American publications. Despite this general neglect by mainstream publishing, poets Ronald Tanaka, Mitsui Yamada, Garrett Hongo, Geraldine Kudaka, and James Mitsui have all had volumes produced by university or small presses.

Edited by the Anthology Committee, *Ayumi* (Journey) is perhaps the most comprehensive collection of Japanese American writing to date, spanning four generations of Nikkei (Americans of Japanese ancestry) in this country: Issei, Nisei, Sansei, and Yonsei. As its introduction states, "Ayumi is the ongoing journey . . . to sing our connections." By bringing together some of the finest, most important voices in Japanese American literature, this anthology represents a bold challenge to the institutional racism of mainstream publishing as well as a lasting contribution to the multicultural literature of this country.

Most of the Issei (first generation Japanese American) selections are written in the form of journal entries or autobiographical reminiscences and are rather brief in length. In view of their hardships, one has to assume that most Issei had little time to write at all. Of the poetry by the Issei, the senryu and tanka are most effective, making precise, compact use of words: "hay spread for / movie viewing / beneath spring stars" (Hokko) and "thorns of the iron fence / pointed inward / toward camp" (Kyokusui). While the first poem takes nature as its theme with a wry modern twist, the second conveys well the pain and confinement of the camp experience in which 110,000 Japanese Americans were imprisoned in ten American concentration camps during World War II. What distinguishes the senryu and tanka is their stringent economy of expression. Although a variety of themes reoccur in many poems (the shock of internment, observations of daily camp life, remembrances of Japan, expressions of loneliness, isolation, and exile, of conflicted loyalties, and Buddhist perception of transience), these themes are rendered with an economy and precision that make them affecting.

A poem from "Japanese Poems on Angel Island Detention Station," translated by Kiyohi Hama (Karl G. Yoneda), turns upon the irony of a name: "Angel Island—what a beautiful name / But there was no angel here / Only nameless prisoners of immigration." In San Francisco Bay, Angel Island served as an entry station for Japanese and Chinese immigrants at the turn of the century. One of the poems carved into the walls of the barracks where the immigrants were detained, it is an anonymous message to the world recording the mistreatment of newly arrived Asian immigrants with the truth and immediacy of one who experienced it.

Yoshio Yao's "A Pilgrimage to Tule Lake, May 25, 1974" evokes the harsh conditions under which the internees were forced to live with a close attention to detail: "Vast and withered fields, / a dried lake bottom, / where I was once evacuated / and lived for the duration," and "Like dirty crows, / we were forced to live under low roofs."

Finally, Yoshihiko Tomari's poem gives the reader a sense of the daily costs and hazards the Japanese American immigrant faced in order to survive in this country: "After his funeral / I found out he had used a false name / to enter the country." These poems gain their quiet strength through simple, direct statement and clarity of image.

> Through the thirties and forties Japanese-American writers produced their own literary magazines. Even in the internment period, Japanese American literary journals sprang up in the relocation centers . . . The question of Japanese-American identity, the conflicts between Issei and Nisei, yellow and white relations, black, white, and yellow relations, and the war were all examined and re-examined in camp newspapers, literary magazines, diaries, and journals . . . The Japanese-Americans did write of the camp experience, but were not published outside the confines.[3]

The Nisei (second generation Japanese American) section features some of the most consistently realized work in the collection. Born and raised in the United States, the Nisei were bilingual American citizens, a fact that the federal government chose to ignore when it imprisoned them in the camps. But in some ironic sense they had more opportunity to create an authentic Japanese American literature. In this section we see more poems and stories and fewer autobiographical selections.

Hiroshi Kashiwagi's poem "Haircut" deals with familial emotions in a minimalist style:

> papa
> you used to
> cut my hair
> rice bowl style
> carving
> big ears for
> juicy spitball
> targets.

The poet recalls suffering through the private but commonplace ritual (I, too, can recall being given such a haircut) while feeling a quiet pride for his Issei father when he chases away a white *Sacramento Bee* reporter.

Mitsuye Yamada's "In the Outhouse" is extraordinarily powerful expressing disgust and revulsion for the camp experience:

> I have this place to hide
> the excreta and
> the blood which
> do not flush down
> nor seep away. They pile up
> fill the earth. I am drowning.

After exploiting their labor in agriculture and other fields, the American government exiled the Nikkei to areas of barren desert. Yamada captures well the sense of unbearable shame and humiliation of that time. Poets Kashiwagi and Yamada both use spare, stripped-down language and short lines to produce a voice taut with irony and anger.

Yasuo Sasaki's "Spoilage" expresses strong antiwar sentiments with biblical allusions:

> There is spoilage
> in God's granary,
> for warfare
> takes its toll
> even in wheatfields—
> where chaff remains chaff,
> and injured grains
> are gathered.

James Masao Mitsui's "Nisei: Second Generation Japanese American" possesses the precise but impressionistic quality of Japanese landscape painting:

>Farmers in Kyushu are caught by the floating clouds,
>caught square in the middle of their fields,
>squinting to see who it is
>standing there on the dirt bank, the mud
>in the soft rain, soft as the leading edge of a cloud.

His "Destination: Tule Lake Relocation Center May 20, 1942" is a photographically exact portrait of an Issei woman waiting on a train to leave for the relocation center:

>The fingers of her left
>hand
>worried two strings
>attached
>to a baggage tag flapping
>from her
>lapel.

Mitsui's poem reminded me of Dorothea Lange's photographs of the evacuation, that sense of loss and apprehension at what was to come.

Poet Iwao Kawakami uses the stylistic technique of the camera eye popularized by John Dos Passos as a method of distancing while at the same time recording an event in our buried history. "The Paper" is based upon an incident in which an Issei man was attempting to re- trieve a wind-blown paper along the barbed-wire fence in Topaz and was shot and killed by a guard.

Poetry predominates over either fiction or autobiography in the Sansei and Yonsei (third and fourth generation Japanese American) section, perhaps because most Sansei and Yonsei writers find the form of poetry more usable as a way of "saying something" than either fic- tional narrative or the autobiographical essay.

Jonny Kyoko Sullivan's "Obasan" (Grandmother) is a precise, con- trolled, sharply imaged poem in five sections. Clearly, it is one of the finest in the anthology, containing vivid, memorable images which convey both remembrances of growing up in Japan and the awkward, tentative experience of returning "home" years later: "My bones are wild herons / trapped in your kimonos" and "And when I kissed your cheek, / the smooth dark jars of your eyes / broke into astonished frag- ments." Sullivan's "Sagimusume: The White Heron" is also excep- tional.

While Sullivan uses sharp, particular images to evoke her "Obasan," the narrator of Momoko Iko's "1963: Obasan Makes Peace" has a tough, street-wise voice. Momoko Iko shares this emotional toughness with Nisei writers Mitsuye Yamada and Hiroshi Kashiwagi.

Janice Mirikitani's "For My Father" is an unsparing portrait: "word-less / he sold / the rich, / full berries / to / hakujin / whose children / pointed at our eyes" and later, "Father, / i wanted to scream / at your silence." As much an indictment of white racism as of her father's un-communicative behavior, Mirikitani's poem is among the most polit-ical in the anthology.

Lonny Kaneko's "Renewal: Algona, Washington" and Lawson Fusao Inada's "My Father and Myself Facing the Sun" delineate relationships between the poets and their Nisei parents in a gentle, devotional tone. Kaneko evokes his mother's life on a farm in the Pacific Northwest with evidences of decay and urban blight, not "renewal," everywhere: "Be-hind us, the ribs of the barn / bowed by rains and dry rot, invite air." But still, she speaks of her own hardship and the need to retain one's identity:

> And when we cross parking lots sparkling with rain,
> my mother's aging face rises out of the darkness.
> She says to her grandchildren,
> "Look for your own faces.
> They rise out of the past like old wounds."

Inada conjures a sublime landscape with the figures of the poet's fa-ther, the poet himself, and his children alongside a lake:

> He is much the smooth, grass-brown slopes
> reaching knee-high around you as you walk;
> I am the cracks of cliffs and gulleys,
> pieces of secret deep in the back of the eye.

While Inada's poem shares a representational quality with James Masao Mitsui's "Nisei," Inada uses the "I," placing the poet firmly in his landscape and thus personalizing the poem.

Karen Tei Yamashita's "Maceio Maceio" gracefully describes her fa-ther fishing in the ocean: "Waves grapple at his knees and / spume his majestic cape, / sputtering behind." This action works as a counter-point to the brutally exact description of an urubu, "a tailless black turkey," feeding upon the poisonous baiacu: "Together they encircle her, / flapping black shadows / poke at the fixed eyes, / pierce the bloated throat." The poet's fascination with this ritual dance and her use of the feminine pronoun suggest an identification with the baiacu: "Drunken salary men in Tokyo / dip her raw pieces / in shoyu and play / fugu roulette. There are expensive ways / to die." By shifting between the twin poles of grace and violence, "Maceio Maceio" is a dark, complex poem which casts a cold eye upon death.

Tillie Olsen has described Mitsuye Yamada's work as "hard wrung poetry." This stringent quality is also present in Momoko Iko's "Obasan." Kyoko Sullivan's poems suggest the binds and constraints inherent in Japanese women's sex roles, while Janice Mirikitani dramatizes sexist and racist stereotypes. And Karen Yamashita's poem seems to identify with the violence of nature to an unusual degree. Japanese American women poets, then, are depicting and challenging traditional gender-defined roles or simply exploding them with taut expressions of rage. Thus, this instinctive concern with women's experience and oppression often bridges generational barriers between Nisei and Sansei women poets.

As a Sansei writer, I believe this anthology is continuing proof of the Japanese American literary tradition. Work by the Issei offers glimpses and illuminations of what those of my grandparents' generation felt and thought in their own language, a language that most Sansei have little command of. Thus, their work brings me closer to those unvoiced histories of our grandmothers and grandfathers.

Some of our best, most prolific writers are Nisei and some continue to write even now. While growing up in New York City, I sensed the effects of the internment on my parents as a weary silence, of speech withheld, of emotions so hurtful that they must be held within at all costs. Nisei poets Mitsuye Yamada and Hiroshi Kashiwagi give passionate voice to those emotions which makes the impact of their poems cleansing—an art that redeems us.

The Sansei and Yonsei poets I admire affect me in other ways, for their poetry indicates possible directions as to where my own writing may lead. Many Sansei and Yonsei find themselves in the predicament of being thoroughly Americanized yet desiring to reclaim their cultural past, however distant and elusive it might be. In Jonny Kyoko Sullivan's work, her exploration of the complexities of identity merged with an extraordinary gift for the image makes her poems doubly exciting to me. But more specifically, I think her work, its tone and sensibility, is indisputably Japanese American.

Finally, the history of Nikkei in the United States from the immigrant experience to the Asian American movement of the present moment can be found in *Ayumi*. Because our history was not told in textbooks and our writers were not even mentioned in literature classes, for a long time I felt that my own experience was outside history. This anthology further dispels the myth that Japanese Americans have not contributed to the multicultural literature of this country.

While some Issei poets worked in traditional Japanese poetic forms and some Nisei and Sansei poets might have been influenced by the Imagist Movement, I would hesitate to place those poets in either tradition. They belong to, and extend, the tradition that is their own. In his "Tribute to Toshio," Lawson Inada says, "Does one merely 'admire' whom one is descended from? There is an abiding love involved, a pride in where the elder has been, what he has done, and from there do we reach out to the world."

Notes

1. Lawson Fusao Inada, *Before the War* (New York: William Morrow and Co., 1971).
2. Frank Chin, Jeffery Chan, Lawson Inada, and Shawn Wong, eds., *Aiiieeeee! An Anthology of Asian American Writers* (Garden City, N.Y.: Anchor Press/ Doubleday, 1975).
3. Ibid.

Documentaries and Declamadores

Puerto Rican Poetry in the United States

> If only they
> had kept their eyes open
> at the funeral of their fellow employees
> who came to this country to make a fortune
> and were buried without underwears[1]

With this startling image from his long poem *Puerto Rican Obituary*, Pedro Pietri documents the life of his community at the same time that he seeks to raise awareness—to open the eyes of his "fellow employees"—in that very community. This is a dual responsibility frequently accepted by Puerto Rican poetry in the United States, a unique, neglected poetry reflecting the life of its community rather than the life of an educated elite, the focus of so much "mainstream" poetry.

The presence of Puerto Rican poets in the United States can be traced back to the 1860s, according to Efraín Barradas, critic and professor of Spanish at the University of Massachusetts-Boston. The first major figure to emerge, however, was Clemente Soto Vélez, who by the 1950s was no longer writing solely for an audience in Puerto Rico but also for what Barradas calls "a future reader." Soto Vélez, a leader of the independence movement in Puerto Rico who spent eight years in federal prison as a result of his fierce advocacy, a visionary who invented his own phonetic Spanish alphabet, published several books from his exile in New York, including the landmark *Caballo de Palo*

(The Broomstick Stallion) in 1959. Still writing and speaking today in his eighties, Soto Vélez has been instrumental as well in providing guidance and support to many younger writers in the Puerto Rican community.

The most important context for contemporary Puerto Rican poetry in the United States remains the great migration from the island in the 1950s and 1960s, a migration so massive that approximately one-third of the population left Puerto Rico during this time.[2] Roberto Márquez, Caribbean scholar at the University of Virginia and former editor of the influential journal *Caliban,* sees this migration as "class homogeneous: a group of displaced labor was coming here," pushed off the island by the political machinations and economic failures of Operation Bootstrap, the industrialization of Puerto Rico which ultimately benefited North American corporations far more than the majority of Puerto Ricans. From this group of displaced labor emerged the first two poets of the migration: Víctor Hernández Cruz and Pedro Pietri. The poetry of Hernández Cruz, surreal, insistently musical, and bilingual, gained the poet considerable attention by the age of twenty, when his book *Snaps* was published by Random House. Pietri, whose *Puerto Rican Obituary* is probably the best-known and certainly one of the most powerful poetic works to arise from the Puerto Rican community, according to Roberto Márquez "represented the first generation, beginning to write literature out of that experience." Blending humor and rage with genuine verbal inventiveness, a true "street" poet, Pietri's natural eloquence concerning conditions in his community and the reaffirmation of that community won him an enormous following.

By the early 1970s, the self-proclaimed "Nuyorican" literary movement had developed. Originally a derogatory term used against New York Puerto Ricans by Puerto Ricans on the island (that is, neo-Rican, or not really Puerto Rican at all), "Nuyorican," when applied to poetry, came to mean a combination of English and Spanish, frequently in a street idiom, aimed at a bilingual/bicultural audience and reflecting the language as well as the experience of that audience. Some proponents of the poetry such as Miguel Algarín even claimed that a "new language" was being invented; and indeed, says Roberto Márquez, "we'd done something to the language which was not there before." Said Algarín in his introduction to the anthology he co-edited with Miguel Piñero, *Nuyorican Poetry,* published in 1975: "Nuyorican is at its birth. English nouns function as verbs. Spanish verbs function as adjectives . . . Raw life needs raw verbs and raw nouns to express the action and to name the experience."[3] As poetry, the language was clear, direct, and concrete, usually meant to be read aloud, even chanted. The bilingual nature of the poetry encouraged agile wordplay across languages. Witness the Víctor Hernández Cruz pun:

> There will be a Sun
> Risa
> on your lips[4]

The poet blends the Spanish words *risa* (laughter) and *sonrisa* (smile) with the English word "sunrise," a feat which can be appreciated only by an audience familiar with both languages.

The poet and the audience in the Puerto Rican community were, and still are, closely linked. This linkage has deep philosophical roots. In the words of Louis Reyes Rivera, a well-respected New York poet and publisher of Shamal Books, "there is no distinction between the reader and the writer. Without someone to clean streets and sew garments, there would not be someone with time to write poetry." The language used by the poet, maintains Rivera, "reflects what the people themselves have done with language in their everyday use."

The English which has increasingly replaced Spanish as the dominant mode of communication for Puerto Rican poets in this country is often non-standard English and as such owes a considerable debt to the black community. Roberto Márquez provides the context: "El Barrio [in New York] is called Spanish Harlem for a reason. It shares a lot of space with the black community." Sandra María Esteves, another leading Nuyorican poet and director of the African-Caribbean Poetry Theatre, adds: "the Puerto Rican community has merged with the black community in terms of how we are treated by the dominant society . . . The black community here has been dealing with language issues for a long time. That provides a focus for us to deal with the English language."

Black words and music have their strongest influence on the rhythm of Puerto Rican poetry. Louis Reyes Rivera: "In non-standard English, there's more attention to rhythm than meter. One syllable lines can be complete. A series of one syllable lines can be a cutting edge, staccato-like. We end up taking a series of natural sounds—guttural sounds—

and 'spleeeeeing' our way through it. It's a record of what we call hypertension: the paranoia, the pain cutting loose."

Puerto Rican poetry has an oral tradition which antedates its contact with the black community in the United States, though that contact clearly strengthened the tradition of poetry as spoken word. The *declamador*, a dramatic public performer of memorized verse, has held forth in Latin American plazas for centuries, Puerto Rico included. In New York, the oral tradition ranges from Jorge Brandon, an old-style declamador nearing eighty who still recites on street corners, to Georgie Lopez, who, at the age of nine had his oral poems transcribed for the *Nuyorican Poetry* anthology because, according to editor Algarin, he could neither read nor write:

> georgie lopez will be the DDT against
> the rats[5]

Two other factors involved in the development of the oral tradition are the speech patterns and music of the Puerto Rican community itself. Efraín Barradas: "It comes from the community. People sit on stoops, or stick their heads out the window, and talk." Salsa, the hybrid Afro-Caribbean music which fully evolved in New York, is also credited by many with having an impact on Puerto Rican poetry as sound. In fact, the music, in all its variations, is often referred to in the poetry by Hernández Cruz ("The Cha Cha Cha at Salt Lake City Bus Terminal") and numerous others.

The themes of which the poets speak again reflect the migration experience and the many complexities that experience entails. There is, first of all, the theme of Puerto Rico. Barradas defines this as "the [literary] myth of Puerto Rico as paradise." Roberto Márquez sees the myth as "an unavoidable necessity . . . It's comparative. That's paradise compared to here. That's where I belong because I obviously don't belong here." Waves of migrants have "transmitted their sense of return to their offspring." In the poetry, the myth of Puerto Rico as paradise surfaces in imagery of the island's natural world: the mountains, the rivers and the sea, the warm climate, the vegetation. This tendency is found, for example, in the work of Hernández Cruz, who has written dreamlike poems about green bananas falling from the sky onto an urban landscape, or people popping out of mangoes. These images acquire a transcendent power when set off against the harsh conditions faced by Puerto Ricans in the United States. Hernández Cruz, trapped in a cold tenement, remembers an uncle

> Who never left his hometown
> We'd picture him sitting around
> cooling himself with a fan
> in that imaginary place
> called Puerto Rico.[6]

By referring to Puerto Rico as "imaginary," the poet doubts the myth at the same time he revels in it. And indeed, sometimes the myth is contradicted, as with Miguel Algarín's "A Mongo Affair":

> Don't fill me full of vain
> disturbing love for an island
> filled with Burger Kings[7]

Just as Puerto Rico is a major theme in the poetry, so too is the subject of the Puerto Rican. The Puerto Rican cultural character is seen as essentially good; this perspective clearly acts as a reinforcement of the Puerto Rican identity, threatened on the mainland by Anglo stereotyping in the media, schools, the workplace, and elsewhere, as well as the dilution or loss of Spanish and other cultural characteristics. According to Sandra María Esteves, "who is a Puerto Rican and what is a Puerto Rican" are ongoing concerns for the poet on the mainland. When that question is answered, the response is often based on the "reality of Puerto Rican culture, a mixture of Indian, white, and black, even within one family." Thus, continues Esteves, "diversity, and the need for respect among cultures" becomes a recurring subtheme in the poetry. Esteves addresses both the identity crisis of the mainland Puerto Rican and her own African cultural roots in the poem "Puerto Rico, I," where she speaks to the island directly, like a person:

> How can you say I am not your child?
> You are my black mother who teaches
> Me to see in the darkness where
> there exists only music[8]

In poems such as this, Esteves and Louis Reyes Rivera have assured that the black aspects of the Puerto Rican self are recognized.

Most often, the poetry returns to the sense of self held by the poet and the audience, their shared identity affirmed. Pedro Pietri, in "Love Poem for My People," writes:

> if you want
> to feel very rich
> look at your hands
> that is where
> the definition of magic
> is located at[9]

Perhaps the most striking characteristic of Puerto Rican poetry in the United States is its element of protest. At times, this protest manifests itself merely by description of surroundings: when Pedro Pietri writes of funeral parlors and liquor stores proliferating in his neighborhood, that and similar observations based on simply looking out the window may be interpreted as political. The daily enemies of the community are depicted in turn: the landlord, the boss, the police, the pusher, the cold, and even the city itself, be it in the form of bad public hospitals and welfare systems or the apparent soullessness of the metropolis. Exploitation on the job and its debilitating effects on the spirit draw Pietri's ire in the now-classic "Puerto Rican Obituary":

> They worked
> They were always on time
> They never spoke back
> when they were insulted
> They worked
> They never took days off
> that were not on the calendar
> They never went on strike
> without permission
> They worked
> ten days a week
> and were only paid for five
> They worked
> They worked
> They worked
> and they died[10]

Narrative poetry is frequently employed to document, and protest, incidents which would otherwise be left undocumented, as with

Rivera's "Burning Embers," about a police killing, or Esteves' "Lil' Pito," about a child who fell from a broken window. "Lil' Pito" is replete with the precise, authentic details which characterize the use of poetry as documentary:

> I got to the hospital to see
> Rosa standing with a piece of
> Rotten window gate in hand[11]

Thus, the awareness of the audience/community is raised with respect to a particular event, from the perspective of that community, so unlike the point of view reflected in the media, if indeed the media were to cover these events at all. In this way, the traditional role of poet as community historian is perpetuated in the barrio.

According to Rivera, "all mores, sexual, religious, political, moral, are questioned and re-questioned" in the poetry. He comments that the poetry is "sometimes left-leaning, but not consistently enough to be of the left." However, certain poets with a more developed political awareness, such as Rivera, Esteves, Algarín, José Angel Figueroa (in poems such as "Cowboynomics"), and others have produced a definite anticolonial strain in their work, a natural outgrowth of the history and political status of Puerto Rico. Rivera writes in "Grito de Lares" of "enemy soldiers romping" through Puerto Rico:

> in the name of
>   someone else's right
>   to juicy slabs of stolen produce[12]

The poet is tying together centuries of colonial occupation, first under Spain and later under the United States, recalling an earlier rebellion—the "Grito de Lares"—and hoping for another. This kind of anticolonial statement represents Puerto Rican poetry at its most politically universal. In a logical extension of the anticolonial position, a variety of Puerto Rican poets have written about Central America and South Africa as well.

Women's issues have also been addressed by Puerto Rican poets in the United States. Contemporary poets are inspired by the example of Julia de Burgos, who lived in New York during the 1940s and 1950s, leaving behind such well-known poems as "A Julia de Burgos":

You are only the prim ladylike lady;
not I; I am life, strength, woman . . .

You curl your hair and paint your face; not I;
My hair is curled by the wind, my face is painted
by the sun[13]

Today, the work of Sandra María Esteves ranges from a depiction of woman as life-giver in "A Celebration of Home Birth" to the defiant rejection of female servility in "From the Common Wealth." Rosario Morales and Luz María Umpierre write from a consistently feminist perspective. Umpierre's "Rubbish" succinctly states her position:

I b-e-g yul paldon, escuismi
am sorri pero yo soy latina
y no sopolto su RUBBISH.[14]

Not coincidentally, Puerto Rican poetry in the United States has been almost completely excluded from the mainstream. This is nowhere more evident than in the area of publishing. Only one Puerto Rican poet in this country has ever had a book published by a major commercial press: the previously mentioned Víctor Hernández Cruz with Random House. Many accomplished poets—Rivera, Esteves, and Susana Cabanas among them—must self-publish their books. Awards and grants have also been difficult to come by, though Esteves has twice been awarded grants through the New York State Council on the Arts, while Miguel Algarín and Tato Laviera have each received the Before Columbus Foundation American Book Award. Many reasons are offered for the near-total absence of the Puerto Rican poet from the broader community of poets in the United States. Roberto Márquez: "in historical terms, the Puerto Rican just got here . . . Where are the Nuyorican Paul Robesons, Richard Wrights? They're just beginning to form." Says Sandra María Esteves, "It's a manifestation of the colonial mind. Hispanics get excluded from the mainstream at every level: in the job market, in educational institutions, everywhere Puerto Ricans are not allowed to participate as equals." Louis Reyes Rivera sums it up simply by saying that "nobody wants to be reminded that they're wreaking havoc on others." But Efraín Barradas believes that "it's good that the poetry has been excluded. It's provided the possibility of development. It would have otherwise been completely absorbed, assimilated . . . You wouldn't have a corpus called Nuyorican poetry."

There is a consensus among those involved that the Puerto Rican community must develop its own literary institutions. Several small or university presses currently emphasize Puerto Rican poetry. Foremost among them is Arte Publico Press, based at the University of Houston and headed by a Puerto Rican, Nicolás Kanellos. Other presses, such as the Bilingual Press, Waterfront Press, and Ediciones del Norte, though not Puerto Rican–run, have published a good deal of Puerto Rican writing. Where the Puerto Rican community has been quite active is in the area of organizing and supporting reading series. In New York alone, readings have been sponsored by the Museo del Barrio, Grupo Moriviví, the African-Caribbean Poetry Theatre, and the Nuyorican Poets' Cafe.

Yet Puerto Rican poetry in the United States has grown beyond the borders of New York City. The presence of Rosario Morales in Cambridge, Juan Sáez-Burgos in Boston, Naomi Ayala in New Haven, David Hernández in Chicago, and Víctor Hernández Cruz in San Francisco testify to the sweep of the Puerto Rican diaspora and the persistence of its voice.

The prognosis for Puerto Rican poetry in the United States is mixed. Undoubtedly, the fate of the poets is intertwined with that of the Puerto Rican community itself, and they may continue to be excluded from the mainstream as a consequence of identifying with that powerless and resource-poor community. On the other hand, according to Kal Wagenheim, editor and publisher of the Puerto Rican–oriented Waterfront Press, there is cause for optimism: "I certainly do think there's a future. The potential is out there. It's up to the writers and publishers to figure out a way to reach a young and growing community . . . a dispersed community, with its own needs." Louis Reyes Rivera considers it the writer's responsibility to assure that "the literature is there and you yourself made sure it didn't go away." However, the future is probably best summarized by three lines from a poem called "News from the Front," by Sandra María Esteves, which personify the humor and toughness of the people she w ites for and about:

> We lost graffiti battle no. #3
> but reinforcements are on the way
> from lexington avenue.[15]

Notes

Quoted comments from Efraín Barradas, Sandra María Esteves, Roberto Márquez, Louis Reyes Rivera, and Kal Wagenheim were taken from interviews conducted by Martín Espada in November and December 1985.

1. Pedro Pietri, *Puerto Rican Obituary* (New York: Monthly Review Press, 1973), p. 10.
2. Ann Nelson, *Murder under Two Flags* (New York: Ticknor and Fields, 1986), p. 98.
3. Miguel Algarín and Miguel Piñero, eds., *Nuyorican Poetry: An Anthology of Puerto Rican Words and Feelings* (New York: William Morrow and Co., 1975), p. 19.
4. Julio Marzán, ed., *Inventing a Word: An Anthology of Twentieth-Century Puerto Rican Poetry* (New York: Columbia University Press, 1980), p. 169.
5. Algarín and Piñero, *Nuyorican Poetry*, p. 42.
6. Víctor Hernández Cruz, *Tropicalization* (New York: Reed, Cannon, and Johnson, 1976), p. 62.
7. Algarín and Piñero, *Nuyorican Poetry*, p. 55.
8. Sandra María Esteves, *Tropical Rains: A Bilingual Downpour* (New York: African-Caribbean Poetry Theatre, 1984), p. 25.
9. Pietri, *Puerto Rican Obituary*, p. 78.
10. Ibid., p. 1.
11. Esteves, *Tropical Rains*, p. 30.
12. Efraín Barradas and Rafael Rodríguez, eds., *Herejes y mitificadores: Muestra de poesía puertorriqueña en los Estados Unidos* (Rio Piedras: Ediciones Huracán, 1980), p. 74.
13. Angel Flores and Kate Flores, eds., *The Defiant Muse: Hispanic Feminist Poems from the Middle Ages to the Present* (New York: Feminist Press, 1986), p. 79.
14. Barradas and Rodríguez, *Herejes y mitificadores*, p. 108. The Spanish in this verse translates into "but I am Latina and do not tolerate your RUBBISH."
15. Sandra María Esteves, *Yerba Buena* (New York: Greenfield Review Press, 1980), p. 82.

In Search of a Muse
The Politics of Gay Poetry

Something unprecedented happend on June 27, 1969. The patrons of the Stonewall Inn—a Greenwich Village gay bar—did not disperse quietly, as the police, after a routine raid, expected them to. One small homosexual population, mostly "Puerto Rican transvestites and young street people," fought back, first with cobblestones, bottles, and coins, and then with an uprooted parking meter which became a battering ram. It managed to trap a number of policemen inside the Stonewall. Flames suddenly appeared in the bar and reinforcements had to be called in—to rescue the police.

Thus began three nights of rioting that have been immortalized—in the hearts and minds of gay and lesbian people around the world, at least—as the Stonewall Rebellion. If Stonewall doesn't constitute the *beginning* of gay liberation (in *Sexual Politics, Sexual Communities* John d'Emilio details the decades of gay and lesbian activism that prepared its way),[1] it certainly precipitated a heating up of organized insurgency in political as well as other arenas. One of those arenas was the cultural.

Gay identities were fleshing themselves out. Just so gay poetry was coming to be. Or was it? In 1982 the *Advocate*, the most widely distributed gay newspaper in the world, wanted to know. Cultural/Associate Editor Mark Thompson commissioned the two essays which follow—Steve Abbott's reflections on West Coast gay poetry and mine on its East Coast complement. They were published together—along with interviews with poets Richard Howard and Paul Mariah and snippets from the work of James Merrill, Edward Field, James Broughton, James Schuyler, Thom Gunn, and Robert Gluck—in a special issue of the *Advocate* which questioned the existence of a "gay muse."[2]

Abbott considers lesbian as well as gay male poets in his survey, which

267

comes equipped with a historical overview. The division I find among East Coast "gay" poets—between politics and art—seems to me paralleled in novelist and cultural commentator Edmund White's antithesis (in *States of Desire: Travels in Gay America*) between gay political radicals and moderates.[3] "Radicals," according to White, "would call for a thorough change of national (and international) institutions and ways of living. The moderates would want gays to swim into the mainstream. Whereas the radical goal is to transform society, the moderate goal is to enter it." And if the question I pose ("What hope is there that the two tiers will become one?") is mirrored in White ("Are the goals incompatible?"), my guarded optimism probably comes from him too. "Yes, of course" the goals are incompatible, he declares, "but at this moment, at least, I see no reason the two groups can't work together." My hope of a cultural reconciliation? Such as it is, it seems to rest with "Lady Day, the woman in us all."

R.K.

East by Rudy Kikel

Three strikes were against me. Was I out? I certainly hadn't got to first base. At least that was how I felt as I began receiving responses to a "gay poetry" questionnaire I had sent to some twenty East Coast gay male poets and critics, some of whom I knew personally and some of whom were slated to read their work at "Glad Fridays," the visiting gay writers' series I organized in Boston at the gay bookstore Glad Day. First off, I had asked my correspondents if they *were* gay poets. And while they were about it, is there an East or West Coast gay poetry? One from New York City, Boston, Washington, D.C., Philadelphia, or the South? What, by the way, did they think of the notion promulgated and defended by *Gay Sunshine* editor Winston Leyland that there has been "especially since Stonewall" a "Gay Cultural Renaissance" that has been "of equal importance to other literary movements (such as the Beat) of the second half of the 20th century"? Other comments?

The first notion to fall was that of my generic word *poet*. Ian Young, the Canadian poet—er, writer—who lives part-time in New York City, didn't like it: "When someone says to me, 'Come and meet so-&-so; he's a poet,' my first reaction is either 'Poor wretch!' or 'Isn't everyone?' 'Poetry' sounds, unfortunately, anachronistic and pompous. Rather like being a marquis or a G-man. I write other things as well and would rather be known as just a writer."

So much for *poet*. Then Edmund White chipped away—working from left to right—at my second term, *gay*: "I think that before one can answer the question is there a gay poetry, one must first ask, are there gay people, a question Michel Foucault has raised again in the last few years. . . . Foucault has argued that *homosexuality* itself is a Victorian term invented by heterosexuals in order to 'medicalize' sexuality in general and homosexuality in particular. Previously, one might have been a doer of homosexual acts, one might have made love *homosexually*, but one was not oneself *a* homosexual (the word was an adverb but not a noun or even an adjective). Have we allowed desire to be quarantined, by medicalizing it?"

My notion of a "Genius of Place" fared little better than "poet" or "gay." It started to crumble—in my own eyes—in the light of poets' deliberate attempts, perhaps in deference to my silly questionnaire, to prop it up. So Tom Meyer allowed that a "sensuality" he saw as his "aesthetic" had been "nourished" in the South (he lives in Highlands, North Carolina)—"though I'm not much clearer than that about its influences." And Chasen Gaver ventured that in Washington, D.C., "more poems are written about interpersonal questions than about 'abstract' ideas" as a "reaction to the abstractions of everyday life in a city that compiles data for the rest of the nation." But poets Meyer and Gaver would probably be the first to agree that "sensuality" and "interpersonality" are not exclusive to their regions.

Some poets, I thought, do what *I* do—entertain fantasies not so much about where I live but about other places, ripe for projection because they are more mysterious. So Ron Schreiber, who doesn't think the work of the Boston poets he knows are gay "could be grouped together in anything but mutual sexual preference," offered this proposition about San Francisco: "Longer hippydom, slower pace, small city—I suppose these and other things (like proximity to big nature) make many S.F. poets different from poets on this coast." What is mysterious can also be ominous; other-place projections can be negative ones. Asked if there were a West Coast poetry, Bostonian Walta Borawski replied, "Yes, but I've never liked it." Sometimes a poet's projection justified staying in place: Meyer feels he needs "an epicurean tension that I can't find possible on that other, laid-back coast."

And as if to balance the ledger, negative West Coast fantasies about the East Coast were *themselves* entertained by an East Coast writer. Asked if there were an East Coast poetry, J. D. McClatchy suggested I "ask a poet—or better yet, a poetoid—who lives in San Francisco. They've made up the conspiracy, and the tiresome code words: *academic, elitist, repressive, obscure, smart, crafted.*"

White, the traveloguer of gay America, offered the only full-scale dichotomy and, I thought, a measured one, constituted as it is of two equally desirable ambiences: "East is more formal, more reserved, more given to traditional verse patterns, more indebted to the visionary strain of Emerson and Wallace Stevens, whereas West is more casual, more demotic in its allusions, more given to the William Carlos Williams tradition." But these are "large and rather vague regional differences," White writes—to be qualified, it is to be presumed, in the particular. And after all, when they were asked to list influences on their own East Coast work, poets Schreiber, Jack Anderson, Felice Picano, and David Eberly listed Oriental poetry or Williams among them. "Think of William Carlos Williams as 'West Coast,'" Borawski muses: "Impossible."

How are we to think of *anybody* as anywhere! That's the problem with a poetry of place. Cross-fertilization, first off, obscures the model, as Tim Dlugos argues: "So San Francisco poet Steve Benson is a language-centered artist with as many connections to New York as to the West; Dennis Cooper's own work is heavily influenced by New York, not the traditional Bukowski poetics of his native Los Angeles; Allen Ginsberg," who is often identified with New York City, "invented Beat Poetry while living in San Francisco." Then, what place do we give credit for a poet's achievement, that of his origin, a stop on the way, or his eventual destination? Robert Frost was born in California (Charley Shively reminds me), Frank O'Hara in Worcester, Massachusetts. Finally, even when a poet believes "literature cannot help reflecting the milieu from which it springs," as Anderson does, he is struck by diversity of style in the work of the regional poets with which he is familiar—as Anderson is in the work of O'Hara, John Ashbery, and James Schuyler, "original" members of the so-called New York School. No wonder Jonathan Williams ("O dear o dear, R.K., I fear you have asked the wrong poet"), in response to my questionnaire, cited lines from another poet, Robert Creeley: "There is no such thing as place, except as it exists within a given man."

Of course one way the notion of place survives is when it is qualified, as here by Picano: "I don't think geographical location means much in poetry . . . but *social* location does." And as if to illustrate Picano's point, here is veteran New York poet, librettist, and publisher Kenward Elmslie: "N.Y.C. was great because of the special friendships possible in it—with Frank O'Hara, John Ashbery, et cetera. Jimmy Schuyler too. And certain painters like Alex Katz. And Joe Brainard. Anne Waldman. Vermont is great (half-a-year at a time) because of the extreme isolation and independence this gives me. Not only is there no gay scene involving other poets, there's NO scene—at least none I'm part of."

None of the tags in my questionnaire escaped scrutiny, qualification, or criticism by some poet or critic. Least of all did the combination term *gay poetry*. At least with *East Coast, gay,* and *poetry* (taken singularly) there was little problem of definition. Everyone seems to agree about where the East Coast is! Is poetry "gay" when it's written by a gay man about his "personal life" (as Joe Brainard implies), on gay subjects or themes (Picano), or when it's addressed to a gay audience (critic Robert Martin)? Definitions abounded and often determined a writer's embrace or rejection of the phrase. So Elmslie, who thinks he "would have to write much more about sex" than he does to be considered a gay poet, feels he is a "poet, period." And Anderson "can't help being a gay poet" because a gay man who writes poetry *is* one, in his view, "no matter what themes" he may explore.

The sands kept shifting around me, or self-definitions did. Was some pattern emerging? I noticed this: how often discussion of the subject of "gay poetry" elicited statements of commitment—to something or other. The something was culture. Poet Alfred Corn's responsibility is to "writing," he said, no matter what labels or rubrics others applied to his work; for Corn, furthermore, "if you place constraints of any sort on an artist, you weaken the enspiriting example of self-realization that surely has been at the heart of all liberation movements." The other was politics. Schreiber's calling himself a "gay poet" is a "political statement and an affirmation of [himself] as a member of an oppressed minority," which has the advantage of "freeing a writer not to have to worry about the issue, from pronouns to anything else" in his life.

Two opposing positions seemed to define themselves in the carpet of my correspondence, constituting, I would suggest, that carpet's emerging "figure," which depicted a conflict between politics and art. Concerning the root of the problem, poet critics Shively and McClatchy—one with a Ph.D. from Harvard, the other with one from Yale—are not far apart. (Schreiber: "Be wary of academics with theories, however.") McClatchy thinks a "gay artist is put into an unusual relationship with the English language, whose diction, syntax, and range is heterosexual, like most of our literary heritage." Here is Shively on language's "heterosexual" diction and syntax:

> Grammarians instruct us that every sentence is composed of a subject and a predicate. Basically the subject fucks the object; fucking (the verb of action) is the most important part of the sentence. Everything in the sentence is subordinate to this fucking. Adjectives are considered inconsequential ornaments, and careful (male) writers are warned to use them sparingly if they don't want to appear faggy or effeminate. Likewise, avoid adverbs and anything gaudy. With objects or lesser indirect objects you can do anything you want; the more forceful your thrust the better. "Simple" sentence structure is considered the most manly form in American construction. And you are advised to avoid the passive voice at all costs. Concentrate on the action: Dick runs; Sally is watching; and no dykes or faggots appear. (Puff is actually a drag queen, but that too has been suppressed.)

Thus far, McClatchy and Shively just might find areas of agreement, but they soon diverge. Here is Shively: "To be free, faggots must destroy the very language we speak and write. Because that language (and the culture it embodies) are at the very core oppressive and heterosexual." Where Shively counsels subversion ("linguistic terrorism"), McClatchy sees a creative challenge: "Any poet learns to twist language for expressive purposes; for a gay artist this is a more difficult and exhilarating business." Shively, whose remarks along with much of his poetry are in the counterculture periodical *Fag Rag* (see Fall 1978) and are specifically addressed to a gay audience, is convinced that conventional art encourages racism and sexism and that "we faggots need to avoid traditional forms altogether and keep searching among the avant-garde works for ways out of the linguistic binds." But for McClatchy, whose "Establishment" credentials are impressive, "unless poetry by gays identifies itself with the imagination and with the major traditions of English verse—instead of with a political struggle or soft-core literalism—there is no chance of its surviving, or of revising any reader's sense of what poetry can do and see and feel."

Both of these positions reflect real fears: of being culturally absorbed (Shively), of being historically erased (McClatchy). And both reflect disturbing risks taken. The risk of a political art is that it will no longer *be* art. In his often reprinted 1975 essay on "The Poetry of Male Love," Ian Young is not so much a "linguistic terrorist" as Shively, but he admires the new poets of "gay liberation" for tending to "identify more with the gay community than with the literary community" and for being "in the main more interested" in what Young calls "a life-oriented poetry than in academism, technical 'experimentation' for its own sake, or purely literary concerns." But according to sociologist Peter Berger in *Facing Up to Modernity*,[4] when members of a youth culture, in order not to be complicit in a corrupt "system," become permanent members of a counterculture and forgo "the higher positions in modern society," what results is "downward social mobility" for the dropouts and "room at the top" for someone else. Are some gay poets, too, in the interest of a "correct" politics and a new gay community, deserting the "purely literary" field and forgoing niches in literary history like those a perhaps less politically savvy past generation of poets, our pre-Stonewall poets, have secured for themselves? Martin, for one, thinks that "gay poetry written for gays alone is the stuff of Consciousness Raising—probably very useful but not really art." More poignant still is the vision of gay poets deserting literary fields for a "community" that may not be there! McClatchy tells of recently meeting

> a gay poet from San Francisco. He is frank, sweet, committed. He has publised a book of poems—wistful lyrics, with no capital letters, and line-drawings of demure rimmings and flowered crotches. (In other words, like most gay-identified poetry written today, it smacks of the '40's. Auden had enough sense to compose his "Platonic Blow" in light verse—and then to suppress it!) The poet had also written a play—based, he said, on The Street ("the only true gay community"). When the play was produced,

he offered free tickets to the hustlers on whom he'd based his characters. None showed up—and he is still, sadly, perplexed. That is because he, like too many gay poets, does not recognize his true audience, or confuses it with his "material."

On the other hand, the risk in a "pure" literature is that it will pass over political realities. In his pathbreaking book *The Homosexual Tradition in American Poetry*, Robert Martin claims gay poets "have no longer felt an impetus to establish a connection between their sexuality and their political views" because "being homosexual is no longer likely to make one lose one's job."[5] "While this may have resulted in a loss of political fervor," Martin concludes, "it has also meant an extension of the forms of gay poetry." Literary concerns—an "extension of the forms"—are thus linked to a diminished need for surveillance. But here is McClatchy, putting us on political guard and divorcing us from "purely literary" concerns *again*, perhaps despite himself:

> I taught at Yale, in the English Department, for several years. One expects a certain percentage of gays in any English Department—or rather one counts on them: they're usually the best teachers. At Yale, with an English Department of nearly a hundred, there were three gays on its faculty, and I was the only one out. That statistic says something about a hiring (and firing) policy. I know, not just because of the statistic but because I tried to propose a course called "Homosexuality and Literature." Oh, I eventually taught the course, and it was duly listed in the catalogue. . . . it took me *two years* to fight through committee-opposition to get the course approved—and, some years later, after I'd been let go by Yale, I was told by sympathetic insiders, that my being gay (or, in their words, "pushy about it") got me canned. One is glad to be gone from such an atmosphere—*and* glad to know why. I wouldn't want to pretend it isn't tough on all sorts of people, but I'd still insist that it's easier to *be* cruel to gays.

Shively, I would say, is more solicitous of his "gayness" than he is of the full resources of poetry, while McClatchy's defense of poetry might be at the expense of some radical implications—*in his work*—of "gayness." (Unless every break with silence is itself radical!) "I have written gay poems," McClatchy says, "but I am *not* a gay poet. Some poems are 'responsible' to my sexuality, many others are not. All of them, I hope, are responsible to language and form." Of course the phrase *gay poet* is not entirely fissionable: none of my correspondents defend only one and not the other of its constituent terms. Corn, who has reason to believe heterosexual readers find his poems "useful," is "very much in favor of gay liberation," while Eberly, who writes "first for a gay audience," doesn't see that commitment as literarily disruptive: for him the term *gay poetry* is a "political term, not a creative or critical one." Certain questions, however, continue to be answered in opposite ways: Should poetry sacrifice its traditional "universality" for a political commitment? Must poetry not reflect the light to which "gay liberation" has opened our eyes? The confrontation between politics and art, I would argue, is one that Stonewall has only intensified for gay men writing poetry on the East Coast. It may even have occasioned two *separate* poetries, audiences, and lines of access to publication. Ed Hermance, the proprietor of Giovanni's Room, Philadelphia's gay bookstore, writes about his city's "two-tiered" gay poetry scene:

> On top is a goodly group of people who would prefer to be called poets. For whatever reasons they don't like to read for specifically gay audiences, and they prefer that their books appear in the feminist rather than in the lesbian and gay section of our bookstore. They help run *The American Poetry Review, The Painted Bride Quarterly*, and the *Philadelphia Poets Newsletter*. They review for the *Philadelphia Inquirer, The New York Times*, et cetera. A lot of them are in my opinion very good. They even write gay poetry. . . . The more fundamental tier is formed of the rabble-rousers and movement people.

What hope is there that the two tiers will become one? Not much. Nor is it required. There is, however, a surprising area of agreement. Shively thinks "the introduction and selections of Louise Bernikow's anthology *The World Split Open* should encourage anyone trying to write poetry outside the straitjacket. Bernikow includes selections from Blues singers Ma Rainey, Bessie Smith, Ida Cox & Memphis Minnie." And he adds: "What would John Wieners or Frank O'Hara be without Billie Holiday?" What were the influences on McClatchy's poetry? "Milton, Keats, Crane, Stevens, Merrill, Hollander, Corn. And singers too, like Billie Holiday." Indeed, according to White,

> in self-styled "gay poetry," no matter where it's written in America today, there are striking similarities of tone, design, subject matter. The gay poem is most often a love lyric, addressed to the

beloved—a confession or an avowal or a lament or an elegy. The most influential models seem to me the early love poems of Auden and the Rae Dalven translations of Cavafy and the lyrics of pop songs, especially sad old ballads of the Billie Holiday variety.

Perhaps that is the place to start, or to keep going: with Lady Day, the woman in us all. With Billie Holiday and with the dedication and enthusiasm of Jack Anderson: "It is often difficult to write of gay themes without sounding mannered, awkward, hesitant, 'dirty,' preachy, or merely 'camp.' Yet to try to find a vocabulary and to build a gay poetic tradition can be a very exciting and necessary undertaking. Certainly, if this derives from a post-Stonewall gay 'Renaissance,' then I am proud to be even a small part of it."

West by Steve Abbott

"A gay poem is a poem that sleeps with other poems." Chuckling over this tongue-in-cheek definition by William Barber a few years ago, I began thinking of the deeper questions it raised. Does such a thing as "gay poetry" actually exist, and, if so, what is it? To what extent, if any, have gay poets helped shape the social or imaginative identity of the West Coast gay community?

Over thirty gay poets—young and old, men and women, and representing a cross section of ethnic backgrounds—responded to these questions with a great diversity of viewpoints. Harold Norse, termed "the American Catullus" by an earlier *Advocate* critic, feels gay poetry definitely does exist and that its role is "to affirm the reality and naturalness of homoerotic love."

Lyn Lonidier, whose first book was entitled *Lesbian Estate*, says, "I think we must now create a whole new vocabulary that goes beyond categories such as gay and straight, feminist and sexist." Today Lonidier calls herself an "allsexual." Lesbian poet and publisher Noni Howard tends to agree: "Most gay writing fails because it doesn't have the qualities of universal art. With a few exceptions, such as Judy Grahn, Adrienne Rich, James Broughton, and Robert Duncan, gay poetry is sectarian and deals only with its own issues."

Responds Robert Gluck: "That's like saying to Isaac Bashevis Singer,

'Isaac, how about some Gentile stories?' Better to start with the experience of our own community. Then, through this experience, we bring in the rest of the world. If there is a universal, that's how good writing gets to it."

Aaron Shurin, one of the founders of gay male poetry in the early 1970s, sees not just one kind of poetry today but many. "Diversity is the key to our evolutionary strength," Shurin says. "I'm part of the gay community, but I'm part of many other communities as well. I think my writing reflects this." But before we can explore the diversity of gay poetry in 1982 or speculate on its future directions, we must first consider its long, rich history.

Few walking past the Sunset library in San Francisco would recognize the name Charles Warren Stoddard carved in its stone facade. Stoddard was a poet protégé of Bret Harte in the 1870s and later a secretary for Mark Twain. One of America's first openly homoerotic writers, Stoddard carried on a lively correspondence with Walt Whitman.

Although Whitman never came west himself, he gave warm encouragement to young avant-garde feminist and homosexual writers who did. Homosexual? Actually, no positive term for same-sex love existed in Whitman's day, so in *Democratic Vistas* he attempted to create one. "Adhesive love," he called it, "that fervid comradeship . . . at least rivaling the amative love hitherto possessing imaginative literature, if not going beyond it."

Though Whitman's vocabulary never caught on (the term *gay* later appeared in a story published in 1926 by lesbian poet Gertrude Stein, born in Oakland), he prophetically realized that those inclined to same-sex love were a nascent community and, as a counterpart to heterosexuals, were necessary for "the spiritual health of America's democracy." Whitman sang the beauties of same-sex love in his own poetry and exerted great influence on later West Coast gay poets such as Duncan, Norse, and Thom Gunn, to name a few.

Elsa Gidlow wrote openly of lesbian love in the 1920s, but even as late as the early 1950s, when lesbian and homosexual poets such as Duncan, Broughton, Madeline Gleason, Jack Spicer, and Robin Blaser wrote openly of their sexuality, there was still no thought of this being "gay poetry." "I remember Robert Duncan wearing eye make-up and jewelry in those days," Broughton recalls, "but 'gay poetry'? We just didn't think in those terms. We were just writing about our lives."

This was after Duncan's controversial essay "The Homosexual in Society" had appeared in the magazine *Politics* in answer to charges that his poetry was somehow "unmanly." Duncan had grown up in Bakersfield, California, attended UC Berkeley, and lived for a time in New York City, where he was part of Anais Nin's circle. He returned to California and became one of the leaders of the San Francisco Renaissance poetry movement.

As always, West Coast poetry was more experimental, bold, and sexually open than that back east. Duncan was the first to use the word *cocksucker* in a poem. In 1955 his play *Faust Foutu* was performed at Gallery Six; the script called for Duncan to strip naked as he delivered lines such as these:

> . . . In the wet hairy pits of sweat I address you, in the meaty, fruity, fish-sopping odours of sex, I adore you. By cunt, by mouth, by cock, by ass-hole I invoke you. Eternal sexual garden. By suck, by lick, by taste, by tongue, by smell, by nose, by sweat, by piss, by spittle, by shit, O eternal Magician of the ages, I invoke you. . . .

Duncan claims that when Allen Ginsberg saw the play he got the idea to strip during readings of his own poem *Howl*, which was first read at Gallery Six a year later.

More than anyone else, perhaps, Ginsberg thrust homosexuality onto the map of public consciousness in America. *Howl* exploded poetry out of small bohemian salons and into court (the first printed edition of the poem was seized by the police for being obscene) and finally into the pages of *Life* magazine. In the mid 1960s, he traveled through India, Europe, and much of America giving poetry readings.

In 1967, as the editor of a campus literary magazine, I invited Ginsberg to the University of Nebraska in Lincoln for a reading. Over five thousand people crammed into the Student Union Ballroom to hear him, many of them fraternity jocks just looking for a reason to stomp this "dope-smoking, antiwar, fag poet." Ginsberg completely won them over.

Never again would I think of poetry as boring or irrelevant. Never again would I equate homosexuality with cowardice. Despite the guilt over his sexuality implied in some of his writing, the image of Ginsberg bravely facing down that crowd of macho thugs with nothing but the sincerity and beauty of his words would later give me the courage to come out publicly myself.

Meanwhile, San Francisco was giving birth to a new movement, the hippies. *Vanguard*, edited by Keith St. Clair in the Haight-Ashbury neighborhood, and *Sebastian Quill*, edited by Jim Mitchell in the Western Addition, appeared briefly to celebrate poems of same-sex love. Then, in 1969, *Manroot* was born, and in 1970 *Gay Sunshine*. Both went on to become internationally famous presses for gay writing.

Following the 1969 Stonewall riots in New York City, self-proclaimed "gay poets" across urban America began working collectively in gay liberation groups. In Wolf Creek, Oregon, *RFD*, a magazine for gay men living in the country, appeared. Lesbian magazines and presses also flourished: *The Ladder, Country Women, Calyx, Sinister Wisdom, The 13th Moon*, Diana Press, and Shameless Hussy Press are just a few.

In San Francisco itself, Paul Mariah became the crusading voice for "gay poetry" in the late 1960s and early 1970s. Tede Matthews and lesbian poet Pat Parker remember Mariah as a significant gay voice in the Bay Area poetry scene. Being more spread out geographically, Los Angeles had no concentrated poetry community in the early 1970s, but Leland Hickman remembers Joseph Hansen, Robert Peters, and George Drury Smith (who had just started Beyond Baroque) as poets who emphasized gay content in their work.

The zenith of West Coast gay male poetry occurred in the mid to late 1970s. On the occasion of his second gay poetry anthology, *Orgasms of Light*, Winston Leyland filled Glide Memorial Church for a Gay Sunshine Benefit. Along with established poets such as Ginsberg and Norse, younger gay poets such as Gluck and Dennis Cooper, who had just started his *Little Caesar* magazine in Los Angeles, riveted the crowd of over one thousand.

Lesbian poets such as Grahn and Susan Griffin, who read separately from men at this time, drew large, enthusiastic crowds of women to their readings. Said Grahn at the Left Write Conference in San Francisco last year: "Left organizations were hopelessly sexist. [We] joined women's consciousness-raising groups, but when discussion of our lesbianism paralyzed our straight sisters, we dropped out and . . . formed, defined, and acted out lesbian separatism. For the first time we had a voice of our own and we used it loud and clear. We were a mixture of races and classes and used separatism as a *tool*, not as a way of life."

San Francisco gay readings in the late 1970s began to include lesbians and gay men on the same lineup, but not without some discussion. Margaret Sloan strongly criticized a "drag" poem read by Matthews at a gay benefit organized during the fight against the Briggs initiative. Duncan and Karen Brodine defended Matthews' poem. A year later, pandemonium broke loose at a gay reading organized by Howard and David Emerson Smith over a poem read by Norse. Norse was accused of being racist and imperialist.

"I'll admit I didn't have a very highly developed feminist consciousness in some of my earlier poetry," Norse says, "but I've never been racist or imperialist." Anyone who knows the whole of his work or has looked carefully at the poem in question would have to agree. Equally disturbing is a recent effort by a group of white socialists in Los Angeles to get Grahn's *Work of a Common Woman* removed from the Los Angeles Public Library on the grounds that the book is racist. Lesbian poets of color have rightfully come to Grahn's defense.

In the early 1970s, the lesbian and gay community found it necessary to confront greater American society with one voice; the militant "gay is good" theme in poetry was perhaps a historic necessity. Now that the gay and lesbian movements have grown more powerful, gay and lesbian writers are exploring and emphasizing greater diversity.

While this is positive, in that it gives poets more leeway to examine what being gay or being human means, it also makes it more difficult for gay writers to reach their audience. A strong network of women's centers and bookstores has kept lesbian poets in touch with their audience, for example, allowing Rich to draw over one thousand people to a recent reading she gave in San Francisco, but many gay male presses and magazines have either folded or have had to cut back on the amount of poetry they publish.

Both younger and older gay poets express concern about this. Says poet-critic Robert Peters: "At one time I thought gays would be attentive to their own culture as a manifestation of superior gifts. But I don't see that that has happened. Few turn up at poetry readings. Books of gay poetry don't sell well—stack sales up against *Meat* and *Flesh*, for example." Peters notes that while there's a vibrant gay student group at UC Irvine, only one or two gay men enrolled in his gay lit course. Most who attended were straight women.

Avotcja, a black lesbian poet whose first book, *Ache*, is forthcoming from Howard's New World Press, feels the main support for her work comes from the Latino and black communities. "I'm not sure I can depend on white gays," Avotcja says. Part of the reason for this is racism, she feels, and part because of "self-hatred on the part of many gays."

Notes Los Angeles poet Peter Cashorali, "My general impression is that nobody reads poetry or is even aware that it's a form that contains life." At the same time Cashorali feels a poem celebrating cruising or gay domestic life should make gays "feel more substantial to read about their private lives." Brodine agrees, adding: "Coming from a rural background, I was in isolation until I discovered there were words for my feelings, and thus my feelings could become real."

Arizona poet/editor Will Inman concurs. "We need to help homosexuals get beyond guilt and low self-esteem," he says, but he fears the "suicide" of gay ghettoization as an equal danger. "I'm afraid I feel there's as much selfishness and narrowness among gays as among any other element in society. Urging emphasis on our differentness more than on our humanity only plays along with our emptiness."

Gay poets have attempted to solve the problem of audience by creating new groupings or audiences within the greater gay community, by connecting to sympathetic nongay audiences, or both.

Cooper, whose first book *Idols* was a poetry best-seller, has brought together a post-Stonewall generation of poets in his magazine *Little Caesar* and his anthology *Coming Attractions*. Publishing younger East Coast poets as well as older, famous, nongay poets whom Cooper likes, *Little Caesar* also features spunky essays on rock music and film. But Cooper still believes gay poets have a duty to build community, and he is thinking of starting a reading series in the hustler section of Hollywood known as Boystown.

Aleida Rodriguez and Jacqueline di Angelis have teamed up to give a voice to lesbian poetry in Los Angeles with their exceptional magazine *rara avis*. Along with Eloise Klein Healy and others, they put on events at the Women's Building in downtown Los Angeles. Paul Monette, Clifton Snider, and Gavin Dillard are among the gay male poets active in the Los Angeles area.

In San Francisco, Matthews and Randy Johnson helped found Mainstream Exiles, a collective of lesbian and gay artists, musicians, and poets. Besides sponsoring readings, art shows, and workshops, they plan to publish a poetry anthology soon. Matthews also runs a reading series at Modern Times Bookstore, which features a large number of lesbian and gay poets.

Eric Allyn recently advertised another gay writers' network in Bay Area gay papers. Over forty people have attended its first four meetings at the Valencia Rose Cafe. Subgroups meet to discuss play writing and fiction as well as poetry; according to Loren Rhoads, about fifteen people attend the poetry subgroup. Some network members have attended workshops that aren't manifestly gay, but "when you have gay theme pieces, it's more comfortable to discuss them in a gay group," Rhoads says. Groups that support lesbian poets include the Feminist Writer's Guild and the Women Writer's Union.

Other gay poets prefer working alone and don't care to center their writing around the subject of sexuality. Ronald Johnson is one such in San Francisco; Robert Crosson another in Los Angeles. "I am cautious," says Crosson. "I distrust politics, any politics. I am suspicious of fashion. Gay rights is imperative. That has nothing to do with poetry. Poetry to me is a private affair."

Gunn would more or less agree. While some of his poetry concerns gay subject matter and he has given several interviews to gay publications, Gunn prefers not to be labeled as "a gay poet for the same reason I don't want to be labeled a nature poet or a city poet. I'm an everything poet."

Whether working alone or in groups, West Coast gay poets are exploring many new forms and directions. "The gay poet is the keeper of mythology and also the theorist of the future," says Jim Washington, who has performed his work to music. "Some poets have the ability to imbue personal symbols with a mysterious perfume projecting new connections."

Some of the new connections are political, and some involve technology and theater. Shurin, Steve Benson, and Richard Irwin have incorporated slides, film, tape recorders, music, spontaneous raps, or theatrical settings to extend their poetry beyond the format of the "traditional reading." Irwin has become an important promotor of performance art in the Bay area.

Bruce Boone, however, thinks the devices of Postmodernism, if "not rooted in the social origins of language" are often ambiguous. "The point is not to speak *for* but *through* one's community," Boone said in a

recent interview in *City Arts Monthly.* Boone feels the new project for
gay writers is to incorporate "the aspirations and indignations of those
with whom [we are] engaged in an ongoing dialogue."

Randy Johnson thinks "lesbian and Third World gay poets will be
heard more in the future" and notes "the increasing exploration of
eroticism" in lesbian writing. Brodine also foresees "an increased forging of connections" between radical feminists, feminist men, and
writers of color. "Only in activism, in a willingness to stand together
on the picket line, have our words of courage taken the substantial,
real edge. I think it could happen a whole lot more." Peters sees a "vast
improvement in poetry by gays. It used to be that much of it sounded
like insipid high-school boy turn-on stuff."

Despite the advances gay poetry has made in recent years, homophobia and even censorship from straight critics and editors are still a
problem. Almost all lesbian and gay writers I talked to had experienced
at least one such incident.

While openly gay writers such as Grahn, Ginsberg, Aleida Rodriguez, and Peter Orlovsky have received NEA grants, most have not.
When Bruce Boone queried NEA as to why he was denied a grant, two
of the four panelists judging his work alluded to its homosexual content. One comment read: "Very well written story about the breakup of
a love affair which we learn halfway through is a homosexual one.
Unfortunately, it is at that point the broad appeal a narrative such as
this one might have becomes severely limited." The sole criterion for
the awarding of grants is supposed to be "the literary quality of the
manuscript submitted."

Houghton-Mifflin wanted a manuscript from Leland Hickman, but
when they saw more of his work, they decided it was "too sexual" (90
percent of the material was gay, says Hickman). When Hickman's
Great Slave Lake Suite came out from Momentum Press, it was nominated by the *Los Angeles Times* for a poetry prize in the 1980 Book
Prizes. The book later received several homophobic reviews, inspiring
Cashorali to comment, "Whenever I hear heterosexuals talking about
gays, I have visions of peasants with pitchforks."

David Trinidad has never been physically threatened at a reading, as
Hickman has, but he says that once, when he was reading poems on
the radio, a woman phoned the radio station and complained his
poems were obscene. "As I hadn't used any of the words ordinarily

considered obscene," Trinidad says, "I assume it was the subject matter—in this case gay—that she considered offensive."

But most gay poets refuse to be intimidated by homophobia. Says
Native American Paula Gunn Allen: "I get homophobia and racist
responses and all sorts of crap, but I get even more empowerment and
validation from those audiences/editors who hear me and use my work
in their lives, criticism, and classes." Cooper finds his work "is taken
pretty seriously on its own terms by straights, that the sex in the poems
seems universal"; he adds that he feels "gratified and honored by letters
I've gotten from young gays who've said that *Idols* had a profound effect
on their self-acceptance as gays."

Despite all the difficulties and aesthetic disagreements, gay poets
will no doubt continue to write, and San Francisco and Los Angeles
will no doubt continue to be the major centers of writing and publishing activity for West Coast gay and lesbian poets. In the words of Aaron
Shurin: "Gay poetries will continue as long as the issue of homosexuality remains embattled in the society at large, which will probably be
a long time. After that there will only be poetry. Ultimately we have a
community of souls, or hearts, and the poet's light lights up matters of
deep integrity in living. The free reign of the imagination can only
further unlock all [closet] doors."

Update 1985

Much has happened in Bay Area gay poetry since I wrote this
survey. A number of new gay magazines have surfaced. My own, *Soup*, while
not exclusively gay, has featured interviews, poems, and fiction by numerous
West Coast poets such as Robert Duncan, Robert Gluck, Dennis Cooper,
Karen Brodine, and others. *Soup 3*, a translation issue, brought forward the
work of gay writing pioneers René Crevel (France) and Eric Muhsam (Germany) to an English reading audience for the first time.

In 1983, Bryan Monte began *No Apologies*, which connected new and
older Bay Area gay writers to Vancouver poets formerly of Jack Spicer's circle
(for example, Robin Blaser, George Stanley). Also, the work of lesbian poets
Dodie Bellamy, Judy Grahn, and Marilyn Hacker appeared along with that of
gay male writers.

When Monte won a graduate creative writing fellowship to Brown University and moved his magazine back east, his associate editor Kevin Killian

began *Mirage*. Issue one was a festschrift to John Weiners on the legendary poet's fiftieth birthday and in celebration of his *Collected Poems* (Black Sparrow) edited by Raymond Foye. Dodie Bellamy guest edited an issue on new experimental writing by women.

Sam D'Allessandro is typical of the new, younger gay writers in that he works in both poetry and prose. His narratives have a cinematic rather than lineal or logocentric drive. "I like to see something that seems definite dissolved by a look from a different angle," D'Allessandro says. "I like people to take stands but I don't like it when they put answers on things that don't have answers."

Notes

1. John d'Emilio, *Sexual Politics, Sexual Communities* (Chicago: 1983).
2. *Advocate*, May 13, 1982.
3. Edmund White, *States of Desire: Travels in Gay America* (New York: Dutton, 1980).
4. Peter Berger, *Facing Up to Modernity* (New York: Basic Books, 1977).
5. Robert Martin, *The Homosexual Tradition in American Poetry* (Austin: University of Texas Press, 1979).

Breaking Out with the Pen
Poetry in American Prisons

Few experiences are as jarring as legal incarceration. Stripped by the state of your possessions, isolated from contact with the everyday world, you become one virtually reborn—or at least cast into a place which, like Dante's Purgatory, is halfway between your final death and the memories of your former life. There, removed from the familiar sights and sounds of your former life, those memories may take on a life of their own. Small wonder that the experience of prison throughout history has turned men of action into introspective writers, transforming the soldier Cervantes into the creator of Don Quixote and prompting the violent Thomas Malory to recreate the chivalrous dreams of Arthur and his knights. The relatively modern term "penitentiary," in fact, comes from the Quakers' idea that a person isolated in a cell can consider the deeds of his or her life, repent, and change for the better.

Though the prisons of contemporary America are a far cry from both the dungeons of medieval Europe and that first concept of the penitentiary as a collection of monastic cells, they are still separate realities from the American culture most of us know. Although there is a great deal of truth in the old prison maxim that "Everything you can find on the street—from drugs and booze to sex—can be found in the joint," it is also true that none of those things are quite the same in a prison as they are on the street. Even a good part of the everyday language spoken by men and women behind bars differs from that of the majority society, though that majority society continually is absorbing (in small doses) words and phrases which originate in the constantly changing body of prison slang. While teaching writing workshops in an upstate New York prison in the late 1970s I helped Michael Baynard, one of my inmate students, put together a small dictionary of prison slang. Here are a few entries:

> *Ace:* nickname for a male. Best friend; a first-rate person; one's lover.
>
> *Ain't got one of somethin' and two of nothin':* I have no money.
>
> *A shot (or "A shot at life"):* chance to make parole.
>
> *Bogart (used as a verb):* to forcibly take something, to bully, to act in a forceful manner.
>
> *Booty Bandit:* a man who craves intercourse with boys.
>
> *Bozo-fro:* an Afro hair-do with a bald spot in the center caused by hair loss.
>
> *Back up and live:* a profound threat.
>
> *Box:* carton of cigarettes; food package sent to someone in prison; tape player.
>
> *San Dusty:* death. (San Dusty Express: instant death.)
>
> *Sap Rap:* words which sound good but have no real meaning.
>
> *Short:* a car; a cigarette.
>
> *Skid bid:* a "short" sentence. (In city jails, a year or less. In state prisons, five years or less.)
>
> *Slam:* prison.

As those random samples indicate, the world within the walls is a complex and often violent one. It is, especially when one considers the current images of law-breakers which we see each day in the newspapers, in the movies, and on TV, hardly a place where one might expect to find poets.

Poetry, however, sent me to prison, not as an inmate, but as a teacher. A few months after the infamous Attica riot and massacre of September 1971, I began teaching a workshop at Great Meadow Correctional facility. From the start I found men who were incredibly responsive to contemporary poetry, even though most of them had no previous experience with it. (Of the more than one hundred men who were part of the workshop over the period of eighteen months, ninety percent had never completed high school, nearly all of those with diplomas had received them through High School Equivalency examinations, and only three had ever attended a college class on the outside.) Within a few months, those in my first class were not only reading contemporary poems and responding to them with warm intelligence, they were writing poems themselves that were both powerful and publishable. I was impressed but wondered if I was being objective until I brought in as a guest someone who had just finished teaching at the New School. "These guys are better than the average college class!" he said.

Like most workshops which dozens of other American writers (including Carolyn Forche, Richard Shelton, Galway Kinnell, John Cheever, and Carol Muske) have conducted in prisons throughout the country over the past decade, that first class of mine was an interesting cross-section of prison types and prison life. The only things they had in common were that they had volunteered to take the workshop and they had an intense desire to express themselves. Of the twenty men, four were white and the rest black. Martin, one of the white inmates, was a Jewish anti–Vietnam War activist jailed for trying to bomb a bank. (He would later, after his release from prison, publish an article about his time in prison in *Crawdaddy* magazine.) Another of the white students, Chip, was a drug addict and wrote science fiction poems and stories. The best dramatic poet in the class, Stephen, had belonged to the Black Panthers. Kihiem, who specialized in ironic verse, was doing time for the murder of a policeman. Eight of my students had been at Attica during the riot and four were still recovering from the gunshot wounds they received when the state police stormed the prison, shooting both inmates and hostages alike. (I still have the rough manuscript which Henry, an older black inmate, gave me for safe-keeping. It contains his account of the Attica rebellion and insists in its last pages that he and a group of thirty other level-headed and more mature black inmates were about to retake the prison from the hotheads to free the hostages and hand back control to the guards before "somebody got crazy and people got hurt.")

In the decade and a half since that first workshop I have taught and visited writing workshops in prisons from Maine to California and corresponded with many serious, dedicated writers in prison from every state in the Union. I have read, published, and helped place in other books and magazines hundreds of poems by inmate and ex-inmate writers. I've compared notes with other writers who've conducted workshops in correctional facilities and found that all of us discovered certain things to be true about the effect of contemporary poetry on people in our prisons. Poetry often deeply touches their lives as soon as they begin to read it. When they begin to write it, poetry becomes an act of personal liberation and a validation, not just of their creativity but of their essential humanity, a humanity diminished or denied by incarceration. "When I'm writing poetry," one of my first inmate students said to me, "I'm not in prison." For some inmates, in fact, poetry has been a means to change their lives. Although talent—whether in prison or in the outside world—is neither a guarantee of success nor some sort of indication of moral virtue, there does seem to be some positive correlation between involvement in writing workshops while in prison and success in returning to society and staying straight after being released from jail. Reformation and personal virtue aside, some of the most powerful poetry I have seen in the last ten years has come out of prisons and has been written by men and women who had no experience with and no interest in poetry prior to being jailed. It may be that, contrary to the dictum that "poetry makes nothing happen," reading and writing poems is a powerful force for bringing out the hidden creative potential, for transformation and growth.

It is, of course, ironic that poetry should be so popular in our prisons. We live in a time which has been described as "post-literate." Television (which is found in prisons, too) has taken the place of reading. Commercial publishers are generally uninterested in poetry. Thus, it may come as a shock to hear that men and women labelled as dangers to society, people who never completed high school in most cases, are deeply committed to both the reading and the writing of contemporary poetry. But it is true. From 1973 to 1985, my wife, Carol, and I operated a program (supported, until the Reagan Era, by the National Endowment for the Arts) which sent donated literary magazines and books of poetry to prison inmates on request. Every six weeks mailings went to over five hundred inmates all over the country on an ever-changing mailing list. We received back thousands of letters (and poems) from them. Here are a few excerpts from some of the letters in our archive which spoke directly of the effect of poetry on their lives:

> I never knew this world [poetry] existed. May Allah bless you for letting me know about it. (Salaam A., Florida State Prison, 1974)

> The books of poetry you sent me have become a lifeline to sanity. (Michael P., Walla Walla State Prison, 1978)

> I'm beginning to see, through poetry, that there are still people in America who care, who won't see me as an animal or sub-human. (Jose L., Marion Federal Prison, 1980)

Certain forms of poetry, though this may not be generally known, have been present in American prisons for many decades. The most common is the "toast," a storytelling, usually humorous poem. These long, memorized toasts are rhymed and syncopated. They are closely connected to Afro-American oral traditions but were recited by black and white inmates alike throughout the United States (although the toast tradition seems to now be dying out in prisons). In a sense, these poems are a sort of prison oral history. They tell of tricksters (some-times human, like Shine, sometimes animal, like the Signifying Monkey) who are able to survive by using guile and down-home com-mon sense to deceive those more powerful but less clever. The best-known of America's contemporary poets who began writing while in prison is Etheridge Knight. His first book, *Poems from Prison*, was pub-lished in 1968 and praised by Gwendolyn Brooks as "a major an-nouncement." A veteran of the Korean War, he became addicted to drugs as a result of the morphine he was given while recovering from his wounds and eventually ended up in prison. He began writing his poems in jail before the advent of prison writing workshops, and the influence of the toast tradition can be seen in his work. His poem "I Sing of Shine" (anthologized in Dudley Randall's landmark 1971 an-thology from Bantam, *The Black Poets*) is a direct tribute to the hero of numerous toasts, Shine, the black man whom folk traditions say sur-vived the sinking of the Titanic by being smart enough to swim. It begins with these lines:

> And, yeah, brothers,
> while white/america sings about the unsink
> able molly brown
> (who was hustling the titanic
> when it went down)

> I sing to thee of Shine
> the stoker who was hip
> enough to flee the fucking ship . . .

At this writing, only one major critical study has been published on contemporary writing from American prisons. First published in 1978, *Prison Literature in America* by H. Bruce Franklin traces inmate writing directly back to the slave narratives. The prison, Franklin says, is just a modern version of the slave ship and the plantation. Michael Hogan, a brilliant ex-inmate poet and critic who began writing in the 1970s in the Arizona State Prison workshops taught by Richard Shelton, disagrees with at least part of Franklin's contention. In his article "Some Further Observations on the Convict as Author," published in *New Letters* in 1979, Hogan points out that Franklin's thesis seems to leave out the large part of the prison population which is not black. Writing from prison, Hogan says, is not just a reaction to slavery. It is more complicated than that. In some ways, prisons are a microcosm of American society. The experiences which shape the perceptions of the inmate poet are not that different from those encountered in majority culture. The inmate poet, though, is more clearly on the cutting edge. What is done today to us in the prisons, Hogan says, may be done tomorrow to those of you who think yourselves to be "free."

While in prison, Hogan edited a superb anthology of poems from the Arizona prisons, *Do Not Go Gentle* (Blue Moon Press, 1977). In his introduction to the book he said:

> Many of these strong and beautiful poems have appeared previously in magazines and chapbooks. But I see these poems primarily as weapons of psychic survival and only incidentally as good literature. Each man represented in these pages fought to preserve his identity, his existential wonder, his joy at being alive in the world, his rage at being imprisoned. In doing so he gave courage to others who might have abandoned the fight, might have succumbed as so many before them had, to the darkness of not seeing, not feeling . . .

The winner, while in prison, of a National Endowment for the Arts Poetry Fellowship, Hogan does not, however, fall into the trap of imagining—as did some of the "revolutionaries" of the 1960s—that all prisoners are noble. One of his closest friends in prison, inmate poet

Charles Schmidt, was murdered by other prisoners who bore him an old grudge. Though his strongest identification is with those locked in, Hogan is still able to see the keepers as human. The following lines from his poem "Spring" show both his clarity of vision and his exact touch with image:

> Ice has been cracking all day
> and small boys on the shore
> pretending it is the booming of artillery
> lie prone clutching imaginary carbines . . .
>
> Old cons shiver in cloth jackets
> as they cross the naked quadrangle.
> They know the inside perimeter is exactly
> two thousand eighty-four steps
> and they can walk it five more times
> before the steam whistle blows for count.
>
> Above them a tower guard dips his rifle
> then raises it again dreamily.
> He imagines a speckled trout
> coming up shining and raging with life.

Two decades ago, before the advent of writing workshops in correctional facilities, most of the published writing from prisons tended to be letters, autobiographies, or novels. Many of those books were written by inmates who wanted to both express themselves and make money. Today, with far more poetry being written in prisons and a good deal of it being published in literary magazines (which usually pay only in copies), the average inmate writer is much less mercenary. In fact (as most poets everywhere know), a major commitment to writing poetry is pretty much a *de facto* statement that you are *not* in it for the money. Unlike the isolated inmate working at night in his cell to hand write a novel (which might end up being confiscated by the warden), many of the prison writers of today are in workshops approved of (if not blessed by) the prison administration and conducted by practicing writers. Interestingly, it appears that the worst prison troublemakers often become the best writers. Further, after entering a workshop, they no longer cause trouble in the prison. In California, where a statistically sound study has proven that arts programs in the prisons are cost-effective because they create a safer and more stable environment in the prison with a consequent decrease in spending for such things as guard overtime, the state department of corrections budgets close to a million dollars a year for arts programs in the prisons. Two years ago, in fact, the warden at San Quentin said something like, "Things are pretty tense down in C Block. Looks like we'd better get a poetry workshop going in there." One result of such prison writing workshops has been to not only channel formerly destructive energy into creative channels, but also to produce writers whose work may sometimes be as polished and professional as that of students in graduate writing programs.

Although many workshops have been terminated or threatened because of funding cuts, there are still long-standing programs continuing in more than a dozen states and new ones being started. In Arizona, workshops in the prisons were begun with state funding and coordinated for years by University of Arizona Professor Richard Shelton, whose own poems sometimes reflect the experiences of teaching in prisons. In Pittsburgh, Pennsylvania, the Academy of Prison Arts was founded by inmate writers, coordinated by a civilian employee of the Western State Penitentiary, and funded through grants from the National Endowment for the Arts. In Maine, workshops were started in the state prison by James Lewisohn, a published poet before his incarceration (he was sent to prison for the shooting of his wife—a death which many facts indicate to have been the result of criminal negligence rather than murder). At Attica Prison in New York State workshops have been offered as part of the college program run within the walls by the Consortium of the Niagara Frontier. Florida, Oklahoma, Texas, South Carolina, Alaska, New Mexico, Connecticut, and Ohio all now have or had in the recent past creative writing workshops in their prisons. Since less than 5 percent of the total U.S. prison population of about half a million are women, the majority of inmate poets who've been published are male. Writing workshops have been made available to women inmates much less frequently than to men, but when such opportunities have arisen women have been quick to respond. Carolyn Baxter, a veteran of Carol Muske's poetry workshops in the Riker's Island Prison, and Diana Bickston, who studied with Pamela Stewart in the workshop in the women's prison in Arizona, both have published books of poetry. Here are a few lines from one of Bickston's poems "For Zorro":

when I read a poem that i feel
like a taste or smell, lingering to be tried once more,
i want to write, as if to answer in mouthfuls
words i could not say . . .

One of the strongest long-standing workshops in an American prison is called "Bright Fires." Founded by Jean Samuel and Sharon Stricker, it still operates in the California Rehabilitation Center for Women. One of several literary magazines published in American prisons, *Poppy*, is edited and published on a yearly basis from the Bright Fires workshops. (Other inmate-edited literary magazines include *Empire* magazine from the Arthur Kill Correctional Facility on Staten Island and *Sentences* from the New Haven, Connecticut, city jail.)

In March of 1980, a graduate student at the University of Colorado, Emmanuel Diel, completed a master's thesis on writers in prison published by the small press and little magazines. His bibliography listed more than seventy individual published volumes and anthologies of poetry by inmates. Today, six years later, that list would be more than twice as long. Of the sixty inmate writers I included in *The Light from Another Country*, my anthology of poetry from American prisons (published in 1985), all had already published individual poems in magazines or anthologies and more than half had published books. Yet almost most every one of those men and women had not written—or read—poetry before entering prison.

Some continue to view the work of writers in prison as little more than a literary curiosity, despite the fact that much of the current poetry from prisons is moving and highly crafted, despite the fact that a large part of the poetic output of American inmates makes no mention of prison and is being published because of its excellence, not its origin. The only fair way to judge the work produced by that varied community of men and women in our nation who have been legally defined as outcasts is to use the same criteria you use to judge all good writing. You may find, as I have found, that there is a special energy in a surprising percentage of the poetry from prisons, that the poems—even when they focus on the specific and narrow details of prison life—are also about *all of us*. You may come to believe—as I do—that if such a community of letters can spring to life in the blighted atmosphere behind the high concrete walls and razor wire, a profusion of poets as unexpected as flowers in a field of glaciers, then there may be hope for us all.

Literary Reputation and the Thrown Voice

In Kingsley Amis' side-splitter *Lucky Jim*, we find the hapless hero agonizing over the first sentence of his unwritten and long-delayed dissertation. "In considering this strangely neglected topic . . ." he writes, but he can get no further. He chants the phrase over and over as he questions whether he really has a topic and whether its neglect is all that strange. His ill-chosen topic, "The Economic Influence of the Development in Ship Building 1450–1485," makes his loss for words understandable, but part of Jim's discomposure lies in approaching a subject from the angle of its neglect. To use this strategy is to cast oneself in the role of the attentive discoverer—the exceptional one who did not neglect—but the approach may easily backfire by strengthening the associations between one's topic and its neglect, especially in the case of the so-called neglected author whose name might be already too well associated with an insufficiency of reputation. Similarly, attempts to elevate an "underground" artist may prove self-defeating. The mere use of the tag may push him deeper into that vaguely subversive netherworld. The hazards of the "neglect approach" may be reduced by first turning attention to the processes by which literary reputation is created or stifled.

Notions of literary neglect and recognition are nettlesome because they involve so many extraliterary factors. Posterity may be viewed as the final arbiter who confers repute according to the criterion of durability, but the reputation of a writer within his own time is calculated by a more complex set of reckonings. More often than not, a writer achieves contemporary reputation when he finds himself situated at a graph-point where talent, cultural fashion, publishing-world pull, and even image all intersect. The possibility of a purely literary determination of reputation is severely reduced by the sociological, cultural, and economic factors at play. Bitterly aware of these complications, Wordsworth remarked that the original poet must "create the taste by which he is to be enjoyed."

The question of poetic reputation today is vexed by public obliviousness to poetry and by the fact of the media-flooded global village which offers the possibility of a scope of recognition unknown to previous ages. Of course, the concern over writerly fame is an ancient one. One of the conventional subjects treated in medieval religious tracts was "pride of authorship," a literary version of the first deadly sin; but until the nineteenth century artistic renown as we think of it today hardly existed, especially among poets. Whatever reputation poets enjoyed was limited to a coterie of upper-class people who were wealthy enough to buy books and educated enough to read them. Only with mass literacy and the growth of a culturally avaricious middle class in the nineteenth century did the possibility of wider recognition arise. No poet before Byron—who said he awoke one morning to find himself famous—luxuriated in what we would call celebrity status. And since then only Tennyson, laureate and favorite of Queen Victoria, achieved in his own lifetime a broader national fame. If poetry continues to be ignored by the public, perhaps no other poet will ever match Tennyson's contemporary renown. What American poet has been lifted by reputation out of the circle of the literati? One thinks of Ginsberg and his beat flamboyance and of Frost reciting at Kennedy's inauguration, the wind almost blowing the pages out of his old hands. Within our celebrity-obsessed culture the desire for fame can become a psychological disorder, a disease of the ego. Andy Warhol's dry prediction that in the future everyone would be famous for fifteen minutes suggests a dystopia in which the mass media's democratic ideal of "equal time" is married to universal narcissism.

At the center of the issue of poetic reputation is the seeming hegemony of that curious phantom which has no address or phone number, the Poetry Establishment. Like other unincorporated establishments (art's, academia's) poetry's is both everywhere and nowhere. It is not composed of a board of directors (though there are boards and committees and prize-granting groups within it), nor does it have an official membership. The closest one can come to locating the Poetry Establishment is to say it is defined by a canon, a body of acknowledged work. Just as the Church and the academic establishment draw a chalk-circle which embraces canonical texts and excludes apocrypha, so too the authority of the Poetry Establishment seems to rest on a body of "authenticated" poets and their works.[1] The canon, of course, is always changing. Works once considered "heretical" (or more often the case with poetry, ignored) sometimes receive an imprimatur. The reverse occurs but less frequently; canonical works are cast out, their authors "defrocked" and consigned to a state of illegitimacy. No work or author can be sure of a tenured position within the institution—remember that Saint Christopher, patron saint of the dashboard, was himself decanonized—and no work or author outside the canon can ever be certain of being admitted. The canon changes—books and authors entering and exiting through revolving doors—by mysterious processes, but a real canon nonetheless exists. Like the Church, the Poetry Establishment honors some of its dead by conferring a kind of sainthood. Lacking England's Poets' Corner in Westminster Abbey where the Greats are interred, this country maintains a Poetry Hall of Fame, invisible but as tightly controlled as the one in Cooperstown. Robert Frost is American poetry's Babe Ruth.

Neglect by the Poetry Establishment becomes its own kind of reputation, the reputation of a poetry-singer for being himself unsung. Poets may become somewhat well known for *not* being well known. This kind of antireputation is bred and maintained within the hyperactive world of Small-Press-Little-Magazine publication whose growing dimensions are reflected by Len Fulton's burgeoning directory. There are many poets active and well known within this literary demimonde, many poets who could be examined as case studies, but the work and reputation of California-based poet Robert Peters seem particularly exemplary. Author of over twenty books of poetry and several volumes of contemporary criticism, an active public reader (whose readings have become theater) and relentless contributor to small periodicals, Peters has established himself as a general among the rank and file of the small press world, but according to a paradoxical formula it is his stature in this world which keeps him from gaining wider acceptance.

There may be a few specialized and almost self-inflicted reasons why a poet of Peters' talent and output has not been "Nortonized"—surely, the Norton anthologizers comprise the closest thing the Poetry Establishment has to a synod. His salty and outspoken criticism, collected in two volumes of *The Great American Poetry Bake-Off*, has acquired a sort of infamy for its reckless iconoclasm and its off-beat, irreverant voice, a style Peters has called "informal and funky." Here he pulls the tails of sacred cows, dismantling their reputations and offering ready insights into their sexual posturings. As a literary columnist for *Margins* Peters used as a by-line "The Big Bad Wolf"—someone waiting to ambush you on your way to grandmother's house and eat all the poems in your basket.

From an establishment point of view, Peters' career presents other embarrassments. Although his first book of poems, a moving and risky elegy on the death of a son, was shot from the big guns of W. W. Norton, Peters used small presses for most of his subsequent volumes. This is a departure from the hierarchical logic by which one is expected to make only upward moves on the ladder, leaving the small presses behind once one has been knighted by a big house. After all, the mayor doesn't run for dog catcher in the next election. What's worse, Peters has committed the unpardonable sin of self-publication in a volume with the uncloseted title *Love Songs for Robert Mitchum*, a collection of hilarious, kinky homoerotic fantasies. Sure, Emerson did it but Emerson was Emerson. Just because no one wants this dance with you doesn't mean you should get up there and dance with yourself.

Another reason why Peters' work has not garnered a wider reputation is the sheer diversity of his output. His books jump through a range of disparate genres, styles, voices, and forms. Turning from one volume to another, the reader has to readjust his compass to a new direction. Such unclassifiable versatility may frustrate readers who expect a steady predictability in their poets. His early works tend to maintain an autobiographical focus. *Songs for a Son* is the response to his child's death which compelled him to begin writing poetry at the age of forty. *Bronchical Tangle, Heart System,* and many poems in *The Sow's Head* revisit Peters' boyhood on a Wisconsin dirt-farm. Here begins one of Peters' most obsessive themes: the betrayal of creatures by their own mortal guts, a theme spelled out in stark biological or, better, visceral language. In a poem about the butchering of a sow,

We shaved her hair,
spun her around, cut off
her feet and knuckles,
hacked off her head
slashed her belly
from asshole down through
bleached fat throat.
Jewels spilled out
crotches of arteries
fluids danced and ran . . .
The liver, steaming, monochrome,
quivered with eyes. [2]

But later Peters abandons autobiography for the unnerving surrealism of *Holy Cow: Parable Poems*, the comic found-poems of *Pioneers of Modern Poetry*, and the literary parodies and burlesques of *The Poet as Ice-Skater*. This almost playful diversity and experimentalism quiets down only in Peters' more recent poetry at the point where he appears to discover his true form. The final section of *The Poet as Ice-Skater*, "Byron Exhumed," is a series of monologues spoken in reaction to Byron's death by a mixture of real and fictitious characters, including a sensitive Harrow schoolboy, Byron's wife, and the church sexton who tends the burial plot. Here Peters begins his work in the form which was to determine the shape and substance of his four subsequent books, the extended biographical monologue. His exploration of this form, which has extended the frontiers of the monologue genre, amounts to a major contribution to the body of American poetry and points to an enlargement of his poetic reputation, his deserved canonization.

The four full-length books in this monologue form are *The Gift to Be Simple*, spoken in the person of Mother Ann Lee, founder of the Shakers; *Ikagnak, the North Wind*, spoken by Elisha Kent Kane, the Arctic explorer; *Hawker*, whose speaker is Robert Stephen Hawker, an eccentric Cornish vicar; and *Picnic in the Snow*, written from the point of view of King Ludwig of Bavaria, the mad castle-builder and patron of Wagner. Enriched by Peters' research into the life and times of his subjects, each work is a series of poems delivered in the voice of the central character.

The intentions behind the use of this form seem similar to those of Browning, whose name is almost synonymous with the genre. Like other Victorians, Browning was reacting against the mode of personal confession which the Romantics before him had conceived and popularized. Browning's own evasion of Romantic directness involved a double maneuver, a retreat into the past (usually the Italian Renaissance), and a rhetorical displacement of the author by a dramatic speaker. Browning's sympathies and preoccupations are detectable in the monologues (he is fascinated with his aesthetic villains and failed artists), but by avoiding direct address he gains a measure of objectivity. Retelling replaces telling. The other replaces the self.

Peters' work within this genre also reflects a dissatisfaction with the limitations of the confessional style and the weary modern "I" who has long dominated the poetic stage. By now the neo-Romanticism of Lowell, Plath, Merrill, and their followers has pushed self-portraiture to the point of exhaustion and has spawned a mob of self-haunted speakers, hypersensitive gadflies relentlessly present in every line. The substitution of a historical speaker for the poet's self provides an escape from the claustrophobic enclosure of his own ego. This is similar to the relief sought by Yeats and Pound in their adoption of masks and personae and by Eliot, who defined poetry as an escape from personality; but in the dramatic-historical monologue, the speaker is both a tone of voice to which the poet ascribes rhetorical independence and the embodiment of an alien consciousness. Peters' speakers are drawn from the nineteenth century, a kind of historical childhood to moderns, and they imply a disaffection with our own age, a period Peters has dubbed "lower-case times," in which capitalized abstractions no longer carry meaning.

The Victorian monologue is a flow of talk which catches a character at a single dramatic juncture. The assumption here is that each moment in a person's life contains his being; each utterance is like a soil sample. Start someone talking and soon you will know his essence, for life is a continuous act of self-revelation and speech is the entrance to the soul. But Peters' expansion of the genre into a sequence of speeches takes into account growth and change. Browning's characters, forever themselves, never change but only stand more revealed, to paraphrase Charles Olson. Peters' characters move through stages of development like characters in novels. Browning's characters are synchronically frozen, often exposing themselves in their first sentence; in Peters' monologues the process is cumulative and accretive. Each poem displays one facet of the gem of being. Speech touches on narrative, poetic biography, verse history.

The first of these monologue books, *The Gift to Be Simple,* traces the life of Mother Ann Lee, daughter of a Manchester blacksmith and founder of the Shakers, that quasi-mystical departure from Quakerism which espoused celibacy, communal sharing of property, virtual economic self-sufficiency, and the public confession of sins. The poems, most of them uttered in her voice, follow Ann Lee's development from her girlhood through her religious involvement, her subsequent persecution and imprisonment, and her seventy-eight-day crossing to America to establish Shaker communities. The poems bring us into contact with a woman who is simple in her piety, tormented by carnality, and heroic in the fervor and spiritual zeal that led her to believe she was the Female Christ. What makes this contact so direct and evocative is the employment of a language rinsed of modern usage and faithful to the vocabulary and idiom of the times. Many poems have an almost nursery-rhyme simplicity:

> Ann at twilight, Ann
> at dawn, Ann with her
> meager playthings on
> the lawn, a stick doll
> tucked into her pocket
> a polished hen bone for
> a locket, and on another
> string a miniature tin dog
> with a tin ball in his mouth.[3]

There is even a Shaker alphabet book included:

> A is for Apse and Altar and Aisle, as A is for
> Ant, Angel, Apple and Ann . . .[4]

The language becomes more heated and complex as Ann's obsession with God takes hold. Her first sex with her husband is an assault which she sublimates through a religious vision:

> He strokes my back, bites as he pumps
> to a pitch. As he falls, there is a

luminous angel: his feet are curly
and he blows a horn. His hair
is silver, his wings are rainbow-
stained. He loves me! He loves me!
My angel loves me![5]

After four of her children die in infancy she is visited by terrifying
visions, one of a choir of people burning,

Their mouths
are eaten through above the
lips, blue gums, their heads
are turtles, chinless, leather
and green[6]

and another of Adam and Eve engaged in animalistic sex, a shocking,
anti-Miltonic picture. To exorcise these sinful confabulations she taps
wood slivers under her fingernails, binds her breasts with thongs, and
seals her vagina with mud and dung, all the while praying, shaking,
hallucinating Christ. The book concludes peacefully with Ann's arrival in America and her anticipation of Shaker life there: the "impec-
cably plain" white houses of the communities, orchards, gardens, and
workrooms which will produce buckles, pails, tubs, cheese hoops, oval
boxes, hand-crafted furniture, and Shaker inventions such as the
straight broom and the washing machine. All of this productivity will
be realized in the new Zion.

Peters seems to invade Ann Lee's spirit by an act of possession. The
poems were composed near one of the few surviving Shaker communities, and Peters got into the habit of paying regular visits to her grave.
There is an otherness to Ann's voice and a fidelity in the language to
her historical milieu. But at the same time Peters does infuse these
monologuists with his own tensions and obsessions. Perhaps what
these works finally present are double characters, half-themselves,
half-Peters; in other words, explorations of Peters-Lee, Peters-Kane,
Peters-Hawker, Peters-Ludwig. By grafting his feelings onto theirs and
throwing his voice into history, Peters performs an eerie act of ventrilo-
quism by which two voices, two consciousnesses, converge and become indistinguishable.

Ikagnak documents Dr. Elisha Kent Kane's doomed voyage to the
Arctic, where his ship became imprisoned in ice; he was forced to walk

for eighty-four days back to civilization with a handful of survivors. Based on Kane's journals, the poems capture the painful drama of survival in a cryptlike landscape of glacier and ice. Some poems focus on the practical matters of living in this hostile environment: how to control a dog-team, how to defrost a cheek, how to kill a seal, capture a duck, or share an igloo with fourteen sleeping Eskimos. But as the expedition's situation deteriorates, the poems present a saga of hardship in stark, unsentimental language. Crew members die off from gangrene, scurvy, hunger, or mere exposure to this brutal place; the survivors, who are subsisting on boiled bear paws, whale tongues, and the meat of their dogs, sprinkle snow for dust on the graves. Kane, a doctor, performs amputations with a saw ("A foot thuds to the floor. A rush / of dogs: the whips, the whimpering") and describes the guts of his creatures hit by scurvy:

> Hematoma in the
> gastroenemius and
> gluteus muscles. Swollen gums,
> thickened skin-layers. Fatty
> changes in liver, spleen, kidneys
> and heart.[7]

As a historical work, *Ikagnak* resurrects an almost forgotten American explorer-hero whose funeral in 1856 "was second only to Lincoln's in grandeur," and as a tale the book reads like a poetic version of Piers Paul Read's gripping *Alive*.

In *Hawker*, Peters assumes the identity of Robert Stephen Hawker, a Cornish vicar who tended a church on the vertiginous cliffs of England's west coast where shipwrecks were common. Dressed in a "claret cassock, old yellow wool pancho, fisherman's boot and a bright red hat," this odd Victorian would recover the bodies of sailors washed ashore and anoint and bury them in his churchyard. He would invite farm animals to church services, and at night he would play mermaid by festooning himself with seaweed and singing by the shore as he caught moonlight in a mirror. When his wife died he took up opium to assuage his grief; his own decline was punctuated by bouts of hallucination and paranoia.

The Hawker poems begin with the vicar's ruminations on the everyday business of the vicarage, then move into his mystical communings with his patron Saint Morwenna and his obsession with the corpses of sailors, and end with his vividly frightening opium visions. Some of the best poems show Hawker's concern with such matters as the running of his parish school, the hiring of a new verger, diseases of swine, his wife's baking, the ailments of his parishioners, and his friendship with Gyp, a pet pig who followed him everywhere. In precisely paced language, Peters captures the innocent daftness of the vicar, who sees

> An oak-tree branch, snow crammed,
> with a dozen merry elves in a row,
> in German leather pants
> and buttons as large as ox eyes.
> Tasselled mutli-colored caps . . .[8]

as well as his Franciscan love for the creatures of God's world. Hawker combines a rural saintliness with a kind of tender mania. He drops violets and robins' eggs on the grave of a friend and feeds his parishioners cabbages and whortleberries; he is stimulated by erotic visions of angels and tattooed sailors. Like Ann Lee, Hawker is a spiritual over-reacher and a stranger-than-fiction exotic; but behind the quirks and aberrations lies an example of humanity standing on the sheer cliff-edge of a holy madness. The volume ends with a bold rhetorical switch whereby Hawker becomes aware of Peters' presence and addresses him in prose, assessing his book and scolding him for implying that Hawker was homosexual and for being too ornate in his description of Hawker's opium pipe.

Picnic in the Snow, spoken in the voice of King Ludwig II of Bavaria, best expresses Peters' attraction to sexual and artistic eccentricity. Ludwig is famous for his castle building and his sexually ambiguous role as Wagner's friend and patron. His extravagant architectural legacy, now a draw for tourists, consists of a half-dozen castles—some on the scale of Versailles—which blend Gothic, Baroque, Teutonic, and Byzantine styles with Ludwig's own penchant for fantasy, manifested in several elaborate artificial grottoes featuring cast-iron stalactites, waterfalls, mechanical lighting effects, swans, painted scenes from Wagner's operas, and shell-shaped boats in which Ludwig would be rowed by servants as he soaked up the atmosphere. He visited one of the castles only once for a period of ten days.

The monologues are notable for mapping the Bavarian landscape, its mountains and flower-bordered lakes, and for penetrating the king's mind, which was torn between the political pressures of running the country and his compulsive love for the fantasy-land of operatic performance. The poems explore Ludwig's dreams:

> I believe
> the salt of my own blood is a swan's.
> The sweat of my palms has the fragrance of
> feathers. I ruffle the surface of lakes,[9]

and his difficult boyhood in a bizarre family which included an aunt who maintained the belief that she had swallowed a glass piano. Ludwig's subjects grew infuriated over the king's lavish spending, the neglect of his royal duties for aesthetic pursuits, and the cultivation of his own vanity—he noted that "if I didn't have my hair curled every day, I couldn't enjoy my food." Declared insane, he was imprisoned and later died mysteriously, his body found floating in the shallow water of Lake Starnberg.

Taken as a group, these monologues express a fascination with the possibility of pursuing a personal vision to its extreme, whether the grail be purity, heroic adventure, God, or aesthetic opulence. Each character crosses the boundaries of social sanity and moves into an uncharted tundra of the spirit. The poems are reenactments of these characters' wild exertions rather than disengaged commentaries on them. As acts of exhumation, the poems fit these historical characters with flesh and return to them their voices. And while they speak always within their own times and cultures, they speak also out to ours.

The importance of Robert Peters' poetry rests on the fact that it modifies poetic language and breaks new artistic ground. By combining playful rhymes with painfully serious matter, he has returned new tonal possibilities to poetry. By fully exploiting the metaphor of the body, its epidermal shape and vulnerable interior, he has provided a fresh code for the expression of feeling. By historicizing and enlarging the scope of the dramatic monologue, he has revitalized an important genre and implied its almost limitless potential. No doubt others will rush into the fields he is now clearing.

Peters is currently writing a new monologue sequence in the person

of Elizabeth Bathory of Hungary, known in her time as the Blood
Countess, a madwoman who believed she could preserve her youthful-
ness by bathing in the blood of virgins. Her victims were locked in a
metal cage equipped with inward-pointing spikes, and she would stand
naked below showering in their blood. Over six hundred virgins died
in the name of her beauty before they walled up Elizabeth in her castle
in 1611.[10]

Notes

1. Frank Kermode draws a similar analogy in "Institutional Control of Interpretation," reprinted in *The Pushcard Prize V: The Best of the Small Presses*, 1980–81
   edition, pp. 107–123.
2. *The Sow's Head and Other Poems* (Detroit: Wayne State University Press, 1968),
   p. 86.
3. *The Gift to Be Simple: A Garland for Ann Lee* (New York: Liveright, 1973), p. 3.
4. Ibid., p. 12.
5. Ibid., pp. 22–23.
6. Ibid., p. 43.
7. *Ikagnak, the North Wind: with Dr. Kane in the Arctic* (Pasadena: Kenmore Press,
   1978), p. 34.
8. *Hawker* (Greensboro: Unicorn Press, 1984), p. 10.
9. *The Picnic in the Snow: Ludwig of Bavaria* (New Rivers Press, 1982), p. 21.
10. Robert Peters' Selected Poems—*Gauguin's Chair*—was published by the Cross-
    ing Press, Trumansburg, N.Y., in 1977. Recent books include *Hawker* and *Kane*
    (Greensboro, N.C.: Unicorn Press, 1985).

Contemporary Appalachian Poetry

Sources and Directions

At the beginning of 1960, you could have counted the important Appalachian poets on both hands. Since then, over seventy collections of Appalachian poetry have appeared; anthologies and little magazines have featured it; and scholars have written essays about it. This sudden flowering is impressive and, because some of the earlier poets are out of print, may seem miraculous. But it has its roots in work that came before, in individual voices, and in what they expressed for the region as a whole.

Ballad of the Bones, Hounds on the Mountain, Song in the Meadow—the titles of these books of Appalachian poetry from the thirties and forties reveal its origin in closeness to the earth and love of song. These collections by Byron Herbert Reece of north Georgia and James Still and Elizabeth Madox Roberts of Kentucky are rooted in tradition, formally as well as thematically. They contain sonnets, ballads, song cycles, and carefully reined free verse, often with a biblical cadence. While they employ less dialect than Ann Cobb's groundbreaking *Kinfolks: Kentucky Mountain Rhymes* (1922), they show a kinship to those poems, to Roy Helton's *Lonesome Waters* (1930), and to Jesse Stuart's *Man with a Bull-Tongue Plow* (1934) in that they wish to examine and most often to preserve the stories and values that have been islanded within the culture as a whole. As James Still writes in "White Highways":

To the broad highways, and back again I have come
To the creek-bed roads and narrow winding trails
Worn into ruts by hoofs and steady feet;
I have come back to the long way around,
The far between, the slow arrival.
Here is my pleasure most where I have lived
And called my home.[1]

Still's "homing place" is quiet in the world's sense, a cove away from the scream of machines and rapid transit, but it is lapped in music: "The dulcimer sings from fretted maple throat" ("Mountain Dulcimer"). We hear "the mellow banjos of the hounds' throats" and "shrill notes of a sheep's horn billow down the mountain" ("Fox Hunt"). Most importantly, the human songs are handed down and sung, and the *song* comes to symbolize identity, not just personal but cultural, the unbroken strand of life. Byron Herbert Reece not only writes of those singing the ballads, but also casts many of his poems in the ballad mold, emphasizing the timelessness of his themes, the beauty of song, and its power of renewal. "Mountain Fiddler" begins:

I took my fiddle
That sings and cries
To a hill in the middle
Of Paradise.

The fiddler tunes up, prepared to play to the emptiness around him. But, after the first few notes, "a crowd of wings" comes toward him and a voice says:

"Our halls can show
No thing so rude
As your horsehair bow,
Or your fiddlewood;

"And yet can they
So well entrance
If you but play
Then we must dance!"[2]

Song is a loom for weaving together the joys and sorrows of the earth, for shaping the human story. And narrative threads its way through the lyrical work of these poets, as though the ballad has not yet split into written forms of lyric and narrative. Notice how the light dance of rhythms in "When Daniel Was a Blacksmith" by Elizabeth Madox Roberts prepares us for a new look at the story of Daniel Boone and plays against the heaviness of our standard image of him. In form and fable quality the poem is reminiscent of Blake:

> When Daniel was a Blacksmith
>
> .   .   .   .
>
> He fitted for the dray horse,
> He shod the little wild colt,
> And shod the dappled gray.
>
> .   .   .   .
>
> And the wild beasts in a thousand hills,
> And in a thousand valley prongs,
> They lifted up their quivering ears
> To hear his anvil songs.[3]

Roberts, best known for her fiction (*The Great Meadow*, 1930), is a central Kentucky native whose work often deals with Appalachian themes and experiences. In "Love in the Harvest" she writes of "a song in the meadow and a song in the mouth."[4] Certainly her fellow poets—Still, Reece, Cobb, Helton, and Stuart—find in nature's song, the "song in the meadow," the impulse for human expression, the "song the mouth." Jesse Stuart makes this relationship explicit in his introductory poem to *Man with a Bull-Tongue Plow* (1934), a collection which further illustrates the strain of romanticism in Appalachian poetry. If his proclamation seems defensive or willfully provincial, consider that he was launching his poems on the same stream as Hart Crane and T. S. Eliot. A literary world which had seen *The Bridge* (1930) and *Ash Wednesday* (1930) was not likely to praise the "farmer singing at the plow":

> .   .   . I can sing my lays like singing corn,
> And flute them like a fluting gray corn-bird;
> And I can pipe them like a hunter's horn—
> All of my life these are the songs I've heard.
> And these crude strains no critic can call art,
> Yours very respectively, Jesse Stuart.[5]

Louise McNeill's *Gauley Mountain* (1939) marks a change in this pattern of poets singing the land, for its impulse is more narrative than lyrical and the story of the land emerges through the stories of the people. The relationship between the two is still crucial, but the emphasis has changed. With the focus on story comes a new concern with character, not just of heroes or ballad figures, but of everyday people. Here is an exchange between the Gauley mail rider and a Washington postal clerk, based on a letter that once hung on the wall in a West Virginia post office. The first stanza establishes that the mail carrier has been asked why his mail was three months late during the winter. Note how in his rejoinder the mountaineer's tall-tale humor works to give him the last word:

> Jed Kane
>
> . . .
>
> . . . "Respected Sir,
> You ask the reason and this be her—
> If the gable end blowed out of hell
> Straight into the drifts of a snow that fell
> Last fall on the ram's horn point of Cheat
> It would take till Easter for brimstone heat
> To melt a horsepath. So I remain
> Your obdt. svt., Jedson Kane."[6]

The poem with which *Gauley Mountain* closes brings the human stories, with all their urgency, to rest in the hill's shadow, but there is evidence already of the difference human values are making in the landscape:

> Now they have bridged the canyon of the Gauley
> And built a lock above the Swago shoal
> . . . .
> Along the shore where passing Mingo warriors
> Built drift-wood fires to parch Ohio maize
> Coke ovens glare red-eyed upon the darkness
> And belch their cinders at the fevered days.
>
> ("The River")[7]

The uneasiness evidenced in this poem increases as we come closer to our own time, and the relationship between nature and song in Appalachian poetry changes more profoundly. It is not just that the poets are disconnected from the land (though some are, and clearly that is the movement of the culture), it is that the land no longer presents itself as a constant, the hub of the wheel of seasons, of present and past, of birth and death, struggle and fulfillment. Improper road building, damming, and timbering as well as the onslaught of strip mining have changed the land and the lives lived on it dramatically. Lifting up one's eyes unto the hills becomes less comforting when the hills stand in need of help. Folksinger Jean Ritchie chronicles the change in "Black Waters":

> O the quail, she's a pretty bird, she sings a sweet tongue;
> In the roots of the tall timbers she nests with her young.
> But the hillside explodes with the dynamite's roar,
> And the voices of the small birds will sound there no more;
> And the hillsides come a-sliding so awful and grand,
> And the flooding black waters rise over my land.
>
> Sad scenes of destruction on every hand;
> Black waters, black waters run down through the land.[8]

Alongside the exploitation of the land has come an accelerated modernization of life in the mountains. The speed and scale of this change, along with the economic roller-coaster of coal production and increasing industrialization, make for a very unstable way of life. As Mike Clark explains in his foreword to Voices from the Mountains, "The real story of Appalachia today is the attempt by mountain people to retain the humanistic elements of the old culture and at the same time to adapt to the pressures and demands of a technological society."[9]

As in James Still's "White Highways," the road is often seen as both a symbol and an agent in this transformation. Billy Edd Wheeler, West Virginia poet, playwright, and songwriter, whose Song of a Woods Colt appeared in 1969, gives one version of this in "The Coming of the Roads":

> O look how they've cut all to pieces
> Our ancient poplar and oak
>
> . . . .
>
> We used to curse the bold crewmen
> Who stripped our earth of its ore
> Now you've changed and you've gone over to them
> And you've learned to love what you hated before
>
> Once I thanked God for my treasure
> Now, like rust, it corrodes

And I can't help from blaming
Your going
On the coming
The coming of the roads. [10]

Kentucky poet Lee Pennington captures a more ambivalent attitude, this time toward the railroad, which hauls away the life-product of the Harlan County train watchers and gives only longing in return:

I have seen them down at the crossing,
their eyes dug out with silence,
their mouths hanging caves on faces
and their feet tapping rhythm of train horn blow.
                              ("Train Horn")[11]

The movement of contemporary Appalachian poetry, then, is from a rooted, traditional body of work to a more volatile, politically active, and varied offering. Not that there was not political awareness before, most obviously in Georgia poet Don West's *Clods of Southern Earth* (1946), a collection which exposes the condition of workers in factories, on sharecropped farms, in the mines, and in the steel mills, where West himself worked. But the political considerations which inspired songwriters like Florence Reece had not been a major source of poetry in the mountains. From the mid-sixties on, not only labor movement questions but also the old interest in and involvement with the land demanded more political thinking. It became clear that Granny had to walk uphill just to throw water off the back porch, and, as Jim Wayne Miller, poet, critic, and one of the central voices of the seventies, tells us, possession of a small farm turned into a counter-cultural act:

Sometimes a whole farm family comes awake

. . . .

to find their farm's been rolled up like a rug
with them inside it. . . .

. . . .

It's a ring, a syndicate dismantling farms

. . . .

disposing of them part by stolen part.

Parts of farms turn up in unlikely places:

. . . .
One missing farm was found intact at the head
of a falling creek in a recently published short story.
One farm that disappeared without a clue
has turned up in the colorful folk expressions
of a state university buildings and grounds custodian.
A whole farm was found in the face of Miss Hattie Johnson,
lodged in a Michigan convalescent home.
        ("Small Farms Disappearing in Tennessee—*Headline*")[12]

Given these opposing forces at work in Appalachian life—the long-lived isolation which preserved ignorance along with strong family ties, the volatile coal economy with its exploitation of human and natural resources, the accelerated modernization and the accompanying loss—it is not surprising that its poetry offers varied and often contradictory visions. While one can say that in general it is less traditional in form, less given to the use of dialect, and more diverse in voice and rhythm than the poetry which led up to it, it is difficult to characterize more specifically than that. Two things can safely be said. First, it most often concerns itself with revaluation or reclamation of the past, which includes a strengthening or at least an exploration of the bonds between generations. Second, its strong tie to the land has continued, whether in the pastoral work of poets like Jeff Daniel Marion, Robert Morgan, Fred Chappell, and Maggie Anderson or the more consciously political poems of Jonathan Williams, P. J. Laska, Mary Joan Coleman, and Bob Snyder.

This recognition of the bond between generations (usually the speaker in the poem and someone older), while it may be celebratory, painful, angry, or a combination thereof, is a way of remapping the land, reforesting so that the past does not erode into floods of present isolated ego. We see examples of this in the work of two young West Virginia poets, Bob Henry Baber and Mary Joan Coleman, who were part of the Soupbean Collective, a group of writers at Antioch College/Appalachia in Beckley, West Virginia.[13] A stubborn integrity, a continuity, is handed down in Baber's "Roofing for Aunt Pearl." Her relatives think she is too old to live out in the country by herself. They want her to move to town, but she tells them:

". . . I'm Cold Knob born,
Cold Knob bred,
'n' when I die, by God,
I'm gonna be COLD KNOB dead!"[14]

Exploring one's connections with the past is a kind of self-discovery
and definition of wrongs as well as a delineation of what is valuable.
This is evident in Mary Joan Coleman's description of her father's relationship with the world in "the man of stones":

my father wrote a poem forty years ago
about laying stones for a wall

. . . .

i knew if my mother would take the hatchet
from the pickled bean shelf in the cellar
and strike his breast the steel
would ring upon solid rock,
i have read his statement of stoning
a hundred times since childhood

. . . .

we seldom speak; but in the vacuum
i often hear the undeniable
crumble and groan
of old stones shifting.[15]

Where Baber's and Coleman's poems have the active quality of film,
Tennessee poet and editor Jeff Daniel Marion's work is closer to still
life. Contemplative, generally low-toned, his poems approach the past
and the joining of generations in a different way from Baber and Coleman, but the poets share many of the same concerns. Marion writes in
"Ebbing and Flowing Spring":

Coming back you almost
expect to find the dipper
gourd hung there by the latch.

. . . .

"Dip and drink," [Matilda would] say,
"It's best when the water is rising."

. . . .

You waited while
Matilda's stories flowed back,

seeds & seasons, names & signs,
almanac of all her days.

. . . .
Moons & years & generations
& now Matilda alone.
You listen.

. . . .
. . . before you know it
the water's up & around you
flowing by.

. . . .
This is what you have come for.
Drink.[16]

"This is what you have come for": the past as a source or way to a source of life is accessible in "Ebbing and Flowing Spring" at least in the rhythms of the earth, of the rising water. The speaker is able to carry out the commands of the past because basic facts of the landscape have remained constant and he has kept his life tuned to them. A life tuned to the stripped landscapes of eastern Kentucky or West Virginia is apt to produce more jagged lines. The threat of overburden is constant, as many protest songs tell us. Mike Kline's "Strip Away," based on "Swing Low, Sweet Chariot," is particularly effective:

Strip away, big D-9 Dozer,
Comin' for to bury my home,
I'm a-gettin' madder as you're gettin' closer,
Comin' for to bury my home.[17]

The wedding in this song of an old hymn of hope with a vision of future hopelessness is significant, an effort to graft present powerlessness onto the strength of the past and thus regain power. And some power lies in declaring the truth, whether or not action is possible. This is a recurring message in the poetry of P. J. Laska, West Virginia writer, socialist critic, and editor of *The Unrealist*. His "Follow-up Report from Farmington" deals with the devastation resulting from deep mining, reminding us that the enemy is more subtle than dozers or the enormous power shovel called Big Bertha:

> First the high school cracked,
> one whole wing separated
>
> . . . .
>
> The basements of the houses
> began to crumble
>
> . . . .
>
> The field on the hillside
> behind the cemetery opened up
>
> . . . .
>
> Bethlehem Steel wouldn't pay anything
> because those worked out sections
> under the town
> filled up with water,
> and now nobody can go down there
> to prove that they pulled out
> those pillars of coal
> they were supposed to leave standing . . .[18]

The force of this poem is its revelation of a truth that victims know but can do nothing about. The situation is a little more hopeful in Lillie D. Chaffin's "Old-Timer to Grandchild," despite its recognition that to some extent mountain people have signed on the dotted line of their own destruction:

> [Our kinfolks] let some Philadelphia lawyers
> tell them they could sell the yoke
> and keep the egg. . . .
> . . . And now the yoke owners
> are claiming their gold, and squashing
> the shell. . . .
> . . . Let folks talk about our
> backward ways. . . .
> . . . If forward's now,
> then I feel sorry for the ones who'll
> never know. But you will remember
> a little bit. You tell them birds
> do fly low before a storm.[19]

The hope here is in the communication of values from one generation to another, as in Marion's and Baber's poems and in the warning of the last two lines.

While it is evident that people cannot "go into backup" on any large scale, at least not unless the economy collapses, they can offer a personal resistance by declaring the truth, as in "Farmington" and "Old-Timer," and by "holding onto their rights, both mineral and otherwise," as Lee Howard says in the dedication of her book *The Last Unmined Vein* (1980). The speaker in the title poem refuses to sell coal from under his farm "to make steel in Ohio / turn on the lights in New York City / and heat houses in Detroit" because he knows the consequences. And he has figured out how to make selling hard for his children, too:

> I done got my marker
> and laid out the lines for my grave
> right smack in the middle
> of that vein
> They gonna have to chip out the coal 6 foot by 6
> and then put her right back on top of me
> and that will be the end of that[20]

The best the speaker (and the poet) can do is "remind them / of what it's gonna cost them," the speaker by his own dead body and the poet by the body of her work.

That the acceleration of change in the mountains is also an acceleration of loss is clear. Why this change and loss should result in a burgeoning of poetry in the last decade is not so obvious. If there are ten names that must be mentioned in discussing Appalachian poetry up to 1960, there are at least thirty of significance since then, most of whom published primarily between 1969 and 1980. There are complex reasons for this. Along with the increased political awareness characteristic of the nation as a whole in the sixties came the growing consciousness of Appalachia as a region, a realization from within that its distinctiveness and importance were being distorted and sold in the "Beverly Hillbillies" market and praised and misunderstood by outreach programs, governmental and religious; that the people, like the land, were being stripped of their ore. From the outside, Appalachia attracted mercenaries and missionaries; from the inside, Appalachians wondered if the War on Poverty were being waged against them, if their lives were both quaint and deplorable, like the little shellacked outhouses sold in Mountain Kraft stores. A cultural crisis resulted, and it is still going on.

Poetry, so often considered impractical, a luxury, is in fact a natural human response in dealing with this loss and distortion of value, because poetry is a valuing process. Through its intense selectivity in imagery, in rhythm, in sound, and in word, poetry imparts value; its light shines on the few things chosen till they become luminous, radiating a truth long locked within. North Carolina poet Robert Morgan, whose books *Zirconia Poems*, *Red Owl*, and *Groundwork* span the seventies, has many poems which illustrate this process. Language circles, analyzes, polishes, and explores in "Stove":

> The stove is an extra digestive tract,
> a vehicle for translating
> the ancient vegetable
> heat to the present.
>
> . . . .
> The stove is motor.
> Tobacco juice ferments in the bucket of ashes.
> Later the heat returns and vanishes
> through the coals.
> The campfire dies while the hunters
> are off hunting.
> A sour wet silence pours down the stairwell.[21]

By the sheer act of naming, poetry declares what is lasting and eases the mortality of people and places it is concerned with. By rendering us speechful, poetry incants us, and the incantation both recognizes and bestows value.

The obvious question is, why poetry? Isn't this valuing process part of all literature which is essentially, however desperate, an act of affirmation? Certainly, but poetry is the logical vehicle here for many reasons. To begin with, its intensity matches the feeling of crisis and its immediacy—it is not, after all, as time-consuming as fiction—matches the urgency of the situation. Poetry dresses the wound on the spot rather than waiting for the tests, prep, and major surgery of a novel. Poetry is also a natural development of expression in a song- and story-fed culture.

More importantly, poetry is rooted in paradox, and paradox is as indigenous to Appalachia as the coal: wealth and poverty (personal, cultural, ecological), beauty and ugliness, the stereotype with its wink of truth. The violent good neighbor, loving father who puts a fork in his boy's arm at the dinner table. Steady, wise hill farmer who would like to burn up all the kids in the university before they burn it down themselves. Straightforward corruption—revivalist who saves a new wife every night. People so poor their new baby sleeps in the box of their color TV, people starving to death behind the wheel of a car, people whose lives are up on blocks, gutted, rusted out. All these leaves and seeds of paradox fall down that steep air and rot into rich ground where poetry can take hold, for the energy of poetry lies in language and paradox. The force of metaphor comes from its wedding of like and unlike to make something new without destroying the separate identities of the old. It is easy to see how this approaches the dilemma of Appalachia itself.

Poetry offers, then, some healing, a map of relatedness amid the fragmentation and isolation of modern life and the template sameness that is its deadening connector. Furthermore, its recognition of paradox, its mission work among the irreconcilable forces in our lives, is a form of healing. And to the extent that *to name* and *to tell* are to know and thus to control, poetry gives us a measure of power over those forces.

Notes

This article first appeared in the *Kentucky Review* 2, no. 2 (1981).

1. James Still, *Hounds on the Mountain* (New York: Viking Press, 1937), p. 45.
2. Byron Herbert Reece, *Ballad of the Bones* (New York: E. P. Dutton, 1945), p. 56.
3. Elizabeth Madox Roberts, *Song in the Meadow* (New York: Viking Press, 1940), p. 98.
4. Roberts, *Song in the Meadow*, p. 26.
5. Jesse Stuart, *Man with a Bull-Tongue Plow* (New York: E. P. Dutton, 1934), p. 3.
6. Louise McNeill, *Gauley Mountain* (New York: Harcourt Brace, 1939), p. 40.
7. McNeill, *Gauley Mountain*, p. 98.
8. Jean Ritchie, "Black Waters" (New York: Geordie Music Publishing Co., 1967).
9. Mike Clark, "Appalachia: The Changing Times," foreword to *Voices from the Mountains*, collected and recorded by Guy and Candie Carawan (New York: Knopf, 1975), p. ix.

10. Billy Edd Wheeler, *Song of a Woods Colt* (Anderson, S.C.: Droke House, 1969), p. 106.
11. Lee Pennington, *Scenes from a Southern Road* (Smithtown, N.Y.: JRD Publishing Co., 1969), p. 45.
12. Jim Wayne Miller, "Small Farms Disappearing in Tennessee," in *Voices from the Hills: Selected Readings of Southern Appalachia*, ed. Robert J. Higgs and Ambrose N. Manning (New York: Frederick Ungar Publishing Co., 1975), pp. 350–351.
13. Baber's book, *Assorted Life Savers*, appeared in 1976 and Coleman's *Take One Blood Red Rose* in 1978, but both poets' work had appeared earlier in the Antioch/Appalachia literary magazine *What's a Nice Hillbilly Like You . . . ?* and in works published by the Southern Appalachian Writers Cooperative, which they helped to found. SAWC sought to form a network of writers in the region in order to overcome the problems of isolation, the reluctance of publishers, and the obstacles to truth telling which they all felt. In 1977 they published *Soupbean: An Anthology of Contemporary Appalachian Literature and New Ground*, an anthology co-published with *Mountain Review*, the Appalshop magazine out of Whitesburg, Kentucky. In 1978 SAWC published *Mucked*, a collection of writings and photographs in response to the 1977 flooding of Appalachia.

    While the Soupbean poets are no longer a group, SAWC is still holding on, most recently with the help of the Appalachian Poetry Project, a year-long effort, supported by a grant to the University of Kentucky's Appalachian Center from the Witter Bynner Foundation to encourage poetry in the mountains. To date, the project has held seventeen reading/workshops in a five-state area. Many of these were led by old Soupbean and SAWC poets whose work appears in the most recent SAWC publication, *Strokes: Contemporary Appalachian Poetry* (1980).
14. Robert Henry Baber, *Assorted Life Savers and Poems from the Mountains* (Beckley, W.Va.: Troy Baber, 1976), p. 32.
15. Mary Joan Coleman, *Take One Blood Red Rose* (Cambridge, Mass.: West End Press, 1978), unpaged.
16. Jeff Daniel Marion, *Out in the Country, Back Home* (Winston-Salem, N.C.: Jackpine Press, 1976), p. 65.
17. Mike Kline, "Strip Away," in *Voices from the Mountains*, p. 36.
18. P. J. Laska, *Songs and Dances* (Prince, W.Va.: Unrealist Press, 1977), p. 30.
19. Lillie D. Chaffin, "Old-Timer to Grandchild," in *Mucked*, ed. Bob Henry Baber and Jim Webb (Williamson, W.Va.: Hesperus Press, 1978), unpaged.
20. Lee Howard, "The Last Unmined Vein," in *The Last Unmined Vein* (Washington, D.C.: Anemone Press, 1980), pp. 50–51.
21. Robert Morgan, *Red Owl: Poems* (New York: Norton, 1972), p. 46.

Poetry at the Periphery

There are those for whom Appalachian culture is no more than "a region of the heart." The metaphor here is one of emotion and feeling rather than one of perception of reality. The suggestion is that Appalachian culture is more past than present and more desire than fulfillment, and that therefore it is accessible only as folk culture. I suggest a different approach to Appalachian culture, one that links the folk and heritage concepts to the idea of a living people's culture. What I mean by "people's culture" is significantly different from mass culture and something clearly distinct from the elitist culture of modernism. In Appalachia it includes the surviving part of that native folk culture that once gave a degree of identity and unity to life in these mountains. The important question for my purposes is whether these remnants and the tremendous enthusiasm for them will develop a living value in the present, and whether "the mountain experience" and the "things Appalachian" will encompass reality as well as history. At this juncture I think it is the poets of the region who are pressing this question upon us, and what follows is my attempt to explain the significance of their work.

Side by side with the pursuit of heritage and regional self-consciousness, which has been largely a scholarly, intellectual effort, there has been a virtual explosion of activity on the part of writers and poets of the region. One critic has written recently that "poems are pouring out of the region as if a sensitive nerve had been touched." He wonders whether all this activity will ultimately be classified as a famous literary movement. My own view is that something more basic, more revolutionary than a mere interest in literature is behind this upsurge. The outpouring of poetry in Appalachia in the past decade is part of a larger development which we have begun to see in the cultural life of the country. I would argue that in the past decade Appalachian poets have been at the forefront of a significant change emerging in American cultural life, a change that constitutes a major break with the past and with the cultural hegemony of urban modernism.

To substantiate this rather large assertion I offer the following brief survey, which will probably not convince anyone but may enable me to get a foot in the door. An urban cultural hierarchy has been in place in this country since at least the early fifties, probably since the war period. Politically, it has been decidedly right wing, or very conservative, as has been the dominant politics of the nation. In the early fifties what survived of a left-wing cultural opposition was driven into hiding by a right-wing hysteria that came damn close to elevating another Hitler (some say he later came to power only to be dethroned by newspaper reporters).

This cultural opposition has been slow in its return to public life. The "Beat Movement," which began in the fifties, was not left wing. It was hardly political at all. It was, however, opposed to the formalism and careerism of the established poets clustered around American universities. This urban cultural hierarchy had at the time enough power to reduce any cultural movement that rejected its standards of taste to the status of a *peripheral* phenomenon.

And this is what happened, in spite of the media interest in the Beats. The net effect of nonrecognition and ridicule was a status of cultural pariah for a whole group of writers whose literature and lifestyle flouted the dominant cultural values. Donald Hall's influential anthology of American poets, originally published in 1962, contained only Gary Snyder among the Beats, no blacks, and few women. The upheavals of the sixties brought a change to this picture of the contemporary scene. In the second edition of his *Contemporary American Poetry* (1972), Hall added more poets, including Allen Ginsberg, whom he admits having misjudged. More importantly, though, he included two black poets and was turned down by a third (Amiri Baraka, then Leroi Jones).

This little background survey illustrates what is an obvious truth to many, that social forces are the strength of cultural forces. It is also a truth that is borne out by developments of the seventies. The seventies have seen a continuation of social upheaval in America centered around the family and racial and ethnic identity. Toward the latter part of the seventies there has also appeared a lot of poetry to which the Canadian poet Tom Wayman has given the label "New Realism." In the United States there are an increasing number of little poetry magazines that feature what we could call "new realism" poetry in a broader sense than Wayman's. Some of the ones I have seen are *Quindaro* (Kansas City), *Cultural Correspondence* (Providence, Rhode Island), *Working Cultures* (Washington, D.C.), *West End* and *Nostoc* (Boston), *Main Trend* (New York), and *The Unrealist*. Also, established literary journals like *Minnesota Review, Praxis,* and *Left Curve* all feature poetry which embodies social and historical perspectives.

An anthology of the seventies would also have to take account of the rise of regionalism in American culture. The poetry upsurge in Appalachia is contemporary with a revival of poetry in other regions of the country. Regional markets for poetry are evident all across the country, and these markets are in fact part of the mainstay of the small press publishing business. As a result certain poets have a large following in the area in which they live and publish but are not known or attract little interest outside that area. The "region" can be entirely ersatz in this sense. Away from the urban centers we find poets taking localism more seriously than as a literary game, some to the point of becoming consciously regionalist. It is difficult to imagine the work of Vincent Ferrini apart from the Gloucester's fishermen and the Cape Ann area of Massachusetts. In his latest book, *Know Fish*, Ferrini returns to the Italian-English dialect of his immigrant parents and writes some of his best poems. David Budbill, a regional poet in Northern New England, is another example of a poet who uses dialect. In his book, *The Chain-Saw Dance*, he writes of the people of the northern Appalachian mountains and reproduces some of their speech.

This sort of thing is going on outside the national literary network. California, New Jersey, New York, Washington, D.C., and its suburbs, even Hawaii have all seen anthologies of their poets. In some cases they have more than one. So far, it has been in the heavily populated urban areas of the country that the money has tended to concentrate.

We can look at what is happening in the country culturally from the side of the old, which is breaking up, or from the side of the new, which is just beginning to appear. What is breaking up is the cultural life, its ability by controlling the production of art to define the standards of perception and taste, as well as the modes of enjoyment, in American society. What has appeared on the horizon to replace it is the regional focus of populist cultural developments that threaten to break down the traditional hierarchy in the arts and perhaps create new hierarchies in its place. The bureaucratic scaffolding for such regional hierarchies is already in place in many states. One's reaction to this cultural dialectic is likely determined by whether one's politics are populist or elitist. Those who lament the passing of the old order talk about the seventies as "a decade of dispersal" and argue, for example, that Robert Lowell is the last of the great American poets because of the scattering of cultural focus and the fracturing of the national audience. Daniel Bell, the sociologist who pronounced the end of ideology in the fifties, argues in a recent book that American society is experiencing a crisis of values and that the most pressing problem is the loss of a center. He and others are concerned to reestablish the central clearinghouse concept of culture even if it takes a new ideology to do it. But the reaction of elitists to the breakup of the cultural core cannot be better illustrated than in the flap which saw CCLM (Coordinating Council of Literary Magazines) in an uproar when a grants board of the latter, dominated by elected small magazine editors, voted to disperse their monies in equal amounts to all applicants. With action equal to their conviction, this CCLM grants board refused to sit in judgment of the relative merit of the various diverse literary magazines around the country and thus refused to play the role of Pro-Tem Cultural God that had been allotted to them. For this betrayal of elitist trust and bureaucratic authority, this grants board of CCLM was roundly criticized, castigated, and ridiculed, although many editors of small magazines were delighted.

So the fight is on. The arts are no longer divorced from politics. And although Congress continues to appropriate large funds for the arts without much debate, the day of floor fights may not be far off. In a recent article entitled "Post Post-Art—Where Do We Go from Here?" Douglas Davis described our cultural situation as a problem of perception. We are "tumbling into infinitely complex sub-sets . . . older, tighter structures are decentralizing, spreading . . . [and] we do not clearly perceive the premise behind the action." Davis sees elitist culture as poised at the end of modernism without being able to define what is "post-modern." This is a humbling experience for Davis, who concludes that "small has to be beautiful now." What I find interesting is that Davis takes for granted that the end of modernism means the end of progress. *Après moi, le déluge.* "Each of the great Modernist states," he says, "is breaking into component parts, the reverse of the Global Village metaphor." As though he had looked into an abyss, Davis is engaged in the desperate search for a new metaphor to stem the tide of decentralization "before we're engulfed." Those whose politics are of a populist bent are likely to view what is happening as a positive development which opens up new possibilities. The thought that never seems to occur in these decline-of-the-West discussions is that decentralization brings with it the possibility of genuine people's culture.

The unity of art and life that occurs in folk culture is utopian to modernists (with their conception of art as commodity and museum pieces) and they are unable to take it seriously. Yet from the Appalachian vantage point, in which the remnants of a real folk culture are still immediate, it can be taken seriously. And those who do take it seriously will have a very different attitude to what is happening to modernist culture.

In a wide sense culture is the shared beliefs which inform our work and its shaping of physical existence. Cultural pluralism allows many shapes and elaborations as real. The cultural imperialism of mass culture resulting in a bureaucratically controlled consumption cannot permit any real pluralism because it would mean the end of the mass market in many areas of life. This imperialism has taken its toll on the psyche of the population. The results are evident in the alienation and unreality that people experience and in the proliferating psychological and religious attempts to counter the meaninglessness of everyday life.

The cultural life of a people cannot be successfully controlled or managed unless the power to shape life, *poesis* as the Greeks called it, is taken away from the people. *Poesis* lies at the basis of culture. It is the origin of all art, literature, drama, and even of language and thought itself. Originally, the folk artist only embodied and articulated what was the common creation of the whole people, *their style of life*. The people created the form of life, the artist recorded it.

For the purposes of power what matters is that *poesis* come under the control of an elite. This is an old story. Written language for the few and the illiteracy of masses over the centuries gave us a hieratic ideology which says that the power of *poesis* is the special gift of the few. In modern culture it is known as the gift of genius. What is creative in the culture is supposed to exist in their work. The living culture of the folk, with its union of art and life, is broken up into an elite producing the "high art" of novel experiment on the one hand and a mass culture entertainment industry on the other. Both are virtually empty of any real content.

The elitist "high art" defends itself against the charge of emptiness and irrelevance by the argument of art for art's sake, which says that the value of the work lies in how well it deals with its own challenge and not in any articulation of human meaning and truth. The argument uses the autonomy of art as an ideological defense. It says that the absence of the human dimension is not a permissible criticism. So long as there is something novel in the work to serve as evidence of genius, any reference to human reality is inessential. It sees no struggle between form and content or between reality and unreality because everything takes place on the side of the individual's imagination.

But the dues have to be paid somewhere, and they are paid through loss of meaning. Obscure, meaningless, and trivial works of art come to predominate and art is alienated from the people. The proliferation of novelty in a void is a necessary consequence of the theory and its practice. And since the only judgment of any importance about the merit of these works concerns their intrinsic qualities, we naturally have to have a captain-critic to tell us whether a new work is metal or dross.

It turns out that the problem with modern culture is the *cult*; that is, the hieratic clique. Historically, the tendency has been for the cult to dislodge the spontaneous genius of the people and install its own rules, which had something secret and mysterious about them. Now the opposite appears to be taking place. People's ignorance about the power of *poesis* within themselves and the cultural heritage of fear and self-deprecation that comes with ignorance is giving way everywhere to interest in the arts. Also, in Appalachia the emergence of oral history, folklore, and heritage studies has begun to reclaim some public space and funds for what was once a flourishing people's culture. The decentralization toward regionalism is a positive development, full of possibility for bringing together art and life in the region.

Folk culture and people's culture are not identical in concept, but I think they are closely interrelated. They are on a continuous line and I think it can be shown that what survives of the folk is part of people's culture. Both are populist conceptions of culture that reverse the elitist form. They are not derived from theory or ideology but arise in response to real needs. They develop around the interchange of artists and craftsmen with the people. If Appalachian poetry is seen as inclusive of mountain folk, blues, gospel, and grass songs, as well as the songs of work and protest, then I think we can document this continuous line. It's not something that I could attempt here, but it is something that should be attempted.

There is a tendency in modern poetry and modern criticism to pooh-pooh the song, to downgrade its aesthetic value as poetry. Modern poetry anthologies don't usually include songs that had popularity over the period covered by the anthology. I think this highlights the antilyrical, antipopulist bent of modern poetry. In the days of the oral tradition, prior to the book revolution, song was the main form for the poem to take. I'm not suggesting that the new Appalachian poets should all start writing songs. The song is only one form of poetry, and the limits of the musical form resulting from use of rime and fixed beat make it inappropriate for certain purposes. My point is that *thematically* the early Appalachian poetry, whose form is the song, is closely linked to the new poetry coming out of the hills. The folk themes and the political themes are inseparable because our people's lives have been and are now filled with struggle.

In the past the Appalachian poetry of song was an organic part of a genuine folk culture. The modernist break has been felt as the break *from* the lyric form. This break was progressive in that it opened up new forms for poetic work, but the price was paid in terms of alienation because its avant garde experimentalism tended to downgrade the folk as passé and to set modern poetry apart from people's culture. It remains to be seen whether Appalachian poetry, which is now consciously finding itself, will become an integral part of that collectivity that the folk represents in a way that modern poetry could not. To become part of the life of the people it will have to be a poetry in which the poem responds not merely to the challenge of itself but responds to the felt but perhaps unarticulated needs of the people. What makes poetry valuable to the people is not the novel linguistic inventions but the experience of the people that is articulated.

The *poesis* at the basis of popular culture is both real and repressed. We can think of the removal of this repression as the liberation of poetic power on the part of the people and as the fulfillment of the idea of art. It is an idea that traces its beginnings in the old work songs, whose practical function in one way or another assisted the laborer or assuaged his pain. Think of the prudential advice offered in "The Miner's Lifeguard,"

> Union miners stand together
> Heed no operator's tale
> Keep your hand upon the dollar
> and your eye upon the scale.

Or the humor appropriate to the absurdities of mining low coal as in Turner's "Hignite Blues,"

> Bumps all along to skin your back
> You lay your wire and hang your track.

Or of the surreal quality of the dream in which freedom is symbolized by a sea-gull in "Coal Loadin' Blues,"

> Thought I heard a sea-gull
> Way down in the ground;
> Must've been those miners
> A-turnin' that coal around.

Real freedom—free time and free mind—is the fulfillment of the idea of art. It is a revolutionary break to get poetry away from the cult and back into the life and consciousness of the people. In his last work German philosopher Herbert Marcuse wrote that "the truth of art lies in its power to break the monopoly of established reality . . . to *define* what is *real*." What he seems not to have seen is that art only has this power when it is in the hands of the people.

Appalachian people's culture is a real possibility for our generation. We have now the opportunity to nurture the growth of that organic relation between past and present, between poetry and people.

David Walls' core-periphery model has done much to reshape our thinking about the region. The limitation of the core-periphery model lies in the fact that in the present situation it is economically applicable but rapidly becoming culturally inapplicable. Culturally, the core is disintegrating at the same time that the Appalachian "periphery," along with other regions of the country, is experiencing a cultural renaissance. It is possible for the cultural core of American capitalism to become so weakened that there will no longer be any justification for speaking of Appalachian culture, or that of any of the other regions, as peripheral. Theoretically, then, we should remember that there is no periphery without a core.

Of course, the break-up of the "core" does not imply that a regional people's culture will emerge in its place. Other changes in the cultural superstructure are consistent with the continued functioning of American capitalism, even in its more or less dysfunctional "late" or post-Keynesian stage. One cannot say, for example, that the economics of American capitalism rules out an elitist cultural dispersal. The economic base of capitalism *is* consistent with the development of cultural pluralism under the control of regional elites. The important thing for capitalism is that a bureaucratic society of controlled consumption be preserved.

Is it not understandable, then, that in Appalachia the money flows in the direction of cultural heritage programs and not in the direction of contemporary programs which nourish a living people's culture and that would, in the words of the French philosopher Lefebvre, "create a culture that is not an institution but a style of life." The practical obstacles to people's culture have to do with where the money goes and where it doesn't go. State and private investments have been lavished, even squandered, on the collection and preservation of the remnants of folk culture in museums, libraries, and heritage centers. Heritage is a safe investment so long as it does not materially affect the present. A contemporary people's culture, on the other hand, is risky. Just how risky is stated with the exhortation of a mountain preacher in a recent paper by Cratis Williams when he says that Appalachians are a people "who have risen from our long fast in the mountains, the agony of our neglect and abuse, and the sharp thorns of perfidy that have been our anguish, and are now shaking our hides and flexing our muscles as we reach for the control box that determines our destiny." To the extent that this assessment is true, the "periphery" will turn out to be more like the front lines. Its truth value makes it dangerous to the established order because it identifies the fate of a culture with the *action* of the people. This is an important and far-reaching perception.

Socially and politically, a division takes place when there is serious talk about reaching for the control box. We know that the control box is ultimately outside Appalachia, but a good many in the region who support the folksy heritage concept of culture are tied in with those whose hands are on the controls. The controllers will permit a plurality of ethnic identities, their agents will give grants to assist in their development. What they will ridicule and condemn is the possibility that these identities should have *a living value in the present*, one that possesses real social power such that the people of the region gain control over their destiny.

Our self-consciousness has brought us to a crucial juncture. Now is the time to invest in contemporary work in an unparalleled manner. Heritage and "roots" are not enough for a *living* identity. We need to take another look at folk culture and recognize that the folk are the people of the present, in need of a living culture. Folk culture must extend into the present as people's culture. If it doesn't, we will lose it all.

Bibliography of Publishers, Journals, and Anthologies

The following is a list of presses, magazines, and anthologies in which the work of American poets discussed in the essays can be found. Because some of the work may be difficult to locate through conventional channels, we have included addresses so that material can be ordered directly from the presses. And, since there is no single anthology in which a range of representative work is collected, we have mentioned a number of anthologies and collections by way of a beginning. Some of the titles have been suggested by our contributors, some are our own choices, others have been culled from *The International Directory of Little Magazines and Small Presses*, edited by Len Fulton and Ellen Ferber. (This very useful volume can be ordered directly from Dustbooks, P.O. Box 100, Paradise, CA 95969. It is updated periodically.)

Books mentioned in individual essays are cited only in the essays' endnotes. Small presses that also publish magazines are included in each magazine's entry. Where clarification seemed necessary, we added a brief annotation.

Many university presses emphasize the work of writers within their region. Among them are the University of Arizona Press, the University of New Mexico Press, the University of Indiana Press, the University of Pittsburgh Press, and the Navajo Community College Press. We would advise the reader to examine the university and community college lists for relevant texts. And, of course, bookstores which specialize in poetry can be an invaluable resource.

For the time being, anyone interested in locating the works of the full spectrum of American poets must see the task as a search. We can only hope that the reader will find the process enlightening and the results exciting.

Presses and Journals

A, a journal of contemporary literature. A Publications, Box 42A510, York Station, CA 90042 (Third World publishers with Native American preferences).

Afro-Hispanic Review. 3306 Ross Place N.W., Washington, D.C. 20008.

Akwekon: A National Native American Literature and Arts Journal. Mohawk Nation, Rooseveltown, NY 13683.

Alice James Books, 138 Mt. Auburn St., Cambridge, MA 02138 (emphasis on publishing poetry by women).

American Book Review. P.O. Box 188, Cooper Station, New York, NY 10003 (includes reviews of books from small, regional, Third World, and women's presses).

American Indian Culture and Research Journal. American Indian Studies Center, 3220 Campbell Hall, University of California, Los Angeles, CA 90024.

American Indian Quarterly. American Indian Studies Department, University of California, Berkeley, CA 84127.

Appalachian Consortium Press, University Hall, Appalachian State University, Boone, NC 28607.

Azalea. 306 Lafayette Ave., Brooklyn, NY 11238 (published by and for Third World lesbians).

Aztlán: International Journal of Chicano Studies Research. Chicano Studies Research Center Publications, UCLA, 405 Highland Ave., Los Angeles, CA 90025.

Bilingual Review. Bilingual Press, Office of the Graduate School, SUNY-Binghamton, Binghamton, NY 13091 (Spanish/English, Hispanic culture in the United States).

Black American Literature Forum. Indiana State University, Parsons Hall 237, Terre Haute, IN 47809.

Black Maria. Metis Press, Inc., P.O. Box 25187, Chicago, IL 60625 (material by and about women).

Black Oyster Press, P.O. Box 8550, Chicago, IL 60680 (feminist).

The Black Scholar: Journal of Black Studies and Research. The Black Scholar Press, P.O. Box 7106, San Francisco, CA 94120.

Blue Cloud Quarterly. Blue Cloud Abbey, Box 98, Marvin, SD 57251 (poetry by Native Americans).

Boletín Anglohispano. Bola Publications, 8769 Devon Ave., Hesperia, CA 92345.

Bridge: Asian American Perspectives. 32 E. Broadway, New York, NY 90002.

Café Solo. Café Solo Press, 7975 San Marcos, Atascadero, CA 93422 (includes prison poets, Spanish literature).

Calamus Books, Box 689, Cooper Station, New York, NY 10003 (work by or about lesbians and gay men).

Callaloo. Department of English, University of Kentucky, Lexington, KY 40506 (creative literature by black writers and critical works about black literature).

Calyx: A Journal of Art and Literature by Women. P.O. Box B, Corvallis, OR 97339 (special issue of Native/Latina work, *Bearing Witness/ Sobreviviendo,* published 1984).

Carta Abierta. Relampago Books Press, Center for Mexican-American Studies, Texas Lutheran College, Sequin, TX 78155.

Common Lives/Lesbian Lives. P.O. Box 1553, Iowa City, IA 52244.

Conditions. P.O. Box 56, Van Brunt Station, Brooklyn, NY 11215 (feminist with emphasis on writing by lesbians).

Contact/II: A Bimonthly Poetry Review Magazine. Contact II Publications, P.O. Box 451, Bowling Green Station, New York, NY 10004 (multicultural, special issue—*Asian American: North and South,* vol. 7, no. 38/39/40 [Winter/Spring 1986]).

Crossing Press, 17 W. Main St., Box 640, Trumansburg, NY 14886 (multicultural list).

Exquisite Corpse. 630 Lakeland Drive, Baton Rouge, LA 70802 (eclectic— poetry, articles, reviews, criticism).

Fag Rag. Good Gay Poets Press, Fag Rag Collective, Box 331, Kenmore Station, Boston, MA 02215.

Feminary. 3543 18th St., San Francisco, CA 94110.

The Feminist Press at the City University of New York, 311 East 94 St., New York, NY 10128.

Feminist Studies. c/o Women's Studies Program, University of Maryland, College Park, MD 20742.

Firebrand Books, 141 The Commons, Ithaca, NY 14850 (feminist).

Focus: A Journal for Lesbians. Focus Collective, 1151 Mass. Ave., Cambridge, MA 02138.

Gay Presses of New York, P.O. Box 294, Village Station, New York, NY 10014.

Gay Sunshine Journal. Gay Sunshine Press, P.O. Box 40397, San Francisco, CA 94140.

Greenfield Review. Greenfield Review Press, RD 1, Box 80, Greenfield Center, NY 12833 (the Greenfield Review Press has a multicultural list and runs the Native American Distribution Project as well as publishing the Prison Writing Review).

Hambone. 132 Clinton St., Santa Cruz, CA 95062 (black periodical).

Helicon Nine: The Journal of Women's Arts and Letters. P.O. Box 22412, Kansas City, MO 64113.

Heresies: A Feminist Publication on Art and Politics. Box 766, Canal St. Station, New York, NY 10013.

Ikon. Ikon Press, P.O. Box 1355, Stuyvesant Station, New York, NY 10009 (feminist political, cultural magazine with writing by lesbian, Third World, and working-class women).

Indian Truth. 1505 Race St., Philadelphia, PA 19102.

Inside/Out. Time Capsule Inc., GPO Box 1185, New York, NY 10116 (publishes only incarcerated writers).

Kalliope, A Journal of Women's Art. 3939 Roosevelt Blvd., Florida Jr. College at Jacksonville, Jacksonville, FL 32205.

Kitchen Table: Women of Color Press, Box 2753, New York, NY 10185.

The Laurel Review. West Virginia Wesleyan College, Buckhannon, WV 26201 (encourages writing from Appalachia).

Lector. P.O. Box 4273, Berkeley, CA 94704 (Hispanic-related material).

Long Haul Press, P.O. Box 592, Van Brunt Station, Brooklyn, NY 11215 (feminist).

Lotus Press, Inc., P.O. Box 21607, Detroit, MI 48221 (emphasis on black poets).

Magic Circle Press, 10 Hyde Ridge Rd., Weston, CT 06833 (has done special project on poetry of women in prison).

Melus (The Journal of the Society for the Study of the Multi-Ethnic Literature of the United States). Department of English, University of Southern California, Los Angeles, CA 90007.

Minor Heron Press, P.O. Box 2615, Taos, NM 87571 (emphasis on Southwestern Hispanic and Native American poetry and fiction).

Motheroot Journal. Motheroot Publications, 214 Dewey St., Pittsburgh, PA 15218 (women's press, journal reviews small press books by or about women).

Moving Out: Feminist Literary and Arts Journal. P.O. Box 21249, Detroit, MI 48221.

New Victoria Publishers, 7 Bank St., Lebanon, NH 03766 (women's press).

Obsidian: Black Literature in Review. English Department, Wayne State University, Detroit, MI 48202.

Pacific Bridge. P.O. Box 883903, San Francisco, CA 94188 (gay Asian).

Parnassus: Poetry in Review. 205 West 89th St., New York, NY 10024.

Primavera. 1212 E. 59th St., Chicago, IL 60637 (feminist).

rara avis, Books of a Feather. P.O. Box 3095, Terminal Annex, Los Angeles, CA 90051 (includes women of color, lesbians).

Revista Chicano-Riqueña. Arte Publico Press, University of Houston, University Park, Houston, TX 77004 (Hispanic literature).

Seal Press, Box 13, Seattle, WA 98111 (feminist).

Second Growth: Appalachian Nature and Culture. P.O. Box 24, East Tennessee State University, Johnson City, TN 37619.

Seven Buffaloes Press, Box 249, Big Timber, MT 59011 (publishes *Black Jack*, *Valley Grapevine*, which focus on regional and rural writing).

Sez: A Multi-Racial Journal of Poetry and People's Culture. Shadow Press, P.O. Box 8803, Minneapolis, MN 55408.

Shamal Books, G.P.O. Box 16, New York, NY 10016 (multicultural list).

Shameless Hussy Press, Box 3092, Berkeley, CA 94703.

Signs: Journal of Women in Culture and Society. Center for Research on Women, Serra House, Stanford University, Stanford, CA 94305.

Sing Heavenly Muse!: Women's Poetry and Prose. P.O. Box 14059, Minneapolis, MN 55414.

Sinister Wisdom. P.O. Box 10234, Rockland, ME 04841 (feminist and lesbian writing).

South End Press, 302 Columbus Ave., Boston, MA 02116 (publishes books which aid the day-to-day struggle to control life).

Southern Exposure. Institute for Southern Studies, P.O. Box 531, Durham, NC 27702.

Spawning the Medicine River. Institute of American Indian Arts, Santa Fe, NM 87501.

Spinsters, Ink, 803 De Haro St., San Francisco, CA 94107 (feminist).

Steppingstones: A Literary Anthology toward Liberation. Steppingstones Press, Box 1856, Harlem, NY 10027 (especially Third World and black).

Strawberry Press, P.O. Box 451, Bowling Green Station, New York, NY 10004 (Native American).

Sunbury Press, 22 Catherine St., Basement Workshop, New York, NY 10038 (women, Third World, working class).

Suntracks. English Department, University of Arizona, Tucson, AZ 85721 (Native American).

Third World Press, 7524 So. Cottage Grove Ave., Chicago, IL 60619.

13th Moon. P.O. Box 309, Cathedral Station, New York, NY 10025 (particularly interested in feminist and lesbian work; vol. 7, nos. 1 and 2, is a double issue on working class experience).

Tulsa Studies in Women's Literature. 600 S. College, Tulsa, OK 74104.

The Universal Black Writer. P.O. Box 5, Radio City Station, New York, NY 10101.

Vanguard Books, P.O. Box 3566, Chicago, IL 60654 (literature reflecting current social struggles).

West End Press, P.O. Box 291477, Los Angeles, CA 90029 (politically progressive).

Whetstone. San Pedro Press, 212 Clawson St., Bisbee, AZ 85603 (Native American, Southwest).

Woman Poet. Women-in-Literature, Inc., P.O. Box 60550, Reno, NV 89506.

The Women's Review of Books. Wellesley College, Center for Research on Women, Wellesley, MA 02181.

Women's Studies Quarterly. The Feminist Press, Box 344, Old Westbury, NY 11568.

Wood Ibis. Place of Herons Press, P.O. Box 1952, Austin, TX 78767 (Chicano, Hispanic, Native American, among others).

Anthologies

Algarin, Miguel, and Miguel Piñero, eds. *Nuyorican Poetry: An Anthology of Puerto Rican Words and Feelings*. New York: William Morrow and Co., 1975.

Allen, Terry, ed. *The Whispering Wind, Poetry by Young American Indians*. New York: Doubleday, 1972.

Amburgey, Gail, Mary Joan Coleman, and Pauletta Hansel, eds. *We're Alright but We Ain't Special*. Beckley, W. Va.: Mountain Union Books, 1976.

Astrov, Margot, ed. *American Indian Prose and Poetry*. New York: Capricorn Books, 1946.

Baber, Bob Henry, George Ella Lyon, and Gurney Norman, eds. *Common Ground: Contemporary Appalachian Poetry*. Charleston, W.Va.: Jalamap Press, 1985.

Bambara, Toni Cade, ed. *The Black Woman, An Anthology*. New York: New American Library, 1970.

Baraka, Amiri, and Amina Baraka, eds. *Confirmation: An Anthology of African-American Women*. New York: Quill, 1983.

Barradas, Efraín, and Rafael Rodríguez, eds. *Herejes y mitificadores: Muestra de poesía puertorriqueña en los Estados Unidos*. Puerto Rico: Ediciones Huracán, 1980 (bilingual).

Bernikow, Louise, ed. *The World Split Open: Four Centuries of Women Poets in England and America, 1552–1950*. New York: Vintage, 1974.

Bierhorst, John, ed. *In the Trail of the Wind*. New York: Farrar, Straus and Giroux, 1971.

Bly, Robert, ed. *News of the Universe: Poems of Twofold Consciousness*. San Francisco, Calif.: Sierra Club Books, 1980.

Brant, Beth, ed. *A Gathering of Spirit: Writing and Art by North American Indian Women.* Rockland, Maine: Sinister Wisdom Books, 1984.

Bruchac, Joseph, ed. *Breaking Silence, an Anthology of Contemporary Asian American Poets.* Greenfield Center, N.Y.: Greenfield Review Press, 1983.

_____. *The Light from Another Country: Poetry from American Prisons.* Greenfield Center, N.Y.: Greenfield Review Press, 1984.

_____. *Songs from This Earth on Turtle's Back, Contemporary American Indian Poetry.* Greenfield Center, N.Y.: Greenfield Review Press, 1983.

Bulkin, Elly, and Joan Larkin, eds. *Lesbian Poetry: An Anthology.* Watertown, Mass.: Persephone, 1981 (distributed by Gay Presses of New York).

Chapman, Abraham, ed. *Literature of the American Indians.* New York: Meridian, 1975.

Chiang, Fay et al., eds. *American Born and Foreign.* New York: Sunbury, 1979.

Delgado, Abelardo, ed. *Chicano: 25 Pieces of a Chicano Mind.* Denver: Barrio Publications, 1969.

Epringham, Toni, ed. *Fiesta in Aztlán.* Santa Barbara, Calif.: Capra Press, 1981.

Fisher, Dexter, ed. *The Third Woman: Minority Women Writers of the United States.* Boston, Mass.: Houghton Mifflin, 1980.

Frumkin, Gene and Stanley Noyes, eds. *The Indian Rio Grande: Recent Poems from 3 Cultures.* Albuquerque, N.M.: San Marcos Press, 1977.

Gibson, Donlad B., ed. *Modern Black Poets.* Englewood Cliffs, N.J.: Prentice-Hall, 1973.

Green, Rayna, ed. *That's What She Said, Contemporary Poetry and Fiction by Native American Women.* Bloomington, Ind.: Indiana University Press, 1984.

Henderson, Stephen. *Understanding the New Black Poetry.* New York: William Morrow and Co., 1973.

Hicks, Granville et al., eds. *Proletarian Literature in the United States: An Anthology.* New York: International Publishers, 1935.

Hobson, Geary, ed. *The Remembered Earth, an Anthology of Contemporary Native American Literature.* Albuquerque, N.M.: University of New Mexico Press, 1981.

Howe, Florence, and Ellen Bass, eds. *No More Masks! An Anthology of Poems by Women.* New York: Doubleday Anchor, 1973.

Japanese American Anthology Committee, ed. *Ayumi: A Japanese American Anthology.* P.O. Box 5024, San Francisco, CA, 1980.

Katz, Janet, ed. *I Am the Fire of Time, Writings by Native American Women.* New York: Dutton, 1977.

Keller, Gary, and Francisco Jimenez. *Hispanics in the United States: An An-*

thology of Creative Literature. Tempe, Ariz.: Bilingual Press, Arizona State University, 1980 (vol. 1), 1982 (vol. 2).

Kenny, Maurice, ed. *Wounds Beneath the Flesh, 15 Native American Poets.* Marvin, S. Dak.: Blue Cloud Quarterly Press, 1983.

Kherdian, David, ed. *Settling America: The Ethnic Expression of 14 Contemporary Poets.* New York: Macmillan, 1974.

Leyland, Winston, ed. *Orgasms of Light: The Gay Sunshine Anthology.* San Francisco, Calif.: Gay Sunshine Press, 1977.

Lourie, Dick, ed. *Come to Power: Eleven Contemporary American Indian Poets.* Trumansburg, N.Y.: Crossing Press, 1974.

Lowenfels, Walter, ed. *From the Belly of the Shark.* New York: Vintage, 1973.

Matila, Alfredo, and Iván Silén, eds. *The Puerto Rican Poets.* New York: Bantam, 1972.

Miles, Sara et al., eds. *Ordinary Women, Mujeres Comunes, an Anthology of Poetry by New York City Women.* New York: Ordinary Women, 1978.

Moraga, Cherríe, and Gloria Anzaldúa, eds. *This Bridge Called My Back: Writings by Radical Women of Color.* Watertown, Mass.: Persephone Press, 1981.

Niatum, Duane, ed. *Carriers of the Dream Wheel, Contemporary Native American Poetry.* New York: Harper and Row, 1975.

North, Joseph, ed. *New Masses: An Anthology of the Rebel Thirties.* New York: International Publishers, 1969.

Randall, Dudley, ed. *The Black Poets.* New York: Bantam Books, 1971.

Simon, Myron, ed. *Ethnic Writers in America.* New York: Harcourt Brace Jovanovich, 1972.

Steiner, Stan, and Luis Valdez, eds. *Aztlán: An Anthology of Mexican American Literature.* New York: Random House, 1972.

Stetson, Arlene, ed. *Black Sister: Poetry by Black American Women 1746–1980.* Bloomington: Indiana University Press, 1981.

Troupe, Quincy, and Rainer Schulte, eds. *Giant Talk: An Anthology of Third World Writing.* New York: Random House, 1975.

Young, Ian, ed. *The Male Muse: A Gay Anthology.* Trumansburg, N.Y.: Crossing Press, 1973.

———. *Son of the Male Muse: New Gay Poetry.* Trumansburg, N.Y.: Crossing Press, 1983.

Biographical Notes

Steve Abbott studied poetry with Karl Shapiro and John Berryman and has taught writing at Emory University. He has published three books of poetry and edited *Poetry Flash* from 1979 to 1985 as well as the magazine *Soup* from 1980 to 1985. He has read at the One World Poetry Festival in Amsterdam and the Village Voice Bookstore in Paris. He taught a gay poetry workshop for the James White School in Wisconsin and currently teaches writing at the University of San Francisco.

Kathleen Aguero is the author of a collection of poems, *Thirsty Day* (Alice James Books, 1977), and has a new collection, *The Real Weather*, from Hanging Loose Press. A recipient of a Massachusetts Artists Fellowship in poetry, she has also published reviews. She has taught writing and worked in the Poets-in-Residence Program for many years and is now working as a children's librarian. She lives in Somerville, Massachusetts.

Juan Bruce-Novoa currently teaches in San Antonio, Texas, in the Foreign Languages Department of Trinity University. His books include *Inocencia Porversa/Perverse Innocence* (poetry); *Chicano Authors: Inquiry by Interview*; *Chicano Poetry: A Response to Chaos*. His articles, reviews, and fiction have been published in major journals in the United States, Latin America, and Europe. He is currently developing an international association of scholars to focus on Latino cultures of the United States.

Joseph Bruchac and his wife are editors and publishers of the multicultural literary magazine *The Greenfield Review*. His own books include collections of poetry, novels, and retellings of Native American folk tales. His newest, *Iroquois Stories*, was published in 1986 by the Crossing Press and his book of interviews with American Indian poets will be published in 1987 by the University of Arizona Press.

Billy Collins has published two books of poetry: *Pokerface* (Kenmore Press) and *Video Poems* (Applezaba Press). His work has appeared in periodicals such as *Paris Review, Field, Ploughshares, Rolling Stone, Florida Review,* and *Sierra Madre Review.* He teaches at Lehman College in New York.

John F. Crawford has taught at seven U.S. colleges and universities, worked as a journalist and a typesetter, and served as editor and publisher of *West End* magazine (1971 to 1976) and West End Press (1976 to present). His press has published such writers as Meridel LeSueur, Thomas McGrath, Don West, Sharon Doubiago, Wendy Rose, Cherríe Moraga, and Nellie Wong: forty-three volumes in all, of which twenty-five are in print. He is currently lecturer in English at the University of New Mexico.

Martín Espada is the author of *The Immigrant Iceboy's Bolero* (Waterfront Press) and *Trumpets from the Islands of Their Eviction* (Bilingual Press). Espada has been awarded a 1984 Massachusetts Artists' Foundation Fellowship and a 1986 National Endowment for the Arts Creative Writing Fellowship. He notes that "Documentaries and Declamadores" was written, not by a scholar or critic, but from the perspective of a participant-observer in the community of Puerto Rican poets here in the United States.

Marie Harris is the author of two volumes of poetry: *Raw Honey* (Alice James Books, 1975) and *Interstate* (Slow Loris Press, 1980). She works as writer-in-residence for the New Hampshire Council on the Arts and is a partner with her husband, Charter Weeks, in Isinglass Studio, an industrial advertising agency.

Rudy Kikel writes frequently for the gay press—the Los Angeles *Advocate*, Philadelphia's *Gay News*, and Boston's *Bay Windows*—on subjects ranging from gay male poetry to lesbian powerlifting. He's the arts and entertainment editor of *Bay Windows* and one of that newspaper's two poetry editors. His book of poems, *Lasting Relations*, was published in 1984 by Sea Horse Press.

Annette Kolodny, professor of literature at Rensselaer Polytechnic Institute, is the author of *The Lay of the Land: Metaphor as Experience and*

History in American Life and Letters (1975), *The Land before Her: Fantasy and Experience of the American Frontiers, 1620–1860* (1984), and many prize-winning articles on feminist criticism and American women writers.

Lynda Koolish's work has appeared in *Signs, The Women's Review of Books, Feminist Studies, Sinister Wisdom,* and elsewhere. Indiana University Press is publishing a collection of essays by contemporary American women poets which she is editing called *What Moves Me Brings Me to Myself.* She is currently revising a book-length critical study of contemporary American feminist poetry and is at work on a book on the slave narrative tradition in Afro-American women writers from the Harlem Renaissance to the present.

P. J. Laska lives near Seattle. He is working on his second novel.

Paul Lauter directs "Reconstructing American Literature," a project funded by FIPSE, the Lilly Endowment, and the Rockefeller Foundation aimed at changing the teaching of American literature so that it reflects the full range of voices in American culture—women as well as men, minorities as well as whites. He is currently coordinating editor for a new two-volume anthology of American literature to be published by D. C. Heath in 1989. He edited *Reconstructing American Literature,* a collection of syllabi and course materials. He is co-author of "The Impact of Women's Studies on Curriculum and Campus" (NIE, 1980), author of "Race and Gender in the Shaping of the American Literary Canon," *Feminist Studies* (1983), and a theoretical study directed to the marginalization of women and minority American writers.

George Ella Lyon works as a writer and teacher in Lexington, Kentucky. Her publications include *Mountain,* a chapbook (Andrew Mountain Press, 1983), *Father Time and the Day Boxes,* a children's book (Bradbury Press, 1985), and *Common Ground,* an anthology which she co-edited with Gurney Norman and Bob Henry Baber (Jalamap, 1985). Her play, *Braids,* was produced in April 1985 at Transylvania University through the support of the Kentucky Arts Council.

Adrian Oktenberg is currently working on a novel set in the sixties. Her work appears frequently in *The Women's Review of Books* and other feminist publications.

Richard Oyama was coordinator of the Basement Writers Workshop, an Asian American community arts organization in New York, from

1974 to 1978. He co-edited *American Born and Foreign*, an anthology of Asian American poetry, published by Sunbury Press in 1979. His poems, essays, and critiques have appeared in *downbeat, Greenfield Review, Bridge, East Wind, Sunbury, Time Capsule*, and numerous other publications.

Raymond R. Patterson teaches at the City College of the City University of New York. He is the author of two collections of poems, *26 Ways of Looking at a Black Man and Other Poems* and *Elemental Blues*.

Carmen Tafolla is a writer and educator. The former director of the Mexican American Studies Center at Texas Lutheran College, head writer for the bilingual children's TV series *Sonrisas*, and presently associate professor of women's studies at California State University, Fresno, she is currently on leave doing full-time writing on a novel and several collections of poetry in Flagstaff, Arizona. Among her publications are three books of poetry and a book on racism, sexism, and Chicana women entitled *To Split a Human: Mitos, Machos y la Mujer Chicana*.